STEEL INFIDELS COMPLETE SERIES SET

DEZ BURKE

STEEL INFIDELS COMPLETE SERIES SET

Available for a limited time only, this 5 book box set contains the complete Amazon Top 20 bestselling *Steel Infidels* series.

Contained inside this box set:
1. Safe House (Steel Infidels Series Book 1) (Flint Mason)
2. Liberated (Steel Infidels Series Book 2) (Flint Mason)
3. Steel Justice (Steel Infidels Series Book 3) (Jesse Mason)
4. Thunderclap (Steel Infidels Book 4) (Sam Mason)
5. Take Down (Steel Infidels Book 5) (Toby)

Cover by: Coverluv
Cover Model: Leo Taylor
Cover Photography by: Allan Spiers
Inside Book Photography by: Travis DesLaurier, Leo Taylor and Allan Spiers
Formatting by: Violet Haze

Acknowledgments

Writing the Steel Infidels Series has been one of the best experiences in my life. The characters are part of my family now and will always hold a special place in my heart. I don't want you to worry! You'll see them again when you least expect it. I love them all too much to let them go forever.

If you have any questions about the books please email me at dezburke@aol.com or find me on Facebook at Dez Burke. I'm on there every day and love hearing from my readers! To sign up for my newsletter go here: http://eepurl.com/wxERT

Please note this book is for Adults 18+ and older due to adult situations and language.

New York Times and USA Today bestselling author

SAFEHOUSE

by

DEZ BURKE

Several years before, Flint Mason committed the unthinkable, he left town and turned his back on his brothers and the Steel Infidels Motorcycle Club. When his best friend is murdered by a rival MC, he returns home determined to exact his own personal revenge. Veterinarian Dr. Kendra Shaw has never ignored an animal in need. So when a call comes in about an injured eagle she doesn't think twice about going alone to a secluded cabin to meet the caller. What she finds there sets her on a shocking path she never imagined...

SAFE HOUSE PROLOGUE

The elderly judge banged his gavel on the stand and stood up, signaling the end of the court session. Public defender Flint Mason smiled and leaned over to shake his client's hand, a young Hispanic woman whom the jury had found "not guilty" of charges of child endangerment.

Like most of his clients, her verdict was based on how well the jury understood her desperate situation. Faced with the difficult choice of making her three small children walk two miles with her to the nearest grocery store or leaving them alone for an hour, she'd chosen what she thought was the least dangerous option.

Unfortunately, her neighbor had called the police and now here she was, left to the mercy of a jury who was most definitely not made up of her peers. The young woman seemed slightly confused and Flint realized she didn't understand she was free to go.

"It's okay," he said, taking her arm to usher her out of the courtroom. "You can go home now."

Relief broke across her tired face as his words finally sank in. "Gracias!" she cried, squeezing him in a quick hug before hurrying out the front door of the courthouse.

Flint rubbed the back of his neck and headed to the closest drink machine. Thankfully, Maria Lopez's case was the last one on his docket for the day. He'd defended five clients in court since early that morning. Two were found guilty and got sent back to the county jail while the other three were free to go. He figured that was pretty good odds, considering the fact that he barely had time to read their files before representing them as their court-appointed attorney.

The truth was, most of the time his cases fell into a gray area of guilt anyway. After two years of working for the Public Defender's office, he really didn't want to know if his clients were innocent or guilty. He'd learned things were much easier that way. Always assume the client was innocent, make sure they didn't tell him otherwise, and do his job without asking too many questions.

Some days Flint couldn't remember the reason why he'd chosen to be a public defender. Years ago, he'd been young and idealistic; he thought he could change things and make a difference. Now he wasn't so sure. The system was broken and he was just another spoke in its wheel.

He grabbed a soft drink out of the machine and checked his cell phone. The screen blinked with three missed calls and several voice messages. Flint swore softly. He never gave out his cell phone number to clients, and only a handful of people knew it. He quickly checked his voicemail and listened to the first message.

"Hey Flint, it's Jesse," the deep-voiced caller said, as if he wouldn't recognize his own brother's voice. "Call me. It's urgent."

The next message said the same thing. Flint checked the three missed calls...all from Jesse as well. With a growing dread, he played the last message. "Flint, it's Jesse again. Listen man...it's about Tommy. I hate like hell telling you this over the phone but since you aren't returning your damn phone calls, I don't have a choice." Jesse's voice cracked. "They got him, Flint. Those son of a bitch Liberators finally got him." There was a long pause and Flint wondered if Jesse had hung up before he continued. "His mom set the funeral up for Sunday. You need to come home, Flint. Tommy would want you there. We all do."

Flint clicked his phone off. He leaned his forehead against the cold cement wall of the hallway for a moment before rushing into the restroom and splashing water on his face.

Breathing deeply, he struggled to get his emotions under control and failed. "Goddammit!" he yelled at his reflection. "Motherfuckers!"

He leaned over the sink and drew in several deep breaths.

Why did it have to be Tommy?

Of all the members of the Steel Infidels motorcycle club, Tommy was the one Flint was the closest to. They'd grown up together as childhood best friends and then had ridden together side by side for years before Flint had left town.

He wondered if Tommy had ever forgiven him for leaving the motorcycle club. Now he'd never know. And now he would never have a chance to patch things up with one of the few people in the world he'd ever truly cared about.

Once again, the Liberators had destroyed something dear to him. Anger rushed over Flint, filling him to the brim with an overwhelming desire for revenge. There was no way in hell he was going to let them get away with this.

Thirty minutes later he arrived at his tiny apartment. Rushing inside, he quickly threw a few clothes together into a duffel bag. He searched through his closet until he found what he was looking for: an old pair of faded jeans, white t-shirt, leather boots, and a black leather jacket that he hadn't touched in years.

Closing his eyes and inhaling deeply, he held the jacket to his nose. The smell of the leather brought back memories, so sharp and vivid he could almost touch them. Memories of home, family and friends, memories of good times and bad.

He stripped off his dark suit, blue tie, and long-sleeved starched white shirt. Carefully concealed underneath the business attire was the hidden link to his past; a large black ink tattoo covering his back and upper shoulders.

It read simply in big bold letters:

"Steel Infidels"

It was time for Flint to go home.

1

Six months later...

Flint never looked back once the decision was made to return home to the Steel Infidels. Surprisingly, after the funeral, the motorcycle club accepted him readily back into the fold, breaking one of their firmest and most steadfast rules - if you left the club, you never came back.

He knew the vote to allow him back in wasn't unanimous. Of the twelve remaining voting members of the MC, there were two votes against him: Rocco, a convicted felon and owner of a shady car repo business and Danny, his brother.

Flint wasn't too upset about it. He suspected the main reason Rocco voted against him was because of his deep mistrust of anyone involved in the legal profession. Allowing a lawyer into the club's most private and secret dealings would be a bitter pill to swallow. And unfortunately, Rocco wasn't smart enough to appreciate how much the club could use Flint's expertise in the legal field, especially considering some of their more recent activities.

Flint hoped the brothers would eventually come around. The strength of the MC depended on the solidarity of its members. While the majority ruled in voting situations, every individual vote was still taken solemnly and seriously.

The other ten members had voted yes more out of loyalty to his older brother, Jesse, the current president of the MC, than to him. There was no doubt that at some point, the crew would demand Flint to prove his loyalty to the club. When that day came, he would be expected to do whatever task was given to him without question or hesitation. He was ready and willing though he knew the task might be brutal and would definitely be illegal.

He'd made the mistake of turning his back on the MC once. No matter what, he wouldn't let them down again.

The receptionist knocked gently on the door before opening it a crack and sticking her head inside. "Dr. Shaw, you have a phone call."

"I'm a little bit busy here, Jan," Dr. Kendra Shaw replied. She grimaced as the hawk she was holding tried to dig its sharp talons into her hand. "Squeeze in here. I could use another set of hands to help hold Malone while I examine him. He's looking for any opportunity to shred my fingers if I let him."

Jan moved quickly to the veterinarian's side and held the hawk's feet firmly while Dr. Shaw examined his wings.

"The caller sounded panicked," Jan continued. "He claims he has a bald eagle corralled in his shed with a suspected gunshot wound to his wing. He wanted to know if you can come pick it up."

"A bald eagle?" Dr. Shaw replied. "That's unusual for North Georgia. How much do you want to bet it's really a vulture? He can't bring it here himself?"

Jan shook her head. "No. He said it's flopping around and he doesn't want to risk injuring it more. He's on hold since he insisted on speaking with you directly."

Dr. Shaw let out a tired sigh. "They always do." She carefully turned the hawk over and placed him back into his carrier. "There you go, boy. Jan, you can take him back out to the raptor aviary," she said before washing her hands and picking up the phone.

Never in her life had veterinarian Kendra Shaw been able to turn away from an animal in need. This time wasn't any different. After the phone call, she'd dropped everything, rearranged her schedule for the afternoon, and jumped into her truck to go pick up the eagle.

Usually, people brought the injured wild animals and birds into the Shaw Wildlife Center themselves. Occasionally, she had to go out and get them. Most of the time the pickups were animals people were afraid to touch for fear of rabies, like raccoons, skunks, or foxes. Every once in a while, she'd receive an oddball call about a baby black bear or orphaned coyote pup.

A bald eagle wasn't something she treated often, so she didn't hesitate about offering to drive over herself for this one. She tried to think back. It had been at least a couple of years since she'd had an injured eagle come in for rehab. She hoped this one wasn't hurt too badly. There would be hell to pay if she found out who shot him. Not to mention probable jail time and a huge fine as well. The phone number of the U.S. Fish and Wildlife was on her speed dial and she would be in contact with them the minute she returned to the clinic.

She downshifted the gears in the truck as the gravel road going up the side of the mountain grew steeper. Light sleet pelted the windshield. According to the weather report she had checked before heading out, a winter storm was due to blow in later.

She wasn't concerned. If things went well and the eagle was cooperative, she would have plenty of time to get him safely into the heated carrier in the bed of the truck and head back to town before the roads became slick.

In any case, she hoped the cabin wasn't too much further up the mountain. The male caller had given her very specific directions on how to get there, but she hadn't expected it to be so far out in the middle of nowhere.

It had been at least ten miles since she'd seen another house. The gravel road had first turned to dirt then gradually narrowed to one lane barely big enough for her truck. Like most of the mountain roads in rural north Georgia, there weren't any guardrails preventing cars from sliding off the side of the road with a single wrong move.

After carefully maneuvering the truck around a couple more tight switch-backs, she spotted the rustic log cabin tucked into a small clearing. She pulled up in front of the house and leaned over to grab her medical bag. Before getting out, she took a quick glance around the premises. She didn't see a shed. Surely she didn't miss it on the way up?

The oak front door swung open before she made it to the top step of the porch. A tall, burly man with a scraggly beard in a black leather jacket stepped outside to greet her.

"Thank you for coming in such a hurry, Dr. Shaw," he said, not meeting her eyes. "I appreciate it. Come on inside."

"Where's the eagle?" she asked, suddenly feeling uneasy. It occurred to her that in her haste to rescue yet another animal, she had agreed to meet a strange man in an isolated cabin. Miles and miles from anyone. *Smart move, Kendra,* she berated herself. "Is he still alive?" she asked.

"Yeah, he's okay. Let's go in by the fire and warm up a minute. I'll tell you how I found him," the man replied, motioning for her to walk through the door in front of him.

Kendra smiled politely and tried not to show her irritation or unease. As a general rule, the Good Samaritans who found injured animals always wanted to tell her the whole story about the animal before they handed it over. They seemed to feel the need to tell her the tiniest details of everything they'd done for the animal so far as well as all the research they'd found on the Internet. When every minute counted to save an animal's life, it could be a tad bit annoying at times. She always tried her best to be patient though, knowing their hearts were in the right place.

"It's probably better if you take me straight to him," she said firmly. "There's a storm blowing in and the sooner I can safely transport him back to my clinic, the sooner I can take care of his injuries and hopefully save his wing. You can call me later to check on him if you like. I'll give you my cell phone number. I don't mind if you do."

"Alright," he said, stepping inside and shutting the door behind them. "Let me get my gloves."

Kendra took two steps inside the small cabin and stopped dead in her tracks. "What the hell is going on here?"

2

It took her only a heartbeat to register the fact that she'd been lied to. A group of men in black leather boots and jackets stood by a small couch pulled close to the fireplace. One of the men she recognized as Tom Brewer, a member of the Steel Infidels, a well-known motorcycle gang in town rumored to be involved in several illegal activities.

A few months back he'd brought her an abused pit bull that he'd snatched from a man's backyard. The poor dog had been chained up in the hot sun for days without adequate food or water.

Kendra hadn't asked any questions at the time and had been grateful to Tom for bringing the dog in. It had taken a while, but eventually she'd been able to nurse the dog back to health and had even found a nice home for him with a couple of kids.

Later she'd read in the town's newspaper that someone had beaten the hell out of the dog's owner in what the newspaper had called a "random act of violence." She'd suspected Tom Brewer and the Steel Infidels had been behind it, and to be honest, she was glad. The man deserved much worse in her opinion. No punishment was bad enough for an abuser of innocent animals.

A closer look at the group revealed another man wearing nothing but jeans and steel-toed boots sprawled out on the couch. From what she could see, the bare-chested man was positively lethal when it came to the looks department...and seriously injured.

He was a mass of hard-packed muscle and looked to be in his late twenties with a dark tan and jet black hair. Blood spilled from a wound in his left arm, dripping through the makeshift tourniquet and onto the wood floor. A large black tattoo with the motorcycle gang's emblem wrapped across his back and upper shoulders.

Kendra's mind raced as she tried to get a handle on the situation. She couldn't possibly imagine what had transpired in the cabin and didn't want to know. Getting tangled up with the Steel Infidels was something only a fool would do. And nobody had ever called Dr. Kendra Shaw stupid.

"Well gentlemen, I guess I can assume there's not an injured eagle in here after all," she said before turning and heading back towards the front door.

Damn! Too late.

The heavyset man who had let her in was now blocking her exit.

Kendra drew in a deep calming breath before whirling around. "Okay, somebody had better tell me what is going on here. Who called me?"

Tom Brewer cleared his throat. "I made the call, Dr. Shaw. I'm sorry for lying to you like that to get you up here. We didn't know what to do and we needed help. Fast." He waved a hand toward the injured man. "Flint took a bullet in the arm. We didn't know who else to call." He shrugged helplessly and looked away.

Kendra's eyebrows shot up. "How about 911? That's always a good first choice. Jesus Christ, Tom! I'm a vet, not a doctor! You need to take him to Union General right now."

She hurried to the injured man's side. Not only was his skin unnaturally pale underneath his tan, his breath was also shallow and erratic.

"When did this happen?" she asked.

"An hour or so ago," Tom answered. "We were on a run to pick up some supplies over in Towns County. When we came back through the valley, an ambush was waiting for us. They opened fire and caught Flint in the arm."

Kendra held up her hand to stop him from talking. She had enough sense to know the less she knew about the details, the better. Getting involved in the Steel Infidel's business was a very bad idea.

She turned back to the injured man and quickly assessed his injury the best she could. "The first thing we need to do is stop the bleeding and clean the wound to prevent infection. Then we'll need to load him into my truck. Unless you guys have a vehicle parked somewhere that I didn't see?"

Tom shook his head. "No ma'am, we all rode our motorcycles up here. Even Flint."

Kendra couldn't believe the injured man rode all the way from Towns County and up the mountain on a motorcycle with a bleeding gunshot wound in his arm. He obviously must have a high tolerance for pain. Or maybe he was drugged up. Probably high as a kite on something. That would explain it.

Or it could be attributed to an intense flood of adrenaline hitting him when the shots were fired. She'd heard of cases where people didn't realize they had been shot until much later due to the ability of adrenaline to mask pain.

A tall man with dark brown hair moved to the front of the group and knelt beside her. One glance at his worried face told her he must be related to the injured man. The resemblance was uncanny though this man was a little older.

"I'm Jesse," he said, reaching out to shake her hand. "Flint's brother. What do you need to stop the bleeding?"

"Some clean towels or dishcloths if you have them." She quickly removed the bandage around Flint's arm. She knew the men probably didn't realize the tight tourniquet they had applied would begin to cause irreversible tissue damage in another hour. Then again, bleeding to death was worse.

She frowned when she saw the seriousness of the wound. "The bullet is still in there and it looks really bad. I'll wrap it up as best as I can to stop the bleeding then we need to hurry. Someone should call the hospital to let them know we're coming in with him."

Jesse laid a firm hand on her arm. "That's going to be a problem, Dr. Shaw," he replied quietly. "Flint can't go to the hospital. You're going to have to take the bullet out and stitch him up here. That's why we called you."

Kendra leaned back on her heels and blinked at him in confusion. "What are you talking about? Look, buddy," she replied. "I don't *have* to do anything. I don't know who the hell you and your buddies think you are, but you can't trick people then expect them to do whatever you tell them to. What do you mean he's not going to the hospital? Are you crazy? He's been shot! For the last time, I'm not a medical doctor! Do you want him to lose the use of his arm? He's lucky the bullet didn't nick a major artery or he'd already be dead. Honestly, I'm not qualified to treat him. That is the God's honest truth."

Flint groaned in pain and struggled to sit up before slipping back into unconsciousness. Kendra pushed her fingers through her long black hair and exhaled a breath. Being asked, or in this case, probably being forced to treat a person wasn't a situation she'd ever been faced with before. As far as she was concerned, it wasn't worth losing her veterinarian's license over.

The law was the law. Period. She wasn't licensed to treat people. Legally, she shouldn't touch him. If something went wrong, he could sue her. And rightly so.

"For God's sake!" she said, pointing to Flint. "Take a good look at him. With friends like you, this guy doesn't need enemies." She glared at Jesse. "Or family."

"Haven't you ever treated an animal with a gunshot wound before?" Jesse asked. "Surely you must have. Plenty of times."

Kendra sighed. "Of course I have. But it was under anesthesia with IV fluids and monitors going to keep the animal stable. It's obvious your brother is in terrible pain. Explain to me why you aren't willing to take him to the hospital? Is it because of insurance? Because if it is, they still have to treat him in an emergency even if he doesn't have any. This is crazy. I'm calling an ambulance myself." She pulled her cell phone out of her jacket pocket and started dialing.

Jesse ripped the phone from her hands and turned it off before sliding it into the inside pocket of his leather jacket. "Sorry. Can't let you do that. We didn't want to involve you in the details, but it looks like there's no other way to make you understand our position here. A rival motorcycle club, the Liberators, have put a hit out on Flint. Six months ago, they murdered one of our crew in a shootout over in Tennessee. So they mean business. They'll have every hospital for miles around staked out watching for us to bring him in." He shook his head. "It's not safe. The next time Flint might not be so lucky. We can't take a chance. Not with my brother."

Kendra wondered if he might be telling the truth. She'd heard rumors of gang activity going on in the area but hadn't ever paid much attention to the gossip. Occasionally, in the summer, she would see a group of motorcycles riding down Bardsville's main street. As far as she knew, they weren't doing anything other than making a lot of obnoxious noise.

She stood up and dusted off the seat of her pants. "I don't like this. I don't appreciate being lured here under false pretenses and I don't like being put in this kind of position. I'm not licensed to treat people and could lose my veterinarian's license if I lay a hand on him. Besides, don't you realize doctors are required to report gunshot wounds to the police department?"

"That's only for doctors, right? Not vets?" Jesse replied. "Since you're not a medical doctor, it doesn't apply to you."

He had a valid point.

Damn it!

Flint moaned again. The undeniable pain in his voice pushed Kendra into a quick decision.

"If I do this, it has to stay between us," she said. "Not a word to anybody. Not another soul. And you all owe me. Big time. Do you understand?" She looked around the room, slowly making eye contact with each man to let them know she wouldn't be intimidated. Leather jackets and beards didn't scare her. After glancing at Jesse for guidance, they all nodded.

"Please," Jesse pleaded quietly. "I'm begging you to help him. We'll be in your debt if you do."

"Alright, I'll help him," she snapped irritably. "But give me back my phone. I have other patients, you know. The clinic might need to get in touch with me. And don't worry, I promise not to call 911. Not unless he takes a turn for the worse. Then all bets are off. I'm not going to let a man die on me because of some stupid gang war."

Jesse reluctantly pulled the phone from his jacket and handed it back to her. "Tell us what to do," he said.

"First, we need to get his pain level under control before I try to clean the wound." She rummaged through her medical bag and found only animal medication. Not even a bottle of ibuprofen. "He needs something stronger than what I have. These medications aren't approved for human use."

"We might be able to help you with that." Jesse motioned to the big man who was still guarding the front door. "Get the stuff, Rocco," he ordered. Rocco hurried out of the room and came back a minute later with two large grocery bags. He dumped the contents of both bags onto the coffee table.

"Good heavens!" Kendra exclaimed as bottles of prescription vials rolled around the table. She picked them up and read the labels: codeine, hydrocodone, morphine, Percocet, Vicodin, Oxycotin, Ativan, Xanax, Valium. Upon closer inspection, she noticed the labels included names of people who obviously weren't standing in the room. She recognized one name, Rosa Smith, a little old lady who called her a couple of times a year to come out and check her horse's hoofs.

"Where did you get these?" Kendra demanded, knowing the answer before she asked. The black market for painkillers wasn't exactly a big secret.

Jesse had the decency to clear his throat and look away before answering. "Some of the elderly people on fixed incomes in the community need cash, so we buy their unused medications." He shrugged as if it wasn't a big deal. "They would just flush them down the toilet or throw them away anyway. It's a win-win situation. For everybody."

"You buy them to resell on the black market," Kendra stated. She continued cleaning Flint's wound while she talked. "To junkies? To people hooked on painkillers?" The thought was horrifying.

"No, not necessarily," Jesse answered. "Quite frequently it seems we have a need for them ourselves. Like now."

Kendra let out a short humorless laugh and rolled her eyes. "I can well imagine." She chose the strongest painkiller in the pile and shook out three pills. "Can someone get a glass of water? I need to get these pills in him before I try to remove the bullet and stitch him up. It's going to hurt like hell and he'll need something strong to take the edge off."

Kendra leaned over and placed the back of her hand against Flint's forehead. She tried and failed to ignore the faint whiff of cologne that held a sexy hint of heat and leather.

"His name is Flint?" she asked for clarification.

Tom nodded.

"Flint! Wake up." She shook him gently, attempting to bring him to long enough to swallow the pills. "Come on buddy! You need to open your eyes so I can give you something for the pain. Then I'll knock you out again the best I can."

His eyes flickered for a moment then closed again. "Flint! Open your eyes," she coaxed. Suddenly, his eyes opened and she stared into the greenest eyes she'd ever seen; tantalizingly deep and penetrating. She hesitated for a moment, completely caught off guard. "That's it. Now open your mouth. I'm going to give you some pills and then I want you to swallow a couple sips of water."

Beads of sweat popped out on his forehead and slid down his face as he fought against the pain to stay conscious. "Someone get me a cold rag!" she yelled. The men scattered, eager to do something to help.

Kendra placed her hand behind his neck and propped him up a little. Flint opened his mouth wide enough for her to place the pills on his tongue. She held the glass to his lips and encouraged him to drink. "Don't choke. Make sure you swallow all three pills. Trust me, you'll be glad for it later."

Flint opened his eyes again for a split second, making contact with hers for an instant before sagging heavily against her.

"He's out again," Kendra said. "I need to scrub my hands and put on a pair of gloves. Then I'll need a couple of you guys to hold him down in case he comes to again while I'm working on him. Let's do this as fast as we can while he's unconscious. It will be much easier on him that way."

She worked quickly to clean the wound and remove the bullet. He was lucky. The injury was bad, but it could have been so much worse, even lethal if the bullet had landed just a few inches lower. Flint twitched and jerked in pain while she worked, but he didn't regain consciousness. Once the wound was cleaned to her satisfaction, she deftly stitched him up with the supplies from her bag. After bandaging his arm, she walked into the kitchen to throw away her gloves and wash her hands.

Jesse followed behind her. "Someone needs to make sure he gets the painkillers every three hours," she instructed him. "Don't wait for the pain to hit him first. You have to stay ahead of it. Also, if at all possible try to get him to eat a few bites of something so the painkillers don't make him sick. Give me your phone number and I'll call to check on him in the morning. Obviously you already have my number."

Jesse tucked his hands into his pockets before speaking. "Dr. Shaw, we have another problem," he said. "While you were working on Flint, Tom got a call from one of our other club members in town. The Liberators hit us in two places at once. They threw a Molotov cocktail through the window of my younger brother's tattoo parlor. Luckily, nobody was hurt. The authorities are there now asking a lot of questions that Sam doesn't know how to answer. We need to get back to town to take care of it before things escalate further." He let out a long breath. "We all have to go. Now."

Kendra stared at him in shock then threw up her hands in disbelief. "You're all going to go and leave him here by himself? What if he gets sick and throws up or goes into shock? He's unconscious! Someone needs to stay here to look after him. I don't think you understand how serious his injury is."

"I was really hoping you might be able to do that. You know, just stay here for the night and take care of him. You would know what to do if something went wrong. And with your expertise, you could take much better care of him than we could anyway."

Kendra's mouth opened then closed. Was he insane? What the hell was he thinking? That she would be willing to drop everything and hang out overnight in a secluded cabin with a criminal she didn't know? Yeah right, like that would happen in a million years. If they wanted someone to look after him, they could call one of their groupies.

Kendra was already shaking her head. "Look, this is not my problem and definitely not my responsibility. I did what you asked because it was an emergency situation. I fixed his wound and stitched him up. Any other person in their right mind would've called both 911 and the cops. You're asking way too much from me."

She glanced over at Tom, who was sitting silently at the kitchen table. "I know I owe you for rescuing that dog and bringing him in, but come on. This is crazy. You've crossed so far over the line here already.

I'm not kidding when I say I could very well lose my license if someone found out about this."

Jesse nodded gravely as she spoke. "I know what we're asking. We all do. That's why I'm willing to make it worth your while. Have you heard of the charity ride the Steel Infidels always put on in the spring?"

Kendra shrugged. "Not really, but go ahead." Personally, she'd always wondered if motorcycle gang charity drives were scams. Or at the very least if the gangs were skimming most of the donations off the top. She'd bet good money they were.

"Our club's bylaws allow us to choose any charity we want to donate the funds to," Jesse explained. "Basically it's a goodwill gesture on our part for the community. So I have a proposition for you. What if we agreed to donate the money from the ride this year to the Shaw Wildlife Center in exchange for your help?"

"Seriously?" Kendra answered, suddenly much more interested. "How much money do you usually raise on a charity drive?"

"Twenty thousand minimum. Think of how far that would go in your center. Last year we wrote a check to the children's burn unit for twenty-three thousand dollars."

Whoa! Kendra's mind started churning. Twenty thousand dollars would take the center out of the red. The wildlife rehabilitation center was currently funded solely by donations and by her vet practice that shared the same building. There were times when the center barely had enough money for raw meat for the carnivores, much less any specialized housing facilities.

She thought of all the things twenty thousand dollars could do for the center. A donation that large would help build a huge outdoor aviary for the orphaned and injured raptors that came in every year. Plus the money might even cover the cost of a deer facility to allow the baby fawns to acclimate to the weather before being released back into the wild.

On one hand, she absolutely loathed the thought of getting involved with a motorcycle gang up to their necks in illegal activities. On the other hand, the money would help feed a lot of animals when baby animal season rolled around in the spring.

This wasn't the first time Kendra had been faced with difficult choices where animals were concerned. And this time, like every other time, no matter the consequences, she chose the side of the animals. Right or wrong, it didn't matter.

She didn't hesitate. "Okay, I'll stay," she said firmly. "How long do you need me?"

Jesse heaved a long sigh of relief. She noticed he was quite a handsome man in a bad boy sort of way. Though not as devilishly good-looking as his injured brother.

"As long as you can spare," he replied. "Flint needs to stay here where he is safe and out of sight for a couple of days at least."

"You're lucky it's a Friday and I don't have any big plans. A few of my staff are on duty at the clinic all weekend to take care of the animals, but I'll need to be back at work on Monday morning. Three nights at the absolute maximum and that's it. No more. Two would be better. One of you fellows better be back up here bright and early to check on him no later than Monday morning."

Jesse reached out to shake her hand again. "Thank you so much, Dr. Shaw. You don't know how much this means to us. Especially to me."

Kendra shook his hand and dropped it quickly. "Let's get something straight," she interrupted. "I'm not doing it for you. I'm doing it for the wildlife clinic. As long as you come through with your end of the deal, we'll all be fine. Don't even think about screwing me over."

"Don't worry, my word is good," Jesse replied.

"Good. Before all of you hightail it out of here, I need you to answer me one more question."

"What's that?"

"How do you know the people who shot Flint, the Liberators, aren't going to come up here looking for him? If they knew your route before, wouldn't it be plausible they would know where to find him now?"

"Don't worry," Jesse replied. "This is a safe house. Nobody outside our club knows about it. You'll both be safe here, I promise. I wouldn't leave him here unprotected if I didn't believe that."

"A safe house?" Kendra echoed. She didn't realize such things existed in real life but then again, she didn't make it a habit to hang around people who might need one. "Who owns it?"

"A man who owes us a big favor. That's all you need to know. Trust me, the least you know about our business, the better off you'll be."

"No doubt," she agreed.

Kendra followed the men out the back door of the house and watched as they climbed onto their motorcycles and roared off in single file. She waited until they were out of sight before walking back to her truck. After unlocking the glove box, she pulled out a pistol and the extra box of bullets she always kept stowed there.

Kendra hoped Jesse was right about the Liberators not knowing where to find Flint. In any case, the pistol made her feel a little safer. On second thought, so would the shotgun hidden underneath the front seat.

Looking like a gunslinger from the Wild West, she carried both guns into the house and locked the door behind her. After placing both guns on a table by the door, she sent up a small prayer that the weekend would go by quickly and without incident.

3

Kendra's cell phone beeped incessantly, waking her up out of a restless sleep and alerting her to the fact that it was time to give Flint his pain medication once again. She yawned and checked the time. Three a.m. She was already exhausted and the night wasn't even half over yet.

Thankfully, Flint had slept peacefully most of the evening and into the early hours of the morning. As for herself, sleep was harder to come by. Eventually she dozed off, curled up close by him in a reclining chair.

She watched Flint's sleeping figure sprawled out on the couch and couldn't help but wonder how he got involved with the Steel Infidels in the first place. His brother Jesse would probably have been a huge influence on him. And she remembered Jesse mentioning a younger brother Sam, who ran a tattoo parlor. So there were at least three brothers in the gang, maybe more.

Kendra had always been a person who tried not to judge others without knowing their circumstances first. For some reason, this time it was proving difficult. Sure, the economy was tough and jobs were hard to come by, but in no way did that justify breaking the law or selling drugs.

She wondered how low Flint was willing to go to make money. Steal cars? Cheat old people? Sell drugs? Murder? Who knew? These were the kind of questions that were none of her business.

Kendra stretched her tired muscles and walked into the kitchen. Leaning against the counter, she checked her cell phone for the hundredth time out of habit. No calls. Too bad she didn't know Flint's last name or she would already have checked out one of the numerous mug shot websites. She suspected they would be able to tell her plenty about how many times he had been arrested and for what. If she really wanted to know.

After eating a bowl of the butter pecan ice cream she'd found in the freezer, she walked back into the living room and turned on the lamp. Kneeling beside the couch, she whispered, "Flint, wake up. It's time for your pain medication." She gently touched his uninjured shoulder. "Flint."

Before she had a chance to react, he grabbed her with his good arm, dragging her across his body and pinning her tightly underneath him.

"Who the fuck are you?" he growled, using his body weight to hold her down. "Who sent you? The Liberators? Is that who you're working for?"

"What? Get off me!" She pushed futilely against his chest and tried not to reinjure his arm. Oh dear God! He was probably hallucinating from the morphine. Maybe she shouldn't have given him so many without knowing his medical history. Maybe she shouldn't have agreed to this ridiculous arrangement in the first place. This was bad.

"Flint, it's me, Dr. Kendra Shaw," she answered, trying to get him to focus. From her medical training, she knew people who were hallucinating or on drugs could be very dangerous. "Don't you remember what happened? You were shot and I fixed you up. Your brother Jesse was here. Don't you remember riding up here on your bike with Jesse and Tom?"

Flint's green eyes glittered dangerously. He shook his head as if he didn't believe her. "You're lying," he said, tightening his grip on her wrist, which he held above her head.

"Flint! Listen to me. You're going to hurt yourself. And me. Let me go." She stared back into his eyes, willing him to snap out of it. She couldn't ignore the feeling of his hard muscles suddenly pressed against her breasts. She saw the uncertainty flicker in his eyes. She ought to do something to stop him, she told herself frantically.

Kendra's hands settled on his chest and instead of pushing against him, she grew conscious of the thudding beat of his heart beneath her fingers. She realized hers was probably racing just as fast. A tremor slid down her spine. She stared up at him with wide eyes, speared by the sudden burning gleam in his gaze. What she saw there unnerved her and yet still she couldn't pull away.

Damn! What the hell was wrong with her? One look into those damn green eyes and he made her feel weak with a longing that both shamed and excited her. Why was this man getting to her? Even as his head began to descend slowly on hers, Kendra made no move to protest.

"I don't care who you are," he added huskily, right before his mouth swooped down and crushed hers.

Flint's kiss hit her like a tidal wave. The taste of his lips gave her a mad rush so intense that for a second she forgot how to breathe. Without hesitation, she slid her open palms down his back, feeling the strong muscles underneath her fingers. She knew this was so wrong. Touching him, feeling his skin beneath her hands. But for one brief moment in her life, she wanted to simply feel without thinking about the consequences.

Just one time.

What possible harm could come from that?

Kendra's eyes fluttered closed and she made the biggest mistake yet; she parted her lips for his probing tongue. She heard his throaty growl of pleasure as her tongue clashed with his and sensed how his muscled body hardened in response against her ample softness. She responded back with a fiery heat of her own, knowing he probably wouldn't remember any of it in the morning.

This hot, sexy man wanted her.

The instant the thought registered in her mind, he abruptly broke the kiss and rolled off her. Kendra stared blankly at him, her mind still muddled by the kiss and her reaction to it.

He sat up and winced in pain. "Jesus Christ! Why didn't you stop me?" He rubbed a hand through his black hair. "For a moment there I was confused. I thought...I don't know what the hell I thought. Shit! My arm hurts like a son of a bitch. Where's my bike? And my crew? I need to get back to the clubhouse." He tried to stand up and swayed unsteadily on his feet.

Kendra scurried off the couch and slid an arm around his waist. "Hang on, buddy. Sit back down before you fall and hurt yourself."

He brushed her hand off him. "Where's Jesse? I need to go."

"Jesse is fine," Kendra replied. "He left earlier this afternoon with the rest of the guys. Everybody is okay. You were the only one who was hurt. Now, sit back down. Please." She guided him back to the couch and pulled the blanket up around his bare chest.

Flint searched her face as if he was trying to put the pieces all together. "Are you a doctor?" he asked.

"Sort of," she answered. "I'm a veterinarian. I own the Shaw Vet Clinic and the Shaw Wildlife Center in town."

His forehead creased in a sudden scowl. "I don't understand. Why are you here? Are you somebody's old lady?"

She laughed out loud at the absurdity of the question, knowing he wasn't insulting her age but merely asking if she belonged to one of the other club members. "Old lady? Are you nuts?" She waved her hand down her full-figured body. "Do I strike you as the type of woman who would be some motorcycle guy's old lady? That would be a quick way to throw eight years of college down the drain."

After looking her over from head to toe, Flint frowned and shook his head. "No."

"Well, that's good, I guess," she said. "You had me worried there for a minute. Here's what happened while you were out cold."

Kendra quickly gave him a brief rundown of how Tom had lured her there under false pretenses. "You were injured pretty badly. So I'm your nurse for the weekend," she finished. "Whether you like it or not."

"I don't need a fucking nurse," Flint muttered before leaning back against the sofa cushions and closing his eyes.

Kendra sighed. Flint was hot and sexy as hell, but he was clearly going to be a royal pain in the ass. "I can see that, tough guy. Now, swallow these damn pain meds and go back to sleep so I can get some rest."

He didn't answer since he was already dead to the world again.

"The things I do for animals," she muttered, shaking her head at the fine mess she was in.

4

Flint opened his eyes and tried to focus. Shit! Why did he hurt all over like a fucking linebacker had thrown him against a brick wall? He pushed himself upright and breathed deeply to fight back the waves of nausea rolling over him.

He tried to recall the previous day's events, but his memory was a little fuzzy. The crew had ridden over to a neighboring county to discuss setting up a buy with a distributor for a huge shipment of alcohol. Shelby County, where the MC was based, remained one of the few two hundred or so dry counties in the entire United States.

Local politicians refused to approve beer, wine, or liquor licenses to any business inside the county limits. This opened up a golden opportunity for groups like the MC to become modern day bootleggers and make tons of cash - if they were willing to break the law in the process. The MC considered the rewards to be worth the risk.

Over the years, they had grown the business and now kept a steady supply of customers stocked with their favorite alcoholic beverage. The customers never questioned it or even seemed to mind paying the fifty percent mark up. Considering the cost of gas and the fifty mile round trip to the nearest liquor store, the citizens of Shelby County were getting quite a deal. Or so the MC crew members always told them.

Flint's arm throbbed. The last thing he remembered clearly was riding alongside Rocco as the group cruised two-by-two back through the valley. Gunshots had come out of nowhere, with the loud booms reverberating off the sides of the mountains. Then a searing white-hot pain had exploded in his upper left arm, tearing through the muscle.

Instinctively, they'd all sped up and kept riding, knowing to stop meant certain death. Flint hadn't let on to the others that he was hurt until they'd made it safely through to the other side of the valley.

Flint remembered pulling over and arguing with Jesse on the side of the road. Jesse wanted to take him to the hospital. Flint knew that not only would the emergency room personnel be required to report the shooting, but there was a chance whoever was after them would show up at the hospital as well. The last thing the MC needed was to be involved in a shootout in a public building where innocent people could be caught in the crossfire.

For once in his life, Jesse had listened to him. Instead of taking him to the hospital, he had called in a big favor and secured the safe house instead.

Everything was a blur after they'd arrived at the cabin. Flint didn't remember stowing his bike away or even walking inside. Not being able to recall the previous night's events made him uneasy. He didn't like feeling vulnerable.

He glanced around the small room for his leather jacket, which held his cell phone and his gun. It was missing, along with his shirt. After taking another deep breath, he stood up and waited a moment for the dizziness to pass.

Holding on to the furniture for support, he made his way carefully across the room toward the kitchen. He figured there had to be a phone somewhere in the cabin that he could use to call Jesse and find out what was going on. When he reached the doorway to the kitchen, he stopped in confusion.

"Who are you?" he asked, staring in shock at the full-figured curvy woman in tight jeans and an even tighter white sweater peeking into the refrigerator.

Kendra whirled around and rolled her eyes. "Oh no! Don't tell me we're going to go through this again? Oh my God!" She threw up her hands in frustration. "I can't believe I got myself into this mess! Jeez, you'd think I gave you a date rape drug or something the way you're acting." She put her hands on her hips. "Just so you know, we've been through all this once already in the middle of the night. Here's the short version this time. I'm Kendra, your nurse for the weekend. Period. The end. Now stop asking the same old questions and wasting my time." She turned back to the refrigerator and started moving containers around to see what was on the back shelf.

When he didn't move, she glanced back over her shoulder. "And sit down! If you fall, I'm not sure I can pick you up. I can carry a small calf, but a full-size man, dead weight and passed out on the floor might be another story."

Flint didn't argue and instead sank down into a chair at the kitchen table. Little by little, bits and pieces of the previous day's events were starting to come back to him. He reached up and winced in pain when he touched the thick white bandage covering his wound. Through the thick fog in his brain, he vaguely remembered Kendra being at the cabin the night before. "You patched me up?" he asked.

"Yep! Didn't want to," Kendra said. She walked over and pulled out a chair to sit beside him. "I was *persuaded* by your brother, Jesse. Personally, I thought you should've gone to the emergency room. Cleaning up a bullet wound is not something I do every day." She put her elbows on the table and leaned closer to peek at the bandage. "Is there any way I can convince you to go see a doctor this morning? Maybe an urgent care facility would be willing to double check your stitches. It would make me feel a whole lot better if you would. My work will probably leave a big old nasty scar."

Flint leaned back in his chair. "I can't do that."

"No surprise there," Kendra muttered. "Thought it couldn't hurt to ask." She let out a tired breath and stood back up. "Do you want some coffee, Flint? The cabin doesn't have any creamer so it has to be black."

Flint nodded and gave her a small smile. "Thanks. The stronger, the better."

Kendra poured him a steaming cup and placed it in front of him. He watched as she moved around the kitchen, gathering ingredients. Then she cracked a few eggs into a bowl and starting beating them. "Don't worry, the eggs are still good," she explained as if he might be worried she would feed him rotten eggs. "I couldn't find much to work with in the pantry except for a block of cheese and a jar of mushrooms for an omelette. Do you feel up to eating a few bites? Pain medicine can make you feel pretty crappy on an empty stomach." She chatted on nervously while she dumped the mushrooms and chunks of cheese into the eggs.

It suddenly occurred to Flint that she might be afraid of him. He wondered how Jesse had convinced her into staying the night. His brother wasn't past using strong-arm tactics to get what he wanted or needed.

"So do you want to try to eat something?" Kendra asked again. She threw a quick glance at him before looking away quickly.

To Flint's surprise, he was hungry and beginning to feel a little better with the exception of the burning, throbbing pain in his arm. "Yeah, I can eat," he mumbled.

"Really?" She suddenly smiled at him; a genuine smile that lit up her whole face and caught him by surprise. "That's good. I hated pumping you full of all of that medicine on an empty stomach. I can't take the stuff myself. After breakfast I'll give you a couple more pain pills. After all, it's not like we're going to run short or anything."

He caught the hint of sarcasm in her voice. "What do you mean?" he asked, afraid of the answer.

"Your pals left behind bags and bags full of prescription bottles for you."

He closed his eyes and groaned inwardly at her comment. The club shouldn't have involved her. No matter how badly hurt he was, there was no excuse for dragging an innocent woman into their problems.

Even worse, what made them think she could be trusted? Jesse had better have a good explanation for bringing her into the situation.

The sooner he got the hell out of there and back to town, the better.

"Where's my bike?" he asked casually. "I hope it's not outside in the sleet."

Kendra poured the omelette mixture into the hot pan and swirled it around before answering. "It's in the back. It's covered and should be fine." She shot him a curious glance. "You aren't thinking of leaving, are you?"

"Yeah, I need to get back to town. My crew needs me."

She flipped the omelette over then slid it onto a plate. "Here you go." She handed it to him along with a fork. She looked at him for a long moment. "Before you get any bright ideas, I'm going to go ahead and tell you that I've hidden your keys."

He started to protest, but she held up a hand to stop him.

"I don't want to hear it. I risked my vet license to help you. I also pumped you full of narcotics to take away your pain. I'm not letting you roar out of here on your bike with all those drugs that weren't prescribed to you floating around in your system. Besides, how are you going to handle a bike with your arm in that condition? Not to mention the sleet. I'm sure the roads are slippery this morning."

Flint was surprised, shocked really. He wasn't used to being told no, especially after rejoining the Steel Infidels. Most people went to great lengths not to cross the MC. Maybe she didn't realize what he was capable of. He slowly placed his fork beside his plate and fixed her with a cool stare, hoping to intimidate her into backing down.

It didn't work.

She didn't even break his gaze. Instead, all she did was look back at him with those soft eyes and blink with those long eyelashes of hers.

Well hell! This might be harder than he thought.

"I'll be fine driving," he said. He shrugged as if it didn't matter. "And I'm not going to take any more of the pain pills, so..."

"So nothing. Wait until they start wearing off and we'll talk about this again. You probably don't remember, but I gave you the last one three hours ago. You're going to be hurting very soon, but hey, it's up to you, tough guy. Can't say I didn't warn you. Either way, you're not getting your keys back until I feel like giving them to you."

Kendra turned and went back to making another omelette. Flint smothered a grin at her unexpected sauciness and took the opportunity to admire her ample backside while her head was turned away from him.

He didn't understand all the details yet of exactly who she was and why she was there. The only thing he knew was that the weekend sure as hell wouldn't be boring.

5

After breakfast, Kendra ushered Flint back to the couch to check his wound for infection and to change the bandage. They'd settled into an uneasy truce. Kendra suspected it wouldn't last long. Flint didn't strike her as the type of man who would be happy hanging out doing nothing for the weekend, especially once he found out about the trouble at his brother's tattoo parlor.

Trying to keep him in the cabin was going to be a bitch. Considering his injury, she thought he would be conked out on the couch all weekend. The fact that he wanted to leave so soon undermined her chance of getting the money for the clinic, and that was a big problem. She'd made a deal with Jesse to stay and take care of him until Monday morning, and by God she meant to keep it - one way or the other.

If it ended up being a battle of wills between her and Flint, she didn't have any doubt as to who would come out the victor. Mr. Motorcycle Man didn't have any idea how determined she could be when she set her mind to something. If push came to shove, she could always knock him out with pills.

A desperate action like that would be underhanded and low, her conscience argued. Then again, it would be better than letting an impaired man drive, her sensible side countered back. And if he left, the

Steel Infidels wouldn't have any reason to give her the donation for the clinic.

Not only was she fighting an inner battle with herself, she was also finding it almost impossible to concentrate on wrapping Flint's bandage while he was watching her face so intently.

"Worried about my skills?" she teased. "If you're not, you should be. I tried very hard to explain to your brother that I'm not qualified to treat you."

Flint grinned. He was such a mix of angel and devil when he flashed that white-hot smile. "I'm not worried, darling," he replied, letting the endearment slip off his lips as smooth as butter.

Kendra's eyebrows shot up and she laughed. Aha! So he thought he could charm her into giving him back his keys. Oh yes. She'd met men like Flint before; the kind of men who women fantasized about when they were all alone. The type of man who merely needed to smile to have a girl reaching around to unhook her bra. Kendra didn't doubt that Flint could have a woman unzipping her jeans before she even realized she'd fallen underneath his spell. If she wasn't real careful, it could happen to her too.

It had been a long time since she'd dated anyone special. Sure there had been a casual date here and there, always ending with a quick kiss goodnight and a pissed-off guy standing on her front porch with a closed door in his face.

Casual sex wasn't something she messed around with. To her, it wasn't worth the time or effort to fall into bed with a man she barely knew or even liked. And if they weren't willing to take the time to woo her, and they usually weren't, then so be it. Like her grandmother always said, "there are much worst things than being alone." After watching some of her girlfriends get cheated on or in miserable marriages, Kendra knew this to be true.

And after all, she had the animals to keep her company and she was plenty busy enough at the clinic. Most nights she was so tired she hit the bed right after taking a shower. Lonely wasn't a word in her vocabulary, which meant the sexy man flirting with her wouldn't get under her skin, no matter how much she might be physically attracted to him.

"The wound looks good," she said. "You're healing nicely and faster than expected. These stitches are a little crooked though."

"Does that mean I'm free to go, Doc?" he asked, flexing his arm.

"Nope," she replied firmly. "Not yet."

"What does your husband think about you staying here with me?"

Kendra laughed. "Lucky for you, I don't have a husband. If there was, I don't think he would be pleased, do you?"

Flint gave her another rakish grin. "Probably not. If you were my wife, I wouldn't let you out of my sight."

Kendra rolled her eyes at him. "There you go again. Have you heard from Jesse?"

"I left him a message. I'm sure he'll call me back as soon as he can."

Kendra taped a new bandage to his arm and started to stand up. Flint grabbed her hand, keeping her on eye level with him.

"I need to ask you something," he said, suddenly serious. "Did I kiss you last night or was that an erotic dream?"

Kendra's face burned with both shock and humiliation. She couldn't have been more mortified that Flint remembered their kiss. And even worse, her reaction to him. She had been so sure he wouldn't remember it. God! This was so embarrassing.

At first she thought about lying. Then she decided brushing it off would be the best thing to do.

"Yes, you did," she answered. "But you were whacked out of your head, so it's fine." Kendra waved her hand as if it didn't mean anything. "No big deal. It's okay. I'm sure you thought I was someone else."

Flint studied her face carefully for a moment then shook his head. "No, I don't think so. I wouldn't have thought you were someone else."

"Oh? And why's that?"

"Because there is no one else."

Before Kendra could reply, Flint's phone rang in his pocket, effectively cutting off their conversation.

"Jesse?" Flint answered. "What's going on? Is everybody okay?"

Kendra grabbed her overnight bag from the table and headed for the bathroom to give Flint some privacy for his call.

Flint waited until Kendra was in the bathroom and out of hearing range. "Jesus Christ, Jesse!" he said tersely into the phone. "What the hell were you thinking bringing Dr. Shaw into this? We don't even know her!"

"Calm down, Flint," Jesse answered. "Look, we didn't have a choice. You were unconscious and bleeding all over the place. What were we supposed to do? Tom wrapped your arm up the best he could but we didn't know how to get the bullet out. We're not a bunch of fucking nurses! What if we had nicked an artery? We couldn't get the bleeding to stop and calling Dr. Shaw was the best idea we could come up with. You don't realize how bad it was yesterday. You weren't even conscious half the time. And don't forget, you're the one who insisted on not going to the hospital in the first goddamn place!"

Flint ran a restless hand through his hair. "I know, alright. I know. You don't have to remind me. But come on, she's a well-known veterinarian in town. Bardsville only has two vets, so you can bet everybody in the whole damn county knows her. Besides maybe the mayor, would there have been anybody with a higher profile you could have chosen to involve in our mess? And now that she knows about the safe house, you can bet it's not safe any longer. "

"She's cool, okay? Trust me. I can read people. After all, she fixed you up and then agreed to stay. How bad could she be?"

Flint snorted. "She told me how you tricked her. The only thing I don't get is how you convinced her to stay. I can tell by the way she looks at me that she thinks I'm a lowlife criminal. She might even be afraid of me. I make her very nervous."

"Nervous? Really?" Jesse seemed surprised. "She didn't strike me as the nervous type at all. Just the opposite in fact. What the hell did you do to her?"

"Me? Nothing!"

"I can tell you Dr. Shaw wasn't the least bit intimidated by me and the crew, so you must be doing something weird to freak her out."

Flint started to argue and decided to drop it. "So how did you convince her to stay?" he asked again.

"I offered to donate the proceeds from the charity run in the spring to the wildlife clinic. She wasn't real keen on hanging around until I made it worth her while. If you take the time to think about it, you'll see it's a good deal all the way around. By giving Dr. Shaw the donation this year, we're basically buying her help and her silence in the future. Understand?"

Jesse was right. The plan was a smart one. His older brother was president of the motorcycle club for a reason. "Yeah, I get it," Flint said after a moment "That was a smart move. You want to tell me what I'm supposed to do here all weekend though? I need to get back to town and she hid my damn keys."

Jesse burst out laughing. "She's afraid of you, huh? Sounds like Dr. Shaw has your number, little brother. From what I've seen, you should be afraid of her. Seriously, you need to sit your damn ass in a chair and stay put. At least for a couple of days until we can figure all this out. I have enough on my plate right now without worrying about you. At least the Liberators don't know about the safe house."

"Did they do something else? What's going on?" Flint knew his brother well enough to know he was keeping something from him.

"They tossed a Molotov cocktail through the tattoo shop window. The good news is they're idiots and the bottle didn't break on impact so there wasn't a firebomb. The bad news is the front window was smashed and the cops were there all last night asking too many questions."

"Fuck! Is Sam okay?"

"Yeah, he was in the back office with a customer when it came through the window. There's some damage to clean up, but nothing we can't handle without you. So I'm telling you to stay put. I'm not asking. Not as your brother, but as president of the MC. Do not leave the cabin until I okay it. You hear me?"

"I hear you," Flint finally muttered.

"Good. By the way, how is your arm feeling this morning?"

"Hurts like a motherfucker. Thanks for asking," Flint added sarcastically.

"I figured. Don't fuck this up with Dr. Shaw. We need her on our side, so play nice. I'll call you soon."

"You do that," Flint answered before hanging up.

Don't fuck it up with Dr. Shaw.

He frowned. The warning had come a little too late.

6

Kendra dropped her bag on the bathroom floor and dug through it for a fresh change of clothes. Luckily, she always kept a spare set or two in her truck. After years of delivering breeched calves, she'd learned an extra change of clean clothes could come in handy. After being up most of the night checking on Flint, she desperately needed a hot shower to help her unwind and loosen up her tired muscles.

Minutes later, she stood under the shower spray, letting the hot water run over her body. No matter how hard she tried, she couldn't shake the image of Flint's face lowering to kiss her. Or the feel of his taut muscles under the Steel Infidels tattoo that stretched across his back and shoulders. Kendra closed her eyes as she replayed the kiss they'd shared in the middle of the night.

Even now, she couldn't understand her strange reaction to Flint. Had she no pride? How in the world had she given in so easily to Flint's kiss...his touch? Maybe it was from lack of sleep, she reasoned. Or more likely the fact that she hadn't been that physically close to a hot, virile male in a very long time. If that was the case, she seriously needed to get out more.

She had acted spontaneously and completely out of character. It was a mistake she wouldn't be making again. After all, she was an educated woman and respected in the small community. What would her staff or clients think if they knew she was making out with a stranger in the middle of the night? And not just any stranger but a member of a motorcycle gang for heaven's sake!

As long as she kept her cool and didn't let it happen again, it would go down in her mind as a temporary lack of judgement. It was understandable, she told herself, considering the stressful situation the MC had placed her under. Maybe she was having a touch of Stockholm Syndrome or something. All she needed to do was keep her distance from Flint and not let him get to her. Piece of cake. She could do it.

Feeling a little bit better about everything and much more in control again, she stepped out of the shower and reached for a towel hanging on the rack.

Kendra bit back a loud yelp.

"Flint! What the hell? You ever heard of knocking?"

Flint stood in the open doorway and appeared to have been there for a while. He was leaning casually against the frame as he regarded her with narrowed eyes.

How had she not heard him? How long had he been standing there watching her through the sliding shower doors without saying one word? She hastily wrapped the towel around her body and tucked in the ends.

He broke the silence at last with a mild-toned, "Need help drying off?" He straightened his lithe frame from the door.

Kendra had no intention of responding and started to walk past him. She jumped back when his arm came up, but it was only to prop it across the doorjamb so that he blocked her exit.

"Do you mind?" she asked steadily, her eyes fierce as they held his.

"No, I don't mind," he replied, intentionally misunderstanding her request to move his arm. "I'll spend hours drying you off if you want me to. Not a problem. At all. I have all the time in the world."

He smiled suddenly, a devastating smile that melted the hard lines of his jaw and made his eyes light up. Kendra really wished he wouldn't look at her like that. She didn't know what to think when those intense green eyes skimmed over her body, missing nothing.

It took superhuman effort not to drop the towel right then and wrap her arms around his neck. To run her hands down his chest and over his shoulders. To trace every stroke of the Steel Infidels tattoo on his back with her tongue.

Good Lord! She refused to even think about how much she wanted to be thrown down and taken hard and fast by him on any available surface, including the tile bathroom floor.

It made no sense. She normally had a whole lot more self-control. He was making her insane. She'd made it to the top of her class in veterinary school and took great pride in being a structured, disciplined person in both work and her personal life. Now Flint was gazing at her and it was like he could tell exactly the effect he was having on her. And that made Kendra want to flee from the room and him as fast as humanly possible.

Maybe her raw desire showed in her eyes. Or maybe he was used to women falling all over him. It could be that he sensed the tingling shiver that went through her whenever he looked at her.

"Why do I make you so nervous?" he suddenly asked. "At first I thought you might be afraid of me, but that's not it, is it? Jesse said you weren't the least bit intimidated by my crew and they're much scarier than I am."

A moment later, he lifted a hand to smooth a knuckle across her cheek. Kendra's strangled breath caught in her chest.

"You're very beautiful," he murmured very thoughtfully, those eyes gliding over her face. "Eyes the prettiest I've ever seen." His words were simply hypnotic. She could only watch, immobilized, as his head slanted low, aiming for her mouth.

Kendra could not believe this was about to happen. Again. So much for resisting him.

But God help her, she couldn't stop it. She couldn't do more than melt into him as he devoured her lips. His tongue began a slow, sensual assault the moment she let him into her mouth. Kendra moaned and trembled when she felt his hands move under the towel and cup her ass. His touch was possessive, heated, famished. He cupped the curves of her ass and tugged her tighter against his hard, overpowering masculinity.

Their lips crashed together so hard Kendra knew her lips would feel the bruises later. Her fingers dug into his hair and rifled through the silken strands. But then moments later her senses returned and she gasped, letting go of his hair and straining against him. He pulled away slowly, resting his hands on her hips as Kendra slowly opened her eyes.

Her eyes were glazed and confused, her sensuous mouth even more swollen and enticing. Kendra was completely losing it. Her gut told her Flint was a man with the potential to lead her deep into forbidden territory, and he was proving her right with every passing second.

He seemed to see right through her to her fears and worries, and he gently touched her swollen bottom lip as he said in a gentle tone, "It's all right, doc. Relax. It's not my style to force myself on women. Which means the next time I touch you or kiss you, you're not going to want me to stop. When that happens, I'll start here," he murmured thickly.

Kendra looked down and gasped as his fingertips grazed over her now rock-hard nipples through the towel. She'd never felt them get so big and stiff, aching with need. Her own body was betraying her. She arched at his barely-there caress across her breasts.

She lifted widened eyes to his face and found his gaze fixed on her heaving breasts, heavy now and filled with want that she was sure he could detect even beneath the terrycloth towel. She met his gaze. She felt one thing, but her brain told her another. She couldn't let this happen. Not now. Not ever. This wasn't her style and he wasn't her type of man.

"I'm sorry," Kendra said before hurrying out of the room, embarrassed once again for giving in so easily. Whatever was happening between them, it was opening a side to her she'd never known; a submissive part that found it so easy to yield to a man with the will and passion strong enough to control her every response. Flint was that kind of man. She knew it instinctively. The knowledge both scared and thrilled her to the bone.

Flint wondered if Kendra had any idea how difficult it was for him to let her go. The luscious feel of her ass in his hands as he'd kissed her had made his brain almost short-circuit. What was it about her?

He hadn't meant to be a peeping Tom and spy on her in the shower like a pervert. His intention had only been to ask her something through the door. But when he found it slightly ajar, he couldn't help pushing it open. Once he'd caught sight of her naked body behind the shower doors, his feet refused to turn and walk away.

All he could do was stand there completely mesmerized and watch as she soaped her heavy breasts and between her legs; all the places he would pleasure with his tongue if he ever got the chance. His reaction to her was immediate and overwhelming, his erection so painfully hard he thought he was going to explode.

He'd wanted her the moment he'd opened his eyes, delirious with pain, and found her leaning over him. He'd already kissed her twice, and who the hell knew what else he was capable of doing if she kept looking at him the way she did? Hell, sex was all he could think about since he'd set eyes on her. When she had stepped out of the shower wrapped in only a towel, it took every bit of control he possessed not to rip it off her body, bend her over the bathroom counter, and take her from behind.

There was no doubt that this woman brought out his primal streak, and holding back was making him feel like he could implode at any moment. She didn't have a clue as to her effect on him. He'd meant it when he told her she was beautiful. She really was even though she was different from his usual preference, which leaned toward petite, blonde and thin.

He loved the way she wore her hair, the wild, long dark mane framing her features. There was a calm intelligence about her that turned him on along with that curvy, full-figured body of hers. Not to mention her heavy breasts and the wide hips that knew how to fill out a tight pair of jeans. She was tall for a woman but only barely reached his shoulder. He loved cupping her large ass. Damn, that was one piece of her he could certainly form an obsession over.

And Kendra wasn't like any of the groupie bimbos that hung around the clubhouse. She didn't mind letting a man know that she possessed a mind of her own. He'd noticed that first thing when she told him about the keys. He would never let her know it, but that single action turned him on as much as it pissed him off. She was most definitely a woman of strong character who wasn't afraid to speak her mind.

The more he thought about her, the angrier he grew inside. Whatever attraction he felt for Dr. Kendra Shaw, he needed to get over it fast. A nice, decent woman like her would never go for a man like him. Maybe she would have liked the man he was once striving to be six months ago. A man with integrity and principles. Certainly not the way he was now and would probably always be.

Nothing more than a common outlaw.

It took a while for Kendra to work up the nerve to join Flint in the kitchen. He was seated at the small dining table enjoying a second cup of coffee. He looked up but didn't speak when she walked past him to the coffee maker.

"Flint, about what happened earlier..." she began and couldn't continue.

Flint raised his eyebrows. "You mean in the bathroom?" he asked innocently.

Kendra turned away from him to look out the window over the kitchen sink. Sleet was beginning to stick to the trees and power lines. The winter storm was turning out to be worse than predicted.

Flint leaned back in his chair and crossed his arms. "So you want to tell me why you ran out of there like a bat out of hell?"

Kendra ripped a paper towel from the roll and nervously wiped down the edges of the sink. "I don't know. I guess I was afraid of what might happen if I stayed," she replied in a soft voice, unable to meet his intense gaze.

He drew in a sharp breath as if she had slapped him. "You're afraid of me?" he asked incredulously. "Jesus!"

She let out a long sigh and turned to look at him. "No," she replied. "No, of course not," she said more firmly. "I'm not afraid of you, Flint. It was more a matter of being afraid of me...of my doing something rash and out of character."

"And that's a problem because...?" he asked, his voice calmer now and his eyes suddenly twinkling.

She shrugged, embarrassed by her admission. "I'm not an impulsive person and you caught me off guard. That's all."

He raised his eyebrows, clearly not buying her story.

"Listen, Flint," she continued. "The bottom line is I don't do casual sex. Ever. I need a mental and emotional connection first. And if that's not happening and I'm not feeling it, then the physical part just isn't worth it to me." She smiled to take the sting off of her words. "After all, I'm sure you have plenty of pretty girls hanging around the clubhouse who would be more than happy to have you. What do you call them? Old ladies or something like that? They probably find the tough guy biker act of yours very appealing."

"And what about you, Kendra?" he asked, suddenly serious again. "Do you find it appealing?"

Kendra opened her mouth to lie. To make a joke and laugh it away as if that was the most ridiculous thing she'd ever heard. And normally it would be. She wasn't into the whole dominant alpha male thing. Or had never been in the past. But if she was to be honest with herself, she would admit this time the answer was different.

Hell yes, she found him immensely appealing. The thought of Flint being in control, persuading her to do things sexually beyond her normal comfort zone, was an erotic fantasy. A fantasy she couldn't stop thinking about. It was driving her crazy. She shook her head to clear her thoughts.

"That's not the point," Kendra snapped. She had a feeling Flint knew exactly what she'd been thinking.

He grinned. "What is the point then?"

"Admit it, Flint. You probably wouldn't look twice at me if we weren't holed up in this cabin together. It's obvious I could stand to lose a few pounds and I don't wear makeup or fix my hair in a fancy style. I'm here and I'm convenient. That's all this is. And don't try to tell me I'm your type because I'm not buying it. Not for a second. If we had met at the grocery store or in my vet clinic, I seriously doubt you would give me a second look or ask for my number. That's all I'm saying. I'm not an idiot. And I won't be used for sexual entertainment."

Flint sprang from his chair with the sleekness of a panther and stood inches from her. His eyes flashed with emotion before he grabbed her with his good arm and pulled her close to his chest. She struggled in his grip, but he was too strong for her as he stared deeply into her startled face. Her heartbeat increased alarmingly at his closeness and Kendra wondered if she would ever be immune to his overwhelming magnetism.

"You really believe that?" he demanded angrily. "That I would sleep with you only because you're stuck here with me? That I wouldn't still want you if we'd met another way? How can you not understand how desirable you are to me? Do you know how incredibly difficult it was to let you walk away wrapped only in a towel? When I saw you in the shower, it took my breath away...you took my breath away."

When she didn't answer, he let out a long sigh and abruptly turned her loose.

"I'm sorry, darling," Flint said simply.

Kendra sent him a sharp look. "For what?" she asked.

Flint shrugged and looked away from her. "For getting you involved in all this. You're a smart woman and seem like a really good person. I let Jesse have it over the phone for dragging you into this mess. It never should have happened. And I do wish we could have met in different circumstances. Like you said, in the grocery store or at your vet clinic. Normal every day circumstances." He let out a short laugh and ran a hand through his hair. "Though I'm not sure normal will be showing up any time soon in my life."

He stuck his hands in his jeans pocket and leaned back against the kitchen counter. "I know it could never work," he said quietly before turning and leaving the kitchen.

Kendra stood there for a moment, stunned by his words.

No, a relationship with a man like Flint would never work out.

Or could it?

Did she dare to find out?

7

Flint hurried back inside the cabin and slammed the heavy oak door behind him. He shrugged off his leather jacket before slinging it over a chair by the door. "God! It's cold out there," he said, rubbing his hands together to warm them up. "From what I could tell, the road is completely iced over. Looks like you're going to be stuck with me for a while longer. Even if I had my keys back, I wouldn't make it more than a few feet." He shook his head, sending a few snowflakes flying to the floor.

Kendra was curled up on the sofa with a blanket, checking messages for the vet clinic on her cell phone. She finished typing a text message to one of her clients and hit send. "Or you're stuck with me," she teased back. "However you want to look at it. I have to warn you, I can be pretty cranky at times. Especially if I don't get my morning cup of coffee. Or lunch. Actually, I'm at my most crankiest if I have to skip lunch. Must be low blood sugar or something. "

Flint grinned. "Is that a fact? I'll have to remember to feed you. Maybe I should make a sign that says "Don't Forget to Feed the Tiger." He walked past the table where her pistol and shotgun were partially tucked under her coat. "I've been meaning to ask you about this. Two guns, Kendra? Pardon my pun, but isn't that a little overkill?"

Kendra looked up from her phone and shrugged. "Yeah, maybe," she replied. "I feel better with the guns in here than in the truck. After all, someone shot you. Who is to say they won't come here looking for more?"

Flint frowned, a flash of concern crossing his face before he quickly hid it. Damn! Why hadn't he given more thought to keeping Kendra safe? He always knew there was a chance the Liberators would come after him, but until now the thought hadn't occurred to him that Kendra might be in danger as well. All because of him.

Kendra immediately picked up on his change of mood. "You're worried too," she said perceptibly. "Aren't you?"

"Not really," Flint replied. "There's no need to be worried. Jesse assured me that nobody knows where we are except for our crew, and they can be trusted. Hopefully the temperature will warm up tomorrow and we can both leave. We need to get you back to town so that you can take care of all of those sick animals."

Kendra nodded in agreement. "Isn't that the truth! There's always plenty of work to do. It seems like I never get caught up. There's always another sick animal to examine."

"Mind if I sit with you?" Flint asked, plopping down on the other end of the sofa before she replied. He pointed to her cell phone, where she was rapidly typing another text message. "Is the vet clinic open on weekends?"

Kendra shook her head. "No. Technically, the vet clinic is closed on the weekends. I'm usually on call twenty-four hours a day for emergencies though. If someone needs help with a mama cow that's having a hard time giving birth, they can't wait around for business hours to call me. It's the nature of the business. Long hours and low pay."

"You go out to their house?" Flint realized he didn't like the idea of Kendra going to a stranger's house alone. Especially after seeing how easily she could be tricked into meeting a man about an animal in the middle of nowhere. Didn't she realize there were bad people out there? He felt strangely protective of her but didn't dare show it.

"Barn usually," she corrected. "Or pasture. It's not like they can load the big animals up and bring them to me. It's not so bad though. Spring and summer are the busiest months. In February and March the majority of the calves are born, so that keeps me busy. Then starting in mid-April, all of the orphaned baby birds and mammals start flooding in to the wildlife clinic. From April until the first of October, the clinic is crazy. We work fourteen hours a day, seven days a week."

"Wow! Sounds intense. How do you get paid for that?"

Kendra laughed. "We don't. Not for the wildlife rehab stuff. It's all volunteer based. I have a terrific group of wildlife rehabilitators who come in several days a week to help out. We wouldn't be able to keep the clinic open without them since the clinic survives solely on donations. I assume your brother mentioned he offered to give the clinic the proceeds from the charity ride in the spring?"

"Yeah," Flint answered. "He told me how they practically strong-armed you into taking care of me. I really do feel bad about that," he added sincerely. "We'll make it up to you, I promise. The MC will deliver on the money for your clinic. You have my word. If it had been my decision, I would have found another way. What they did was wrong."

Kendra's eyebrows shot up in surprise that he would go against the MC.

"Jesse and I don't always see eye to eye on how to handle things in the club," Flint explained. "He's more of an 'act first, apologize later' kind of guy, and I'm more strategic. Methodical. We usually end up in the same place, we just choose different ways to get there."

Kendra quietly turned off her phone. "What about your other brother, Sam? What is he like?"

A shadow crossed Flint's face at the mention of his younger brother. "Sam is stubborn, rebellious, and at times completely out of control."

"Sounds like you two don't get along very well."

"We get along well enough, I suppose," Flint replied. "Considering what we've gone through. Sam still harbors some hard feelings toward me over something I did many years ago. It's taking me a long time to regain his trust. I understand so I'm willing to give him as much time as he needs."

Kendra frowned. "What on earth did you do?"

"I left," Flint replied simply. "I turned my back on my brothers, my dad, the MC, and left town. I moved to Atlanta for a few years and got a job. Started a brand new life. Basically, I abandoned everyone when they needed me the most. Sam never forgave me for that."

"What made you leave? Did something happen?"

Flint let out a long breath. He honestly didn't know why he was telling her all this. Normally, he didn't share personal information about himself with anyone. With Kendra, it was almost like once he started talking, he couldn't stop. The words flowed over each other in a hurry to get out.

"We'd lost our mom to breast cancer," he began. "The years before her death were pretty rough on everybody. Watching somebody you love get sicker and weaker by the day...it was hard. Up until then, we had always been a close-knit family. When she passed away, it took a heavy toll on all of us. None of us knew how to deal with our pain. Before long, Dad was drinking too much. Jesse and I started hanging out with the motorcycle club to take our mind off the situation at home. We left Sam all alone to deal with an alcoholic who could be abusive at times. He was only sixteen and too young to join the MC. He felt abandoned when I left town."

Kendra reached over and gave his leg a comforting pat. "I'm sorry about your mom," she said. "And Sam."

"I regret like hell not being there for Sam when he needed me the most," Flint continued. "I was only twenty at the time and barely more than a teenager myself but still...I should've seen that Sam needed his older brothers. Needed me."

"You're being too hard on yourself," Kendra said softly. "Like you said, you were young too. And going through the pain of losing your mom. Taking care of someone else's needs probably wasn't high on your list of priorities at the time."

He shook his head. "That's not a good excuse. Leaving Sam there to deal with Dad was too much for a kid to handle. Thank God for Jesse. When I left, he stepped up like a man and started helping out around the house. He was the brother I should have been."

Flint had never told anyone his feelings of guilt where Sam was concerned. He'd never even admitted it to himself until after the phone call came about Tommy's death. For years, he'd managed to keep a distance between himself, his family, and the MC.

After moving to Atlanta, he'd eventually enrolled in college more as a joke than anything else. He never expected to do so well. Many years later, he found himself working for the Public Defender's office and was quickly on his way to earning a name for himself. Not one time had Flint ever regretted the hard choices he'd made. Not until Tommy's death.

"So what's it like now between you and Sam?"

"Strained." Flint let out a humorless laugh. "Tense most of the time. He resents anything and everything I say or do."

"Jesse said he owned a tattoo parlor."

"Yes, he does. The Liberators hit it last night as well."

"Was there a lot of damage?" Kendra didn't let on that she already knew about the attack.

"Enough," Flint replied. "The plate glass window on the front of the store was broken when they threw the Molotov cocktail through it. That's about it. The bottle didn't explode and ignite a fire, thank God. The Liberators were sending us a message. That's why I'm so eager to get back to town. To help Sam repair the shop and put it back together. Plus it's our primary source of income, so we need to open for business as soon as possible."

Kendra blinked in confusion. "Wait a minute! You said "our" source of income. Are you a tattoo artist too?"

Moment of truth.

In a split second, Flint realized he didn't want her to know the truth about what he did, or used to do, for a living. He didn't want her to know he had been a respected attorney who defended poor clients. For some reason, he felt a compelling need for her to like him as he was now. For what he was now.

Good or bad, it wouldn't be fair to let her believe he was something better than he was.

"I dabble," he replied, a smile playing around his lips. "I can do a pretty mean tat." Which wasn't an outright lie. He'd done hundreds of tattoos in his life. It just wasn't what he had gone to college for four years and then on to law school to learn how to do. Though compared to the money he made as a public defender, he might have been better off doing tattoos from the beginning.

"Have you ever thought about getting one?" he asked casually.

Kendra laughed and shook her head. "I can honestly say that no, I've never considered getting a tattoo. Don't they hurt?"

"Not too bad if the person doing them is experienced and fast."

Flint quickly slid over. Turning her around slightly, he tugged the hem of her sweater up. Kendra jumped when his fingers touched her lower back. He traced an outline slowly, delicately with both hands.

She gasped. "What are you doing?"

"A hummingbird," he murmured thoughtfully. "Small and colorful with its wings outstretched in flight. Delicate and beautiful."

"What?" she asked again as his fingers continued to draw the imaginary hummingbird.

"Let me design a tattoo for you. I'll do something special. And I promise to do it as fast and painless as possible."

"Oh, I don't know," she replied hesitantly. "I don't see myself as a tattoo kind of gal."

He caressed his thumbs over the small of her back once more before removing his hands and pulling the hem of her sweater back down. "Then maybe it's time to start seeing yourself differently, darling," he drawled in that deep Southern accent she was beginning to find irresistible.

Kendra didn't show it, but she was secretly pleased with his suggestion of a hummingbird tattoo. How could Flint possibly know that hummingbirds held a special significance to her? Her recently deceased grandmother adored the tiny birds and had told Kendra to watch for her on the wings of a hummingbird after she died. In her memory, Kendra had hung at least fifty hummingbird feeders on her farm the previous summer, spread out among all of the flowering bushes and trees.

Flint settled back on his side of the couch and stretched out his long legs. He tapped the toes of his black leather boots together. "Do you live close to the clinic?"

Kendra smiled. "I own a place not too far from town," she replied. "I live in an old farm house with a big front porch. The house is tiny, barely big enough for one person. I love it though. In the evenings, I can sit on my porch and watch the sunrise go down over the mountains. It's relaxing."

"Do you have a lot of pets? I bet you have about ten. Or twenty."

"Believe it or not, I don't have any pets of my own. The hours are so long at the clinic and I never know when I'm going to get called out on emergencies. There's always a baby or injured animal of some kind that I end up dragging home with me most nights. What about you? Do you live close by?"

"I live about ten miles away. In a big house with Jesse and Sam." He laughed at her dubious expression. "I know, I know. I hate to admit I'm living with my brothers and about half of the crew on a temporary basis. We have what we like to call an open door policy. Their old ladies have a tendency to throw them out of the house occasionally."

Kendra made a face. "I'm picturing a big frat house with keg parties and drunk sexy girls in tight shorts. Am I right?"

"Why don't you come over some time and find out for yourself?" he challenged.

She shook her head slowly. "No, I don't think so. The party scene isn't for me. I like it quiet and peaceful."

"Who says I don't? Something tells me you're making presumptions about me based on the MC."

Flint was right. She had been making assumptions about him based on his involvement with the motorcycle gang. She was stereotyping him without giving him the benefit of getting to know him first. It wasn't like her to be so judgemental. She wasn't giving him a fair shake and he'd called her out on it. She respected him for that.

"You're right," she admitted grudgingly. "I probably have been doing that." She shrugged, unsure of how to explain it to him. "You're in a motorcycle gang and even though I don't know much about them, what I do know isn't great."

Flint drew in a deep breath before explaining. "For starters, we're a motorcycle club, not a gang. A big, big difference there. The MC is a way of life and more like a family to me than a club. They took Jesse and me in after Mom died and gave us a place to feel secure. Like we belonged somewhere. When I look back on those times, there were a million bad places I could've ended up if it hadn't been for the MC. I owe them so much."

She nodded. "I get that. I really do. But what about the other stuff? The illegal things?" There, she'd said it. The elephant in the room was now sitting right between them. She needed an answer to the one thing that had been bothering her since she walked into the cabin. "How do you explain that?"

A troubled, dark cloud came over his face. Instantly, Kendra regretted her words and wished she could take them back. She'd stepped over the line with him.

"You know I can't talk about any of that," he answered regretfully. "All I can tell you is that the people on my crew are good guys." He touched his chest above his heart. "Deep down inside. We're not perfect by any means, and maybe not by other people's standards. But they're loyal and they would protect my back. I would do the same for them. That's all I'm going to say."

Flint stood and walked over to check the pile of firewood beside the hearth. "We're running low. I'll go get some more logs from the woodpile on the side of the house."

Kendra started to offer to go help him and decided she would be better off not to. Flint had shut down the moment she mentioned the MC's illegal activities. She felt like kicking herself. She was surprised at how he had really opened up to her about his brothers and his dad, especially since she got the distinct feeling it wasn't something he shared with just anyone. There was so much more to Flint than she realized or expected. He had trusted her and she'd thrown it back in his face.

After a moment's hesitation, she reached into her pocket and pulled out Flint's keys. She placed them on the table so that it would be the first thing he saw when he walked back in.

The remainder of the day passed quickly. Flint spent his time checking in with Jesse and Sam while Kendra counseled anxious clients through various animal emergencies. In between calls, they sat on the couch together and talked about anything and everything. Without the distraction of a television or books, there was nothing left to do in the cabin to ease the awkwardness of the silence but to entertain each other.

By the end of the day, the thought occurred to Kendra that she hadn't spent so much time getting to know another man in a long time. Most of the dates she had been on the past few years had been centered around movies, sporting events, or even dinner in a fancy but very quiet restaurant, none of which were conducive to intimate conversations.

To her surprise, Flint was funny and had a wicked sense of humor that she found irresistibly attractive. He entertained her with stories of the crew and their various misfortunes with the old ladies in their lives. She could listen to him talk for hours with his deep Southern drawl with a touch of Tennessee twang.

The time passed quickly. When nightfall came, Kendra realized they would need to discuss sleeping arrangements. The cabin was tiny, with only a bathroom, a small kitchen, and a living area. From the bare furnishings, it was obvious the owner only used it as a hunting retreat rather than a vacation home.

After being forced to sleep sitting up in the recliner the night before, she wasn't eager to try it again. Being the alpha male he was, she knew Flint would readily give up the couch for her to sleep on.

She walked into the living room where he was busy stoking the fire for the night. "Flint, I hate to be a party pooper," she began. "But I'm exhausted and need to get some shut eye before I fall over."

"I'm sorry for keeping you up all night." Flint moved toward the couch. "Here, let's pull the sofa bed out for you," he said. "I saw some sheets for it while I was prowling around in the closet by the door."

A sofa bed? Well, that made sense, especially since there wasn't a separate bedroom. "I didn't know it made out into a bed," Kendra said. "You would have been much more comfortable last night if I'd known that."

He let out a rueful laugh. "Don't worry, I was comfortable enough with all those pain pills. Or at least I think I was from what I can remember."

Kendra sucked in her breath. Oh God! Please don't let him bring up the kiss again, she prayed. Together, they took the cushions off the couch and pulled out the bed frame. After retrieving the sheets from the closet, Kendra made the bed up.

"I'll sleep in the recliner chair tonight," Flint said to ease the awkwardness. "You've had your turn."

Kendra was too tired to argue. After changing into a long flannel shirt that hung almost to her knees, she crawled under the blanket.

Flint turned off the lamp and pulled his chair closer to the fire. "What is your family like?" he asked in the dark.

"They're great," Kendra replied. "My mom and dad dote on each other. He retired last year from the textile mill where he worked his entire life. My mom is a stay-at-home mother and she spent her life taking care of all of us. I have two older sisters who still try to boss me around. They all live right across the state line in North Carolina."

"Sounds nice."

"It is. My parents sacrificed a great deal for me to go to veterinarian school. They always encouraged me not to give up even though money was so tight. Many times I almost dropped out. My parents are the best. I wish you could meet them." The thought slipped out before she could catch herself. Oh crap! Did she really just say that?

"Me too," Flint replied softly. "Me too, Kendra."

"My dad took a second mortgage out on their house to loan me the money to buy into the vet practice. Dr. Henson wanted to retire and he preferred someone local to take over his clients. There aren't a lot of veterinarians willing to work in a small country practice so I got lucky. I went on every vet visit with Dr. Henson for two years before he trusted me enough to turn the business over."

"I remember Dr. Henson," Flint said. "He was a good man."

"Still is. He comes by the clinic every so often to check on me." Kendra tried and failed to stifle a big yawn.

"You'd better get some sleep. No more questions from me tonight."

Flint leaned back in the leather recliner and watched Kendra as she slept on the sofa bed. The fire had died down, and now there was only a soft glow bouncing off her hair from a few flickering embers. He reached over carefully and tucked back a strand that had fallen over her face. She stirred in her sleep but didn't wake up. Instead, she mumbled something he couldn't make out and pulled the blanket tighter around her.

He liked looking at her when she wasn't on guard and defensive. Kendra was truly gorgeous in a natural way, without a speck of makeup and her hair a crazy mess. He knew she didn't believe him when he'd told her that she was beautiful. She probably thought he was simply another scumbag trying to sweet talk her panties off.

Which, if he was honest with himself, wasn't too far from the truth. On both counts.

Kendra must have unconsciously felt him staring at her because she suddenly opened her eyes. "Flint?" she said sleepily. "Is something wrong? Are you okay?" She propped herself up on one elbow and blinked at him.

He smiled in reassurance. "Everything's okay. I'm fine. Go back to sleep."

She sat up and pulled the blanket up around her neck. "Jesus! It's freezing in here. Did the furnace go out?"

"We lost power about an hour ago," he answered. He stood up and threw another log into the fire. "I heard a pine tree snap under the weight of the ice and then the transformer blew. I figured I'd better hurry and build the fire back up before the temperature started dropping in here, but I didn't want to wake you."

She frowned at his bare chest. "Where is your shirt? Is your arm hurting?"

"Some," he admitted grudgingly, stretching his sore muscles. "The shirt was rubbing the bandage so I figured I'd feel more comfortable with it off."

"I hope you took something for the pain," she said with concern. "It's barely been a little over twenty-four hours since you were shot. Trying to be a tough guy by suffering isn't very smart."

"You're right, and I did." He sat back down in the chair, crossed his arms over his chest to keep warm, and closed his eyes.

Kendra smiled and lay back down after fluffing her pillow. After a moment, she threw the blanket to the side and patted the space beside her. "Flint, I can scoot over. There's plenty of room for both of us. You look miserable and cold sitting in that chair."

Flint didn't hesitate or give her time to change her mind. He gingerly stretched out next to her, careful not to take up too much of her space or accidentally touch her.

After a couple of minutes in silence, Kendra whispered hesitantly, "Flint?"

"Yes," he replied.

"No hanky-panky, okay?"

Flint laughed out loud, a deep rumbling sound that shook the sofa bed. "Goodnight."

"Night, Flint."

He knew she was smiling in the dark.

8

Kendra woke up some time later to discover Flint's injured arm wrapped across her breasts, holding her tightly. His bare chest was pressed close against her back while his warm breath stirred the hair on her neck. She hesitated for a moment, unsure of what to do.

Kendra carefully lifted his arm in an attempt to slide out from under him without waking him up. When she shifted, he instinctively tightened the grip on her in his sleep. She sighed and closed her eyes, resigned to her fate. After all, being snuggled up with a hot guy in a freezing cold cabin wasn't exactly the worst thing in the world, she reasoned. In fact, she couldn't remember the last time she'd felt so warm and safe. She didn't see any harm in enjoying it while it lasted.

A soft kiss on her shoulder stirred her awake a little while later. She smiled, certain it was an erotic dream until she felt another. Oh Jesus! Her stomach tightened as Flint slid the flannel shirt from her shoulder and continued pressing gentle kisses down her upper arm. She deliberately slowed her breathing and pretended to still be asleep while her mind and heart raced.

Flint's lips moved up and nuzzled the back of her neck. An uncontrollably delicious shiver slid down her spine. What on earth did he think he was doing? She had explicitly said no hanky-panky. A warm hand slid under the bottom of her shirt and rested on her waist. Kendra suddenly became distinctly aware of the heat and weight of his arousal prodding her hip.

Of their own will, her breasts swelled in aching need beneath the flannel shirt. Could Flint sense how hard and erect her nipples were? Did he know how much they needed to be pinched and sucked? To be rolled between his finger and thumb and tugged on hard until she cried out and begged for more?

In the past, Kendra had never had the courage to tell a man what she needed and wanted in bed. She always hoped they would just know. Unfortunately she'd always been wrong.

Until now.

Flint slid his hand, palm flat, up her stomach. He stopped right below her heavy breasts.

"I know you're awake," he whispered in her ear, sending chills through her body. "I can feel your heartbeat racing underneath my hand."

"Flint, we shouldn't..." she began before being interrupted by his hand moving up to cup her full breast and squeeze it hard. Oh God!

"Shh....don't say anything," he murmured in her ear. "I love your breasts. Full and heavy with big, fat nipples begging to be sucked. You don't know how much I've wanted to do this every time I looked at you today." She gasped as he circled his open palm around and around on her sensitized tit. An involuntary moan escaped her lips when he pinched and pulled on the elongated nipple. Just as she had wished. She moaned again when he twisted the nipple between his fingers. He tugged a little roughly, drawing the tip out and making her gasp in want and need.

"Your nipples are so very responsive," he continued. "Exactly the way I like them."

He suddenly removed his hand from her shirt and shifted her around so she was lying on her back. He sat up beside her. "Unbutton your shirt," he said, his expression unreadable.

She hesitated, not quite sure where the situation was heading.

Flint looked at her without saying a word, only watching and waiting. Kendra realized he was forcing her to make a decision...to stop or to go forward. It was her choice and he wasn't going to make it for her.

She licked her lips hesitantly then reached up to undo the top button of her flannel shirt. Then the next. Flint watched her quietly with hooded eyes. When she suddenly felt shy right before undoing the last button, he urged her on. " Don't stop," he said, his voice husky with desire.

When she undid that button, Flint reached out with both hands and pushed the shirt to her sides. He rubbed both nipples with the back of his knuckles until they stood up, hard and erect. Grasping locks of her hair gently, he fluffed them forward so that they fell in waves over her breasts, barely covering her nipples.

He leaned back and stared at her exposed body.

"What?" she said self-consciously. "Is something wrong?"

"No, everything is perfect," Flint replied. "I'm memorizing how beautiful you look so I can sketch you later when I'm alone."

Kendra's breath caught in her throat. Damn! That was the nicest thing anyone had ever said to her.

Without warning, Flint swooped down to seize one hard nipple into his mouth. He alternated between breasts, sucking and nipping her tits, teasing and tormenting. Kendra held on tight to his silky hair. He captured one nipple in his mouth and after rolling his tongue around on the nub, sucked hard on the surrounding breast. Kendra gasped and slid her hands down over his shoulders and back. Jesus! She loved the feel of this man.

"You like that?" he said, more of a statement than a question, already knowing her answer.

"Yes," she answered. "Oh, yes." She knew he needed to hear her say it.

While his mouth sucked on one breast and one hand squeezed and massaged the other, his free hand slid down her belly. Her breath shortened and quickened as he touched the lacy rim of her panties. Flint ran his fingers along the edge and then moved them between her thighs. His fingers slid under the silky panties, first on one side then the other, never touching the heated mound in between. Kendra squirmed and writhed underneath him, begging him with her body to touch her where she so desperately wanted. Her fingers clenched in his hair and he growled in approval at her ferocious grip.

"Open your eyes, Kendra," he commanded hoarsely, raising his head to look at her.

She opened her eyes to find his intense green eyes locked with hers. "I want to watch you," he said. He slid a finger inside the rim of her panties then up into her pussy all the way to the knuckle.

"Oh," she cried, raising her ass to meet his hand. She moaned again when he slid a second finger into her snug slickness. Her muscles tightened around his fingers, hungry for any form of penetration.

"God! You're so fucking wet and tight," Flint murmured against her breast. "Just as I knew you would be."

He finger-fucked her hard, one...two...three times with her panties still on, each time more forceful than the last. She grabbed onto his arms with both hands and cried out with each thrust. She bucked into his hand and felt shamed by the sounds her mouth and body were making as he drove in and out of her with his fingers.

"Take off your panties," he ordered.

Kendra quickly slid them over her ass, down her legs, and off her ankles.

"Now spread your legs for me. Wide."

Kendra quickly obeyed, spreading her legs wider to give him better access. The thrill of being dominated and controlled sexually was something she had never experienced before. She liked it more than she ever would have believed. To be told what to do and how to do it while being pleasured in return.

Flint stroked her outer pussy lips with his fingers. He licked his thumb and sought out the tiny nub of her clitoris. He rubbed it hard. Kendra gasped and arched her back.

"Tell me you want it, Kendra," he coaxed. "Tell me," he said again when she didn't answer. He teased the opening of her pussy before shoving a finger deep inside. Her pussy walls tightened around him. "Is this what you want?" he asked again, thrusting into her with a second finger. "If you don't tell me, I'll stop," he warned, momentarily stilling the movements of his fingers.

"Don't stop," she panted. "Yes, I want this." She bucked up against his hand, drawing his fingers in as deep as they would go. He began roughly plunging in and out of her pussy, almost lifting her ass off the sofa bed with each thrust. Reaching up, he rolled a hardened nipple between his thumb and finger. Kendra gasped, her breath uneven and shaky.

She gave up trying to hold back any more sounds of bliss. She couldn't stop writhing and she suddenly felt him push her thighs wider apart. He withdrew his fingers and his tongue dived right into her slit, causing her to erupt in a series of moans. His relentless tongue lapped at her clit over and over.

Oh God! She couldn't wait another second. She wanted Flint inside her now, fucking her hard and fast.

And as rough as he liked it.

If he liked it that way.

She didn't know. Didn't care.

Never had she wanted a man so bad and so urgently.

Kendra reached for his belt buckle and hurriedly undid it. She unzipped his jeans and slid her hand inside to wrap around his hard, velvety length. His cock bobbed and jerked at her touch. Kendra circled his cock firmly and stroked the full length all the way down to the base and back up. He groaned, straining into her hand. Damn! He was thick and long. And rock solid hard.

She caressed the slit at the top and felt drops of pre-cum moisten her thumb. She rubbed it all around the bulbous knob, causing him to close his eyes and groan in pleasure this time.

"Kendra, what are you doing to me?" he murmured. "Are you sure you want to do this?" he asked.

She tugged his jeans down even further in a hurry to get them off and replied, "Trust me. I've never wanted anything more."

Things went crazy fast.

Flint quickly kicked off his jeans then pressed her down on the sofa bed, covering her body with his. He kissed her with a wild dangerous hunger, his lips lightly touching hers before he deepened the kiss, his tongue demanding entry. His masculine hardness nudged intimately into her soft spots.

Kendra's breath caught as her hands rested on the unyielding hardness of his chest. She clung to him, feeling like the world was spinning around them. She parted her lips and he pressed her impossibly tighter against him, sliding into her mouth.

Whimpering, Kendra curled her arms tighter around him, burying her fingers in his hair and pulling him closer as she kissed him back with equal abandon. Her breasts strained and tingled against his chest, her heart hammering in time to the drumming in her ears. Dazed with need, Kendra arched against his body.

Reaching between their bodies, she encircled his cock with her hand and stroked his hard length. She could only imagine him inside her, filling her cunt, stretching her wide with his cock. She stroked faster, wanting him to feel the same desperate need she felt. His cock grew and hardened until it was pulsing with want. He moaned wetly against her mouth.

"Do you feel what you do to me?" he whispered, his lips now trailing her ear. "I've never felt so hard. Never wanted anyone this damn much." He continued whispering in her ear about how dripping wet she was and how he wanted to slide into her tight pussy and fuck her every way he knew how. They were both breathing fast. As soon as he began talking in her ear, Kendra had dissolved into a gooey mess.

He slid down her body and rained kisses down her stomach. At her parted legs, he stopped to raise his head.

"You can still say no. Just say the word."

Kendra stared into the deep pools of his eyes. Wanting Flint might be wrong on so many levels, but none of that counted for a damn thing at the moment. Kendra had denied herself too many things for far too long. Denying herself Flint was one sacrifice she wasn't willing to make.

"I want you deep inside me. Now. I can't wait any longer."

Flint moved at lighting speed. After quickly retrieving a condom from his jeans pocket and donning it, he gently grabbed her legs under her knees and wrapped them around his waist. Grasping his cock in one hand, he stroked the entrance to her moist, swollen pussy.

"Ready, darling?" he asked one last time. He settled his lower body in the cradle between her thighs and Kendra felt the head of his thick, long cock probing against her pussy lips.

Kendra grasped his shoulders. "Yes! Goddammit! Yes!"

With a one long forceful thrust, he plunged into her pussy and embedded himself in her up to his balls. Kendra's mouth opened in a soundless 'O' and for a fleeting second, she forgot how to breathe. Flint drew out slightly then pushed in again, deep and hard, with a loud grunt, stretching her pussy walls to their limit.

Kendra loved that he wasn't gentle or hesitant. He had read her signals correctly and knew exactly what she wanted. This was what she'd always craved, a man who instinctively knew she needed it rough, wild, and primal. Giving it to her as hard as he wanted and needed without holding back for fear of hurting her. She could take it. She wanted it wild and crazy. During her dating days, she'd had enough dull boring sex to last a lifetime.

She grasped his ass with both hands, clenching the firm, smooth muscles and pulling him in deeper if that was even possible. His thrusts were now rapid, rough, and intense. Her large tits jiggled with each stroke until they were swinging wildly between their sweat-slicked bodies. Unable to even speak, Kendra gasped out loud every time he rammed into her core.

"You feel so fucking good," Flint groaned, the sweat on his forehead and the tightness of his jaw revealing how much self-control he was exerting. "So tight and hot around my cock."

The thought occurred to Kendra that if this was controlled, she couldn't imagine what fucking Flint would be like when he was out of control. She was eternally grateful she'd kept up her Kegel exercises. She deliberately clenched and unclenched her pussy walls around him, milking him.

"Oh Jesus!" he said. "If you keep doing that, I don't know how much longer I can last. You're killing me."

He leaned in close, his bare muscled chest rubbing against her heaving breasts. He moved now with long, slow, powerful strokes, filling her completely, owning, claiming. Bending his head, he nipped her tit sharply with his teeth and she cried out, bucking her hips to meet his thrusts while her breast arched into his mouth.

"Don't hold back," he said. His uninjured arm was braced close to her head and she could see every bicep tightening as he strained for control.

He suddenly withdrew and flipped her over on her stomach. "Get on your knees, baby," he said, hooking his hands underneath her and pulling her ass backwards. "Lean on your elbows."

Kendra quickly obeyed. She leaned forward on her elbows and offered herself up to him for the taking. To do with whatever he wanted.

"You have a gorgeous ass," he said before kneading the lush curves with both hands. Spreading her ass cheeks wide, he nudged the tip of his cock at the entrance to her pussy. She let out a long breath of anticipation. Before she had a chance to brace herself, he grabbed her hips with both hands to hold her still and thrust deep into her pussy with one long, powerful plunge.

In this position, his huge cock felt like it was splitting her apart. "Oh Jesus!" she cried out. "Oh God, that's deep!" He pulled out almost all the way and slammed into her again, the force this time flattening her into the mattress.

He lifted her back up again. "Try to stay on your knees." She struggled to do what he asked, her walls screaming with bliss as he slammed into her with rugged thrusts, each plunge taking him as deep as he could possibly go.

Flint didn't say a word as he fucked her savagely, his fingers digging into her ass, his breathing ragged. She knew in the morning her body would be aching. She didn't care. He was taking her to a place she'd never been before and she loved it. God! How she loved it. He penetrated her so deeply she could feel his balls banging against her ass.

On and on he fucked her mercilessly. She could tell by the tenseness of his body that he was close to orgasm. She hoped to God it felt as good for him as it did for her. Any moment now she would be unravelling.

"Come on baby," he urged. "Come for me." He reached underneath her and grabbed a swinging breast. He squeezed her nipple and the sweet mixture of pleasure and pain was enough to send her barrelling over the edge.

"Flint! Oh God!" Damn, but he knew which buttons to push. Kendra felt a rush of overwhelming tightness before her cunt exploded in a series of contractions. The intensity of her orgasm was overwhelming and powerful.

He groaned and held perfectly still deep within her while she milked him with her contractions. "That's it, baby," he murmured. "I can feel you coming around my cock." He pumped into her several more times before he exploded with a loud roar. He thrust into her one final time, shuddering as his orgasm took over him completely.

Flint pulled Kendra onto his chest and wrapped his arm around her. After several minutes, their breathing finally began to slow. He stroked her arm idly and pressed a kiss against her forehead.

"I'm sorry I was so rough," he said. "I didn't hurt you, did I?"

Kendra smiled and traced a finger down his chest. "No, you didn't hurt me."

He let out the breath he'd been holding. "The instant I slid inside you, my brain went haywire. All I could think about was sinking deeper into your body. And once I started, I couldn't get enough. I promise next time I'll take my time and be extra slow and gentle."

Kendra propped herself up on one elbow and pressed her finger against his lips. "Don't say that, and please don't change a thing. I liked it wild and crazy." She hesitated a moment. "You made me feel wanted."

He crushed her to his chest. "You're wanted more than you'll ever know."

Kendra suddenly noticed the bandage on his arm had slipped out of place and was hanging half-off. "Oh no! Flint! I'm the one who should be apologizing! What about your arm? Did we hurt it?"

"Some," he admitted. "But believe me, it was worth it. You can make it up to me though if you really want to," he added teasingly.

"Oh? How's that?"

"Since I probably shouldn't be exerting my arm so much, next time you should be on top. Just the thought of watching you slide up and down on my cock is making me hard all over again."

She laughed and buried her face in his chest.

"If it will make you feel better," she agreed. "We don't want to hurt your arm any more than it already is."

He brought her head closer to his and touched her lips gently this time before he finally said, "Oh, it would make me feel a lot better."

Flint didn't sleep a wink the rest of the night. After everything he'd been through the past several months, he was so afraid that if he closed his eyes, the one good thing in his life would disappear. As long as he stayed awake, he could still feel Kendra's warm breath against his chest and her nude body snuggled close to his. It wasn't worth a few hours of shut-eye to lose it even for a second.

Being with Kendra had been unbelievable. Mind-blowing really. One touch, one taste of her, and he'd lost all control. His brain had short-circuited until all he could feel was white-hot desire and an unquenchable thirst to be buried deep inside her. And she'd felt it too. Of that, he was sure.

Instead of telling him to slow down or be more careful, she had taken everything he gave her willingly and eagerly, no matter how wild or rough it got. She was sexy as hell and didn't even know it. Where Kendra was concerned, he was insatiable.

He couldn't let her go.

He stared at the wooden beams lining the ceiling. How in the world would he ever convince her to give him a chance? A real chance, not just a one-night stand or sex every now and then.

He wasn't a fool and knew exactly what he was up against. Kendra was educated, smart, and a genuinely good-hearted person. Not to mention being a well-respected veterinarian that probably ninety percent of the people in the county knew.

Whereas Kendra thought he was a two-bit criminal...a bad guy. She didn't have any reason to think otherwise. And sometimes he was. The MC knowingly broke the law every day.

The only reason they'd met was because the Liberators had attempted to murder him. He couldn't imagine what she honestly must be thinking about the whole situation. What if deep down she found him disgusting and repulsive? Doubts dogged him. There was no way what they had shared could last any longer than one night. It was over before it ever had a chance to get going. The realization filled him with a deep aching dread about the future.

But something at the back of his mind kept niggling at him, saying "what if?" What if she was willing to take a chance on him? And then what? Would he even be able to keep her safe? The thought chilled him to the bone. What if the Liberators found out about Kendra and tried to get to him through her? They certainly wouldn't be above hurting a woman to destroy him.

His thoughts and deepest fears went round and round in his mind. There had to be a way to have it all. He was a talented lawyer and had been known in the Public Defender's office for being able to work through difficult problems methodically and analytically. He told himself this situation was no different. All he needed to do was calm the fuck down over potentially losing Kendra and think of a solution.

Eventually the answer became clear. If by some miracle he was able to convince Kendra to give him a chance, the threat from the Liberators would have to be eliminated immediately and permanently. No matter what the cost.

The MC would have to take them out. Every fucking last one of them. There would be no survivors. It was time for him to step up beside Jesse and take a leadership role.

If Kendra stayed with him, the only way he could keep her safe was to not rest until every last Liberator was dead.

It was time for the Steel Infidels to go to war.

9

The next morning, Flint stepped up behind Kendra, who was brushing her teeth at the bathroom sink. He wrapped his strong arms around her and leaned down to nuzzle her neck.

He breathed in deeply. "You smell good," he murmured into her ear.

Kendra laughed and rinsed out her toothbrush. "Like mint?" she replied. She caught his eyes in the mirror and stilled for a moment. Good Lord! She could get used to this - sharing bathroom space with Flint in the morning after a night of hot sex. His black hair was tousled where she'd run her hands through it so many times she'd lost count.

She would never tire of touching him, of running her hands over his hard tattooed muscles. Not even in a million years. Being with a man like Flint could be dangerously addictive, and that thought scared the hell out of her.

"Kendra?" he said, his tone suddenly serious.

"Hmmm...."

He pushed the thick hair off her neck and kissed the sensitive spot behind her ear. "Do you want to be my girl?" he asked.

Kendra smiled teasingly at him in the mirror. "Your girl? You mean like in sixth grade, want to go steady sort of thing?"

Flint nibbled on her ear. "Sort of."

Kendra leaned back into him and wrapped her arms around his. "I'll admit I haven't been active in the dating scene much in the past few years, but don't couples usually date awhile first? You know, go out on a few dates, then eventually get around to talking about being in a monogamous relationship and only dating each other?"

"Probably," Flint replied. "I suspect that would be how other people would do it."

Kendra lifted her eyebrows. "And we're not like other people?"

Flint turned her around in his arms so she was facing him. "I think you already know we're definitely not like other people. I realize this is sudden and crazy fast. All I know is that the thought of you being with another man, like you were with me last night makes me feel..." He hesitated for the right word before finding it. "Murderous."

He placed his forehead against hers and slid his hands down to cup her ass. "So I'm asking you again," he said. "Will you be my girl?"

Kendra slid her hands up his chest and traced the beginnings of the tattoo on his shoulders. "What exactly does that mean? Your girl? I need more clarification."

Flint laughed, the deep rumbling vibrating against her breasts. "It means it will be you and me, darling. Just you and me. You would be my girl and I would be your guy." He placed a slow, warm kiss on her lips. "Your only guy," he added for emphasis.

Damn, how she liked the sound of that. Flint. Her guy.

It was weird how her whole world had changed in a weekend. She'd spent a lifetime being the good girl, the responsible girl who made the best grades and worked harder than everyone else. Never letting go or being free with her actions because of how other people might look at her or disapprove.

She needed something wild and crazy to shake up her comfortable and boring life.

She wanted to live, and more importantly, to feel alive.

She wanted Flint. And even more than that, deep down Kendra realized she needed him.

"How do you see this working out between us?" she asked, still a tad unsure and hesitant. "You have to admit our lives are so different. What about our families and our friends? How will we fit into each other's lives?"

Flint shook his head slowly, rubbing his forehead against hers. "I don't know, darling," he replied honestly. "All I can tell you is that I play for keeps. All you have to do is trust in me and I will do whatever I have to do to make it work. Give us a chance. That's all I'm asking."

Kendra stared into his compelling eyes and realized that he meant every word. He was willing to try and by God, so was she.

Kendra placed her hands tenderly on both sides of his face. The green eyes that dazzled her from the very first instant looked back at her now, worried and waiting.

"I'll be your girl," she answered with a smile. "Whatever happens, we'll figure it out."

Flint felt a dark and heavy load lift from his shoulders with her words. Kendra was giving him the chance he so desperately needed. He couldn't imagine what he'd done lately to deserve it, but he was sure as hell glad. Maybe his karma had built up from his years as a public defender. He certainly wasn't going to waste a second questioning why.

Flint took her arms and linked them behind his neck before leaning down and claiming her lips. Her lips felt as soft and juicy as he'd remembered. His heart thudded as she opened her mouth eagerly to his ravenous onslaught. Kendra tasted like no woman he'd ever kissed before. It drove him mad and immediately had him so hard and thick he throbbed.

He wanted her. Desperately.

"Kendra," Flint said with a groan as he tore his lips from hers moments later, his breathing ragged. "You're making me insane. I don't know how you do what you do to me. Please don't ever stop."

He slid his hands underneath her shirt and heard the quick catch of her breath. Instead of stopping him, she placed her hands over his and guided them up her stomach until her heavy breasts filled his hands. She closed her eyes and moaned.

He felt her nipples peak into hard, tight tips as he grazed them with his fingertips.

"The things I want to do to you, Kendra." He nibbled her ear and told her how deep and hard he wanted to fuck her. How she drove him crazy with need. How she made him so hard and stiff he couldn't get enough of her sweet, tight pussy.

Flint's hands let go of her breasts to strip off his jeans, revealing every tight and hard toned muscle. Kendra stared in awe. There wasn't a trace of fat; he was all ripped and rock solid. She was having a hard time wrapping her mind around the fact that this man...this incredibly hot, sexy male wanted her as his. For keeps, he'd said...

He turned to step into the shower, leaving Kendra with a view of his broad upper back and shoulders covered from one side to the other with the Steel Infidels tattoo and his tight, perfect ass. All she could do was stare. His raw masculinity left her breathless.

After turning on the water and adjusting the temperature, he turned and held out his hand to her. The look on his face spelled an intent that sent a coil of need tightening within her belly. Oh shit! Her hair would get all messed up and his bandage couldn't get wet. All the reasons why she shouldn't strip off her shirt and step into the shower with him ran through her mind.

Screw it! No way in hell was she turning him down. A woman would be insane to even think about it. She tugged her flannel shirt over her head and took his hand. Flint smiled and drew her under the water with him.

He pulled her close and turned her around so that he could leisurely soap her back, his warm hands lathering the slippery bar over her shoulders and down her arms. He drew her back against him and reached around to soap her stomach and down between her legs. Kendra closed her eyes and braced her arms against the tile wall of the shower for support.

Flint put down the bar of soap and massaged her breasts, kneading their fleshy mounds and tugging on the nipples. "Have I told you how much I love your big nipples?" he mumbled into her shoulder.

"Yes," Kendra gasped. "But you can tell me again."

"Good," he replied. "Because I love talking about them. There are so many ways to describe your nipples. Rigid...swollen... turgid... irresistible." With each word, he squeezed the tips and rolled them between his finger and thumb. Kendra melted into him, afraid her legs were going to crumble out from under her.

Flint nibbled on her neck, moving one hand from her nipple and down her stomach. His hand slid further still and cupped her sex, pressing her back against him. Kendra whimpered when his fingers parted her swollen, wet pussy lips. He found her clit and rubbed it in circles. "Oh God! Flint," she panted.

Trapped between the tile wall and his rock-hard body, Kendra felt her senses swim, overwhelmed by his male dominance. Tucked between the globes of her buttocks was the unmistakable length of his straining erection and he felt even harder, bigger than she remembered. Kendra writhed against him. The carnal movement caused him to swell even thicker. She wantonly pushed and undulated her ass into Flint again.

"Are you wet yet, Kendra? Because I'm already rock-hard for you," Flint growled with his lips in her ear. If her pussy wasn't already soaking wet with desire, it would have been after his words. She loved it when he talked dirty.

He moved her slightly to the side and out of the direct spray of the water. Kneeling down behind her, he spread her ass cheeks wide with his hands. His tongue settled over her slit before lapping up and down her wet entrance. Kendra's thighs trembled and she was grateful when he tightened his grip on her ass to hold her steady. Flint stroked her cunt with his tongue like he couldn't get enough of her.

"Oh!" she cried out. "Flint! What are you doing?"

Instead of answering, he buried his face deeper into her ass and worked his tongue into her pussy. Kendra's mouth opened in soundless ecstasy as he swept his tongue from her pussy lips all the way up to her ass.

She gasped when he licked her there, not expecting something so carnal and wickedly taboo. Flint was driving her insane. She didn't want it to stop. Kendra ground her ass into his face and moaned in appreciation.

Flint stroked a finger into her cunt and drew her hot juices up to lubricate her ass. He lifted his head and slowly inserted a finger into her tight anal ring, bit by bit, giving her time to relax and adjust before going all the way in. Kendra gasped at the delicious feeling of fullness. Damn! No man had ever done that to her before. She was amazed at how good it felt. Flint continued to take her places she'd never been sexually. She bit her lips to keep from crying out.

"Don't hold back," he gritted out. "Every sound you make drives me fucking insane."

Everything faded except for the feel of Flint's hands as he fucked her ass and pussy forcefully with his fingers. At that moment, nothing mattered to Kendra but the unbelievable sensations Flint was invoking in her. When she thought she couldn't stand up a minute longer without crumbling into a heap, he withdrew his fingers and nudged her feet further apart.

Flint bent her slightly forward with her hands against the tile wall. "Spread your legs, sweetheart," he said. "I can't wait a second longer." Before he finished his sentence, he had already thrust himself into her slippery, hot pussy with a loud grunt. With another short thrust, he was buried all the way up to the hilt.

Kendra cried out loudly this time at the deep contact, the sound echoing off the tile walls. Her pussy gripped his cock and Flint groaned deeply in appreciation. He began to move, fucking her hard with powerful, long thrusts. His arm wrapped around her stomach so she wouldn't slip.

Kendra closed her eyes, hearing nothing but the sound of Flint ravaging her pussy, his labored breathing as he fought to maintain control, and the loud smacks of his cock into her juicy wetness.

"I can't believe how fucking good you feel!" Flint muttered, his thrusts becoming more primal and savage. "You're driving me out of my mind." He sank in as deeply as possible and they both gasped for breath. "Tell me what you need," he said before leaning down and biting her shoulder sharply. "Anything you want."

"Just fuck me, Flint," Kendra panted out between breaths. "Hard and fast."

He slammed into her roughly, causing her breasts to swing wildly. "Oh yes, that's good," Kendra gasped. "That's it," she babbled, almost out of her mind with the overwhelming sensations racking her body. "Oh God!"

Flint slid his hand down her stomach and parted her pussy lips to reveal her clit. Flint rubbed the sensitive nub vigorously while ramming into her from behind with loud grunts. He increased the pressure on her clit while murmuring in her ear. "Scream my name," he urged, his hips moving faster. "Scream my name when you come for me."

One more powerful thrust and her orgasm hit her. "Flint!" she yelled, unraveling in a pool of bliss. "I'm coming! Flint! Fuck! Fuck!"

That was all it took for Flint to become completely undone. He came deep inside her with a loud shout, his cock throbbing and twitching with each pulse. Kendra's pussy walls clenched and unclenched around him, milking him until there was nothing left.

Instead of pulling out, he stayed deep inside her. "Don't move," he whispered. "I'm not ready to let you go." Nuzzling her neck, he reached up to lovingly caress her breast. "Not ever."

They remained snuggled tightly against each other until the water eventually became cooler. Kendra giggled. "You realize any second now we're going to be hit with ice cold water," she said. "We should probably get out and dry off before that happens. I'm not a fan of cold showers."

"There may be lots of cold showers in my future," Flint said. "Unless I can convince you to stay in bed with me all day long." He rocked against her and she felt his cock growing hard again inside her. "I told you I can't get enough of you," he growled into her hair. "Seriously. I'm insatiable where you're concerned."

"The feeling is mutual," Kendra replied. She yelped when the water suddenly turned ice cold. Flint laughed, finally withdrawing from her with a regretful sigh. He stepped out of the shower and she followed right behind him. Grabbing a couple of towels, he threw her one and wrapped the other around his waist. Droplets of water dripped from his hair and slid down his chest. Kendra stared, mesmerized.

Flint's cell phone buzzed in his jeans, which were lying on the floor. "Shit!" he said. "Ignore it."

The phone buzzed again.

"It's okay," Kendra said, quickly towelling off. "You'd better check it. The call might be important."

Flint sighed and pulled the phone out of his pocket. "Jesse?" he answered. He held the phone between his ear and shoulder while he tugged on his jeans. "What's up?" He listened quietly for a moment.

"When? Now? Jesus Christ! You know the road up the mountain is one way, right? How far away are you? We're leaving now."

Flint clicked the phone shut and grabbed Kendra's hand. He half-pulled, half-dragged her out of the bathroom.

"We need to hurry. Put on your clothes and grab the guns. Does your truck have a four-wheel drive?"

Kendra looked bewildered. "Yes, of course, but why do you need to know?"

Flint grabbed his shirt off the back of a chair and slipped it over his head. "The Liberators know where we are. They're on their way here now." He shrugged into his leather jacket and patted the side pocket for the pistol he always kept there. "Jesse and the rest of the crew are heading this way, but they're about twenty-five minutes away. We need to get off this fucking mountain before the Liberators get here."

Kendra's eyes grew wide. "The road is iced over. And it's barely wide enough for one vehicle in some places."

"I know. That's why I asked about the four-wheel drive. Give me your keys, I'm driving."

Kendra reached into her purse and threw him the keys. She already had her coat on and was heading for the door. She picked up the pistol and shotgun from the table. They hadn't been touched since she'd placed them there.

Flint held the door open for her. "You know how to shoot both guns?" he asked.

"Damn right I do," she answered firmly. "My Daddy taught me how to shoot a gun when I was ten years old."

"Kendra, if you need to use them, don't hesitate."

Kendra struggled to fight down the cold fear settling around her chest and threatening to choke off her breath. The Liberators were on their way to kill Flint.

Her guy.

Though she had never knowingly harmed another living creature, she understood in a heartbeat what needed to be done. She moved the safety on both guns to the off position. She already knew they were loaded.

To protect Flint, she would kill.

Without thinking or hesitation.

She glanced around the cabin one last time. Things would never be the same again.

"Let's get the hell out of here."

Keep reading! *Liberated*, the second and final installment of Flint and Kendra's story is included on the next page.

New York Times Bestselling Author

LIBERATED

by

DEZ BURKE

LIBERATED PROLOGUE

Kendra struggled to fight down the cold fear settling around her chest and choking off her breath. The Liberators were on their way to kill Flint.

Her guy.

Though she had never knowingly harmed another living creature, she understood in a heartbeat what needed to be done. She moved the safety on both guns to the off position. She already knew they were loaded.

To protect Flint, she would kill.

Without thinking or hesitation.

She glanced around the safe house one last time. Things would never be the same again.

"Let's get the hell out of here."

1

Kendra ran to the truck and climbed into the passenger seat. She tucked the shotgun underneath the seat and checked the pistol again to make sure it was loaded.

"Put your seatbelt on," Flint said. "Things might get rough."

Kendra quickly obeyed as Flint backed the truck out of the driveway and pulled onto the mountain road.

"Be careful and watch the road," she warned. "The roads are probably slick as glass and there are a couple of places where the road narrows down to barely one lane."

"I'll be as careful as I can be considering the situation," Flint replied, reaching over to squeeze her leg. "Don't worry, darling. I've been driving on these mountain roads my whole life. My daddy put me behind the wheel of a truck when I was only eight years old."

"That's good to know." Kendra fingered the pistol. "What exactly are we up against here? Any idea how many Liberators are headed this way?"

Flint shook his head. "No idea. Could be five or six or as many as thirteen. With the road conditions being so bad, at least we know they won't be on their Harleys. And they're going to have a hard time making it up the mountain road unless they have a four-wheel drive truck. I wouldn't be surprised if they're waiting to ambush us at the bottom. Sneaky little shits."

Kendra bit her bottom lip and considered his words. "That's probably true, but only if they know we're on our way down. Otherwise, there's a very real chance we're going to meet them head on. Who tipped Jesse off anyway?"

"He didn't have time to tell me. If I had to guess, I would say it was a gal who used to be sweet on Jesse. She hung around our club a lot when she was younger. Leah is with one of the Liberators now, but she's always had a soft spot for Jesse. If she thought he was in danger, she would let him know."

"He trusts her?" Kendra frowned. "What if she's double-crossing him to flush you out of the safe house?"

"I can't see her doing that. She always held on to hope that Jesse would eventually come around. Hell, I even thought that they might get together a time or two. Either way, I couldn't stay holed up in the cabin forever so let's try not to freak out yet. Hopefully we have a good head start on the Liberators. In another twenty minutes, we'll be off this mountain and back on the main road. I'll call Jesse when we get to town and arrange for him to pick me up somewhere so you can go on home. Where you'll be safe."

Safe.

At the moment, Kendra would give anything to feel safe again. And to know that Flint would be safe as well. *How would that ever happen,* she wondered? The Liberators had already tried to kill him once, and here they were days later trying for a second time. She knew if she let herself think about it, the panic would begin to overwhelm her. She drew in a deep breath and forced herself to calm down. It wasn't as if she wasn't accustomed to tense, stressful events. In her job as a veterinarian, adrenaline-pumping situations were part of a normal work day.

This was different though. Flint's life was on the line. Maybe her own life, too.

After a moment's hesitation, she reached down under the seat and carefully pulled out the shotgun. She propped it up between her knees with the barrel pointing toward the top of the truck.

Flint glanced over at her and then did a double take. "What the hell are you doing?" he asked. "Put that thing away! You already have the pistol."

"A shotgun can blow a bigger hole," Kendra answered. "And my aim doesn't have to be as good with a bigger gun."

Flint blew out a long breath. "Good point, as long as you know what you're doing. Just don't let it go off in the truck. This is a fine vehicle and it doesn't deserve a hole in the roof." He frowned and slowed down even more. "This next stretch of road looks tricky."

He tapped the brakes gently and slowed the truck to navigate around a tight, slippery turn. Kendra held her breath as the truck's back tires suddenly began sliding on the icy road.

"Damn it!" Flint cursed.

The back tires continued to spin uselessly. The truck slowly began sliding inch by inch toward the edge of the road. Kendra looked out the window at the steep drop off down an embankment on her right.

Why the hell didn't they put guardrails up?

"Watch out!" she yelled. "We're right on the edge over here."

"Come on! Come on!" Flint muttered over the sound of the back tires spinning on ice and going nowhere.

"I'm not kidding, Flint! Stop gassing it for a second. We're about six inches from going off the road and there's a steep drop off over here. I can't take this! I'm getting out of the truck. This is making me too damn nervous."

The truck stopped sliding for an instant. Kendra opened the truck door and stepped out carefully. She swung the door wide so Flint could see out her side of the truck and down into the deep gully below. "See how close we are to going over the edge?"

Flint frowned and pushed a hand through his black hair. "Alright, you come around and drive. I'll get out and push from behind."

"You're going to push the truck with a gunshot wound in your arm?" Kendra asked with a dubious expression. "I don't think that's a good idea."

Flint winked at her and flashed that wicked grin she found so appealing. "I think I've already proven I'm up to any task," he said. "Now hurry and come around. I'll push with my right shoulder, not my left. So don't worry, I'll be fine. We don't need to waste time arguing about it."

Kendra hurried around and climbed into the driver's seat. Flint moved to the back of the truck. "When I say go, you give it a little gas and I'll push. If I yell stop, then stop. Got it?"

"Got it."

"Okay, go!" Kendra pressed down on the accelerator while Flint pushed from behind. The tires spun but didn't catch. "Stop!" Flint stepped from behind the truck. "Let's try it again. Give it a little more gas than last time and I'll push harder." Flint ducked his head down and leaned his shoulder against the truck again. "Go!" he yelled.

At the same instant Flint yelled for her to gas it, a blue SUV swerved from around the other side of the curve. Kendra could tell from the two men's facial expressions in the front seat of the SUV that they were as surprised to see her as she was to see them.

The Liberators! Oh shit!

She didn't doubt it was the rival motorcycle club.

Flint was behind the truck and angled slightly away from them so they hadn't spotted him yet. And with his head lowered to push, she realized he probably hadn't seen them either. The ridiculous thought went through her head that maybe they wouldn't recognize him and would keep on driving. After all, they weren't expecting Flint to be on the side of the road with a woman in a truck. Their plan was to catch him by surprise at the safe house. They probably were hoping she wouldn't pay much attention to them in case she could identify their faces later.

She glanced in her side view mirror and realized Flint was wearing the Steel Infidels leather jacket. Oh Lord! There was no way in hell the Liberators wouldn't notice that. Flint's head was still down with his shoulder against the corner of the truck.

The bearded men in the SUV stared at her as they drove slowly past. She could make out shadows in the back seat but couldn't tell how many more men were in there.

Redneck assholes! Obviously they weren't the type of men to stop and offer help to a damsel in distress stuck on the side of the road. Kendra would have been very pissed off if she wasn't so scared.

Flint lifted his head to see why she wasn't following his instructions at the same moment the Liberators drew even with the back of the truck.

Kendra watched him glance up and make direct eye contact with the driver of the SUV.

If you need to use the guns, don't hesitate.

Flint's words back at the cabin rang in her head. Taking a deep breath, Kendra grabbed her shotgun from the seat and swung open the driver's side door. She would always remember everything that happened next as if it unfolded in slow motion.

The driver of the SUV instinctively slammed on his brakes hard when he recognized Flint. The SUV fishtailed briefly on the icy road before coming to a stop several feet past them.

"Kendra!" Flint yelled. "Get down!"

Kendra heard the Liberators shouting at each other before all four doors of the SUV flew open and men began piling out. Kendra barely had time to register the reflective glint of a handgun in one of the men's hands before she fired. Her first shot shattered the back window of the SUV in a loud explosion of breaking glass. Her next shot hit the driver in the leg.

"Goddammit!" he yelled, grabbing his thigh and crumpling to the ground in a heap of agony.

A Liberator who was crouched behind the SUV peeked his head up and fired, taking off her truck's side mirror that was mere inches away. Kendra screamed and jumped back then unloaded her rifle in the direction of the SUV, hitting tires, windows, and flesh. She wasn't sure what she was shooting at or whom she was even hitting. Nor did she give a damn.

She hadn't been kidding when she said the shotgun would make bigger holes. She had also intentionally not mentioned to Flint that her aim had never been great to begin with. It wasn't like she was a hunter, for God's sake. The only thing she'd ever shot was soda cans off the top of a metal trash can. Her best course of action was to keep shooting in hopes of disabling the Liberators long enough for her and Flint to escape, even if they had to go into the woods on foot.

"Kendra!"

Flint fired several shots with his pistol then rushed to physically block Kendra's body with his own before shoving her back into the truck. "Dammit, get down!"

Kendra didn't argue with him. Instead, she crawled across the floorboard of the truck and opened the glove compartment to grab some more shells. After reloading her gun, she opened the passenger door and slid out the other side. "No!" Flint shouted when he saw what she was doing. "Get back in here! Fuck!"

Before she had a chance to shoot again, a flurry of bullets rained down on the SUV. She watched in shock from behind the truck as one by one, the Liberators fell onto the ground, their forms twisting and jerking as bullet after bullet entered their bodies. The gunfire went on for what seemed like forever until it finally stopped. For a brief second, there wasn't a sound and nobody moved.

An old pickup roared toward them. In the heat of the gun battle, she hadn't noticed that Jesse and several other members of the Steel Infidels had arrived. Jesse jumped out of the truck and ran over while Tom Brewer and the rest of the crew rushed to the SUV to finish the job.

"Are you okay?" Jesse yelled. "Anybody hurt?"

"We're okay," Flint replied. He scrambled across the truck seat to reach Kendra on the other side and grabbed her in a big hug. "You scared the living shit out of me," he murmured into her hair. "Please don't ever do that again. I thought my heart was going to stop when you stepped out of the truck with your gun. Don't you realize they could have killed you?" He hugged her to him even tighter as if he never wanted to let her go.

Kendra closed her eyes and sank into his warmth. She could feel his heart racing wildly underneath her cheek. Now that it was all over and the adrenaline rush was leaving her body, she didn't feel so good. She was grateful that Flint was there to hold her up because her legs were beginning to tremble.

"Are you sure you're okay?" he asked. "Why in God's name did you do that?"

"Do what?" she muttered against his leather jacket.

"Get out of the damn truck and start shooting. If something had happened to you, I never would have been able to forgive myself. You should have stayed down in the floorboard of the truck where it was safer."

Kendra leaned back so she could look at him. "They were going to kill you, Flint. We both know that. I didn't have time to think about it. I knew the moment they spotted you that it was on. They drew their weapons first."

"I'm not saying it wasn't justified. I just don't understand why you put yourself at risk to protect me. I never would have wanted you to do that. Not ever."

"You're my guy," she simply said as if that explained everything.

Flint let out a long sigh and kissed her forehead. "Yes I am."

"Thank God Jesse and your crew got here when they did," she said, her voice shaky now. "I'm not sure what would have happened otherwise."

"From what I saw, you were handling things extremely well all on your own. My money would be on you over the Liberators any day. I bet they about shit in their pants when you unloaded the shotgun into their SUV. Will you be alright here a minute while I go talk to the guys?"

She nodded.

"I want you to stay in the truck. Don't look over there at the bodies and don't go over there. Do you understand?"

"I understand."

"Good. Let me go talk to Jesse. I'll be back in a few minutes."

2

Flint tucked Kendra into the passenger seat of the truck and made her promise one more time not to go over to the SUV. When he felt sure she would stay put, he walked over to check out the situation. There were four dead bodies on the ground. All of them had been shot multiple times.

Jesse immediately pulled him aside, out of earshot of the rest of the crew. "We need to get this mess cleaned up fast and move everybody out of here. The gunshots could probably be heard from miles away. I'll have the crew take care of the bodies and dump the SUV. Your job is take care of Dr. Shaw."

Flint frowned. "Take care of her? What exactly do you mean?"

Jesse looked at him like he was off in the head. "You need to make sure she doesn't breathe a word of this to anybody. She's a witness to everything that went down here today. I don't care what you have to do to make sure she doesn't talk. Just take care of it. We can't have any loose ends." Jesse turned to walk away.

Flint grabbed his arm. "What do you think happened?"

"It's fucking obvious. You ran head on into the Liberators, shot the hell out of their vehicle, and took out a couple of guys before we got here. I don't know how you did so much damage to their truck though."

Flint nodded slowly. "Yeah, that's about how it all went down. Don't worry about Kendra. I'll make sure she doesn't say anything. Are they all dead?"

"If not, they will be," Jesse replied, very matter-of fact.

"Four down," Flint noted. "That means there are nine left to go."

Jesse raised his eyebrows. "What are you saying?"

"The all out war between the Steel Infidels and the Liberators is back on. I'm sick and tired of them attacking and us defending. We need to go on the offensive and take them all out. Every single fucking last one of them. It's the only way. This is never going to be over until we do. As soon as we can get the crew together, we need to take a vote before the council."

Jesse looked surprised, shocked even. "I thought you were always the one who was against the violence. You said the bloodshed between the Liberators and Steel Infidels had to end for the sake of the MC. You've always said that. For years."

Flint shrugged. "I changed my mind," he said firmly. "Funny how little things like two murder attempts on your life can change your perspective. Things are different now. Call for the vote. It's way past time we dealt with this and put it behind us once and for all."

Jesse clapped him on the back. "Yes sir, little brother. Glad to have you back. Now go take care of the doc."

Flint took one last look at each of the bodies on the ground before heading back to Kendra. He was glad to see she hadn't moved. "Are you still doing okay?" he asked.

She tried bravely to smile. "I'm a little shook up, but otherwise I'm fine. Are they all dead?"

Flint looked away, unable to meet her eyes. "Yes."

"Did you know any of them?"

"You mean personally?" he asked, then shook his head. "No, not anyone in this group. Wouldn't recognize them if I met them on the street. I knew plenty about them though."

Kendra started to say something, then stopped. She chewed on her bottom lip a moment before working up the courage to ask the question that had been bothering her. "Did I kill anyone? You need to tell me the truth."

Flint grabbed her hand and linked his fingers through hers. "Kendra, look at me. You didn't kill anyone. I promise. With the exception of the driver that you hit in the leg, I'm not sure you even shot anybody else. There were a lot of shots fired, and most of them came either from my gun or from the crew. Don't start worrying about this. I can see it's already messing with your head. You need to put those thoughts out of your mind right now. But just to be on the safe side, you need to give me your shotgun."

Kendra looked confused. "Why?"

"I think it would be best if it didn't stay in your possession. At least for now. Is it registered to you?"

Kendra shook her head. "I don't think so."

"Where did you get it? Think back because this is important."

Kendra thought for a moment then shrugged. "My uncle gave it to me several years ago. He owns a sporting goods store on the outside of town. It may have even been my Grandpa's. I really don't know."

"Okay. It really doesn't matter as long as it is not registered or traceable in any way back to you."

Kendra looked up at him with her big brown eyes. "I'm in big trouble, aren't I?"

"No," Flint replied firmly. "You didn't do anything wrong. You're not going to be in any trouble and if you ever were, I would protect you. You acted in self-defense. They drew their weapons first. You said so yourself."

"I assume we're not calling the police?"

He shook his head. "You know why we can't. That's all the more reason why you should get out of here as fast as you can. I don't want someone spotting your truck. If anyone asks you what happened to your side mirror, tell them you slid off the road and hit a mailbox. Do you want me to drive you home or can you make it by yourself?"

"I can do it," she replied "I'm sure Jesse needs you more here."

"Okay, let me get the crew over here to push you out and get you on your way. Go very slow, and if you get stuck on an icy spot, just wait for us. We'll be down the mountain real soon right behind you. Hand me the gun and all of the shells that go with it."

Kendra dutifully handed the gun to him along with the extra box of shells.

Flint propped the gun up on the side of the truck. "I'm so sorry," he whispered. “Come here.” He slid his arm behind her and pulled her close one last time. “I promise everything is going to be okay,” he whispered in her ear. He touched his lips to hers for one brief moment before letting her go and waving the crew over.

3

Kendra didn't waste any time once she reached the bottom of the mountain road. She turned the truck toward Bardsville and headed to the wildlife clinic rather than going straight home. She needed to be around animals and her staff members, not sitting at home by herself fretting over things that couldn't be changed.

The decision to shoot had been easy.

Kill or be killed.

Protecting Flint had been her main focus so she hadn't hesitated when it came time to pull the trigger. Unfortunately, the aftermath was proving to be a little more difficult to deal with. She found it ironic how the movies never accurately portrayed the horrifying thud of bullets tearing through flesh and bone or the gaping wounds the bullets left behind. Or how a person gasped for breath when their lungs filled with blood, causing them to technically drown in their own fluids.

Kendra knew it would be a long time before she could forget those things.

If ever.

She was known around town as a savior of animals, and now she wondered if she would also be known as a killer of people. Oh sure, Flint had tried to make her feel better about things, trying to reassure her that the bullets from her gun hadn't killed anyone. But how did he know for certain? How would she ever know for sure that she hadn't murdered another human being? Would the doubts in her mind circle around and around until they eventually drove her crazy?

The MC would destroy all of the evidence. Of that much she was certain. Jesse and the crew were already loading the dead bodies into the back of their truck by the time she had left the scene. She hated to think about what would happen next. Would they bury the bodies? Burn them? Would the men's family members ever know what happened? Or would the women who loved them wait at home forever for their man to return?

She wished she knew exactly where all of her shots had landed. But in the end, she wondered if it would really make a difference. The final result would remain the same. There had been a gun battle between two rival motorcycle clubs, and four men died.

Rather than hiding in the truck and waiting for it all to be over, she had instead chosen to be a willing participant. It had been her choice and hers alone to grab the gun. Nobody forced her to pull the trigger. Not once, but several times.

On the other hand, Flint was safe and alive. At least for now. She had protected her man when he needed her to. Of course he wouldn't have asked her to do it or even wanted her to. But Flint would live to see another sunrise because of her. And that's all that really mattered when it came right down to it.

She always did what needed to be done, and this time was no different than any other.

She took a deep breath.

Whatever happened, there would be no regrets.

4

Flint walked into his house and headed straight for the refrigerator. He grabbed a cold beer and unscrewed the top. After taking two long swigs, he pulled out a chair and sat down at the kitchen table. He rubbed his tired eyes then leaned back and closed them for a second.

He was physically exhausted and mentally whipped. What a fucking nightmare the last few days had turned out to be. The mess with the Liberators was bad enough, but to drag an innocent woman like Kendra into all his shit was unforgivable.

He still couldn't fathom how the day's events had gone downhill so quickly. From making love to an amazing woman in the shower to watching her almost get killed right in front of his eyes. It made him physically ill to remember watching Kendra stepping out of the truck and into the path of the Liberators' bullets.

Everything had happened so fast, catching him completely unprepared and off guard. It never should have happened. He was a smart man. Why didn't he think ahead and at the very least warn Kendra that the Liberators could come up on them at any time? He hadn't wanted to frighten her and so he downplayed the seriousness of the situation. By trying to protect her, he had instead placed her in incredible danger.

He'd made a big mistake and hadn't given Kendra enough credit.

She was a tough woman and could've handled whatever came their way. She had more than proved that today.

What if something had happened to her? He couldn't bear the thought of harm coming to Kendra because of him. Because of his choices. When he had looked into the Liberators' eyes, his first and only thought had been of Kendra. Of how he could possibly keep her safe. The thought never occurred to him that she was thinking the same thing about him. His mind still couldn't wrap around the reasons why.

He would never forget the overwhelming feeling of horror that engulfed him when he saw her step out of the truck and take aim. Time had stood still and his heart ceased to beat. Unable to stop her in time, he'd watched helplessly as the events unfolded.

And when he was finally able to make his way to her and push her back into the truck for safety, what did she do? She snatched up more shells and crawled out the other side of the truck! If he could have grabbed her at that moment, he would have cheerfully wrung her neck.

God! Kendra was exasperating and infuriating. And he wanted her desperately, madly. More than he had ever wanted any other woman before. The feelings he had for other women in the past never came close to this. She was everything he could have ever hoped for in a woman. Even as terrified as he was for her today, he couldn't have been prouder. He knew deep inside it was so much more than a physical attraction. He burned for Kendra.

But he couldn't have her.

In his heart, he knew that to continue the relationship would be wrong. She deserved so much better than him. Kendra deserved more than to be drawn into a life of firebombs, shootings, and murders. A life of being afraid and always watching over her shoulder.

Flint didn't want her to ever feel afraid again. Not like today.

He wanted her to be able to go out on vet visits with an open, trusting heart like she always had before. Without having to worry if the Liberators might be waiting for her in a secluded barn or even back at her house. Just the mere act of being with him would put her at risk.

Back at the cabin, Kendra had told him about how hard she had worked to get through college and then vet school. She loved her family, her job, and her life working with the animals. For him to come in and steal some of that joy away because of his involvement with the Steel

Infidels wasn't right. A few days with him and her life had already been turned completely upside down. And now that the war with the Liberators was cranking up full force, it was only going to get worse. He hated to think what the next few days or weeks would bring. None of it would be good.

He had to end it with Kendra before it went any further, even if it killed him to do it. The thought ripped his heart out. Being with her felt so right. But he knew the longer it went on, the harder it would be to break it off. His feelings would only grow stronger with time.

With any luck, maybe Kendra had come to the same conclusion. She couldn't have been thrilled about everything that had happened the last few days. From being pressured into taking care of his gunshot wound to being caught in the middle of a gun battle, she would probably be very relieved for Flint to end it so she wouldn't have to.

Flint hoped so. Walking away from a woman like Kendra would be a next to impossible thing to do. Depressed and dreading the task ahead of him, Flint drained his beer and grabbed another one.

When Jesse came into the kitchen a little while later, Flint was still sitting at the table with his eyes closed.

"Hey buddy," Jesse said, clapping him on the shoulder as he walked past him to the refrigerator. "Any beer left for me?"

"Maybe," Flint answered. "Everything taken care of with the SUV?"

"For now," Jesse answered. "We were able to get it over to the chop shop. They'll have it in a million unidentifiable pieces by the end of the day. Luckily, there weren't many people out on the roads because of the ice. What about the Liberators? Everything okay on your end?"

Flint nodded. "The bodies will never be found. Ever. We made sure of that."

Jesse studied him for a moment without speaking. He grabbed a beer and joined him at the table. "So, you want to tell me what's going on with you and the doc?" he asked.

Flint leaned forward and began peeling the corner of the paper wrapping of the beer bottle. "What do you mean?"

Jesse raised his eyebrows. "Don't shit me. I can see something's going on. You two were as thick as thieves up on the mountain. You like her?"

Flint let out a tired sigh. "Yeah, I like her. She's great. Too good for me."

Jesse didn't argue with him or try to convince his brother otherwise. He'd had his share of women trouble because of the MC, too. Serious relationships and the motorcycle club rarely went together smoothly.

"Funny thing," Jesse said. "I had a chance to take a good long look at the SUV and the bodies before you hauled them away. I'm not an expert by any means, but from what I could tell, there were a whole shitload of bullet holes that couldn't have come from your pistol. Want to tell me what really happened up there before we arrived?"

Flint blew out a long breath and shook his head. "I can't."

Jesse stayed quiet for a moment. "You realize the MC can't protect her if we don't know the whole story. I'm not an idiot. I saw you take the shotgun away from her and slide it under the seat of my pickup. I assume those extra bullet holes came from her gun?"

Flint knew Jesse was absolutely right. His brother should know about the sacrifices Kendra had made for the MC. Keeping secrets always seemed to cause more problems later on.

"We were stuck on an icy patch of road," Flint began. "I went behind the truck to push while Kendra took the wheel. I had my head down, so when the Liberators came flying around the curve, she spotted them before I did. By the time I saw them and they recognized me, she'd already grabbed the shotgun. When they piled out of the SUV and pointed their guns at me, she started shooting. Long story short, Kendra saved my life."

Jesse leaned back in his chair and took another sip of beer. "Fucking unbelievable. Why the hell did she do that?"

Flint threw up his hands. "I don't know. She was protecting me, I guess. Act first, think later kind of thing. I doubt she really thought it through. It all happened so fast. If she hadn't started shooting, there's no doubt they would have killed us both right then and there."

"She got a lot of shots in with her gun. You understand what I'm saying?"

"She killed one of them?" Flint wasn't surprised.

"Maybe more than one," Jesse answered. "Honestly, how the hell am I supposed to know? A shotgun blows a big ass hole and there were lots of them. Who knows whose bullet did the final deed? It might have been her or any one of us. As long as you took care of the bodies and destroyed the evidence, we'll never need to know. And more importantly, she'll never need to know."

Flint leaned his elbows on the table and put his head in his hands. "This keeps getting worse by the minute. Does anyone else know this about her?"

Jesse shook his head. "Nah, I doubt it. When we arrived, the doc was behind the truck. I didn't see her fire a shot, so my guess is nobody else did either. And you know Rocco and the rest of the crew never pay much attention to details. They probably didn't even notice it. Nobody mentioned it. We were all too busy cleaning up the damn mess and dumping the evidence to think too much about the doc."

"Nobody else can know about this," Flint said. "Especially not Kendra. She thinks she shot the driver in the leg and that's it. She can never find out that she might be responsible for any of the fatal shots."

"She won't hear it from me, I promise," Jesse agreed. "It certainly wouldn't help the MC, and she might even feel guilty enough to turn herself in and spill everything. That would be a fucking disaster. What are you going to do about her anyway?"

"End it. Being with me is shit. She needs to get out while she still can."

"I'm sorry to hear that," Jesse said. "You're right though. It's probably for the best. I haven't had the best luck in the world with women either. No matter what you decide, the Steel Infidels still owe her for everything she did to help us out. Make sure to tell her the proceeds from the charity drive will be there for her wildlife clinic in the spring. And tell her thank you from me. For everything."

"I will," Flint said. "That's the least we can do."

"I've called a meeting tonight at the clubhouse and asked everybody to be there. We need to update all of the crew about the Liberators and take a vote whether to go on the offensive or not. Are you absolutely sure this is best for the MC?"

"It is," Flint replied firmly. "Unless you have a better idea? They're going to keep coming at us until we stop them once and for all."

"I'm shit out of ideas. I've been raring to go full force at them every day since they murdered Tommy. Nothing too bad can happen to them as far as I'm concerned. The only reason I've been holding back is because of you and Sam."

"I know. I've been thinking about this, and we have to be smart this time. Not like in the past. The MC has to go at it a different way. A way that can't be traced back to us. We're not a bunch of deadbeat drug addicts who dropped out of high school. We're on a whole different level than the Liberators, and there should be a way for us to take them out and still keep our hands clean. There's more than one way to put the Liberators out of business without another big shootout somewhere."

"Since you're the brains of the operation, do you want to head this up?" Jesse asked. "All you have to do is say the word, and I'll make sure the crew backs you up one hundred percent. It'll be just like old times. You're the brains and I'm the muscle. It's always been that way."

Flint laughed. "Yeah, we always made quite a team. I knew no matter what kind of mess I got myself into when I was young that you'd always run over and help me fight my way out. The two of us together were invincible. It's not us I'm worried about though. What about Sam? We have to protect him. I don't want him getting hurt or tangled up in this mess."

"He's one of the crew, too," Jesse reasoned. "Just like us. He's all grown up now and we can't treat him differently from the others. He would hate us for it, and the other crew members would disrespect him if we did."

"He's our little brother, for Christ's sake! That makes him different. And you know that after everything Sam has been through with Dad, we can't dump more shit on him. Help me figure out a plan to keep him safe. And don't give me that bullshit about treating him the same as Rocco or Tom. I know deep down inside you feel exactly the same way as I do."

"You're right, I do. But Sam can't know about this or he'll hate us both."

"You mean instead of just me?" Flint asked.

"That's not what I said."

"It's what you meant. I know how Sam feels about me and how I abandoned him. All the more reason I'm not throwing him under the wheels of the Liberators now. I won't let him down again. We need to agree to keep Sam out of the front lines in this fucking mess."

"No argument from me," Jesse said.

"No argument about what?" Sam asked as he strolled into the

kitchen. He shrugged off his jacket and tossed it across the back of a chair. "How is your arm doing, Flint?" he asked over his shoulder before opening the refrigerator. "Dammit! You motherfuckers drank all the goddamn beer!"

"Here, you can have what's left of mine," Flint said. He stood up and handed the half-empty bottle to Sam. "See you both tonight at the clubhouse."

Sam looked at the beer a second before taking a sip. "Thanks a lot, asshole!"

Flint laughed. He shot a quick look at Jesse, who imperceptibly nodded back.

Sam would stay safe. The brothers would make sure of it. And Kendra would never know she most likely murdered someone.

So many secrets to juggle.

5

The Steel Infidels' clubhouse smelled musty, like sweat and stale beer. The hangout was an old renovated warehouse in a rundown industrial park on the outskirts of Bardsville. Only a few years before, the industrial park had been a bustling place with boot factories and textile plants. One by one, the manufacturing businesses had outsourced their work overseas until all of the factories had eventually given pink slips to their workers and closed up shop.

With the economy being so bad, there weren't any new businesses coming in to take over the empty spaces. The man who owned the property had been thrilled to rent out one of the buildings and a back section of the property to the Steel Infidels. It gave the MC privacy, plenty of room to hang out, and a secure place to park their motorcycles and extra vehicles.

A couple of men in the crew were trained carpenters, and it hadn't taken them long to turn the warehouse into a biker's version of an ideal motorcycle club hangout, complete with billiard tables, posters of naked girls on the wall, and mismatched couches and chairs.

The crew had even taken the time to remodel a couple of the old bookkeeping offices into small, drab-looking bedrooms. The term "bedroom" was used loosely since the rooms mainly consisted of a donated bed and a couple of rolling office chairs. Over the years, all of the crew, including Flint, had spent the night there at one time or the other, either to sleep off a drunk or to have a place to hook up with a girlfriend away from their old lady's prying eyes.

When Flint walked in, he immediately noticed the clubhouse needed a good floor-to-ceiling cleaning. After the meeting, he would have to give a strict lecture to the handful of new prospects whose responsibilities were to keep the place looking halfway decent and clean. He'd been away only a couple of days and they were already slacking off. Since they were competing with each other for a place at the voting table, he knew a few stern words would be enough to whip them back into shape.

He glanced around the room, making sure there wasn't anyone there that he didn't know. Strangers weren't allowed in the club, but occasionally a nomad or a member of another friendly motorcycle club would drop by to visit and catch up with the crew.

Flint wasn't surprised to see a few young women milling about the pool tables and a couple more hanging out with the guys throwing darts. The Sweet Butts were as much a part of the motorcycle club culture as the crew's black leather cuts and motorcycles.

Flint didn't find any of the current girls appealing, though he was probably the only guy in the MC to think that way. The girls hanging around the clubhouse were easy on the eyes and eager to please, the main requirements of being one of the MC's Sweet Butts or party girls. With a snap of a crew's fingers, any of the girls would be willing to get down on their knees to give a blowjob or anything else a member wanted.

All for the privilege of being one of the Steel Infidels' girls.

Some of the other motorcycle clubs in the state, mostly renegade one-percenters, recruited young girls right off the street. They were mostly runaways hooked on meth or new hookers. Occasionally, they even bought the girls outright from their pimps to keep and do with as they pleased. It made Flint sick to think about the young girls being sold into a version of modern day slavery. Most people didn't realize such evil things existed in the good old United States of America.

He'd heard rumors that the Liberators were one of the groups who were holding young women, either by force or by keeping them so strung out on drugs they didn't want to leave. As far as he was concerned, that was one more nail in their coffin and another reason to permanently wipe them out.

The Steel Infidels didn't have to stoop so low to get their girls. The pretty young women lined up for the opportunity to swing their legs over the seat of a crew member's bike. If one of the girls fell out of line or caused too much trouble among the other girls, the MC would simply kick them out and bring in another. With women being the way they were, there was always a mess of some kind being stirred up, usually caused by jealousy over preferential treatment by the crew or one girl fucking another girl's man. As a result, the clubhouse always had a steady stream of fresh new faces.

The less than stellar treatment of women in the MC had been around much longer than Flint. And while he didn't agree with it, it wasn't his place to question it or try to change things. Not if he wanted to remain in the MC.

As long as the girls were of legal age and were there voluntarily, he would keep his mouth shut. The girls were a huge perk to most of the crew and one of the main ways to keep them vested in the club. A steady supply of willing pussy was enough to keep most of the men willing to do almost anything to keep their place at the table.

"Hey handsome." One of the short blonde Sweet Butts sidled up to Flint and leaned into his arm. He deliberately averted his gaze from her D-cup sized breasts that were threatening to spill up and over her low cut blouse.

She pressed closer against him. "I heard you were hurt," she said. "Need someone to make you feel better?" She placed a hand on his arm and rubbed it suggestively. He looked down at the long fingernails painted with garish red nail polish and wished he was somewhere else. Anywhere else. With Kendra. "Nobody is using the back room," the blonde added, tilting her head toward the door of the tiny bedroom.

Flint gave her a polite smile. "Nah, I'm good," he replied. "Thanks for the offer, Brittany. I'm sure one of the other guys could use some cheering up though. It's been a hell of a hard day." He extracted himself from her grasp as quickly as he could and hurried across the room to join Rocco and Tom at one of the pool tables.

"Is everyone here?" Flint asked. He glanced around the room and quickly took a count of the voting members. Everyone was there except

Jesse. He frowned. It wasn't like his brother to be running late. Even as a kid, Jesse was always ten minutes early for everything.

"If you ain't early, you're late," was always one of their Dad's favorite sayings. The brothers all still followed their Dad's advice out of habit more than anything else. Old family habits died hard.

"Anybody heard from Jesse?" Flint asked around. "He should've been here by now."

Tom shook his head and pulled at his beard. "Last I heard from him was about an hour ago. He said he was on his way."

Flint nervously checked his watch and his cell phone again. When another fifteen minutes went by without word from Jesse, the rest of the crew started getting restless too. Not only was Jesse late for the meeting, he was also late for an important vote. As President of the Steel Infidels, it was his responsibility to bring the meeting to order and call for the vote. There wouldn't be a meeting without Jesse.

Forty-five minutes later, Jesse rushed in, looked haggard and upset. Flint hurried across the room and met him at the door. "What happened?" he asked. "Tell me."

"They found a body," Jesse said. "My source at the police station contacted me a little bit ago about a call that came in. She was found dumped on the side of the road. A tall woman with long red hair."

Flint immediately knew why Jesse was upset. "You think it's Leah?"

"My gut says it is," Jesse answered. "The Liberators wouldn't think twice about killing her if they found out she tipped me off about the planned raid on the safe house. And now that four of their guys are missing, they have to know it was us. It's my fault if something happened to Leah. She was trying to protect us."

"No, it's not your fault," Flint argued. "Going with the Liberators was her choice, not yours. She could've stayed here as a Sweet Butt for as long as she wanted. Hell, she might have been the MC's queen by now. Everyone loved Leah. Don't blame yourself. You're not responsible if it turns out to be her."

"Dammit, I still feel responsible!" Jesse replied. "I couldn't give Leah what she needed. I tried, but I could never feel the same way for her as she did toward me. I'm the reason she couldn't stay with the MC."

"That may be true, but hooking up with the Liberators was a crazy move on her part. Knowing Leah, she probably did it in the beginning to make you jealous and then couldn't get out. When is your source supposed to call you back?"

"Anytime. He works as a dispatcher, so he'll know something the minute the call comes in. The police are already headed to the scene now. It's not too far out of town on Highway 98."

"I'll round up the guys and tell them what's going on," Flint said. "Why don't you go have a drink to calm your nerves while you wait for the call? There's no hurry on the meeting. We've got all fucking night if we need it."

Jesse's cell phone rang as Flint turned to walk away. He stopped and waited.

"Are you sure?" Jesse said into the phone. "How did she die?" He listened for a moment. "Let me know if you find anything else," he said before hanging up.

Flint stepped toward him.

"It's Leah," Jesse said. "They have a positive ID. The Liberators left her purse with her driver's license on the dirt beside her. They dumped her on the side of the road like a piece of trash."

"How did they do it?" Flint hated having to ask the question. He hoped it was quick and painless. Knowing how revengeful and ruthless the Liberators could be, he doubted it.

"Sounds like they beat the shit out of her first then shot her in the head."

"Aww shit! Motherfuckers! I'm sorry. If this is anyone's fault, it's mine. She died because she was trying to save me."

"I swear to God I'm going to kill all those motherfuckers," Jesse said. "Gather up the guys and get them to the table. I'm calling for a vote now."

Flint quickly made his way around the room, alerting the crew to the updated situation. Jesse grabbed a bottle of bourbon from behind the bar and carried it into the voting room. He took a big swig and passed it to Rocco on his left, who took a swig and passed it on as was the custom.

When the almost empty bottle made its way back around to Jesse, he placed it in the middle of the table with a loud thump and called the meeting to order. The crew didn't ask questions, only listened as he explained what they were voting on and why. Jesse also reminded the crew the vote had to be unanimous in order for it to pass.

When Jesse finished, he stood. "All in favor of declaring war on the Liberators, say aye."

Flint rose to his feet. "Aye."

Rocco stood and voted, followed by Tom, then Rocco's brother. One by one they went around the voting table. The final vote came down to Sam, the youngest member of the Steel Infidels.

He took a deep breath before standing then grinned widely. "Aye!"

"Hell yeah!"

The loud cheers went up in the room.

"About fucking time we did something about the Liberator bastards!" Tom yelled, clapping Jesse on the back. "We've let them shit on us for far too long."

"Before everybody gets too excited, we need to talk about the plan," Jesse said. "Sit back down and listen to what Flint has to say."

6

Kendra checked her cell phone one last time and crawled into bed. It was after midnight, and she hadn't heard a single word from Flint. Not even a text message. It wasn't as if she expected him to be calling her every ten minutes, but a quick call to see how she was doing would've been nice. For all he knew, she could be freaking out over the shooting. A little comfort and reassurance would go a long way, even for a tough girl like her. She pulled the covers up to her chin and stared at the ceiling.

Was she crazy to be wrapped up in him so soon?

Maybe he was already having regrets. Or maybe she didn't meet the approval of the other guys in the Steel Infidels. She knew she wasn't exactly biker chick material. Hell, for all she knew, being with a girl like her could be against their rules. The MC probably had very strict protocol for being one of their girls. Most likely blonde, big-breasted, and brainless. Guess that ruled her out. At least on the blonde and brainless part anyway.

The loud roar of a motorcycle pulling into her driveway startled her. She jumped out of bed and looked out the window. It was too dark to see anything. Her first thought was that it could be the Liberators, though why they would only send one guy didn't make sense. Especially on a very noisy bike.

Kendra inched her way in the darkness to the living room. She was afraid to turn on the lights because whoever it was would be able to see her through the windows. She crouched down behind the couch and carefully crawled across the room. Her pistol was in her purse on a table by the door. Damn! She needed to start keeping it close by on the bedside table at night.

Just before she reached her purse, three loud knocks sounded from the door. "Kendra! Are you home? It's Flint!"

What the hell? She felt like killing him. She ran to the door and threw it open.

"Flint! What are you doing here? You scared me half to death! Haven't you ever heard of a phone? It's after midnight. Normal people are asleep by this time."

Flint gazed at her for a second without saying a word. Kendra was dressed for bed in a white t-shirt without a bra and black sweatpants. Probably not the sexiest outfit in the world to most people, but to him she'd never looked more beautiful.

He had intended to come over and end it gently. Once and for all. On the ride to her house, he'd convinced himself it was for her own good and something that needed to be done. One look at her and all his best intentions disappeared. Damn! How would he ever have the strength to walk away from this woman?

"Who ever said we were normal?" he asked with a wry smile. He let out a tired breath and leaned against the door. "Are you going to invite me in?"

"What are you?" she joked. "A vampire that needs permission to step across the threshold of a house?"

"No...something far worse. We need to talk."

Kendra frowned at his serious tone. "Come on in then." She stepped back to allow him inside her living room then reached over to switch on a lamp. "How did you get your motorcycle off the mountain? Are the roads still icy?"

"We loaded it into the back of Jesse's truck and brought it down the mountain that way." He didn't mention the fact that there were four dead bodies in the back of the truck as well. "The roads in the valley are all clear now after the rain we've had the last couple of hours. It's safe to drive."

"How is your arm?"

"Throbbing. It'll be okay."

"Let me grab my bag and I'll change the bandage."

He touched her arm. "It's fine."

"So what's going on?" Kendra asked. "Did something else happen?"

Flint hesitated. He wanted to tell her everything, or at least as much as he could without giving away too many details of the Steel Infidels' business. He knew if he told her about Leah's murder and the MC's decision to go to war with the Liberators that maybe she would understand why it could never work out between them.

Why it had to be over.

Why there could be no other choice but to end it now.

Flint looked down into her troubled brown eyes and his resolve started to weaken. He reached over and fingered a long strand of wild, tousled hair that had fallen out of place. Swallowing hard, he began, "Kendra..."

She reached up and placed a gentle hand on his cheek. He closed his eyes, and for a moment they stood there in silence without either of them moving.

"Don't say it," she whispered. "Don't say it's over before it's even begun. I can see it on your face."

"I have to protect you, Kendra," he said hoarsely. "I can't go through another ordeal like today. Watching you be put in danger because of me. We have to end this between us. Tonight. Please tell me you understand." He shook his head slowly, his green eyes piercing hers. "I don't want to do this. God knows I don't want to. You're the best thing that's ever happened to me. Which is all the more reason why this can't be. I don't deserve someone like you. My life is all screwed up right now."

"Do you believe in fate, Flint?"

He let out a humorless laugh and ran a hand through his hair. "No, I don't believe in shit. I used to believe in a lot of things. Not anymore. If you believe in things, then you start to have hope. When you have hope, all you do is set yourself up to be shattered later on down the road."

"Maybe someday I can change the way you feel about that," Kendra said. She stepped closer and wrapped both arms around his waist under his leather jacket. He fought to ignore the delicious soft weight of her full breasts pressing against his chest and the sweet smell of her shampoo. He needed to stay strong to get through this and she was making it so damn hard.

"You don't think it's weird how we met?" she asked, her head against his chest. "Think about it. What would be the chance of that? Even if our paths had crossed another way, would we have given each other an opportunity to get to know what was really inside? We were brought together for a reason. I can't help but believe that. We can't just throw it all away because we're scared."

Flint started to speak and she interrupted him. "Don't deny it. It's okay to be scared. Even for a big, tough guy like you. I know you're worried and afraid...for me. I get that."

Flint pulled her close and bent down to nuzzle her neck. "I'm not just scared," he murmured. "I'm fucking terrified. I feel like I can't even breathe. I've never been put in a position like this before. The Liberators can hurt me most by hurting you. I feel so goddamn vulnerable. You're absolutely right, and I'm not afraid to admit it. I'm scared and I'm worried sick for you."

"Nothing is going to happen," she reassured. "I'm a big girl. I can take care of myself. And I promise to be more careful when I go out on vet calls if that's what you're worried the most about. I'll screen my calls and can even take a volunteer or a vet tech out on calls with me."

Flint wanted to believe her. How he wanted to believe she would be safe and things would be okay. That they could continue on like a regular couple and go to movies or grab a burger without packing a weapon and looking over their shoulders every few seconds.

"I know you're tough," he said, smoothing down her hair. "And can handle yourself just fine. But you're also a big-hearted person and trusting. And that's what scares the shit out of me. What if the Liberators found some way to trick and hurt you? Hell, look what we did! When Tom Brewer called, you drove straight up to the cabin without thinking twice about it. What if one day the Liberators are on the other end of the telephone line asking for your help?"

"They don't even know who I am, do they?" she asked. "Aren't they all dead? Nobody else saw me. And not a single person in my life knows the truth about where I was this weekend. So only your crew knows about my involvement with the Steel Infidels. And you trust them implicitly. There's nothing to tie me to what happened today or to the MC."

No, nothing except a shitload of bullet holes from your shotgun in four men and a SUV.

Flint didn't dare say what he was thinking out loud. He realized Kendra hadn't completely thought things through carefully. And for the time being, maybe it was better that way. She was depending on him and the MC to destroy the evidence and as far as he knew, they had. Or at least the biggest and most damaging pieces, the bodies of the Liberators and their SUV.

He knew they had probably left plenty of evidence behind at the scene. Bullet holes in trees, tire tracks, boot prints, and no telling what else. First thing tomorrow he needed to go back up there and carefully go over the area inch by inch. He should probably take a couple of the crew with him, though they might accidentally leave more evidence than they cleaned up. It would have to be only Jesse and him. At least his experience as a lawyer had taught him what he needed to look for and how to clean up a crime scene.

Kendra was right about one thing. There weren't any Liberator witnesses left alive to personally connect her to anything.

"Still thinking about leaving me?" She reached for his belt buckle and started to undo the clasp. "Stop worrying. At least for tonight."

"Kendra, what are you doing?" he muttered. He placed a hand over hers to stop her from going any further. "We're not finished talking about this. This isn't resolved."

"As far as I'm concerned, it is," she answered. "After everything that happened today, I need your arms around me tonight. Please, don't go."

She unsnapped the top button of his jeans and slid her hand inside. The instant her hand touched his cock, it hardened and lengthened in her grasp. She encircled it with her hand and stroked down then up again.

Flint groaned against her hair. "Oh Jesus! You're making this impossible. Please, I'm asking you to push me away. Tell me to get the fuck out of here and I'll go. I should turn around and walk out that door right now. Instead, all I can think about is how much I want to bury myself deep inside you and never turn you loose."

"I won't tell you to go," she replied. "Stay with me tonight. Then if you decide to leave later, at least you'll know what you'll be missing."

With a defeated groan, Flint crushed his lips against hers in a desperate kiss. He closed his eyes tight and drank in her sweetness until his head reeled. Knowing she had foolishly risked her life for him made him crazy inside. And yet here she was now, her lips soft and eager against his. However, it didn't make his heart ache any less.

All of the emotions and feelings he had tried so hard to keep in check came flooding out. He knew he should be telling her now about Leah's murder and the plan to go to war with the Liberators. But the words refused to come.

It would have to wait.

Please God, he silently prayed to a deity he wasn't even sure he believed in. *Please don't make me regret being so weak.*

Kendra had no idea how much he needed *her*. He must've been insane to think he could turn around and walk away. How could he forget about her and let that be the end forever?

He picked her up and wrapped her legs around his waist. "Bedroom?" he growled.

Kendra tilted her head. "In there," she said.

Flint carried her into the darkened room and laid her on the edge of the bed.

"Is there a lamp in here?" he asked. "I want to be able to see every inch of your gorgeous body. No sex in the dark for me. Ever. Not with you. I don't want to miss a thing."

She rolled over and clicked on the lamp beside the bed.

"Much better," he murmured. He grabbed the hem of her t-shirt and pulled it over her head. "Your breasts take my breath away every time," he said. "I love how luscious and heavy they are."

"You don't think they're too big?" Kendra asked, always having been self-conscious about her oversized breasts.

"God no!" he answered incredulously. He cupped each breast in his hand and tested the weight. "They're perfect. Better than perfect. And your nipples..." He sighed as he rolled both protruding nipples between his thumb and forefingers. Bending his head, he kissed one before switching to the other, using his tongue to lave the big tips that hardened to buttons.

Kendra's hands reached for him again. He groaned as she slid his jeans off his hips, his eyes glittering darkly as he waited for her next move. She gazed up into his eyes and flattened her palms on his muscular chest. Her hands moved from his pecs to his abs, touching each sinewy muscle that seemed to ripple beneath her fingers. She let her fingers graze his nipples.

Growing bolder, she wrapped her hand around his cock, causing him to seize his breath and arch up into her. As she stroked her hand up and down his hardened shaft, he groaned out loud and placed his hand over hers, guiding her.

When she licked her lips and lowered her mouth to his bulbous tip, he grabbed both sides of her head and made her look at him. "You don't have to do this, sweetheart," he said. "It's not expected or demanded."

Kendra slowly and purposely closed her lips around his cock and sucked the tip as an answer.

"Oh fuck!" Flint moaned, his hands fisting her hair.

Kendra closed her eyes and slid her lips all the way down to his balls and back up again. His hands in her hair guided her movements as she increased the tempo.

"Your mouth feels so fucking good," Flint told her hoarsely. "Look at me, baby."

Her eyes flew open. She stared into his green eyes, mesmerized by the burning hunger in his gaze as he began to move. He thrust in and out of her mouth, holding the back of her head steady. His eyes burned into hers, holding her captive as he fucked her mouth, owning her completely. Saliva dripped from her lips as she widened her mouth further to take him even deeper. She let him thrust into her at the ragged pace he set. He started to jerk faster and then suddenly he was tugging her off him, swearing loudly.

"If I don't stop now, I'm going to come in your beautiful mouth," he said. "And the only thing better than coming in your mouth would be coming inside your hot, tight pussy."

He pushed her back on the bed and dragged her down until her ass was right on the edge with her legs hanging off. "I need to be inside you so fucking bad." He tugged her sweatpants and panties off in one smooth move and tossed them on the floor. Burning with the need to plunge himself inside her as soon as possible, Flint spread her legs wide.

Kendra licked her lips in expectation.

He entered her with a long, smooth thrust, not breaking eye contact and sinking deep into her hot slickness. Kendra gasped as he began to pump his hips, his hands gripping her thighs. She was so wet and hot. He gritted his teeth and forced himself to focus and not lose control too soon.

It wasn't going to work. Not so soon after having her sweet mouth wrapped around his cock.

Fuck!

With a deep groan, he pulled out and flipped her over to straddle him as he settled back on the pillows. Positioned on top of him, she pressed her thighs into his sides and straightened up on her knees. Kendra leaned forward and splayed her hands over his chest with her pussy settled over his groin.

"Still want to leave?" she asked, now in control.

"Never," was his reply. "Nothing could drag me away."

His reverent gaze feasted on her naked body displayed in front of him. He reached up and traced a hand from her swollen lips down to her full breasts and over her stomach. "Every inch of you is exactly perfect for me," he said.

Face to face, he watched her expressive brown eyes as she reached between them and positioned his cock at her entrance. She stroked her pussy lips with the head, gasping at the friction of his hard flesh against her softness. In one smooth motion, she lifted herself up a few inches and impaled herself onto his cock until she had him buried totally inside her.

For a moment, it was unthinkable for either of them to move. He held her still, almost afraid to breathe, wanting to savor the sensation of being held so snugly inside her. Then she braced her hands on his chest and rode him, rising up and sinking down again and again.

Flint gritted his teeth against the sweet agony of having her curvy body fucking him, her large breasts swaying in his face. He leaned forward and took a nipple into his mouth, causing her to cry out in pleasure.

Damn, she drove him mad.

Kendra's body tensed above him and began to clench. He felt her juices dribbling down from her slick cunt and onto his balls and inner thighs as her orgasm rippled in waves within her.

She cried out as she spasmed uncontrollably. Flint felt her contract around him and he held her tight as she collapsed onto his chest, panting for breath. With his cock still inside her, he rolled her over on her back and continued to pump in and out of her. Her moist pussy seemed to be sucking him in and he couldn't hold back much longer.

He roared out her name as he came, spilling his hot seed into her. He continued to pump inside her until he was completely spent. She kissed his shoulder softly and smoothed her hands down and around the Steel Infidels tattoo on his back.

Cupping the back of her head, he drew her up to meet his lips in a tender, sweet kiss. His eyes held hers and it suddenly became more than just physical pleasure for both of them. They saw it mirrored in each other's eyes.

What they felt for each other would never be over.

Ever.

7

Kendra arrived early at the wildlife clinic. Being out of the office on Friday afternoon and the entire weekend had put her behind on her paperwork. She hated to think about the stacks of lab results she had to go through and the calls that needed to be made to anxious animal owners. She put on a pot of strong coffee in the clinic's tiny kitchen and headed out back to the wildlife enclosures. The sun was barely up and the air was crisp and cold.

She checked on the raptor aviary that held a couple of injured hawks before peeking in on a barn owl that was fast asleep. It was the job of the first person who arrived at the clinic each morning – to walk around all of the outdoor pens and aviaries to make sure a predator hadn't dug under or squeezed their way in during the night.

All of the enclosures were wrapped in 1/8-inch chicken wire to prevent predators from digging under, but occasionally a snake would manage to squeeze through the tiniest opening, usually a crack around the door or underneath a shingle. Unfortunately, once they got inside the enclosure and ate whatever prey they were after, the snakes were then too fat to go back out the same way they came in.

Whoever was unlucky enough to be working the first shift would have to pick the snakes up with a shovel and carry them out to the far edge of the property to be released unharmed. The snakes were never killed of course. It would defeat the whole purpose of the wildlife clinic to kill an animal that was only trying to stay alive.

After everything she had been through over the weekend, Kendra was grateful to see that at least all of the animals were safe, though hungry and eager to be fed. She hurried back inside the clinic and pulled out a few frozen mice from the freezer to be prepped for the raptor's breakfast. The paperwork would have to wait a little bit longer. There were too many hungry mouths to feed, and that always came first.

She smiled to herself as she made up the different bowls of food. It felt good to be back at work where she belonged and doing normal everyday things again. To not have to worry about crazy, violent men with guns. Or dead bodies. Or crimes to cover up.

In the middle of the night, Flint had told her about Leah's murder and what the MC planned to do about the Liberators. After hearing how they had killed Leah, any remaining shred of remorse over shooting the Liberators disappeared. They didn't deserve her guilt, not after everything they had done.

It was difficult not to dwell on the situation. She had to trust Flint, Jesse, and the rest of the crew to take care of the Liberators. At this point, there really wasn't anything left for her to do but try to be careful and pray for the MC's safety.

Kendra forced her mind to think about something else. After a long night of being curled up close to Flint and talking about anything and everything, he had kissed her goodbye and slipped out of bed well before daybreak. The day had started out well and she felt good. She wouldn't dare let herself wonder how long it would last.

She was a tad worried though about something silly. Flint had casually mentioned an upcoming cookout at his house on Sunday and had invited her to attend. He'd explained it was a monthly social event for members of the Steel Infidels and any friends or family they wanted to bring along. Everyone was welcome, from the crew to family members to the groupies who hung around the clubhouse.

While normally she would be thrilled to meet a new boyfriend's family and friends, this was a completely different situation. She didn't know how to act around Jesse or the crew after the incident with the Liberators on the mountain.

She wondered what the proper protocol would be in a situation like that. Was she not supposed to say a word and pretend it never happened? Was it okay to talk about her doctoring Flint up at the cabin but not the shootout and murders of four men?

The whole idea made her nervous and uneasy. She didn't like secrets or covering stuff up. It went against everything she believed in. Honesty was important to her. In this case though, the alternative was much worse.

She also didn't know what Flint had told the other members of the MC about her, if anything. If he wanted her to go to the cookout, she would, even if deep down inside she was dreading it.

8

As soon as Kendra arrived at the house Flint shared with his brothers for the cookout, he immediately pulled her into the kitchen. While no one was looking, he backed her up against the sink and planted a warm soft kiss on her lips.

"Thank you for coming," he said, smoothing her hair away from her face. "I missed you."

She looked at her watch. "It's been all of nine hours since you were in my bed this morning." Since leaving the cabin, Flint had spent almost every night at her house.

"I know. Doesn't mean I didn't miss you." He turned her loose and swatted her butt. "And I'm really glad you're here now to help me." He waved a hand around the clean but disorganized kitchen. "We could use a woman's touch around here."

"I can see that," she replied. "What do you need me to do?"

Flint pulled several packs of hamburger meat out of the refrigerator along with tomatoes, onions, and a couple heads of lettuce. "Ladies choice. Make the hamburger patties or cut up the vegetables."

Kendra washed her hands and grabbed a package of meat. "I'll do both since I'm sure you have plenty of other stuff to do. Who is in the charge of the cooking?"

"Jesse and Tom man the two grills," Flint replied. "It's been that way for years. We all have our little jobs to do. As you can tell, I'm the one always stuck working in the kitchen while everybody else is out there drinking and having fun."

Kendra rolled her eyes at him, knowing he was exaggerating.

Jesse rushed into the kitchen. "Flint, you got those hamburger patties ready yet?" he yelled. He drew up short at the sight of Kendra. "Hey, doc! Didn't know you were already here. Glad you could make it. Hope you're keeping Flint straight. He's falling behind on the job. We got hungry bikers out there and nothing to feed them."

He grabbed a beer from the refrigerator. "C'mon buddy, show some hustle," he said over his shoulder as he headed back out. "Everybody will be here soon, and you know how this crowd gets when they're hungry."

"So does the crowd get unruly if you don't feed them?" Kendra asked with a laugh.

Flint made a face. "I guess you could say that. It's more a matter of they tend to drink too much and the alcohol goes straight to their heads without something in their stomachs. That's why we like to keep them fed, fat, and happy."

"Good to know! Thanks for the warning."

It didn't take Kendra long to realize she shouldn't have been so worried about the cookout. The few members of the Steel Infidels who had met her before greeted her like an old friend with kisses on the cheek, and the new ones Flint introduced her to seemed genuinely glad to meet her. They all wandered into the kitchen to say hello to Flint and to check her out, she suspected.

To her relief, nobody mentioned anything about the Liberators or the safe house. If that was the way they wanted to handle things, it would work out just fine with her.

Before long, someone cranked up the stereo and an old rock song started playing. Kendra handed Flint the last plate of hamburger patties to take out to Jesse.

"Somehow I didn't see the Steel Infidels as being a Southern rock kind of biker club," she teased. "And what's with the stereo? What is this, the eighties? And vinyl records for God's sake! I didn't realize those things were still around anymore. At least ones that weren't scratched all to pieces."

"The Steel Infidels are a little bit of everything," Flint explained. "Rocco and Tom are pushing forty-five years old on one end and then we have Sam, our youngest member in his mid-twenties. So you're likely to hear a mixture of all kinds of music when we're together, even an occasional Willie Nelson country tune. We all learned a long time ago not to criticize each other's taste in music. Caused way too many fistfights." He laughed at the memory. "Now everybody gets their turn. The only thing you can count on is that the music will be consistently loud."

He leaned down to kiss her cheek. "I'll be right back. Stay put while I run these burgers out to Jesse," he said.

While he was gone, Kendra covered the platter of lettuce, tomatoes, and onions with plastic wrap then wiped down the counters with a paper towel. She didn't notice the two women who had walked into the kitchen until she turned around to open the refrigerator. She jumped slightly.

"Sorry! Didn't mean to startle you," one of the women said. She was clearly the older of the two and looked to be in her early forties, with long brown hair that was turning grey around her face. She stuck out her hand and gave Kendra a warm smile.

"I'm Myrtle and this is Sarah," she said, pointing to the younger woman. "We heard rumors that Flint had a woman hidden back here in the kitchen, so we had to come meet you."

Kendra smiled back and shook both of their hands. "Kendra Shaw."

Myrtle studied her face a moment. "You look so familiar. Have we met somewhere before?"

"I'm a veterinarian with the Shaw Wildlife Clinic," Kendra explained. "Maybe you brought an animal in to the clinic?"

Myrtle nodded. "I know where I've seen you before. You helped out at one of the dog vaccination clinics, didn't you? My Mama couldn't afford to get all the shots for her little Lhasa Apso so I took her to one of the annual clinics you offered at the Civic Center. She sure did appreciate that by the way. Living on a fixed income, she really couldn't afford to pay out three to four hundred dollars for her dog's shots. Fifty dollars was a very reasonable amount for everything y'all did."

Kendra was pleased to know someone who needed it had taken advantage of the low cost vaccination clinic. It was one of several community events she held throughout the year, an easy way for her to give back to the local people who supported her and keep their pets healthier as well.

"I'm so glad it helped out," Kendra replied. "How's her dog doing now?"

"Feisty and mean as ever," Myrtle replied with a smile. "Those Lhasas can be that way, you know. Spoiled little stinker that he is. Tries to bite my foot every time I go over there to visit." She leaned back against the kitchen counter and looked Kendra over good. "Well, I'm thrilled Flint has finally found someone decent to hang around with."

When Myrtle noticed Kendra's surprised expression, she immediately started backpedalling. "I didn't mean he had brought around girls before that weren't decent," she explained. "I just meant I was glad he finally found a good woman." She leaned in closer and whispered conspiratorially. "Don't tell him we told you, but this is the first time Flint has ever brought any gal to one of our get-togethers."

"Really?" Kendra asked, both surprised and pleased.

"It's not for a lack of female admirers," Sarah added with an impish grin. She was in her late thirties with curly strawberry blonde hair. A tattoo of a dragon ran down the length of her right arm. "Those damn Sweet Butts throw themselves all over Flint and Jesse. They're picky about their women though. In fact, I don't recall seeing Flint with a woman since he's been back in town."

Kendra's ears perked up at that tidbit of information. In their conversations, Flint had been vague about how long he'd been gone from Bardsville and when exactly he'd returned.

"Now, Flint's brother, Sam, is another story," Sarah continued. "He loves the girls and Lord have mercy, they sure do love him. He's quite a little devil, that one is. I just hope to God he carries lots of protection and uses it."

Myrtle rolled her eyes. "Ain't that the damn truth!" Both ladies burst out laughing.

Flint walked back into the kitchen and frowned. "Oh no! What are you two ladies up to now?" He gave Myrtle a quick peck on the cheek and then did the same for Sarah. "What kind of no-good lies are you filling Kendra's head with? I hope you haven't told her too many bad things about me."

The two women giggled. "Nothing that's not true," Myrtle kidded. It was obvious from the fond way the women looked at Flint that they thought the world of him.

"That's exactly what I was afraid of," Flint replied. "Don't believe anything these ladies say," Flint warned Kendra. "Come on, darling," he said, taking Kendra's hand. "Sam's here and I can't wait for you to meet him." He tugged her toward the doorway.

"Hey Flint!" Sarah called out as they walked away. "Don't let this one get away. She's a keeper if you ask me."

Flint grinned back at them. "Yes, ma'am. Don't I know it!"

"What nice women!" Kendra said as they walked hand-in-hand through the living room. "I have a feeling they're protective of you and were checking me out. To make sure I was worthy. It's obvious they care a great deal about you."

Flint chuckled. "I'm sure you passed with flying colors. After all, who wouldn't like you? Myrtle and Sarah are a couple of the club's old ladies. They've been around for years. They're like mother hens, trying to boss us guys around all the time. It usually works too because we're all so scared of them."

He pointed to a handsome young man in his early twenties with sandy blonde hair and blue eyes standing in the middle of a group of girls across the room. "There's Sam. Doing what he does best. Flirting with the ladies."

"Dang!" Kendra replied. "He's quite a looker, too. All of you brothers are. Your parents must have had very good genes."

"Do I need to be jealous?" Flint said, suddenly serious.

Kendra gave him a curious look and laughed. "No! Of course not. Where did that come from?"

"That's good," Flint replied with a wry smile. "When we were younger, I had more than one girlfriend fall for Jesse after I brought her home to meet the family. After a while, I learned to stop bringing my girlfriends home."

"Probably because he was older and therefore more mysterious," Kendra said. "Trust me, I only have eyes for you." Flint seemed genuinely relieved at her answer, and she wondered if there was more to the story than he was letting on. There seemed to be a lot of undercurrents going on between the three brothers that she hadn't quite figured out yet. She hoped Flint would tell her some day.

Sam looked up and grinned when he saw them. "So you're Kendra?" he said, reaching out to shake her hand. "I'm Sam, otherwise known as the baby brother."

"And the talented tattoo artist too, from what I hear," Kendra added.

"Yeah, that's me."

"Sam has built up quite a steady clientele," Flint said. "He specializes in tattoos for women in...private places." He wriggled his eyebrows for emphasis.

The Sweet Butts hanging on both sides of Sam giggled.

"Oh goodness!" Kendra exclaimed. "I'm afraid to even ask exactly what that means. You don't have to tell me. I'll let it stay a mystery."

"You want one, Kendra?" Sam offered with a wink. "I'll give you a special price. Family discount and all that."

"Hell no," Flint answered curtly "Absolutely not. Hands off, Sam," he warned. "Besides, I already have something very unique for Kendra in mind. I'll do it myself."

Sam lifted up his beer bottle and laughed again at Flint's expression. "Just teasing you, bro. That's all." He turned back to Kendra and lowered his voice. "I'm not so sure I would let him do a tattoo on me. I'm much more experienced, so when the time comes...."

Kendra frowned. "I thought Flint worked at the tattoo parlor with you?"

Sam slapped Flint on the shoulder. "That's a good one. Fuck, Flint! What the hell you been telling this woman?"

Suddenly Kendra felt stupid, like everyone was in on a joke but her. A worried look crossed Flint's face and he quickly hid it.

"So now you've met the infamous Sam," Flint said jokingly before sliding an arm around Kendra's waist. "Let's go see how Jesse and Tom are coming along with those burgers. Sam, will you make sure all of the picnic tables and chairs are set up out back on the screened-in porch? It looks like just about everybody is here and we'll be ready to eat in a few minutes."

"We'll help Sam," one of the young, blonde Sweet Butts replied. She linked her arm with Sam's and giggled again. Kendra resisted the urge to roll her eyes dramatically at the young woman and to suggest she might want to put some more clothes on. It was the dead of winter and the girl was dressed in a low-cut pink tank top to show off her ample boobs. Kendra knew she had to be absolutely freezing to death. Then again, maybe that was the point, judging from the look of the erect nipples poking through her shirt.

Sam threw his arm around another girl's shoulders and hugged both girls tightly. "Come on, ladies. Back to work."

Flint settled down beside Kendra on a bench pulled close to one of the many picnic tables spread around the large porch. Portable heaters kept the area warm and cozy.

"So what do you think?" he asked, handing her another beer.

"Think about what?" she replied.

"Us. The MC. The cookout. This whole thing. What are your thoughts?"

Kendra pondered his question for a moment before answering. "I like it," she replied honestly. "I like the feeling of family and camaraderie among the group. Everyone has been super nice to me, and most of them went out of their way to make me feel comfortable. They didn't have to do that and I really appreciate it. Today has definitely changed my idea of what a motorcycle club is all about."

"Thank you for saying that," Flint said, squeezing her hand underneath the table. "I'm glad you were able to see this side of the MC after everything that's happened. We're like one big family. It seems most of our troubles stem from that since when someone messes with one of us, they mess with the whole MC, but we aren't about to change the way we are."

"No, and I wouldn't want you to."

Flint sighed and stretched his long legs. "Today has been just about perfect. Having you here with me, along with my brothers and the rest of the crew. Good company, good food, good music, and good beer. I couldn't ask for anything else. I'm truly a blessed man. This is the happiest I've been in a long time."

Kendra laid her head on his shoulder. A few of the crew had already drunk way too much whiskey and had wandered outside. They were dancing their best version of an Irish jig around a big oak tree in the front yard. She heard Myrtle yell at one of the men to stop fooling around and get back inside before he hurt himself. When he didn't, Myrtle stormed out of the house, grabbed his arm, and dragged him back in.

Life was pretty good.

She could definitely get used to this.

9

"Oh shit!" Flint said suddenly. He let Kendra's hand go and jumped up from the bench.

"What is it?" she asked in alarm.

A police car slid quietly into the driveway and stopped. Two police officers stepped out of the car and walked down the hill toward the house. Flint's heart leaped into his throat.

Jesus Christ! Please don't let them be here for Kendra.

His worst fucking nightmare was coming true.

Again.

Flint hurried outside to greet the officers, with Kendra following right behind him. Out of the corner of his eye, he saw Jesse moving their way, too. Flint suspected Jesse was probably thinking the exact same thing he was, along with the rest of the crew. That the police had found out about the Liberators. He only hoped to God they didn't know about Kendra's involvement.

Flint put on his calmest, most professional lawyer face. "Evening officers," he said politely. "What's going on? Is there a problem? We might've gotten a little loud with the music, but we'll turn it down if someone called in a complaint. We're about ready to send everyone home anyway. We'll call it a night."

By this time, a crowd had come out of the house and gathered silently behind him. No one said a word. Miraculously, even the drunk guys seemed to have sobered up instantly. Amazing how the sudden appearance of the police could do that.

"We're not here about the party," the officer replied. "We're here looking for Jesse Mason," he said.

Jesse stepped forward beside Flint. "I'm Jesse Mason," he replied. "What can I do for you?"

The second officer pulled out a pair of handcuffs from his back pocket. "Jesse Mason, you're under arrest for the murder of Leah Andrews."

"What???" Flint and Jesse both yelled in shock at the same time. In every scenario either could have imagined, being arrested for Leah's murder wasn't one of them.

The officer pulled Jesse's hands behind his back and slipped on the handcuffs. "You have the right to remain silent," he began. "Anything you say can and will be used against you in a court of law."

"This is crazy!" Jesse yelled. "I would never hurt Leah in a million years. It was those goddamned Liberators. They killed her! Not me. Motherfuckers!" Jesse struggled with the police officer.

"Jesse!" Flint warned. "Goddammit! Be quiet!"

"You have the right to an attorney," the officer continued as if he didn't hear Jesse. "If you cannot afford an attorney, one will be provided for you. Do you understand the rights I have just read to you? With these rights in mind, do you wish to speak to me?"

"Fuck no! I don't wish to speak to you."

Flint moved toward Jesse, and the officer held up his hand to stop him.

"Back away, son," he ordered. "Unless you want cuffs on you, too." He waved at the crowd of bikers gathered around. "And that goes for the rest of you. We don't want any trouble. Let us do our job and we'll all be fine."

"I'm Flint Mason, his attorney," Flint continued. "I'll be representing him." He turned to Jesse. "And as your attorney, I'm telling you to behave and shut the fuck up. I'll take care of this."

The police officer looked Flint up and down, taking in his leather boots and tattoos. "You expect us to believe you're his lawyer?" he asked incredulously before shrugging. "Don't guess it matters one way or the other to us if he's fool enough to hire somebody like you as his attorney. Guess those online schools are also churning out lawyers these days."

"Jesse?" Flint said again, ignoring the officer's insults. "You listening?"

Jesse took a deep breath to calm down and nodded back at him, letting him know he understood. He wouldn't be talking to the police. Not a word without Flint there by his side to guide him through the interrogation process. He wasn't stupid, just angry as hell.

"Alright, let's go," the officer said, leading Jesse up the hill to the police car.

"I'll be right behind you!" Flint called out. "I'll meet you at the police station."

Flint whirled around to grab his keys from inside the house and saw Kendra's stunned expression. For a split second, he had been so caught up with Jesse's arrest that he had completely forgotten about her and the fact that she didn't have a clue about him being a lawyer. She would think he'd lied to her, which wasn't exactly true unless she counted it as a lie of omission. Knowing her, she might consider that every bit as bad.

Shit!

He needed time to explain his actions and the reasons why he hadn't told her everything. Unfortunately, he didn't have time. Not even five minutes at the moment. Jesse didn't deserve to spend one more minute in jail than was absolutely necessary and he would do everything he knew how to get him out as soon as possible.

With it being so late in the evening, Jesse would probably have to spend at least the night in jail. Flint would need to contact the bail bondsman and make sure he was on standby if he could get Jesse's bail set at a reasonable amount when he went before the judge in the morning. Of course, with a murder charge, that would be unlikely. His mind whirled with all the things he needed to do and think of as Jesse's lawyer. No matter what, he couldn't fuck this up.

"Kendra." Her name came out as an anguished plea. "Wait a second."

Her eyes were wide with confusion and mistrust. "You're his attorney?" she asked. "What the hell does that mean? How is that possible? I don't understand. You work at the tattoo parlor, right?"

Flint felt like the earth was shifting underneath him. First Jesse, now

Kendra. Everything was going to hell. He should've known the warm, happy feeling was too good to last.

"It's a long story and one that needs some time to tell," he said. "Can you trust me enough to wait until I can explain it all to you before jumping to conclusions?"

She threw up her hands and looked away. "I don't even know what to say."

To Flint's surprise, Sam stepped up beside her. "Kendra will be fine here with me. I'll make sure she gets home safe and sound. You need to go and take care of Jesse. He needs you. I'll take care of your girl. Don't worry."

Flint reached up and squeezed Sam's shoulder. He knew this was Sam's way of offering an olive branch and making peace with him. It meant more to him than his younger brother would ever know.

Flint let out a long breath. "Okay," he said. "Can you make sure one of the crew follows her home? I need to get to the police station before Jesse loses his temper again and starts talking. They'll use every tactic they know to make him lose his cool. And with Jesse, it doesn't take much for him to go off anyway. I'd better hurry. Thanks, Sam."

He grabbed Kendra quickly and kissed her firmly on the lips. "I'll make this right," he said. "I'll call you as soon as I can."

Kendra's drive home from the party went by in a blur. Sam kept his word and sent one of the few crew members who wasn't dead drunk to follow behind her and make sure she got home. He waited until she unlocked the front door and waved back at him before he took off.

Kendra felt like crying when she finally made it inside her own house where nobody could see her. But she wasn't the crying type, so she didn't. Crying never solved a damn thing and it wouldn't make her feel any less hurt at the moment, either.

She couldn't imagine ever being more shocked or surprised. Watching Jesse be arrested for the murder of the woman who had tried to help them was bad enough, but when Flint had stepped up and announced he was Jesse's attorney, she felt like she'd been hit with a brick.

Flint was a lawyer? How was that even possible? He would've had to spend several years in college and then law school. She thought he'd been gone from Bardsville for a couple of years, not a decade. Even crazier was the thought that the Steel Infidels had allowed a lawyer to be a member of the MC. Wouldn't there be tons of conflict of interests there to consider? The ethical boundaries Flint was crossing must be incredible.

It hurt her to think that in the time they'd spent together, Flint had never felt it important enough to mention he was a practicing attorney. In fact, he'd clearly led her to believe he was a tattoo artist who worked with Sam. He'd lied to her and now she felt betrayed and sick inside.

She never should have trusted him so quickly. After all, what did she really know about Flint Mason except what he'd told her? Which if today's incident was any indication was all a pack of lies.

She rubbed her temples. Crap! Wouldn't you know it? A damn migraine was coming on. Like she didn't have enough problems at the moment. She reached for her prescription migraine medication and took one with a sip of water. The headaches always hit when she least needed them and when she most needed to think clearly.

All of their conversations kept circling around and around in her head. Had he ever said outright he was a tattoo artist, or had she jumped to that conclusion? The more she thought about it, the more she realized he had never actually come right out and said what he did for a living or mentioned how he made money. All he had said was that he could do a mean tattoo and then offered to do a hummingbird tattoo for her.

She hadn't asked too many personal questions because she figured he was a private person and couldn't talk about the MC's business anyway. The few times she had started to ask about the tattoo parlor, he had changed the subject and asked about one of the coyote pups that had just come into the clinic or a Blue Jay with a broken wing. If she had been paying closer attention, she would have realized he was uncomfortable talking about his job. Probably because he knew he was covering up a lie. But why? It didn't make any sense.

In her heart, Kendra knew there must have been a good reason for him not to tell her he was a lawyer. It certainly wasn't anything to be ashamed of and in fact, he should've been proud of his accomplishments. Unless he'd been disbarred, which he obviously wasn't if he was able to represent Jesse.

Kendra spotted her laptop sitting on the table. She'd been so busy lately that it hadn't been turned on in weeks. Any quick emails to her clients were usually done on her cell phone while rushing between animal checkups. She wasn't much of a computer person and felt like it was a useless time drain most of the time.

Except for the very first night at the safe house, she hadn't sincerely considered Googling Flint's name to see what she could find. And then once they were solidly together as a couple, she had felt too guilty to be spying on him like that. Almost as if it would be a huge invasion of his privacy to dig into his online background. After all, she wouldn't want him poking around in hers. Though her life was so boring there wouldn't be anything to find, except maybe a few old photos of her with braces and glasses she'd rather nobody see.

Taking a deep breath, she walked over and flipped open the laptop. As the computer booted up, she realized the main reason she hadn't done this before was because she was afraid of what she might find. Oh sure, she could pretend like she was protecting his privacy and all that bullshit, when the honest truth was she didn't want to find out anything that would make her care for him less.

When the screen finally popped up, she entered his name.

Flint Mason.

Now or never. She hit the search button and held her breath.

An hour later, she sat back and rubbed the back of her neck where the migraine had spread. She'd found out plenty about Flint Mason and had all she needed to know. Instead of the arrest records or other bad things she halfway expected to find, she instead found pages and pages of court cases where he'd represented innocent people as a public defender.

From clearing a grandmother about to be evicted from the only home she'd ever known because her grandson was selling crack in the parking lot of the apartment building to defending a young mother accused of child endangerment because she'd left her kids alone while she ran to the grocery store. The Internet was full of his cases where he'd defended poor innocent people who couldn't afford a big time lawyer on their own.

From the timeline she'd mentally put together, it appeared Flint had spent the last several years working his way up in a public defender's office in Atlanta. She knew enough to know the hours were probably long and the pay pretty low for the qualifications he had and the time he put in. She wondered what made him go into the field in the first place. And more importantly, what made him leave a job that he was obviously good at to come back home and hang out with a motorcycle club?

There were so many unanswered questions about Flint. So much she wanted and needed to know.

She felt like such a bitch. Flint had asked her to trust him and she'd turned away from him in a huff. He deserved better than to be treated in such a way. She wiped away the tears she couldn't hold back any longer and grabbed her purse. It wasn't too late to set things right.

10

Flint and Jesse were seated at a wooden table in the police station's interrogation room with the two arresting officers. They'd been there for hours, with neither side making headway in either direction. The cops kept asking questions which Jesse refused to answer while Flint kept demanding that they turn over whatever evidence they had on Jesse and the cops refusing to hand it over.

Finally, after it was obvious the interrogation was going nowhere, the cops offered up the information Flint had been waiting all along for them to divulge. The arrest had been made based solely on Leah's cell phone records, which contained several calls and a text message between her and Jesse on the day of her murder.

The room went silent while Flint read the evidence file. "Can I have a moment alone with my client?" he asked when he was finished.

"Sure," the officer said, sliding back his metal chair. "I could use another cup of coffee anyway." The officers stood up and left the room.

Flint scooted his chair closer to Jesse. "You want to tell me now about the phone calls? Why the hell didn't you mention this before?"

Jesse shrugged and ran a hand through his hair. "I didn't realize it was important. We both know the Liberators killed Leah for warning me they were on their way to the safe house. It never occurred to me that I would be a suspect in her murder. I didn't realize it was important."

"You didn't think the cops would check her cell phone records?" Flint asked.

"I'm not that stupid," Jesse replied. "I thought she was using a burner phone. I can't believe she was calling me on her real cell phone. What does a prepaid phone cost? Ten bucks?"

Flint shook his head in disbelief. "Even the Sweet Butts would have more sense than that, but it's done now. Tell me about the calls."

"After Leah called to warn me that the Liberators were coming for you, she panicked," Jesse said. "She called me several times that night because she was terrified they would figure out what she'd done. She seemed agitated and not like herself. Or at least not like the Leah I knew years ago."

"You think she was doing drugs?"

"I heard through the grapevine that she was doing meth. Don't know for sure. Something was different about her. I begged her to get the hell out of there because I knew they'd kill her if they suspected that she was a rat. I thought if I could convince her to meet me that I could talk her into leaving the Liberators for good. After I sent the last text message asking her to meet me, I never heard from her again. You know the rest of the story."

Flint didn't speak for a moment, thinking about Leah's battered body being dumped on the side of the road. He couldn't imagine what she must've gone through before they finally killed her.

"The Liberators probably found her cell phone," he said. "Dammit! How could she have let that happen?"

"Leah was a sweetheart, but she wasn't the smartest gal in the world," Jesse replied. "And she wasn't thinking clearly if she was high. It makes me sick to think about what they did to her because she was helping us."

"Obviously you can't come clean to the cops about what you two were talking about because that would lead straight back to the safe house and everything that happened on the mountain. How many text messages were there?" Flint knew any text messages would be used as direct evidence against Jesse.

"Only one," Jesse answered. "The text message asking her to meet me. I'd been calling her for hours and couldn't get an answer, so I sent her a text."

"That wasn't too smart on your part either," Flint said. "So there are no other text messages going back and forth between you?"

"No, I'm sure of that. Just the one. From me to her."

"Okay, that's good to know," Flint said. "If I had to take an educated guess, I would say the police don't have enough real evidence to charge you or even hold you at this point. I don't know what the hell these cops were thinking, dragging you in here with only phone records as evidence. I'm pretty certain I can get this thrown out in the morning as soon as you go before the judge. Are you sure there's nothing else you haven't told me?"

"I swear," Jesse replied. "You know everything I do."

Flint stood up and slapped Jesse on the back. "I'll take care of this. You're going to have to spend the night in jail since it's so late on a Sunday evening, but by tomorrow night you'll be back in your own bed. Or somebody else's bed. Whatever makes you happy."

Jesse tried to smile. "I knew all that damn lawyer stuff of yours would come in handy some day."

Flint rapped twice on the door to let the officers know to unlock it from the outside so he could leave. He turned back to Jesse. "You probably never noticed or needed to care up until now, but I'm a damn good lawyer. And I can be fucking brilliant in court when I set my mind to it. You don't need to worry."

Jesse grew serious. "I noticed. I never said it out loud, but I'm proud of you. Always was, so go get me the fuck out of here. I'm counting on you."

"I got this. See you in the morning."

By the time Flint had filled out all the paperwork, it was already late. He hated like hell leaving Jesse in jail overnight, but there wasn't a damn thing he could do about it until the morning. Jesse was tough and he'd make it through the night just fine. It wasn't as if this was the first time he'd been arrested either, though the offenses were usually stupid misdemeanors like public drunkenness or disturbing the peace. Never anything serious enough to keep him in the slammer for more than a day or two.

Flint had already contacted a bail bondsman he knew and had everything ready to go if he couldn't convince the judge to dismiss the charges first. His connections from the public defender's office were definitely paying off now when he needed them. Never in a million years would he have foreseen having to represent his brother on a murder charge.

Flint zipped up his leather jacket and stepped outside the police station. He headed for his motorcycle parked in the far end of the lot. Even at a police station, he knew better than to park his bike close to any of the other cars. Too many times he'd found his bike lying on its side where a car had "accidentally" backed into it.

Even now, some idiot had parked their truck right beside his bike, even with all the empty spots closer to the building. The truck's door opened and a shadowy figure stepped out. Flint automatically felt for the pistol he normally kept in his inside jacket pocket then remembered he had left it at the house since he couldn't be caught carrying a weapon into the police station. The person turned and he caught sight of her hair under the pale glow of the streetlight.

Kendra!

He ran the last few steps then drew up short when he reached her side. "What are you doing here?"

She tugged her coat tighter around her. "I needed to see you. And to check on Jesse, too. How's he doing?"

"He's okay for now," Flint answered. "Unfortunately, there's no way I can get him released on bail tonight. It will have to wait until morning after he goes before a judge."

"Will he be in a cell by himself?"

"I hope so. I'm not worried though. Jesse has quite a reputation, and I would be surprised if anyone in this town has enough nerve to mess with him in there."

"How about you?" Kendra asked in a soft voice. "Are you doing okay?"

"Much better, now that you're here."

She looked away, unable to meet his eyes. "I'm sorry," she said simply. "You asked me to trust you and give you time to explain. I was hurt and confused so I acted childish."

"Kendra, you don't ever need to apologize to me for anything. I should've told you the truth right upfront."

"Why didn't you?" she asked, the hurt coming through in her voice. "I don't understand why you felt you couldn't tell me you were a lawyer. And a damn good one too, from what I've read. You let me go on believing you were a tattoo artist. I felt like you had tricked me. For the life of me, I can't figure out why."

Flint sighed and leaned back against the hood of her truck. "This is going to sound really stupid, and you probably won't even believe me."

"Yes, I will," Kendra reassured. "Just tell me."

"I'm not that person anymore," he tried to explain. "A guy who puts on a business suit and goes to work every day at the courthouse. Defending clients who may or may not be innocent. I made a decision to leave all that behind and come home. To rejoin the Steel Infidels and to be there for my brothers if they needed me. My life is so different now." He hesitated, struggling to come up with the right words. "I didn't tell you because I needed you to like me for the man I am now. A bad guy. An outlaw. Not the good guy I tried to be before. No matter how much I might want to be, I can't be that guy anymore. It would be wrong to fool you into thinking I was something more than I am."

Kendra moved closer and wrapped her arms around his neck. "What am I going to do with you, Flint? You're killing me here. You are a good guy. Why can't you see that? Maybe not the same type you were before. But still every bit as good inside here." She touched his heart. "Where it counts the most." She smoothed his hair back from his forehead. "I like this man. Just the way you are now. You don't need to change anything for me."

Flint was still worried. "There are so many things I want to tell you," he said. "To explain why I left my job in Atlanta and came back home. I just need a little more time and I promise I'll tell you everything you want to know."

"Even about the Liberators?" she asked.

Flint hesitated. "Yes, that too." She deserved to know everything.

More importantly, Kendra was giving him another chance.

He rubbed the corner of her eyelid with his thumb, where a smudge of mascara had smeared.

"Have you been crying?" he asked, already knowing the answer.

Even the thought that he could make his beautiful Kendra cry ripped his heart out.

"I'm okay now," she answered truthfully. She sank her hands into his hair and pulled his face closer. "But you can make me feel much better. I know what I need."

Flint's head loomed lower and he covered her mouth with his in a kiss so passionate and fierce it made her head spin. His hands cupped her ass, massaging the heavy globes and pulling her up on tiptoe to ravage her mouth possessively. He was as masterful as ever, taking everything and giving even more. After a moment, he pulled his lips away and shot a quick glance around the parking lot.

"Over here," he said. Flint took her by the hand and tugged her to the other side of the truck, out of the direct glare of the streetlight. He opened the passenger door and backed her up against the seat then switched off the interior light. Lifting up her thick hair, he blazed a path with his mouth from her jawline to the base of her neck, burying his nose there and drinking in her essence.

"The things you do to me," he groaned, pulling her tighter against him so she could feel the straining erection in his jeans. "I'll never get my fill of you. Not in a million years."

Her breath hitched in her throat because she felt exactly the same way.

Using both hands, he pushed her shirt and bra up. Grabbing her breasts, he fondled and massaged the large orbs forcefully, stimulating the nipples until they enlarged into hard aching thimbles.

Without warning, he whipped her around in one smooth motion so that she faced the truck seat. Jerking down her pants, he nudged her feet apart with a booted foot and placed his left hand in the small of her back.

God! He was making her hot and soaking wet!

She never knew what to expect from Flint or what he might do. His wild impulsiveness turned her on, especially when he became dominating and a little rough.

"Tell me what you want," he murmured, leaning close to her ear.

His words sent a shiver down her spine. Without waiting for a reply, he leaned down so that he was almost covering her body with his and rammed a finger deep inside her cunt, then followed that up by sliding another finger in. With a sawing motion, he savagely finger-fucked her pussy, with her legs and body hanging halfway out of the truck.

"Tell me what would make you feel better," he whispered again. "Anything. I'll do it."

Before she could answer, the sound of voices broke through the silence. Two police officers had left the station and were walking to their patrol car parked at the other end of the lot. Flint peeked up through the window to see which car they were heading toward.

"We're going to get caught," Kendra said in a panic. She struggled to move away from him so she could pull up her pants. Being arrested for public indecency was the last thing either of them needed at the moment.

Flint grabbed her with his free hand to prevent her from moving. "Be quiet," he ordered. "Stay down where they can't see you." He waited only a split second before sliding his fingers almost all the way out and plunging them in again, filling her completely.

"Oh Jesus!" she moaned in pleasure, knowing that no matter what the consequences would be, he wasn't going to stop. This was sweet torture.

"Shh..." he whispered again in warning.

Kendra bit her lip to keep from crying out and buried her head in the truck seat as he jammed his fingers all the way in to the knuckle. When she couldn't keep from moaning again, he pressed his hand against her mouth to stifle the sounds.

Flint furiously ravaged her with his fingers, keeping up a steady pumping motion. Kendra loved the sheer eroticism of their act, knowing the police were mere feet away. When he suddenly removed his fingers and shifted his weight, Kendra twisted her head around to look at him.

"I'm going to fuck you raw," was all he said in a low voice.

God! Yes, please.

Kendra let out a willing whimper of surrender.

He quickly unzipped his pants and brought his long cock out with one hand. The next instant, he lined himself up behind her and thrust himself into her slick, slippery pussy. All it took was one long powerful stroke and he was buried into her up to his balls.

From somewhere behind her, she heard him mutter, "Oh fuck..." before shoving deeply in and out of her cunt, filling the truck with the sounds of their lust.

His powerful thrusts pitched his body against hers, strong enough to push her into the truck seat with each plunge. She listened to the sounds they made as he fucked her, the ragged hiss of his breath, the wet sounds from her cunt every time his cock slammed into her, and the sound of his skin smacking against the back of her thighs and buttocks.

Only a few cars down from them, the chattering voices droned on. Occasionally, one of the officers would laugh loudly. *How could the policemen not hear them?* Kendra wondered.

It was hot wild sex, primitive and primal.

Flint buried his face in the back of her neck, his breathing now uneven and choppy. She vaguely heard him grit out her name, but she was so past conscious thought her head was buzzing. Flint must have felt how tightly her walls gripped him because he groaned deeply, kneading her hips so hard she could feel the imprint of each finger.

Unable to catch her breath, she was helpless to hold off the shuddering sensations racking her body. The sweet pleasure swelled within her until she was bursting with the force of her orgasm.

As Kendra's pussy walls begin pulsing around his cock, she involuntarily cried out again. He grabbed her hair and twisted her head sideways so he could capture her lips in a kiss, sealing off her sounds of passion

With one last thrust, his cock jerked and swelled then filled her cunt with hot cum. She felt him throbbing inside her, pulsing with heat. He continued to stroke inside her until he was completely spent and exhausted.

"Don't pull out yet," Kendra whispered.

"I could stay inside you forever," was his answer.

After several minutes, he slid out and zipped himself up. He helped her do the same and tugged her closer to him. He pointed to the now empty parking lot. "I guess our spectators are gone," he said. So caught up in their passion, neither of them had noticed when the policemen had driven away.

Kendra laughed. "We're damn lucky we didn't get caught. Will you come home with me and stay the night?" she asked, unwilling to pull away from his warmth just yet.

"I would love to, darling," he replied, rubbing a hand up and down her back under her sweater. "But I can't. Sam is probably waiting up for me to fill him in on what's going on with Jesse. And I need to make sure I have something clean and suitable to wear for Jesse's court appearance in the morning. I can't go into court dressed in jeans and a t-shirt."

"You own a suit?" Kendra asked with a laugh.

Flint chuckled. "I own lots of expensive suits, ties, and dress shoes. For God's sake, don't tell any of the crew about it though. If you do, I'll deny it."

"I'm finding it very hard to visualize you as a lawyer. It's going to take some getting used to."

"Don't get too used to it," Flint said, suddenly serious. "This is a one time thing. I don't have any intention of going back into the legal field. I'll do what needs to be done and that's it. Once this is over with Jesse, I'm hanging my suits and ties back up."

"Did you leave your job in Atlanta because of the Liberators?" she suddenly asked.

"Yes," he answered after a moment. "They murdered Tommy, my best friend in the MC, in a shootout over in Tennessee several months ago. When that happened, I had to make a choice."

"You mean to be on one side of the law or the other?"

"In a way," he replied. "And now Jesse is sitting in jail. I'm hopeful the judge will drop the charges. All they have on him are phone records. Leah and Jesse had talked several times by cell phone, and he texted her asking to meet a few hours before she was killed. That's why he's the number one murder suspect right now."

"You can't let the Liberators get away with this."

"We don't intend to," Flint answered. "The MC is going to annihilate them. To wipe them off the face of the earth. To put their club out of business completely."

"How bad will it get?"

"Possibly as bad as you can imagine," he admitted. "And it won't happen overnight. This kind of thing could take months, even years.

The war with the Liberators has been years in the making, and it may take that long to finish it once and for all."

"How are you ever going to end it?"

He pulled her closer against his chest. "There are some things you can't know. It's better and safer for you that way. All I can tell you is that the plan has been put into motion. There were thirteen men in the Liberators. Four were killed on the mountain. That leaves nine to take care of. "

"Are you going to murder them?" Kendra whispered.

"That's one option, no doubt," he replied honestly. "It's not the only way to wipe out their club though. It doesn't always have to be a shootout with bullets flying. I'm a lawyer, remember? And they're involved in some very nasty underworld shit. Not just drugs and gun running. The word on the street is that they're holding underage girls, keeping them doped up and passing them around like property. To wipe them out, all we have to do is make sure every member is off the street, either dead or in prison for a very long time."

"You're close to getting them, aren't you?"

"I hope so. That's why I need to keep a close eye on you for a while. Either me or one of my crew. That okay with you?"

"I guess so," she agreed. "If it means you'll keep your mind on what you're doing and not worrying about me, then of course I'll go along with it."

"Okay then. Let's get you on home. I'll follow on my bike to make sure you get there and I'll let you know how things are going with Jesse as soon as we know something in the morning."

Kendra grabbed his hand. "Stay safe, baby."

"I will, I promise. I have too much to lose now."

11

Kendra lifted up the last of the three baby squirrels and tucked it into the laundry basket filled with soft towels. Since no one else had volunteered to take the group home for the night, it looked like the job was up to her. She really didn't mind. Taking care of the baby squirrels for the evening would keep her mind busy and off worrying about Flint and Jesse.

She'd been wondering all day about what was going on with Jesse's court appearance and so far hadn't heard anything. In the past few days, she'd learned one thing about Flint. He might not call and check in with her often, but if he said he'd call, he would.

"Dr. Shaw?" A volunteer poked her head into Kendra's office. "There's someone here to see you."

"A client? I thought we were through with vet appointments for the day. I don't see anyone else on my schedule."

"No, not a client." The young girl grinned like she had a big secret. "Maybe he's a salesman. I don't know. Trust me, you'll want to make an exception and see this guy. Shall I send him in? Then I'll need to head on home."

Kendra rolled her eyes. "Sure. Why not? It's not like I have anything else in the world to do except waste time with a copier salesman," she muttered as the young girl hurried back out the door.

After checking the thermometer lying in the basket with the squirrels, she decided they might not be warm enough for the ride home. She grabbed a pink heat disc from the shelf to put under the towels and headed for the kitchen to stick it in the microwave. A knock on the door stopped her. The door swung open before she had a chance to call out.

Kendra turned around, expecting to see a slick-haired salesman in thick black glasses and carrying a briefcase. Instead, Flint stood in the doorway, wearing a pair of designer sunglasses and a twelve-hundred dollar suit.

Hot damn! He was sexy as hell, gorgeous, and all hers. Her tongue practically rolled out of her mouth.

"Hey, darling."

His honeyed tone hit her right in the gut. Two words had never held such thick, unspoken promise. He stepped inside and kicked the door shut behind him. An electric current passed between them as their eyes met, primal and dangerous. His eyes traveled slowly over her ample curves.

Kendra flew across the room and threw herself into his arms. Fisting her long hair tight with one hand, he slammed her back against the wall, pinning her wrists above her with one hand and pressing his lips against hers in a hungry deep kiss. His muscled strength, the way he moved so quickly and precisely like a panther stalking his prey, thickened the haze of desire fogging her senses. His other hand slipped down to her thrust-out breasts in that dominating, possessive way that made her breathless and wet.

She drew away after a long moment, gasping for air. "Wow! What did I do to deserve that? Not that I'm complaining."

"The judge dropped all charges," he replied with a cocky grin. "Jesse's already out of jail."

"What? How?"

"I'll tell you later. Right now I want my prize. Convincing the judge to drop the charges deserves a special reward, don't you think?"

"If I'm your prize, then definitely," Kendra said. She frantically tried to loosen his tie. "You didn't happen to see my volunteer leave the building, did you?"

"Yep, I saw her get in her car and drive away."

"Then it's on, baby."

She whipped the tie off and threw it onto the floor then went to work on the buttons of his shirt. She felt him yank down her scrub pants along with her white silk panties before cupping her ass with both hands and lifting her completely off the floor.

Kendra gave up on his shirt buttons and went straight for his belt and zipper. "We might mess up your expensive suit," she muttered.

"Don't worry," he replied. "I don't plan on wearing it again."

He braced her back against the wall for support and wrapped her legs around his waist. Holding her tight with one arm, he brought out his cock from the gap in his zipper with the other. Kendra was panting, already soaking wet and ready. In one powerful thrust, he rammed deep inside her, driving her against the wall.

Kendra gasped and clung to his shoulders. He gripped her ass cheeks tightly in each hand and forcefully moved her up and down on his long length. Damn, he was so strong. She could feel the power pulsing through his arms, his hands.

"Fuck, Kendra!" he groaned, leaning down to nibble her earlobe. "You're like a drug to me. The more I have, the more I need. I dream of your sweet, tight pussy every night then I wake up rock hard, aching with need and wanting you even more."

Kendra closed her eyes and gave herself up to the sweet sensations of his cock plunging into her, deeper with every thrust. Flint held her with one arm and slid a hand under her shirt and bra to clutch her heaving breast with the other. He pinched and twisted her begging nipple, stretching the elongated tip until she cried out.

She moaned, flinging her head back.

He drilled into her again and again, holding her steady, forcing her to give herself over to his control completely. She felt helpless as he spread her ass cheeks even wider to allow deeper penetration.

Kendra clung to him desperately, reaching for her release. His thrusts became wilder, more primal as he grunted and drove into her faster and harder. Her pleasure was bordering on pain, but she didn't care. Flint was animalistic and unrepentant, with every lunge ramming her against the sheetrock.

Flint knew she wanted it, loved it, and craved the wild power fuck as much as he did. He bent down to kiss her lips with such force, their teeth clashed. He never slowed down or eased up, grinding against her clit while inside her his cock stroked as rough and deep as physically possible.

"I can't hold out much longer," he gritted out between strokes, his breathing harsh. Reaching down, he rubbed her clit with his thumb, sending her over the edge. Waves of contractions racked her pussy, each one stronger than the last. She grabbed him tighter, her nails digging into his arms. When it was over, she went limp with bliss and exhaustion, with only his muscular tattooed arms holding her up.

"Fuck!" he cursed as he climaxed, his face intense and inches from hers. Kendra loved it when he lost control with no restraint, no limits. Just wild unleashed passion without boundaries or holds. He bit her neck as he convulsed into her.

It was a long time before their breathing slowed enough to move. Neither one of them wanted to be the first to break the mood by speaking. Finally, he backed over to the closest office chair and sat down, still cradling her in his arms.

"I'm a grand prize winner," he said, nuzzling her hair.

"Have I ever told you how extremely sexy you are in a suit?" Kendra asked. She snuggled closer and ran a hand through his damp hair. "I can't believe you didn't have a million women after you when you were working in Atlanta."

"No, I didn't have time for that then."

"And you do now?"

He hugged her closer. "I'll make time."

"So tell me how you managed to get Jesse out of jail."

"Two things," Flint answered. "My flair for dramatics in court and the fact that they didn't have enough to charge him with in the first place. I convinced the judge that the DNA evidence found on the scene would clear Jesse anyway, so why waste time looking at the wrong guy? I'm not sure how much of it the judge bought, but he agreed the cell phone records weren't enough for now to charge him. I'm sure the police officers will have a new asshole chewed by now."

"Sam and the crew must be so happy and relieved about this."

"They are," he said emphatically. "And that's why I'm here. To invite you to come over to the house after work tonight to celebrate. It will be only a few of us, not the big group that was there yesterday."

Kendra frowned. "Darn it! I can't! I have to babysit."

Flint raised his eyebrows. "Kids?" He sounded a little horrified.

"No, not real children," she explained. "Baby squirrels." She pointed to the basket in the corner with the squirming babies. "They need to be fed often, so I can't leave them alone that long."

"So bring them with you. You can put them upstairs in my room where it will be quiet and feed them whenever you need to."

"Alright then," she said. "I'll need to run home really quick and change clothes then I'll be right over."

Flint lifted the hair from her neck and trailed a line of kisses down to her shoulder. "Or we could just stay here all night. In your office." His growing erection stirred against her hip.

"Are you insatiable?"

"Only where you're concerned."

"Later then," Kendra teased. "I'm sure the crew are all dying to see you and celebrate, so you'd better get going."

She slid off his lap and walked over to pick up her panties and scrub pants from the floor. She wriggled back into them then picked up his tie and tossed it to him. He caught it and stuffed it in his pocket before tucking himself back into his pants and zipping it up. He picked up his sunglasses where he'd dropped them on the table and slid them on.

"Don't forget your squirrels," he said with a grin on his way out.

Kendra sighed and snatched up the laundry basket. "I won't."

12

One month later...

The line of police cars arrived at the Liberators' hangout in the middle of the night with their sirens screaming and lights flashing. With search warrants already in their hands, they didn't take time to knock. Instead, the officers kicked down the front door and busted in with guns drawn.

"Police! Get your hands up!" they screamed as they charged from room to room, clearing the building. Three of the Liberators' crew were passed out dead drunk in the main room, piled up on the ratty sofa and on the floor. They didn't move or wake up when the cops entered the room. An assortment of drug paraphernalia, coke, and meth sat on the coffee table along with half-empty whiskey bottles. A big screen television was turned to a cable pay-per-view porn channel.

Two of the police officers quickly handcuffed the Liberators right where they snoozed while the other cops searched the adjoining rooms. It wasn't until they reached a double-bolted locked door that they knew they'd hit the jackpot. The biggest cop in the group stepped forward and landed a strong kick to the area right below the doorknob. The wood splintered into pieces. A young girl inside the room screamed in terror.

"Shit! Look at this!" one of the cops said, rushing into the room.

Two frightened girls clad only in bras and panties huddled together on the floor in a corner. They looked to be no more than sixteen, clearly undernourished with visible track marks on their arms. Another teenage girl was tied spread-eagled to the bed. A professional video camera was set up on a tripod, with a cord running from the camera to a laptop on a small desk.

The policeman hastily untied the girl on the bed and helped her to sit up. "Who did this to you?" he asked.

She started shaking uncontrollably. "I can't tell you," she choked out. "He'll kill me."

"His name is Roy," one of the girls in the corner whispered. "They call him Big Roy."

The other cop knelt down in front of the girls on the floor. "You know his last name?"

The girls shook their heads reluctantly.

"What does he look like? Anything else you can tell us?"

"He's really tall with reddish hair," the same girl offered. "And he has a tattoo of a snake on his arm with his name."

"Did he force you to have sex with him?"

They both nodded.

"With anybody else or just him?"

"Lots of men," she said. "I don't know their names. Sometimes he would videotape it. Other times a bunch of them would watch and take turns."

The cop wiped his tired eyes and stood up. "Call dispatch and have them send a couple of the female officers out here to take these ladies to the hospital." He turned back to the girls. "We're going to make sure you're taken care of. Big Roy will never hurt you again. You have any idea where he is now?"

"No," the girl answered. "He was here earlier and said he'd be back. We were afraid to go to sleep."

Another police officer walked into the room. "The building is clear. We didn't find anyone else. Only the three guys out there."

"If they can stand up, arrest them and take them out to the police cars. If not, drag those assholes out by their boots. If their heads happen to hit a few rocks on the way, then so be it."

All thirteen members of the Steel Infidels were gathered in the voting room. Flint had been given the task of clearing out the clubhouse of any Sweet Butts or prospects hanging around for the night, so only the crew remained.

In the voting room, nobody talked. They were all waiting patiently for Jesse's phone to ring. He had called them all together as soon as his source at the police station contacted him to say the raid on the Liberators was on. It was the middle of the night, but they didn't care. No way would any of them have missed this.

Already jittery and on edge, they jumped when Jesse's cell phone finally rang.

"How many were arrested?" Jesse asked the caller. "What about the girls?" He listened a few more minutes. "Thanks for calling to let me know. If there's anything I can do for you, I will. Thanks again."

The crew looked at Jesse expectantly.

"They found the girls," he said. "Just like we knew they would. Three underage girls no more than fifteen or sixteen locked up in a back room. As we suspected, Big Roy was forcing them to have sex with different men and making porn movies. Unfortunately, only three of the Liberators were there at the time. They've been arrested."

"And Big Roy?" Flint asked. The President of the Liberators ran a tight ship. All orders came straight from him, and nothing happened without his approval.

Jesse shook his head. "They didn't get him. They've put an APB out for him, so they will, eventually."

"Unless we get to him first," Flint said. "Cut off the head of the snake and the body will die."

"How many Liberators does that leave to take care of?" Rocco asked. Rocco had many talents, including being able to completely chop up a car in a matter of hours. However, he wasn't known for being sharp with numbers.

"Six," Flint answered. "Four dead on the mountain, three arrested today. That leaves Big Roy and his closest team of five."

"Big Roy is mine," Jesse said firmly. "As most of you know, we go way back and have a long history. This is my score to settle. I want to get to him before the police do."

Flint nodded. "Understood. Let's make it happen."

EPILOGUE

Kendra crossed her arms and eyed the motorcycle with distrust. "Not even a hint of where we're going?" she asked.

"You'll figure it out soon enough," Flint said with a grin. "Put this on." He handed her a helmet and she slid it over her head before climbing onto the motorcycle seat behind him. "Hold on tight because I drive fast."

"Like I don't know that!" She wrapped her arms around his waist and scooted closer. "But don't worry, I will. I'm still not quite used to all this biker stuff. Tell me again what is so terribly wrong about riding in a regular vehicle like a car or a truck?"

Flint didn't answer. Instead he laughed, a deep rumbling sound she loved so much. He revved the engine. "You all set?" he asked over his shoulder.

She pressed her cheek against his jacket. "I'm ready. Let's go."

He swung the motorcycle onto the highway and picked up speed. Riding behind Flint on the motorcycle had taken a little getting used to, but now Kendra looked forward to their weekend rides with the Steel Infidels. There was something about being out on the open road with the fresh air that she found quite thrilling.

At first, she would instinctively tense up every time they went around a tight curve until eventually she learned to relax, lean with the bike, and enjoy the ride.

She had even made a few good friends in the motorcycle club, women who were either serious girlfriends or wives of some of the crew. The ladies had been quick to accept Kendra into the fold and never seemed to question Flint's choice for a girlfriend. From the very first get-together where they'd pulled Kendra aside and told her a few things she needed to know until now, they'd hung right by her side.

The pretty young girls who made up the Sweet Butts weren't high on Kendra's list of favorites though. She realized they were an integral part of the motorcycle club, mostly there for eye candy more than anything else. Or at least as far as she knew. Flint never said much about them, but she didn't worry since Flint had made it clear he wasn't the least bit tempted by their big boobs or their loose morals. The best thing about the Sweet Butts were that they seemed to change frequently so if there was one you didn't particularly like, she would probably be gone soon anyway.

Kendra tried to be nice and polite to the girls at the very least, but she'd found that trying to have a real friendship or even a deep conversation with most of them was almost impossible. They were there for the male bikers, not to make girlfriends.

As long as they kept their hands off Flint, everything would be fine. They could look all they wanted. After all, what normal female wouldn't want to stare at Flint? But the second they laid a hand on him, there would be hell to pay.

After the police had dropped all charges against Jesse, Flint had begun to slowly relax and show a side to her that she hadn't seen before. She knew the MC was still going hard after the Liberators even though she wasn't privy to the details. Flint felt it was safer that way. She'd read in the local newspaper that several men had been arrested, and even though the article didn't mention the Liberators by name, she knew it had to be them.

"You doing okay back there?" Flint yelled over his shoulder, breaking into her thoughts.

"Yeah, I'm good."

"You want to see how fast this baby can go?" he challenged.

"No, not really," she replied with a laugh, knowing he was going to show her anyway. She tightened her grip on his waist and leaned up to peek around his shoulder. They were on a flat stretch of highway in a valley between two mountains. She could see at least a mile ahead, if not more. Of course Flint wouldn't be able to turn down a perfect opportunity to speed.

Flint opened the throttle full blast and the speedometer crept up. When the needle went over 100 mph, she shut her eyes and said a silent prayer. She trusted him completely, but it still unnerved her a little bit. To think there was nothing between her skin and the asphalt if they had an accident. At least she would die happy. Or at least that was what she told herself.

There would always be a little bit of holding back and timidness in her. She wasn't a risk taker or an adrenaline junkie like Flint. But there was no way in hell she was going to ask him to slow down. Just as he needed her calming and steady presence, she needed his thrill. In a weird way, they completed each other, two oddball parts to equal a decent whole.

Flint lived to ride. To feel the engine underneath his body, the wind in his hair. It was as much a part of him as breathing. To love Flint meant accepting every part of him, especially the wild and sometimes reckless man she had fallen for in the very beginning. And she did love him. More than she ever would have thought possible. There wasn't a single exact moment where she knew she'd fallen in love with Flint. To her, it seemed as if her love for him had always been there. Forever.

As they rode deeper into the mountains, it didn't take Kendra long to guess where they were headed – the safe house where they'd first met. As to why he was taking her there after all this time, she couldn't guess.

Flint turned off the highway and started up the dirt mountain road. The last time they'd been there, the road had been icy and dangerous. Now yellow jonquils and pink blooming mountain laurels dotted the woods beside the road. Except for some times when she'd catch Flint flexing his injured arm to work out the soreness, there was no evidence left behind of their time on the mountain.

Flint didn't stop or even slow down when they reached the stretch of road where the shootout with the Liberators had occurred. Neither of them ever mentioned the incident anymore, and as far as she knew the whole thing was in the past where it would hopefully stay. The spot looked completely normal, with nothing amiss to indicate four men had lost their lives there.

Kendra had never once regretted her actions and had eventually made peace with the fact that one of her many bullets may have ended a life that day. Flint was breathing and alive because of her. She was grateful every time she heard his heart beat underneath her cheek at night. If she had to do it over, she would make the same decision again a thousand times over. To think she might have lost him forever was a terrifying and sickening thought.

When they passed the spot they would never forget, Flint reached back and squeezed her leg reassuringly. His touch said he knew exactly what she was thinking.

It didn't take them much longer to reach the cabin. Flint pulled the bike around the back of the house and parked it underneath the shed. He slid off and undid his helmet, suddenly grinning from ear to ear.

"What are you up to, Flint?" Kendra asked, hopping off behind him and stretching her tight leg muscles. "The safe house, huh? Are we hiding from somebody? Please tell me we're not going through that again."

He took her helmet from her and locked it in the compartment. "Not this time. Come on." Flint grabbed her hand and led her around to the front porch.

"How did you get use of the cabin?" she asked. "Someone still owes the Steel Infidels a big favor?"

He flashed his mischievous grin again and chuckled. "You could say that."

After unlocking the door, he moved aside to let her in. She walked a few feet inside the door and stopped. "Wow!" she said. "This looks different than I remembered."

The cabin had been completely redecorated. The sparse furniture of the hunting cabin was gone, replaced by warm colored rugs and comfy looking chairs. A large bed covered with a handmade patchwork quilt took up the space where the old sofa bed was before. An ice bucket with a bottle of champagne and two glasses sat on a table in the corner. A fire had already been laid in the fireplace, waiting to be lit.

Kendra walked around the room, noticing all the homey little touches someone had taken the time to add. A photo frame sat on the fireplace mantel. She went over and picked it up, expecting to see the cabin's owner or his kids. Instead, it was a photo of herself holding a baby Ruby-throated Hummingbird in the palm of her hand. Flint had taken it with his cell phone a couple of weeks before. She turned toward him and held it out. "What's this?"

"My favorite photo of you," he replied. "I wanted to put it on the fireplace mantle where I could see it often."

She rolled her eyes. "I know what it is. What is it doing here in the cabin?"

He shrugged. "I thought the cabin could use some personal touches. It was pretty bare before."

"*You* thought?" she repeated, confused. "What are you? An interior decorator now, too? I'll admit finding out you're a lawyer threw me, but an interior decorator? That's a stretch, though not completely unbelievable. I've discovered you're a man of many talents."

"So, do you like the changes?" He waved a hand at the room.

She raised her eyebrows at him. "Okay, stop right there. What's going on? I can tell you're up to something."

Flint walked over and opened the closet door. He pulled out a big box with a bright red ribbon. "Here, I have a present for you," he said, handing her the box. "Sit on the bed and open it."

She tentatively took the box from him and sat down on the quilt. She bounced up and down a couple of times on the mattress, testing the firmness. "Oh, this bed is much better than the sofa bed that was here before. I feel kind of like Goldilocks, a little girl who wandered into the wrong cabin."

"Are you going to open the box or play around on the bed all day?" Flint teased, plopping down on the bed beside her.

Kendra giggled like a teenager and hastily untied the ribbon. She opened the box top and stared at what was inside. "Oh my goodness! What is this?" Kendra pulled out a heavy black leather jacket and held it up. The jacket was almost identical to the leather cut Flint wore, complete with the Steel Infidels logo. The only difference was the huge black letters on the back that read: "Property of Flint."

Flint burst out laughing at her expression. "Are you going to give me a chance to explain what that means before you go all women's rights and stuff on me?" he asked.

She held the jacket up to her nose and smelled the new leather. "I love the jacket," she said. "I really do. This is beautiful." She hid a smile. "Sure, go ahead and tell me why my new jacket says I'm your property."

Kendra already knew the significance of the jacket and exactly what the "Property of Flint" meant in the world of motorcycle clubs. She just wanted him to tell her in his words. And to watch him squirm a little in the process.

He took a deep breath, wanting to get it right. "When a woman becomes a Steel Infidel's "old lady", it's a serious commitment," he explained. "It's not a casual hook up or something to be taken lightly. Even though the jacket says "Property of Flint", that's not really what it means."

Kendra raised her eyebrows but didn't say anything.

"It's more of a symbol of respect for you," he continued. "When you wear this jacket, it means you are part of the Steel Infidels. The MC is bound to protect you the same as if you were one of our crew. If you ever get into any kind of trouble, they will be there for you, always. Even if something were to happen to me down the road. The Steel Infidels protect their own. And if you accept and wear this leather cut, you'll be part of the Steel Infidels family, too."

"Is it okay if I sew a patch on your jacket that says 'Property of Kendra'?" she asked with a straight face.

He shook his head and smiled, realizing she was messing with him. "That's not the way it works, darling."

"I know, I'm only teasing you," she replied. "I always like to be prepared, so I did some research on my own about this. Plus, Sarah and Myrtle pulled me aside one night at the clubhouse and talked to me about it as well. They wanted to make sure I understood it was a sign of honor, not servitude, to be an "old lady" in the club. I truly love the jacket and I will wear it everywhere."

Flint ran a nervous hand through his black hair. "Whew! I was worried there for a minute. Try it on then! Let's see if it fits."

He stood up and held up the jacket. Kendra turned around and slid her arms into the sleeves. He zipped her up and patted the shoulders. "So how does that feel? Is it the right size?"

Kendra smiled up at him. "It's a perfect fit." She shivered. "I feel so sexy in this jacket. Now all I need are some black leather boots to go with it. And maybe a pair of red leather biker gloves."

"I'm sure that can be arranged," Flint replied. "I foresee a shopping trip to Atlanta in our near future. Maybe we can make a weekend out of it. Go to the zoo and the aquarium while we're there. Anything you want to do."

Kendra rose up on her toes to kiss him. "Thank you, Flint. I'm really touched by this. It means a lot to me. I love the MC and all the guys. The Sweet Butts not so much, but maybe they'll grow on me."

Flint wrapped his arms around her waist. "Did you check the pockets? The jacket has inside pockets too, with zippers for your cash and credit cards. Or pistols. Whatever."

Kendra stuck her hands into the deep pockets. She glanced up at him, startled, with her mouth open wide as she pulled out a little ring box from the right pocket. Her eyes started to fill with tears even before she opened the box.

"Now don't cry, darling," he said, taking the ring box from her hands. "How are you going to see what's inside if you're all teary-eyed?"

He flipped open the ring box and turned it for her to see inside. The ring was simple, like her. A solid gold band and a solitary diamond. Perfect. Nothing too flashy. And the diamond stone was set deep and securely so none of the raptors or parrots in her care could pick it out with their beaks if they tried. She'd lost more than one piece of jewelry to the sneaky little devils.

Flint took the ring out of the box and held it between his thumb and forefinger. He started to speak then stopped, suddenly unsure of what to say. "Kendra, if this is too soon..."

"No! Are you crazy?" Tears were falling steadily down her cheeks now. She shook her head. "It's not too soon."

Flint knelt down in front of her and took both her hands in his. He gazed up at her with those intense green eyes she had fallen in love with the very first instant she looked into them. She'd suspected she was a goner on that day, and she had been right.

"I love you, Kendra," he began. "I've loved you from the very first moment when I opened my eyes, delirious with pain, and saw an angel with wild black hair leaning over me, tending to my wounds. As my grandpa would say, I was smitten with you from the very beginning. All

I could think about was making you mine. The first night after we made love on the sofa bed, I stayed awake until sunrise trying to figure out how to convince you to give me a chance. Just one chance. That's all I could hope for. And more than I deserved."

Kendra sniffled and smiled at him through her tears.

"You're strong and beautiful," he continued. "You're both my steady rock and my soft place to fall. I know I don't have much to offer you in the way of material things or money, but I will love you forever. I will always be there for you and I will never knowingly let you down. So, Kendra Shaw, will you make an honest man out of me and marry me? Preferably as soon as possible? Maybe this summer?"

Kendra sniffled again and laughed giddily. "Yes!" she replied. "Of course I'll marry you."

Flint sighed in relief, letting out the deep breath he'd been holding. He slid the ring carefully onto her finger and stood up. "You'll always be my girl?" he asked. It was the same question he'd asked her months before in the safe house.

"I said I would be your girl then, and I haven't changed my mind," she replied. "I will never change my mind. I love you, Flint. With everything I have. Being your wife would make me the happiest woman in the world."

"Should we open the champagne and make a toast?" He tilted his head toward the ice bucket.

"Wait a minute!" Kendra exclaimed. "You still haven't explained about the cabin."

"It's not 'the cabin', it's now 'our cabin'."

Her eyes grew wide. "You bought this place?"

"The owner found himself in a tight spot and was looking to sell. I made him an offer." He held up his hand. "I know what you're thinking and the answer is no, I didn't strong arm or pressure him in any way. He overextended on some real estate and needed to liquidate some of his assets. When I heard this was one of his properties going up for sale, I jumped on it."

"How did you get the money?"

Flint shrugged. "While working in the public defender's office, I made decent money. Not great money, but it was okay. I stashed everything I could. I worked all the time so I didn't have that much to spend it on. By making a few decent investments in the stock market at the right time, I was able to earn enough for a solid down payment."

Kendra drew in a shaky breath. "I'm having a hard time taking all this in. I love this place, and to think that it's yours now."

"Ours," he corrected. "It's our cabin now. I did a little bit of fixing up in here already. To surprise you more than anything else. I was thinking we might add on a bedroom in a year or so. Use this place as a weekend retreat when you can get away from the wildlife clinic or a place to bring our little ones in the summer."

"Little ones? Already thinking that far ahead?" Kendra was surprised and pleased. Flint had never mentioned one word about having kids before. Coming from a close family herself, she couldn't wait to have a bundle of kids running around the house someday. Whenever Flint was ready.

"Maybe in a couple of years?" he replied. "Hopefully soon the threat from the Liberators will be completely eliminated and we can all breathe easily again. I would hate to bring a baby right into the middle of a biker war. A baby would give them leverage. The timing isn't right yet because it isn't safe."

"I couldn't agree more," she said, sidling up closer. "Besides I'm not ready to share you yet with anyone else, not even a little munchkin. I want to be selfish and keep you all to myself." She leaned into him suggestively. "I do need a little more clarification about one thing though."

"What's that?"

"Does 'Property of Flint' mean you can do anything you want to me?" she asked in her sexiest voice. "Anything at all?"

He slowly unzipped her leather jacket. "Anything. You okay with that?" He slid his hands down and cupped her ample ass.

"Even if it's dirty and very, very bad?" she whispered.

Flint swallowed hard. "Especially then."

"And I can never say no?" she purred. "I can never refuse anything you want me to do?"

"You can never refuse me," Flint said, playing along with her sexy game.

"One more question," she said.

"Let's hear it."

"Are there rules in the MC about what you can do and not do while wearing a leather cut?"

Flint laughed in spite of himself. "Do you have something specific in mind or is this a general question?"

"Turn around and close your eyes until I tell you to open them."

"I thought I was the one who was supposed to be making up the rules."

"Would you just be quiet and turn around?" she said, slipping out of her sexy voice and giggling.

Flint sighed and turned around. It was only a couple of minutes, but it seemed like forever before Kendra said, "Okay! Open your eyes."

Flint whirled around with a silly grin on his face, which quickly changed to something else. "Holy fuck, Kendra!"

Kendra was stretched back on the pillows holding two glasses of champagne and wearing absolutely nothing except the leather cut. She had unzipped it halfway so her heavy naked breasts bulged through the opening. The jacket stopped at her waist, leaving her freshly waxed pussy bare to his gaze.

She held up a glass. "Shall we make a toast before you have a taste of your property?"

Three quick strides and Flint was beside her on the bed. He grabbed one of the champagne flutes from her and drained the contents in one long swallow, then placed the glass on a table beside the bed. "The toast can wait," he growled, unzipping the leather cut the rest of the way and spreading it wide open with the palms of his hands. "I want my taste now."

He grabbed both of her full breasts in his hands and massaged the nipples with his thumbs, pinching and fondling. Bending his head, he kissed and licked every inch of her tits. Kendra had already gulped down her champagne and ditched the glass. She curled her hands in his hair and writhed with pleasure.

Kendra threw her head back and pushed her breasts harder into his face. When he licked lightly on one nipple then the other, she gasped and held him tighter. Flint's tongue suddenly bit hard on one nipple while kneading the other breast roughly. He sucked hungrily on the tight bud, lavishing it with ravenous attention that soon had it aching and hard. Kendra melted into him, her body squirming as he moved his attention to the other breast. He tugged the nipple into his mouth with an insistent pull.

"You like that?" he murmured.

"Oh, yes," she moaned.

He slid down her body and guided her knees gently apart. Kendra leaned back on her bent elbows, using them to support her as his wide shoulders settled in between her legs.

His mind couldn't decide whether to look or to touch or do both. He could see her beautiful skin as she willingly opened herself up to him, her waxed pussy already glistening. He loved how responsive she was to his every touch, how her breath hitched and caught when he hit the right spots.

Flint leaned in close to breathe in her heady scent and caress the calf of her leg. To think he had almost walked away from this. What a fool he would have been. He slid his hand up the thigh, closer to the juncture between her legs. Moving his hand from her inner thigh, he pushed a finger into her waiting slit.

"Flint!" Kendra said, reaching down with both hands to grab his shoulders. She feverishly ran her hands down his arms and back up.

"You're dripping wet," he said. "I can't wait to taste you."

Flint put a hand on both of her knees, forcing her legs apart even wider. He lowered his head and sucked on her juicy pussy lips then wrapped Kendra's legs around his shoulders so he could drive deeper into her with his tongue.

He licked and licked, feeling like he could never get enough of her to satisfy him. Her hot cunt tasted even better than he'd remembered. Spurred on by her writhing and her tight grip on his hair, he buried his tongue into her slit as deep as it could go.

Flint wanted to drive her wild, to have her grinding her hips uncontrollably into his face. He didn't ever want her to doubt how she drove him mad with desire and how insatiable he would always be for her. And only her.

He looked up to see her watching him, her lips parted and her brown eyes almost glazed black with lust. "Touch your tits for me," he said huskily. "Squeeze your fat nipples."

Kendra touched her breasts hesitantly at first then cupped and pinched her tits while he watched from between her legs. Her inhibitions lost, she did as he asked, eager to please him any way he wanted. She rubbed her breasts and squeezed the round tits together, twisting and pulling the hard nubs as he tongued her deeper.

Flint bit back a groan as he dug his face closer into her pussy. He spread his mouth wider, letting his tongue sweep from her clit to the sensitive nerve endings of her ass. She bucked hard into his face and he grabbed her thighs, pinning her down. He held her tightly and forced her to succumb to his oral assault. She whimpered with her hips undulating underneath his hands and tongue.

He couldn't get enough of her taste. It was intoxicating and overwhelmed his senses, the way her sweet juices spilled onto his tongue. His head roared with desire.

"Open more for me," he whispered hoarsely. "You're wet and so fucking sexy."

She spread even wider for him and grew more vocal, moaning his name and driving him close to madness.

As always, sex with Kendra was wicked and hot.

Flint sucked on her clit, sending her into a quivering frenzy. He continued building up the pressure by flicking his tongue faster around her hooded button. She bit hard on her bottom lip, so close to orgasm. She closed her eyes and gasped as Flint lapped at her cunt, her fingers pulling hard on his hair as she ground herself into his face, coming in waves of contractions.

Fuck! How he loved her.

He didn't move from her inner thighs until he felt the last tremor of her climax had finally passed. Quickly stripping off all his clothes, he threw them into a pile on the floor and moved back between her legs.

"If I don't fuck you now, I'm going to explode," he said. He placed the tip of his cock at the entrance of her pussy and thrust in deep and hard. "It's a good thing we have all night because there are so many things I want to do to you..."

"Kendra! Wake up! Hurry!" Flint grabbed her shoulder and shook her gently awake.

Kendra rubbed her eyes with the back of her hand. "What is it? Is it the Liberators?" She looked at the clock. It wasn't even six a.m. yet. "What's wrong?"

"Nothing's wrong," Flint replied. He grabbed her t-shirt from the floor where she'd tossed it the night before. "Put this on. I want to show you something, but hurry so we don't miss it."

She tugged the t-shirt over her head and stood up. Flint grabbed the quilt from the bed and pressed it around her. "I'll wrap you up in this so you don't get cold. Come outside on the deck."

Kendra followed sleepily behind him, dragging half the quilt on the floor behind her. They stepped out on the tiny wooden deck that looked over the valley below them. The sun was barely coming up over the mountain ridge.

Flint tugged the quilt tighter around her and snuggled her against him. "Shh...be quiet and you'll hear it."

She leaned back against him, happy to be enjoying the early morning air but not quite understanding exactly what he thought was exciting enough to drag her half-naked body out of bed before daylight. After a minute of standing there barefoot in the cold and not hearing anything, she turned to go back inside.

"How about a hot cup of coffee?" she suggested.

"Wait!" He tugged her arm and turned her back around. "There! See? There's two of them circling the tallest tree on the ridge."

"What are you talking about?" she asked.

Suddenly, the loud and unmistakable scream of an eagle pierced the silence, followed by the sound of his mate.

"Oh my God! It's a pair of eagles!" Kendra jerked the quilt loose and ran to the railing where she could see them better. "There hasn't been an eagle spotted in the county in several years. I can't believe this! Isn't that a big nest over there on the top of that tree?"

Flint squinted and looked to where she pointed. "It must be. At first I thought they were only a couple of big hawks. When they kept circling closer and closer, I was finally able to see they were eagles."

Kendra stood there, grinning from ear to ear. "Thank you for waking me up," she said, going back to Flint and snuggling up to his warmth. He threw the quilt around her shoulders again and held her close.

"Stay snuggled up close to my body," he said. "I don't want you to catch a cold. I knew you wouldn't want to miss seeing them. Even if it meant dragging you out of bed."

"You can drag my butt out of bed any time to see an eagle in my backyard."

They stood there in silence, watching as the eagles circled and swooped over the valley. "Look at them fly," Kendra said. "They look so free, with not a care in the world. Soaring above the mountains, loving life, building a nest for their babies."

Flint rested his chin on the top of her head. "Hopefully, one of these days very soon we'll feel like that, too. Without a care in the world."

"You mean free?" she asked, pulling back to look up at his face.

He grinned. That sexy, devilish smile that made her heart skip a beat every time he turned it on her.

"I believe the word I'm searching for is 'Liberated'."

Kendra nodded in understanding and smiled. "Yes."

Liberated.

The End

If you would like to be notified of new releases sign up for my mailing list here. Keep reading! Jesse's story *Steel Justice* is up next!

Steel
Infidels
STEEL
JUSTICE
DEZ BURKE

One taste of her sweet lips and I swore I'd make her mine...

Bikers, babes, and booze. Three things I lived for, all in one dirty package when I decided to throw my brother's bachelor party at the Panama City Bike Rally.

Then she came along and screwed up everything.

The plan was simple. Familiar. Take her home, wreck her for other men, then kick her to the curb by daylight, spent and breathless.

It would've been the perfect night making her scream my name if she hadn't hidden one little fact.

She's Big Roy's property, and he owns her. The Prez of the Liberators MC is used to getting what he wants, and he won't let her go without a fight.

Neither will I.

I'll see him burn in hell before I let him touch her ever again...

PROLOGUE

JESSE

"Are you sure you're ready for this?" I whisper to my brother, Flint.

The taped music begins to play and he nods.

"Let's do it then," I say.

He starts walking down the aisle, lined by white chairs with blue bows, with me close behind him.

We reach the end and turn around to face the group gathered for Flint and Kendra's wedding. All members of the Steel Infidels are here, along with most of our families and friends.

The music stops and all eyes turn to Kendra standing at the end of the aisle. A big smile lights up Flint's face when he sees her. As the music plays, she slowly makes her way between the rows of guests. She reaches out to squeeze her mother's hand, who is sitting on the front row.

When she stops walking, her father leans down to kiss her cheek and places her hand in Flint's. Kendra takes a deep breath then lets out a nervous laugh.

The wedding officiant, chosen primarily for his love of motorcycles, begins the ceremony by welcoming the guests and reminding us all why we are here. He was asked to prepare a few words for the wedding, and I suspect they're going to be on the corny side.

"When you say I love you, what you are saying is, 'hold on tight, the ride is long,'" he begins in a deep, solemn voice.

I resist the urge to smile. Damn! Guess I was right.

After quoting a few more lines combining an odd mixture of motorcycles and weddings, he holds out his hand to me for the rings. I reach into my pocket and pull out two plain gold wedding bands and pass them to him.

A look of relief crosses Flint's face. Did he really think I would forget to bring the rings? I'm disappointed. He should have more faith in me.

No way was I fucking this up.

Unlike me, Flint is one of the solid good guys. A tough guy on the outside covering up a big old heart of gold. After everything he has been through the past few months, he deserves a happy ending.

There's nothing I won't do to make sure that happens.

The officiant takes the rings and places one each in Flint and Kendra's hands. He turns to the bride, who looks absolutely beautiful in her white wedding dress. In keeping with Kendra's down-to-earth personality, she chose a simple dress with a single strand of pearls. No fancy frills or layers of lace for her.

Flint would have preferred a traditional biker wedding with a motorcycle procession, leather jackets, and a bottomless beer keg. Kendra shot down that idea in a hurry.

So here we all are, standing in their decorated backyard located high on a mountain, dressed in uncomfortable clothes and sweating like pigs.

Kendra told me she was worried about looking fat on her big day. She shouldn't have. The baby bump is barely visible. If I didn't know to look for it, I wouldn't even suspect it was there. She sniffles and then laughs, wiping away a tear threatening to spill down her cheek and ruin her makeup.

I don't remember ever seeing her look so happy. From the corner of my eye, I catch Flint starting to get choked up by emotion, too. I grab his shoulder in a sign of brotherly support.

Come on buddy, you can do this.

Standing on my other side is our younger brother, Sam. He is grinning from ear to ear and rocking back and forth on the balls of his feet. Last night, I reminded him not to lock his knees and pass out like a dumbass during the ceremony. Now I realize I should have also explained that it wasn't okay for him to bounce around like a jumping bean either.

What the fuck is he grinning about anyway?

I hope to God he isn't about to do something stupid. I won't put it past Sam to pull one of his pranks right in the middle of the wedding. For once, I hope he has enough sense to behave himself. I shoot him a stern look just in case he has something on his mind.

"Be still," I whisper out of the side of my mouth.

He nods and stops moving.

The officiant glares at me and continues with the ceremony.

"Kendra, do you take this man to have and to hold, to lean with him when he leans and ride when he rides?" he asks.

Kendra gazes up into Flint's face and smiles. "I do."

"Flint, do you take this woman to share the open road, to protect and to ride with today and for eternity?"

"Hell yes!" Flint says without hesitation. The audience, consisting mostly of bikers, erupts in a cheer. "I mean, I do," he quickly adds. "I do."

"Please join hands." The officiant beams at the smiling couple. "By the power vested in me by the State of Georgia, I now pronounce you husband and wife! Flint, you may kiss your bride."

The crowd breaks out in applause.

Flint takes a step forward and pulls Kendra toward him for a kiss.

A shot rings out.

Then another.

For a split second, I freeze. My mind is telling me that a gun has accidentally misfired. Maybe some idiot forgot to put on the safety.

My gut tells me I'm dead wrong.

A big splotch of red appears on Kendra's wedding gown and begins spreading. The color both horrifies and mesmerizes me at the same time.

More shots ring out. Flint knocks Kendra to the ground and covers her with his body. A music speaker near the front row explodes.

All hell breaks loose.

We're all here. Ripe for the picking.

Every member of the Steel Infidels MC, Kendra's family, our family, close friends, and even some members of other friendly biker clubs.

As President of the Steel Infidels, this is my fault. All blame is on me. I never should have allowed this to happen. Gathering us together in a big group provides the perfect opportunity for someone with a grudge to strike against us.

I should have stood firm and not given my approval for a big wedding. Especially after everything that went down at the bike rally in Panama City.

Happy endings aren't meant for us. Shouldn't I know that by now?

Movement at the edge of the driveway catches my eye and I spot him.

The red-headed motherfucker I've spent months trying to find.

Big Roy, President of the Liberators.

My sworn enemy, the only person in this world that I want to kill with my bare hands.

I take off after him with Sam right behind me. By the time I reach my motorcycle, the handgun I normally keep tucked in the back of my pants is already in my hand.

The fight with the Liberators is ending today.

One way or the other.

1

TRISH

Three weeks earlier in Panama City, Florida...

I frown at my reflection and lean closer to the mirror to apply a coat of bright pink lipstick. Between the heavy makeup and false eyelashes, I barely recognize the face looking back at me.

"I bet if you lost ten pounds you'd bring in more bucks," says a surly voice from behind me. "You should lay off the potato chips and donuts."

I turn to glare at my brother. He is casually sprawled out on my hotel bed, watching me get ready for work as if he didn't have a care in the world.

"Go to hell, Ty. And get your dirty boots off my bed."

He doesn't move and instead takes a long drag on his cigarette. He blows the smoke in my direction, knowing this will piss me off.

"Do you really have to smoke in my room?" I ask, waving a hand to thin out the smoke floating toward me. "You know how much I hate the smell. Now I'll reek like cigarettes and so will my clothes."

"Since you're working in a bar, you'll be stinking to high heaven by the end of the night anyway. What fucking difference does it make?"

I let out a tired sigh. He is probably right. It didn't mean I wanted him smoking in my room. Truth is, I don't want him in my room period, smoking or not.

My brother is a jerk.

The less time I spend with him, the better off we both will be. All we do is argue constantly when we're together anyway.

I smooth down the short blue jean skirt that barely covers my butt and plump up my white bikini top one more time. My boobs look pretty good I think, and they're all mine. Not that the customers will care one way or the other. All that matters to them is cup size.

Fake or not.

The bigger and bouncier, the better.

Placing a red, white, and blue cowboy hat on my head, I turn this way, and then the other, checking out my reflection in the mirror one more time. I need something else to give the outfit a little more jazz. Maybe a pair of dangling hoop earrings.

The sexier I look, the more tips I will make.

A sad fact of life.

"What do you think about the hat?" I ask Ty. "You know how bikers love anything patriotic. It's a nice touch, don't you think?"

He grunts. "I doubt the hat makes a damn bit of difference one way or the other. As long as they can see your ass cheeks and tits, it won't matter what you're wearing. You could have a paper bag over your head and they wouldn't care. T and A is the name of the game. Everything else is decoration."

"Why do you always have to be so nasty? The owner of the bar told the girls to show up every night looking halfway respectable. This is the best I can do with what I have to work with."

Ty lifts his eyebrows. "If that is your best, then you need to do better," he says. "In any case, don't come back tonight without five hundred bucks in your pocket. We've got bills to pay."

I shoot him an incredulous look. I hope he is kidding. I know he isn't.

"Five hundred? Are you crazy? I can't make that much money as a beer bucket babe. Not even during a bike rally. You know all of our money comes from tips. Bikers can be tight-fisted."

He taps his cigarette on the white plastic ashtray sitting on the bedside table. Stray ash floats to the floor and melt tiny holes in the carpet. He doesn't even notice.

"That's because you're lazy," he replies. "I've heard some of those girls make five thousand bucks a week at the bike rallies."

I shake my head and sit down on the foot of the bed.

"Maybe at Sturgis, South Dakota, or Daytona Beach. The Panama City Bike Rally doesn't draw half the crowd of those rallies. I'll be lucky to bring in two hundred a night at the most." I glance around the room. "Have you seen my black boots? They were on the bed."

"Yeah, I threw them on the floor. They were in my way."

I look down under the dingy bedspread and reach for the knee-high leather boots. I tug one on and then the other. My feet are aching before I even pull up the zippers.

The boots, with their three-inch spiked heels, are incredibly painful to stand in all night. If I had it my way, I would be working in a pair of worn-out tennis shoes. Too bad old shoes aren't considered sexy.

When I start to stand up, Ty suddenly reaches over and grabs my upper arm. He squeezes until I yelp.

"Stop it!"

I tug at his hand. It doesn't budge.

"Let me go, Ty."

I turn my head away from the stale smell of cigarettes and alcohol on his breath. By tomorrow, a big purple bruise will appear and I'll have to cover it up with makeup. Bruises aren't a turn on and will make me look cheap.

"I said five hundred," he warns. "And I don't want to hear any excuses from you. Frankly, I don't give a flying fuck what you have to do to make it either. If you can't bring in the money opening beer bottles, then find another way. Show them your tits if you have to. You like to put on airs and act all high and mighty, but you ain't too good for that. Don't forget where you came from. A two-bit meth whore, that's where."

I know arguing with my brother won't do any good. The only reason he dragged me along with him on this trip to Panama City is because he thought we would have an opportunity to make some extra bucks.

For *me* to make some extra bucks, it turns out. Not him.

Easy money, he had said. Piece of cake.

Yeah right.

Easy for him to say that, too.

He isn't the one standing on his feet for fourteen hours straight a night. My official title at the Silver Shark Saloon is a "beer tub babe." A cute name for girls in sexy outfits who spend the night popping the caps on beer bottles as fast as they can while flirting and teasing with the customers for tips.

My hourly wage, if it can be called that, is a measly two dollars and thirteen cents. The real money comes from working the customers for dollar bills. A five if I'm really lucky.

I hate the job.

It disgusts me to have to put up with drunken bikers eyeballing my body like I am less than nothing, talking about my tits and whispering filthy comments in my ear.

Telling me what they want to do to me and asking what my nightly rate runs. Or, if they are really cheap, my charge to go behind the building for fifteen minutes.

I'm not a hooker. As far as I know, none of the girls are.

Not that this makes a difference. The men seem to think we're all for sale. As if everything in the world is right there for their taking, to be bought and sold during the bike rally.

Whatever they want or need.

The more I know about bikers, the less I like them.

"I told you already, Ty. I can't make that much money tonight."

Sure, I know we are running short on funds. What else is new? We are always low on money. God forbid Ty would go out and do something worthwhile for a change to make some cash. Why was it all up to me?

Ty gives my arm one last tight squeeze then slams his fist against the headboard. I can't help but flinch. His moods are so unpredictable and keep me on edge.

"Shut up!" he yells. "I've already told you a hundred times. We need the damn money so you're going to put your sweet ass to work and make it. Remember how I took you in when you had nowhere to go? And look at how you repay me, by giving me a hard time when I ask you to do one little thing."

"I'm working, aren't I? I just can't make that much."

"Yes, you can. It's time you start earning your way around here. I'm sick of hearing your complaining. You're beginning to sound just like that worthless piece-of-shit mother of ours. Always whining. Why she couldn't do this, or couldn't do that, while she let her kids almost starve to damn death. It's time to grow up, Trish. Face the real world."

His words sting more than I let him see.

"I'm not like her."

My voice sounds much softer than I mean for it to. I hate myself for sounding weak. Never in a million years will I turn out like my mother, an addict and a sorry excuse for a parent.

"Really?" he answers sarcastically. "Then start acting like it. Everybody needs to pull their weight around here, and that means you. Me and the boys are doing everything we can to put the Liberators back together, so I don't need your shit right now. Got it? If you're not willing to contribute, then you can just get the fuck out. I don't have time for this."

"Where will I go?"

The words slip out before I can stop them. His threat scares me. With no money, family, or friends, I don't have many options.

"Well, that's your damn problem, isn't it? When you get it figured out, you let me know. In the meantime, don't come back here until you have a wad of fucking cash in your hand. You understand? I'm not running a damn charity. Get out of my sight."

"Gladly."

Grabbing my purse, I hurry out of the hotel room. Once outside the building, I head down the street in the direction of the Silver Shark Saloon. Luckily the bar is close enough for me to walk to so I don't have to bum a ride from Ty or one of the other motorcycle club members.

As I walk down the crowded Panama City beach strip, past the numerous tattoo parlors, candy shops, and t-shirt tourist traps, his threat is still on my mind.

Where will I go if he throws me out?

This is a good question, one that I don't have an answer to.

Ty never lets me keep more than a few dollars of the money I make with the odd jobs I pick up here and there. Usually it goes to booze or spare parts for the motorcycle. Never for anything I want or need. The last two months has been absolute hell living with him and the rest of the Liberators.

To make things worse, we're always slipping around trying to keep a low profile since the FBI is still looking for Big Roy, the President of the MC.

In a way, I hope the Feds find him soon. The man gives me the creeps. I see the way he looks at me when he thinks I'm not paying attention. If he ever corners me or catches me by myself, I am in deep trouble. There's no doubt in my mind.

I'm not even sure Ty would stand up and protect me if it came to that. I don't kid myself where my older brother is concerned. I know he doesn't care about me.

Not really.

The only reason he took me in was because the few Liberators that are not in jail needed someone to help cook and clean up after them. Most of their old ladies split after the Feds raided the club and arrested most of the crew. The ones that are still hanging around can't even make decent coffee, much less an edible sandwich.

On the other hand, Ty *did* take me in when I had nowhere else to go, and my brother is the only real family I have left. In my way of thinking, this must count for something.

Our mother isn't technically deceased, though she might as well be. Between the drinking and the meth, she is more dead than alive. For years, I tried my best to take care of her. When the abuse, drugs, and constant stream of men coming in and out of the house became more than I could handle, I split and never looked back.

I ran from one living hell straight into another.

Occasionally at night when I'm all alone, I dream of a normal life.

A life with a man who cares about me. A little house with a yard, and maybe someday a couple of kids. A dog would be nice too, a yellow Lab that likes to chase tennis balls.

For now, it is all just a distant dream.

Someday, somehow, I will find a way out.

Too bad for me, it won't be today.

2

JESSE

I step inside the packed bar and take off my sunglasses. It takes a minute for my eyes to adjust to the dark building after coming in from the blinding sunlight of the beach.

Looking around, I check out the enormous two-story club. Bikers from all across the southeast are lined up at the two bars running the length of both sides of the room. A few of their faces I recognize, some of them friendly, and others definitely not.

I blow out a long breath. How the hell am I going to find my brothers and the rest of the Steel Infidels in this mess? I manage to squeeze my way through the crowd to an empty spot at the closest bar and order a whiskey, straight up without ice.

As I size up the various motorcycle clubs scattered around the tables, I'm hoping there won't be trouble this week during the bike rally. At the bare minimum, there will probably be a few fights breaking out between rival clubs. If that happens, I won't be surprised if the Steel Infidels are caught right smack dab in the middle of it.

My crew can't seem to stay out of bar brawls, and I suspect they secretly enjoy beating the shit out of people. As long as there aren't any fatal shootings or stabbings and nobody gets admitted to the hospital, I'll consider the week to be a raging success.

"Jesse Mason!" a loud booming voice calls out from behind me before a heavy hand clamps down on my shoulder. "Where have you been hiding? I thought you would show up yesterday, son."

I turn around and grasp the man's hand to shake.

"Roger! Good to see you. There were a few last-minute things to take care of before I could leave town, so I'm running late. I'm here now and ready to party. How have you been?" I wave a hand at the noisy room. "Business must be great. This place is so crowded that you couldn't squeeze ten more people in here."

Roger is the owner of the Silver Shark Saloon, a bar catering to the party crowd in Panama City, Florida. The centrally located bar on the beach strip is *the* happening place to be during the bike rally and known by everyone as party central.

"Business is going gang-busters," he replies with a chuckle. "I love it when the bike rally is here. You guys sure know how to party. Thank God bikers aren't like those cheap-ass spring breakers coming to town with nothing but fifty bucks in their pocket and a hard-on."

He grabs a toothpick from the bar and sticks it in his mouth. "Money is money, but sometimes I wish those spring breakers would go somewhere else for a change. They're beginning to get on my last nerve."

I laugh and down the rest of my whiskey in one swallow. "I bet they are. So have you seen my brothers and the rest of the MC? We're all supposed to meet up tonight. I'm sure they're here somewhere and have most likely started the party without me."

Roger tilts his white golf cap back on his bald head and points across the room to where three scantily clad girls are dancing on a long wooden bar. "Last time I saw them, they were hanging around in that general direction."

I watch as one of the girls leans over to give a bearded biker a full view of her braless breasts straight down the front of her tight white t-shirt.

"Well, that's not a surprise," I say. "The Steel Infidels never miss a chance to ogle the ladies. You didn't happen to mention anything about the bachelor party to Flint, did you?"

"Hell no," he replies, clearly insulted. "You told me it was a surprise bachelor party, so mum's the word. The private room, booze, and strippers are already arranged. All you guys need to do is show up the night of the party ready to see some pussy."

"Strippers too? Wow, you are a man with connections. I thought I would have to round those up myself."

"Don't you worry about a thing. I've got you covered. Every year I bring in a group of traveling strippers for the rally. You'll be glad to know I checked them all out personally from head to toe. Or should I say tits to pussy. I think the Steel Infidels will be pleased with my choices."

He leans closer.

"And if you need anything else, let me know. I have to warn you though. The cops are hanging tight this week. The word on the street is that there's going to be trouble."

"What kind of trouble?" I motion for the bartender to bring me another whiskey. "I was hoping for a quiet, no-drama week for a change. I have a gut feeling Flint is only going to get married once, so I want his bachelor party to go smoothly. For us, that means no arrests, no drunk driving, and no trips to the emergency room."

"I wouldn't worry much about it," Roger says. "The rumors are flying that there might be a couple of the one-percenter clubs showing up. Trying to settle some scores left over from that mess in Waco."

He shakes his head in disbelief.

"What a fiasco that turned out to be. Most of those bikers are still sitting in the county jail out in Texas. The authorities don't know what to do with them. If you ask me, they should throw them all in a cell together and the problem would be solved in a hurry. Think of all the taxpayer money they'll save."

I shrug it off. "The MC doesn't have any beef with the one-percenters. As long as they stay out of our way, we'll stay out of theirs. Now if any of those fucking Liberators show up here, that will be an entirely different story."

"Did something go down with them?" he asks. "I haven't seen them around yet this week and hope I don't. That Big Roy is one nasty son-of-a-bitch. I don't need his kind of business."

I hesitate before answering. Roger is a friend, but not a confidant. The decades-old feud between the Steel Infidels and the Liberators is a known fact. What isn't widely known are the brutal events that have gone down over the past few months.

After the Liberators murdered one of my crew members and shot Flint, the MC made the decision to permanently take them out.

By whatever means necessary.

Unfortunately, we were only partially successful. Several Liberators were killed during a shootout. A few others were arrested for the prostitution of young girls for sex and pornography.

Even after all this, the leader of the Liberators, Big Roy, and his top crew members managed to escape. Someone from the police department tipped them off before the raid. Being the fucking cowards they are, they let their newest members take the fall for the club.

The Liberators have been in hiding for months now. Nobody has seen or heard from them. Or if they have, they sure as hell aren't talking.

The thought of Big Roy still out there somewhere eats at me like a festering wound every single day. I know he will show his ugly face sooner or later. He isn't the type of man to hide out in a mountain cabin forever because he likes terrorizing people too much to lay low for long. When he comes out of hiding, I'll be there waiting for him.

Roger doesn't need to know any of this though. I believe in sharing information only on a 'need to know' basis.

"Nothing major happened," I finally answer, downplaying the situation. "Same old shit, you know. The FBI is looking for them, so I highly doubt they will show up here. You don't need to worry about it."

"Good to know. I don't want any trouble this week."

"That makes two of us."

Flint spots me trying to make my way through the crowd and waves me over to join the rest of the MC. From the flushed looks on their faces, I guess the other members of the Steel Infidels are already on their fourth or fifth drink.

I'm a little surprised and pleased to see that Flint has obviously imbibed his fair share of alcohol, too. Now that he is engaged, he tries to keep the partying down to a minimum.

At least when his fiancée, Kendra, is around.

I know better than anyone that there is still a wild streak in my brother that can never be fully tamed. Kendra probably senses it as well. To her credit, she loves and accepts him the way he is without trying to change him. She is a great asset to the club and has shown her loyalty many times over. Flint is damn lucky to have her.

I don't know many women who would be willing to put up with us. The life of an old lady in a motorcycle club isn't easy. There are rules to follow and a strict chain of command. The men run the show and the ladies follow with no questions asked. It is either put up or get out.

The motorcycle club always comes first.

No matter what.

"Any alcohol left for me?" I ask. "Or did you boys drain the bottom of the barrels already?"

The men step aside to make room for me between them. I turn to Flint. "I see you've already had a couple."

He laughs and lifts the glass. "I'm making the best of my limited time left as a single man. Time is slipping away like the sand in an hourglass. I can't waste a second."

I clap him on the shoulder. "That's the spirit. Kendra is going to make you toe the line once you two are married. So you had better drink up while you have the chance."

Flint drains his glass and slams it on the bar. "You're right, and I couldn't be happier about it."

I take a mental count of the group and notice one member is missing. Not surprisingly, it is our other brother, Sam. He is the youngest member of the MC and at times can be completely out of control. Sam loves the ladies more than anything else in this world, and they love him. This makes for a continuous shit heap of drama where he is concerned.

I've been woken up in the middle of the night more times than I can count by women on our front doorstep crying over Sam. If it gets much worse, we may be forced to move to a secret location deep in the caves of Afghanistan.

"Where the hell is Sam?" I ask. "I thought he rode over from the hotel with you guys."

"Oh, he did," Flint answers with a slight slur to his voice. He turns around on the bar stool to look for him in the crowd. "He's here somewhere. Look for a cluster of women with big titties and you'll find Sam tangled up right in the middle."

"Speak of the devil. Here comes the little shit now."

Sam wanders up with two big-breasted blondes, one hanging tightly onto each of his tattooed arms. He pulls back and punches my shoulder hard in greeting. I resist the urge to rub the stinging spot.

"What took you so long to get here, Jesse?" he asks. "Sorry, we had to start the party without you. We tried to wait for you, but you know how it is." He shrugs in explanation. "Time is wasting and all that."

I try not to stare at the large breasts of the girl closest to me. Damn! She isn't wearing a bra, and her tight red t-shirt is doing little to conceal her ample tits and hard nipples.

"Who are your friends?" I ask as she slides a little closer. As usual, Sam isn't wasting any time hooking up. Some things never change.

"This is Molly and Christina," Sam answers, pointing to one and then the other. "Or is it Christina and Molly? My apologies girls, I get confused by your beauty. They're in town all week for the rally."

"We're with a group of traveling strippers," Molly explains. "Next week we'll be moving on to Daytona Beach. It's a fun gig. We get to go different places and do all kinds of different things."

Oh, I bet you do.

"Sounds like an interesting job," I say with a polite smile.

"We're here for the Miss Panama City Bike Rally contest tonight."

She giggles for no reason, and I gulp as her breasts threaten to spill out of her shirt. "First prize is a thousand bucks, so we signed up as soon as we heard about it. The contest should start in a half hour or so. You should all stick around and cheer for us."

"Don't worry, we're not going anywhere," Sam says. "We wouldn't miss it for the world. Would we, guys?"

The rest of my crew grin and quickly agree. "Oh, no. We'll be right here," they all say. "Cheering for you gals."

I turn back to the bartender and order another round of drinks for everyone.

The bike rally is already off to a terrific start.

3

JESSE

"Good God almighty! Look at the tits on that one." Sam points to the first contestant stepping up on the stage for the Miss Panama City Biker Rally contest.

The contestant is a typical biker gal: long jet-black hair, a couple of tattoos on her shoulders, and a pierced navel. She's wearing hot pink shorts that ride three quarters of the way up her hefty ass and a pink bikini top that barely covers her dark nipples.

Definitely not my type.

The crowd of wasted bikers obviously think differently. They push closer to the stage, whistling and clapping as she struts around in her ridiculously high heels. At one point, she wobbles and for a second it looks like she might twist her ankle.

"Damn! She's going to fall flat on her ass," I say to Sam, who snickers. "Whoops! No, she's up on her feet again. Good save."

The chick recovers quickly. To cover up her clumsiness, she turns her back to the audience and bends over dramatically, giving the men closest to her a glimpse of skin barely concealed by a thin line of fabric.

"That will score her some big points with the judges," Sam says. "They've already forgotten she almost tumbled off the stage. Who needs beauty and grace when you can show a little pussy instead?"

"Let's give it up for Trixie!" Roger barks into the microphone from the side of the stage. "Hell of a way to start the contest. Right, gentlemen?"

The men roar their approval. The next contestant, a carbon copy of the first, only in a different outfit, begins to shimmy and dance her way across the wooden platform.

Bored, I turn away from the contest.

I've seen it all before.

Dyed hair, fake tits, pussies shaved the exact same way.

Why do women all want to look exactly alike? Don't they realize men need variety in their life?

The other girls are patiently waiting for their turn by the side of the stage. They chat with each other as they smooth down thickly sprayed hair and adjust their bikini tops to show the maximum amount of cleavage.

None of them interest me either.

Too bad, because I'm horny as hell and am counting on getting laid tonight.

What catches my eye is the girl standing behind a huge cooler of ice and beer set up near the corner of the stage. She is tall with long brown hair and shapely legs that go on forever. My eyes follow those legs up from her high-heeled leather boots to the curvy ass in a blue jean skirt. A flag-themed cowboy hat sits on her head.

Her tits, barely covered by a white bikini top, are large, pillow soft, and obviously real. Even from way back where I'm standing, I can tell they're not pumped full of stiff silicone shit. I can't help but imagine what it would feel like to sink my teeth into the lush globes and roll the thick nipples with my tongue.

My cock stirs against my jeans.

Oh yeah, I'm interested now alright.

I wonder how much sweet-talking it will take to talk her into going back to my hotel room after work. I'm already thinking of how tight her pussy will feel when I sink balls deep inside.

Maybe I'll ask her to leave the cowboy hat on while I fuck her hard from behind. Those sexy-as-hell black leather boots should stay on, too.

If I had to guess, I'd say she is the type of gal that will act all coy and tell me no at first.

I won't let a little thing like that stop me.

I'm a man who loves a challenge and besides, I haven't found a woman yet that wasn't eventually willing to spread her legs wide for me. And after one good fuck, they always come back begging for more.

Finding a woman to fuck isn't my problem.

Finding a woman who keeps my interest the next morning definitely is.

The girl smiles and laughs while she hastily pops the tops off bottles of beer and hands them to waiting customers. Dollar after dollar falls into her tip jar. It is almost full and the night isn't halfway over.

When the last customer in line steps away, her smile instantly drops. I watch her tuck a strand of brown hair behind her ear and adjust the cowboy hat. Her whole demeanor changes when she isn't putting on a show.

I'm intrigued by her even more now.

She clearly doesn't belong here. Any fool could see that.

Whereas the other girls exude dirty sex, she projects almost a sense of innocence and purity. Not something you expect, or even want to see, working at a bar loaded with bikers.

I bet she thinks she looks sexy with her high-heeled leather boots and short skirt. And she does, in her own way.

Hot as hell in fact.

Just not in the way she thinks. She reminds me of a juicy, ripe Georgia peach waiting to be plucked from the tree.

I start making my way across the room, telling myself I need another beer. Truth is, I want a closer look at those sweet tits.

Other men obviously have the same idea, and a long line quickly forms in front of her. A man wearing a muscle shirt with a red bandanna wrapped around his head leans forward for a better view down her bikini top. I want to slap the shit out of him and choke him with his bandanna. If he does it again, I might do exactly that.

The girl keeps up a steady stream of flirty banter with the men who reach the front of the line. I notice she is careful to treat them all the same, thanking each one politely for their compliments, even the lewd ones, and laughing at their jokes.

The girl is good at her job. No wonder her tips are piling up.

The longer I watch her, the more I want to sling her over my shoulder and take her back to the hotel. Or upstairs, if there is an empty room, or even a broom closet. I'm not picky about the location. As long as I can get a good angle, I'm pumped and ready to go.

Finally I reach the front of the line and it's my turn to order. She looks up at me and smiles. It seems genuine, though the smile doesn't quite reach her eyes.

I never have any problem getting ladies to do exactly what I want them to. There's nothing to make me believe this pretty gal will be any different.

For some reason, the thought leaves me slightly disappointed. Occasionally it might be nice to have to work for it.

Love them and leave them wanting more is my rule.

Take her home, do the dirty, and kiss her goodbye. Hell, if she's a fantastic lay, I might even buy this one breakfast.

"Hey gorgeous," I say, suddenly and inexplicably at a loss for anything more clever.

"Hey yourself," she responds. "How many bottles of beer do you need?"

"Just one."

She pulls an ice-cold beer out of the cooler, pops the cap, and hands it to me. "You're a big drinker, I see," she says with a wink. "That will be five bucks."

I hand her a ten-dollar bill so she can see me put the five in change into her tip jar.

"I'm usually a whiskey man," I explain. "I'm only ordering beer so I'll have an excuse to see your beautiful body up close and personal."

"I appreciate that," she says. She smiles politely and looks over my shoulder at the next customer.

"What can I get you?" she asks the man standing behind me.

Damn! Did she really brush me off that fast?

I blink in surprise and turn around to face him.

"How many beers do you need?" I ask. "I'm buying if you'll move along quickly."

He laughs and slaps me on the back. "You got it, buddy. I'll take two."

I fork over more money and she hands him the bottles. "Hope you get lucky tonight," he says before walking away.

For a brief moment, we're alone. I know it won't last for long. Not unless I want to keep buying beer for a line of guys all night. I better make my move fast. Like Sam says, time is wasting.

I lean closer.

"So I was wondering, what you are doing after work tonight, sweetheart? Got any big plans that can't be cancelled?"

She rolls her eyes at me. "You were wondering, huh? You and about a hundred other guys in here. No offense, but you're not the first person to ask me that exact same question tonight."

"Since that isn't a valid answer, I'm not taking it as a 'no.'"

With a sigh, she turns away to start jamming beer bottles further down into the ice. She almost seems pissed at me. I can't figure out why, since I haven't done anything.

Yet.

"Sorry, *sweetheart*, I've already got plans," she replies with a sarcastic emphasis on the 'sweetheart.'

Guess she doesn't like to be called endearing names. Most women eat that shit up. I wonder what her issue is.

"Doing what?"

She straightens up and hesitates for a split second too long. "Well for starters, I have to go home and make lunch for my three kids to take to school tomorrow. They're all in elementary school and are quite a handful. You know how it is...homework, stomach flu, lice. You name it, they've got it."

I grin and take a sip of the cold beer. She is a terrible liar. "How old are they?"

"Five, six, and eight."

"So you started popping out babies at the age of what...twelve?"

She doesn't miss a beat. "I look young for my age. Everyone says so."

"Is that really the best excuse you can make up for not going out with me? At least let me take you to grab something to eat after work."

"And where would that be at two o'clock in the morning? Last call isn't until one forty-five, and then we have to clean up. I appreciate it though. Truly. The answer is still no."

She smiles again to soften her words and to convince me to give up quietly and move along without making a scene.

I'm a little surprised at how fast she is shutting me down.

This isn't going as well as expected.

"So why aren't you up there in the beauty contest?" I ask, pointing to the last contestant up on stage. "You would win. Hands down. There wouldn't even be a contest."

Compliments always work to warm up the ladies.

She laughs out loud at the suggestion. "No way. Prancing around on stage isn't my thing."

I take another swig of beer. "Glad to hear it."

She lifts her eyebrows and gives me her full attention. "And why do you say that?"

"Because I wouldn't be able to stand all those assholes looking at my girl. If you were mine, I would keep you all to myself."

Before she has a chance to reply, I turn and walk away without a backwards glance.

I'll let her chew on that little tidbit for a while.

She'll come around looking for me before the night is over.

They always do.

4

TRISH

"*His girl?*"

What did he mean by that?

From the moment his muscular tattooed frame started making its way toward me through the crowd, I knew he was trouble.

Big time.

Nothing worse than a badass biker with an attitude.

I've met plenty of guys like him before, arrogant assholes used to getting their own way. None quite so good-looking though with his jet-black hair and mesmerizing blue eyes.

Or as sexy.

Raw masculine energy radiates off him in every direction. It is all I can do not to be caught up in it like a spider web. I suspect most women aren't so lucky.

I don't know what his deal is and don't want to find out. My gut tells me to stay far away. There's plenty enough crap in my life without adding the temptation of a sexy-as-hell tattooed biker to the pile.

By the time my fourteen-hour shift is over, I am dead tired. Every step hurts on the walk back to the hotel. The first thing I'm going to do when I reach my room is soak my tired feet in cold water. Then I'll take a hot shower to wash off all the grime and the stench from the bar.

A soft bed or even a hard, uncomfortable hotel room bed will feel so good. I'm already dreaming of crawling under the sheets and passing out for a solid eight hours, maybe more.

I climb the two sets of metal stairs leading up to my hotel room and reach for my key card. The flickering glow of the television light shines through the curtains. I frown. Ty must have left it on when he left the room earlier. At least I hope he is gone. I am not in the mood to be dealing with him tonight.

Stepping inside the door, I sling my purse on a chair and reach to switch on the main light. The sight of a big, red-headed bearded man sitting on my bed startles me.

"Big Roy! Jesus Christ! You scared me half to death. What are you doing here?"

The President of the Liberators Motorcycle Club is the last person I expect to see waiting for me in the dark room. Ty must have given him a key. I'm going to chew my brother out good. I can't believe he did this to me.

Big Roy hits a button on the remote control to mute the pay-per-view porn channel he is watching. He looks at me for a long minute without answering. "I'm waiting on you, darling. I hear you have something for me. Hand it over."

I hesitate, confused. Normally I turn over all of my earnings directly to Ty. I don't have a clue as to what happens to the money after that point. I always assumed most of it went to Big Roy and the club. I never ask questions because I wouldn't get straight answers anyway.

"Okay," I say, reaching for my purse since saying 'no' to Big Roy isn't an option.

"Throw it to me," he orders.

I toss him the purse and wait while he digs out my wallet. He quickly counts the thick, folded stack of bills.

"Two hundred?" he says with obvious disappointment. His eyes narrow dangerously. "That's it? Ty told me you would be bringing in more every night."

I shrug as if it's no big deal. "The beauty contest was going on tonight at the bar, so it slowed down beer sales. Plus I was stuck working near the side of the stage where the men couldn't see the action while they were waiting in line."

I sit down in the chair and begin unzipping my boots. "I don't have a choice about where in the bar they set up my beer tub. I have to take whatever they give me. The girls who have worked there longer get first pick on the better locations."

Big Roy gives me a doubtful look. "You wouldn't be holding out on me, would you? Because there could be bad consequences if you are."

"No, of course not," I lie.

I try my best to look indignant at the accusation while at the same time thinking of the two hundred dollars folded neatly in the back pocket of my jean skirt.

For a second, I consider handing it over, too.

No, it's too late now. He would know I intended to keep it for myself and there would be hell to pay.

My heart pounds loudly in my chest. I focus on keeping my voice steady and my breathing calm. It won't do to let him smell fear.

"Where is Ty?" I ask. "Is he passed out drunk again in his room? I'm getting worried about his drinking."

"No, he's out doing something for the club. Why? Are you scared to be alone with me?" He laughs as if the thought amuses him.

Yes.

Terrified.

He wants me to be scared of him. In fact, he wants everyone to be scared of him. Big Roy rules by fear and force. I've seen him in action often enough to know.

I don't answer his question out loud. No matter what I say, it will come out wrong. If I say I'm not afraid of him, he'll tell me I should be. If I say I am afraid, it will make me look weak, and he won't like that either.

What a fool I've been. To foolishly believe I was immune to the danger because I was his VP's little sister. The best thing for me to do is try to placate him for now and hopefully he'll leave me alone.

"Tips should pick up tomorrow night at the club," I say. "Tonight was a light crowd. The other girls were talking about how most of the bikers aren't due in town until tomorrow for the long weekend." I try to smile. "I have a few new ideas to spice up my look. I'll try harder," I offer, hoping to sound convincing.

Big Roy stands up and crams the wad of money into his pockets. "For your sake, I sure hope so," he says. "I don't like to be disappointed. Make sure it doesn't happen again."

He walks past me to the door and I hold my breath, waiting and praying for him to leave. If he reaches a hand out to touch me, I'm screwed.

In more ways than one.

He steps out the doorway then turns around. My heart drops.

"Just so you know," he says. "It's already been decided. From now on, you're going to ride with me as my old lady. Tomorrow you'll need to move your stuff into my room."

The floor threatens to fall out from under me.

"I left a porn channel on for you," he adds. "Maybe you can pick up some tips. We can try them out later." He gives me a nasty wink and walks away.

I quickly shut the door, throw the deadbolt, and lean back against it.

I'd rather be dead than let Big Roy touch me.

Ride as his old lady?

No way in hell.

I've picked up enough biker slang to know that 'old lady' means he wants me to be his woman and share his bed. The thought of Big Roy crawling between my legs makes me want to vomit.

I can't imagine where he got the crazy idea that I would be willing to have sex with him. Not one time have I ever given him any encouragement. No flirting, no chatting, no sly smiles in his direction. Then I realize what I want has nothing to do with this.

Big Roy wants, therefore he gets.

Period.

End of story.

I wonder how long Ty and Big Roy have been planning this behind my back. Would Ty really be willing to prostitute his own sister?

I am so stupid.

I should have known this could happen.

In the back of my mind, I always hoped Ty would step up and protect me if one of the club members made a move on me. Like any decent big brother would do. And maybe he might have, if the pursuer had been anyone other than Big Roy.

According to Ty, Big Roy walks on water. The best day of his life was when Big Roy nominated him as his VP. There is no way Ty will go up against him now on anything.

Even if Big Roy wants to have sex with his little sister against her will.

I am hurt.

No, more like devastated.

Any shred of family connection is gone now. Tears threaten to fall and I wipe them back. Damn it! I will not cry. My asshole brother isn't worth it. My whole life is turning to crap.

I grab a duffel bag and start stuffing my belongings into it as fast as I can. I can't stay here any longer. No matter what happens, being Big Roy's old lady isn't part of my plan.

Not now, not ever.

Before I'll let him touch me with those fat, dirty hands of his, I'll murder him first myself. Or tip off the Feds to where he is hiding. Smiling at the thought, I quickly brush it off. Even I'm not dumb enough to do that. Not unless I have a death wish.

I look longingly at the bed and consider lying down for just a minute to rest my eyes. I'm so exhausted and wish I could wait until morning to leave. A shower and a few hours of sleep would make me feel so much better. When I'm this tired, I can't think straight.

The risk isn't worth it.

Big Roy could change his mind and come back for me any second. I can't take the chance he'll decide I need to become his 'old lady' tonight.

I pack up everything and decide to intentionally leave a few of my things behind: a hairbrush, some makeup, and dirty clothes strewn around the room.

If Ty drops by in the morning to check in with me, maybe he'll think I've run out to pick up coffee and donuts for the men. The same thing I've done every day for the past two months as part of my club duties.

My brother will figure it out soon enough. My days of fetching coffee for the Liberators are now officially over. They can get their own damn coffee and donuts from now on. And I don't need my brother's help any longer if this is way he's going to treat me.

I open the door quietly and peek out, checking to make sure the coast is clear. I hear drunken laughter coming from a few doors down. It sounds as if they're all inside Big Roy's room.

With any luck, I can make my getaway without being spotted. I ease the door shut and tiptoe down the stairs, trying not to make a sound on the metal steps.

I can't get caught now. Not with a bag with most of my things. There's no telling what Big Roy might do if he catches me trying to make a run for it. I hold my breath and try not to let my mind go to dark places.

Up until this point, I honestly believed that hanging out with the Liberators was my choice. That I could freely choose to leave at any time and go on my merry way whenever I felt like it.

Not anymore.

Big Roy thinks he owns me, and he isn't going to let me go without a fight. I know this now, and it terrifies me.

I run across the street and make it two blocks before I realize I don't have any idea where I'm going. For the first time in my life, I'm all on my own. Alone and with nothing except what I'm carrying with me.

On the bright side, at least I have the two hundred dollars in my pocket and a job for the rest of the week. First thing in the morning, I'll talk to the owner of the bar to see if he has any additional jobs I can do. Maybe he'll let me come in to work early to set up tables.

All I have to do is make it through tonight. Surely I can survive one night?

5

JESSE

"What the fuck is going on with this traffic?" I yell to Flint, who is riding beside me on his motorcycle.

He throws up his hands. "Bike week, man," he replies.

Even in the middle of the night, the strip along Panama City's beachfront is lined with bumper-to-bumper traffic; mostly motorcycles interspersed with only a few cars and trucks.

All of the bars in town have closed for the night, so there is nothing left for bikers to do but pile into the streets to show off their motorcycles. From the hordes of people lining the packed sidewalks to the inebriated bikers trying to keep their bikes upright, it seems everyone is doing their best to keep the party going until the sun comes up.

Nobody sleeps much during bike week. The event only happens once a year, so nobody wants to miss a minute of the action. "I can sleep when I get home," people always say.

Flint and I are leading the Steel Infidels' pack of thirteen motorcycles, with Rocco and Sam bringing up the rear. We all drank more tonight than we should have.

I hope the rest of the guys are sober enough to make it the short distance back to the hotel. Not that we are doing any actual driving at the moment. More like walking our bikes along with the heel of our boots in the traffic.

Hell, walking might be faster.

The good news is, as long as my crew doesn't pass out and tip their bike over, nobody will get hurt tonight. Guess I shouldn't be bitching about the stalled traffic, considering how wasted most of them are.

Up ahead, I spot a cowboy hat bouncing along with the crowd of people on the sidewalk. I do a double take. Surely it isn't the beer tub babe from the bar? What the hell would she be doing wandering around the streets this time of night?

I motion to Flint to get his attention.

"Take the crew on back to the hotel," I yell over the roar of motorcycles. "I'll catch up."

"Where are you going?"

"Tell you later."

I pull off to the side to allow the other members of the Steel Infidels to go by. I wait until they pass me before I begin slowly trailing behind the cowboy hat.

It's her, alright.

She's wearing the same clothes she had on at the bar, except now she is carrying a big heavy bag slung over one shoulder.

I pull the bike up alongside her.

"Hey gorgeous! Where are you going?"

She doesn't speak or even acknowledge that she hears me. Instead, she looks straight ahead and keeps walking.

"Wait up a minute! Where are you headed? I can give you a ride."

No response.

Fuck! She is one tough cookie.

Not to be deterred so easily, I pull ahead then run the front wheel of the bike up on the sidewalk in front of her, blocking her path.

"Jesus, man!" says a man walking close behind her. "What the hell are you doing?"

"Fuck off," I say.

He gives me a long look, as if he's considering confronting me further. Thinking better of it, he walks around me without another word.

She abruptly stops walking and crosses her arms in irritation. She obviously isn't as pleased to see me as I had hoped.

"What the hell do you want?" she asks. "I already told you 'no' a half dozen times. I'm not interested, get it? Nothing personal. Please just leave me alone." Her eyes are shooting daggers at me. She looks even hotter when she is mad.

"I thought you might need a ride," I explain. "That's all. The bag you're carrying looks awfully damn heavy. Hop on the back of my bike and I'll deliver you wherever you want to go. Where are you staying?"

"None of your damn business," she replies, a little out of breath from the walking.

Her breasts are heaving, and I can't help but stare at them. She's still wearing the white bikini top as before with an unbuttoned short-sleeved jacket over it.

"What if I said I'm making it my business? Look around. Everyone else is partying and having fun. You, on the other hand, look like you're about to burst out crying any second. What the hell are you doing out here in the middle of the night?"

She waves a hand in front of my nose.

"Do you mind looking at my face instead of my boobs when you're talking to me?" she says. "That is, if you really want an answer. As far as I know, they don't respond to questions."

I grin at her. "So what do they respond to?" I tease, reluctantly tearing my eyes away from her tits.

"Is your filthy mind in the gutter all the time?" she asks with a disgusted look on her face.

I start to reply with an even dirtier comment about the things I could do to make her tits respond then stop when I notice the dark circles under her eyes. She's clearly on the verge of falling over from exhaustion.

I feel a tinge of regret for teasing her. This might not be the time or the place.

"I'm sorry, okay? Let's start over. You're obviously beat and I'm offering you a ride. No strings attached. What do you say?"

She lets out a tired sigh and slings the bag off her shoulder on to the ground.

"Not that it's any of your business, but I had a falling out with my roommates, so I split. I'm trying to find a cheap hotel with a vacancy and I'm not having much luck. Everything is booked up for bike week. I've already checked every hotel on this end of the strip, so I'm going to keep walking until I find something."

"Where is your car?"

"Obviously not here."

The thought of her not having a sure place to go in the middle of the night or even a reliable way to get there worries me. Even so, I'm willing to bet there is more to her story than she is letting on. I also suspect there is a guy involved that she isn't telling me about, a guy that will soon be history if I have anything to say about it.

"So what's your plan?" I ask. "To walk the streets until you're ten miles from the strip? Everything is booked solid. Most people made their reservations a year ago. You look exhausted. Come on. I'll take you back to my room where you can grab a shower, change clothes, and get a couple hours of sleep."

She puts her hands on her hips and gives me a dubious look. I take it as encouragement to keep talking.

"In the morning, I'll take you out to breakfast and we'll figure out something. I know your boss pretty well. I'll talk to him and see if any of the other girls needs a roommate. Roger will help you out. I'm sure of it. He's a decent guy."

She doesn't answer right away.

I can't tell if she's considering my offer or if she's getting ready to tell me to go to hell and never show my face near her again.

A deep boom of thunder rumbles in the distance, far out over the ocean. I cock an eyebrow at her.

"My generous offer is about to expire in ten seconds. I suggest you make a decision quickly. I'm not a fan of riding in the rain, and I'm guessing you aren't either."

"I'm not having sex with you," she blurts out.

I burst out laughing. "Suit yourself. I don't remember asking you to. I wouldn't have sex with you anyway. Not even if you got down on your knees and begged. I have high standards to uphold."

A smile tugs around her lips that she quickly hides. "Glad to get that settled then," she says.

I feel a tiny glimmer of hope. There might be a chance with her after all. Reaching for her bag, I securely strap it to the back of the bike. Surprisingly, she doesn't protest or argue with me. I rev the throttle.

"Climb on, if you're coming. I don't have all night to stand around chit-chatting."

She hesitates, still unsure if she's making the right decision. I can't blame her. She's taking a big risk riding off with a stranger. For all she knows, I could be a serial killer.

I'm not kidding myself. If she wasn't desperate, going with me wouldn't be an option. I'm usually not a man to take advantage of a woman's bad situation. Sometimes though, like now, it's the only way to move things along quickly.

"I don't even know your name," she says. "This doesn't feel right."

"It's Jesse Mason, and now you know."

She takes a deep breath. "Okay. I'm Trish, short for Patricia."

After sliding a leg over the back of the bike, she tentatively places a hand on each side of my waist.

"You had better hold on tighter than that, Trish," I say to her over my shoulder. "Sorry I don't have a helmet for you. The beautiful state of Florida says we don't need one. I'll drive careful so you won't have anything to be scared of."

She grips me tighter and my cock starts to swell.

"It's okay," she breathes into my ear. "I'm not afraid of motorcycles. Bikers, however, are a whole different story."

When we reach the hotel, my crew is waiting outside for me in the parking lot. They raise their hands in greeting and openly stare at the pretty girl riding behind me.

Trish slides off the bike and quickly tugs down her short skirt. Sam lets out a low whistle of appreciation.

"Cut it out," I say curtly. "That's enough."

He blinks in surprise and the rest of the crew breaks out into laughter. For a reason I don't understand myself, I want the guys to know this girl is different and not like the low-class broads we usually pick up.

I won't tolerate any disrespect toward her.

"Come on, let's go inside."

I take her bag and point toward the door to my room located on the street level. I usher her in and turn on the lights.

Trish takes two steps inside and goes dead still when she sees the oversized king bed in the center of the room.

"Don't start freaking the fuck out now," I say. "Trust me. I've never had to force a woman in my life to have sex with me, and I don't have any plans to start now."

She raises her eyebrows at me. "Never had to force a woman, huh? I can believe it. You have some smooth moves, I'll give you that. Doesn't mean I'll fall for them, so don't get any ideas."

"At least you noticed. That's a start."

Moving past her across the room, I throw open the door to the bathroom. "You can put some of your stuff in here on the sink. There should be plenty of fresh towels, soap, and shampoo. I'm going to check in with my crew. Give you some privacy while you take a shower and change."

She nods and I turn to leave.

"Jesse?"

"Yeah?"

"Thank you."

"Don't mention it. Saving ladies in distress is my specialty. I have a business card and everything. It's a booming business these days. I'm thinking about starting up franchises in other cities."

She frowns and chews on her bottom lip.

"Look, you didn't save me. I was doing perfectly fine on my own. I would have found a place eventually."

The words had no sooner come out of her mouth when a big streak of lighting popped, followed by a roll of thunder that shook the building. The power flickered off for a moment before coming back on.

I hide a grin. "If you say so."

There isn't any reason to argue. We both know her situation was looking dire when I came along. I'm just glad I did.

For both of our sakes.

"I'll be back in a little bit."

I leave the room to give her a chance to settle in. Sleeping arrangements are going to be tricky. My cock has been rock hard from the time she climbed on the bike and pressed her breasts close against my back. Lying next to her all night and not touching her sweet body is going to take every bit of willpower I possess.

I'm not sure I'll be able to make it through.

It will be a testament to my strength if I can.

After enduring an hour of good-natured teasing from the men, I head back inside. Between the lingering effects of alcohol and my own wishful thinking, I've almost half-convinced myself that the girl waiting for me in my hotel room wants a good hard fuck as much as I do.

Maybe that's her intention all along.

To play coy and act disinterested when in fact she wants nothing more than to wrap her legs over my shoulders and pull me deep into her tight pussy.

The sight of her body snuggled sound asleep under my sheets erases that thought quickly. Well hell! Looks like I'm not getting lucky tonight after all. Not unless I want to be a great big asshole and wake up a woman who is dead to the world.

She looks peaceful with her dark hair spread out on the pillow. My fingers itch to run through the long strands. I imagine how it would feel wrapped around my cock.

She's right.

My mind is in the gutter most of the time.

At least when she's around.

With each breath, her long eyelashes flutter on her cheeks. Without the disguise of heavy makeup, she looks even sweeter and more innocent than before.

I reach over to pull the sheet up higher around her. On her upper arm, just below the sleeve of her t-shirt, is a dark purple bruise. A fresh one too, newly formed. Maybe even from today.

White-hot rage fills me.

Someone hurt her, and it wouldn't have been at the bar. Roger takes good care of his employees, and he would never let a girl be manhandled. All an employee has to do is whisper a hint that a customer is out of line and security will throw them out on their ass in an instant.

No questions asked or explanations given. So it had to have happened somewhere else before she came into work.

Who did this to her?

The thought of a man grabbing her arm and squeezing it hard enough to make a bruise that ugly makes my blood boil.

Tomorrow, I'm going to get answers.

And when I find out who hurt her, I'm going to make them pay.

6

TRISH

The sensation of a warm hand settled on my stomach slowly invades my brain, breaking through the deep dreamy fog of sleep. I open my eyes slowly and blink.

It is still dark outside and eerily quiet. No sounds of motorcycle engines revving or drunk people yelling.

Where am I?

The naked body snuggled close behind me is warm and hard. The only thing I want to do is close my eyes and sink back into sleep. Just for a few more blissful minutes.

Suddenly, the memories of the previous night's events flood back in a rush.

Oh crap!

I remain perfectly still so as not to wake up Jesse. The man who I now realize is spooned close with his hand on my waist.

Surprisingly, he is a man of his word.

He didn't attempt to put the moves on me last night or even try to kiss me. A tad disappointing. Not that he would have been successful. Still, the effort would have been nice.

I meant what I said. No way was I sleeping with him. A one-night stand isn't something I would consider doing. Not even for a man as drop-dead gorgeous as Jesse.

For a brief moment, I wonder what would happen if I turned over and wrapped my hand around the thick cock pressed against my ass. It would be so natural and easy to go with the flow.

Until it was all over.

And I was left with nothing but regrets.

Stop thinking about it, Trish. Don't even go there.

I must have been totally wiped out to not wake up when he climbed into the bed next to me. Vaguely, I remember trying my best to stay awake while waiting for him to return. I closed my eyes for just a second, and that is the last thing I remember.

Now I need to slip out and leave before he wakes up.

It will be awkward if we're both here in the morning, making polite small talk and feeling weird around each other. He'll have questions for me that I don't want to answer. He might even offer to take me to breakfast, where we'll sit across from each other in a greasy diner and tell lies about our life over bacon and eggs.

Or if not lies, then at least not the whole truth.

What can I say about my life anyway? Oh, by the way, I've been hanging out with a motorcycle gang who is on the run from the Feds. The president wants to bang me, so I split in the middle of the night. Now I am two hundred dollars away from being homeless and broke. You want me for a girlfriend? I'm a great catch.

Jesse would be out the door so fast he'd leave skid marks on the carpet.

It's time to end this little adventure before it even begins.

No need to start something I can't finish, and certainly no reason to drag someone else into my disaster of a life.

I carefully remove Jesse's arm from across my body and slide out of bed. I don't take time to do anything except slip on my shoes and grab my bag.

At least I knew better than to unpack any of my things. It was a nice gesture for him to offer sink space. Most men wouldn't have thought of such a thing and instead would complain about a woman's stuff cluttering things up.

At the door, I turn to look back at him one last time.

What on earth am I doing? Leaving a naked, sexy hunk of man in a warm bed all alone?

Full of regret, but knowing I am doing the right thing, I slip out the door and leave him behind.

7

JESSE

I wake up with a start and discover she's gone without a trace. Can't say it surprises me. Trish is skittish as hell and running from something. This morning was when I was going to find out exactly what that something is.

A man for certain.

A man with a very bad temper.

Might be a dead man if he ever crosses my path.

I've never had much tolerance for men who physically abuse women. Picking on someone smaller and weaker is for pussies. I've beaten the shit out of plenty of men for doing less than bruising up a woman.

The thought strikes me that she might have run straight back to him, whoever he is, full of apologies and promises to do better. I hope for her sake that she didn't.

An image of the mottled bruise on her arm pops into my mind. If nothing else, I kept her safe for the night. Whatever happens today is completely up to her. If she's fool enough to go running back to him, then there's not much I can do to stop her.

I roll over and instinctively reach for my wallet on the bedside table. Looking inside, I check to see if anything is missing. When chicks sneak out in the middle of the night, they usually take something that belongs to me with them.

Money, cigarettes, knives.

One time even a pair of my leather gloves.

You name it, fucking broads will steal it if it isn't tied down.

All of my cash is here. This really doesn't surprise me either. Trish didn't strike me as the type of gal to rob and run. Not her style.

Doesn't matter.

It would have been nice if she could have hung around longer, but I have enough on my plate today dealing with MC business without worrying about some girl and her problems. These days I try to keep my life as drama free as possible. It isn't always easy to do, especially where women are concerned.

A knock comes at the door. I hear a keycard slide into the lock before Sam opens it and sticks his head inside.

"Where's your lady friend?" he asks, looking at the empty bed. "Gone already?"

"Yeah, she split," I answer. I pull on a pair of jeans and slide the wallet into my back pocket.

"You struck out?" Sam claps his hands together in surprise. "Hot damn! That's a first. You're losing your touch, big brother."

"I wouldn't call it that. The girl has issues, and I haven't got time to deal with them right now. I'm meeting with the Rebels today to hammer out a distribution deal. Want to ride with me?"

"Sure," Sam replies. "Don't have anything better to do except prowl the beach for babes. They'll still be here when I get back. Bros before hoes, and all that."

"Speaking of hoes, who else have you invited to Flint's bachelor party? Roger told me to let him know by tonight how much booze we'll need and how many strippers we want working the party."

"Just a few guys. All friends of the MC. You know them."

"Try to keep it under fifty guys. We don't want things to get out of hand. Let's not screw this up. We only get one chance to throw our brother a bachelor party he won't forget."

Sam grins. "Or won't remember."

"Either way, let's make sure he has a fucking blast."

8

TRISH

Things are definitely looking up.

Here I am, less than twenty-four hours from breaking away from the Liberators, and I have a better job and hopefully a new place to stay.

Jesse was right about Roger being a decent man. When I told him about my housing situation, he offered to give me extra hours before my regular shifts setting up the bar.

He also tipped me off that several of the other girls rent a big townhouse together. With his encouragement, I approached the group, and they were thrilled to have an extra person to split the rent. The more the merrier, they said.

I'm beginning to let myself think about the future beyond this week. If Roger would be willing to hire me permanently, I might be able to stick around Panama City for the rest of the summer. Save up enough for a decent car and decide what I want to do with my life.

All of my adult years, I've been so caught up with taking care of my mother and her addiction problems that I've never thought about what I want to do. It's past time I give it some serious consideration.

The annoying crackle of the bar's loudspeaker turning on jolts me out of my thoughts.

"Hello, beautiful ladies!" Roger's voice rings out over the bar. "Are all stations ready? The doors will open for business in three minutes. Knock 'em dead tonight."

After checking my station one last time, I stick a few more beer bottles into the large cooler and tighten up my bikini top in preparation for opening.

"Good luck, Trish!" a girl calls out from across the room.

"You too, Jessica." I smile and wave back at one of my new roommates. It feels good for a change to have female friends and be almost normal.

I plump up my boobs and apply a final coat of lip gloss.

Bring it on, gentlemen. I'm ready for you.

The bouncers unlock and swing open the wide oak doors. The bikers who have been waiting outside in the hot sun begin to pour in and make their way to the multiple bars.

If the initial crowd is any indication, business is going to be very good tonight. Now that I'm working for myself and not handing over all the money to Ty, I bet I *can* make five hundred dollars a night if I really try.

9

JESSE

It is almost midnight before Sam and I make it to the Silver Shark Saloon. The bar is crowded again tonight, with bikers squeezed in tight from one wall to the other. In the middle of the room is a roped-off stage for special activities.

Sam nudges me and points to the pink blinking neon sign hanging from the ceiling announcing the next event - 'Ladies Chocolate Pudding Wrestling at Midnight!'

I do a double take at the sign to make sure I read it correctly.

"Wonder how long it took Roger to come up with that idea?" Sam asks. "Too bad the rest of the crew couldn't make it tonight. Just look at what they're going to miss. I bet they will be pissed."

"Nobody forced them to start drinking shots of tequila before lunch," I say. "They're a bunch of pansy asses and should learn to pace their drinking. Like us professionals."

Sam and I had hung around the hotel all evening hoping the rest of the Steel Infidels would sober up enough to come with us. When it began to look like a lost cause, we left them passed out in their rooms and decided to carry on without them.

I scan the room and wonder if Trish is working since I haven't been able to get her off my mind all day. If not, I don't have a clue how to get in touch with her.

This is an unusual dilemma for me, and one I'm not sure I like. Broads always leave me their phone number, either scribbled on a note left by the bed or scrawled in bright red lipstick on the bathroom mirror. If I'm out at a club, they'll whisper in my ear and slip a piece of paper into my back pocket. Women go out of their way to make sure I know exactly how to reach them later.

I keep the numbers of the girls I like well enough to see again in a bowl in my kitchen. Sometimes if I'm feeling horny and keyed up late at night, I'll pick out a number, give her a call, and have her come over for a quick fuck. When I don't ask them spend the night, they always act indignant and pissed off like they didn't know the score beforehand.

No matter what, I never make the mistake of letting them find out my cell phone number. It only took me a few times to learn my lesson about that the hard way.

"What are u doing?" they'll text first.

Then "where R U?"

After the third unanswered text, they'll start with the, "R U OK? Call me! I'm worried."

Screw that needy shit. The last thing I want is a woman texting me all day long with constant updates. My rule is after three text messages, I block her number.

Cut the bitch off, just like that.

Except now I'm wishing I had broken my own rule and given Trish my cell phone number last night.

Damn it.

Worry tightens in my gut. What if something bad has happened to her? How would I even know? I should have handled things better with her somehow.

Relief hits me when I spot her working at a busy location on the other side of the bar. Roger has her set up again as a beer tub babe. He's a smart businessman and knows a good thing when he sees it. She probably sells more beer than any other girl in the place.

I check out her outfit. Damn! She looks totally fuckable in her white shorts and red polka dot bikini top. I notice she's still wearing the cowboy hat, except tonight she has on white tennis shoes with lacy socks instead of the leather boots. To me, she looks even sexier than the night before.

She bends over to grab a beer out of the tub of ice, intentionally giving the customers a good look at her ass. If she were my old lady, I wouldn't let her do that shit.

Not for any amount of money.

I meant what I told her about keeping that spectacular view all to myself.

"Let's go grab a good spot," Sam suggests, tilting his head toward the stage where the contest is about to begin. "We don't want to miss the show. You know how I love chocolate pudding. Maybe Roger will ask for volunteers to lick the girls clean afterwards."

I laugh, suspecting Sam is only half kidding. Knowing Roger, he might put the pudding-covered girls up for auction to the highest bidder after the contest is over.

"You go ahead," I say. "I need to check on something first. Save me a place."

Sam follows my line of vision across the room to Trish. "You mean check on someone? Fuck! Your girl is smoking hot tonight. Too bad you didn't get some of that ass when you had the chance. I bet she is one nice piece of pussy. Since she's obviously not interested in you, due to her cutting out before daylight, mind if I give it a shot? I'll bet you a hundred bucks I won't strike out like you did. Watch and learn, brother. You'll see how it's done."

Sam takes three steps in her direction before I roughly grab his arm and jerk him back. He bends over laughing.

"Gotcha!" he says, slapping me hard on the back. "You should have seen the look on your face. Jesus Christ, Jesse! You need to chill the fuck out. What has you so wound up tonight? Her? Thought you said she was a shit load of problems that you didn't have time for. You have a thing for her, don't you?"

"I said she has problems, not that she is the problem."

Sam shrugs. "Same fucking difference. Women are a shit heap of trouble. Are you really going to give her the chance to smack you down again? If so, you are a glutton for punishment, brother. It's a bad idea if you ask me. Life is too short to spend chasing one piece of tail. Look around this room. Lots of options to choose from."

"Maybe," I answer. "There's no harm in giving it one more go. See what happens."

He looks doubtful at the thought of my success. "Suit yourself, dumbass. Keep in mind there's lots of available, willing women here tonight. No reason for us to go back to the hotel empty-handed. What's the point of bike week if it's not to fuck a different broad every night? Or in my case, two. Maybe more if I get lucky."

Sam is right.

Why am I wasting my time worrying about a woman I don't even know? Trish had her opportunity and she blew it. I should consider myself lucky for dodging the bullet with a woman who had issues as deep as hers.

"You, my brother, make an excellent point," I say. "Lead the way. I'm right behind you. What are you in the mood for? Blondes or brunettes?"

Sam grins back at me. "Is there a new rule that says we have to choose?"

10

TRISH

My shift is almost over and there is still no sign of Jesse. I know it's dumb, but somehow I expected him to show up looking for me. The fact that he doesn't care enough to drop by puts a damper on my night. He probably hasn't given me a second thought. In fact, he was probably relieved when he woke up to find me gone.

What good is a girl who won't put out?

No good at all.

Especially to bikers who like their women pliable and willing. I wish I could explain to him why I left in such a rush. Unfortunately, there's no way I can tell him the truth about what is going on between me and the Liberators. If I mention one word about Big Roy to anyone, I will be putting both myself and them in danger.

I wouldn't do that to Jesse.

All I can do is push him out of my mind. Thinking about him isn't doing me any good at the moment, and there are plenty more important things for me to worry about, like money for groceries and having a roof over my head to start.

I redo my ponytail and check out my tip jar for the umpteenth time. At least the tips are good tonight. For the most part, the customers have been tolerable too, except for a few who whispered crude dirty jokes in my ear. I giggled right along with them as if I thought they were hilarious when I really wanted to knee the guys in the balls.

All part of my job though.

Some bad behavior is only to be expected after the bikers have been knocking back drinks for hours. Even if those drinks are considerably watered down according to the bartenders.

I smile at Jessica as she walks past carrying a heavy tray of drinks. She rolls her eyes and nods toward the stage.

"Thank God the pudding contest is almost over," she says. "Those girls better be getting paid lots of dough for what they're having to put up with. I wouldn't roll around in that nasty mess for a whole boatload of money."

"That's for sure."

Between customers, I glance over at the stage to see what's happening. Two bikini-clad women are pretending to wrestle while slipping and sliding on a layer of dark chocolate pudding.

It's all for show, and they're not very convincing. I have to admit it *is* pretty hilarious to watch. Especially knowing the two girls are sisters and have been practicing their wrestling moves all day.

One of the sisters yanks the other's hair, who screams for effect. To get even, she picks up a handful of the gooey pudding and smears it all over her sister's big breasts. The crowd around the stage goes crazy.

"Show us her tits!" a man yells. "Rip off her top!"

The girls are struggling to keep it together and not laugh. When one falls out of character and giggles, the other smacks her so hard on the butt that it leaves a bright red mark.

"Oh yeah! Give it to her! Smack that juicy ass!"

Of course the men would love the rough stuff. Whatever the girls are doing seems to be working, so I guess that's all that matters. I hope Roger is paying them well. After watching for a few minutes, I'm just thankful it's not me up there being degraded and rolling around in dessert.

My eyes land on a tall, dark-haired man standing two rows behind the stage. Snuggled close beside him is a blonde girl with long hair extensions trailing down her back. His tattooed arm is thrown casually over her shoulders.

Jesse!

So he is here after all, and he didn't even take the time to find me.

Now I'm pissed off.

Realistically, I don't have any right to be mad since I was the one who walked out on him without an explanation.

Still, it stings a bit.

Actually more than a bit.

He could have at least asked me why I left without saying goodbye. I could kick myself in the butt. I should've known Jesse wouldn't waste any more of his time on me. A few hours later and he's already moving on to platinum blondes with fake boobs.

The type of girl I can't stand.

The blonde giggles up at him and leans closer, melding her body close to his. An urge strikes me to run over there and yank her long hair extensions right out of her head. Bet she wouldn't look so pretty then.

"What the fuck do you think you're doing?" a loud voice snarls, startling me out of my thoughts.

I whirl around, and my heart drops at the sight of my brother. When did he show up?

"Ty! What are you doing here?" I ask.

He reaches into the tip jar and pulls out all of the money.

"What the fuck does it look like I'm doing? Getting what is due me, that's what. Did you really think you could just walk out on Big Roy like that? You are an embarrassment to me and stupider than I thought. He sent me here to bring you back. Said you needed to be taught a lesson."

Bring me back?

"What do you mean? I'm not a prisoner, for God's sake! I can leave anytime I want. I thought you would be glad to get rid of me. All I've heard from you lately is what a burden I am to you. So now, I'm not. I'm out of your hair for good."

Ty lets out a humorless laugh. His hand snakes out and grabs my jaw.

"Nobody, and I mean nobody, walks out on Big Roy. The Liberators own you now. What part of this equation don't you understand?"

11

JESSE

For the past hour, I followed Sam's advice by flirting with the ladies and downing never-ending shots of tequila. I'm doing my best to have fun and it just isn't working. Time after time, my eyes wander across the room to search out Trish.

I wonder if she has been watching for me too.

Who knows?

The girl is too damn hard to figure out. I'm not sure I have the time or patience to try.

When I see her glance my way, I throw an arm around the girl standing next to me. I don't know her, but she doesn't seem to mind. Instead of pulling away, the blonde looks up at me and giggles.

It was a dick move even for me, and I don't know what made me do it. Guess I wanted to gauge Trish's reaction.

Her face drops when she spots me. I can't tell if she's disappointed to see me or upset about another girl hanging onto my side.

I'm already regretting my impulsive action when a customer approaches Trish. He looks vaguely familiar. Something about the way he moves or his haircut.

I can't place him. I know it will bother me until I figure it out. Too bad he isn't wearing a leather cut. The patches would tell me immediately which motorcycle club he rides with.

While I'm racking my brain trying to remember where I've seen him, he casually reaches into Trish's tip jar and takes out her money.

What the fuck!

I drop my arm from the blonde's shoulders and start pushing my way through the crowd of men packed in like sardines around the stage.

"Hey babe! Where are you going?" the blonde calls out after me in a confused voice.

I ignore her and keep moving.

So this must be the guy, the man who left bruises on Trish's arm.

Things are about to get fucking real.

He doesn't have a clue I'm coming for him.

If he did, he wouldn't be so stupid. I'm still pushing through the crowd when he grabs Trish by the jaw and holds her face tight in his hand. Her expression says it all. She's terrified.

I'm not close enough to hear what he's saying. Whatever it is, it will be the last thing the motherfucker ever says to her.

Fury boils up inside me. This man made a big mistake showing up here.

It feels like it takes forever to reach them, though I know it is only a few seconds. Trish sees me right before I wrap my arm around his throat from behind and jerk him up, lifting his feet completely off the ground. Her eyes widen as I squeeze with all of my strength.

He immediately lets go of her face. I apply more pressure. He gasps and pulls at my arm.

"Drop the money, motherfucker!" I yell.

He tries to pry my arm from around his neck. His face is turning red.

"Drop it, I said!"

His left hand opens and the wad of dollar bills fall to the floor. He kicks back at me and struggles to break free. I'm much bigger and stronger, so he doesn't stand a chance. Plus I'm energized with anger now. I can play this game all night.

"Stop it, Jesse!" Trish yells. "Please stop!" She runs around the big cooler of beer and pulls at my arm too.

Why the fuck is she telling me to stop?

The bouncers watching the room suddenly notice the commotion and three of them rush toward us. One grabs me around the chest to hold me back while the other two wrench my arm from the asshole's neck.

"He stole her tips!" I yell.

The bouncers don't let go of me. Instead, they turn to Trish.

"Is that right?" one of them asks.

She hesitates for a long moment then nods without looking at the bastard who robbed her. "Yeah, he took all of the money in my tip jar."

The bouncers turn me loose and grab him by the arms instead. "Let's go, buddy. The night is over for you."

"You stupid fucking bitch!" the guy spits out. "You're going to regret this!"

The bouncers tighten their grip on him in case he's thinking of breaking free and going after Trish again. There isn't any doubt he is angry enough to do her bodily harm given half a chance.

She opens her mouth and starts to reply when Roger comes barging over, interrupting her.

"What the hell is going on over here, Jesse?" he asks angrily. He waves his arms around and points to the stage. "I'm up there on the stage trying to run a damn contest, and I see you and this guy brawling over here like a couple of high school kids. You know I don't put up with any biker fights in my bar. Not even from you. We go way back, but if you've got a beef with somebody, you better take it outside and as far away from my club as you can get. The 'no fighting' rule includes the parking lot, too."

I hold up my hands. He keeps sputtering and I know better than to interrupt.

"I'm not letting my place turn into no damn Waco with motorcycle clubs shooting and stabbing each other. I can't have that kind of publicity. It's not worth losing my liquor license over."

"Calm down, Roger. This isn't my fault," I explain. "That asshole stole Trish's tip money, and I made him give it back to her. By excessive force. That's all. I'm not trying to start any trouble."

He glances over at Trish. "Is that what happened?" he asks.

She nods vigorously. "He was only trying to help me out. I'm sorry if it caused a disturbance."

He still looks doubtful. "My customers know better than to steal tip money. In all of my years running this place, I've never had that happen. What's really going on? Honey, if this guy is your pimp, then I don't want no part of it. My bar isn't that kind of establishment. You seem like a sweet gal and all, but it might be best if you pack up your stuff now and leave." He nods to the bouncers and turns to walk away.

I grab his arm.

"Whoa! Hang on a damn minute," I say. "Don't blame her. You're punishing the victim here. She didn't do anything wrong."

He looks back and forth between us. "Ah, shit! I need a cold drink. It's hot as hell in here with all these bikers." He takes off his baseball cap and wipes the sweat dripping off his bald head then signals to the bouncers. "Get that fucker out of here and make sure he never comes back in. That goes for his friends too, if he has any."

"This isn't over!" the guy yells back at Trish as they drag him away. "I promise you. You ain't seen the last of it." He turns to glare at me. "You either, asshole! I know who you are. You better be watching your back!"

I don't have a fucking clue what he is talking about.

"Sorry for getting all worked up." Roger says, clapping me on the back. "The bike rally always makes me a little jumpy. The damn spring breaker kids are bad enough, but at least they don't want to kill each other. Most of you bikers are carrying guns in your pockets and knives in your boots. I love the money you boys bring in, but damn I'll be glad when this week is over."

I try not to smile. He tells me this same story every year.

"You know you love us," I say. "Admit it. The rally is the highlight of your year. Think of how boring life would be if we weren't around to liven things up."

He laughs, and I know all is forgiven. "Maybe you and the rest of your club," he says. "Some of the other MCs, not so much. They're all a bunch of assholes as far as I'm concerned. Like that guy." He points to the man who is still fighting and struggling with the bouncers as they drag him toward the door.

"Do you still want me to leave?" Trish interrupts in a timid voice.

Roger turns to her and sighs. "No, honey, looks like it wasn't your fault after all. Sorry the bouncers didn't get over here sooner. I could use ten more of those guys." He motions to the cash on the floor. "Gather up your money and hurry on back to work. The boys will be thirsty and wanting their beers now that the wrestling contest is over. Jesse, I'll catch up with you later. And for God's sake, try to stay out of trouble, will you? At least for a few more days?"

"Don't worry, I will."

Roger isn't listening. He is already walking away, muttering something to himself about fucking bikers.

Trish squats down and begins picking up the dollar bills off the dirty floor. I bend over to help her.

"Are you okay?" I ask.

I gently tilt up her chin. Her big brown eyes are pooling with tears that threaten to spill over.

"Did he hurt you? I saw him grab your face. You want me to go beat the shit out of him? Just say the word and it's done."

She sniffles and shakes her head, wiping away a tear with the back of her hand that is sliding down her cheek.

"No, I'm okay. Honest. Maybe a little shook up. That's all."

I hand over the money and help her stand up. "You want to tell me who that son-of-a-bitch is or do I have to go outside and pound it out of him? Either way, I'm going to find out. And after that, we're going to have a real serious talk. I don't want him messing with you again."

A panicked look crosses her face and she touches my arm. "Please don't do that," she says. "I'll tell you."

I cross my arms, thinking this is going to be good. "Alright, let's hear it then."

She takes a deep shaky breath. "He's my brother," she finally says.

"Your brother?" I echo.

I'm stunned.

Whatever I was expecting her to tell me, it sure as hell isn't this. I thought for certain the man was her ex-boyfriend. But her brother? This doesn't make any sense.

"Are you shitting me?"

"No, it's the honest truth."

For some odd reason, I believe her. "What was your brother doing here? And why did he steal your money?"

She shrugs as if it's nothing. Like it's perfectly normal for a brother to rough up his little sister. I wonder what kind of a family life they must have had when they were younger to screw up their sibling relationship so bad.

"I owed him some money, so he came by to get it. It's nothing."

I don't like the sound of this. At all.

"Does your brother normally take your money?"

She runs a nervous hand through her long hair. "No, not always. He's just a little upset with me. Look, there's no reason to make a big deal out of this. I'm fine, so you should let it go." She looks up at me, pleading with her big eyes. "I'm asking you to just drop it. Okay?"

"You're asking the wrong person, sweetheart," I say. "I'm not a man that lets things go."

Suddenly a thought occurs to me. Now things are starting to make more sense.

"He threw you out, didn't he? You were staying with him somewhere, the two of you got into a fight last night, and then he kicked you out. Is he the roommate you had a falling out with?"

"Not exactly, but close enough, I guess."

So I'm still not getting the whole picture. "How did you get the bruise?" I point to her left arm.

She glances down at the purple spot that is now carefully concealed with makeup. If I didn't know it was there, I would have thought I imagined it.

"What are you talking about?" she asks. "What bruise?"

"The big ugly bruise on your upper arm where someone grabbed you. You think I didn't notice it when you were asleep in my bed last night? I looked at every square inch of your luscious body, so you can bet I didn't miss a thing. Especially not a nasty bruise."

"It was a dumb accident. I'm clumsy and bumped it against the side of the bathroom door. You know how tiny hotel room bathrooms can be."

She's lying and still trying to protect him. This pisses me off more than ever.

"Is that right? Funny how those bathroom doors can jump out at you when you're not looking. Your brother mentioned something else. He said he knew me. You want to tell me what he meant by that?"

"I don't know," she says. "I was wondering the same thing. I doubt he meant anything by it. He was angry, so you shouldn't pay much attention to what he said."

"Maybe he knows me because of the Steel Infidels," I suggest. "My motorcycle club. We might have run into each other at another bike rally or charity ride somewhere. I've met lots of bikers the past few years."

12

TRISH

TRISH

S*teel Infidels???*

"The Steel Infidels?" I ask, my voice coming out in a squeak. "You ride with the Steel Infidels?"

Did I hear that right? Oh dear God.

"Yeah, I'm the President of the MC. Thought you knew that. Come to think of it, we didn't have time to discuss it."

"No, I must have missed that somehow."

I screwed up big time.

Of all the men in the world I might have managed to get involved with, why did it have to be one of the Steel Infidels?

For months, the feud between the Liberators and the Steel Infidels is all Ty and Big Roy have talked about. How the Steel Infidels caused all of the Liberators' problems and even murdered some of their crew members in a shootout.

Over and over, they rehashed the same stories while their anger festered and grew. Eventually I got so sick of hearing them that I tuned everything out. Now I wish I had paid closer attention. At least about what they were planning to do for revenge.

Even back then, I wasn't stupid enough to believe everything they said. The stories were all their version of the events, and I suspect Jesse would tell it from a whole other perspective.

This is a nightmare.

Every time I think my life can't get any worse, it does.

What have I done? Why didn't I ask Jesse what club he was riding with when I had the chance? Or check out his tattoos more closely?

Another idea occurs to me. Maybe there is more than one Steel Infidels chapter. The Hell's Angels has chapters all across the United States. I might be getting all panicked for nothing. There are thousands of bikers in town. It can't be the same club. Even my luck couldn't be that bad.

"Where is your club from?" I casually ask.

"North Georgia," he answers.

My luck *is* that bad. So it is the same motorcycle club. A ball of dread builds in my stomach. I suddenly feel physically ill.

He narrows his eyes and looks closely at me. "Are you sure you're okay? What's with the questions about the MC all of a sudden? You have a thing against bikers?"

Yes, definitely.

"I was wondering how Ty might know you. That's all."

"Well, when you figure it out, you let me know. He looked familiar to me too. I know I've seen him somewhere. It's bugging the hell out of me."

From the corner of my eye, I see a crowd of thirsty customers heading my way. "I need to get back to work before I get fired," I say with a weak smile. "Thanks again for sticking up for me."

"Anytime. I'll catch up with you before you leave tonight. You still owe me a damn good explanation about why you slipped out this morning. Don't think I've forgotten about it. We need to talk."

"Sounds good," I reply with no intention of meeting him later or any other time.

Now that I know who Jesse is, I have to stay as far away from him as I can get. Pitting Jesse and Big Roy against each other isn't something that I want to be responsible for.

This time it's not me I'm worried about.

It's Jesse.

13

JESSE

"What was that all about?" Sam asks when I join him and his harem of girls again. "I was on my way to give you a hand when I saw Roger storming over to break it up. You didn't look like you needed my help anyway. That motherfucker didn't stand a chance against you."

"No, he didn't," I agree. "Someone should have warned him I was a linebacker in high school."

"So who is he?" Sam asks. "Anyone I know?"

"Maybe. Turns out he is Trish's brother. He looks familiar to me. He said something about knowing me and that I should watch my back. Did you recognize him?"

"No, I didn't get a good look at him though."

The blonde girl who I had left so abruptly before smiles when she sees I am back.

"Hey stranger," she purrs, placing a manicured hand on my arm. "Don't be running off like that again. I was getting lonely over here all by myself."

Shit! I forgot all about her. Now I have to ditch the chick.

"Sorry," I say. "I'm not in the mood for company tonight. Maybe another time?"

She pouts her lips, clearly disappointed. "Your loss," she says with a flip of her hair.

I look at Sam over the top of her head and he winks.

"You can hang with me, darling," he says to the girl, draping an arm around her waist and pulling her close. "My brother is much too dull and old for you anyway. You need a real man to keep you happy."

The girl seems pleased, even if it means sharing Sam with another girl. Maybe that's what she is into. If so, more power to her and to Sam.

My brother is truly a piece of work. Watching him in action wears me out sometimes. Maybe I am getting too old for this.

"Listen up, people! Last call for alcohol!" Roger's voice barks over the loudspeaker. "The bars will be closing in ten minutes. No extensions per county law."

"Are you ready to head on back to the hotel?" I ask Sam. "We should probably check on the crew and make sure everybody is still breathing."

Sam drains his glass and places it on the table. "Yeah sure, I'm more than ready. I've been waiting on you. Say the word and we're out of here."

He stands and grabs the elbow of the girl sitting next to him to help her up. She leans against him unsteadily.

"I'll be just a minute," I say. "I need to ask Trish if she wants a lift anywhere."

"In that case, we'll meet you outside in the parking lot," Sam says. "This pretty lady is coming home with me." He hugs the girl tighter against his chest so she can keep her balance.

I start to say something to Sam then decide to keep my mouth shut. Pretty wouldn't be the exact word I would use to describe his date at the moment. Her once-smooth hair is now sticking up in all kinds of directions and streaks of mascara are smeared under her eyes. She doesn't look nearly as attractive as she did two hours ago when she walked up to Sam and plopped her big tits on his arm. I hate to think what she'll look like in the morning, hung over and without makeup.

Not for me to judge.

I've fucked worse plenty of times. Beauty is only a light switch away.

In the dark, it doesn't always matter what a girl's face looks like as long as her pussy is tight.

"What about her?" I ask, pointing to the chick I dumped earlier. She is sitting with her head on the table, either half-asleep or passed out, I can't tell for sure.

"Leave her," Sam says. "We didn't bring her, so not our problem."

"Fine by me. I'll meet you outside. Don't ride without me."

I head toward Trish's beer tub. The customers have kept her busy for the past hour. Since I didn't want to give Roger another reason to fire her, I kept my distance.

Now I don't see her at all. The steady line of customers has disappeared as well. Where did she get off to so fast?

Due to the ruckus earlier, I had completely forgotten to ask her if she had found a place to stay. Hopefully she isn't planning on wandering around the streets all night again. Especially when there is a warm, comfy bed with an empty spot just waiting for her. When I find her, I'll offer to take her back with me again. And this time I might get lucky.

I stop a waitress as she walks by. "Do you know where the beer tub girl has gone to?" I ask, pointing to the empty cooler.

"She closed down a few minutes ago," she answers. "It's been a long night. She may have already left."

"Thanks."

I search the room hoping to spot Trish's cowboy hat. Just when I am about to give up hope of finding her, I see her slip out of the building. By the time I reach the door, half the bar is spilling outside with me. Nobody hangs around for long after last call. No alcohol, no party.

It is pitch dark outside and the floodlights do little to light the parking lot. Throngs of bikers are wandering across the asphalt in search of their bikes. There's no way I can find her in this moving sea of drunk people.

I'm about to turn around and go meet up with Sam when I see her walking along the far edge of the lot. Trish is heading straight toward a man leaning against a motorcycle.

Fuck! What is she doing?

I speed up to narrow the distance between us. When I get closer, I recognize the man as her brother. Is she crazy? Why on earth would she agree to meet him out here in the dark after what happened tonight? He obviously has some kind of mental hold on her that I don't understand. I hang back just out of sight to watch what happens.

Trish opens her purse. After taking out some money, she offers it to him. Her brother laughs and then grabs her wrist. When she tries to pull free, he deftly twists it behind her back. A move he's obviously done many times before in her life.

She struggles with him only for a second before I make my move. I don't care if he is her brother. She shouldn't have to put up with his bullshit.

I barrel into his side going full speed, knocking both him and his bike over onto the pavement. Trish screams as I start throwing punches at his face. A bone crunches when my fist connects with his nose.

I don't give a fuck what their back story is or why she feels compelled to put up with a deadbeat brother. I'm not a psychiatrist, but I can recognize an abusive relationship. She can't see clearly enough to make the right decisions where her brother is concerned.

When I think he's had enough of a beating and some of my anger is gone, I pin him down by the throat. "If you ever touch Trish again, I'll kill you," I threaten. "Nod if you understand what I'm saying."

He spits out a mouthful of blood and a broken tooth. "You don't fucking scare me, Jesse," he says with a sneer. "The Liberators are back, asshole. You're a dead man. You hear me? A dead man. You and all of your pussy ass brothers too."

The Liberators?

No wonder he looks familiar.

The night is full of surprises. And in this case, an odd bit of good news. If the Liberators are back, it means they're out in the open again.

Where the Steel Infidels can find and kill them.

I grab him by the collar and hit him hard one more time. The punch knocks him out cold. Satisfied with the job, I stand and wipe off my bloody hands on my jeans.

Trish doesn't say one word. She stands there with her arms crossed, shaking and trying not to cry.

"You're with the fucking Liberators?" I hiss through clenched teeth. "And you said nothing to me about it? What was your angle? Surely you must know of the feud between the Liberators and the Steel Infidels?"

"No," she vehemently denies. "It wasn't like that. I would never *be* with the Liberators. I didn't have anywhere to go and my brother let me stay with him in exchange for helping them out with stuff. I would never choose to be part of their group. I hate them."

I'm not fully convinced. Her excuse sounds pretty lame. Nobody could hang around the Liberators for long without realizing exactly what they were all about.

I take her arm. "Either way, you're coming with me," I say. "This is only the beginning. You're not safe now that they know you're involved with me."

She slings off my hand. "We're not involved," she argues. "We only just met. I can't go running off with you again. I've found some new roommates so I have a place to stay. At least for a few nights until I can find something more permanent."

"Listen, sweetheart, we're involved whether you like it or not," I say firmly. "Where's your stuff? Go back in and get it. I need to find my brother Sam to tell him what is going on. I'll wait for you at the door. Don't take too long in there either. We need to go now."

Trish starts to argue and thinks better of it. "There's something else you may need to know," she says after a long minute. "The reason I split is because Big Roy told me he was going to make me his old lady. He wanted me to move my things into his hotel room this morning."

"He did what?"

The thought of Big Roy's hands on Trish fills me with a murderous rage. I swear to God I'm going to kill that son-of-a-bitch.

"Were you going to do it?"

"No! Of course not!"

"I'll see that red-headed motherfucker in hell first before I ever let him touch you. I promise you that. Go get your things."

14

TRISH

I'm too upset and exhausted to put up an argument about going back to Jesse's hotel with him. Of the different alternatives, it seems like the best option at the time.

I dash back inside the bar and grab my bag from the break room. On my way out, I tell one of the girls that I unfortunately won't be making it to the condo tonight. I was really hoping things would work out with them. For a brief few hours, things almost felt normal.

My mind is whirling as I hurry back outside to meet Jesse. Things keep happening so quickly and I don't have time to adjust. Just when I think I have things figured out, at least for the next twenty-four hours, something else happens to flip my plans upside down.

Agreeing to meet Ty in the parking lot was a mistake. I know that now. God only knows what I was thinking. I shouldn't have looked at his text messages after he was thrown out of the club, much less replied to them.

Old habits die hard.

He said he only needed a couple of hundred bucks. I stupidly thought that giving him the money would be a cheap way to get rid of him and get him off my back.

What a bad decision that turned out to be.

My plan was to give him the money and tell him to never bother me again as long as he was riding with the Liberators.

My brother wasn't always an asshole. There was a time not so long ago when we were almost friends. I refuse to believe the brother I used to know is gone forever. Big Roy and the Liberators changed him. I hate them for what they've done to Ty.

When Jesse attacked him, I felt ripped right down the middle. For the first time in my life, someone was actually protecting me for a change. It felt good and was definitely something I could get used to.

At the same time, it hurt to see my brother getting beaten to a bloody pulp, even if Ty didn't have any qualms about hurting me when it suited him.

"Did you get all of your things?" Jesse asks when I walk out. He is leaning against the building, waiting for me, just like he said he would be.

"Everything I own is in here," I answer, patting the green duffel bag.

"If you need anything else, we can pick it up at the store tomorrow," he offers. "Let's get out of here before your brother wakes up and calls the Liberators for backup." He takes my arm and quickly ushers me away from the building.

I glance back over my shoulder toward my brother, who is still lying on the ground at the edge of the parking lot. The crowd has thinned out and the few remaining customers aren't paying him any attention. Probably assuming he is passed out drunk or high on drugs.

"Shouldn't I call an ambulance or something?" I say. "What if he is badly hurt?"

"Trust me, he'll be fine," Jesse says. "A busted nose, maybe. That's all. It's nothing that a couple of painkillers and Band-Aids can't fix."

I abruptly stop walking. Now I'm starting to feel bad about leaving my brother alone and bleeding on the ground. I always take care of people. Leaving someone behind who needs me is not easy.

"I should at least go back to check on him," I say. "Wait here. I'll be right back." I turn around and start walking toward Ty, who is already stirring.

Jesse grabs the strap of my bag and jerks me back. "Damn it, Trish! You really don't get this, do you? Haven't you been paying any attention? Don't you realize what kind of men the Liberators are? Do you think they are just playing around or joking about the things they are involved with?"

His tone is grim. He's furious with me.

"Less than six months ago, I attended the funeral of a young woman the Liberators murdered and dumped on the side of the road like a bag of trash. She was Big Roy's old lady, by her choice. She was also an old friend of mine from high school. She warned us that the Liberators were on their way to ambush my brother, Flint. They killed her for that. And she's been an integral part of their club for years."

"I'm sorry," I say, my voice faltering. "I didn't realize."

"What do you think they will do to you? A new girl who they don't know or care about? Do you think for one second that they give a shit about you? That they wouldn't hesitate to rape or even kill you if it suits them? When Big Roy said you were going to be his old lady, he meant one way or the other. In his eyes, he doesn't need a woman's permission to take what he wants. And right now he wants you."

I'm shocked by everything Jesse is telling me, yet I don't need any verification or proof. In my gut, I know every word is true.

"I feel like such a fool," I stammer. "I didn't know about any of these things. They didn't talk much around me. And when they did, Big Roy always blamed everything on the Steel Infidels."

From the corner of my eye, I see Ty pull himself up to a sitting position.

"Well, you know now and that ought to be enough," Jesse says. "I don't want to hear any more argument. Let's get out of here. Your brother is coming around."

He hustles me around the corner where his brother Sam is waiting by the two motorcycles.

"Where's the girl?" Jesse asks.

"I gave her money for a cab and sent her home," Sam answers. "If the Liberators are in town, we've got bigger problems to deal with than chasing pussy. She would just be a distraction for me tonight."

"Good decision," Jesse says as he slings my bag onto the back of the bike.

"I've already called Flint and told him to round up the rest of the crew for a sitdown when we get back to the hotel," Sam says. "He's rousing everybody and making coffee, so hopefully they'll be halfway sober by the time we get there."

Jesse motions to me. "Hop on."

I throw my leg across the bike and wrap my arms around Jesse's waist, at first hesitantly then in a death grip. I scoot up as close as I can get to his hard, muscular body.

I'm not about to let go of this man.

Not now.

Maybe not ever.

"You go first," Sam says. "I'll make sure we're not being followed."

Jesse revs the engine. The motorcycle roars when he pulls out onto the road with Sam right behind us.

The short distance to the hotel flies by in a blur. The rest of the Steel Infidels are waiting for us when we ride into the hotel parking lot a few minutes later. Some are a little wobbly and unsteady on their feet, but at least they all made the effort to be there.

Jesse slides off the bike, pulls out his keycard, and hands it to me. "Go ahead and get settled in," he says. "Don't wait up for me. I don't know how long I'll be."

As I walk by the group, one of the men who is a spitting image of Jesse, only younger, throws up a hand at me in greeting, and I nod as I hurry past. Must be his other brother.

Once inside the hotel room, I head straight for the shower.

What a night this is turning out to be.

It seems like forever before Jesse returns. By the time he opens the door and steps inside, I've worked myself up into a frenzied state of anxiety.

I'm freaking out, not only over the situation with Big Roy and my brother, but also because I can't imagine spending another celibate night lying next to Jesse. I don't know what he expects from me or how long I can continue to hold him at bay.

Or even if I want to try.

I'm so confused and a mental wreck inside.

"Everything okay?" I ask, worried by the serious look on his face.

"Nothing for you to worry about," he says, giving me a reassuring smile. "You're safe here with me. To get to you, Big Roy will have to go through thirteen big men first. My crew knows that protecting you is our top priority right now."

"You told them about me?"

He throws me a curious look. "Of course I told them. How could we keep you safe otherwise? We work as a group, a family. What hurts one of us harms us all. If I'm ever not here, any of my men will protect you the same as I would. You understand? You're under our protection now."

He moves to sit down on the bed beside me, leans back against the headboard, and stretches out his long legs.

"Not really," I say, confused. "Why would they do that? I mean, all I have done is make things worse between you and the Liberators. Why would your men care one way or the other what happens to me?"

He takes my hand in his and rubs his thumb along the back. "They care because I care. This mess with the Liberators isn't your fault. Bad blood has run between us for years. You happened to get caught up in it, that's all. Don't blame yourself. At least now they've finally come out of the shadows where they've been hiding. The Steel Infidels has an opportunity to make things right once and for all."

"This is all a bit much for me to take in," I say, still feeling partially responsible for everything. "Whenever I overheard the Liberators talking about feuds and fights, I always thought they were greatly exaggerating things and telling tall tales. Now I'm finding out it's all real. Like stuff you see on television, except worse."

Jesse chuckles softly. "The life of a biker isn't always easy," he says. "Especially for our women." He continues slowly stroking my hand. "There's something I need to ask you. Whatever you say won't change things between us."

"Okay," I say hesitantly. "What is it?"

"Are you willing to tell me where we can find the Liberators? We need to know where they're staying."

I let that sink in for a moment. Of course he would need to ask me this.

"What about my brother?"

Jesse lets out a long breath and looks away. "I'm not going to lie to you. He's a big fucking problem. I can't promise you he won't get hurt. I would be lying to you if I did."

"But he..."

"You need to remember, Trish. He made the choice to stick by Big Roy, even after knowing everything he's done in the past and what he wants to do to you now."

"He's still my brother," I say emphatically. "The only sibling I have."

"I get it," he replies. "I have brothers too. It doesn't change the circumstances. We can strike first or wait for them to come after us. Either way, you're not going to be able to stop the inevitable from happening. The bottom line is if they come here, you'll be in more danger than if we go after them. I would rather have the upper hand than sit around on our asses waiting for their move."

Jesse lets go of my hand and waits silently while I think it over. If I tell him where the Liberators are, I'll put my brother in danger. If I don't, I'll be endangering myself, Jesse, and the men who have agreed to protect me.

Once my decision is made, the words tumble out rapidly. "We were staying at the Beachcomber on the other end of the strip." I need to tell him everything before I lose my nerve. "It's a rundown dive of a hotel. There are six guys total: Big Roy, Ty, and four other members. They're all carrying guns."

Jesse pulls out his cell phone and rapidly sends off a text, I presume to one of his brothers.

Oh God! What have I set in motion?

"They have guns? Well, so do we," Jesse says with a cocky grin. "What?" he asks when he catches the shocked expression on my face. "I said that to reassure you, not scare you. Every biker in Panama City is packing weapons of some kind. Do you know how to handle a gun? If not, I'll teach you. Every woman should know for their own protection."

Hell no, I don't want to handle a gun!

I wonder what strange dimension I've stepped into.

"No, I don't want to know," I say firmly. "I'm scared to death of guns. They make me nervous. I'm not touching a gun."

"That's only because you aren't comfortable around them. Once you learn how to handle one safely, you won't be afraid anymore."

"Do you honestly think I'm in enough danger that I should learn how to use a gun?" The thought worries me. "Or are you just trying to scare me?"

"I would never scare you unnecessarily. I only want to keep you safe. Whatever it takes to do that."

His cell phone beeps and he checks the incoming text before snapping the phone shut.

"Your crew is going after the Liberators, aren't they?"

"Not tonight, and definitely not without me," he says firmly. "Flint and a couple of the guys are taking a ride over to the Beachcomber to see if their bikes are still there. I wouldn't be surprised if the Liberators have already moved locations after hearing from your brother."

I can't help but be relieved that a confrontation between the two clubs won't be happening tonight. I need time to catch my breath.

"You must think I'm crazy to still love my brother," I say, feeling as if I should apologize. "He's not all bad. I know it's hard to understand after seeing how he treats me."

Jesse puts an arm around my shoulder and tugs me closer to him. His body is hot. I want to lay my head on his shoulder, close my eyes, and melt into his warmth.

"No, it's not so hard to understand. My Dad isn't always the nicest guy in the world either. You can't choose your family though, and you sure as hell can't help how you feel."

He reaches up to brush my hair back from my face. "Are you upset about staying here with me again tonight? I know it isn't your first choice of accommodations, but it's the only way to keep you safe."

I give in to the urge to put my head on his shoulder. Immediately, I feel safer surrounded by his warmth.

"My plans seem to change every five minutes lately. I'm not upset. Uncomfortable is a better word. I hope you realize that I'm normally not like this. I don't do one-night stands or hookups with strange guys I've just met." I look up at him and realize I can't think straight when I'm gazing into his blue eyes. "This isn't the real me. I don't want you to get the wrong idea and think I'm some cheap woman without morals."

"I suspected that all along," he teases, his eyes twinkling. "Tell you what. I'll go bunk with Flint tonight in his room. He's right next door. Give you some breathing space. You need time to calm down and get some rest. The last twenty-four hours must have been tough on you. We don't need to rush things. There's plenty of time. No hurry."

He leans over and softly kisses my lips then ruffles my hair. "Things always look brighter in the morning." He stands and walks to the door. "Lock the deadbolt behind me. Don't open the door for anyone and keep the lights dim so nobody can see in through the curtains. If you get scared, you can always bang on the wall and I'll hear you. If you need me, I'll be here."

Is he really leaving? Just like that?

"Jesse, wait," I call out as he turns the doorknob. "Don't go. I don't want to be alone tonight. Stay with me."

He pauses at the door, turning reluctantly to face me. He shoves his hair back with his hand. "If I stay, this is only going to go one way. We both know it. There's no way in hell I can spend another night next to you without touching your gorgeous body. I have willpower, but I'm not a damn saint. I don't want you to feel pressured into anything."

I pat the bedspread beside me in invitation.

"Fuck," he swears, looking like he is about to turn and leave anyway. Then without warning, he is striding to the bed and stripping the sheets from my fingers. I yelp in surprise.

He doesn't touch me and instead leans his arms on either side of my body. The atmosphere stills around us. Without tearing his eyes from mine, he says, "Tell me to leave, Trish, and I'll go. If you tell me that fucking you is something you don't want, I'll respect your wishes. I'm not Big Roy, and I won't force a woman into being with me. There's nothing more that I want and need right now than to make you mine. But you have to want it too. As much as I do."

I shiver at the intense heat in his eyes and suddenly feel shy. What if he's disappointed in me? My sex life up to now has been limited and unsatisfying.

"I'm not experienced like those other women," I whisper.

His harsh expression softens at my words. "I know," he says in a gentler tone than before. "I want you so much I feel like my cock is going to explode, but I can wait until you're ready." He blows out a long breath and touches his forehead to mine. "That's a lie. Please tell me you're ready now."

His tortured words make my heart trip. I know exactly how he feels.

No way can I wait another second either. I'd been waiting since the first second I caught a glimpse of his tattooed muscular body making its way toward me at the bar.

The solid weight of his body holds me down and keeps me from moving or bolting out the door. Not that I want to. My fingers itch to sink into the dark waves of his hair. Instead I fist the sheets on either side of me as his hot breath fans my earlobe. I feel the tension in his every muscle as he strives to stay in control.

"I want to take you now," he says. "Pin you to the bed, spread your thighs as far apart as they can go, and fuck you senseless. But tonight we're going to go slow...really slow," he adds softly. "I want this to be a night to remember."

He kisses me right behind my ear. My skin feels hot and I can barely meet his gaze. He chuckles at my shyness, leaning down and closing the distance between our lips.

"Do you have any clue what you do to me?" he murmurs before covering my mouth possessively in a kiss. Our breaths mingle as I eagerly open my lips wider. Long minutes pass before he draws away slightly, just enough for me to try to catch my unsteady breath. I feel his smile as he kisses my bottom lip.

"You make me rock hard just by looking at you. Every man in the bar wanted you tonight. I was in agony watching them and knowing what they were thinking." His mouth moves to kiss along my jaw line and continues lower. "They were thinking of all the things they wanted to do to you. Just like I was. And now I am."

I shiver at his words.

"They were wondering how it would feel to touch your breasts," he says, tugging my shirt up over my head. He stares at my breasts for a moment in pure wonder before cupping each full globe in his hands and thumbing the nipples. "And how responsive your nipples would be." Dipping his head, he captures a nipple in his mouth and tugs hard. My fingers clench in his hair and he growls his approval.

"I promise it will be so good," he whispers in my ear. "I will spend all night pleasing you."

He moves his hand lower, and I hold my breath as he slides his hand further down my stomach. Embarrassed by the moan that escapes my mouth, I grab his hand. This is moving too fast and I'm not sure what I'm getting into.

"Jesse, wait," I say.

My hand closes around his wrist as he slides his hand under my panties, parts my swollen lips, and pushes his middle finger deep inside all the way up to his knuckle. I hear him grunt softly as I instinctively grind against his hand, shocked and amazed by how delicious his finger feels. I close my eyes and shudder when he slides a second finger in and strokes my snug tightness.

"Tell me what you want," he says, running his lips along my throat. "What you need from me."

I can show him faster than I can possibly say it.

Reaching for his belt buckle, I hurriedly undo it, unzip his jeans, and slide my hand inside to wrap around his hard length. He groans and strains against my hand.

"We're reaching the point of no going back," he says hoarsely. "Are you sure?"

I nod and stroke my hand down the length of his cock as my answer.

"Thank you Jesus!" he says.

He stands up by the edge of the bed and quickly strips off his clothes. I'm speechless as I gaze up in awe at his deeply tanned, muscular body. A large Steel Infidels tattoo runs across the front of his chest. Several smaller tattoos cover his neck, shoulders, arms, and back. I try not to stare, but I can't help checking out the thick, long erection between his legs too. Thank you Jesus is right.

Grasping my ankles, he pulls me down the length of the bed then quickly grabs my panties and tugs them off. Immediately he covers my entire body with his. I close my eyes and slide my hands down his back. Damn! His muscular ass feels delicious underneath my palms.

Urgently, he claims my lips before leaving a trail of kisses between my breasts and down my stomach. When he reaches my legs, he pauses and looks up at me with blue eyes hazy with desire.

"Open your legs," he coaxes. "I want to see your pussy spread wide for me."

I swallow and try hard to fight back against the timidness welling up in me. If he only knew how pathetic my sexual experience has been. The desire to please him is stronger than the need to protect my modesty, so I pull my knees up and spread my legs wide apart just like he asked.

"Breathtaking," he says, before moving between my legs and placing his cock at the entrance to my pussy lips.

In an instant, he penetrates me, leaving me gasping from sweet agony. With barely a pause, he sinks in.

"Damn! You are so fucking wet and tight," he says, lifting his face from my neck to gaze at me. "I could stay inside you forever. This feels so good."

"I know," I say.

"I need to move, sweetheart," he says softly. "And I need you to tell me it's okay. I can pull out or keep going. All you have to do is say no and I'll stop. Just say the word."

He holds completely still, letting me adjust to his width.

"No, I want you," I say, pulling him deeper as I feel him start to withdraw. "It feels too good to stop now."

"You want it slow and easy?" he murmurs as he starts moving.

"Yes," I whisper.

Shallow at first with a smooth, steady rhythm, Jesse takes me, allowing only a few inches of his cock to slide in and out until my body relaxes. He pumps in steady strokes, sliding and stroking, making me feel him deep inside.

Everything he gives, I have no choice but to take and keep taking. He rocks in deeper and harder while intently watching my every expression. Leaning down, he kisses my lips again, then my throat, before moving lower and capturing my nipple in his mouth.

"Is it good?" he asks huskily.

His hoarse voice breaks through my daze. Not trusting my voice, I speak instead with my body, my legs locking around his sides tightly while my hips move almost imperceptibly beneath him, urging him on.

The next second he pulls out slightly again and then thrusts more powerfully, jolting me back against the pillows. He is buried so deep inside me now. Beads of sweat break out on our skin, making us slide slickly against each other.

My nails rake down his muscular back as the pressure mounts deep inside me until I'm writhing and frantic, impatient for more. My teeth sink deep into his neck when I suddenly cum in a rush.

Jesse groans as my whole body spasms uncontrollably around his hard cock and I lose control over my muscles as they ripple and contract.

"Trish," he breathes when my body goes perfectly still.

I open my eyes and gaze up at him. Bringing him into focus is difficult. There is strain on his face from holding back. He isn't even breathing hard, though the sheen of perspiration on his forehead shows how much effort it is taking for him to slow things down for me.

"I can't hold back much longer," he says.

Linking my arms behind his neck, I whisper to him, "It's okay. Let go."

I hear the hitch in his breath as he quickens his pace. His thrusts grow choppy and I buck my hips up to meet his. His hard cock swells and then starts to pulse deep inside me.

"Fuck!"

He pushes in to the balls and buries his face in my throat while his body shudders in release.

Several minutes later, we're both still breathing raggedly. He rests his forehead against mine, his chest heaving, while his elbows are braced at my sides to support his weight.

"I don't want to move," he says. "I could stay like this forever."

With a regretful sound, he slides out of me and rolls off. I glance over and he is staring up at the ceiling with a dazed look on his face. Turning his face toward mine, he reaches out and touches my cheek with his finger.

"You're unbelievable," he says. "Everything I could have wanted and so much more."

Pulling me to his chest, he holds my face in his hands and stares into my eyes.

"Promise me you'll be here in the morning. No more running away this time. I need to hear you say it. Promise me."

No way am I leaving him again.

"I promise."

15

JESSE

Trish is still fast asleep when I slip out of the room. After the night we spent together, she needs all the rest she can get. My gut told me that fucking her would be something special. What I didn't expect is for it to be mind-blowing spectacular.

Something about her brings out my protective streak. Maybe because her brother is such an asshole. Or maybe because when she looks at me with those soft brown eyes, I want to make sure they never have a reason to fill with tears again.

It's been years since I've had deep feelings for any girl. Being with Trish is stirring up something I had forgotten existed, and it worries me.

I have to be careful not to let my personal feelings for her cloud my judgment where the Liberators are concerned. If her brother gets hurt or even killed in the crossfire, then so be it.

I try not to think about how devastated Trish will be if that ever happens.

Or if she will ever forgive me.

I knock on Flint's door to see if he is up yet. He swings the door open wide and rubs his eyes groggily with the palms of his hands.

"Jesus Christ, Jesse! What time is it?" he asks.

"Time to get your lazy ass up and out of bed. We need to work on a plan." I move past him into the messy hotel room.

Flint yawns. "Don't call me lazy, dickhead. I was out all night checking out the Liberators' hotel while you were next door fucking around. You were, right?"

"Were what?"

"Fucking," he says with a straight face.

"None of your damn business."

He chuckles. "Oh, so that's how it is now." He cocks his head and gives me a closer look. "You've got a serious thing for her, don't you? Don't worry. Your secret is safe with me. There's no point in trying to fool me though, Jesse. I know you better than anyone."

I think about lying and know it will only be a waste of my time. "So I like her," I say with a shrug. "No big deal. Nothing for you to get a hard on over. Women come and go."

Flint clears his throat. "Considering I haven't heard of a single girl actually spending the entire night with you since I came back to town, I do think it's a big deal. What happened to your famous 'fuck them and send them packing before daylight' rule?"

"She's only sticking around for a couple of days until we get this mess sorted out with the Liberators. After that, who knows? We certainly haven't talked about it, and I doubt she has given it any thought either. I know I haven't. So drop it, okay?"

"Whatever you say. You're the boss man."

Flint rips open a package provided by the hotel containing a prefilled coffee filter. He holds it up for me to see the label.

"This shit says gourmet coffee, but I'll bet you fifty bucks it tastes like ass."

He pours water into the canister and starts the coffee brewing. "How can they make hotel coffee taste so damn awful?"

"You can always stop by the store and buy yourself a bag of decent coffee if you hate it that bad," I suggest.

"Yeah, but that would ruin the whole experience of going on vacation to bike week with you guys," he jokes. "If I buy a bag of good coffee, the next thing I know you'll all be ordering me to make cappuccinos like I'm your own personal barista. Kind of like going camping and bringing along a chef."

He pours a cup of black coffee when it finishes dripping and hands it to me. I take a sip and grimace.

"Damn! You weren't kidding. So tell me what you found out last night at the Beachcomber. Any sign of Big Roy?"

Flint shakes his head. "No. Not that we were really expecting there to be. The brother obviously tipped him off and they all split. We hung around in the parking lot for a bit and asked a few questions. Some bikers there remembered seeing a man with red hair and a long beard. Snake tattoo on his arm."

"Big Roy?"

"Must be. Don't know anybody else that ugly. Nobody knew where they went. The girl at the check-in desk said the rooms were paid in full through the end of bike week. That's all we know right now."

I sit down in a chair by the window and pull up the blinds to keep a close eye on the parking lot. "Since you're the lawyer and the brains in the family, got any ideas how we can flush them out?"

"Sure, I have an idea," he says slowly. "You're probably not going to like it."

"Spit it out. Let's hear it." I already have a clue where this is going.

"We use your girl as bait to lure them out into the open again."

"No," I say curtly. "You're right, I don't like it. Not one damn bit."

Flint holds up his hand. "Hear me out, okay? We wouldn't be putting her in any danger. Well, at least not intentionally. Trish needs to agree to be part of the plan for it to work smoothly."

"And what exactly would this plan be?"

"First, she would have to call or text her brother and create a believable excuse to set up a meeting. Then, we'll put a tail on him after the meet up is over. He's our best link to Big Roy and the rest of the Liberators."

"No fucking way."

"Jesse..."

"Don't start with me, Flint. I'm not asking Trish to do this. You didn't see the two of them together. Her brother is mean as a rattlesnake and plenty capable of hurting her. He doesn't give a shit about his sister. I don't want her anywhere near him."

"What's their story?"

"I don't really know all the details yet. He roughed her up in the parking lot of the bar and left bruises on her arm before that. She hasn't told me what the extent of his abuse is or if he's done anything worse.

Psychologically, he has some kind of weird hold on her. It's not safe for her to be with him. Especially now that she's hanging with us. There's no telling what he might do."

Flint blows out a long breath. "I figured you might feel this way. There's always Plan B then."

I lift my eyebrows at him. "Which is?"

"We go ahead with the same plan without her knowing she's part of it."

"And how do you propose we do that? Wouldn't she need to be the one to contact her brother?"

Flint downs the last of his coffee and pours another cup. "Not if you can secretly grab her cell phone and do it instead. Send him a text from her phone asking to meet him at the bar and then delete it."

"Aww...shit. This plan sucks. You graduate from law school and this is the best you can come up with?"

I lean back in the chair and close my eyes. If I do this, Trish is going to be so pissed at me.

"Even if I delete the text, won't Trish see his response to it?"

Flint hesitates and leans forward to explain. "See, this is where it gets a little tricky and complicated. You need to steal her phone and not give it back. Ever."

"Steal my girl's phone? Boy, you're full of shit ideas this morning, aren't you? Are you still drunk? What if she needs to call me in an emergency and I have her damn phone in my pocket? What good will that do?"

"I've got you covered there too," Flint says. "A lawyer is always thinking ahead. I'll pick up a couple of prepaid burner phones for you at the drugstore. You should keep one of those activated and ready to hand over to her when she realizes her phone is...missing in action."

"I still don't like it. She'll suspect something is up. She's not dumb."

"Did I say she was?" he asks. "You're already making this way too personal, and it isn't like you. We've been chasing after the Liberators for months and you're going to let it all go down the drain for a girl you just met? Quit thinking with your damn dick and get onboard with the plan."

"When have you ever known me to put a girl before the club?"

"There's a first time for everything. How many chances do you think we're going to get to nail the Liberators? We need to finish this. It hasn't been so long ago that you and I stood up in front of the crew and promised them we would do just that. Here is our opportunity and we have to take it. Trust me, the end justifies the means in this case."

He's right. I'm letting my feelings for Trish corrode my judgment. Exactly what I swore to myself I wouldn't do.

"Plan B it is then," I say, standing up. "I'll find a way to grab her phone today. When should I try to set up the meet?"

"Tonight," he replies without hesitation. "After the bar closes. No need to drag this shit out any longer than necessary."

"I agree. Wouldn't it be terrific to never have to think about those bastard Liberators again? Tonight it is then."

Trish is already awake and dressed when I return to the room. I'm disappointed since I was hoping to slide back under the sheets and wake her up slowly with my tongue.

Now that we have a plan, I realize my time with her is limited. Something tells me to make the best of every second. Once she finds out we're using her and her brother as bait, she is going to be furious with me.

I slip up behind her at the mirror and bend down to nuzzle the soft nape of her neck.

"Good morning, gorgeous," I say, wrapping my arms around her waist and inhaling her sweet scent.

She leans back into me and smiles at my reflection. "You're up early. I woke up and you were already gone."

"Did you miss me?" I tease.

She gives me a shy smile. "Maybe a little."

"I promise to make it up to you later tonight if you'll let me," I say. "There are so many things I want to do to you. Just thinking about it is making my dick hard. But first things first. Let's talk about breakfast. Are you hungry? When was the last time you had anything to eat?"

She puts her hairbrush down to think. "I really don't remember. Lunch yesterday, maybe. Now that you mention it, I'm starving."

"Are you up for a ride? I thought we could grab a quick breakfast then take a drive today along the coastal highway. Get away from all the bikers for a few hours. It's a nice ride and I think you'll like it."

"Actually, I would love it. Can you get me back in time for work? I don't want to piss Roger off any more than I already have. I can't afford to be fired."

"I'll deliver you to the bar with extra time to spare," I promise.

"It's a date then. I'm almost ready to go."

She reaches for a ponytail holder and deftly pulls back her long hair. "Which direction are we riding? East or west?"

"I'll let you pick. East will take us to Apalachicola Bay where we can order fresh oysters right out of the bay for lunch. Or we can go west through the pretty little town of Seaside and then on to Destin for fresh fish. Red snapper might be in season, or if not they always serve grouper."

She wrinkles her nose and makes a face.

"Sorry, I'm not a fan of raw oysters. The texture grosses me out. I would love to ride through Seaside. I've seen photos of the town in magazines and it looks beautiful. Can we go west?"

"Anything you want," I say. "Do you have any sunscreen?"

She nods.

"You had better slather it on thick. One of the worst sunburns I ever got was riding on my bike through Florida. Make sure you do your face, arms, and legs."

She pulls out a tube of sunscreen from her bag.

"Here, let me do it," I say.

I squirt a big dollop of sunscreen onto the palm of my hand and start rubbing the lotion on her arms. She winces when I accidentally touch the bruise on her upper arm. I frown and draw back my hand.

"Is this still sore?"

"Only when you touch it."

"You want to tell me how it happened? You never did say."

A sad look crosses her face. "Can we please not talk about my brother today? I want to forget about him for a while if I can. Let's just go have a good time and pretend we're normal people for a few hours."

"Your wish is my command. There's nothing I would like more."

16

JESSE

The bustling town of Seaside is busier than I expected. It has been years since I'd ridden through the pastel-colored town, and it surprises me to see throngs of tourists filling the sidewalks and crosswalks.

Instead of bikers, most of the tourists are wealthy, sunburned families with children, all dragging umbrellas and towels from their rented houses over to the public beach. I don't envy them since they look hot, tired, and cranky.

For some reason, they all seem to be irritated at me. After we receive several hateful glares, I realize the loud muffler on my motorcycle might have something to do with it.

Too bad.

They can just fucking deal.

"What do you think about Seaside?" I yell to Trish over my shoulder.

"I love it," she says back. "The colors of the buildings are so pretty. A picture perfect town. I wonder what it would be like to live in a place like this."

"Probably nice in the winter," I reply. "The spring and summer months would be a bitch with all these tourists walking around. The locals must hate it."

"I bet they like the money the tourists bring in."

"You've got a point there."

Trish spots an art festival going on in the village green space located in the middle of the town.

"Do we have time to stop and look around?" she asks. "I need to stretch my legs for a minute. They're going numb."

"Sure," I say, glad for any opportunity to get to know her better.

The bike ride seemed like a good idea at first, but then I realized we weren't getting much of a chance to talk. It's hard to have a deep, meaningful conversation when every word has to be yelled to the person behind you.

After parking the bike, I take her hand in mine and we follow the other tourists to where the white tents for the art festival are set up. The area between the tents is congested with lots of people milling around.

When Trish's purse bangs my side, I realize this might be the best opportunity to steal her cell phone without her noticing. I had been enjoying the day so much that I almost forgot my mission.

She slows down as we move past a booth selling handmade jewelry. I notice her eyes go to a pair of silver earrings. She reaches down to pick them up for a closer look then changes her mind.

"Do you like those?" I ask.

"They're beautiful," she says. "Unfortunately, with my current financial situation, I can't afford to be looking at jewelry."

Reaching for the earrings, I hold them up to her ear. "I think these earrings will look fantastic on you." I lean down to whisper into her ear where the elderly lady working the booth can't hear. "The earrings and nothing else."

Trish ducks her head. I love her shyness, both inside the bed and out.

"We'll take them," I tell the clerk.

"Do you need a box?" the lady asks after I hand over the money.

I turn to Trish for her answer.

"No, if it's okay, I'll put them on now," she says.

She deftly slips one earring on and then the other.

"How do they look?" she asks, smiling up at me as if she doesn't have a care in the world.

Like we are a normal couple on vacation doing ordinary things;

walking around an art festival and looking at jewelry. Buying drippy ice cream cones or strolling along the beach.

I look at her and for a moment, my heart actually hurts. She's breathtakingly beautiful when she's happy.

If only we had more time.

I know I could keep her happy if we had a real chance.

My mind turns to how much I hate the Liberators. If it's not bad enough that they took important things from my past, now they're taking away my future as well.

Gathering her close, I lean down and kiss her softly on the lips. The embarrassed clerk clears her throat and looks away.

"I think you're the prettiest gal I've ever seen," I say truthfully, brushing a wisp of hair back from her face that has sprung loose from the ponytail. "The earrings look absolutely stunning on you."

While one hand presses against her back, the other slides into her open purse. In a split second, I palm her cell phone and slip it into my pocket.

I'm going straight to hell.

In my life, I've done plenty of bad things, some that I've regretted, and other worse things that I didn't feel a tingle of remorse about.

Right now, stealing Trish's cell phone when she's looking up at me with those big innocent eyes is at the top of my list of things I'll need to repent for some day at the pearly gates.

"Thank you so much for the earrings, Jesse," she says, reaching up to touch my cheek. "I love them."

I feel like a big stinking pile of dog shit.

17

TRISH

Biking along the Florida Panhandle with Jesse is one of the best times I remember having in years. I'm feeling carefree, snuggled close behind him on the bike with the hot sun on my legs and the wind in my hair. The salty ocean air smells fresh and crisp. With every mile, the stress of the past few days melts away more and more.

Being on a bike is peaceful, and peace isn't something I've had much of in my life, especially lately. I can understand why bikers love riding so much.

I wrap my arms tighter around Jesse's waist. He turns slightly and grins back at me. I long to run my hands up and down the hard abs on his chest to feel the smooth muscles I know are there. I resist the urge because I'm afraid he'll let go of the handlebars or be so distracted that he'll run off the road. At the speed we're going, a wreck would be disastrous, if not fatal.

I reach up to touch the earrings to make sure they're still on my ears. His sweet, impulsive gesture to buy them for me brought tears to my eyes, but I didn't let him see. I made sure to blink the tears back before he noticed.

He would probably think I was being silly or overly sentimental. Emotions that most men can't tolerate in women, especially a tough biker like Jesse. I'm too embarrassed to tell him that the earrings were the first gift a man has ever bought me. I'll keep that little secret to myself.

Taking care of an addict mother most of my life didn't leave me much free time for fun or dating. After Ty left home, my mom always needed me for something: putting her to bed when she was wasted, or staying up all night babysitting her because I was afraid she would accidentally set the house on fire if I fell asleep.

Many mornings I dragged myself to high school with little to no sleep the night before. If my teachers suspected anything was wrong with my home life, they never said a word about it.

I didn't date at all in high school, and in the years since, I haven't been on more than a handful of casual dates. Even then, I was never foolish enough to bring the men home to meet my mother. In a small country town, word gets around fast about drug addicts. Everyone knows who they are.

Once the guys realized my situation, they always dumped me without a second thought. I can't blame them. I split too, once I finally worked up the courage to go.

Now there's Jesse, and I'm afraid to let my mind wander further into the future than this week. Last night was filled with incredible, mind-blowing sex. Something that, if I'm honest with myself, probably meant a whole lot more to me than to him.

I'm smart enough to know good sex doesn't mean we are meant to be together forever. Believing we have a future beyond bike week would be idiotic and immature on my part.

So I can't let myself think about it.

There has been enough heartache in my life from my own family. I can't afford to let a man break my heart too, though it's growing increasingly hard to keep my feelings for Jesse tamped down.

Everything he does ramps them up a little more. First protecting me from my brother, then taking me in when I was wandering the streets in the middle of the night, and now buying me earrings. Not to mention the hot sex. My mind keeps going back to that.

Jesse takes a hand off the handlebars and casually places it on my leg.

"Keep your hands on the wheel, buddy!" I say into his ear before placing a quick kiss there, too. "It scares me when you take your hands off the handlebars."

"If you want me to stop touching your legs, you should wear jeans," he says back. "Otherwise I can't resist. And I can drive just fine with no hands. See?"

He lifts both hands and holds them high up into the air.

"Stop! Oh my God, don't do that," I scream, closing my eyes and tucking my head against his back so I can't see if we're about to crash.

I feel the rumble of his laughter through his shirt.

"I'm sorry. I didn't mean to frighten you."

"Are your hands still up?" I whisper.

"No, you can look now."

I don't move my head from his back. "Actually, this feels pretty comfy right here."

"If you keep rubbing up against me like that, I'm going to have to pull off the road and take you behind a sand dune," he warns.

"And what would happen behind this sand dune?" I ask innocently.

"I would rather show than tell," he replies.

"Promises, promises."

My stomach growls loudly, reminding me it has been hours since breakfast.

"How much further before we get to Destin?" I ask.

"Not too much longer," he says. "I know of a little place right on the water by the harbor where we can stop for lunch. The fishermen sell their fresh fish to the restaurants there every day."

"Sounds fantastic. I haven't eaten fresh seafood in forever."

Twenty minutes later, we're seated at a table on an outdoor patio overlooking the Destin Harbor. From where we're sitting, we can see the fishing boats pulling up with their catch of the day. Large brown pelicans and sea gulls perch on the tall wooden poles lining the boat docks at the edge of the water. When the boats come closer, they all stand up and wait patiently for the fishermen to clean the fish and throw them scraps.

Jesse starts to reach for my hand across the table, then suddenly moves around and pulls up a chair close beside me.

I laugh. "What are you doing? Something wrong with that side of the table?"

"Yeah," he says. "You're on this side and too far away. I want to be closer."

He slides a hand down the inside of my leg and scoots my chair over toward him. "Now, that's much better. I like keeping my hands on my girl."

There's that term again. My girl. I like it.

The waitress takes our drink order and hands us menus with ten handwritten items.

"Any suggestions?" I ask Jesse when she walks away.

"Not the chicken."

After we order two mixed seafood platters, I slip off to the restroom to freshen up. When I reach into my purse for my lip gloss, I notice right off that my cell phone isn't where it should be. I unzip all of the extra pockets of the purse in a panic and check those, too. No phone anywhere.

Darn it! I'm always so careful to keep up with my phone and to make sure it stays fully charged. My heart beats fast at the thought of losing it.

Ty is always adamant that I keep the phone turned on at all times in case he needs me to do something for the club. Plus, my cell phone is the only way my mother knows how to get in touch with me.

It takes me a full minute to calm down and remember that Ty doesn't control me anymore, and it might be for the best if my mother can't call me either.

Maybe this is a good thing.

Without my cell phone, I am completely cut off from my family. If they can't reach me, they can't hurt me.

I'm free.

At least until I find my phone.

Jesse stands up and politely pulls back my chair for me when I return to the table.

"Thank you," I say, smiling up at him. "Men don't pull out chairs for women much anymore. It's nice."

"My mom taught all of us boys manners. She said we needed to know how to be true Southern gentlemen. And we all know how, we just don't always show it." He looks sad at the thought of his mom. "I'm afraid she wouldn't be very happy with her boys these days."

I'm surprised by his comment. "Why do you say that?"

He shrugs. "Like most mothers, she wanted us to make something big of ourselves. Something besides running a motorcycle club, of course. She wouldn't have considered that to be a real or honorable profession. My mom would have been very proud of Flint though."

"Is that the man who looks just like you, only younger?"

He nods. "Flint is a lawyer. He worked in Atlanta for a couple of years and only came back home a few months ago. He's back with the MC now and picks up freelance legal work on the side."

I open two packets of sugar and pour them into my sweet tea. "What do the rest of you do?" I ask, stirring the sugar until it melts.

"Sam and I own a tattoo parlor. Sam does most of the work and I run the business side of things. He's much more artistic than I am. Most of his clients are women, believe it or not. His specialty is tattoos in intimate places. The ladies don't seem to mind letting him get the tools right there, up close and personal. Hell, sometimes I think they actually enjoy it."

"Are you serious? Or are you pulling my leg?"

"I'm dead serious. Ask him yourself next time you see him. Just whatever you do, don't agree to let him give you a tattoo."

"Don't worry," I say adamantly. "I won't. Especially not there. What about the rest of your crew?"

"The MC is involved in a few other ventures too. Nothing much worth talking about. We get by okay. It pays the bills."

I'm afraid to ask and really don't want to know what the Steel Infidels are involved in. For now, I like keeping my head in the sand where Jesse is concerned, and he obviously isn't comfortable with telling me more.

"What about you?" he asks. "Any big plans for the future?"

I let out a long sigh.

"I wish. My mom is...sick, and I spent most of my time looking after her. It's past time I figured out what I want to do with the rest of my life. I just don't know where to start. I've been a caregiver for so long that I feel kind of lost not doing it."

The mention of my mom reminds me of my lost phone. For some reason, I can't stop worrying about it. Most likely because I'm so obsessive compulsive about constantly checking things that I never lose anything. It is still bothering me. I peek down under the table to see if it fell out of my purse and onto the floor.

"What are you looking for?" Jesse asks.

"My cell phone. I lost it. I always keep it in my purse and now I can't find it. It must have fallen out somewhere along the way."

"Damn! I'm sorry," he says. "I don't know what I would do if I lost my phone. I keep everything on there. Was there anything important on it?"

"Not really," I say. "Phone numbers. Most of which I have memorized anyway. That's about it. It wasn't an expensive phone, so that's not what I'm worried about. Not one of those fancy smartphones. My phone is the only way for Ty and Mom to reach me in an emergency. It kind of freaks me out to be cut off from everyone."

He gives me a concerned look. "I thought you were going to stay away from your brother. Isn't that what we agreed would be best for now? We talked about this."

"I know," I reluctantly say. "You're right. Still, in case of a real emergency, I would want my mother to be able to call me."

"I'm sure it will turn up somewhere. Maybe it fell out of your purse at the bar last night? We were in such a hurry to get out of there. I bet that's what happened. I have a couple of extra prepaid cell phones back at the hotel. I'll give you one of those to use until you can find your phone. At least you'll have a phone if you need me for anything."

"You've done enough for me already."

"They're cheap. I would feel much better knowing you have a phone, even if it is an 'el cheapo' prepaid phone. My crew misplaces their phones all the time so I've learned to keep extras on hand."

I don't bother telling Jesse that he doesn't need to explain to me about burner phones. Nobody keeps extra prepaid phones around unless they're making calls they don't want traced back to them. The Liberators always kept extra burner phones, too. For their illegal activities. It's good to know I picked up a few helpful hints while hanging around those jerks. I can't help but wonder why Jesse needs the phones, too.

When the huge platters of seafood arrive, we look at each other wide-eyed and burst out laughing. There is enough fried fish, shrimp, and clams for ten people, not including the fries, coleslaw, and hushpuppies spilling off the plates.

"Why did we order so much food?" I ask. "There's no way we can eat all of this."

"You said you were starving," he says. "Don't you dare go telling me how you're full after eating two bites. You need to put some meat on your bones. Besides, I know you've been skipping meals the past few days."

I pop a fried shrimp into my mouth.

"Don't worry. I'm not one of those kind of girls. I like to eat and I don't mind admitting it. Luckily I'm a decent cook, too. I prefer baking to cooking though. Desserts, cakes, cookies."

"That's good to know, because I love curves in all the right places. Skinny women don't do a thing for me." He points a fork at my plate. "So eat up and fill out those luscious curves some more."

Forty-five minutes later, I give up trying to finish my plate of food. I'm amazed at how much food Jesse can pack in and still be so muscular and fit. After finishing his platter of food, he slides my plate over and eats the rest of it, too.

While watching him eat, I can't help thinking about how fun it would be to cook his favorite food. Ty always complained about my cooking even as he was gobbling it all up. I bet Jesse wouldn't do that. It would be nice to cook for someone who appreciated it for a change.

"Do you work out every day?" I ask. "How do you stay in such great shape?"

"You mean work out in a gym?" He shakes his head. "Nah, I don't have time for that. We all keep in shape by doing work stuff, lifting bikes to change tires, and other things like that."

That figures. A body as fine as Jesse's would be God-given and not made by lifting weights.

He signals for the check.

"We should probably be heading on back. I don't want you to be late for work. Do you want me to drop you off straight at the bar or do you need to go back to the hotel and change clothes first?"

I roll my eyes. Men. They're so clueless sometimes. They must think we wake up looking all pretty with our hair fixed and makeup applied. They have no idea how long it takes us to get ready.

"I should change clothes and fix my hair," I say. "My work outfit is a little different from what I have on now."

I point to my t-shirt, shorts, and flip-flops.

"Nothing too revealing, I hope," he says, suddenly serious.

"Why? Are you jealous? Afraid another man might look at my boobs?"

He grabs my hand and links his fingers through mine. "Yes, exactly that. And your curvy ass too."

"If it makes you feel better, you're the only man I'm letting touch them."

He grins. "Thanks for that and for the mental image. Now the whole ride back, all I'll be thinking about is fondling your tits. And other things. If I start weaving off the road, you'll know where my mind is wandering off to. Are you absolutely sure I can't talk you into the sand dune thing? Because I spotted a few secluded places on the drive up."

I playfully punch him.

"Time to hit the road, big fella, before you get all frisky right here at the table."

"What about on a fishing pier then? Or under a fishing pier? That would be unique."

"Now you're just being weird." I smile at him. "Ask me again sometime and I just might take you up on it."

"You can bet I will."

18

JESSE

"I'll be back before closing to pick you up," I tell Trish before kissing her goodbye at the front door of the bar. "If you need me before then, don't hesitate to call. I'll keep my phone on."

"Don't worry, I will."

She turns to go through the door then runs back over to reach up on her tiptoes and plant a long kiss on my lips.

"Wow!" I say, holding on to her arm when she pulls away. "What was that for?"

"So you don't forget me," she answers.

"As if I ever could."

Once she goes inside and out of sight, I pull her cell phone out of my pocket to send a text to her brother. After scrolling through the past several texts back and forth between him and Trish, I decide a simple, 'I'm sorry. Meet me tonight after work?' is best.

I hit the send button. Now all I can do is wait and hope he is mad enough or curious enough to show up.

I'm not really expecting him to reply to her by phone, if their previous texts are any indication. Most of their conversations consisted of Ty ordering her to do something and Trish replying with, 'okay.' Reading the texts pisses me off all over again. I wish there was a way to get her away from him for good. I don't like that he is a part of her life.

If I have any say about it, he won't be for long.

"Any word?" Flint asks me for the hundredth time. He leans back against a light pole, pulls a cigarette out of a pack, and lights it.

We're sitting at the far end of the parking lot under a street lamp with a busted out lightbulb. From our vantage point, we can see everyone walking through the lot while we're safely hidden in the shadows. If Ty shows up, we'll see him.

"Nope," I say, checking Trish's cell phone again and shaking my head. I give him a curious look. "Does Kendra know you smoke?"

"Nope," he replies. He blows a ring of smoke up into the air. "And she won't. Will she?" He turns to stare at me.

"Not from me. I wouldn't want to be near that conversation. Kendra is going to kick your ass all the way from Georgia to the Mississippi River when she finds out."

"I'll quit before then."

"That's what they all say."

"Think the brother will show up tonight?"

"I don't know. I hope so. If not, it means they smell a rat or they've decided to go underground again and not show their faces. It can go either way."

Flint flips open his cell phone. "Sam just sent me a text saying there is no sign of the brother or any of the Liberators inside. He's going to approach a couple of the friendly biker groups and give them a head's up about the situation in case we need them."

"I don't think we have to worry about the Liberators getting to Trish inside the bar. Roger swore to me that he wouldn't let Ty back in after I told him he was part of the Liberators. He hates that club almost as much as we do. I've got Rocco keeping a close eye on Trish just in case though. We don't want any surprises."

"They've ambushed us before."

"You don't need to remind me," I say dryly. "There's not a day that goes by that I don't think about it. I can't believe you actually convinced Kendra to marry you after that mess at the safe house."

"Me either. Who would have thought that getting shot was the luckiest thing that ever happened to me? When I opened my eyes that day and saw her tending to my wound, I honest to God thought I had seriously died and gone to heaven. She was like an angel in the bright light."

"That's because you lost so much blood that you were loony tunes and fucking out of your head. I'm glad you were enjoying it, because it scared the shit out of the rest of us. You probably wouldn't be standing here if Kendra hadn't decided to hang around and sew you up. God, she was so fucking pissed at me. I mean really spitting mad."

"Can you blame her? You threatened her and basically forced a veterinarian to perform medical care on me. She could have lost her vet's license."

"I don't see how. What were we going to do if she screwed up your stitches? Sue her? I was desperate. I couldn't just let you bleed out. I would have done anything to keep you alive. And you would have done exactly the same for me or Sam. I will always be in her debt for that. And now that she's taking you off my hands, I'm in double debt to her."

Flint flicks ashes onto the ground and stamps them out with his boot. "I'm pretty confident she's forgiven you. After all, she got me out of the deal, and I'm one hell of a consolation prize."

"Are you sure you're up to being a married man? The wedding is less than a month away. You still have time to back out if you have any doubts."

"Are you kidding?" Flint says. "We would already be married if it were up to me. Hell, I would have dragged her to the justice of the peace as soon as she said yes. Except she wants a wedding and a dress. All that girlie stuff. If she wants a big wedding, then by God I'm going to give her one."

"I'm just fucking around. Wanted to see what you would say. Better you than me though. Getting married is a big commitment. I can't imagine ever being ready for something like that."

"Never say never," he says. "Look what happened to me. When Kendra came along, it hit me like a fucking tornado. One day I didn't know her and the next I couldn't imagine being without her."

"That's you, not me. I'll always have the club to think about."

"The MC isn't everything, Jesse."

"It's all I've got."

Two hours later, we're still hanging around the parking lot bored to death and waiting. Last call is already over, and most of the bar patrons are piling out unsteadily to head for their bikes.

"What time are you supposed to be picking up Trish at the door?" Flint asks.

"In ten minutes."

"She didn't think it was suspicious that you're not at the bar tonight? What did you tell her you were doing instead?"

"MC business," I reply. "I told her you and I were brokering a deal with another club. She didn't question it. I think she was relieved that I wouldn't be hanging around watching her work. Truth is, I'm not sure how much of that I can tolerate anyway. Flirting with the customers is how she makes her tips. Yet every time a man looks at her tits or ass, I want to punch his face in."

"Yeah, I wouldn't like that either if I was in your position. I hope you realize you're getting off on the wrong foot with her if you have any intentions of taking this further."

"What are you talking about?"

"Lying to her. Stealing her phone."

I cross my arms and glare at him. "Are you fucking kidding me? This dumbass plan was your idea. Remember? Incidentally, it doesn't seem to be working. He's not going to show. Otherwise he would have been here by now."

"Think the Liberators are on to us?"

"No. They're running scared again. We might have missed our best opportunity to take them down."

I spot Trish coming out the front door.

"Let's go. There she is, and brother dearest is nowhere to be seen. Act normal, okay? Don't let her know anything is going on."

"Me act normal? I'm not the one lying about everything."

"You know what I mean. Text Sam and let him know we're heading back to the hotel. The plan is a no go for tonight."

I slip up behind Trish and slide an arm around her waist. "Hey beautiful," I say. "Ready to go?"

She slumps tiredly against me.

"More than ready. What a long night! My feet are killing me. I swear, I don't know if I can take another step. Where is your bike?"

"Not far."

I drop my arm from her shoulder and lean over.

"Hop on my back and I'll carry you piggyback style."

She smiles at my silly suggestion.

"I'm not going to let you carry me, Jesse. Don't be ridiculous. I'm too heavy. If I can stand all night, I can certainly walk a few more feet."

"Come on. You're light enough and I'm strong. It will give me a chance to show you what a manly man I am."

Giggling, she jumps up onto my back. I stagger and I pretend like I'm about to drop her, and she laughs again. I'm glad my attempt to lighten the mood is working. Might as well enjoy what is left of the night.

She grabs me tighter around the neck.

"I missed you," she whispers.

"Music to my ears. Can you show me how much when I get you back to the hotel?"

19

JESSE

The ride back to the hotel seems to take forever. Trish keeps teasing me by sliding her hand down my stomach and over my belt buckle. I finally have to grab her hand and hold it tight in mine to get her to stop.

I know she's playing and doesn't have any idea how incredibly distracting she is being. One small mistake on a bike and we're both going to end up on the pavement. I would never forgive myself if I had an accident with Trish riding with me.

I'm in such a hurry to fuck her that I don't wait for the rest of the crew who are following behind us to catch up. When we get inside the hotel room, I slam the door shut and shove her against it.

"Hang on a minute," she says, pushing against my chest. "I have to take a shower first. There's no way I'm letting you touch me when I smell like smoke and spilled beer."

"You really think I care?" I ask, burying my face in the space between her ear and neck.

"Maybe not, but I do," she says. "Don't you want me smelling nice and clean?" She untangles herself from my arms and quickly slips around me. "I won't be long."

She points to the bed as she walks past it. "Make yourself comfortable while you wait, Mr. Mason."

Hurrying off to the bathroom, she goes inside, shuts the door, and turns on the shower.

Make myself comfortable? I wonder how she thinks that will be possible with a hard-on so thick I need to unzip my jeans. One touch of her body, and all I can think about is sinking deep inside her again and again.

She's like a drug that I can't get enough of. The more I get, the more I crave. Trish is driving me mad, and the worst part is that she doesn't even realize it.

I strip off my shirt and walk to the bathroom door. The shower is still running. Damn! I pace the room back and forth like a caged tiger. How long has she been in there? Three minutes? Surely that's long enough to rinse off. I can't wait any longer. Opening the bathroom door, I step inside and rip back the shower curtain.

"Jesse! What the hell!" she yelps while instinctively trying to cover her breasts.

I reach over and turn off the water.

"Come on. Out you go. You're wasting water. Haven't you ever heard of water conservation?"

I grab a towel to throw on the floor for her to step on and another to wrap around her.

"Who are you? Greenpeace?" she says as she steps out of the shower. "I still have soap on me."

I smile at her confused expression. She can't tell if I'm serious or joking about the water. Leaning forward, I wrap the towel around her and pull her to me. "Got you now," I tease, tugging the towel tighter so she's caught against my body. "No escape for you, naughty water waster."

"I'm going to get you all wet," she protests, spreading her hands against my bare chest. "And soapy."

"A problem soon to be rectified."

I take the edges of the towel and start drying her off. First her shoulders and arms, then I slide the towel lower and gently swab the soap from her lush breasts. A water droplet slides down the rounded globe and hangs on the tip of her nipple. I lean down and lick it off slowly.

God! She's irresistible.

"You need a warning tattoo that says slippery when wet," I tease.

She glances up with a slightly embarrassed look, and I chuckle at her bashfulness.

"Sorry. I didn't mean that as dirty as it sounded." I swallow hard as her large nipples harden right in front of my eyes. "Or on second thought, maybe I did."

I kneel down in front of her, putting my face on the same level as her belly button. Shifting the towel down, I rub her ass dry, then her upper thighs. When I reach her stomach, I drop the towel, unable to resist the temptation any longer. With a loud groan, I bury my face in the waxed mound between her legs.

"Your skin is so warm and smooth," I say, inhaling deeply.

I close my eyes tight and drink in her sweetness until I'm reeling. My brain fogs over as her utter sexiness goes straight to my head. She's like a straight shot of tequila, only a hundred times more potent.

"Damn, you smell so delicious," I say, kissing my way over her hip bone and down her inner thigh. "I know you'll taste even better."

She grabs my shoulders with both hands for support. "Jesse, what are you doing?" she asks unsteadily, her voice so soft it's almost a whisper. Her firm, heavy breasts rise and fall with shaky breaths, the nipples still wet and engorged.

I don't break eye contact with her as I firmly push open her thighs, baring her to my gaze. She moves one foot slightly and willingly opens herself to me, her pussy already glistening.

"You know I will do anything to please you, right?" I say.

She nods and timidly moves her legs wider to give me access. I spread her damp folds apart with my thumbs and slam my tongue deep inside her.

Her dripping wet pussy tastes intoxicating. I close my eyes and bury my tongue deep into her slit, savoring her moistness against my face. The powerful sweet flavor drives me over the edge, getting me so hard and thick that I'm throbbing. Above me, I hear her whimper my name.

I'm torn between wanting to drown my face in her sweet nectar and taking her now against the bathroom wall. When she grabs a fistful of my hair and grinds her pussy into my face, it makes my choice easy.

There's nothing I want more than to drive her wild and make her loose all control. Anything less than hearing her scream my name won't be enough.

"You're melting for me, baby," I murmur, moving my tongue to flick at her clit. Sliding my hands around, I cup her ass cheeks, massaging them beneath my large hands and holding her steady.

"Oh God," she says, breathing hard now.

I lick faster over her clit and look up to see her staring down at me, lips parted and eyes hazy with lust. Her whole body is tight and I know she is almost over the edge. With a hoarse groan, I dig my face deeper into her pussy. I want to feel her cum all over my face.

"Jesse!"

She grips my head tighter and rides my tongue through an endless, powerful release. I forget how to breathe as her orgasm spasms wildly around my nose and tongue, her hot juices spilling into my mouth. Desperately I try to drink it all in like a starving man, her smell, her taste, the sound of her voice calling my name. Never has eating a woman's pussy ever felt so damn amazing. Grasping her ass tightly, I brace her up with my arms so she doesn't collapse on the tile floor.

Shit! I'm in so deep. How the fuck did this happen?

I can't imagine what I could have ever done in my wretched life to deserve Trish being here with me at this moment. All I know is that I'll do anything it takes now to make her stay.

When her breathing slows, I stand up and scoop her up in my arms like a tiny child. Kicking the door wide, I make my way to the bed and place her gently on the edge.

Trish links her arm behind my neck and pulls my lips down to hers for a long kiss. "Now it's your turn," she says, locking her eyes with mine and running her tongue slowly along her moist lips to lick off her own taste.

The erotic gesture hits me like a taser straight to my cock. Damn! She's so fucking sexy. I can't remember ever needing any woman as bad as I want her.

"The question is, why are you still wearing pants?" she asks, grabbing my belt buckle and sliding it loose.

"Good question," I say, whipping the belt loose from the loops and stepping out of my jeans. My long, hard cock springs free and bobs in front of her face.

She smiles up at me with a sensual gleam in her eyes. Leaning down, she cups my balls in one hand and encircles my hardened cock with the other. With her thumb, she rubs the slit then licks off the pre-cum on the bulbous tip.

"Oh Christ!" I mutter, summoning every bit of willpower I have not to grab her head with both hands and shove my cock deep down her throat. I swear to God she's killing me. She has no idea how much effort it is taking me to stay in control.

"Do you want more?" she asks, opening her mouth wide and sliding the entire length of my cock between her lips.

She moves her hands to grip my ass, pulling me as far into her mouth as I can possibly go. Her nose touches my stomach and my cock hits the back of her throat. Black spots float in front of my eyes. I fight like hell to keep from loosing it completely.

She doesn't flinch or gag as she slides my cock all the way out to the tip and takes it again and again. The sight of her lips wrapped around my cock is the hottest thing I've ever seen in my life. I blink back the sweat dripping into my eyes. If I'm not careful, a couple more thrusts and I'll be spurting wads of cum down her throat.

Fuck! I need to take a deep breath and slow this down before it's over way too soon.

"As much as I love the feel of my cock in your sweet mouth, I want to be inside you even more," I tell her, sliding out of her mouth and pushing her down on the bed. "Right now, I want you on top, riding my cock where I can see your beautiful tits and face." I stretch out onto my back and drag her over my chest.

She straddles me with her hands on my chest for balance, her knees resting on either side of me. Reaching up, I pull her long hair forward and down over her breasts, loving how the strands barely brush her nipples. With my knuckles, I stroke the curve of her breasts and catch the nipples lightly between my fingers.

She arches her back and leans into my touch. "You don't need to ask me twice," she says, reaching behind her to stroke my cock.

I grip her waist tightly, fighting against the urge to lift her up with my bare hands and impale her on my bursting cock. She scoots back and rises up on her knees. With one hand, she guides the tip of my cock to her slippery pussy.

My eyes lock on the scene before me. Face to face, Trish on top, her body flushed with heat, poised above my waiting cock. Her nipples are swollen and rigid, begging for my hands.

Should I look or should I touch? I can't decide.

Lifting her hips, she edges herself onto the tip then sinks down inch by inch until I'm halfway buried deep inside her.

I groan as I hear her swift intake of breath.

She slides the rest of the way down until her ass is bumping on my thighs and my entire cock has filled her to the balls. Moisture from her wet pussy drips down and coats my thighs.

My brain is about to explode.

Fuck taking it slow.

God help me, I can't do it.

I meant to let her take the lead and control the speed, but now that I'm inside her, all I can think about is driving in harder and deeper. With my hands on either side of her waist, I lift her up and thrust back into her. She rides me hard and fast, being careful not to slide off the tip.

With a loud cry, she cums all around my cock, her pussy pulsating and clenching me tighter. Her breasts heave as her whole body shakes. I keep my eyes pinned on her face, not wanting to miss anything.

"That's it, baby," I say. "God! How I love watching you cum."

I give up trying to hold back any longer. A man can only take so much and I'm way past my limit. I thrust one last time and explode deep inside her. She leans forward and clenches tightly around me, milking my cock for every last drop. Our eyes meet and I lose myself in her gaze.

When our breathing slows, I slide my hands down her arms to grip her wrists. Bringing her hands to my face, I kiss her palms then interlock my fingers with hers.

"Don't move yet," I say. "I want to hold onto this sight a little bit longer." Leaning forward, I nuzzle the valley between her heavy breasts.

"Was it okay for you?" she whispers, looking unsure of my answer.

I smile at the ridiculous question and lick her nipple. "If it gets any better, you'll have to call an ambulance to haul me off. Why would you ask something crazy like that?"

Her fingers trace the tattoos running down my right arm. "I've never been on top before," she says. "I didn't want you to be disappointed."

Never been on top? How can that be?

"Disappointed in you? Not going to happen."

Curiosity gets the best of me. I have to know.

"Trish, how many men have you been with?"

"You can't ask me that," she says with a horrified look. "It's against the rules."

"I never play by the rules. Answer me."

"Only two," she finally says, not meeting my eyes. "The first time was in the back seat of a car when I was a teenager. The second was my boss at a fast food joint. I thought he loved me. Turned out he was married with three little kids. So as you can see, my sexual experience is basically nonexistent. I'm sorry."

"You're sorry?" I say, wrapping my arms around her back and pressing her breasts against my chest. "I'm sure as hell not. The only thing you should be sorry for is telling me. Now my head is filled with filthy, dirty ideas. All the things I want to do to you and show you."

She nibbles on my ear and my cock twitches inside her, already coming to life again.

"Make a list," she says. "We'll check them off as we go."

"Honey, I'm way ahead of you. I'm already on number ten."

Feeling completely sated and satisfied, I plump up my pillow and slide an arm under Trish's neck. She murmurs in approval then snuggles closer, throwing her arm over my chest. I pick up a lock of her long hair and drop the strands slowly from my fingertips.

So this is what contentment feels like.

Weird.

But I like it.

More than I ever thought possible.

Normally, five minutes after sex is over, I'm rolling out of bed and looking for a cigarette. Not because I need a smoke, but because I'm desperate for any excuse to put as much distance as possible between me and the girl I've just fucked.

Cuddling isn't my thing.

I never saw the point.

Sex is the point.

Once that is over, my mind is already rolling on to the next item on my agenda: club business, new tires for my bike, raiding the refrigerator, and sometimes even another girl.

Wanting to spend a full night with a woman sprawled on top of me is uncharted territory for me. I don't have time for a woman in my life. There's no place for one. Not with me being President of the Steel Infidels.

I have too many responsibilities to bring a girl into the mix. Not only would it be too damn much trouble, it would also be dangerous. The club has to come first.

Somehow Flint makes it work with Kendra. I'm not my brother though. Not even close. Flint has a sensitive side, so he can give Kendra what she needs. It worries me at times because this also makes him vulnerable. By hurting her, someone can get to him. Nobody can hurt us as long as we don't give a shit.

And now I give a shit too.

The thought pops into my head before I can stop it.

Fuck!

This is no good.

What the hell is happening here?

Trish's hand slides down my chest and rests on my stomach.

"Jesse?" she whispers softly. "Are you still awake?"

"Sure, sweetheart," I say, kissing the top of her head. Her hair smells good and I sink my nose into it. "One of the things you'll discover about me is that I don't sleep much. It's a mental defect."

"What do you mean?"

"My mind won't turn off at night. There's always something to worry about. I've learned it's easier to stay up and keep moving than to lie in bed staring at the ceiling all night. Most of the time I'm too wired to sleep."

"What do you worry about?" she asks.

I sigh. Where to even begin?

"My brothers, mostly. It may seem like they've got it all together, but it hasn't always been this way. Our mom died of breast cancer several years ago and it tore the family upside down. Dad didn't handle it well and started drinking too much. I was already with the Steel Infidels at the time and not around the house much. Flint took off and left town not too long after."

"And Sam?"

"Sam didn't fare as well. He was still in high school and too young to move out. So he was stuck with an alcoholic father who was abusive at times. Flint and I didn't know how bad it was. Sam's tough as nails and not a complainer. He just took it and survived the best he could."

"That is so sad," she says softly. "Parents can certainly screw kids up."

"They sure can. I blame myself for what happened. I was too busy with my own life to pay attention to what was going on at home. I knew Sam was furious with Flint for leaving town. I didn't realize at the time that it was because Flint left him to deal with Dad all alone. When one of Dad's punches landed Sam in the emergency room and the truth came out, I brought him into the Steel Infidels with me."

"Wasn't he too young for a motorcycle club?"

"Definitely. The club bent the rules for him because I asked them to. Looking back, there wasn't much of a choice. I needed him close by so I could keep an eye on him."

"Was he in some kind of trouble?"

"Trouble is Sam's middle name. You've met him. He has a wild streak you wouldn't believe. Nothing is too outrageous or crazy for him to try at least once. The club gives him some stability. And responsibility, too. Without the club, we would have lost him already to something... drugs, drunk driving, bar brawls. In my gut, I know Sam wouldn't be here today without the Steel Infidels taking him under their wing."

"You love your brothers." She says it as a statement instead of a question.

"That I do. My brothers and the club are everything to me. I would cut off my right arm to protect them. Flint is getting married soon, believe it or not. To a veterinarian."

"Really?" She rises up on her elbows to look at me. "I didn't think bikers were the settling down type."

"We're usually not," I say honestly. "Flint makes up his own rules as he goes along. His fiancée, Kendra, is a good person. You would like her."

"It sounds like an odd combination...biker lawyer and veterinarian."

I chuckle, thinking about Kendra and Flint. "You should see them together. They're both book smart and clever as hell. Kendra doesn't put up with shit from any of us. I couldn't have picked a more perfect gal for Flint."

"And what about you? What kind of girl would be perfect for you?"

You are.

I don't dare say it. Can't say it.

Instead I throw things back at her.

"Enough talk about me. Tell me about Trish."

If she notices that I abruptly changed the conversation, she doesn't mention it. She puts her head back on my chest and pulls the sheet up over our hips.

"Well for starters, my family sucks," she says.

"I gathered that much."

"When I said that my mother was sick, I wasn't telling you the whole truth. She's an addict and has been for a long time. I took care of her until I couldn't take it anymore. I felt like I was going down with a sinking ship and that nothing I did made any difference. She loves the drugs more than she loves me or herself."

My arms tighten around her. The heartbreaking hurt is coming off of her like waves.

"You don't have to talk about it if you don't want to. It's okay. I didn't mean to make you sad."

"No, you should know why I'm so screwed up," she says in a resigned voice. "Between Mom and Ty, my family life hasn't been what I would call a positive influence in my life."

"And your father?"

"He left us years ago and I haven't seen him since."

"I'm sorry."

I can't stand hearing the pain in her voice. So much hurt inside the sweetest soul. Suddenly I want nothing more than to take her pain away if only for a little while, in the only way I know how.

Physical comfort might be inadequate and certainly not a permanent fix, but it's the only thing I can offer. For the first time in my life, I wish I knew how to give a woman emotionally what they really need from a man. What I have to give her won't be nearly enough.

Taking her hand, I place it over my strong, beating heart.

"Feel that? It means I'm here now and I'm not going anywhere."

Leaning up, I claim her lips in a kiss.

"Don't be sad. Don't think, just feel," I coax. "Feel me and nothing else."

20

JESSE

I leave a note for Trish and slip out to meet up with the rest of the crew in Sam's room. Since the plan to lure Trish's brother didn't pan out, I decide to go ahead with Flint's bachelor party tonight.

We've already spent too much of our time in Panama City worrying about the Liberators. I don't want those assholes to spoil Flint's bachelor party, too.

"Where's Flint?" Sam asks when I step into his room packed with the rest of the crew.

"I sent him out for donuts so we can finalize plans for his party. Someone should watch for him out the window."

"Do you really think it's a good idea to still throw the party?" Rocco asks. "We can do that any old time. We've got more important things to deal with right now."

I'm not surprised he is the one questioning my judgment. Rocco and his brother, Danny, have never been big fans of Flint. They never truly forgave him for leaving the MC and going off to law school. The only reason they voted to let him back in was because I asked them to as a personal favor to me. The brothers tolerate Flint, but that's about the extent of it.

"Roger has already set aside a room and ordered the booze," I explain. "And I've already given him a non-refundable deposit, so I think we should proceed as planned unless we have a good reason not to. Sam and I have also invited several other bikers from friendly clubs. It will be a good chance for us to solidify our relationships with them. The party isn't just about Flint. It's about bringing a group of bikers together to relax, let loose, and to have some fun. That's why we're having it here during the bike rally instead of back home."

A few of the crew cross their arms and give me concerned looks.

"Come on, guys!" Sam says in encouragement. "We need to have some fun while we can. We only have two more nights here in Panama City and then it's time to head back home. Back to the old grindstone. I'm voting for the party."

Rocco looks at him in exasperation. "Damn it, Sam! When are you not voting for a party? What about the Liberators? Shouldn't we be spending our time looking for them instead of getting wasted?"

"I understand your concerns," I say. "I suspect the Liberators have gone into hiding again. Big Roy probably flipped his shit when he realized Ty slipped up and exposed them. Plus, Trish is with us now and she knows where they've been living back at their hometown. The Liberators are not going to just sit around and wait for the Feds to come pick them up. My guess is they're long gone."

Sam jumps back from the window. "Flint's coming," he says. "Hurry up and tell them about the strippers."

"Damn it, Sam!" I throw up my hands. "The strippers were supposed to be a big surprise for everybody. Can you ever keep a secret?"

"Too late now. Tell them."

"Now that big mouth here has spoiled the surprise, I'll go ahead and tell you that Roger will also be providing us with several private strippers for the party."

Tom Brewer slaps his leg and stands up. "Why didn't you say so ten minutes ago? This meeting is over as far as I'm concerned. What time do we need to be in the private room?"

"Ten o'clock, and don't be late. Sam and I will make sure Flint is there. Rocco, are you in?"

Rocco slowly nods. I walk over and grab him by the shoulder. "If any shit goes down tonight, back me up, brother. I need you there with me."

He grasps my arm. "Always, Jesse. No matter what. Club first."

21

TRISH

TRISH

"There's something I need to tell you about tonight," Jesse says.

He is sitting on the bed waiting for me to finish getting ready for work. The troublesome look on his face scares me. I stop fiddling with my hair and give him my full attention.

"What is it? Did you find out something about the Liberators? Is it Ty?"

He grabs my hand and pulls me onto his lap. "Nothing like that," he says. "And I haven't heard anything about the Liberators. It's no big deal really, but something I should warn you about."

Now I'm really worried. I pull back to look at him closely. "So tell me."

"We're throwing Flint a bachelor party tonight at the bar. Roger reserved a private room for us upstairs."

I blink at him, not liking the sound of this.

"What kind of bachelor party? I didn't know Roger rented out private rooms for special events."

Jesse makes a face and tugs my hair playfully. "The regular kind of bachelor party. You know, lots of bikers, booze...and strippers."

I remove his arms from around me and slide off his lap. "Okay."

He looks perplexed. "You're upset. What's wrong?"

"Nothing's wrong," I say, my voice coming out more irritable than I mean for it to. The mental image of naked strippers crawling all over Jesse punches me in the gut.

"Is it the strippers? You realize it's just a guy thing, right? It doesn't mean anything. Whooping and hollering over strippers is what men do at bachelor parties. It won't go any further than that, and I didn't hire any hookers if that is what you're worrying about. Can't have a bachelor party without strippers."

He starts talking fast, which is a dead giveaway that he knows this is making me uneasy.

"Lots of our biker friends will be there, too," he continues. "Guys we haven't seen in a long time. It will be a big get-together more than anything."

"Yeah, it's okay, really. I get it." I manage a tiny smile. "I hope you all have a good time."

In my mind, I'm running through a list of girls from the bar who mentioned they're traveling strippers. Ugh! They're all so pretty, extremely well-endowed, and very touchy feely with the customers.

Do they let the men touch them while they're stripping? I have no idea. My experience with strippers is only what I've seen on television. I've heard they offer private lap dances. What does that even mean? Oh God!

Now I'm freaking out without any right to. Jesse hasn't mentioned one word to me about trying to get together again after this week is over. I know he's going home in two days, and I don't know where the hell I'll be.

Jesse gives me a devilish grin that I can't resist and slips up behind me. "You're actually mad about this, aren't you? You're jealous. And so hot when you're angry." He slides his hands around my waist.

I push against his arms and try to get away. "Oh no, you don't. Let me go. I need to finish getting ready for work. I'm going to be late."

"Not yet," Jesse says. "Maybe when you sound like you really mean it." He leans around to kiss me, and I playfully turn my head from his lips. He merely chuckles and presses the kiss to my neck instead, attaching his mouth to the nape of my neck. Tracing his lips over my sensitive skin, he nibbles wickedly.

He slides his hands under my shirt and reaches up to cup my breasts. "Are you worried I'll do this to one of the strippers?" He pinches my nipples hard, and I close my eyes and lean back into him. "Or this?"

Instinctively, he knows what I want as he rotates the flat of his hand over each enlarged nipple then squeezes the oversized buds.

"Just so you know, I've never seen a stripper with breasts as lovely as yours," he murmurs, tugging my shirt off over my head. "Your breasts are real and soft as a pillow. The first thing that went through my head the night I met you is how much I wanted to do this."

Whirling me around, he kisses his way down my neck then catches one hardened nipple in his mouth and tugs hard with a firm insistent pull.

Damn! That feels good.

"I wanted my mouth here," he says, kissing between my breasts, "and then here," nipping my nipple with his teeth. "All I could think about was ripping your bikini top off right there in the bar and kissing my way all the way down from your neck to your pussy. Hell! What am I saying? It's all I still think about. I'm semi-hard every time I'm near you, and when I touch you something in my head fucking explodes."

Jesse buries his face in my neck, and I feel the wall at my back without even realizing he'd shoved me against it.

"Touch me and you'll realize what you do to me," he says, dragging my hand down his front to rest on the bulge under his belt. "No stripper could make me feel this way. Are you wet for me? Because I'm sure as hell hard for you."

I press my hand against his cock through his jeans. "Why don't you find out for yourself?" I say in invitation.

With a pleased grunt, he props me up against the wall and quickly bunches my skirt up above my waist.

"No panties?" he asks in surprise, cupping my ass cheeks with each hand.

"I wasn't finished getting dressed."

"Lucky for me."

He slides his hand between my thighs. "You're drenched," he says, parting my pussy lips and pushing two fingers deep inside me. "Hot and juicy. I love it when you're wet. It tells me how badly you want this too, even if you're too shy to say the words."

He strokes in and out with his fingers, trying to drive me mad, then bites down roughly on my nipple again. Smart man. He knows I love it. My nipples are so hard and swollen they're aching in agony. I squeeze my eyes tight and arch my back.

My body craves him like it's my next breath. Every part of me aches for Jesse in this moment.

I want him. Desperately. Now.

Tugging at his belt buckle, I quickly pull the belt loose and unzip his jeans. I slide my hand inside in one smooth move and encircle the solid hardness. A shudder slams through him, and the hitch in his breathing tells me he's as turned on as I am. I stroke him slowly from his tip all the way down to his balls...once, twice.

His breathing quickens and he grabs my hand to stop me. "You had better not start something you can't finish, little lady," he warns in a voice suddenly thick with lust.

"Oh, this lady has every intention of finishing it," I say, leaning close and whispering into his mouth. "As long as you fuck me now. Hard and fast. Like I know you want to."

"Fuck you?" he growls. "I'll fucking own you."

In one powerful move, he picks me up and throws me so hard on the bed that I bounce.

"How hard and fast do you want it?" he says, quickly tugging my skirt down over my knees and ankles.

Wow! What kind of an animal did I just unleash?

"The best you got," I throw back at him.

He strips out of his jeans and tosses them on the floor along with my skirt. Flipping me over on my stomach, he pulls me back so that I'm positioned on my knees. With his hands, he parts my ass and places the tip of his cock at my pussy lips. For a split second he hesitates, and I realize he's waiting for a signal from me.

"Do it," I urge. "Don't you dare hold back, Jesse."

"Fuck!" he mutters loudly.

All it takes is one high-powered motion and he is buried to the hilt inside me. We both breathe out harshly at the jarring contact. Jesse's hands are heavy on my hips, gripping me so tightly that I can feel the imprints of his fingers.

He lunges in with deep, long thrusts, stretching out each moment as long as he can. I grip the pillow tightly in my hands. This is exactly what

I want. To feel the raw masculine power in those strong, tattooed muscles that Jesse has been holding back from me.

"Is this what you want?" he asks, his voice hoarse with unfiltered lust.

"Yes!" I cry, surrendering completely to his total dominance and possession. My breasts swing and jiggle as he slams into me harder with each pump. The headboard bangs against the wall.

His movements grow more driven and animalistic. The harder he rams into me, the more I love it. I close my eyes and lose myself in the bliss that is Jesse.

I'm so close.

Now I know what pure ownage feels like.

Suddenly he pulls out and twists me over. "I want to see your face when you cum," he says.

He slides his cock back in and pulls my legs up to wrap them around his shoulders. Sweat is rolling down his face. "I'm going in deep this time, baby," he warns before plunging into me further than I ever imagined.

I love the way every muscle in his arms and shoulders flex and the heat of his hot skin pressing up hard against mine. Three thrusts in this position and I'm over the edge. I barely hear his sharp intake of breath as my orgasm contracts and pulses tightly around his cock. When I stop shuddering he begins to move again, his thrusts growing more erratic.

"I can't hold out," he groans, holding my head tightly between his hands and capturing my mouth in a deep kiss as he cums inside me.

His body shudders and finally stills. He gasps for breath and nuzzles his face in the curve of my neck. When his breathing slows, he tightens his grip on me, holding me so close I can barely breathe.

Something is changing with him. I can feel it deep down in my soul.

"You're unraveling me," he says simply, and I know exactly what he means.

22

JESSE

It's after midnight, and Flint's bachelor party is in full swing. With a room full of bikers, booze, and babes, what more could Flint ask for in a party?

The upstairs private room at the bar is packed with all of the members of the Steel Infidels, along with several of our friends from other motorcycle clubs. As promised, Roger delivered the beer kegs and strippers right on time.

Like most bachelor parties, the goal is for everyone to drown themselves in alcohol. While a few guys might get lucky enough to grab some pussy, most are here to drink and look more than touch.

I can't help but smile when I think about Trish's reaction to the party. Without saying one word, she made it perfectly clear she wasn't thrilled about the strippers. Hopefully I convinced her it is all in good fun and nothing else.

With a woman as satisfying as Trish in my bed, I sure as hell won't be looking elsewhere for a quick, dirty fuck. Especially after the red-hot sex this afternoon. My mind and body are still reeling. The more I taste of her, the more I want.

I walk over to speak with Rocco and Tom Brewer, the two oldest members of the Steel Infidels. "Thanks for coming," I say to them. "It means a lot that you are here."

"Sorry about giving you a hard time about the party," Rocco says, looking slightly embarrassed. "This whole thing with the Liberators has me spooked. That's all. You know I wouldn't miss it. Flint looks like he's having fun."

He points his beer toward a straight chair set up in the middle of the room.

I turn around to look and then laugh. "To be honest, I'm not sure."

Flint is sitting in a chair while a group of strippers take turns giving him intimate lap dances. At first he put up resistance to the idea, but after enduring a great deal of teasing from the men and securing promises of no cell phone photos, he finally agreed to take the place of honor.

Now it looks like he might be regretting it. Big time.

A topless stripper with purple-streaked hair has his head squeezed between her oversized DD breasts. From the panicked look in his eyes, I can't tell if he's turned on and enjoying it or if he's about to suffocate from the intense motor-boating.

Sam is standing a few feet away from the action laughing his ass off. It's obvious who is having the most fun tonight. No surprise there.

If nothing else, at least Flint knows his brothers care enough to throw him a party. I wonder if I should go rescue him. When he reaches up with the back of his hand to wipe the sweat dripping off of his forehead, I walk over and hand him a plastic cup of draft beer.

He chug-a-lugs the entire contents of the cup and hands it back. "Thanks. I needed that," he says. "Jesus Christ, Jesse! How many fucking strippers are in this room? I don't know how much more I can take. The last one tried to put her nipple in my mouth!" He wipes his lips with his hand. "Got any mouthwash on you? That was downright nasty, and not in a good way."

The next stripper in line, a petite blonde in only a G-string that covers absolutely nothing, interrupts our conversation by putting her hands on his shoulders and grinding on his groin.

Flint cuts his eyes at me. "You got to help me out here, man."

I touch the blonde's arm and motion for her to move on. "Okay, ladies," I say to the remaining girls. "Let's give the man of the hour a little break before he has a heart attack. I'm sure the other men would love a show, so spread your love out around the room."

The blonde looks slightly disappointed, then her face lights up when she sees Sam beckoning her over.

Flint stands up and scoots the chair out of the way. He takes a deep breath and blows it out. "Whew! That was something," he says, wiping off his lips again with the corner of his shirt.

"That bad, huh?" I ask, unable to hide a smile.

"More like overwhelming," he answers. "I'm not complaining though. I appreciate the bachelor party. Thank you. I know you put all of this together and it means a lot. Seriously."

"I couldn't let my brother get hitched without a party." I squeeze his shoulder. "By the way, you have red lipstick on your shirt."

He looks down at the stain left behind on the white fabric. "Damn! Now I'll have to toss this shirt before I go home. Kendra is going to fucking kill me. The last thing she said to me the morning I left was 'look at the girls all you want, but don't touch, Flint.'"

"Technically, they touched you. Not the other way around. So you're square."

"Oh yeah, like Kendra is going to appreciate the tiny distinction there."

"Don't worry about it," I say. "She'll never know. Come on. Let's go catch up with some of our friends."

We almost make it across the room before we hear screams coming from the bar downstairs.

"What the fuck is that?" Flint turns to me to say.

"We'd better go find out," I reply, already on my way out the door.

Taking the stairs two at a time, we rush down to the lower level. The bar customers are pushing in a wave of panic toward the back of the bar while trying to get away from flickering flames near the front windows and door. A tablecloth catches on fire, spreading the flames further into the room.

"What the hell?" Flint yells.

While we're standing there trying to figure out what is going on, the front window of the bar shatters in a loud explosion of glass as a bottle comes hurtling through.

"Molotov cocktails!" I yell to Flint. "Go upstairs and get everybody in the party out the back. Someone is trying to set the place on fire."

Flint takes off back upstairs and I frantically search the bar for Trish.

She's standing behind her beer cooler, frozen to the spot in confusion and fear. Pushing my way against the crowd of people moving toward me, I finally reach her side and grab her hand.

"Come on! You need to get out of here now! Where's the back exit?"

She points to a hallway behind the bar and I start dragging her that way. A series of loud pops in quick succession rattle the building. I can't tell if it is explosions or gunfire. I look toward the front of the bar and see two security guards with guns raised firing through the blown-out windows into the parking lot.

"Shit! Where the hell did Roger get those bouncers from? ISIS?"

Another security guard runs toward the flames with a fire extinguisher spewing out foam. Trish looks over her shoulder while I keep tugging her toward the back door.

I need to get her out of the building before the rest of the crowd realizes this is the only way out. A fire in a bar full of drunk bikers with one small door isn't a good combination. Trish might be crushed in a stampede.

I throw open the back door and push her out in front of me. "Stay here where you'll be safe. Don't go back in."

Trish grabs my sleeve. "Where are you going?"

"Around to the front of the building. I know who did this."

Before she has a chance to argue, I dash around the corner of the building and head to the front parking lot. The bouncers are outside the building now with their guns pointed at a man lying on the edge of the pavement. His bike is on the ground beside him.

"Oh shit!"

I know him.

23

TRISH

"Jesse! Wait!"

Where the hell does he think he's going? Didn't we just hear gunshots?

If he thinks I'm going to patiently wait here while he goes off and gets himself shot, he had better think again. I hurry after him as fast as I can in my high heels. He's standing at the far end of the building, and it takes me a minute to catch up.

"What's going on?" I ask when I reach him, out of breath. "What's happening?"

"Trish, no. Don't look," he says in an anguished voice, turning and stepping in front of me to block my view.

Too late.

"Ty!"

I tear loose from Jesse's grip and take off running across the parking lot.

"Trish, stop!" Jesse yells from behind me.

I don't stop running until I reach my brother's body sprawled out on the pavement. His eyes are closed and blood is gushing from a gunshot wound in his stomach. The bright red liquid is dripping steadily and pooling into a big puddle onto the ground.

"Ty!" I cry. "Are you okay? Can you hear me? Ty!"

I tug his shirt loose from his pants and pull it up so I can see how bad he is hurt. I gasp when I see his abdomen. So much blood everywhere, and it isn't slowing down.

I place my hands against the wound in a pitiful attempt to stop the bleeding. Immediately, the blood seeps between my fingers and soaks my hands.

"Help!" I scream, looking around in a panic, hoping someone is coming to his aid. The bouncers are still standing there with their guns pointed at us. "Call 911! Why did you shoot him?"

"I'm here," Jesse says, kneeling down beside me.

He quickly dials 911 and tells them to send an ambulance to the Silver Shark Saloon for a gunshot victim before clicking the phone shut.

"He's bleeding so much," I say, my voice catching on a sob. "He's still alive, right? Right? Please tell me he isn't dead! Why did they shoot him? I don't understand."

"Yeah, he's breathing," Jesse assures. "It's shallow, but he's definitely breathing. We need to try to slow down this bleeding until the ambulances get here."

He pulls a rag out of his pocket and nudges my hands away so he can press it against the wound. Red blood instantly soaks through the white rag.

"Damn!" Jesse swears.

He leans over Ty's body to put more pressure on it.

"Please don't let him die, Jesse. Please."

He doesn't look up at me.

"I'll try my best," he says.

I sit down on the pavement and cradle my brother's head in my lap like a little child.

"Hang in there, Ty. You're strong. You can beat this."

Tears flow down my cheeks. I sniffle and try to wipe them away with the back of my hand. In the distance, the wail of sirens lets me know the ambulance is on the way.

"Thank God," Jesse says without glancing up.

In a matter of minutes, an ambulance and fire truck pulls into the parking lot with lights flashing and sirens screaming. I jump up and wave my arms.

"Over here!" I yell. "This way!"

A team of paramedics rush toward us and instruct Jesse to move aside so they can do their job. He quickly stands up and engulfs me in a big hug. His chest is warm and his shirt is now wet from my tears that I can't seem to stop. He rests his chin on the top of my head.

"He's going to be okay," he says, rubbing my back. "I've seen guys live through worse."

"Really?" I ask, knowing he's probably only saying that to make me feel better.

"Sure. He'll be okay."

A male paramedic places an oxygen mask over Ty's face. "What happened here?" he asks.

"I'm not exactly sure," Jesse answers. "Someone threw Molotov cocktails through the front glass windows. A fire started inside the bar and everyone panicked. Shots rang out in the parking lot. That's all I know."

The paramedics give each other a knowing look. "Fool bikers," one of them mutters under his breath.

"Will he be okay?" I ask. "He's lost so much blood."

"He's alive, and that's a start."

The paramedics carefully load Ty onto a stretcher and carry him to the ambulance with me following close behind. They lift him up gently and start to shut the doors.

"I'm going with him," I say, hopping up into the ambulance without waiting for an invitation. "I'm his sister, and he needs me."

Jesse starts to climb in behind me.

The paramedic stops him. "Sorry, only family can ride in the ambulance."

Jesse backs away. "Where are you headed?" he asks.

"St. Mary's Hospital."

"I'll meet you there," Jesse yells to me as the paramedic slams the doors shut and flips on the sirens again.

"Can I get you a cup of coffee?" Jesse asks. "Or something to eat? It's going to be a few more hours before Ty is out of surgery, and you can't go that long without eating. I'm worried about how you're holding up."

I shake my head, feeling numb. There's no way I can think about food right now. Not with Ty on an operating table, fighting for his life.

"I'm not hungry," I say.

I scoot closer to Jesse and put my head on his shoulder. Luckily, the hospital's waiting room is almost empty and we were able to grab a small sofa to sit on instead of the hard metal chairs.

"Rest your eyes," he says, reaching an arm around me and tucking me into his shoulder. "You must be tired. I'll let you know if the doctor walks in or if there's any news."

"I won't be able to sleep. I keep thinking, what if Ty doesn't make it? I can't believe this is happening. This is all my fault."

"No, it's not," Jesse says adamantly. "Why do you think that?"

"If I hadn't created such a mess by walking out on Big Roy, then Ty wouldn't have had any reason to come to the bar looking for me. He was probably there to try to talk me into coming back with the Liberators. I can't think of any other reason why he would show up. He's on an operating table with a big hole in his gut because of me."

Jesse sighs and stretches out his long legs in front of him.

"Trish, you can't blame yourself. It's crazy to think that way. Who do you think threw the Molotov cocktails through the windows and started the fire? The Liberators, that's who. It's their calling card. They did the same thing to our tattoo shop about six months ago."

"What are you saying?"

"We shouldn't be discussing this right now. It isn't the place or the time. You have enough on your mind as it is."

I sit up straighter and turn to look at him.

"No, I want to know. What did you mean their calling card?"

"The Liberators knew we were all inside the bar for Flint's party. Sam has been running his mouth off about it to different biker clubs all week. Maybe he said something to someone he shouldn't. Or the word could have just gotten out. Bikers like to talk among themselves as much as gossipy old women sometimes."

"Are you saying the Liberators were going after the Steel Infidels tonight?"

"Not so much going after us. More like letting us know the feud between the clubs is back on full force again. Not that we ever thought it wasn't. It was a signal that they could get to us whenever they wanted. And as a more personal threat, that they could get to you as well. That's why they hit the bar and not our hotel. Big Roy and the Liberators like to make big, showy statements. It was an added bonus to them that all of the other biker clubs were in the bar, too. Think of it as the Liberators hanging up a 'now open for business' sign for everyone to see."

I rub my forehead where a headache is starting to form.

"Ty wouldn't do something like that. Not if he knew I was inside the bar. Or even if I wasn't. What if the fire had spread? People could have been trapped inside. Me, too. Thank God the security guards knew where the fire extinguishers were and how to use them quickly. It scares me to think how badly it could have turned out."

Jesse doesn't argue with me. He clearly believes Ty is involved. Well, I'm his sister and I know better. My brother has his faults. That doesn't mean he would be willing to kill people or set a building on fire.

"Do you mind if I go down the hall to grab some coffee out of the machine?" Jesse asks. "I'll bring one back for you too. You don't have to drink it if you don't want it."

"Thanks. A hot chocolate would be good."

Not really, but I know Jesse needs to walk around for a minute and stretch his muscles. We've been sitting here waiting a long time, and he hasn't left my side.

While he's gone, I open the bag of Ty's belongings the nurse handed me before they took him into surgery. I check the pockets of his leather jacket and pull out his cell phone. When my hands hits something cold and metallic in the other pocket, I slide my hand back out carefully. It feels like a gun and I don't want to touch it.

I flip open Ty's cell phone. He would be furious if he knew I was prowling through his stuff. I idly scan through his text messages. There aren't too many of them, mostly back and forth with me. The Liberators aren't big on technology.

I start to close his phone when I notice the date of my last text message to him. Yesterday's date. That's weird. That would have been after we had the big fight at the bar and after I lost my phone. How can that be?

I open the message to read it.

"I'm sorry. Meet me tonight after work?" it says.

I don't understand. Why would there be a fake message from me to Ty asking to meet him after work? Who could possibly have something to gain by pretending to be me?

I check the time on the message. Not more than five minutes after Jesse dropped me off at work yesterday.

It was Jesse.

It had to be him. Nothing else makes any sense.

He must have swiped my phone during our ride along the coast. I think back to when he would have had a chance to do it. Since I noticed the phone was missing in the restaurant, he would have taken it before.

I remember his impulsive gift and the spontaneous hug at the art festival in Seaside when he bought the earrings for me. How easy it must have been to slip a hand inside my purse and pull out my phone without me noticing.

Blood rushes to my face and I want to throw up.

Everything is a big lie.

Every word Jesse said to me, every sweet whisper in my ear, every soft caress on my hair. All lies of one form or the other.

He's been playing me the entire time. He is still playing me even now. Acting all concerned about my welfare, and about my brother, who I know for a fact he hates.

I wonder if he knew who I was the first time he walked up to me at the bar and ordered a beer.

Who am I kidding? Of course he did.

Why else would he have stepped in with Ty to take up for me? It was all part of some big Steel Infidels vs. Liberators revenge plan. Everything else was probably just icing on the cake to him. A big game. No wonder he never mentioned a relationship beyond this week.

God! I feel so stupid and naïve. And most of all used.

The things we did together and the intimate sexual moments we shared. Thinking about it now makes me want to crawl away into a hole and hide. And to think I really cared about him and desperately wanted something more. I knew better than to get my hopes up, and I did it anyway.

"Here's your hot chocolate," Jesse says suddenly, settling back down beside me on the sofa.

I'm so upset that I didn't even notice when he walked back into the waiting room. I take the cup from him without speaking.

"Any news?" he asks. "You look upset. I'm sorry it took so long. The damn machine kept spitting back out my dollar bills."

"Can I have my cell phone back now?"

He glances over at me sharply, and I can tell from the surprised look on his face that he knows he is caught. His gaze drops to Ty's cell phone in my hand. I hold up the phone for him to read the message he sent to Ty while pretending to be me.

"Trish..." he begins before I hold up my hand to interrupt him.

"I don't want to hear whatever lie it is you're getting ready to tell me right now," I say. "All I want is for you to give me my cell phone back and for you to get the hell out of my sight."

"Fuck!" He runs a hand through his black hair. "Trish, let me explain."

"What can you possibly say that will make me feel better? Let's lay out the facts here."

I hold up my fingers to count off his bad deeds.

"You lied to me, you stole my phone, you set up my brother, and the end result is that you almost got him killed. And if that's not bad enough, you let me think it was all my fault."

"No, I didn't! I told you it wasn't your fault."

"Yeah, but you sure as hell didn't say it was yours. I realized after reading the text message that you purposely lured Ty to the bar. He went there thinking he was supposed to meet me. You made him believe that I needed him. And he showed up. And as a result, he got shot. How am I supposed to forgive that, Jesse? You tell me."

He leans back and rubs his tired eyes.

"You're right, okay. Yes, I stole your phone and I lied to you. I'm sorry. And I sent him a text asking him to meet you. Only so we could put a tail on him back to Big Roy and the rest of the Liberators. This was always about more than your brother. I never meant for you to get hurt."

He reaches into his back pocket and pulls out my cell phone. Without saying a word, he hands it back to me. I take the phone and drop it into my purse.

"So you admit it then?"

"I'll admit what I did, and that's all I'm admitting to. If you'll read the text again, the meet up was supposed to be for last night, not tonight. Ty didn't come to the bar to see you. Not unless he normally runs a full twenty-four hours late. The only reason he was there tonight was to create mayhem with the Liberators."

Jesse is still lying to me. I shake my head in disbelief.

"Why do you think the security guards shot him?" he says. "Because he was the one who threw the damn Molotov cocktails through the window! Your brother doesn't give a shit about you and the sooner you realize that, the better off you will be."

"I would like you to leave now."

"Damn it, Trish! You're not giving me a chance here. When it comes to your brother, you are so fucking blind. Why is that? Help me understand. I can't get through to you, and it's driving me insane. You're throwing everything away for nothing. He's not worth it."

"If you don't stand up and walk out that door right now, I'm calling security."

He gives me a shocked look.

"And say what?"

"That you're threatening me. Don't think for one second that I won't do it."

He reaches for my hand and I jerk it out of his reach.

"This isn't over," he says quietly.

"You're right. It isn't over, because nothing real ever started in the first place. Now please, just go!"

I bury my face in Ty's leather jacket and will myself not to cry.

"I'll drop your stuff off at the bar unless you want me to bring it here," he says.

"I don't."

"Fuck!" Jesse swears one last time before standing up and walking out of the hospital.

I don't look up because I can't bear to watch him walk out of my life for good.

24

JESSE

Two weeks later back in Georgia...

I pull up to Flint and Kendra's driveway and cut the engine. Every time I visit their home sitting high on top of a steep mountain, my mind flashes back to the days we used it as a safe house.

Now they're planning to hold their wedding here in the very same spot. A chance to make better memories, they said. I'm all for it because this family could sure use some good memories. We've had enough fucking bad ones to last a lifetime.

Flint walks out the front door and motions for me to sit down in one of the rocking chairs on the front porch.

"Have you heard anything from Trish?" he asks when I take a seat.

"No, and I don't think I'm going to," I reply. "She hasn't responded to a single one of my voice mails or texts. I doubt she'll ever forgive me. I'm sure by this time her brother has poisoned any feelings she might have had for me anyway."

"That's too bad," Flint says. "I thought there might be a real chance for you two. I know you cared about her."

I shake my head. "There was never a chance for us. Not really. All just wishful thinking on my part. It's probably for the best. She's too sweet to be tangled up in my shit."

"Hate to hear it. Anyway, I called my contact at the Panama City police department today. I thought I might have a better chance of finding out what is going on from them than the Feds."

I raise my eyebrows. "What did they say?"

"Ty still refuses to take the deal being offered to him. He isn't willing to turn on Big Roy, even if it means a lesser prison sentence for himself. They're going to pay him a visit one more time at the hospital and then they're taking the deal off the table. Either way, as soon as he gets out of the hospital, he's going into police custody. From what I hear, they have one of his hands handcuffed to the hospital bed now. "

I prop my boots up on the wooden banister.

"I'm not sure how I feel about that. While I would love to see one of Big Roy's own men turn on him, I don't like the thought of Ty being back in Trish's life someday either. I can't imagine what she's going through, knowing he's headed off to jail. She must be freaking out."

"How on earth did she not realize all the illegal activities her brother was involved in?" Flint asks.

I shrug. "Hell if I know. She has a blind side where her brother is concerned. That's my only explanation. She knew the Liberators and Big Roy were on the run from the Feds. Somehow she convinced herself that even though Ty was VP of the Liberators, he wasn't involved in anything bad. According to Trish, everything is Big Roy's fault and Ty shits rainbows. It still makes me see red every time I think about Ty trying to set the bar on fire with Trish inside."

"Me too," Flint says. "What kind of a brother does something like that? Do you think Trish realizes he did it even now?"

"I doubt it. Roger told me she's staying with Ty at the hospital. I'm just thankful Roger agreed to let her keep her job. I cashed in a bunch of favors with him for that. The only thing I can't figure out is how Ty ended up being the one who got shot. It's almost as if the other Liberators intentionally left him behind."

"Knowing how Big Roy operates, it might have been part of his plan," he says. "He couldn't have been happy about Ty outing the club to you. Maybe he set him up. Between arson and all the other charges the Feds already have on him, Ty might be going away for a long time."

"I sure hope so. He is one evil son-of-a-bitch. The sooner Trish gets away from him, the better off she'll be."

The screen door slams behind us on the porch.

"Too bad about Flint's little bachelor party being cut short," Kendra says sarcastically as she comes out the door with a glass of sweet tea.

She hands it to me and puts her hand on her hip.

"What?" she says at my surprised expression. "I bet you thought Flint wouldn't tell me about that, didn't you? You are in big trouble with me now, Jesse. Big trouble with a capital T. Strippers, for heaven's sake! I swear, sometimes you're every bit as bad as Sam, and we all know he is beyond help."

I glare at Flint over her shoulder, and he gives me a 'don't blame me, I have to live with her' look.

"Kendra, I swear to you that Flint didn't do anything disrespectful," I say, hoping she isn't mad enough to call off the wedding. "Nothing at all. He acted like a true gentleman the entire trip to Panama City. Scout's honor. And he didn't even like the strippers. He said they were disgusting and..."

"Ugly," Flint interrupts. "Disgusting and ugly strippers. The worst you could ever imagine. They were at least sixty with baggy tits hanging down to their knees." He demonstrates with his hands how low their tits were hanging.

"That's right," I say. "We couldn't afford the younger ones so we had to go with the budget strippers."

Kendra rolls her eyes. "You two are ridiculous," she says. "Besides, why would Flint need naked strippers dancing around when he can have all this?" She waves a hand down her curvy body then bursts out giggling.

"I'm messing with you, Jesse," she says, playfully slapping me on the back. "I know you boys just wanted to have some fun. We can use more of that around here. And when were you ever a Boy Scout anyway?"

She whirls around to wag a finger at Flint. "And you are the worst liar ever. How you ever made it as a lawyer, I don't know. Sixty-year-old strippers, my ass." She points to a motorcycle roaring up the road. "Here comes your brother now. I'll go set the table for dinner."

She opens the screen door, then stops and turns around. "Oh, Jesse, I forgot to mention one last thing."

"What's that?" I ask.

"Next year I'm going with you boys to the bike rally. So plan accordingly."

She laughs as the door slams shut behind her.

Flint looks at me and shrugs. "I had to tell her."

I just shake my head.

"Kendra, you outdid yourself on the pecan pie," Sam says, sliding the pie plate over and helping himself to a third slice.

She beams back at him from across the table.

"Compliments won't get you anywhere, Sam. Except maybe your own pie. I made an extra one for you and Jesse to take back to your house."

"Yes!" Sam says, pumping his fist in the air. "We're hurting for home cooking down at the bachelor pad. Why don't you two come live with us after you get married?"

"Oh no," she says. "I'm not taking care of all three of you brothers. One Mason brother is enough, believe me. I have my hands full trying to keep Flint straight."

"So what's the big announcement you called us up here for?" I ask. "The wedding is next weekend, so I hope you haven't decided to cancel it. There will be some very disappointed people if you do. Even the crew is looking forward to being there."

Kendra glances over at Flint and raises her eyebrows. He slides his chair back from the table and stands up to place his hands on her shoulders.

"Don't you boys think Kendra looks beautiful these days?" he asks.

"Kendra always looks pretty," Sam mumbles with a mouthful of pie without looking up.

"I mean unusually radiant," Flint coaxes. "Take a look at her. Don't tell me you can't see the glow on her face."

I start grinning. Sam hasn't caught on yet.

Kendra bangs her spoon on the table. "Sam, are you even paying attention or are you just dense?" she says in exasperation. "I'm pregnant! That's what we're trying to tell you. We're going to have a baby."

Sam stops chewing and puts down his fork. "You're pregnant? I'm going to be an uncle? For real?"

Kendra laughs. "That's right, so you had better start cleaning up your lover boy act. The baby doesn't need any bad influences growing up."

I reach across the table to shake Flint's hand. "Congratulations, brother," I say, gripping his hand firmly. "You're going to make a terrific father."

I walk around the table and lean down to kiss Kendra on the cheek. "How far along are you, little Mama?"

"Not quite three months," she says. "Since I'm normally a little chunky around the middle, nobody has even noticed." She pats her stomach for emphasis.

"You look great," I say. "I can't believe there's going to be a baby in the family. This is terrific news. Maybe there's hope for me and Sam after all."

Kendra squeezes my arm and grows serious for a moment. "There's hope, Jesse. You just have to believe in it. Your problem is, you don't think you deserve love. That's the only thing standing in your way."

"I believe this calls for a celebration," Sam suggests. "First, a wedding coming up, and then our own little baby Steel Infidel. Flint, where do you keep the whiskey?"

25

JESSE

"Are you sure you're ready for this?" I whisper to my brother, Flint.

The taped music begins to play and he nods.

"Let's do it then," I say.

He starts walking down the aisle, lined by white chairs with blue bows, with me close behind him.

We reach the end and turn around to face the group gathered for Flint and Kendra's wedding. All members of the Steel Infidels are here, along with most of our families and friends.

The music stops and all eyes turn to Kendra standing at the end of the aisle. A big smile lights up Flint's face when he sees her. As the music plays, she slowly makes her way between the rows of guests. She reaches out to squeeze her mother's hand, who is sitting on the front row.

When she stops walking, her father leans down to kiss her cheek and places her hand in Flint's. Kendra takes a deep breath then lets out a nervous laugh.

The wedding officiant, chosen primarily for his love of motorcycles, begins the ceremony by welcoming the guests and reminding us all why we are here. He was asked to prepare a few words for the wedding, and I suspect they're going to be on the corny side.

"When you say I love you, what you are saying is, 'hold on tight, the ride is long,'" he begins in a deep, solemn voice.

I resist the urge to smile. Damn! Guess I was right.

After quoting a few more lines combining an odd mixture of motorcycles and weddings, he holds out his hand to me for the rings. I reach into my pocket and pull out two plain gold wedding bands and pass them to him.

A look of relief crosses Flint's face. Did he really think I would forget to bring the rings? I'm disappointed. He should have more faith in me.

No way was I fucking this up.

Unlike me, Flint is one of the solid good guys. A tough guy on the outside covering up a big old heart of gold. After everything he has been through the past few months, he deserves a happy ending.

There's nothing I won't do to make sure that happens.

The officiant takes the rings and places one each in Flint and Kendra's hands. He turns to the bride, who looks absolutely beautiful in her white wedding dress. In keeping with Kendra's down-to-earth personality, she chose a simple dress with a single strand of pearls. No fancy frills or layers of lace for her.

Flint would have preferred a traditional biker wedding with a motorcycle procession, leather jackets, and a bottomless beer keg. Kendra shot down that idea in a hurry.

So here we all are, standing in their decorated backyard located high on a mountain, dressed in uncomfortable clothes and sweating like pigs.

Kendra told me she was worried about looking fat on her big day. She shouldn't have. The baby bump is barely visible. She sniffles and then laughs, wiping away a tear threatening to spill down her cheek and ruin her makeup.

I don't remember ever seeing her look so happy. From the corner of my eye, I catch Flint starting to get choked up by emotion, too. I grab his shoulder in a sign of brotherly support.

Come on buddy, you can do this.

Standing on my other side is our younger brother, Sam. He is grinning from ear to ear and rocking back and forth on the balls of his feet. Last night, I reminded him not to lock his knees and pass out like a dumbass during the ceremony. Now I realize I should have also explained that it wasn't okay for him to bounce around like a jumping bean either.

What the fuck is he grinning about anyway?

I hope to God he isn't about to do something stupid. I wouldn't put it past Sam to pull one of his pranks right in the middle of the wedding. For once, I hope he has enough sense to behave himself. I shoot him a stern look just in case he has something on his mind.

"Be still," I whisper out of the side of my mouth.

He nods and stops moving.

The officiant glares at me and continues with the ceremony.

"Kendra, do you take this man to have and to hold, to lean with him when he leans and ride when he rides?" he asks.

Kendra gazes up into Flint's face and smiles. "I do."

"Flint, do you take this woman to share the open road, to protect and to ride with today and for eternity?"

"Hell yes!" Flint says without hesitation. The audience, consisting mostly of bikers, erupts in a cheer. "I mean, I do," he quickly adds. "I do."

"Please join hands." The officiant beams at the smiling couple. "By the power vested in me by the State of Georgia, I now pronounce you husband and wife! Flint, you may kiss your bride."

The crowd breaks out in applause.

Flint takes a step forward and pulls Kendra toward him for a kiss.

A shot rings out.

Then another.

For a split second, I freeze. My mind is telling me that a gun has accidentally misfired. Maybe some idiot forgot to put on the safety.

My gut tells me I'm dead wrong.

A big splotch of red appears on Kendra's wedding gown and begins spreading. The color both horrifies and mesmerizes me at the same time.

More shots ring out. Flint knocks Kendra to the ground and covers her with his body. A music speaker near the front row explodes.

All hell breaks loose.

We're all here. Ripe for the picking.

Every member of the Steel Infidels MC, Kendra's family, our family, close friends, and even some members of other friendly biker clubs.

As President of the Steel Infidels, this is my fault. All blame is on me. I never should have allowed this to happen. Gathering us together in a big group provides the perfect opportunity for someone with a grudge to strike against us.

I should have stood firm and not given my approval for a big wedding. Especially after everything that went down at the bike rally in Panama City.

Happy endings aren't meant for us. Shouldn't I know that by now?

Movement at the edge of the driveway catches my eye and I spot him.

The red-headed motherfucker I've spent months trying to find.

Big Roy, President of the Liberators.

My sworn enemy, the only person in this world that I want to kill with my bare hands.

I take off after him with Sam right behind me. By the time I reach my motorcycle, the handgun I normally keep tucked in the back of my pants is already in my hand.

The fight with the Liberators is ending today.

One way or the other.

I wonder how long Big Roy and his crew have been sitting in the woods above the house patiently waiting for the wedding to begin. Probably hours. With all the preparations going on, nobody would have noticed the noise from a few extra motorcycles coming up the mountain. I suspect they hid the bikes on the side of the road and hiked through the woods to find a good sniper spot. When I hear motorcycle engines starting up a little ways down the road, I know I'm right.

"They're on their bikes," I yell to Sam. "We can catch them. They don't know the road."

I roar out of the driveway with Sam on my tail. There are several bad curves on the mountain road, some of which have steep cliffs dropping off on the side.

While it might not be possible to pull close enough to the Liberators to get off a good shot, I know I can force them into taking the curves faster than they should.

In the past few months, I've come up that gravel mountain road often to visit Flint. There have been plenty of times that I've almost spun out myself, so I know exactly how fast to go and still be able to keep the bike on the road.

I motion for Sam to stay behind me. He better not get any ideas to hot shot ahead. There's enough blame on my shoulders today without something happening to him, too.

Speeding up, I lean in with the bike as I take a sharp curve. Big Roy is in my line of sight now. He glances back and sees me.

Good.

I want my face to be the last thing he sees before he dies. And if not my face, the glint of sunlight off of my bike will do too. As long as he knows I'm the one responsible for taking him off this earth.

"I'm coming for you, motherfucker!" I yell into the wind, knowing he can't hear me.

Everything he's done to me and the MC flashes through my mind: killing Flint's best friend Tommy, shooting Flint, murdering his own old lady and my high school sweetheart, Leah. Terrorizing Trish, firebombing Roger's club, and shooting an innocent, pregnant woman on her wedding day.

Only the devil himself could be capable of such evil.

Big Roy is going down this time. The feud with the Liberators has dragged on for far too long.

As we speed along the twisting road, I realize that for my plan to work, I might have to go down with him.

To protect my family and my club, it will be worth it. They all have so much more to lose than I do. Wives, babies, real futures. It is my duty, and mine alone, to protect them. None of them will ever be safe again as long as Big Roy lives. Not even Trish.

Rolling back the throttle, I lean in, determined now more than ever. If I'm going to do this, I only have one chance. The next curve coming up is a tight hairpin. Every second that goes by, I'm gaining on him a little bit more, pushing him to go faster and faster. I can sense him getting nervous now as he realizes I'm willing to risk it all to take him out.

How does it feel to know you're going to die today, Big Roy?

Sam frantically yells at me from behind. He's figured out what I'm going to do too. Fuck! I wish he wasn't here to see this. I've always tried to protect him the best I could. If something happens to me, I know he'll still be okay. Flint and Kendra will make sure of it. I wave for him to pull back and he backs off only a little.

Another few seconds and Big Roy will be coming up on the curve. Like most country mountain roads, there isn't a guardrail. Only a thin patch of loose dirt and a steep drop off down the side.

Time to go full throttle.

I instinctively feel Big Roy's moment of panic deep in my gut when he hears me right on his ass.

For a split-second, an image of Trish's beautiful face pops into my head.

She could've been the one.

Hell! She is the one.

So many regrets.

I never meant for things to end this way.

Now or never.

It's time to meet your maker, Big Roy, and it sure as hell ain't God!

I surge ahead and slam into the back end of his bike going full speed. The impact throws us both up into the air, off the side of the road, and then we're falling down the side of the cliff in a tangle of limbs and bikes, tumbling over and over.

"Jesse!" Sam yells from far away.

Finally, after what seems like forever, I stop moving.

Am I dead? I hurt too damn much to be dead.

I need to get up. I try to push myself to a sitting position. A surge of pain slices through my right arm. Fuck! My arm is hanging limp from my shoulder and is completely useless. I don't know if something is broken or dislocated. Maybe both, the way it feels. Either way, it hurts like a motherfucker. I look around for my bike and see it in a crumpled heap, the front tire and rim bent beyond repair. Shit!

Where is Big Roy? I don't see him, but I can hear him moaning in pain. Damn! The motherfucker is still alive. What do I have to do to kill this fucking bastard? Drive a wooden stake through his heart?

I turn toward the sound. Further down below me, wrapped around a thick pine tree, is Big Roy and his mangled bike. He may be still alive, but from the looks of it, not by much.

I have to finish it.

Rolling over onto my knees, I push up with my left hand. I'm standing now, not steady, but at least I'm up. I take a step toward him and almost fall down again when my ankle gives out under my weight. Shit! A sprained ankle, too. Well, if I'm moving, at least I'm in better shape than he is.

I limp and slide my way down the cliff until I reach his side. Blood is pouring from a nasty hole in his head and both legs are splayed out at weird, crooked angles in front of him. His breath is coming out in wheezy, gurgling sounds. He opens his eyes and looks up at me.

"Lucky for you, the tree broke your fall," I say.

"You fucker!" he mutters.

He reaches for his pocket. I hit him across the face with the gun I'm holding in my left hand.

"Fuck you, Jesse," he says then chokes on a laugh. "Bet you thought the crash would kill me, didn't you? And now you can't finish the job," he says. "Not here. Not now."

I lift the gun and point it toward his head. I'm right-handed, but I can shoot a target at close range with my left.

"And why's that? Remind me."

"You can't kill me. Not with all these people around. The police will be coming up the mountain soon. Probably an ambulance too for that pretty veterinarian. If you shoot me now, everyone will know you did it in cold blood. Not even your fancy ass lawyer brother can get you off for that."

I slowly limp around behind him. "I disagree. Nobody will blame me for blowing your head off. I will be doing the world a big favor."

Now that I'm closer, I can see that he's hurt worse than I thought. Broken legs and a serious-looking head injury. I suspect there's major internal damage as well.

"I've always worried about wrapping my bike around a tree," I say. "All kinds of bad things can happen. Severed spine, broken neck."

He struggles to turn around to face me. "You don't have to do this," he says, sounding desperate now. "We can call it even and drop the feud between the clubs. I'm willing to work out a boundary deal for territory."

"Call it even? No fucking way. You've had this coming for a very long time. Do you honestly expect me to show you mercy after all the things you've done to hurt the people that I care about? I will enjoy killing you. Protecting my family and the MC is the only thing that matters."

"Wait! Listen, I can hear the police sirens coming up the mountain now. Let's talk about this. It's not too late."

Big Roy is right.

The police can't be more than a couple of miles away. As much as I'm enjoying listening to him beg, there's no more time to sit around talking shit.

"You started this, asshole," I say, "and now I'm going to finish it. The only thing I regret is that I can't hurt you more."

Before he has a chance to react, I lean down and wrap my left arm around his neck. With a strong upward twist at an angle, I break his neck. His head rolls limply to the side. I turn him loose and he falls over face first into the dirt.

"Now...we're even."

26

TRISH

"Trish? Are you still here?"

I jump awake at the sound of my brother's voice and swing my legs over the side of the cot tucked into the corner of the hospital room. "I'm here," I say, hurrying over to the hospital bed.

For the past few weeks, I practically lived at the hospital, spending all of my time with Ty when I'm not working at the bar. The nurses eventually took pity on me and pulled in a cot for me to sleep on at night.

Ty is treating me civilly now at least. I don't know if it is because they're keeping him doped up or because he feels bad for everything he put me through. I'm just glad he's not his normal nasty self, so I don't question why.

I pick up a Styrofoam cup from the bedside table, bend the straw, and place it between his parched lips.

"Are you in a lot of pain?" I ask, already knowing the answer.

The doctors aren't giving him enough painkillers to keep the pain at a manageable level. I'm not sure if this is intentional on their part or if they're simply being negligent.

"Yes," he whispers hoarsely. "What else is new?"

He takes a long sip of the water then leans back and closes his eyes.

"Trish, you need to go," he says after a long minute. "For good this time, and don't come back."

"For good?" I ask in surprise. "What are you talking about? You need me here. Who would take care of you?"

"The nurses," he answers, then erupts in a fit of coughing. "Shit!" he swears. "This damn incision is killing me."

I check the hanging IV bag of pain medicine. Empty again. I hit the call button for the nurse. Not that she will pay any attention. They usually don't, and I have to chase them down at the nurses' station where they gather for coffee and goodies brought in by other families. Maybe I should try bribing them, too.

"I'm serious," he says. "It's past time you left and got on with your life."

"What about your life?" I ask. "Why aren't you agreeing to take the deal you're being offered by the Feds? I don't understand why you're being so stubborn. With good behavior, you will be out of prison in a few years."

He grimaces in pain and tries to scoot up in the bed. "I would be dead in prison long before that. Big Roy has lots of friends on the inside. I'm not taking the deal, and I don't want to hear any more about it. You wouldn't understand my reasons, so there's no point in trying to explain."

"But you didn't do the things they're accusing you of." I frown and try to untangle the sheets caught around his legs. "It doesn't seem fair that you go to prison while Big Roy is still out there running around free."

Ty opens his eyes and looks directly into mine. At times he reminds me so much of our father, the little I remember about him before he left us. One day we were a family, the next two little kids left alone with an addict mother.

"Deep down, you must know better than that. None of us are innocent, Trish. Not me, not Big Roy, and especially not Jesse. We're all bad. Real bad. That's what I'm trying to tell you. The best thing for you to do is save up enough money to buy a bus ticket to California or someplace else far away. Get on that bus and don't ever come back."

I touch his hand that the police have handcuffed to the hospital bed.

It seems like overkill. Ty can't move two inches in the bed by himself, much less crawl out of the hospital and escape.

"I can't do that. You're my family."

"If you want any kind of a life, you don't have a choice. I mean it. Don't visit me in prison, don't try to save Mom, and never see Jesse again. Or any other biker as far as that goes. You don't owe any of us jack shit. You understand? Not even Mom. You remind me of that mangy stray dog that kept hanging around our house that summer. Remember him?"

I nod. "I wanted to keep him and you kept chasing him off."

"I know. You think I wouldn't have liked to have a dog and be a normal kid? Hell, I knew we weren't no good for him. We didn't have enough money to feed ourselves, much less a dog. No matter how many times I yelled at him, he kept coming back around. I knew he would be better off with any other family besides ours. Eventually he got the point and never came back. I know you're at least as smart as that stupid dog."

As much as I hate to admit it, I know there is some truth to what he is saying. All of my relationships are toxic.

"The rest of us are already fucked up," he continues. "It's not too late for you. They're transferring me this afternoon to the prison hospital. I don't want you here when they come to get me. So go now."

"What? Why didn't you tell me this sooner?" Everything is happening too fast. "You're not well enough to be moved yet. I'll talk to the doctors and see if they can stall the transfer for a few more days."

Ty coughs again. "Don't waste your breath. They don't give a shit about my health. I'm a criminal, and they can't wait for me to leave."

A nurse pushes the door open and hurries in. "I have some pain medicine for you," she says with a fake smile. We don't talk as she quickly switches out the IV bags. "There is some nausea medicine in here too, so it will make you drowsy," she warns before rushing back out the door.

"I'm staying here with you as long as I can," I say firmly. "A few more hours isn't going to make any difference in my grand life plan. Do you want to try some yogurt?"

I reach for the container and peel back the lid, turning away so he can't see the tears forming. Why are they taking him away so soon? I thought they would give him a chance to post bail or something. We don't have enough money for a lawyer, so he's stuck with a public defender that is doing a terrible job.

Ty starts to say something and stops.

"What is it?" I ask.

The medication is already kicking in. He tries to hold his eyes open and fails. Struggling to stay awake, he mumbles something that I can't catch. I lean closer.

"Ty? I'm still here."

"Just go," he mutters before falling asleep.

Tears roll down my cheeks. How am I going to be strong enough to keep it together when they take him away? I won't be able to. There's no way. Ty knows it too. For once in our lives, he's thinking of me instead of himself. By pushing me away, he's protecting me this time.

For a moment, I thought he was going to apologize. In a way, I'm glad he didn't. An apology would have sucked me right back in again. The truth has always been there. I just didn't want to see it. He's bad and I can't fix him. The only person I can fix now is myself.

Leaning down, I brush the hair back from his forehead. He's already snoring softly. I take a deep breath. This might be the last time I ever see him. He's treated me terribly, but he's still my brother. Like Jesse said, I can't choose my family and I can't help how I feel.

"Goodbye, Ty. I love you."

27

TRISH

"Trish!" Roger yells to me across the bar. "Would you mind running back to the storage room and grabbing a package of red plastic cups for me please? We're running low over here behind the bar."

"Sure."

I drop the towel I'm using to wipe off the tables and head for the storage room. Once inside, I search through the tall metal racks to look for the cardboard box of cups. What a disaster the room is in. How am I supposed to find anything? Maybe I should offer to come in on my day off and organize things. The extra hours would come in handy.

Finally, I spy the cups high up on the top rack. I drag the rolling stepladder over and climb up. Even with the ladder, I can barely reach the edge of the box. I grab onto the shelf and lean toward it.

"Need some help?" a familiar deep voice says below me.

My heart catches in my throat.

I'm afraid to look.

And even more afraid to get my hopes up.

If I look down and it's not Jesse, the disappointment will be more than I can bear. I've spent the past few weeks forcing myself to not think about him.

Every time I remember the night he walked out the door of the hospital, I want to sob. It's taken all the strength I have in me to keep things together well enough to go to work, much less not cry myself to sleep every night.

Letting go of Jesse was the worst decision of my life, one that I've regretted every minute since. With all the stress I've been under lately, I'm probably imagining his voice now. I grip the shelf tighter so I don't fall.

"I have to admit the view is looking pretty fine from down here," he says, a smile in his voice. "Those pink panties of yours are doing things to me that you can't even imagine. Want to come down and check out the effects for yourself?"

It's Jesse, alright.

I let out the breath I've been holding and turn to look down at him. He's standing there in jeans and a solid black t-shirt that does little to hide his ripped muscles.

"Is your filthy mind always in the gutter?" I ask.

Jesse gives me that gut-wrenching smile that turns my stomach inside out.

"Where you're concerned, yes it is, ma'am."

He reaches up a strong hand, and I hesitate only a split-second before taking it and allowing him to help me down the ladder. When I reach the floor, he tugs me close against his chest.

"Jesse," I mumble against his shirt. "What are you doing here?"

"Shh...don't say anything," he says, burying his face in my hair and inhaling deeply. "Let me hold you one more time before you send me away. I've missed you so much."

For a long minute we stand there, holding each other and not moving. I never want this moment to end.

"Did I ever tell you how good you smell?" he asks into my hair. "No, I probably didn't. I meant to. I'm sorry for not telling you those things. I was sure we had more time. That we could take it slow and easy. That I would have all the time in the world to show you how I feel. And maybe at some point to tell you too."

I'm almost afraid to breathe or say anything. I'm scared he'll stop talking or take back the words. Or even worse, laugh and say he's only kidding.

"I came to tell you that you're safe now," he continues. "Big Roy was killed in a motorcycle accident. He'll never hurt you or anybody else. So you never have to worry about the Liberators again. I made sure of that."

"He's really dead?"

A huge wave of relief engulfs me. I didn't realize how much the threat of Big Roy was hanging over me until it was gone. No more looking behind me when I walk down the street or triple-checking to make sure I've locked the doors.

"What about the other Liberators?" I ask. "Won't they pick up the pieces and keep the feud going?"

"Not this time. Cut off the head of a snake and the body dies."

I slide my arms around his waist and look up at him.

"Is that all you came to tell me?"

He gently tucks a strand of hair behind my ear and kisses me softly on the lips. "No, that's not all. Not by a long shot. I want you to come back to Georgia with me."

He tilts my chin up so his mesmerizing blue eyes can stare intently into mine. All I want to do is melt against him and never let go.

"I want you, Trish, and I'm not leaving here without you. No matter how much time it takes. I won't give up. Tell me what I need to say or do to convince you to give us another chance to be a real couple."

As much as I would love to be with Jesse, the thought of being broke and homeless again scares me to death. I finally have a tiny bit of stability in my life, and to think about starting all over again is terrifying.

"How can I go back with you? I wouldn't have a job or a place to live."

"We'll work all that out once we get there," he says. "I need my girl by my side. Not four hundred miles away. I want you to move in with me so that your gorgeous face is the first thing I see every morning and the last memory I have at night." He makes a face and smiles. "In the interest of full disclosure, you would be living with Sam too since we share a great big farmhouse. He's cool though. Once you get settled in, you can take some time and decide what you want to do with your life. There is even a college close by that you can commute to if you want to go back to school."

My mind is already whirling with possibilities. I don't know what to say. I'm afraid to grab onto the hope. There's nothing I would like more than to build a life with Jesse.

"Let me take care of you," he says. "Give me a chance to show you how good we can be together. I know you've been through so much. So that's all I'm asking of you for now. Until you're ready for more. Just be with me. I will take whatever you're willing to give at this point."

He places his hands on both sides of my face. "I know this is fast and I'm rushing things. I'm not going to apologize for that. If there's one thing I've learned lately, it's that there are no promises of tomorrow. Or even the rest of today. I love you, and I need you to know that now. Today. No more holding back, thinking there's more time."

Closing his eyes, he rests his forehead against mine. "Tell me you'll slide on the back of my bike and come back home with me."

This must be a dream.

It has to be.

Fairy tale endings don't happen to girls like me.

How can I possibly resist him?

I reach up and run my fingers through the dark hair at the nape of his neck. He tugs me up against him with his hands gripping my hips.

"I'll need to give Roger a two-week notice," I say.

Jesse raises his head and smiles. His blue eyes are twinkling. "Is that a yes?"

I nod. He grabs me in a bear hug, lifts me off of my feet, and whirls me around.

"You've made me the happiest man alive. Let's get out of here. We can swing by wherever you've been staying and pick up your stuff. With any luck, we can be home for a late breakfast if we leave right now. I don't mind driving in the dark, if you don't mind riding. I can't wait to get you home."

"Whoa! Wait!" I say, laughing and trying to catch my breath. "I can't just leave. I need to help Roger finish closing up the bar tonight. Didn't you hear what I said about giving him notice? I don't want to leave him in a bind. He's been so good to me that I can't treat him that way."

"I have a confession to make," he says in a serious voice. "I hope you don't get mad. I've been talking to Roger about you every single day for weeks. I needed to be sure you were okay. He knew I was coming back for you as soon as I knew it was safe. And when I was able to ride again."

To know Jesse has been thinking and caring about me this whole time chokes me up. Tears spring to my eyes.

"You've been checking on me? I wish I had known. I've never felt so alone as I have lately."

"If you'll remember, you weren't returning any of my phone calls or texts. Any other man might have given up."

I bury my head in his shirt and try not to cry. What if I had driven him away for good? I can't bear to think about how things might have turned out.

"I know, and I'm so sorry. I was confused about Ty and you and everything. And by the time I realized you had been telling me the truth about Ty, I was too embarrassed and ashamed to call you back. I felt like such a naïve idiot. It devastated me to finally accept who Ty really is."

"You love your brother and it clouded your judgment. Luckily, I'm not the type of man to let things go. I told you it wasn't over, and it's not. Not now, not ever. You're mine now. If you'll have me."

"You're the only man I can ever imagine being with, Jesse." Something he said stuck in my mind. "What did you mean about being able to ride again? Did something happen? Are you okay?"

He runs a steady hand up and down my back in reassurance. "Nothing that time couldn't fix. I took a spill on my bike. Dislocated a shoulder, sprained an ankle, and had a few more bumps and bruises. No big deal," he says with an easy smile. "I learned my lesson and I'll take the curves a little slower next time."

"Now I feel even worse to think that you were hurt and I wasn't there for you. What kind of a bad person am I?"

"To be honest, I'm glad you weren't there. I wanted to keep as many miles as possible between you and the Liberators. No regrets, Trish. Okay? Everything now is about the future, not the past. We can start fresh. It's not too late."

A loud rapping on the storage room door interrupts us.

"Trish! You still in there?" Roger yells through the door. "I'm leaving now. Turn off everything and lock the back door to the bar when you leave. Everyone else has gone home for the night."

Jesse winks at me and I stifle a giggle.

"Okay!" I yell back. "I will."

"Jesse?" Roger says after a minute. "I know you're in there too doing God knows what. Can the phone calls stop now? You're worse than my Mama about calling every damn day."

Jesse smiles. "No more phone calls, Roger! I promise."

"Alright then. I'll leave you two lovebirds to continue whatever you're doing. If you make any kind of a mess, clean it up."

We wait silently until we hear the back door of the bar slam shut then burst out laughing.

"I owe that man big time," Jesse says. "I hope I get the chance to repay him someday." He takes my hand and opens the door to the storage room. "Come with me," he says, leading me out into the now empty and dark bar.

"What are you doing?" I ask as he drags me toward the long wooden bar lining one side of the room. "Where are we going? I need to lock up."

"Not yet. From the first night I saw you, I've had this fantasy playing through my mind," he says. "No way am I going to miss the chance to act it out for real."

He suddenly spins me around to face him. In one smooth movement, he picks me up and plants my ass on the edge of the wooden bar with my legs hanging over. I don't know what he is planning, but he already has my whole body trembling in anticipation of his next move.

In an instant, his lips are everywhere, kissing every inch of my face and down along my neck while his hands pull my bikini top loose, exposing my breasts to the cool air-conditioning.

Jesse's harsh intake of breath tells me how much he likes what he sees, his body stilling as he stares down at my breasts. The dark gleam in his eyes sends my heart racing.

"Wow!" he says, stopping for a long moment to look. "I'll never get tired of this view. You take my breath away every single time."

I don't have time to answer before his head swoops down and he encloses a hard nipple in the heat of his mouth.

"Jesse," I cry out, clutching the dark hair that I love so much as his lips seal around the nipple and sucks with urgent tugs.

Nothing has ever felt so good.

The feelings grow more intense with a hand inching up my leg and under my short skirt. His hands cup beneath my ass, half-lifting me off the bar as he reaches for my thong panties. With a strong tug, he rips them right off me and throws them on the floor, followed by my skirt.

"Those are my favorite pair," I scold.

"I'll buy you more, or even better, you can go without. Then I can rub your bare ass whenever I feel like it. Lie back. Those sexy as hell leather boots are staying on."

He lifts my legs to place them over his shoulders while he scoots my ass right to the edge of the bar.

"Perfect," he says, sliding his hands down my thighs. "Just as I imagined. Your pussy is lined up exactly where I want you to be."

I lean back on my bent elbows, using them to support me as he takes his position in between my legs, which he pushes wider apart. His hand slips between my thighs and the next moment his fingers are skimming over my mound.

"You are so fucking wet," he says with a deep groan, sliding one finger then two deep inside. "Did you miss me?" My tightness and heat clasps hold of his fingers, and his breath catches as he feels the sensation.

"God! Yes!" I writhe against his hand and hear him chuckle with pleasure. How I missed him!

"Show me how much. Rub your tits for me," Jesse says, his eyes gone almost black with unadulterated lust. "Make your nipples hard while you watch me."

Shy at first but eager to please him, I squeeze my full breasts together and tug on the large nipples. Without breaking eye contact, he finger fucks me harder, with each thrust almost lifting me off the bar while his thumb rubs my clit.

"You're so unbelievably beautiful to me," he says.

He spreads my legs wider and moves his head between them. My thighs quiver as he rubs his day-old stubble gently against them and kisses his way up my leg.

"I want to taste you," he murmurs. "So many long nights I would have given anything for one more sweet taste of you inside and out. Sometimes I would close my eyes and remember how it felt to bury my face between your legs. Your scent, your flavor. I never dreamed I would get the chance to be with you like this again."

Removing his fingers, he replaces them with his tongue. I buck hard into his face and he clutches my thighs, holding me steady on the bar. I fist my hands in his thick hair and bite down hard on my bottom lip to keep from crying out.

He looks up at me, his eyes mirroring every emotion surging through my body before using first the flat of his tongue and then just the tip to tease me.

Hungrily, I slide my hands from his shoulders down to grip his muscular upper arms. I can never get enough of the feel of his skin beneath the palms of my hand. A lifetime spent tracing the dark black tattoos lining his body will never be enough. I want to lick and touch every symbol, every letter.

I close my eyes in ecstasy as Jesse gives me everything I want and need, driving me to the edge of sanity when he touches my clit with his tongue.

"Open your eyes," he commands hoarsely, raising his head to look at me. "I want to make you cum harder than you ever have so you'll know your gorgeous body was made just for my touch."

He murmurs sexy, dirty words to me, telling me how hot I am and how much he craves one more touch of me. How I am like a drug to his system that he can never get enough of.

Instincts take over, and all I can focus on is Jesse's tongue grinding into my sex with delicious pressure. Now that I know that he is playing for keeps, I relax and give in to all the wonderful sensations flooding my body.

The empty bar fills with the sound of my moans. I'm past the point of being embarrassed by how good his mouth feels. Clutching his hair, I wiggle wantonly beneath his tongue. He nibbles on my clit and I cry out his name as a powerful orgasm hits, sending wave after wave of contractions through my body. When I float back to earth, he looks up at me from between my legs.

"You're a living, breathing wet dream," he says hoarsely. "I would have waited forever to feel you cum on my face again."

Suddenly he slides me backward on the slippery bar. I clutch the edge, afraid I'll fall off the side straight into the bottles of liquor. He chuckles and the sound thrills my heart. I love to hear him laugh.

"I won't let you fall," he says with a devilish grin. "Trust me, I've got you. From now on, I've always got you." In one smooth move, he pulls himself up to join me on the bar then strips off his shirt.

I stare at him, awestruck. His tanned chest muscles are bigger than I remember. My hands quickly spread over his pecs and the large Steel Infidels tattoo running across the width of his chest.

"There's one last part of my fantasy yet to be fulfilled," he says. "Roll over and scoot up on your knees. See that mirror?" He points to our reflection in the long mirror behind the bar. "Don't take your eyes off it."

I catch a glimpse of our bodies. Jesse is shirtless, deeply tanned and sexy as hell. I'm sprawled out on the bar wearing nothing but black leather boots.

"Thank God for your vivid imagination," I say. I turn over, tilt my ass high in the air, and brace myself on my elbows.

"Fuck," he groans, his fingers tightening on my flesh as he gets a full view of what I'm offering up for his taking. "Damn, Trish. That's just...*damn*. You're driving me insane."

I watch in the mirror as he kneels behind me, quickly unbuckles his belt, and unzips his pants. With one hand, he pulls free his large, hard erection.

Oh. My. God.

"I'll never forget how wild and sexy you look at this moment," he says. "No matter how amazing my fantasies were, they never came close to this reality. I need you. So much it's fucking unreal."

He spreads my ass cheeks and fingers me one more time slowly before placing the head of his thick cock against my pussy. Grabbing a handful of my long hair, he wraps it around his hand and pulls my head back slightly. His blue eyes meet mine in the mirror. Just when I think the waiting will drive me crazy, he slides into me in one powerful thrust.

I can't think and can only feel.

Slowly, he begins to move. He draws out inch by inch and then thrusts back in, increasing his pace and intensity. Each time, he sinks himself in to the balls and causes his groin to smack into my ass. I can't take my eyes off the mirror. I love the sight of his cock appearing and then disappearing into my pussy.

Watching him fuck me from behind is wild, erotic, and primal.

"Please tell me this is as good for you as it is for me," he murmurs before slamming into me a bit more fiercely and reaching under me to tweak my nipple in his fingers.

"Better than good," I moan between thrusts. "You're the only man who can make me feel this way."

I'm so close when I hear his deep, rough groans. He angles his hips and plunges deeper than ever. I bump and grind back against him, seeking more. He grabs my swaying tit and massages hard.

"Yes...oh yes!" I cry out in a blend of agony and bliss. Another strangled moan escapes me, and my inner muscles spasm and clench like a fist around him.

His pace becomes a blur of stabbing thrusts, and an instant later Jesse climaxes with me. He lets out a choked curse and grips my hips to hold me tight against him.

I gasp at the visual in the mirror, watching how powerfully he loses control, just like everything else he does. No filters or holding back. Nothing but pure masculine energy pumping into me.

Jesse.

All man.

And all mine.

28

JESSE

"Are you okay, sweetheart?" I lean forward to kiss my way down Trish's spine.

"I may never be able to walk again," she says with a laugh. "Other than that, I'm great."

With a long, regretful sigh, I slide off the bar and adjust my pants. "We need to find your clothes."

"No, *you* need to find my clothes," Trish says. "I'm not running around the bar naked. You lost them, you find them. Last time I saw them, they were flying through the air in that direction." She smiles and points behind me.

I spot her clothes under a table and after retrieving them, hold up the ripped pink panties by one finger.

"Since these aren't any good to you anymore, I'm keeping them as a souvenir." I stuff them in my pocket. "Hopefully the skirt is still salvageable." I toss it to her and she slides it over her boots and up her legs.

"Only you would take home panties instead of sea shells as a souvenir from Panama City," she says. "I'm still missing a piece of clothing. Where's my bikini top?"

I lean far over the bar to look and find it caught on a bottle of whiskey. After handing it to her, I walk around to tie the strings around her neck and back. Unable to resist one last touch, I trail my hands down her sides and grip her waist.

"Let me help you down," I offer, sliding an arm under her legs and scooping her up. Instead of placing her on the floor, I sit down on a bar stool and cradle her tightly in my lap.

Trish gives me a mischievous look. "Let me guess. You have one more erotic fantasy you want to tell me about."

I laugh and shake my head. "No. I'm done for at least another twenty minutes. Are you complaining?"

"Never."

She reaches up a hand to cup my cheek. "I love you, Jesse. Thank you for not giving up on us."

I grab her hand and turn it over to kiss her palm.

How did I ever get so lucky?

Trish is a vision with her long hair spread out all over my chest, her skin still flushed, those big beautiful eyes gazing at me. I could get lost in her eyes and never find my way out again. Not that I would ever want to.

The gorgeous woman curled against my chest loves me.

It's hard for me to believe. I sure as hell don't deserve her love.

Yet deep down inside, I want more.

Need more.

I wasn't being truthful when I told her I would be happy with anything she could give me. At that moment, I would have said whatever it takes to keep her in my arms and prevent her from bolting out the door. So I didn't push or ask for too much too soon.

I know she's scared.

So am I.

I also know I won't be satisfied until she's completely mine in every way. The time we've spent apart has given me plenty of opportunity to think.

I want it all.

Wife, kids, the whole fucking package.

From now on, I'm running my life the way I ride.

Full throttle.

No hitting the brakes.

Leaning down, I grab her lips in a slow, tender kiss. How I wish she could absorb everything I'm feeling, to instinctively know the emotions I can't express in words. From the way she grasps the back of my neck and kisses me back, I realize she understands.

"Marry me," I say.

Her mouth drops open. She blinks at me in surprise. "You want a wife? Now?"

"Yes, I want a wife. And a family. Most of all, I want a life, Trish, with you. I love you and I don't want to wait. Say yes."

"What about the Steel Infidels?"

"The MC will always be a major part of my life. But they can't *be* my life. You're my life now."

"Nothing would make me happier," she says, her eyes shining with tears. "The answer is a great big yes."

EPILOGUE

TRISH

Six months later...

"What's taking so damn long?" Sam asks. "Shouldn't we have heard something by now?" He jumps up to pace the length of the maternity ward waiting room.

It has been over two hours since Flint last ran in to give us a quick update on Kendra's labor. We're all beginning to get a little worried. Kendra was adamant that she didn't want a Caesarean delivery, but the longer the labor drags on, the more likely it seems.

"It takes a long time to birth a baby," I patiently explain to Sam. "Don't worry. She'll be okay. Sit down before you wear holes in the floor."

In the past few months, I've grown close to Sam. He's like the brother that I always wanted and never had. Moving into the big house with both Jesse and Sam seemed a little awkward at first, but it didn't take me long to feel right at home. Once Sam realized I knew how to cook, I became his new best friend.

So now, I have two men to spoil and I love every minute of it. Most evenings, the three of us all hang out together, either watching action movies or going for long rides through the countryside. Sometimes if they're working late at the tattoo shop, I'll pick up a pizza after my nursing classes and take it by to 'my boys,' as I like to call them now.

On weekends, the big house is filled with the rest of the Steel Infidels roaming in and out. Sometimes we'll throw a barbeque or the crew will hang out in the front yard working on their bikes. A couple of the 'old ladies' in the club and Kendra have adopted me, taking me under their wing and showing me the ropes.

For the first time in my life, I'm truly happy.

Life with Jesse is just about perfect. The only thing that will make it better is the pitter-patter of little feet someday. If my recent morning queasiness is any indication, it may be sooner than later. I haven't told Jesse about my suspicions yet since I want to be absolutely sure first.

Jesse removes his arm from around my shoulder and stands up to stretch. "Poor Flint," he says. "I bet he's going nuts in there seeing Kendra in pain and not being able to do anything about it."

"Poor Flint?" I say. "You mean poor Kendra, don't you? No matter how awful Flint feels, it can't be as bad as what she's experiencing."

Jesse reaches down and squeezes my hand. "I know. I just can't help thinking how I would feel if you were the one in there suffering. Not to be able to take the pain away would kill me. It must be the most helpless feeling in the world. I hope that when we have a baby, they'll give you a shot to knock your ass out cold or something."

I roll my eyes at him. "I'm pretty sure they don't drug up pregnant women anymore. You need to be able to push."

Sam stops pacing and looks back and forth between us. "Wait! Are you guys having a baby too?"

Jesse smiles down at me. "Not yet, but we're working on it. Every day and every night."

I playfully slap him on the arm. "Stop it! You're embarrassing me. Sam doesn't need to hear all this private stuff. The walls are thin in the house, you know."

A nurse walks into the waiting room and we immediately stop talking. "The Mason family?" she asks.

We stand up together. "That's us," Jesse says.

"Come with me. You can all go in the room now, but only for a couple of minutes. Mama is very tired and needs her rest."

"Are they both okay?" Jesse asks anxiously. "Mama and the baby?"

Jesse has been worried sick about the health of the baby ever since the shooting at the wedding. The gunshot grazed Kendra in the upper thigh and luckily didn't hit anywhere near the baby. Even with the doctor's continued reassurance, it's been impossible to convince Jesse that the baby is okay. He won't believe it until he sees it with his own eyes.

"Mama and the baby boy are both doing great," she says with a big smile.

"A boy! Just what I wanted!" Sam reaches over to high five Jesse. "I can't wait to teach him how to ride. I wonder if they make little motorcycles for toddlers."

"I sure hope not," I say with a frown.

When we reach the door to the room, I walk a couple more steps down the hallway. I suddenly feel like an intruder and don't want to interrupt the family's private time together. Jesse starts to go in and notices me hanging back.

"What's wrong?" he asks. "You okay? I thought you would be all over this baby stuff. Jotting down notes and asking questions."

"I'm fine. I just don't want to intrude on this special time for all of you. The first baby in a family is a big deal."

"It is a big deal," he says. "That's why I want you here with us." He leans down and kisses my hair. "I love you, sweetheart. More than you'll ever know. When are you going to accept this is your family too, Trish? You're part of us now." He takes my hand. "Come on now. Don't be shy. Kendra will want to see you."

We walk into the birthing room where Kendra is lying in a hospital bed looking completely exhausted. Flint, in green hospital scrubs, doesn't look much better. He gives us a tired smile and walks over carrying the baby.

"Meet your new nephew," he says to Jesse and Sam. "Joshua Mason. Josh for short."

Jesse takes one look at the big, healthy baby boy swaddled in a white blanket, and his blue eyes unexpectedly fill with tears. His strong emotion catches me by surprise, because in all this time, I've never seen him cry. It makes me tear up too. I know he is overwhelmed by relief since he hasn't forgiven himself for what happened at the wedding.

"Here Jesse, why don't you hold him for a minute?" Flint suggests, moving closer with the little bundle.

"Oh no," Jesse says in a panic, holding up a hand to stop him. "I'm afraid I'll drop him."

"You're not going to drop him," Flint reassures him. "Here, put your arms up and keep his head supported." He carefully transfers the baby over into Jesse's tattooed arms.

"Hey Josh," Jesse says softly. "I'm your uncle, Jesse, and this is your Aunt Trish. We're going to spoil you rotten."

Sam pulls out his cell phone and takes a quick photo. "The crew isn't going to believe this," he says. "Big, tough Jesse holding a baby."

"Jesse needs all the practice he can get," Kendra says weakly from the hospital bed. "Trish, I'm counting on you to babysit for us, too."

"Anytime," I say. "I would love to. Just say the word and I'm all yours."

I reach over and gently touch little Joshua's hand. He grasps my finger and holds on tight.

In a flash, I can see all of us together for years to come. On Christmas mornings and Easter egg hunts. Thanksgiving dinners and trick-or-treating with our kids.

Everything I ever wanted is in this room.

Jesse, and a family to love that will love me back.

I've finally found my place.

THUNDERCLAP
NEW YORK TIMES & USA TODAY BESTSELLING AUTHOR
DEZ BURKE

Cover Model: Travis DesLaurier
Photograph by: Scott Hoover Photography
Cover Art by: Kevin McGrath at www.kevindoesart.com

The player has met his match...

Sam...

I admit it. I'm a player.
I adore women and they love me.
I've never met a woman that I couldn't wrap around my body with only a smile and a sexy wink.
Until Lila blew in to town.
For the first time in my life, my tricks aren't working.
I want her and she thinks I'm nothing more than a two-bit thug.
It's time for the player to up his game.

Lila...

I can sketch Sam Mason with my eyes closed.
Every line of his tattoos, every muscle in his arms.
Even the crinkle around the corners of his blue eyes with every easy smile.
I know him well...he's been my mark for weeks.
Nobody said going undercover as an agent for the Alcohol, Tobacco, Firearms and Explosives special units division was going to be easy.
Working my way into the Steel Infidels Motorcycle Club's inner circle will take time.
Then again I'm a patient and determined woman.
Sam Mason may be the sexiest man alive but he's still going down.
This time the player has met his match.

1

SAM

I notice her legs first. Long and firm in a pair of tight blue jean shorts.

Her car is pulled off on the shoulder of the road and she's reaching up on her tiptoes into the open trunk. As I drive past her on the mountain road, I see the front flat tire.

Damn!

What a bad place for a woman to have a breakdown. The nearest gas station is twenty miles away and roadside assistance in the mountains of North Georgia is nonexistent. Since I'm going too fast on my motorcycle to stop, I slow down and make a wide U-turn on the road.

Lucky for her, I know how to fix a flat.

Lucky for me, she's a sexy lady in distress.

A winning combination in my way of thinking.

This might be my lucky day.

I pull my bike alongside her car and unbuckle my helmet. She straightens up from the trunk and gives me a wary look.

"Need some help?" I ask, pointing to the tire and walking closer.

She holds up the heavy jack. I don't know if it's her way of letting me know she has a weapon or if she intends to change the tire herself.

"Not really," she replies. "I can handle it."

She walks around to the front of the car and squats down to look at the tire. Okay, so maybe she isn't bullshitting me.

I grin and give her a doubtful look.

"You can change a tire all by yourself?"

She raises her eyebrows and challenges me with a smile. "Is there something about me that makes you think I can't?"

Other than you're a girl?

I'm not stupid enough to say it.

Something tells me that she might smack me on the side of the head with the heavy jack.

She's not my normal, long-haired blonde bimbo type, but she's sexy as hell. She's tall, almost my height, with long toned legs that go on forever and an ass just begging for me to grab it. Her hair is almost shoulder-length, cut in an edgy, punkish style. I've never seen the color before, an unusual blend of purple and red.

Kind of weird, but for some reason I like it.

My eyes stray to the dangling strings of her frayed jean shorts. I have a strong urge to grab one and pull, before slipping my fingers under the denim fabric to find out if her ass feels as firm as it looks.

From where I'm standing, I can see straight down the front of her low-cut white shirt. It's at least ninety-five degrees on the hot asphalt, and I watch as a drop of perspiration slowly rolls down between her full breasts. I wonder if she would get pissed if I leaned down and licked it off.

I smile at the thought.

Hell!

She might even enjoy it.

"Are you enjoying the view?" she snaps at me with a frown. "Why are you standing there smiling when it's blazing hot out here and I have a flat tire? If you're going to just stare at my tits, you might as well make yourself useful and help me."

I love a girl with sass.

"Yes, ma'am. I don't know why you're getting all testy with me. I offered to help. Move out of the damn way and let me take care of that for you."

She hesitates for a second, and I think she's going to be stubborn and refuse to move. With a loud sigh, she finally stands up and hands me the jack. We switch places and I start working on her tire.

"Where are you headed to?" I ask.

"Bardsville."

"You're about twenty miles away, so I'll follow you into town when we finish up. I want to make sure you get there safe and sound."

"That won't be necessary," she says.

"Sure it is. Do you have a spare?"

She points to the trunk. I stand up, strip off my t-shirt, and wipe my face with it before throwing it onto the roof of her car.

"Nothing like a hot summer day in Georgia, right? The heat is a killer."

She stands there blinking at me with her big green eyes. Maybe I scared her by saying the word 'killer.' She should be scared. It's not safe these days for a woman to be stranded on a lonely mountain road. Anyone could come by and drag her off into the woods. Actually, now that I think about it, that's exactly what I would like to do. Rip her shorts off and back her up against a tree.

Only if she's willing and begging for it though, and from the look she's giving me right now, I'm not betting on that happening anytime soon.

Bummer.

"I have a cooler with drinks," she offers. "I'll get one for you. And thank you for helping me. I appreciate it. The heat is making me grumpy. Sorry for snapping at you."

"My pleasure, darling. I would never pass up a lady stranded on the side of the road without stopping. I'm Sam, by the way."

I wipe my hand off on my jeans and hold it out.

She gives me a reluctant smile and shakes it with a firm grip.

"Nice to meet you. I'm Lila."

She reaches into the back seat of her car, opens a small cooler, and pulls out two bottles.

"Take your pick," she says. "Water or kombucha? Either one is fine with me."

I glance up from the tire and look at the bottles she's holding out.

"Looks like we'll be sharing the water," I say. "You need to throw that other shit away. For God's sake, don't drink it. Can't you see all that crap floating around in the bottom? Something is growing in there, and it looks nasty."

She laughs and hands me the water bottle.

"Kombucha is supposed to have that icky stuff in it. It's good for you."

I shake my head and take a big gulp of water. "No thank you. Water is fine. You're from Atlanta, aren't you?"

She looks surprised. "Yeah, how did you know?"

"I can tell. You're a big city girl and not from around here."

"Is that a bad thing?" she asks, leaning against the side of the car.

I wink at her and turn back to the tire.

"Not to me, it isn't."

2

LILA

I had it all together and under control until he stripped off his shirt.

Why the hell did he do that?

It caught me completely off guard and for a moment, I was actually speechless. Something about the sight of his tattooed, muscular chest threw me in a way I wasn't expecting and certainly couldn't have planned for.

I already knew Sam Mason was a handsome man with baby blue eyes the color of a clear Montana sky and a smile that could make a woman want to drop her pants on the spot.

I've studied his photos.

I came prepared.

Or so I thought.

Looking at still photos of Sam Mason in my office cubicle was one thing. Seeing him up close and in the flesh is something completely different. No way could a photo or even a video capture the raw masculine heat oozing from his every pore.

This job is going to be harder than I thought.

Ten minutes into the operation and I'm already hitting a major hurdle. Sam is sexy, likable, and almost irresistible. The key word being *almost*.

While he works on the tire, I try not to let him see me checking him out. I notice he has recently added a couple of new tattoos that I haven't seen before. I wonder if he'll keep going until eventually his whole body is covered. I wouldn't be surprised since he's a tattoo artist. Personally, I think he has exactly the right amount. Any more and he'll be covering up some very nice-looking muscle.

I don't know why I keep staring besides the fact that now that I'm here, I can't seem to tear my eyes away. The truth is I can sketch Sam Mason with my eyes closed.

Every line of his tattoos, every muscle in his arms.

Even the crinkle around the corners of his eyes with every easy smile.

I know him well...he's been my mark for weeks.

For countless hours, I've stared at photos of Sam and the rest of the Steel Infidels until my eyes blurred. I've memorized their patterns, their habits, what they like to do and even what they eat. From my research, I know the three brothers in the motorcycle club, Sam, Flint and Jesse, are handsome, charming, and *dangerous* as hell.

Nobody said going undercover as an agent for the Alcohol, Tobacco, Firearms and Explosives Special Units division was going to be easy. Worming my way into the Steel Infidels inner circle will take some time. Then again, I'm a patient and determined woman.

There's no doubt in my mind that I can do this.

Sam Mason may be the sexiest man I've ever met, but he's still going down.

This time the player has met his match.

He stands up and reaches for his shirt. I'm secretly hoping he doesn't put it back on.

"All done," he says. "You're ready to go."

"Great!" I clasp my hands together. "Thank you. You're a lifesaver, Sam."

I'm expecting him to ask for my cell phone number any second now. Instead he walks to his bike and straps on a helmet.

"I'll follow you into town," he says. "If you have time, swing by and see me sometime. I own a tattoo shop on the main street in Bardsville. You can't miss it. The Inked Dragon."

Okay.

Not exactly the outcome I was hoping for, but I can work with it. At least he gave me an opening that I can use.

"Sure," I reply. "I'll drop by one day while I'm in town."

I slide behind the wheel and start the engine. After adjusting my rearview mirror, I catch a glimpse of Sam pulling out onto the road behind me.

I reach for my cell phone in the console and hit the send button on a saved text.

Operation Thunderclap is a go.

3

SAM

I drive into the lot of the Steel Infidel's clubhouse and park my bike alongside the others. Toby, the newest patch member of the motorcycle club and my best friend from high school, pulls up right behind me.

"What's up, Toby?" I call out as I unbuckle my helmet.

"Nothing much," he replies. "What's going on? Jesse called me an hour ago and said we were having an emergency meeting."

"Beats me. I've been at the shop all day and haven't had a chance to talk to him. Maybe he decided to vote you out of the MC."

A worried look crosses Toby's face, so I punch his shoulder hard.

"I'm kidding, man! You're my best bud. No way in hell is that going to happen. The MC is thrilled to have you back."

Toby has spent the past few years serving as a Marine in the Middle East. He usually doesn't say much about his time there unless he's rip-roaring drunk. The tales he told me were horrific enough to give me nightmares. I can't imagine what they must do to him.

He's trying like hell to work through some issues he brought back and get his shit together. A few months ago, the MC brought him in as a patch member. Any day now, we'll make him a full member of the MC. He doesn't know, which means I can still tease him a while longer.

We step inside the dark clubhouse where we are immediately greeted by Laura, one of the regular Sweet Butts and my favorite go-to girl for a casual fuck. She flips her long blonde hair over her shoulder and leans into me with her soft tits.

"Are you busy later tonight, Sam?" she asks. "I can hang out here a little while longer if you don't have any plans."

"I'm not sure yet," I reply with a playful swat on her ample ass. "I'll let you know."

She smiles and walks away, apparently satisfied with my answer.

"So what's the deal with her?" Toby asks when she moves out of earshot. "Do you two have something serious going on?"

I laugh at the ridiculous thought.

"Hell no! Are you kidding me? Why? You want her? You can have her."

Toby shakes his head and grins.

"No way. I don't want your leftovers. A girl needs to have a little something more between her ears than that one anyway. Too much empty space."

"If you're going for brains, widen your search beyond the Sweet Butts," I advise.

We head to a big room at the back of the building. The chicks hanging around the clubhouse know the room is off limits to everyone except the thirteen members of the Steel Infidels Motorcycle Club. All major club business and meetings are conducted inside.

We're the last two to arrive for tonight's meeting. My older brothers, Jesse and Flint, are already seated at the head of the long wooden table. The other nine members of the MC are scattered around the room waiting for us. They look up when we walk in.

"Take a seat," Jesse says. "We don't have time for any bullshit tonight."

I pull out a chair beside Flint. The other members stop talking and join us at the table too. Jesse's face looks grim, which makes me nervous. Nothing much rattles my older brother and President of the MC, so this can't be good.

"We're in a shitload of trouble," Jesse begins. "One of Flint's contacts in Atlanta passed us word that we're under investigation again.

This time it's the Alcohol, Tobacco, Firearms and Explosives division. The ATF can nail us on a number of different charges if they start digging. We don't have a clue as to what they have on us yet or how long we've been under their microscope. Flint knows more of the details, so I'll let him fill you in."

"The word on the street is that they're going to send someone undercover to Bardsville to poke around in our business," Flint says. "Whoever they send might even try to infiltrate the MC. For them to allocate this much manpower and time to an investigation means they're confident they can find something solid. Obviously none of us want to go to prison, so we need to get a handle on this quickly and be prepared."

He picks up the large manila envelope sitting on the table and pulls out a stack of photographs.

"Pass these around," Flint says. "I want everyone to take a good look. If someone shows up undercover here, they will most likely be a member of this group. This is the field team of the ATF's Special Agents division. Keep in mind they might change their appearance, so look at the shape of their eyes and facial features. The minute any of these people arrive in town, we need to know so we can cover our asses. Memorize these photographs."

"How many do you think are coming?" Rocco, the oldest member of the MC, asks.

"Maybe a team of two, or it could even be a single agent working alone," Flint replies. "It's a small town, so if more than a couple of people show up and start asking questions, the locals will get suspicious."

Flint passes the photos across the table to Rocco, who starts thumbing through them.

"What are the exact charges they're trying to nail us on?" I ask.

Flint is a lawyer so if anyone knows how much trouble we're in, it would be him.

"The fact that we're selling bootlegged alcohol in a dry county would be the first and the most obvious illegal activity they would go after. And the cigarettes. Not only are we selling without a license, we're also exporting hundreds of cases every week across state lines and not paying sales or excise taxes. I suspect the Georgia Department of Revenue is involved too since the two agencies work together. It's not as if what we do is a big secret. Everyone in this town knows about it. Hell, half of the county's citizens are our customers."

"All it takes is one person to turn us in," Jesse adds. "They probably already have. The alcohol and cigarette operation needs to be suspended until this blows over."

"How the hell are we going to do that?" I ask. "We've been selling out the back of the tattoo shop for years. Toby and I are scheduled to pick up another shipment this week. Where are we supposed to store the inventory? We've made agreements with our suppliers that we can't back out of, and the bottles are going to pile up to the ceiling."

"I don't think we have a choice here," Jesse replies. "Either we temporarily shut it down, or the ATF is going to permanently shut us down. We'll make it work somehow."

"Isn't there another way?" I argue. "Our customers are going to be so pissed when they show up Friday after work and we tell them that we're closed for business. They depend on us."

Flint shrugs.

"They'll have to deal with it. The operation has to be shut down for now. Let's just hope the ATF doesn't know about any of the other stuff."

"Like the guns?" Toby asks with a worried frown.

Jesse and Flint have been grooming him to take over the club's gun running division since he came back to town. With his military experience, he is by far the most qualified man for the job.

"If we shut everything down, we take the chance of losing face with the other MCs, our suppliers, and our distributors," Jesse says. "If at all possible, we need to keep the guns going."

"I agree," Toby says. "We'll need to shake up our schedules though. I'll alert the suppliers tonight."

Rocco finishes with the stack of photos and slides them across the table to Toby. I glance over his shoulder while he leafs through the pile. Most of the photos are of middle-aged men with short hair, glasses, and dull facial features. They look like worn-out tax accountants. Toby slows down to look at a photo of a prim young woman wearing a tan business suit buttoned up to her neck.

"I bet she's a lot of fun," Toby says sarcastically.

I laugh and take a closer look. The woman's long hair is pulled back into a bun. Wire-rimmed reading glasses cover part of her face. She isn't wearing any jewelry or makeup. She reminds me of the girls in the high school Math Club. Then I notice something familiar about her eyes.

I grab the photo out of his hands to take a better look.

No way. It can't be.

"Fuck!" I blurt out. "She's already here. Damn it! I can't believe this."

Flint leans over and snatches the photo from me.

"Who? This girl?" he asks. "How do you know?"

"I've already met her. She had a flat tire up on the mountain and I stopped to help her out. Trust me when I say she doesn't look anything like this now. She's hot and sexy as hell. I wouldn't have recognized her except for her eyes. I'm absolutely sure it's her."

"When was this?" Jesse asks.

"Yesterday," I answer. "I was on my way back from my regular weekly cash drop."

Flint jumps up and runs his hand through his hair, an old nervous habit of his when he's stressed out.

"She set you up," he says.

My mouth drops open and I stare at him in shock.

"No way! What are you saying? That she faked a flat tire?"

"That's exactly what I'm saying. You were coming back from a weekly drop. The ATF must know your schedule. She was waiting for you and you fell right into her trap."

I slump down in my chair. "Well, this sucks," I say. "I can't tell you how upset I am. I was planning on getting a piece of that sweet ass."

"Sam!" Jesse snaps at me. "This is a serious situation. Quit thinking about chasing pussy."

"Never," I say.

"Wait a minute," Flint says. "Hang on. Let's think about this. Obviously the ATF has sent a girl specifically to target Sam. Now that we know about it, we have the upper hand. We can turn this around on them and use Sam to feed her false information."

"So all hope is not lost then?" I ask, leaning forward. "Good. I feel better already."

"We all know Sam has an uncanny ability to seduce the ladies," Flint continues. "Why would this chick be any different? I'm not saying you have to fuck her. Just pull her in with your boyish charm and keep her close. Try to find out exactly what they already have on us. You probably got her phone number, right?"

I shake my head. "No. I was trying to play it cool so I didn't ask for it. I told her to swing by the tattoo shop while she is in town. Want me to try and find her?"

"Not yet," Flint replies. "We need more info on this girl so we'll know what we're dealing with. I don't want to send you into a bad situation running blind. Let me call my guy and see if he has anything else on her."

Flint walks to a corner of the room and places a call.

"So what is she like?" Jesse asks.

I think for a moment.

"Edgy is the best way I would describe her," I say. "Independent, smart-mouthed, feisty. She has this weird-colored hair. Not red, not purple, or pink. Kind of a mixture."

"Magenta," Toby says.

"What the hell is magenta?" I ask. "And big green eyes."

I poke her photo in front of me.

"Her name is Lila, and she looks absolutely nothing like this now."

"You need to think back," Jesse says. "Did she have an opportunity to plant anything on you, like a surveillance device? Did she ask to use your phone or go near your bike?"

I shake my head slowly.

"No. I'm sure about both."

Jesse sighs and leans back in his chair.

"I don't like this one bit," he says. "Especially the fact that they're targeting you. Why would they do that?"

"Who else in the MC would they target?" I ask. "Think about it. You and Flint are happily married with babies. Toby has only been back in the country six months and is new to the MC. Rocco and Tom are old as shit." I look over at the two oldest members and grin. "Sorry, but you know it's true. Donny's old lady has him pussy-whipped, and the rest of the crew are all tangled up with the Sweet Butts. I was the logical choice."

"Plus you're a sucker for a pretty lady," Toby says. "Don't forget that."

"I am, and I'm not apologizing for it either."

Flint clicks his phone shut and walks back to the table.

"I have a little bit more information about the girl," he says. "And honestly I'm more concerned now than ever. Her real name is Delilah Ash. She's twenty-six years old and lives in Atlanta. She was arrested at the age of seventeen for hacking a government website and served a few months in juvenile detention. After that, she went on to Georgia Tech, where she graduated in three years. The government recruited her right out of college and she's been an employee of the ATF ever since."

"Wait a minute!" I say. "She's a hacker?"

"Was a hacker," Flint replies. "She was involved with an older guy who taught her how to hack. Mostly it was minor stuff until they started hacking government websites and leaking secure information online. When they got caught, she took the fall for him because she was a juvenile. She served four months in juvie and he walked away scot-free. She hasn't been in any trouble since then and according to her personnel file, she's an outstanding employee for the ATF. Her specialty with them is surveillance...bugs, tapping cell phones, breaking into security systems. You name it, she can do it."

"She's here to plant surveillance devices, right?" Jesse asks. "So what would be her plan?"

"To get close to Sam," Flint answers. "This would give her easy access to the tattoo shop, the clubhouse, and maybe even your house. If she was hanging around us, she would be able to find a way to monitor all of our cell phones and computers. If we hadn't been warned, she could have easily pulled it off. It would have only taken a few casual dates with Sam to visit all these places and plant the bugs unnoticed."

The room goes silent as everyone absorbs the seriousness of the situation.

"Okay then," Jesse finally says. "If that is what she wants to do, we'll make it easy for her. From this point forward, no one is to discuss club business unless you're in this room or standing naked in the middle of a cornfield. Flint will give everyone new burner cell phones, and we'll switch them out again in a few days. Under no circumstances can we call each other on our regular cell phones or landlines. We have to assume that she will be planting bugs everywhere. We can't let the Old Ladies or Sweet Butts know what is going on, because they won't be able to keep their mouths shut. You got it?"

Everyone nods in agreement.

Flint unlocks a file cabinet in the corner and takes out thirteen prepaid cell phones. He walks around the table and hands out the phones.

"I've already programmed them all with our new numbers to cut down on the confusion," he says.

"Thank God!" I say. "What a mess that was the last time we all tried to switch to burner phones. Twelve new phone numbers to learn."

Flint gives me a stern look.

"I'm concerned that you're not taking this seriously enough, Sam. We're depending on you to pull this off. It's all on you now."

"Okay," I say, throwing up my hands. "I'll be serious. Tell me what you want me to do."

"She's going to approach you again. When she does, act like she's just another girl that you're interested in. Ask her out, flirt, be yourself. We'll let her plant the bugs and then we'll make sure they don't get anything useful on us. Pretend like you believe everything she says. Play along. Act stupid. But whatever you do, don't trust her."

"Damn, Flint! You don't need to tell me not to trust her. I won't. Don't worry. I've got this one hundred percent under control. Personally, I'm concerned about your lack of confidence in me."

A worried look passes between Jesse and Flint.

"What?" I say. "You don't think I can do this?"

I stand up, take my wallet out of my jeans, pull out a hundred bucks, then throw it in the middle of the table.

"Who is a betting man? A hundred bucks says I can get this girl to spread her legs for me within seven days."

The men burst out laughing.

"I'm not taking you up on that bet," Toby says. "No way in hell. I work too hard for my money."

"Me either," Rocco adds.

"Jesse?" I ask.

"Not me, little brother," Jesse says. "I've seen you in action too many times."

All the other men shake their heads as I glance around the table.

"That only leaves you, Flint," I say "Want to bet against me? I'll even sweeten up the pot. Go to two hundred. Come on! I want to win some money. Make a bet with me."

Flint grins and slaps me on the back.

"I would never bet against one of my brothers. You got this. Make us proud, lover boy. Go do your thing."

4

LILA

The noisy diner is crowded with customers, mostly working men with a few senior citizen couples scattered around the room. As soon as I step inside the door, I glance around for Sam and don't see him.

Good.

This means I've beat him to his regular breakfast spot. If he wants to talk to me, he'll have to search me out and make the first move.

"Just one for breakfast, honey?" a curly-haired waitress asks me before grabbing a plastic menu from the reception stand.

I nod, and she ushers me to a large booth by the windows.

"This okay?"

"Yes, it's fine," I say, sliding into the booth with my back to the door. "I'll have coffee to start."

She hands me the menu and hurries off to give me time to scan the artery-clogging choices. Checking my cell phone, I see that I have at least another ten minutes before Sam will show up.

During the week, he sticks to a rigid schedule, usually arriving on his motorcycle for breakfast at the diner at eight. After spending an hour sitting at the counter talking with the local men, he then opens his tattoo shop down the street at nine o'clock sharp.

He's never late and his daily schedule never varies by much.

I would have expected someone in a motorcycle gang to have a little less of a work ethic. Then again, considering all of the illegal businesses the Steel Infidels are involved in, it is probably worth his time in gold to stick to a schedule.

The ATF suspects that Sam runs shipments of alcohol, cigarettes, and guns out of the back of his shop. The Steel Infidels have been on our watch list for a long time.

I grab my computer out of my bag and boot it up. After quickly checking my emails and typing up a quick check-in note to my boss, I load up the morning edition of the New York Times. I'm halfway through reading the front section when I feel a light tap on my shoulder. Without asking for my permission, Sam slides into the booth across from me with a big grin on his face.

He's wearing a black t-shirt stretched tight across his muscular chest. The sleeves barely hide the elaborate skull tattoos covering both upper arms. I would love to ask him what they all mean. Another time, perhaps. When he places his elbows on the table and leans forward, I can smell the soap from his shower.

"I wouldn't have pictured you as a New York Times kind of gal," he says, pointing to my computer.

I shut my laptop and slide it back into my bag.

"It's rude to read over someone's shoulder," I say.

"Not as rude as taking up a big booth all by yourself. Mind if I join you for breakfast?"

He doesn't wait for my answer before waving over the waitress.

"Morning, Sam," she says. "The usual?"

"Yes, ma'am," he answers then waves at me. "What are you having, Lila?"

I hand the waitress my menu.

"Just a bowl of oatmeal for me. Do you have almond milk?"

She gives me a quizzical look and shakes her head.

"Sorry honey."

"Okay. How about coconut milk or rice milk?"

Sam raises his eyebrows and grins at me.

"We don't have that either," she answers with an apologetic smile. "Will skim milk do?"

I frown. "No, that's okay. Orange juice will be fine."

She tucks her pad into her pocket. "I'll be right back with two cups of coffee then."

When she leaves, Sam leans back, crosses his arms, and gives me a slow smile. Damn, he's sexy. I can't let myself think about it, but it's impossible not to.

His sandy blond hair is still damp from the shower and unruly from wearing a motorcycle helmet. A lock of hair keeps falling over his eye, and I have a strong urge to reach over and push it back with my fingers.

"I didn't tell you it was okay for you to sit here," I point out.

"Why? Someone else joining you?"

"Maybe. Or maybe I wanted some peace and quiet by myself. To read my New York Times and drink my coffee alone."

"I make you nervous, don't I?" he says. "Want to tell me why?"

The waitress places two coffee mugs on the table and I take a sip before answering.

"All strange men make me nervous. Nothing personal."

"You're implying I'm strange?"

"Not strange, a stranger," I explain then smile at him. "You might be strange too. Probably are. I don't know you well enough to say."

"Maybe you should stick around a while and find out for yourself. And since we're being brutally honest here, there's something about you that I've been wondering about too."

He uncrosses his arms and leans forward.

"I'm just going to spit it out," he continues. "If it offends you, I'm sorry, but I really need to ask you something. Right now. Before this goes any further, I have to know."

Does he already suspect something about me?

My heart starts pounding. I must be the worst special agent in the history of the ATF if I've already blown my cover.

"What do you want to know?" I say. "Go ahead and ask."

"Only if you promise you won't get mad."

I relax a little. Maybe he doesn't know.

"I can't promise I won't get mad. Say it."

"Okay. But you have to be honest." He leans closer. "Are you one of those kind of women? There, I said it. Just tell me the truth."

I put my coffee mug down and stare at him.

Big mistake.

His twinkling blue eyes immediately suck me in and break my concentration.

"What exactly are you asking me?"

He shrugs and fiddles with the handle of his coffee mug.

"You know what I mean. Don't make me spell it out."

It takes me a minute to comprehend what he is asking.

Oh my God!

He thinks I'm a lesbian.

My first instinct as a woman is to be hurt. I should be thinking about how I've failed at my job and instead I'm wondering what it is about me that made him think that. The whole undercover operation was based on me being someone who might be intriguing enough to Sam to lure him in. And now I find out that he doesn't even find me attractive.

Ouch, that stings.

On so many different levels.

"You think I'm a lesbian?" I ask, my voice rising and cracking.

His loud burst of laughter rings out across the diner, causing several of the customers to look our way. A couple of the men nod at Sam and throw up a hand in greeting.

"Hell no!" he says, still chuckling. "I know better than that, darling. Where on earth did you come up with a crazy idea like that?" He looks around to make sure no one is listening before his voice lowers to a whisper.

"I meant are you a...*vegan*?"

I can't help but laugh. He's messing with me. And he got me good. Lesson learned. I'll have to keep my guard up with him from now on. Sam is a sly, mischievous devil. Somehow my detailed research failed to reveal that vital piece of information.

"Just because I try to eat healthy doesn't mean I'm a vegan." I glance up at the waitress heading our way with our orders. "Looks like you should think about eating a little healthier, too."

I watch in fascination as the waitress unloads Sam's large order of biscuits, gravy, bacon, eggs, and grits. She places my tiny bowl of oatmeal in front of me.

"Please don't tell me you eat like this every day," I say, pointing to his plate.

He frowns at me. "Please don't tell me you're putting two packs of artificial sweetener in your oatmeal. At least I'm eating real food and not chemicals. And just so you know, I don't eat like this every day. Some mornings when I'm feeling frisky, I order blueberry pancakes and sausage instead."

I roll my eyes at him.

"Let's see who is still alive in fifty years," I say.

"So you're planning on sticking around for decades?" he asks. "How long are you going to be in town?"

"As long as it takes to write the magazine articles I'm working on," I lie.

"Oh, you're a writer?" he asks. "Who do you work for?"

Time to spin my cover story of lies.

"I'm a freelance writer for several different magazines. I'm currently on assignment doing a story about Southern traditions. The North Georgia Mountains seemed like a good place to start. So here I am."

Sam looks up from the plate of food he is rapidly devouring.

"Sounds interesting. Where are you staying while you're in town? Do you have family here?"

"I rented a cabin on the lake for a month. Hopefully that will be enough time to get all the information I need. The cabin has a deck with a great view, so it will be like a long summer vacation. I don't plan on working every minute I'm here. Since I'm a freelancer, I don't punch a time clock."

"Good to hear," he says. "Maybe I can help you out with your story. What kind of Southern traditions are you writing about?"

"I haven't decided yet. The magazine has expressed some interest in moonshiners, so I'll probably start there."

Sam wipes his mouth with a napkin and takes a sip of his coffee.

"Moonshine stills are illegal," he says. "Nobody around here is going to be willing to talk to a big city writer. You probably should think of something else to write about. Quilting or canning green beans might be good."

"What if I had a local person to help me out with an introduction?"

"Are you talking about me?" He leans back and looks surprised. "What would make you think I know any local moonshiners?"

"Do you?"

"I might know a couple of people who still make hooch," he says slowly. "If you want the info, it's going to cost you though. If I arrange to make these introductions, you have to go on a date with me this weekend."

Well, that was easy and unexpectedly fast. Things are going much better than planned. I was counting on having to play the cat and mouse game with Sam for a while longer. It was completely on impulse that I threw the moonshiners into the conversation, mostly out of curiosity to see what he would say.

I've heard of reality shows featuring Georgia moonshiners but didn't think they really existed. And if they do, the ATF would be very interested in their activities.

"Is this date going to be an interview for sex?" I ask. "Because if it is, I'm not interested."

He gives me a hurt look.

"Of course not," he says then smiles again. "You've already got the job if you want it. No formal interview necessary."

"I don't want it," I say firmly. "And I'm not looking for a relationship either. Just so you know."

"Good," he replies. "Neither am I."

"So what are you after?"

He reaches across the table and rubs the back of my hand with his thumb.

"You'll find out."

My breath catches in my throat. I pull my hand back out of his reach.

"So how soon can you take me to meet these people?" I ask.

"How about this evening after I close the tattoo shop?" he says. "I'll make a few calls. I'm sure I can set something up. I'll pick you up at your lake cabin at seven. Send me a text with the address and I'll be there."

"You're that confident you can set something up with a phone call?"

"I can be extremely persuasive when I want to be," he says.

I bet.

"Okay then. I'll be ready for you at seven."

"I'll be on my bike, so dress accordingly."

I frown at him. "You don't own a car?"

He gulps down the remaining coffee in his cup.

"Sure I do. I rarely take it out. If you want to go anywhere with me, you have to be willing to ride behind me on the bike."

"Not a problem," I say. "I'm game if you are. Or we can drive my car."

"No way. You ride or you don't go."

"Fine. I'll ride. Are you a safe driver?"

"Guess you'll find out."

He stands up and grabs the tickets for both of our meals.

"See you at seven."

I resist the urge to turn around in the booth so I can watch him walk away. It's hard to take my eyes off him. I hear several people in the diner call out to him as he makes his way to the door, including most of the waitresses.

Sam Mason is a popular guy.

Too bad he won't be hanging around Bardsville much longer once the ATF gets their hands on him.

5

SAM

I arrive at Lila's cabin on the lake at seven o'clock sharp. My Dad always insisted on promptness from me and my brothers, so it's a habit I've never broken. After having the shit beat out of me for being late more than a few times when I was younger, I learned quickly to be where you're supposed to be right on time or early.

Jesse and Flint are both the same way. We never talk about the things that went on in our house. It's better to leave things in the past. Bad memories need to stay buried deep where they belong.

Lila steps out the front door before I have a chance to turn off the bike. She doesn't invite me in and instead waves a hand down her body.

"Am I dressed okay?" she asks. "I wasn't sure what to wear."

I take a long look. She's wearing a pair of white shorts that could be a little shorter in my opinion and a white blouse with ruffles. The blouse is sheer and I can see straight through to the white lacy bra underneath. I would love to slip up behind her, slide my hands under the shirt, and cup her full breasts in my hands.

Shit!

She wore that sexy blouse on purpose.

To tempt me.

I can't forget that everything is a pre-calculated move with her.

"You're better than okay," I say. "You look good enough to eat. But your blouse is a little too see-through for where we're going. The people we're going to visit can be a little unpredictable, and we don't want to stir up trouble. You probably should change into something a tad more...nun-like."

She looks confused and her eyes widen.

"Oh, you mean the moonshiners," she says. "How rough are these people? Are they dangerous?"

"I don't know for sure, so it's better to be safe than sorry." I try not to let my facial expression give anything away. "Some of these backwoods country folks are a little different. They might not appreciate a provocative blouse with a sexy lacy bra underneath the way I do." I stare pointedly at her breasts. "And just so you know, I appreciate it very much. So if the shirt is for my benefit, thank you."

"It isn't," she says in a huff, throwing up her hands in frustration. "I'll be right back."

I admire the view of her gorgeous ass running back into the house. She returns two minutes later in a plain blue shirt that covers up everything.

"Is this better?" she asks.

I make a face.

"Not to me. But I think you'll be glad you changed once we get there."

I hand her a helmet and she straps it on without asking for my help. After I climb on the bike, she hops on behind me and grips my waist without saying a word.

I slide on my sunglasses and hide a smile.

This is going to be fun.

Little Miss Lila is screwing with the wrong person.

Nobody outplays a player, and I'm the best there is.

I run my hand down her smooth thigh before resting it on her knee. She tenses slightly, unconsciously letting me know that she would like to slap my hand away. So I leave it.

"All set back there?" I ask.

"Yeah, let's go."

I drive slowly on the two-lane country road then open up the engine when we hit the open highway. When I glance back in the mirror at her,

I can't tell if she's enjoying the ride or terrified. Either way, she's not going to let me see it.

Everything Lila does is carefully calculated. Behind those clear green eyes, her mind is probably whirling constantly, always thinking of her next big move against me. It freaks me out to think how things might have turned out if Flint's contact hadn't warned us.

When I speed up, she scoots up closer and grips my waist tighter. Her soft breasts press against my back. My cock stirs in interest and I can't help wondering what she's like in bed.

Would she be a nice, polite fuck, technically doing everything right, but leaving me cold in the end? Or would she allow herself to let go and feel without inhibitions?

I'm dying to find out.

I want to shake her up, turn her inside out and see what she's hiding underneath.

Everyone needs a mission.

Her mission is to send me to prison. My new mission is to fuck her so good and so often that when the time comes, she won't be able to complete her mission.

And after that?

Who the hell knows what will happen? If I get too caught up in the forever after details, it will mess with my head and I'll screw up.

She leans close to my ear. Her breath tickles my neck. "How much further?"

"Another fifteen minutes or so," I answer back.

I can't wait to see her face when we get there. She is going to be pissed.

After several more miles, I turn off onto a one-lane road and drive back into the countryside. The road gradually changes from pavement to gravel to dirt.

"Do you know where you're going?" she asks in concern after I swerve around a mud puddle in the middle of the dirt road.

"Almost there."

I make one more turn and then we pull up in front of a small yellow house. The wraparound front porch is covered in flower pots of red geraniums and hanging baskets of purples pansies. An elderly woman steps out of the house and waves to us.

After I stop the bike, Lila slides off and removes her helmet.

"Where are we?" she asks, confused. "I thought you were taking me to see a moonshine still."

I give her a blank look.

"No, you must have misunderstood. I said we were going to see someone who makes *hooch*. And that would be my Aunt Leona. She mixes up a wicked potion of apple brandy. And occasionally plum."

"Your Aunt Leona?" Lila echoes after me. "We're here to talk to the lady waving to us?"

"Yeah, let's go on in. She's looking forward to meeting you. When I told her you might write about her in a big-time magazine, she said to bring you right over."

Lila refuses to budge away from the bike. Her green eyes look perplexed.

"But you said I needed to change my blouse because the moonshiners might think it was too suggestive."

I laugh and shake my head.

"No, I didn't say that. You have a wild imagination. What do you think this place is? *Deliverance*? I knew my Aunt Leona wouldn't appreciate being able to see straight through your shirt. She's conservative and old-fashioned. Aren't you glad now that you changed?"

From the expression on Lila's face, I can tell she's having a hard time keeping her shit together. She can't decide if she should be polite since there's an old lady waving at her or if she should pitch a hissy fit on me like she really wants to do.

I try to keep a straight face and wait patiently while she makes up her mind, knowing it can easily go either way.

"Y'all come on in now," Aunt Leona beckons from the porch.

I take Lila's hand in mine. "We're coming," I yell back.

Lila obviously needs a little push. Otherwise we'll be standing here all night while she tries to figure out how I screwed her over.

"You're going to love my Aunt Leona," I say. "She'll tell you everything you ever wanted to know about making hooch. And I mean *everything*. She loves to talk, especially if she has a captive audience."

Lila plasters a fake smile on her face.

"Great," she says cheerfully. "I'm looking forward to it."

My aunt opens the screen door for us to walk through and winks at me behind Lila's back. She might be old, but she's as mischievous as I am, if not worse. When I called her earlier and filled her in about what was going on, she jumped at the chance to fool a city girl. The last thing she said before hanging up was that "nobody messes with my boys and gets away with it."

I'm actually feeling kind of bad for Lila at the moment.

Not too bad though.

Whatever Aunt Leona is getting ready to do to her, she deserves it.

And more.

6

LILA

I would like to strangle Sam with my bare hands.

We've been walking for fifteen minutes through a hot, hilly cow pasture to reach an apple orchard that I can't even see yet. I'm already out of breath and his aunt isn't winded, though she hasn't stopped talking since we set out. She insisted that I call her Aunt Leona too, which feels awkward and weird.

"It's a good thing you've got your walking shoes on, Lila," she says, pointing to my new, uncomfortable sandals that are killing my feet. I'll be covered in blisters tomorrow and will have to go barefoot for a week.

"If Sam had told me we would be hiking, I would have worn tennis shoes," I reply, giving him a dirty look.

"But that would have spoiled the surprise," he says with a straight face.

Is he screwing with me?

I study his face closely to see if he is joking and can't tell. He would make an excellent poker player. My gut tells me that he set this whole thing up to aggravate me. What I can't figure out is why would he do that? He's the one that asked me out on a date, not the other way around.

I know it isn't my imagination that he led me to believe that we would be going to see actual moonshiners. Not a sweet old lady who makes apple cider vinegar and convinces herself there's alcohol in it.

I hope to God she doesn't expect me to drink it at some point during the visit. When she offers it to me, I'll either say alcohol is against my religion or that I'm diabetic. Neither of which is true.

Finally we huff and puff our way to the top of a hill and she points to two little apple trees on the other side with her walking stick. A herd of black and white cows are standing underneath the limbs. Apples are scattered all over the ground.

She waves a wrinkled hand at the trees. "There's my orchard," she says with a proud smile. "Isn't it nice? Take out your pencil and paper so I can tell you all about how I take care of the trees. We can go sit on the ground in the shade while you take notes."

"Sit with the cows?" I ask.

The white shorts I'm wearing won't be white much longer.

"Oh, the cows won't hurt you," she says. "The worst they might do is stomp on your toes. The black flies hanging around on them can be bad sometimes. They bite."

I hear a sound behind me that sounds suspiciously like a snicker. I whirl around to glare at Sam, who smiles at me.

"Here, take my hand, Lila," he says. "I'll help you walk down the hill."

Yeah, he'll help me alright. Right down into a cow patty.

I ignore his outstretched hand.

"That's Sam for you," his aunt says. "Always being a true Southern gentleman. His mama, who was my sister Melissa, always tried to teach the boys good manners. Isn't that right, Sam?"

"Yes ma'am," he answers politely.

Now there's a story I don't believe for a minute.

I wonder if good old Aunt Leona knows that all three Mason boys are criminals. Nothing more than common outlaws with pretty faces who are currently under investigation by the ATF and state government agencies.

Of course she doesn't. Why would she?

When we reach the trees, Sam points to a clear spot on the ground for me to sit. He plops down beside me, leans back against the tree trunk, and stretches his long legs out in front of him. After picking up a half-rotten apple, he casually rubs it with his shirt and tries to hand it to me.

"Want an apple?" he asks. "I wiped it off."

Do I want to die from e-coli?

"No thank you," I say politely. "I'm not hungry."

He grins, and without taking his eyes from mine, takes a big bite out of it. Juice drips down the side of his mouth until he casually wipes it off with the back of his hand.

Jesus Christ.

With his eating habits, I wondered if he would live to see forty. Now I'm having doubts he'll make it to next week.

Aunt Leona is busy picking up apples off the ground and stuffing them into her apron pockets.

"Do you pick the apples from the trees for your brandy or take the ones from the ground?" I ask.

She laughs as if it's a stupid question. "Whichever ones look the best, honey. I wash them, so they're fine." She points to the notebook I've taken out of my purse. "Be sure to write down that I wash them all very well."

I click my pen and write down 'she washes the apples.'

This is stupid as hell.

Black flies are swarming all around us, and I can't decide if I want to slash my wrists with the sharp knife I always keep in my purse or stab Sam to death with my pen.

As if he knows what I'm thinking, he winks at me and reaches over to squeeze my thigh.

Definitely stab him first.

Two hours later and Aunt Leona is still talking about apple brandy. At least now we're back at the house and out of that godforsaken apple orchard. We've gone over the entire process from beginning to end three dozen times. I've written down pages upon pages of notes to the point my hand is cramping.

"Are you sure you understand everything?" she asks. "It seems like I'm forgetting to tell you an important step. I would hate for someone to try to follow my recipe and get poisoned."

Yes. God forbid.

The whole time we're talking, Sam just sits there as if he doesn't have a care in the world. Smiling, eating pound cake, and teasing his aunt constantly. From the way she's doting on Sam, she obviously loves him a great deal. Her heart will be broken when she finds out what kind of man he really is, not to mention his two brothers.

It makes me sad for her and mad at them. She is such a sweet old lady, and I hate to think what it will do to her when they're arrested. These are the kind of thoughts I can't dwell on. Otherwise it will mess with my head.

I close my notepad and click my pen.

"I believe I've gotten all the information I need," I say. "If I have any questions, I can always call you later."

I can't take this charade anymore and am beginning to feel bad for deceiving her.

Sometimes I hate my job.

Especially when innocent people get hurt and I always end up feeling like it's my fault.

"Well, hang on a minute. You can't go yet." She walks over to the cabinet and pulls out a Mason jar filled with a light amber liquid. "Sam, fetch us some hot toddy glasses," she says, pointing to a cabinet above the refrigerator.

While he reaches for three little shot glasses, she opens the lid on the jar and sniffs. Her eyes immediately water and she pats at them with the corner of her apron.

"Whew!" she says. "Smells strong. Don't worry. You're going to like this, Lila. And I won't let you leave without trying it."

I feel like banging my head on the Formica kitchen table.

Okay, fine.

At this point I'm willing to drink gasoline for this to be over and done with.

Sam places the shot glasses on the table and she carefully fills each one to the rim. After handing me mine, she gives one to Sam and picks up her glass.

"Here's to new friends," she says, holding her glass high.

Sam catches my eye and lifts his glass. His eyes are twinkling in mischief again. He knows this is going to be bad, and he's not doing one damn thing to stop it.

When the devil came down to Georgia looking for a soul to steal, he found one person.

Sam Mason.

And he never left.

"To new friends," he repeats.

"Cheers," I say.

I tilt the entire contents of the shot glass into my mouth and swallow.

I'm on fire.

Gasoline would have gone down smoother. My throat and lungs are burning in agony. I start coughing and choking.

"Don't stand there like an idiot, Sam," Aunt Leona says. "Hurry and get her a glass of water."

She pounds me hard on the back like I'm choking on a piece of steak while I try to catch my breath. What she's doing isn't helping one bit.

"Here, drink this," Sam says. He hands me a glass of water and I try to take a sip in between coughs. "I'm sorry," he says. "I should've warned you. Hooch is stronger than regular liquor. That's why we call it *hard liquor.*"

I nod and drink more water.

Aunt Leona picks up her shot glass, downs it all in a quick swallow, and smacks her lips. "A little bit stronger than last year's batch," she says. "Maybe I shouldn't have let it ferment as long. You want to write that down? Not to leave it in the jug too long?"

I hold up my hand and shake my head.

No more.

"It's getting late," Sam says. "I should take Lila home." He knocks his glass back without blinking then slides a casual arm around my waist. "Are you going to be okay? Should we wait a few more minutes before heading out?"

"I'm okay," I say. "We should probably go. We've taken up far too much of Aunt Leona's time." I reach out and touch her arm. "Thank you. You've been a big help."

"I hope to see you again," she says, still patting me on the back. "Visit me anytime. And be sure to send me a copy of the magazine article when it comes out."

"I will," I lie.

I hate this.

7

LILA

The loud roar of a motorcycle muffler wakes me up. I reach over groggily, switch on the bedside lamp, and look at the clock.

1 a.m.

Who is up at this time of the night? I'm an early morning person, so this is *way* past my bedtime.

Surely not Sam?

He dropped me off at my front door three hours ago. I can't imagine why he would come back. Especially since we had such an amazing fun time at Aunt Leona's.

Not.

I couldn't wait for that little excursion to end.

The motorcycle pulls up in front of the house and the engine cuts off.

Would Sam really come over this late without calling? Yeah, he would.

I tug on a long t-shirt that hangs halfway down my thighs and slip on a pair of panties. Sam doesn't need to know that I sleep in the nude.

He's already knocking at the front door before I reach the kitchen.

"Lila," he whispers loudly. "Are you awake? Lila!"

Why is he whispering?

The nearest house is a half-mile away and he obviously doesn't mind waking me. I open the door and see him leaning against the porch railing. I notice he has a firm grip on the wooden post next to him. He smiles at me as if there isn't anything unusual about showing up at a woman's house uninvited in the middle of the night.

"Hey," he says. "Were you asleep?"

"I *was*."

He looks disappointed.

"Oh...I saw your bedroom light on when I pulled up so I thought you might be still awake. That's why I knocked on the door."

"I'm awake because I heard your motorcycle roaring down the road. The sound could wake the dead."

"I didn't think about that," he says sheepishly. "Sorry. Okay, I'll be on my way then. You go on back to sleep."

He turns to walk back down the porch steps and sways slightly.

"Wait! Sam, are you drunk?"

He glances back at me over his shoulder and laughs.

"No...I'm not drunk. What would make you think that?"

Of course not.

I've never known a single man to admit when they were drunk.

"Let me rephrase my question then. How much have you had to drink tonight?"

He opens his blue eyes wide and gives me his best puppy dog, innocent look. I wonder how many times he's used that expression on other women. Or cops.

"Only a couple of beers," he answers. "Not much."

"Ah...the standard answer. Two beers."

"I'm fine," he says with a wave. "I'll call you."

He walks down the porch steps to his motorcycle, reaches for his helmet, and fumbles it onto the ground.

Great.

"You had better come inside," I say. "You can't drive in this condition."

"Sure I can," he argues. "I'm an excellent driver."

Now he's slurring his words, though I notice he's taking great care to enunciate each word as clearly as he can. He sounds like he's getting more intoxicated by the minute. In my mind, I picture him guzzling down a quart of whiskey then hopping on his bike before the alcohol had time to seep through his system.

"Right now you're a drunk driver who has no business being on the road."

I walk outside in my bare feet and hold out my hand.

"Give me your keys."

He chuckles and jerks the keys high out of my reach.

"I'm not giving a woman the keys to my bike," he says.

Now he's about to piss me off.

"Did you really just say that? Do you want me to knock you on your ass? Give me the damn keys!"

"You're a feisty little kitten, aren't you?" he says.

"Kitten? Keep it up buddy, and I'll show you what it feels like to be shredded by a tiger."

I grab for the keys and he jumps back again. It's all I can do to refrain from kicking his legs out from under him and taking the keys like I know I can. Throwing him to the ground might be a little suspicious since he's bigger and much stronger, so I have to control myself. Few women my size can throw a big man off their feet in three seconds. With all the self-defense and takedown training I've had, it will be easy. One way or another, he's not going back on the road.

"Cut it out, Sam. I'm not playing with you."

Chuckling, he steps back again and staggers against the side of the bike. I grab the handlebars to keep them both from falling over.

"Oh my God! Will you please stop it?"

I haven't dealt with an intoxicated person in a long time. I've forgotten how frustrating it can be to reason with them.

"Are you still sticking to your 'not drunk' story?" I ask. "Because you're not very convincing. You can barely stand up without swaying."

He squeezes two fingers almost together.

"Maybe a teensy, weensy bit drunk," he admits.

"Well, that's a start on the road to recovery," I say. "Where were you tonight anyway?"

"The clubhouse."

"And your biker friends let you leave in this shape?"

"No," he says. "I was the last one there. Except for the Sweet Butts."

Oh yes. The infamous Sweet Butts.

I know all about the group of women who hang around the Steel Infidels clubhouse. Most, if not all of them, are willing to do anything the bikers want to keep their position within the club. Sex, blowjobs, nothing is off limits. The women are passed around among the members and shared like club property. It disgusts me to think about it. It also ticks me off that they let Sam drive when he's clearly wasted. He could hurt someone.

"Why didn't you stay there with them until you sobered up?"

"I wanted to see you," he says simply. "And you weren't there, so I had to come here." He points to the house then reaches out unsteadily to gently touch the side of my face.

I look up at his bloodshot eyes and let out a long sigh. Looks like I've got a drunk for the night whether I want him or not. On the bright side, this might be a golden opportunity for me to pry some information out of him about the Steel Infidel's business dealings.

I decide to switch tactics since strong-arming him clearly isn't working. Taking his hand in mine, I tug him away from the bike. Thankfully he moves with me this time instead of jerking away.

"Let's go inside where we can talk. If you came all this way to see me, you can't just leave. Come on."

To my relief, he allows me to lead him up the steps to the front porch. I open the door and he suddenly stops. Turning around, he tries to pull me back down the stairs.

"You want to go skinny-dipping?" he asks, waving a hand toward the black lake behind the house. "It's hot out here."

This man is driving me batshit crazy.

"Oh, there's a great idea if I've ever heard one. Let's think about this. It's pitch dark, the lake has drop-offs, and you're wasted. You would drown and take me under with you. So the answer is no, we're not going skinny-dipping. Are you out of your mind? The house has air-conditioning, so you'll survive."

Certain he was going to keep giving me a hard time, I put my hand on his back and practically shove him inside the house. Slamming the door behind us, I lock the deadbolt to keep him from running right back out again.

After sitting him down in a chair at the kitchen table, I reach for a bottle of aspirin in the cabinet.

"You're going to have a massive hangover tomorrow."

He shakes his head. "I don't get them."

"Lucky you. So I'm guessing you do this often?"

He doesn't answer me.

I shake out two aspirin anyway and pour him a glass of water.

"Here," I say, handing them to him. "Swallow these and drink the whole glass. Maybe the water will dilute the gallons of alcohol flooding your bloodstream."

Surprisingly, he does exactly what I tell him to do without arguing. When I turn to walk away, he grabs my hand and tugs me down onto his lap. I try to push against his arms and instead of turning me loose, he tightens his grip.

"Do you like sitting in my lap?" he mumbles into my hair.

I hide a smile because encouraging him is the last thing I want to do.

"I don't know, because I've never sat in your lap before."

"Are you sure?" he asks doubtfully.

"Pretty sure I would remember it."

"Maybe I dreamed it then," he says. "Because I like it."

His hand strokes my calf then slides up my bare thigh to rest on my ass. I try to ignore the heat coming off his skin through the thin shirt or how good his muscular arms feel wrapped around my back.

Yeah, I like sitting on his lap. Too much.

Sam leans closer and nuzzles my neck.

"You smell sweet. Like shampoo. And your skin is so soft."

He slides his fingers under the side rim of my panties and caresses my hip.

Oh mercy!

This is good and not good.

It's hard enough trying to resist cocky, devilish Sam. Fending off drunk, sweet Sam with warm, roving hands is even worse. Maybe it's my imagination, but his hands feel like they're *everywhere* at the same time.

I wrap my hand around his wrist to stop him before he goes any further.

"Okay, buddy. Keep your hands above the waist."

He chuckles into my neck and immediately slides his hand up my shirt to cup my braless breast. My nipple responds instantly to his touch, hardening into a thick bud.

Bad choice of words.

He obviously isn't too drunk to catch my slip up and to take advantage of it.

"Sorry, Sam. This is not happening tonight. You're wasted."

I pull his hand out from under my shirt. He grumbles in protest.

"I'm not having sex with someone who is drunk and won't even remember it tomorrow," I explain.

I feel him smile against my neck.

"So you would if I wasn't drunk?" he asks.

"I guess you'll never know now, will you? You just blew your one big opportunity. Any chance with me is gone forever. Getting drunk and coming over here was a bad idea. What can I say? You screwed up."

"Now I'm sad," he says in a pitiful voice.

He really does sound sad. Sam has probably never heard the word 'no' from a woman. Maybe it's time he learned he can't get everything he wants. Resisting him is not going to be a problem for me, so he'd better get used to it.

"Can I have a kiss to make me feel better?" he asks, his voice already sounding cheerful again. His sorrow didn't last long.

"No," I snap back at him.

He nibbles at my earlobe.

"One little kiss," he whispers into my ear. "That's all and then I'll be good. I promise."

Oh, you're plenty good already.

Heat floods through my body. I want to curl up into his lap, slide my fingers through his hair, and hold onto him until the sun comes up.

"Lila," he breathes slowly against my neck, his warm breath sending shivers down my spine. "Kiss me."

He's not going to give up. Sam is trying his best to seduce me, and his plan is working. There's no point in denying what he is doing to me. My defenses are melting underneath his hands and the warm breath in my ear.

I've put myself in a bad situation both personally and professionally.

My job is to get close enough to Sam to place the surveillance equipment and gather information to build a case. Having sex with Sam is not in my job description.

On the other hand, so what if I'm physically attracted to Sam? I'm a grown woman. I can do anything I want, including closing my eyes and leaning in to kiss the sexy man holding me on his lap.

Plus, I'm tired and it's the middle of the night. I can't think straight.

What's the possible harm in one little kiss?

"One kiss and one kiss only," I finally say, caving in.

"That's all I need," he murmurs huskily, right before covering my mouth with his. Strong, warm hands hold my throat, keeping me in place, his grasp gentle yet possessive. The raging intensity of heat that immediately surges between us catches me off guard. Before I realize it, I'm kissing him back, opening my mouth and welcoming his tongue. I melt into him as our kiss deepens into something seamless and primal.

Long minutes pass before Sam draws away just an inch, only long enough to give me time to catch my breath.

Damn that felt good.

"There's your one kiss," I say, my voice unrecognizable to my own ears. "The show's over."

I'm reeling from the aftershocks. Sure, I knew kissing Sam would be good. He's a ladies' man. Of course he would know how to please a woman. With my eyes still shut tight, I feel more than see his smile as he moves his lips against mine.

"Maybe I want more than one," he growls, his grasp on my throat tightening just a fraction as he seizes my lips again with a ferocious frenzy.

My fingers clutch at the back of his neck with my self-control sliding down a slippery slope. His heart is racing wildly underneath my hand on his shirt. It would be so easy to move this into the bedroom.

I would like to.

No, that's a lie.

I would love to.

But I won't.

I meant what I told him. I'm not sleeping with him.

Mustering all the willpower I have in me, I reluctantly break the kiss and pull back. We're both breathing erratically and I'm in a daze. Reaching up, I smooth back a messy lock of his hair that keeps falling down over his forehead.

"You're sleeping on the sofa tonight," I say with a bit of regret. "Not in the bed with me."

"Okay," he mumbles, and he abruptly turns me loose so I can slide off his lap.

"No arguments from you?"

I give him a suspicious look because I'm surprised he would give up so easily. And maybe a tad disappointed too.

"None," he says before adding, "Do you know how to cook biscuits and gravy?"

I stare at him. We just shared the best kiss of my life, and he's thinking about food? Does he really think I'm going to get up early and cook him breakfast? Sam must have balls of steel to suggest such a thing to me.

"Do I look like a short order cook to you? No, I don't know how to cook biscuits and gravy, and I don't want to learn. Don't get any thoughts about hanging around for breakfast. Not even coffee. In the morning, you need to get your hungover butt up early and leave. I've got work to do and I'm sure you do too."

"Trish knows how to cook biscuits," he rambles on. "She's married to my brother, Jesse. She can teach you if you want. Southern cooking, and all that other stuff. You can write about it in the magazine."

Oh my God.

Why did I ever tell him I was writing a magazine article? He is never going to let this go.

From my research, I know that Trish's brother was the vice president of a rival motorcycle club who is now sitting in jail for firebombing a bar in Panama City. Other than that, I don't know much about Trish except that she worked at the bar as one of the beer tub gals.

"I'm sure Trish knows how to do all kinds of fun things that I'm not interested in learning," I say. "So please don't go setting up any cooking classes with me and Trish. You're never going to see this girl getting up early to cook you biscuits and gravy, so you can put it out of your mind and forget it."

He leans his head back and closes his eyes. "Never hurts to ask."

"You can ask, but it's not going to happen," I say. "Are you still listening to me?"

He doesn't answer. Another minute and he's going to be out.

"Don't go to sleep in the chair or you'll fall on the floor and knock yourself unconscious."

I pick his keys up off the table and slide them into my T-shirt's pocket. He can't be trusted to make good decisions tonight. Maybe not any night. Sam strikes me as a spur of the moment guy who never thinks before he acts.

Pretty much the exact opposite of me.

"Stay here and I'll find a blanket and pillow for you. The house came furnished and I don't know where everything is yet. Okay?"

He barely nods.

It takes me a few minutes to find an extra set of sheets and a light blanket. When I walk back into the kitchen with them, Sam is missing.

Now what?

"Sam?" I call out. "Where are you?"

No answer.

I open the door and check to make sure his bike is still parked out front. For a second I was afraid he had a second key hidden somewhere and had taken off. I'm relieved to see he didn't.

I check the living room and the bathrooms. No Sam. Only one room left to check. If he's where I think he is, he's going to be in big trouble. I toss the pillow and blanket onto the sofa and head for my bedroom. So help me, if he has crawled into my bed, I'm going to dump his ass right onto the floor.

The word 'no' means 'no' and it makes me angry when men think I'm only kidding when I say it.

I turn the knob and step inside.

Whoa!

Okay. Maybe I won't dump him out just yet.

Sam is lying on the bed completely naked with his back to me. A muscular arm covered in tattoos is slung over his head, and he is out cold. I consider shaking him awake and decide the view is too good to disturb.

I quietly inch closer to take a look at the large Steel Infidels tattoo stretching all the way from one shoulder to the other on his back. My eyes glide down his spine to the finest looking male ass I've ever seen.

Definitely a 'do not disturb' situation.

After all, who cares where he sleeps? The bed, the couch...the location is merely a technicality. As long as it's not with me, it doesn't matter. I can sleep on the sofa and maybe even curled up in the chair on the other side of the room.

Where I can keep a close eye on him.

For observational purposes only.

He might choke in his sleep or something, so I should definitely stay in the same room. It's not hard to convince myself that the situation isn't so bad and I can definitely find a way to work around it.

Lying in a pile on the floor are his clothes and leather boots. Never one to miss a good opportunity, I slide my hand into his pants pocket and pull out his wallet and cell phone. Not surprising he's carrying a cheap prepaid phone instead of a smartphone. The bikers most likely switch them out often. I turn his phone on and look through his call records and a few texts. Nothing interesting jumps out at me.

The ATF has wiretaps on the home phone where he lives with Jesse. His brother Flint's phone is tapped, too. When the ATF tried to place wiretaps on the other members of the Steel Infidels, the local judge gave us grief about it. Said we couldn't prove enough cause. We don't need to tap the others anyway.

Anything big that happens with the Steel Infidels involves Sam, Jesse, and Flint. No matter what's going on, at least one of them is right in the middle of it. My gut instinct tells me that the newest member, Toby, needs to be kept under surveillance too. His military background as a Marine and his gun expertise concerns me.

I quietly turn off Sam's cell phone and lean over his body to make sure he's still breathing. It would be bad to have a target of an investigation die in my bed.

After putting the phone back into his pocket, I reach for his wallet. One side contains two hundred dollar bills and a few twenties. More cash than I would carry, though not an outrageous amount.

No credit cards in the wallet, only a driver's license with a photo of a much younger Sam. Even then he was a handsome devil. I can't imagine the trouble he must have gotten into as a teenager. Tucked into the other side are two condoms in their foil packages.

Suddenly feeling like a creepy pervert, though I'm only doing my job, I close the wallet and put it back. The condoms gave me a weird feeling. I don't know why. At least he's responsible and careful. That's better than a lot of men. And it's not like I don't know that he's a manwhore already. My research made that blatantly clear.

Even so, the thought of Sam being with other women bothers me a little bit.

Which is dumb.

This isn't real.

Sam needs to stay off-limits.

No matter how much I might enjoy sex with him, it can only screw things up all the way around. No more kissing and no more touching. Nothing says I can't still look though.

And I will.

All night.

After all, who needs sleep?

Certainly not me.

I wake up the next morning in the chair with a light blanket tucked around me. Sam is already gone. He must have taken the blanket off the bed and covered me up with it before he left. His surprising thoughtfulness brings a smile to my face. Maybe his mother taught him a few good manners after all.

The sheets on the bed are a tangled mess. Considering how drunk he was, I'm surprised he moved a muscle. The bed looks like an F-5 tornado tore through it.

I walk over to the bed, pick up the pillow, and bring it to my nose. The scent of the soap Sam uses is still on the pillowcase. All I have to do is close my eyes and I can see him as clearly as if he's standing beside me. Instead of changing the pillowcase, I put the pillow back down on the side of the bed where I normally sleep.

The weeks of research on Sam leading up to the undercover operation must be messing with my head. In a way, I feel like I've known him forever, and yet he constantly surprises me with the crazy things he says and does.

Sam is one sizzling hot mess.

No doubt about it.

I'm dreading making the daily check-in call to my boss, Frank. No matter how much progress I'm making, it won't be enough for him. He rides me during every investigation to push harder and work faster.

The other field agents feel the same way about him.

Frank continues to put us in volatile situations with little to no regard for our safety. According to him, no risk is too great. Which is easy for him to say. He's sitting all comfy behind a desk while we're out sweating undercover in the field.

I call his number and he answers on the first ring.

"Hi Frank, it's me," I say. "Calling in with an update."

"It had better be good," he says in a gruff voice. "My boss is on my ass about blowing taxpayer's money to shut down a group of small-town bikers."

This is the first time I've heard him mention problems with his boss. It wouldn't hurt my feelings if he got reassigned

I quickly fill him in on the progress I've made so far. A normal boss would be pleased by the fact that I made contact with Sam so quickly. Instead he starts pushing me to place the surveillance bugs.

"If you're already hanging out with the guy, you shouldn't have any problem placing the bug in his tattoo shop," he says. "Don't forget that's the main reason you're there. As long as the bugs are installed, we'll get everything else we need."

"That might be too suspicious," I argue back. "I don't have a reason to show up there uninvited yet. These things take time to gain trust. Do you want to get me killed? We just met."

"Stop stalling and set up the bugs," he says. "It should be simple. We only need them in three spots - the tattoo shop, his house, and the Steel Infidels clubhouse. Get them in place now. If you don't have the balls to do the job, I'll send somebody else who can. You got it?"

Frank knows how to get to me. Threatening to send another agent to take over my investigation is about the worst thing he can do. Even the thought of closely working with another person makes my skin crawl. Partners aren't for me. Other agents only slow me down.

I always work alone.

And nobody else from the team knows the Steel Infidels like I do.

There's no way I'm letting someone else take over this investigation. I need to stay in place.

"I can handle it," I say. "One bug at a time though. I'll do the tattoo shop first and then I'll have to work my way up to the other two. Sam isn't going to invite a stranger to his house, especially since he lives with Jesse and his wife. I can't imagine being able to gain access to the clubhouse ever. If I do, it will be a long shot, so don't get your hopes up."

"Do it today," he says. "You're inventive. I'm sure you can come up with a good excuse to go to the tattoo shop. Call me when the bug is in place and the tapes are rolling."

I blow out a long breath.

Might as well get this over with. The bugs will have to be placed sooner or later anyway. No point in dragging this out.

"I'm on it," I say.

8

SAM

It's almost noon and I've already finished two tattoo jobs. Business is going great these days. Once word got around town that I specialize in tattoos for women, I got all the customers I can reasonably handle.

Jesse comes in several times a week to help me with the overload and to take care of our finances. He is more comfortable doing the simpler tattoos and prefers to leave the bigger, artistic masterpieces to me. Trish balked at the thought of Jesse doing tattoos for female customers, so now I take them all. If a customer wants a skull tattoo, they go to Jesse. If they want a cute little butterfly on their ass, they come to me.

My last customer of the morning, a cute blonde in shorts and pink tank top, didn't want to leave after I finished a flower tattoo high on her inner thigh. It's a recurring problem that I encounter quite often. Over the years, I've learned how to say 'no' while at the same time letting the women think I'm saying 'maybe later.' No feelings get hurt, everyone leaves happy, and I have a return customer. I practically had to drag her to the front door and politely push her outside.

The bell on the front door jingles. I look up from my desk where I'm hand-drawing an intricate tattoo for a special customer. Lila steps inside carrying a bag of takeout food. She's stunning in a short white sundress and high-heeled sandals. Her hair is pulled up on one side with a clip. Gold hoop earrings dangle from her ears.

This is the first time I've seen her in a dress, and I'm floored. My cock begins to stir before the door shuts behind her. Dropping my pencil, I hurry over and lean down to kiss her softly on the lips.

She draws back in surprise and then gives me what sure as hell feels like a genuine pleased smile.

"Wow," I say. "You just made my day, beautiful lady. What's the occasion? And why are you dressed up? You look fantastic by the way."

"No special reason," she says. "Except that I felt kind of bad about telling you to get up early this morning and leave before breakfast. I didn't mean that you had to disappear before daylight. What time did you leave?"

"Around five thirty," I answer. "And I owe you a big apology for stealing your bed. When I woke up and saw you curled up asleep in a chair, I was afraid you would never speak to me again. I'm glad you're here. Can I tell you again how much I love the dress?"

"Yes, you can. I usually wear shorts, so I wanted to wear something nice for a change and bring you lunch." She holds up the bag from a deli down the street. "If you have time that is. Am I interrupting anything?"

"Nope, not a thing. My next client's appointment isn't for at least another hour. Come in and sit down."

I take her hand and clear out a chair for her to sit down on. She looks curiously around the tattoo shop's front office.

"So this is where you work your magic?" she asks.

"I do the tattoos in the back. I try to keep things as sterile as possible, so only clients are allowed in that room. I do the consultations in here and the design work."

I run my hand down her arm, amazed at how soft her skin always feels underneath my fingers. I can't stop touching her. She smells good, and it makes me want to bury my face in the soft place in her neck.

"Maybe I can talk you into letting me give you a tattoo one day."

She shakes her head and laughs.

"I don't think so. The permanent nature of a tattoo worries me. I might get bored with having the same tattoo on my body for the rest of my life. Besides, I like to change my look occasionally."

I bet you do.

Like every time you go undercover. Thank you for reminding me.

"Is that so? I would love to see your other looks. Do you have any photos? Did you wear your hair different?"

"Not too much," she answers. "Sometimes I change the color, that's all. I'll show you some old photos another time."

I reach over and finger her hair. "I like you the way you look now. Don't change anytime soon, okay?"

"I'll agree to that," she says. "But only for now."

She checks the time on her cell phone and holds up the food bag.

"I'm taking up too much of your time. I wasn't sure what you liked so I bought three different sandwiches. I like them all, so you pick first."

If she's playing me, it's working. Doesn't mean I can't enjoy it along the way.

"Sounds great. I have some paper plates in the back. I'll go get them."

After rummaging around in my back room for plates and grabbing a couple of soft drinks from the refrigerator, I walk back into the front office.

"Here we go," I say. "Let's eat."

Lila is bent down on the floor near the front desk. She stands up and touches her ear with both hands.

"I dropped the back of my earring on the floor," she explains. "I was afraid I'd lost it. It fell under your desk so I had to crawl on my hands and knees to reach it."

Something in her voice sounds off. Why is she crawling around on the floor when she could've waited two minutes for me to come back and help her look?

"You should have waited on me to get it for you," I say. "I hope you didn't mess up your pretty white dress."

She holds out the palms of her hands, now covered in dust.

"You're right, and you should sweep in here more often," she says. "I need to wash my hands. Can I borrow your restroom?"

I tilt my head to the hallway.

"First door on the left."

The second she steps inside the restroom and shuts the door, I drop down on the floor to search under my desk. I don't even know what I'm looking for.

And then I see it.

Son of a bitch.

A tiny object no bigger than a watch battery stuck on the underside of my desk.

Lila planted a bug.

I'm stunned, though I shouldn't be. The only reason she dropped by in her pretty dress was to gain access to the tattoo shop. She obviously isn't above pulling out all of her underhanded tricks to keep me sidetracked long enough to place surveillance equipment.

Everything she does is a scam.

Wearing a feminine dress and bringing me lunch. Spraying sweet perfume behind her ears and smiling at me like she really means it.

I'm an idiot for buying into her act. Damn! She's too good at her job.

To say I'm furious is the understatement of the century.

I wonder if the bug is already switched on and recording. For all I know, there could be an unmarked white van down the street with ATF agents listening in on our conversation right now.

I hope they are because I'm about to give them something to burn their fucking ears off. Maybe I'll even get her fired. Screwing the person you're supposed to be investigating can't be considered professional conduct, even in her line of work.

I close my eyes and take a deep breath. If I don't calm down, I'll blow this shit sky high right now. And then we'll all be screwed. The MC is depending on me not to fuck up.

Keep it together, Sam.

There's never been a woman that I couldn't wrap around my cock anytime I wanted. All I have to do is stay calm and not let her see that something is wrong. If she wants to play dirty, then so can I.

Low-down-filthy dirty.

Walking over to the front door, I lock it and flip the sign over to say 'closed.' Then I calmly take the sandwiches out of the bag, remove the plastic wrap, and place them on the plates all nice and neat.

"There you are, pretty lady," I say when she walks back into the room. "I assume the 'all veggie, no meat sandwich' is for you?"

She smiles at me. I want her to mean it and instead I feel sick inside.

"How did you guess?" she asks. "But only if you don't want it."

"No, I definitely don't want it, sweetheart."

I place my hands on both sides of her waist and lift her up to sit her on the edge of my desk. Sliding my hands up her thighs, I drag the dress up with them.

"You know what I really want?" I say, speaking loud and clear so that whoever might be listening in on the bug can hear everything. "I want you. Here. Right now. Spread wide on my desk so I can eat your pussy nice and slow. You would like that too, wouldn't you, Lila? My tongue deep in your pussy." I lean down slightly to make sure my voice is picked up by the bug. "Just like we did *last night*."

I hook my fingers underneath the edge of her lacy white panties and start pulling them down.

"Sam! What the hell are you doing?" she says. She pushes my hands away and tries to shove me backwards.

"Don't tell me you don't want it, Lila. You were begging for me last night."

She stares at me in shock.

"What are you talking about? Nothing happened. You were drunk!"

"So were you," I argue back. "We both were wasted after drinking hooch all night."

"No, I wasn't, you idiot."

"That's not the way I remember it. If we didn't fuck last night, then how did I end up naked in your bed this morning? Are you going to tell me I imagined that too?"

Lila's eyes are getting bigger by the second.

"You're insane, and I don't understand where this is all coming from. I came by to bring you lunch. Then you start talking dirty and...this is getting way too weird for me."

She looks up at me with a hurt, puzzled look.

Damn! Now why is she looking at me like that?

She's the one screwing me over, not the other way around.

This is so fucked up.

She suddenly slides off the desk and stands up. "This is a mistake," she says, straightening her dress. "I need to go."

Of course she needs to go. She can't have her fellow ATF agents hear her being screwed over a desk.

"What's the hurry?" I call after her as she walks toward the door. "We were just getting started."

She turns around and gives me a long look.

"Did something happen when I was in the bathroom? You're different. Hard and cold."

"And here I thought I was turning you on."

"If you think that, you've got the wrong girl. I can't do this. Enjoy the lunch. I've obviously given you the wrong impression. My mistake. I won't be dropping by again."

Oh shit! Now I've really screwed up.

She's bailing out already? This isn't part of the plan. Damn it! I went too far.

"Lila, wait!" I say, touching her arm. "I didn't mean to sound crude. My dirty mouth gets me into trouble sometimes. I blurt out words before I think about how they might sound. And I thought, okay, maybe I was hoping, that we did indeed fuck last night. But if you say that we didn't, I believe you and I owe you an apology."

I'm not sure if she believes what I'm saying. She crosses her arms and glares at me.

"So you didn't mean what you just said about wanting to eat my pussy on the desk?"

My mouth drops open.

Did she really say those words?

Damn! That sounds hot coming out of her mouth.

My cock goes rock hard in my jeans. Even now I want her so fucking bad.

I hate her and I want her.

All at the same time.

Or maybe I want to hate her.

This is a confusing situation.

No matter what, I can't let her walk out of here. I need more time.

For some strange reason, I need Lila to be on *my* side.

"Do you want an honest answer to your question?" I ask. "Yes, I meant what I said. I'm a man, and you waltz in here smelling good and looking pretty in your white sundress. And the thought went through my head that I want to do things to you. Right here in my shop. Or tonight or tomorrow. Honestly, anytime that you'll let me. I'm sorry for sounding like an asshole. I'm not sorry for wanting you. So sorry, not sorry."

She's listening and hasn't told me to 'go to hell' yet, which is a good sign.

"I'll promise to watch my filthy mouth from now on. You can start a swear jar and every time you catch me saying an inappropriate dirty comment, I'll put a dollar in it. I'll probably go broke, but if it keeps me out of trouble with you, it'll be worth it."

I see a smile starting around her lips.

She sighs. "Sam, it's not *what* you said, it's *how* you said it. You caught me off guard and it made me feel...cheap and dirty. Like I'm one of the girls that hang around bikers looking for sexual handouts from anyone. Plus you were completely off base about last night. Nothing happened."

She's acting like I hurt her feelings.

Wait? What? How does that make sense?

I don't understand women.

"Lila."

I'm pulling her to me and kissing her before I think about it. The instant our lips touch, my mind goes blank and all I can do is feel. I'm lost in her smell and the feel of her ass beneath my hands. I tell myself I'm kissing her to protect the MC. Deep down, I know I'm kissing her only for me.

My cock swells, throbbing with need against my jeans. I want nothing more than to shove her dress up around her waist and bury my face between her legs. Everything I said to her five minutes ago I desperately want to do now.

I'm sure as hell not going to say one word about it though. This time I'm keeping my damn mouth shut.

Lila immediately responds just like I hoped she would, tangling her fingers in my hair and leaning closer. She can't stop this madness between us any more than I can.

We're doomed.

This is going to end with both of us going down in flames. I can see it coming from a mile away and can't do one damn thing to stop it.

Even worse, I don't want to stop it.

"Sam?" she finally whispers against my lips when we break apart for air.

"Hmmm," I answer, moving her hair aside and kissing her neck.

"Are we still on for dinner tomorrow night?"
"Damn straight. If you still want me."
"I want you," she says softly.
I bury my nose in her hair and breathe in her scent.
I'm getting in so deep.

9

LILA

I drive away from the Inked Dragon then double back around on side streets to an empty abandoned building with a clear view of the shop. The ATF rented the location for a month to give me a place to observe the customers entering the front door.

The back entrance of the Inked Dragon is being watched by a surveillance camera that I placed two weeks ago on a utility pole in the alley. Every few days, I'm supposed to pull the tapes and go through them. I haven't looked at them yet. There's no telling what I'll see. I'm almost afraid to imagine.

The empty building where I'm set up is old, hot, and musty. As soon as I unlock the door and step inside, I head up to the second floor bathroom and change into shorts and a t-shirt. Surveillance work for the most part is tiring and mind-numbing dull. Wearing comfortable clothes will make it a tiny bit more bearable.

At least I'm working alone. Trying to keep a conversation going with another agent for hours takes too much effort and energy.

After positioning an office chair near the window, I pull a pair of high-powered binoculars out of my bag and try to get comfortable.

It's going to be a long day.

The visit with Sam threw me off balance. One minute he was adorable Sam and the next he turned into a man I didn't recognize. Or maybe it is my fault for not recognizing him before as a sex-crazed maniac.

Something felt off after I came back from the restroom.

He seemed almost mad at me for some reason, and his crude language shocked me since it came out of nowhere. Under the right circumstances, I'm sure I would feel differently, but today it simply wasn't appropriate. At least he smoothed things over quickly, obviously feeling bad for messing up.

Truth is I was the one who screwed up and almost turned the investigation upside down. My personal feelings got in the way, and I was close to stomping out of there in an angry huff.

If Sam hadn't kissed me, I don't know how things would have ended between us.

I'm not ready for things to end yet.

Things *will* end at some point, and I'll be leaving town. Getting attached to Sam would be bad for me. Nothing good can come from it. My personal feelings about anything happening here has to stay out of the equation. It's not my job to question, judge, or even try to protect the people I'm investigating. If laws are being broken, then it's my job to gather evidence.

Period.

End of story.

Keeping my personal feelings under wraps has never been an issue before.

I'm a professional and I need to remember that.

I stand up when I see a woman with her head wrapped up in a bright red scarf walking down the sidewalk in front of the shop. Holding the binoculars to my eyes, I focus on her face. She's pale and appears frail.

Could she be a cancer patient?

I put the binoculars down and watch as she walks into the shop. This can't be good. What could a cancer patient be doing going into a tattoo shop? Buying drugs is the only answer. Probably marijuana.

At least I hope that's all it is.

She might need marijuana to fight the nausea from the chemotherapy treatments. And where would a cancer patient go first in this town to look for weed?

To Sam, of course. The same place they would go for everything else illegal they might want.

I sit back and rub my tired eyes.

He's digging a hole for himself that is only going to be harder and harder to crawl out of. Illegal cigarettes, alcohol, guns, and now marijuana added to the list.

I feel like grabbing him by the neck and shaking some sense into him. The Steel Infidels are involved in too much shit, and Sam's head will be the first one on the chopping block when this all goes down.

He has a good business going with the tattoo shop and would be fine if that's all he did. I'm having a hard time wrapping my head around why the Steel Infidels are risking everything. The profit from their businesses must be tremendous if they're willing to go to prison. They all lead simple lives and never make big purchases, so I'm clueless.

The woman stays inside the shop for a full hour before leaving. I watch through the binoculars as Sam walks her to the door and waves goodbye. She steps outside on the sidewalk and takes three steps before turning around and going back. He's still standing in the doorway and she reaches up to hug his neck.

No, that's not weird at all.

Customers always hug their drug dealers.

What in the world is going on with him?

I'm mystified.

There's too much about Sam that I don't know.

10

SAM

I'm pacing back and forth in the shop, still fuming over Lila placing the bug, when a potential customer walks in.

I walk over to greet her. "Hazel, you're back."

She nods and tries to smile. Taking a deep breath, she says, "I'm ready to talk about it. For real this time."

"Great. Come on back to the private room."

Hazel follows me back to the room where I do the tattoos. She looks a little stronger than the last time I saw her. Still pale, but she's put on a few pounds, which is good. A red scarf hides the fact that all of her hair has fallen out due to chemotherapy.

I point to a chair and she sits down.

"Are you still doing chemo?" I ask.

"No, I'm done. For good I hope."

"I hope so too."

She's uncomfortable. I don't blame her since I know how hard this is on the women.

"Okay, first off, you're going to have to show me," I say. "And then I'll tell you what your options are."

Hazel reaches up to undo the top button of her shirt and stops. Her eyes fill with tears.

"It will be alright," I say, trying to cheer her up. "Look, I've seen plenty of boobs before in my life. Hundreds of boobs. Maybe thousands."

"I'm sure you have," she says and tries to laugh. "Not like mine, I bet."

"My mom had breast cancer too. Believe me, I've seen it all."

I stand up and pull out a cabinet drawer. Picking up a stack of 'before and after' tattoo photos, I hand them to her.

She flips through them and her whole attitude brightens up. "You did all these?" she asks.

"And many more."

She takes a shaky breath. "Okay, I'll show you." She unbuttons her shirt and unhooks the front clasp of her bra then pulls it open wide.

Damn.

A double mastectomy that took both nipples. Her chest is a mangled mess of jagged scars. I make a conscious effort to not show what I'm thinking. These poor women get enough horrified looks without me adding to it.

"It's too bad to work with, isn't it?" she says in disappointment.

"No. Are you kidding? Of course not. As far as I'm concerned, you're a blank canvas that I can make beautiful again. You're not doing any reconstructive surgery?"

She shakes her head and tries not to cry. "The insurance won't pay for it. I was wondering if you could tattoo on nipples. I heard you can do that."

"Sure I can, if that's really what you want to do. And they'll look pretty damn close to real, too. But there's another option we should talk about. Take another good look at those photos. I can design a big tattoo on your chest that will cover all of your scars. Something wild and magnificent. You'll be going topless at the beach just to show off your cool tat."

She thumbs through the photos again, then smiles and nods her head.

"That's what I want. Go big or go home, I always say. Can you do horses?"

"I can do anything," I say. "You'll look like a warrior. Because that's what you are, right? You beat breast cancer, so you should be proud and show it off."

"Damn right I'm a warrior," she says. "How soon can you do this?"

"Whenever you're ready. Let's talk about a design."

An hour later, she leaves the shop with a new perkiness in her step. I walk her to the door and she takes a few steps down the sidewalk before turning around and coming back to quickly hug me.

"Thank you," she whispers into my ear.

11

LILA

I obsessively check the time again and take another look at my reflection in the mirror. I've spent far too much time and effort on my appearance for tonight's date. After a great deal of deliberation, I decided to wear another dress since Sam seemed to like the white sundress. Not the most ladylike attire for a motorcycle, but hopefully it's long and loose enough to keep me decent.

Sam didn't say where he's taking me for dinner. After the visit to his Aunt Leona's, I'm almost afraid to find out. There's no telling what might be on the menu. Frog legs, venison, squirrel. Whatever...I'll be ready. The only surprise will be if he takes me somewhere normal.

When I hear a car pull up in front of the house, I hurry to the door. It can't be Sam because he made a point of telling me it's either ride on the back of his motorcycle or don't go at all.

An older model red Camaro with dark tinted windows is sitting in the driveway. The door opens and a black leather boot steps out.

Sam.

I can't believe he actually drove a car to pick me up. Now I'm wishing I had chosen a shorter dress to wear. One that he might have liked better.

What's wrong with me?

I shouldn't care one way or the other what he likes.

Sam slams the car door and runs up the steps. I've noticed he doesn't do anything slow. He's a continuously moving fireball of pent-up energy. He has on his regular jeans and boots, but this time his muscles are covered by a light blue button down shirt that brings out the color of his eyes. I could stare into those eyes of his all night long and never get tired.

"A Camaro?" I ask. "I should have known you would drive a fast car."

He doesn't answer and instead leans down to kiss me lightly on the mouth. I don't pull back and secretly like that he doesn't hesitate or ask me first before kissing me.

"Did you think I would be driving a station wagon?" he teases before pulling me closer to him and kissing me playfully a second time. "Or a mini-van?"

"You're frisky tonight. What's gotten into you?"

"I'm excited about taking such a pretty gal out on a date," he answers. "I'm also very glad that I brought the car since you're wearing a dress. You look beautiful."

He means it. I can tell by the appreciative look in his eyes.

"You're not so bad yourself, handsome," I say. "So why *did* you bring the car?"

"The truth?" he says. "I can't see your face when you're riding behind me. Or hold your hand." He laces his fingers through mine. "Are you ready to go?"

"I'm ready," I say. "I was planning to ask you in for a beer or glass of wine first, and then I remembered this is a dry county. How far is it to the nearest place to buy alcohol?"

"From here, it's about thirty minutes if you go all the way across the North Carolina line, and at least that much time if you drive to another Georgia county."

"Just for a bottle of wine? That seems crazy and way behind the times. What do people do if they want a drink?"

"They go on beer runs," he answers with a laugh. "If you want alcohol, you grab a friend and go on a beer run. Want to go on one?"

"Not really. I'm not desperate for a drink. Are you saying that is the only way to get alcohol in this county?"

Besides buying it illegally from the Steel Infidels, of course.

Truthfully, I would kill for a decent glass of chardonnay. Being in a dry county sucks. Even if this is the Bible belt, banning all forms of alcohol is ridiculous.

"Yeah, it's the only way," he answers. "Don't worry. The place we're going to is 'bring your own bottle,' so I have a little something in the trunk of the car. We'll take it in with us to dinner."

"Wine?" I ask hopefully, then realize I'm being overly optimistic. "Or beer?"

I'm not crazy about beer. If there's nothing else, I'll drink it in an emergency.

"Tequila," he answers with a straight face.

I burst out laughing. "Seriously?"

Only Sam would bring along a bottle of tequila to a first date. This should be interesting. I'm actually looking forward to tonight. Sam makes me laugh, and that's something I haven't done much of in a long time.

"What's wrong with tequila?" he asks.

I can't tell if he's kidding or not.

"Not a thing," I say. "Let's get this show on the road."

He opens the car door for me like a Southern gentleman and helps me tuck my dress inside before shutting the door. By now I've accepted the fact that he actually does have a few good manners.

So he is a good-mannered criminal. I don't think that's going to help him any in the eyes of the law.

After sliding behind the steering wheel, he turns the key in the ignition and reaches over to grab my hand again.

Is he really going to hold my hand the whole time while he drives?

It feels nice and I like it.

Steering with his left hand, he backs out of the driveway and pulls onto the road.

"So where are we going?" I ask.

He winks at me and I melt all over again. A gut punch in the stomach every time.

"Oh, so now you ask where we're going? Lila, how would you like to go to a honky-tonk?"

I smile back at him.

Here we go again.

The restaurant is located high on the top of a big hill with a spectacular view of green mountains in every direction. A large deck overlooks the valley stretching out for miles below.

Sam pulls into a parking spot at the far end of the lot.

"What do you think about God's country?" he asks, waving a hand at the mountains.

"It's beautiful," I say. "I can't imagine what it must be like waking up to a view like this every morning. The traffic in Atlanta gets to me sometimes."

He squeezes my hand. "Ever thought about moving? You could have this every day too. There's nothing that says you can't."

I look over at his handsome face, not at the mountains.

There could be worse things than waking up to the view of Sam every morning.

Wishful thinking won't get me anywhere.

"Don't move," he says. "I'll get the car door for you."

"I'm perfectly capable of opening a car door, Sam," I say.

He laughs. "I know. I'm trying to impress you, so work with me here, okay?"

I roll my eyes and sit there like an invalid while he walks around and makes a big show of opening the door and helping me out.

"Don't forget the tequila," I say, pointing to the trunk.

"I almost did. Thanks for reminding me."

He unlocks the trunk and pulls out a brown paper bag.

"We're brown bagging it?" I tease. "That's a big bottle. Were you planning on us drinking the whole bottle by ourselves? I have to warn you, I'm a lightweight when it comes to alcohol. A little bit goes a long way with me."

Not true.

For some bizarre reason, I can drink most men under the table and not even be the least bit tipsy. Must be my metabolism. This little party trick has come in handy plenty of times when working undercover. It always surprises me what people will do and say if they think I'm drunk. I'm dying to know how long Sam's Southern boy good manners will last if I'm tipsy.

I hope I'm not disappointed.

We walk into the restaurant with Sam holding onto me with one hand and the bottle of tequila with the other. Loud country music is blasting from a room towards the back of the dining area.

"Was this place originally a barn?" I ask, glancing up at the upper level that still looks like a hayloft. I hope the customers don't go up there since only a thin wooden railing would keep someone from tumbling off into the crowd below.

"I believe so," he says. "It's been a honky-tonk for as long as I can remember. If you haven't guessed, we're hurting for good entertainment around here."

"I can see that."

A waitress, an older woman with grey hair and a wrinkle-lined face, greets us.

"You brought a friend this time, I see," she says, winking at Sam.

Is there anyone in this town who doesn't know him?

"Do you want to stay in the dining area or eat in the back with the music?" she asks.

Sam looks at me for an answer.

"Near the music?" I say, knowing that he would always want to be right in the middle of the action.

She leads us through the large crowd of diners to a big cavernous room with tables and a stage. A country music band made up of four long-bearded men is playing a fairly decent version of an old Waylon Jennings song.

"Take your choice of tables," she says, waving her hand at several tables near the stage.

Sam points instead to an empty table set up against the wall.

"As the night goes on, the music gets progressively louder," he explains. "I doubt you'll want to be right in front of the stage."

Sam places the bottle of tequila on the table and pulls out my chair.

"What do you need to go with whatever is in that paper bag?" the waitress asks. "Mixer? Coke? Orange juice?"

"Lime, salt, and shot glasses," Sam answers.

"Oh no," she says. "Let me guess. Tequila again? Will your friend Toby be joining you?"

"Not tonight," he answers. "I'm on a date." He places a hand possessively on my thigh.

"Thank goodness for that. The two of you almost got thrown out of here last time you were drinking tequila." She turns to me. "You need to watch him close and keep him out of trouble tonight. I'll be right back with menus."

Sam slides his chair over closer to me and slings an arm over the back of mine.

"So what did you do last time you were here?" I ask.

He shakes his head and laughs. "I honestly don't remember. Toby might, but I sincerely doubt it. I'll have to ask him. Do you like country music?"

"I like all kinds of different music. It depends whatever kind of mood I'm in."

I never listen to country music.

My musical tastes run wilder and darker. Sam would be shocked to know the last time I listened to live music was in the middle of the night at an underground club. Less than a month ago.

There are lots of things about me that Sam would be shocked to find out.

I hope he never does.

The waitress returns with menus along with a saltshaker, lime wedges, and two shot glasses. "Have fun," she says after placing the items on the table.

Sam opens the bottle of tequila and fills the two shot glasses. He places one in front of me.

"Give me your hand," he says.

I cock my eyebrows at him, and after hesitating a moment, place my hand on the table. He picks it up and curls my fingers into a fist. Slowly, he runs his tongue across the space between the thumb and forefinger on the back of my hand.

Damn. That's erotic.

He lifts his eyes and looks straight into mine. I know just as well what he's thinking and exactly what he wishes he was doing right now instead of licking my hand.

I know because I'm thinking the same thing.

He's not going to say it though. Not after the last time.

Suddenly he grins.

He read my mind. How the hell did he do that?

We're in so much trouble.

Picking up the saltshaker, he sprinkles salt onto my hand and hands me a slice of lime.

"Lick the salt, drink the shot, then bite on the lime," he says.

I've drank tequila plenty of times in my life, but I'm not telling him. It will be more fun to pretend like I know nothing.

"You go first," I suggest for no other reason than I want to watch him lick my hand again.

"I don't use the salt and lime," he says. "I drink the shots straight."

"Oh, come on," I say. "I need you to show me how."

I can't believe how turned on I'm getting just by watching him.

He picks up a wedge of lime. "Okay, if I must. For you, I'll drink my tequila like a sissy. I hope nobody else is watching this. I will never forgive you if one of the other Steel Infidels walks in here."

I can't help smiling as he slowly licks the salt from my hand, downs the shot, then bites down on the lime. As far as I'm concerned, we can sit here doing this all night long. This is the best entertainment I've had in forever.

"Now it's your turn."

He lets go of my hand and moves the saltshaker towards me.

Two can play this game.

Instead of putting the salt on my own hand like he's expecting me to do, I reach for his. Since getting thrown out of honky-tonk for indecent behavior wouldn't look good on my resume, I double check to make sure no one sitting around us is watching.

Bringing his hand to my lips, I run my tongue along the same spot. Then I surprise him by sliding my lips all the way down over his thumb and sucking slowly one time hard before turning it loose.

"Fuck, Lila!" he says and almost jerks his hand away from mine.

Exactly the reaction I was looking for.

I sprinkle the salt on his hand and lick it again. Grabbing my shot glass, I down the tequila and bite the lime.

He grips my hand tighter. "Jesus Christ, Lila! What the hell was that thing you just did?"

I don't answer and instead pour two more shots of tequila.

"Ready to go for round two? Your turn."

12

SAM

An hour later, my body is still reeling and my mind is a white, lust-filled blank.

Lila shocked me when she licked my hand instead of her own, and then my head almost exploded when she slid her lips down my thumb. A jolt of white-hot electricity shot straight through to my cock and I almost turned the table over.

I want her so much it's killing me.

And she knows it.

For the last hour, we've joked and talked while the whole time I keep thinking about how unbelievably fantastic she would feel sprawled naked underneath me. Or her sweet lips sliding down my cock. I can't think straight or keep up with the conversation. I'm so turned on, I'm not even sure what I ate for dinner or how it tasted.

All I can think about is Lila.

The sweet scent of her hair drifts my way every time she brushes it back from her face, and I want to lift it up to kiss my way down the back of her neck. My hands can't stop reaching over to touch her. Thankfully she doesn't seem to mind my hand on her leg or stroking her arm.

I can't get enough.

It frustrates me to know that I'll never have her.

There's no way she's going to sleep with me now or ever. All I can do is dream.

Besides being an ATF agent, Lila is out of my league. Until she came along, I never realized girls like her even existed. She doesn't put up with my shit and isn't afraid to dish it right back to me.

I don't understand why none of my old tricks are working on her. Or maybe they are and she's not showing it. This is a position I've never been in before, and one that I don't like very much.

Either way, I need to up my game.

Again.

I thought I had already done that. And then she upped her game on top of mine.

At this point, I need to accept that outplaying her might not be an option.

Or outwitting her, since she's always a mental step ahead.

The one thing I can do is outlast her.

I won't give up. I'll wear her down and keep trying until she completely shuts me down with no chance at all.

I hope to God that doesn't happen.

If it does, I probably deserve it.

The steady stream of women in my life has been endless and disposable. Not a single girl has managed to keep my attention for more than a few weeks, usually only a few days.

I've lost count of the number of women I've fucked in my life. Many I can't recall at all. My sex life has been an endless blur of pussy and boobs. Tons of fun at the time, yet meaningless and at times, almost unbearably empty.

One night with Lila would be unforgettable.

I'll wait for as long as it takes.

"Do you want to dance?" I ask her after the waitress clears our food plates away.

Lila reaches for the bottle of tequila and starts to pour what would be her fourth shot. I've been keeping close count.

"How about another shot of tequila?" she says. "I'm game if you are."

I place my hand over hers. "I'm driving with a special gal in the car, so no more for me. And I would hate for you to have a raging headache tomorrow. Dance with me, beautiful."

"You're right," she agrees. "We've had enough tequila for one night."

She allows me to take her hand and lead her to the dance floor in front of the band.

"I'm not a good dancer," she says with an embarrassed laugh when I pull her closer.

"That's okay, I'm not either. So it's a good thing this isn't dancing." I lift her arms and place them behind my neck. "This is hugging on a dance floor."

She leans closer into me and runs her fingers along the back of my neck. "I can do that," she says and sways slightly off balance. "Whoops! I'm a little tipsy. Maybe I shouldn't have knocked back that last shot."

I slide my arms around her back and place a kiss behind her ear. "Don't worry, I'll hold you up." Now I'm wishing I'd tried to stop her after the second shot of tequila.

She runs a hand up my arm and traces one of the skull tattoos on my bicep. "I like your tattoos. Do they all mean something special?"

"I'm sure at the time I thought they meant something special. And some of them do. Except for the skulls. They're just there to make me look badass."

"What about the others? What do they mean?"

"It's a long story that I'll save for another time. You might be bored to death. Are you having a good time tonight?"

She leans her head against my chest, and I smooth a hand down the back of her hair. I notice she doesn't use any gel or hairspray, so her hair is silky and soft in my fingers.

"I'm having a great time," she whispers against my shirt. "I could dance with you like this for hours."

I pull her closer and we slowly sway together all the way through the band's set. When the band stops to take a break, she looks up at me without removing her arms from my neck.

"Are you ready to go home?" I ask. "Or do you want to sit down and wait for the band to come back?"

"How about we dance at my place?"

"That will definitely work too. Let's get out of here."

She's a little wobbly and unsteady on her feet as we make our way out of the building. When we reach the car, I lean her up against the side while I unlock the door.

"Are we going to make out in the car?" she asks with an uncharacteristic giggle. "I always wanted to make out in a Camaro."

I wish.

"Not this time, darling. Ask me again sometime and I'll take you up on it."

I turn on the radio for the drive back to her house and Lila starts singing along loudly to the song.

"Your personality changes quite a bit when you're tipsy," I say.

She laughs and keeps singing.

When we arrive at her house, I walk her up to the front door and lean down to give her a light goodnight kiss. No way am I screwing things up by touching her while she's drunk. She might be all up for it now, but tomorrow she'll want to slap the shit out of me.

There's no need to rush things. We have time.

"Aren't you coming inside?" she asks. "You can stay for a minute, can't you?"

"I don't think that's a good idea. You need to go to bed and get some sleep."

Pulling my head down to hers, she reaches up and kisses me slowly.

"Five minutes?" she says.

"Five minutes, and then I need to go."

"Are you going to the clubhouse?" she asks. "To hang out with the Sweet Butts?"

The thought of leaving Lila to be with one of the Sweet Butts is not appealing in the least.

"No, I'll go straight home. Alone."

I help her inside the house and turn on the lights.

"I need to change my clothes," she says while walking toward the bedroom.

When she doesn't return in a few minutes, I go to check on her. She's lying on the bed still wearing her dress. I walk over and nudge her

"You can't sleep in your dress. What do you normally sleep in? A gown? T-shirt?"

"Nothing," she mumbles.

"You don't wear anything to bed?"

"No."

Shit.

Not what I need to hear when I'm trying to be a decent man.

"That makes two of us then."

I walk over to her dresser and pull out a drawer. All of her panties, bras, shorts, and shirts are organized into nice, tidy piles. I avoid touching the lacy lingerie since resisting her is hard enough as it is. Grabbing a soft shirt, I walk back to the bed. She sits up and looks at me groggily.

"Take off your dress and put this on."

I start to offer to help her and decide against it. I'm a man and I'm only human. Only someone with superpowers would be able to resist her with her clothes off, and that's not me. I know my limits and I'm reaching them very fast.

"I'm going to get you a couple of aspirin. They're in the kitchen cabinet, right?"

I vaguely remember seeing her reach for them the other night when I was wasted. The thought crosses my mind that we both should stop drinking if this relationship ever has a chance of moving forward.

New rule. No more alcohol.

She starts tugging up her dress, and I hurry out of the room before it gets to the point where I can't walk away.

In the kitchen, I open and close several of the cabinets until I find the one with her medical supplies. Lila is obviously a health nut. One shelf is loaded with several different kinds of vitamins and supplements along with Band-Aids, hydrogen peroxide, aspirin, and a round pink container of birth control pills.

Out of curiosity, I pick up the packet of birth control pills and open it. The pill for today is still there, which means she forgot to take it. Or she takes them at night before she goes to bed.

A crazy and desperate plan forms in my mind.

When this is all over, Lila isn't going to be able to walk away from me without a backwards glance if I can help it.

I punch out today's pill and drop it down the sink's garbage disposal. This time I'm one step ahead of her. I always wear condoms, so I still have time to think this over carefully before I risk anything. It's probably a stupid and ridiculous idea. For some reason, it makes me feel more in control of the situation to know I have a backup plan if things go bad.

After shaking out two aspirin, I place them on the counter and pour her a glass of water. When I walk back into the bedroom, she's already in her shirt and under the sheets.

"Here's your aspirin," I say, handing them to her along with the water. "We need to stop doing this. No more heavy drinking. Okay?"

She nods in agreement. After swallowing the aspirin, she puts her head back on the pillow. "You're not staying?" she asks.

I swallow hard and don't let myself consider it, even for a split second. If I do, I'll be crawling into the bed beside her before she can blink.

"No, because you'll be mad at me tomorrow if I do. I'll call you in the morning."

I can't trust myself to kiss her goodnight without things going further. I turn to walk away and she grabs my arm.

"Goodnight, Sam," she says in a perfectly clear voice.

Her green eyes suddenly look as bright and alert as they always do. Then it hits me. She's not drunk. She was testing me tonight.

I pull the sheet up to her shoulders and kiss her on the forehead.

"Goodnight, darling."

13

LILA

I'm still working on my first cup of coffee when Sam calls.

"Are you doing okay this morning?" he asks. "I'm calling to check on you."

"Yeah, I'm fine. Thank you for tucking me into bed."

Sam passed my pretend drunk test with flying colors. I was suitably impressed. If things had gone the other way, I could have put the brakes on at any time by pretending to throw up in the bathroom. Works like a charm every time to cool off a man's passion.

"No need to thank me," he says. "I'll do turn down service for you any night of the week."

His deep Southern twang is a nice thing to hear first thing in the morning.

"So...I was wondering how you would feel about coming over to my house tomorrow for a party," he continues. "All of the Steel Infidels will be there, and I would like for you to meet them."

He's inviting me to his house?

"Sure. I would love to meet everyone."

"It's a casual affair, so no need to dress up. I can't wait for you to meet my brothers, Jesse and Flint."

The Steel Infidels President and VP.

"Me either. Are you picking me up?"

"Of course. I'll be there around five. The fun starts early and the party goes on most of the night."

"Sounds like fun. I can't wait."

"See you tomorrow then," he says before hanging up.

I'm not sure how I feel about going to Sam's house, the second location where I'm supposed to place another surveillance bug. This investigation is beginning to make me feel uneasy.

Surely the ATF has other criminals they could be investigating instead of the Steel Infidels? Like genuinely bad people with no redeeming qualities? The fact that I aggressively pushed for this investigation isn't helping me to feel any better.

After finishing a second cup of coffee, I set up my equipment on the kitchen table. I've been putting off the task of going through the surveillance tapes taken before I arrived in town. Sam will be at the shop all day, so this will give me a good chance to sit down and work on it uninterrupted.

I'm barely into the first tape when Sam commits his first crime on camera. A customer walks down the alley and knocks on the back door of the tattoo shop. Sam steps out and money is exchanged. He ducks into the building and then hands him two bottles of alcohol that he doesn't even take the time to disguise in bags. Ten minutes later, another exchange happens and then another.

The tape date is a Friday night, and he's doing more business than most big-city package stores. A truck backs up to the door and Sam helps a man load several boxes into the bed. By the time I finish a week's worth of tapes, my hands are shaking.

I honestly don't know what I expected to find. Maybe I was hoping he wasn't really doing anything illegal. There's enough on the tapes to put him away. And that's without bringing the gun running into the equation.

Things are looking very bad for Sam.

I'm unusually nervous about meeting Sam's family and the rest of the Steel Infidels. I don't know why. It's not like this is my first undercover operation. I've worked plenty of them over the past few years. After the first couple of times, it became easy to put on a mask and be someone else.

This feels different.

When we pull up into the driveway of Sam's house, I see a group of men standing outside the house. I immediately recognize Jesse and Flint standing side by side. Both men are solidly built, with muscles like granite beneath their close-fitting shirts. Jesse is much bigger than I expected, with large muscular arms and a broad chest. He towers over Flint by several inches. They're both deeply tanned with dark hair. I wonder how Sam ended up with his blondish hair and blue eyes.

They look up and smile when they see us walking down the hill to the house.

"You actually brought a date to this shindig?" one of the other men jokes.

I recognize him as Toby, a high school classmate of Sam's and a Marine back at home after years in Afghanistan. He's wearing an Atlanta Braves baseball cap turned backwards. Another blue-eyed, dark-haired, handsome hunk of a man.

Does an ugly Steel Infidel even exist?

If so, I haven't seen him yet.

Sam pulls me over closer to meet Jesse. I take one look at Jesse's eyes and immediately want to step behind Sam to put him between us. If there is one person here who wouldn't think twice about hurting me, it would be Jesse. He is the very definition of silent and deadly.

The ATF has placed him at the scene of several mysterious rival motorcycle gang deaths. Not enough to charge him with anything, but enough for me to keep a close eye on him. He makes me uncomfortable. To underestimate him would be a big mistake.

"Who is your girl?" he asks. When he smiles, his face softens and I relax a little.

"This is Lila," Sam says. "She's from Atlanta." He waves a hand at the group of men. "Lila, meet the Steel Infidels. My two big brothers, Jesse and Flint." He points them out and I pretend like I don't know exactly who they are already. "The big guy with the dorky baseball cap is Toby. Don't pay attention to anything he says about me because he's a big fat liar."

Toby laughs and takes a sip of the beer he's holding. Sam goes on to introduce me to the rest of the Steel Infidels one by one. They all nod politely and smile. If I didn't know better, I would think they were a nice group of Southern boys.

But I do know better.

Appearances in this case can be very deceiving.

"Where are Trish and Kendra?" Sam asks.

Flint nods toward the house. "They're in the kitchen with the kids."

"I can't wait for you to meet them," Sam says. "And my niece and nephew. Missy is only a couple of months old and Josh is a toddler."

He takes me inside the house where his brothers' wives are busy putting out platters of food for the guests. An adorable toddler with dark curly hair is hanging on to a woman's legs. Sam scoops him up off the floor and tosses him into the air. The toddler squeals with laughter and Sam tosses him again.

"Don't come crying to me if he pukes all over your face, Sam," the woman says with a laugh. "I've warned you about that before."

"You wouldn't do that to me, would you, Josh?" he says to the child, who giggles.

"I'm Kendra," the woman says. "And that's my son Josh being thrown around. I'm married to Sam's brother, Flint."

So this is Kendra, the town veterinarian.

"Nice to meet you," I say.

Another pretty young woman walks into the kitchen with a baby in her arms. "And I'm the other brother's wife," she says. "We're Trish and Missy." She holds out the baby's fist to wave at me.

"Missy is a lovely name," I say.

"Jesse and I named her Melissa after his mom," Trish says. "Then Sam kept calling her Little Missy, so the name stuck. It suits her better anyway."

"Sam, why don't you run along outside and play with the boys while Trish and I get to know this gal," Kendra says. "We can use an extra set of hands in the kitchen." She turns to me. "We don't want to let the Steel Infidels get too hungry. If we wait too long to put out snacks, they turn into a bunch of grouchy grizzly bears."

"I know when I'm not wanted," Sam says. "But I'm taking Josh with me." He turns to me. "Will you be alright here for a few minutes?"

"Of course."

"You're not taking Josh outside to hang around all of you dirty-talking guys," Kendra scolds. "Put him back down right this minute."

Sam sighs and hands Josh back over before walking out.

Trish and Kendra seem nice. It makes me wonder how they ever got involved with men like Flint and Jesse in the first place. Especially Kendra, a highly educated woman with a good reputation in a small town.

I guess the saying about 'love is blind' must be true.

I'm still hanging out in the kitchen making small talk with Trish and Kendra when the music outside the house suddenly changes from a slow Willie Nelson tune to loud heavy metal.

Trish sighs and places the baby up against her shoulder to burp.

"Sounds like the boys are starting up again," she says. "Come on, Lila. You don't want to miss this."

Everyone in the house starts making their way toward the doors. I can't help wondering why anyone in their right mind would want to be outside in the unbearable heat when it's air-conditioned inside.

"What's going on?" I ask. "What's happening? Where's everyone going?"

"The men call it basketball," Kendra says with a grin. "We call it foreplay." She laughs and glances over at Trish. "Isn't that right?"

Trish nods. "Oh, yes. You'll see what we mean. Let's go."

When the two women move toward the door, I realize now might be my best chance to place the surveillance bug in the house. Another two minutes and the house will be empty.

"I need to use your restroom," I say. "I'll be right out in a sec."

"We'll save you a spot," Trish says. "Hurry though. You don't want to miss the best part."

I walk to the bathroom and wait until the house is quiet before going back into the kitchen. Slipping the bug out of my purse, I head toward the table. I bend down to attach it when suddenly, through the kitchen window, I hear Sam's laughter ring out loud and clear.

I hesitate and then drop the bug back into the purse.

Damn it.

I can't do it today.

Instead, I hurry outside to join Trish and Kendra at the side yard where a basketball goal is set up on a small concrete court. A few scantily-clad Sweet Butts are placing lounge chairs around the edges of the court while the men toss a basketball back and forth.

"They're going to play a basketball game?" I ask, still confused as to what's happening. "In blue jeans and boots? That's weird and something I've never seen before."

"You'll never catch one of these men in a pair of shorts or without their boots," Trish says. "Grab a lounge chair. We shouldn't sit too close to the court. The guys can get rough, and I don't want them crashing into the baby or little Josh."

I drag a couple of lounge chairs from the stack and set one up in the shade for Trish and the baby. Kendra plops down on the other side of me with Josh hanging onto her legs for support. He starts to fall, and I instinctively reach over to grab his chubby little hand.

Weird.

I can't remember ever touching a baby's hand before. He smiles at me, showing a new tooth, and my heart melts.

"Better watch out," Kendra says. "Josh is teething and he'll eat your hand."

As if right on cue, Josh tries to cram my finger in his mouth. Kendra laughs and pulls my hand free.

"Told you so," she says.

I point at the basketball court.

"How do they split up the teams with thirteen guys?" I ask "Isn't that too many players?"

Trish laughs. "They make up their own rules," she says. "And they reserve the right to change them frequently. Tom is the referee since he's older, slower, and has bad knees. Jesse and Flint are team captains. They each pick a team of six. Five men play and one member will sit on the sidelines and wait to be tagged in. That usually only happens when someone is injured."

"*When* someone is injured?" I repeat. "Don't you mean *if*?"

"We wish," Kendra answers. "When you throw that much testosterone together with no rules, someone usually winds up with a minor injury. Luckily Trish is training to be a nurse and I'm a veterinarian, so we can usually patch them up without sending them off to the emergency room. The only hard and fast rule they follow is 'no hands.' No grabbing or punching allowed. Elbows, body slams, tripping, head butting, and rolling around on the ground are all okay."

I frown, not liking the sound of this. They said the game was going to be fun. Foreplay, Kendra had called it. So far, I'm missing the appeal.

"Alright boys," Tom yells out from the center of the court. "Time for the Prez and VP to pick your teams. Go Jesse. You're up first, big fella."

Jesse steps up and chooses as his first pick the stout, muscular Toby. Flint goes for Sam. The brothers Rocco and Danny are divided up next. The other team members are chosen quickly and then the teams huddle up to pick the two men to sit out first.

"Are the teams split fairly?" I ask. "The men on Jesse's team look huge compared to Flint and Sam's."

"Don't worry," Kendra answers. "Sam and Flint might not be as big, but they're quicker. Trust me, it's even." She picks up Josh and sits him on her lap. "My favorite part is coming up. Prepare to drool. This is what dreams are made of, honey."

She points to the court and my mouth drops open.

Good Lord!

The men begin peeling off their shirts and tossing them to the women lining the court. With the exception of the heavy, out-of-shape referee who thankfully left his shirt on, the basketball court is loaded with bare skin, muscles, and tattoos.

Pure masculine man candy.

I consider taking a photo with my cell phone and decide I'd better not chance it.

"The men used to play shirts and skins until we convinced them that it would be more beneficial for everyone if all the shirts came off," Kendra says with a laugh. "It was one of the rare moments the men actually listened to us. This way it's a win-win for everyone." She shrugs. "The men want to get lucky later and we need visuals so..."

"Well, thank you for that," I say, fanning myself with my hand. "Whew! They're the hottest group of men I've ever seen in my life."

I notice Sam looking around for me in the crowd, and I stand up. His gaze lands on me and he smiles, causing his whole face to light up.

My God.

Why does it always feel like Christmas morning when he looks at me like that?

Quickly running to the side of the court, he tosses me his shirt and I catch it in mid-air. I grin and clutch his shirt in my hands, resisting the urge to hold it to my face and breathe in his scent.

The simple gesture of a guy throwing me his shirt sends my heart racing like I'm fifteen years old. More than a few of the Sweet Butts shoot me evil looks that clearly say they want me to die a quick, painful death, right here and now. Especially a big-breasted girl with long blonde hair in a bikini top and cut-off blue jean shorts.

Flint and Jesse run over, and their shirts come flying by right behind Sam's, landing in Kendra and Trish's laps. They both giggle as they grab at the shirts. It's good to know I'm not the only one this is having an effect on.

"I never get tired of this," Kendra says. She leans across me to tap Trish on the leg. "How about you, Trish?"

"I would happily watch this every day," Trish replies.

"The women have only one rule, Lila," Kendra says. "You're allowed to look at the other men as much as you want, but only touch the man that belongs to you."

"Understood," I say, nodding. "Sounds like an excellent rule to me."

"Now if we can only get those dumbass Sweet Butts to follow the rules," she says with a heavy sigh. "I really wish they wouldn't come to these get-togethers."

I'm surprised. "They put their hands on Flint?" I ask.

From everything I've seen, Flint only has eyes for Kendra. Even now, he's watching her from the other side of the basketball court.

Kendra gives me a shocked look.

"Not if they want to live to see another day, they don't," she says. "Our rule doesn't stop them from flirting. Or dressing like hookers with all their goods hanging out on display. The Sweet Butts are a big part of the biker culture, so we try to tolerate them."

"Barely," Trish says, rolling her eyes. "We barely tolerate them. Kendra and I have come up with a devious plan to find wives for all the Steel Infidels so the Sweet Butts will eventually wither away. Someone needs to drag Sam and Toby to the altar soon because they're the biggest draw. Would you be interested in the position, Lila? We could use some help with our plan."

I'm not sure if Trish is being serious or not.

"We've just met, so I would have to say no at this point."

"No problem," she says. "I'll ask you again in a week. It took me less than that to fall hard for Jesse, and things only get better every day."

"You held out longer than I did," Kendra pipes in. "A weekend stuck in a cabin with Flint and I was a goner. Forty-eight hours and I was head over heels in love with that man. Still am. One thing about the Mason men, when they find the girl they want, they fall hard and quick. With Flint, I realized there wasn't any need in trying to play coy. I knew I wanted him, so I grabbed him and never let loose. And I haven't regretted it for one moment since then either."

"I'll keep all that in mind," I say, halfway wondering if she might have a valid point.

Looking at the three brothers on the basketball court, I can see how it would be very difficult for a woman to resist any of them for long.

I can't forget why I'm here.

The referee pulls a whistle out of his pocket and blows it.

"Here we go," Trish says. "It's show time. Help us watch out for the babies if the game moves this way."

The referee tosses the ball up into the air. The two biggest men on the teams, Jesse and Rocco, both go for it. Jesse tips it to Toby, who gets off the first shot easily and scores. Half the crowd erupts into cheers and the other half groans.

"Uh oh," I say. "How does this game end anyway?"

"Whoever reaches twenty points wins," Kendra answers. "If it were up to me, I would make it ten. The last ten points are always too intense. Look at Flint and Sam's faces. They are so pissed that Toby got past them. The Steel Infidels are the most competitive group of men I've ever seen. Everything is a contest and they all hate to lose. In other words, things are about to get ugly."

Flint passes Sam the ball and he jumps up to take a shot. Danny leaps up to block it and hits him square in the chest, knocking both Sam and the ball out of bounds.

"Isn't that unnecessary roughness?" I ask, frowning. "Why didn't the ref call it?"

"Oh, that was nothing," Trish answers. "You haven't seen anything yet."

It turns out she's right.

As the game goes on, the physical contact between the men increases in intensity. I cringe and hide my face in my hands when Sam goes up for another shot and crashes down hard on the concrete with both Jesse and Toby in a tangle of muscle and limbs. They hit the ground with loud thuds as the breath is knocked out of all three of them.

I'm worried until I see Sam stand up, clap Jesse on the shoulder, and laugh. He's actually enjoying this. Maybe I'm worrying for nothing. Then I notice the large, nasty red scrape on his back covered in dirt and grit.

"Somebody's going to get hurt," I say.

It had better not be Sam.

"Don't worry, you'll get used to it," Trish says with a casual wave of her hand. "They'll be fine."

Trish is sweet, but I'm seriously beginning to wonder if she's a little off in the head. I don't know how she can be so nonchalant.

"Easy for you to say. Jesse is built like a semi-truck. It would take a lot to hurt him. The bigger guys are knocking the shit out of Sam out there."

Trish laughs at my remark. "Sam would be so pissed if he heard you say that. For some reason he isn't playing down and dirty like he usually does. He's probably trying to impress you so you won't think he's a thug. Believe me, he can dish it back to them when he wants to. Sam can hold his own against any man on the court. *Easy.* Don't go feeling sorry for Sam."

I'm not convinced.

The nasty, rough play is making me nervous. I've already bitten my nails on both hands down to the quick in a bad habit that I broke ten years ago.

This is ridiculous.

What do I care if Sam gets hurt anyway?

He's just a man I'm spying on for a federal investigation. It's not like he's a real boyfriend or even someone I'm casually dating.

Trying to reason with myself isn't helping one bit.

Not when that God-awful heavy metal music is blasting, the men are crashing into each other like it's full contact football, and perspiration is dripping down my back from the heat and anxiety.

And yet Kendra and Trish are sitting here so calmly, bouncing children on their laps and smiling like we're at a church picnic.

I'm not cut out for this.

The score draws closer now, sixteen to eighteen with Jesse's team in the lead. Thank goodness. Two more points and this will be over. I'm secretly cheering for Jesse's team just to put an end to this madness.

Sam is closely guarding Toby, who is dribbling the ball with his back to him. Sam laughs and says something to him, most likely talking crap trying to goad him into making a mistake. Toby picks up the ball, whirls around fast, and intentionally elbows Sam hard right in the mouth, knocking him off his feet.

"Foul!" I scream, jumping up out of my chair. "Ref! What the hell was that? He did that on purpose. Foul him out!"

Sam spits out a mouthful of blood on the concrete and then wipes his busted lip with the back of his hand before getting back up. He hears me yelling and glances over to give me a wink to let me know he's okay.

"Sam! Tag out! Go out!"

I'm the only one of the spectators screaming like a crazy person, and I don't care. The Sweet Butts are all staring at me like I've committed an ultimate sin.

What the hell is wrong with these people?

Sam shakes his head like I'm nuts and mouths the word 'no' to me.

I throw my hands up in frustration.

This is insane.

Trish tugs on my arm.

"Might as well sit back down," she says. "They don't like it when we try to interfere. Makes them look weak."

"So we're supposed to sit here and watch quietly while the men beat the crap out of each other?" I ask, not expecting an answer.

Nice.

Well, I'm not in their club, so I don't have to play by their stupid rules.

"You know, I actually don't give a damn what they like or don't like," I say. "Did you not see that? That big guy tried to knock Sam's teeth out. This isn't basketball. This is freaking cage fighting without the cage."

"The big guy is Sam's best friend, Toby,' Trish says. "I'm sure he didn't mean to hit him in the mouth. He's a Marine."

Oh, like Marines are above playing dirty?

The elbow looked intentional to me.

Jesse's team is still passing the ball around to each other. They're all sweating heavily now and look like they're all about to pass out from the heat. Jesse throws the ball to Danny and when he tries to take the shot, Sam slices his legs out from under him with a single swipe of his boot.

I laugh out loud and clap my hands. I guess Sam *can* play dirty after all. Good for him. I'm proud of him.

The thought pops into my head before I have time to censor it.

Oh great.

Now I'm proud of a criminal for playing dirty on a basketball court. The sun must be melting my brain cells.

The men are getting tired and overheated. One shot after another is blocked on both teams. I'm beginning to wonder if the game will ever end. Or if it will end with the men dropping like flies one after the other from heat exhaustion. Rocco goes out with a turned ankle, so Sam's team is out of relief players.

Suddenly Flint makes a quick move and steals the ball. He throws it to Sam and they start working together smoothly, passing the ball back and forth, moving all over the court in perfect sync like they must have done a million times before in their life. Their movements are in perfect harmony, a choreographed ballet of muscles and tattoos.

Kendra reaches over and pats me on the leg.

"Look at our boys now," she says, pointing to them. "Aren't they something?"

I nod slowly. "Yes, they are."

"I believe they've been holding back this whole time," Kendra says. "Flint and Sam don't even look winded. Those two don't always get along but when they do, it's like magic. They don't need words to communicate. Watch them work it out there."

As if I could tear my eyes away.

Sam fakes out Jesse and Toby, who are double-teaming him, and breaks away. Flint spots him open and passes him the ball. In one quick movement, Sam shoots and the ball swishes through the net.

It's over.

Thank you, Jesus.

My nerves are shot to hell.

I jump up again, screaming Sam's name and cheering with the rest of the crowd. The men stand around the court for a minute, joking and clapping each other on the back. One of the blonde Sweet Butts runs up to Sam, who walks away from her without a second glance. He hurries toward me with a broad smile.

When he reaches me, he leans down, grabs my face in both hands, and claims my lips in a long, deep kiss. His mouth tastes of blood and sweat. I close my eyes and drink him in. Nothing has ever tasted so sweet. I wrap my hands around the back of his neck, still holding his shirt in one hand, and pull him closer.

Sam kisses me like no one is watching, holding me so close that I can feel his heart thumping rapidly through my shirt. I'm completely caught up in the moment and never want it to end. I sink my fingers into his damp hair and cling onto him for dear life. Finally he breaks the kiss and wipes the corner of my lips with his thumb.

"I'm so glad you're here," he says.

I look up into his blue eyes and something clicks for both of us.

I feel it and I know he does, too.

Game over.

"Get a room, people," Kendra says from behind me. "For heaven's sake, think of the little children. You're burning their eyes."

Sam drapes an arm around my shoulders and pulls me against his side. "You're just jealous because you're an old married woman now," he teases.

"You obviously don't talk to Flint if you believe that," Kendra says. "There are things that go on behind closed doors at our house that would simply blow your mind."

"Oh really," Sam says. "I'm all ears. Tell me more."

"No way," Kendra says. "It's private, and don't you go asking Flint about it either."

"What are you keeping private?" Flint asks. He walks over and leans down to pick up Josh. "Hey little buddy." Josh babbles baby talk and reaches a hand up to pat Flint's face.

"I'll tell you later," Kendra says when Flint ruffles her hair. "And don't you go putting your sweaty hands in my hair."

Flint laughs, but doesn't move his hand. "Where do you want them then?"

Kendra shakes her head. "Men."

Trish tries to fold up her lounge chair with one hand before Sam takes it from her. "Like I said, I'll ask you again in a week, Lila," she says, winking at me behind Sam's back.

"Ask you what?" Sam asks when she walks away.

"Nothing," I answer, handing him my water bottle. "Drink this before you fall over from dehydration. And we should go inside so I can put some antiseptic on your scrapes and clean up your busted lip."

"No need to do that," he says, wiping more blood off his lip with the back of his hand. "I'm fine."

"Of course you would say that, tough guy."

I step around behind him to peek at the ugly scrape on his back. Reaching up, I gently try to wipe off some grit and he flinches.

"You don't look fine. I have bandages back at my place. I can fix you up there."

He looks disappointed.

"You want me to take you home? You're tired of me already?"

No way.

"I was thinking you could use some tender loving care. For your wounds."

He grins down at me and interlaces his fingers through mine.

"Now that you mention it, I'm feeling pretty banged up. I think I need medical attention. Or any kind of attention. Let's go."

When we reach his bike, he hands me my helmet.

"I didn't ask you before," he says. "How fast do you like to ride?"

"That depends. How fast can this bike go?"

"Want to find out?" he challenges.

"You bet I do."

"I knew it," he says. "Hold on, darling."

14

SAM

Once we reach the open highway, I quickly ramp up the bike's speed. Lila grips my waist tighter but doesn't yell for me to slow down like other girls usually do.

"Are you okay back there?" I yell to her.

"I'm good. Is this the best you can do?"

I chuckle and squeeze her hand on my belt.

Where has this girl been all my life?

"There's a long straight away in the road coming up. Hang on!"

I take a curve faster than I should with her on the back and then it's nothing but us and an empty, open road as far as I can see. Pulling back on the throttle, I watch as the speedometer rapidly creeps up higher than I've ever driven on this road.

Somehow I instinctively know that Lila loves the thrill as much as I do. I've been chasing adrenaline all my life, and my guess is she has too in different ways.

We're a match made in heaven.

Now all I need to do is make her see it.

When we reach the maximum speed I'm willing to go with her, I glance in my mirror and catch a glimpse of exhilaration on her face.

And I know without a doubt.

Whatever it takes, no matter how dirty I have to play, I'm keeping this woman by my side forever.

Lila unlocks the doorknob lock on her front door and then sticks the key in the deadbolt. The lock is stuck and won't turn. I lean against the doorjamb, watching her struggle with it in amusement. She's locking it instead of unlocking.

"Why did you lock the deadbolt too?" I ask. "This is the country, not the big city. You don't need two locks. One lock on a door is enough. If they want to break in, a second lock isn't going to stop them."

She tries the deadbolt again and this time drops her key ring. I scoop them up and hand them to her.

"Your hands are trembling. Did I drive too fast?"

She lets out a nervous laugh. "No, I'm just in a hurry to get this damn door open," she says, hitting the door in frustration with the palm of her hand.

I take the keys from her. "Let me do it. Otherwise, we'll be standing here all day. You keep locking it back."

She's not the only one in a hurry to get the damn door open. I smoothly fit the key into the deadbolt and swing the door wide for her to walk through.

"After you," I say.

She tosses the keys on the kitchen table and walks over to the refrigerator. Bending over at the waist, she peeks inside. "Do you want..." she starts to ask.

I walk up behind her and spin her around.

"Yes, I *want*."

I'm fed up with holding back. I can't keep my hands off her a minute longer, not with the way her curves are begging for my touch. I hold her face firmly between my hands and stare down into her beautiful eyes.

"I want *you*. If you're going to tell me no, you had better say it now and you had better say it fast. Once you let me touch you, I might not be able to stop."

Lila slides her hands behind my neck. "Then it's a yes," she says without hesitation.

Damn.

So much promise in one little word.

Reaching down, I slide one arm around her legs and the other around her shoulders. Picking her up easily, I head to the bedroom with her clinging tightly to my neck.

I'm kissing her hungrily before we make it to the bed. My mind is telling me to take it slow and easy. My cock is telling me to fuck her every way possible and then do it all over again until we're both too exhausted to move.

I place her on the bed and cover her with my body. Her hands curl tightly in my hair and she parts her soft lips, opening her mouth to draw me in. My brain fogs over as I drink in her taste.

I'm almost frozen by indecision. I can't decide where to touch first.

Too many choices.

Before this night is over, I want to touch and taste it all. As many times as she'll let me.

I slide my hand up her side to cup her full breast through her thin shirt. I apply more pressure with my fingers until I can feel them sinking through the fabric to the soft, luscious tit beneath. She gazes at me, her eyes clouded with desire, and I sense in a flash what she needs.

Lila doesn't want it slow and easy. She's as hungry as I am. She wants it raw, hot and fast.

I've never wanted a woman so much in my life.

"Do you have any idea what you're doing to me?" I whisper in her ear. Her sweet smell is intoxicating and I can't resist trailing my lips down her neck. "I've dreamed of touching you just like this."

She smoothes her hands down my back and tugs my shirt out of my jeans. "You're not the only dreamer," she says. "Help me take your shirt off."

I sit up and tug my shirt up over my head. Her hands immediately reach for me to drag me back on top of her.

"Hang on, darling. I'm stripping you naked right now. And I have to warn you...I might talk dirty. So if you're still keeping score, I'll sign over my paycheck to you at the end of the week."

"I'll give you a free pass this time," she says breathlessly and holds her arms up so I can hastily remove her shirt and lacy white bra. I toss her clothes on the floor.

"I should be doing this slower," I say in apology. "But I'm in a big fucking hurry to get my hands on you in case you haven't noticed." I grasp the waistband of her shorts and she lifts her hips to wiggle out of them. All that is left is white silky panties that cover absolutely nothing.

One look and I can't breathe.

For my sanity, I'm leaving them on for now.

"Don't slow down on my account," she says. She slides the palms of her hands eagerly up my chest and over my pecs. "I've been dying to touch these muscles since the first day I met you on the mountain. You don't know how close I came to jumping you right there on the road when you took off your shirt."

"Why didn't you?"

"No good reason that I can think of now."

I know why and it doesn't matter anymore.

"Since we're being honest, I wanted to drag you off into the woods and fuck you behind a tree."

She laughs, and I stare down at her in mesmerized wonder. Her exposed body is gorgeous with breasts that are full, soft, and real with oversized nipples. I want to feel their thickness and taste them with my tongue. Lowering my head, I swoop down to seize one thimble-sized nipple in my mouth. Immediately the responsive tip hardens between my lips.

She feels amazing in my mouth.

My cock is already rock hard and throbbing. I tug her nipple a little roughly with my teeth, drawing the tip out.

I'm not going to be able to keep it together enough to slow this down.

I want to savor every moment, yet I'm dying to slide between her legs and feel her tight pussy clenching around me. Luckily I have plenty of stamina and if she's willing, we can go as slow as she wants the second and third time around.

Trying to slow down right now is fucking impossible.

But I know every moment with her has to count.

Every kiss, every touch.

Lila's fingers grip my shoulders as I alternate breasts, sucking and teasing the nipples. Her heartbeat is racing fast underneath my lips and her breath hitches as I trail my lips down the valley between her swollen breasts.

If I thought I was in deep shit before, it was nothing compared to now.

I've tasted heaven and I'm not going back.

No way.

Any other woman would be settling and I'm not doing that *ever* again.

I move back to her lips and lower my body so that her soft breasts are pressed directly against my chest. The intense skin-to-skin contact throws me off balance. Lila murmurs my name and strains her body against mine as our kiss deepens.

I've never known the taste of a woman to be so intoxicating.

Lila is opening up and giving me everything I desperately want to take. No holding back. My blood is pumping like crazy, rushing to my cock and making me wonder if she is going mad the same way I am.

Only one way to find out.

I slide my hand down her stomach and under her panties. She sucks in a breath as I skim over her waxed mound. So sexy and smooth.

Perfect.

Her panties are coming off now. So much for my self-control. I hook my fingers on both sides and drag them down her legs and over her ankles. A split-second later, my hand is back between her thighs.

"You're burning hot and wet. Spread your legs wider for me."

She moves her legs further apart and I seek out the soft, warm flesh of her pussy. I look up to see her biting on her lower lip. Her cheeks are flushed with heat and her eyes are closed.

"Lila," I say. "Open your eyes and look at me."

Her eyes fly open and lock onto mine.

"Beautiful," I whisper hoarsely.

I see everything I ever wanted deep in her eyes.

Without breaking eye contact, I push into her soaking wet slit, sliding in two fingers at once. Her body shudders and she grabs my arm. She's so snug around my fingers. It's going to be a tight fit.

"Oh!" she cries out when I thrust in deeper. "Sam..."

The sound of my name on her lips thrills me. I rub her clit in a circular motion with my thumb while slowly ramping up the speed of my pumping fingers until she's writhing on my hand. The thought of being able to watch her cum excites me beyond belief.

I want to be buried deep inside her when that happens for the first time.

She surprises me by suddenly reaching for my belt buckle and unfastening it. Unzipping my pants, she slides her hand around my hard cock.

"Fuck!" I swear.

I'm unable to breathe as she slowly strokes up and down. Her touch has me paralyzed and I can't move.

I never want to move.

I have it so bad for this woman.

"Sam," she breathes in a husky voice that I barely recognize. "Why are you still wearing clothes?"

"Hell if I know."

She removes her hand. "Do something about it."

I stand up and quickly remove my jeans and boots. Lila watches my every move and then I see her eyes drop to my erection.

"Like what you see?" I ask.

"Come here and I'll show you," she says, her green eyes dancing.

I move back onto the bed and lower my body to cover hers completely. Her body is soft and lush under mine. I prop myself up on my elbows so I won't crush her, and my cock bobs hungrily against her stomach.

Shit.

I'm not going to be able to stay in this position for long.

"Are you sure about this?" I ask, not wanting to push her. "I swear I'll make it good for you. Anything you want, anything you need. Just say the word. I'm all yours."

It no longer matters to me how we came to be together. Now that I've had a taste of her, nothing else matters but keeping her right here in my bed.

"Tell me what *you* want," she purrs in my ear.

My balls tighten at her words and my vision clouds over.

Where do I start?

"Touch me," I say, nibbling on her earlobe. "I need to feel your hands on me. Anywhere. Everywhere."

She reaches for my arm, trailing her fingers along my biceps, then both hands are skimming over my shoulders, down my back, and over my ass. Her hands hungrily explore my frame everywhere.

"I love the feel of your body underneath my palms," she says. "When you fell asleep in my bed, I sat up for hours just looking at you. Wanting to touch every tattoo, every muscle, and knowing I couldn't."

I close my eyes and bury my face in her soft hair.

My God. She's killing me.

"Touch me all you want, sweetheart. I'm a touchy feeling guy and my hands are always going to be all over you."

In response, she slides her hand between our bodies. I arch up slightly to give her access. Her small, delicate hand encircles my cock and I blow out a long breath as she strokes slowly.

My willpower is evaporating fast.

I reach for the condom on the side of the bed and quickly roll it on.

Lila opens her arms and I move back over her, settling between her legs. She looks so beautiful with her hair fanned out over the pillow.

"I can't stop kissing you," I say.

My lips lightly touch hers before I deepen the kiss, demanding entry into her soft mouth. Lila curls her arms around me, parting her lips and allowing me in. She kisses me back, burying her fingers in my hair and pulling me closer.

Reaching down, she encircles my cock with her hand and rubs the tip at the entrance of her hot pussy. I moan against her mouth and whisper in her ear how hard and fast I want to fuck her. How I'll do anything to make her cum over and over. I tell her that I've never wanted another woman as much as I want her.

I break the kiss only so I can watch her face when I slide into her.

"Ready?" I ask.

She nods.

With one long thrust, I push all the way into her pussy. Drawing out slightly, I push in again harder all the way up to my balls, stretching and filling her. Lila gasps and grabs my ass with both hands, pulling me in further. Her soft body undulating under mine is heaven on earth.

"You're incredible," I say.

And I mean it.

Her pussy feels fucking amazing. So tight, hot, and moist. Like it was created just for me.

I lean down closer and tease her nipple with my teeth. Moving now with long, deep strokes, I'm touching all her secret spots and claiming her as mine.

I fight like hell to keep control.

It's taking all the strength of will I have not to flip her over and slam into her mercilessly from behind. Beads of sweat break out on my forehead and I grit my teeth. I move slowly for as long as I can, burying myself in her tightness and rocking in and out with slow, steady movements.

Lila rakes down my back with her fingernails, her breath coming in pants. I slant the thrust of my hips slightly and she moans in delight against my mouth.

"Do you like that?" I murmur.

"*Oh yes*...right there."

Now that I had found the perfect angle to drive her over the edge, I'm not stopping. She gasps again and I snap. A mindless rhythm overtakes me and I pound into her fast and deep.

"Oh God!" she cries out. "Sam, don't stop."

I feel her start to ripple around my cock, her muscles spasming in release. Her entire body jerks uncontrollably underneath me as she keeps calling my name. If she's trying to drive me insane, it's working.

I completely lose it.

I ramp up the depth and speed of my thrusts. She grabs my hair and drags my face up so that our lips clash at the very moment I cum deep inside her. I groan against her mouth as she holds me tight with her pussy muscles until the very last shudder is gone and I'm spent.

"I don't want to move," I say into her ear minutes later. "Ever." I collapse on top of her, and she leisurely moves her hands up and down my back.

"So don't," she whispers. "Stay right here."

"How did you get this scar?" Lila asks me much later. "A knife fight?"

She runs a finger gently across the long, jagged scar running across my left shoulder, then dabs antiseptic on the scrape below it.

"Shit!" I yell. "That stings."

"I'm sorry. I don't want it to get infected."

She blows on the scrape and the sting goes away.

"Nothing as exciting as a knife fight," I tell her. "It was a belt buckle."

"What? Someone hit you hard enough to leave a deep scar like this? Who did it?"

I lift my head off the pillow and turn around to look at her.

"Do I have to talk about this?"

"I want to know who did it and when it happened, that's all," she says with a worried look. "You don't have to tell me anything else. Unless you want to."

"My dad, and it was years ago when I was a kid."

Lila grows quiet.

"Did it happen often?" she finally asks.

"Often enough, and that's all I'm going to say about it."

"Do you still see him?"

"Not me. Flint and Jesse go by to check on him occasionally. I hold grudges for a long time and I don't forgive easily. Maybe someday I'll feel differently. Can we please not talk about this?"

I roll over on my back and reach for her.

She puts the bottle of antiseptic on the bedside table and snuggles down onto my chest.

"So what did you think about my family?" I ask.

Lila hasn't invited me to spend the night, so I keep talking about anything and everything. Whatever I have to do to keep the night from ending.

"The party was probably a bit overwhelming with so many people," I continue. "The MC likes to have a big get-together at least once a month at our house."

She doesn't answer. Her hesitation tells me that she's being careful about what she's getting ready to say.

"I liked your family," she says. "Kendra and Trish were both super nice to me and went out of their way to make me feel like part of the group."

Her voice sounds wistful and almost sad.

"That's the way those two are," I say. "It seems like they've always been a part of my family. Sometimes I wonder how Jesse and Flint got so lucky to find women willing to put up with all their shit."

I can't help thinking about how the girls are going to react once the truth comes out about Lila. They will hate her with a vengeance. They're both fiercely protective of the people they love.

"And what about the kids?" I ask.

"Josh is super cute," Lila says with a laugh. "He tried to cram my whole hand in his mouth and bite me. Kendra warned me and I didn't believe her. His little teeth are sharp."

"They're both going to be spoiled rotten, especially Missy in a family full of men," I say. "I can't wait until Christmas this year. Missy will be too little to enjoy it, but Josh will be old enough to play with toys."

She pulls her head up from my chest and looks at me.

"You really like kids, don't you?"

"Yeah, I love kids. I hope to have a bunch one day. At least three. I plan on having a great big family. What about you?"

"I've never given it much thought. Any thought at all, actually. I don't know." She shrugs. "I never saw myself as a parent." She idly traces a tattoo on my arm with her fingers.

"Why? Too permanent for you?"

The comment sounded nastier than I meant for it to.

Her eyes fly back to my face.

"Where did that come from?"

"Gut feeling, I guess. Not every woman wants a pack of kids to weigh them down."

"No, it's not that. I don't have any siblings and my family is small. There aren't any nieces or nephews or even little cousins that I see on a regular basis. I don't know how to take care of kids. I might make mistakes and screw them up for life."

"I doubt that. Where do you go on holidays then? Don't you have any family to be with?"

"I usually go over to my parents' house and have dinner with them. I was an accidental late baby, so they're older." She sighs. "And I was way too much for them to handle. By the time I hit my wild teenage years, they were in their late fifties and didn't know how to handle me."

So all Lila has are two old parents. Then again, maybe she's lying and really has a huge family. At this point, I still shouldn't trust anything she says one way or the other.

"Would you like to come back over tomorrow night for dinner?" she asks, changing the subject. "I'll cook."

I'm relieved. I wasn't sure how things were going to be between us after tonight.

"Oh, I don't know," I tease. "It would depend on what's on the menu."

"How about grilled steaks, sautéed mushrooms, and a baked potato? Can you make it by eight o'clock? Or later is fine too. Whatever is good for you."

She's talking fast, like she's afraid I'll turn her down.

"I wouldn't miss it. I'll be here right on time."

"You're such a stickler about being punctual," she says.

"True, but how do you know that?"

"Lucky guess, that's all," she says to cover up her mistake. "You always show up when you're supposed to. I like that trait in a man."

Her slipup throws me and makes me wonder how deep her research into the Steel Infidels goes. She's obviously dug into my personal habits. Are all the Steel Infidels under close scrutiny?

What if the ATF is looking at Kendra and Trish too? The ATF might think they're involved in our business dealings. Of course they aren't, because we would never mix up the women in anything illegal. The risk is too great and the kids need their mothers.

How many people are going to get hurt in this mess before it ends?

Lila reaches for the sheet at the foot of the bed and tugs it up over us. "Will you stay with me tonight?" she asks. "I don't want you to leave."

I thought she would never ask.

"Wild horses couldn't drag me away from you."

15

SAM

I pull out a chair and silently sit down beside Toby at the clubhouse. He glances over at my swollen lip and bursts out laughing.

"Damn, Toby!" I say. "Did you really have to elbow me so hard?"

"See? I knew you would get pissed off." He throws up his hands and lets out a frustrated sound. "That's why I didn't want to do it. You kept saying 'hit me, hit me' and I did. And now you're mad as a wet hornet."

"I said hit me, not knock my fucking teeth down my throat."

Toby laughs and tilts his baseball cap back on his head.

"You should have made that more clear. Don't tell a Marine to smack you around unless you mean it. It was your dumbass plan, not mine. You wanted to get a reaction out of Lila and you did. So quit your bitching. No pain, no gain."

"The main thing is did it work?" Jesse asks from across the room. "I saw her jump up and start screaming at Tom. I thought for a minute there she was going run out on the court and beat somebody up. I wasn't sure who she would go after first. Tom for bad refereeing or Toby for elbowing you. Trish said she tried to calm her down and couldn't."

"It worked out okay," I say casually.

"What exactly does that mean?" Toby asks. "Did she let you fuck her or not?"

"That's none of your damn business."

Rocco plops down in a chair on the other side of the table, gives me a long look, and then takes a swig of whiskey out of a bottle.

"I believe it is our business," he says. "Weren't you the one who tried to get us to bet against you a week ago? We're not letting you off that easy. Did you fuck her or not?"

I feel like an asshole for making the bet in the first place. Thank God Lila doesn't know about it.

"I would've won the bet, so it's a good thing that nobody bet against me," I finally admit. "Good for you that is, bad for me. Or actually it was good for me, so things worked out all the way around."

Rocco leans back and roars with laughter.

"You sly son of a bitch. I knew it! You banged her right after the basketball game, didn't you? Man, she was looking hot to trot. I bet she was one sweet piece of pussy."

"Knock it off, asshole," I blurt out.

"Knock it off?" He gives me a curious look. "You always tell us every juicy detail of your sexual adventures. Even when we yell at you to shut the fuck up and cover our ears because we can't stand to hear any more. And now you say nothing? Spill the details. Was her cunt nice and tight? What about her breasts? They look firm and real. Were they real?"

It's all I can do to restrain myself from reaching across the table and grabbing Rocco by the throat. Flint is watching us intently from across the room.

"Oh shit!" he suddenly says, walking toward us. "We're all fucked. Sam likes her. That's why he's not giving up the details. He likes this girl who is trying to send us all to prison. Damn it, Sam!"

"What?" The men all yell at the same time.

"No way," Toby says. "Tell us it isn't so, bro. Since when do you give a shit about any girl?"

"I like her," I say with a shrug. "No big deal. Or I would if she wasn't a damn ATF agent. What's the harm? Hopefully she'll like me too and will shut down the investigation. I don't see what the issue is here. I thought this was what we agreed for me to do. To stay close to her and feed her false info until the investigation is over."

Flint sits down beside me, which means I'm about to get a stern brotherly lecture. I always hated those when I was younger. Still do in fact.

Especially coming from Flint.

"The issue is that she's playing you," he says. "Not the other way around. Don't trust her, Sam. I don't know how many times I have to say it so you'll listen. She's getting under your skin. I can see it, and it's frustrating the hell out of me. I'm going to remind you every fucking day until she goes away. I want these words to be the last thing in your head at night and the first thing every morning. *Don't trust her.* Say it like a mantra. Whatever you think you've got going on with this chick isn't real. She is fucking you over."

"And what if she isn't?"

I regret the words immediately.

"See what I mean?" Flint says to the other guys. "Sam just proved my point. This was a bad idea. Lila is too good at her job."

"I can make this work," I say. "Why can't you trust me on this? The original plan is working right on schedule. I don't know what else you expect me to do. I've already fucked her."

Damn. That sounded crude.

Whatever Lila and I shared, I sure as hell wouldn't describe it that way. Not now. Never in a million years.

"Sam, let me tell you a story," Flint says.

Everyone around the table groans.

"Oh God, no," I say, banging my forehead on the table. "Please not another one of your longwinded stories that go nowhere."

Flint doesn't pay any attention to me. Not that I expected him to.

"Do you remember the Bible story of Sampson and Delilah from Sunday School when we were kids?" he asks.

I give him a blank look.

"Is that a serious question? If so, the answer is vaguely. Sampson had long hair and Delilah was a hooker. Am I right? What the fuck does this have to do with anything?"

"Nah, I don't think Delilah was a hooker," Rocco says, rubbing his beard. "She was a conniving bitch though. I see her more as a sexy woman with long black hair and big tits. Wearing like a silky see-through dress. Pink or gold. And a scarf covering part of her face so that only her mysterious dark eyes are showing."

"With no underwear," Toby adds. "She definitely wouldn't wear underwear. Then again, I don't think any of the women wore panties back then. We were born in the wrong era, boys."

"I like where you're going with this," I say. "In my mind, she would be wearing lots of gold jewelry and use black eyeliner in the corner of her eyes like Cleopatra. And have pretty feet in strappy leather sandals."

"This gives me an idea," Toby says. "I wonder if we could talk the Sweet Butts into dressing like Cleopatra for a night? We could tell them we're holding a toga party, except they'll be the only ones dressing up."

Toby and I both crack up at his idea. The Sweet Butts would probably go for it. They'll do pretty much anything we ask them to.

"Did Sampson and Delilah fuck?" Rocco asks. "Or was it only implied?"

"Definitely implied," I say. "The wording is probably something like 'loin to loin,' which always makes me think of pork chops. Not sexy at all."

"It's the Bible," Flint says in exasperation. "What do you expect? It's not supposed to be sexy. Do you guys want to hear this story or not?"

I nod at him. "Sure, let's hear it since you seem so damn determined to tell it."

"Okay then, back to Sam and Lila. I mean Sampson and Delilah."

I cut my eyes over at Toby and he grins back at me.

"Since you all seem to know parts of this story, I'll recap the highlights. Delilah was a beautiful temptress who seduced Sampson with her feminine wiles. She convinced him to tell her the secret of his strength so that she could destroy him."

"His long hair?" I guess. "Ha! See, I know that one."

"Right," Flint says. "She was playing Sampson the whole time just like your Lila is playing you. One night when he was sleeping with his head in her lap, she cut off all his hair. He trusted her and she betrayed him."

"I can see how devastating that would be if he had luxurious hair like mine." I flip my hair back from my forehead to make my point.

"What if she shaved your head in your sleep?" Toby says. "That would suck."

"Do you really think she'll cut off my hair?"

"No, don't worry," Toby says. "She'll cut your dick off first."

"The hair isn't the point, you idiots," Flint says. "The point is that he fell for her and she was fucking with him all along just to find out his secrets. He refused to see her for what she really was. Do you see any other similarities here, Sam? Like maybe Lila is seducing *you* to find out all of the Steel Infidel secrets?"

"Yeah, of course I get it. I'm not stupid. How does the story end?"

"The Philistines, who are the bad guys in the story, put Sampson in prison. Eventually his hair grows back and he brings down the pillars of the temple with his tremendous strength, crushing himself and a whole bunch of Philistines."

"What happens with Delilah?" I ask.

"The Bible doesn't specifically say."

I lean back in my chair and cross my arms.

"I believe I can speak for all of us here in saying thank you so much, Flint, for the uplifting, *cliffhanger* story. My day would have felt incomplete without it. Rocco, slide that bottle of whiskey over this way. I need a fucking drink. Or two."

Rocco pushes the whiskey over to me and I take a long swig and then another.

Jesse laughs and grabs the whiskey bottle from me to take a drink, too.

"I feel sorry for little Josh," Jesse says. "For having to listen to Flint's stupid shit stories every day of his life."

"You're all going to feel sorry for Sam and for the MC when this thing goes south," Flint replies. "Can we at least talk about what he should be doing to help things out? Besides sliding between her legs. We need to get ahead of this situation."

"What do you have in mind?" Jesse asks.

"Sam should check Lila's cell phone and see who she is calling and how often. Is she reporting in to the ATF every day? Once a week? How much time do we have left to turn this around? Read her text messages. Does she have a computer?"

"A laptop," I answer.

"Try to get into it."

"She's a hacker," I remind him. "There's no way I'm getting into her computer."

"She never leaves it open?"

"Not unless she wants me to read what's on the screen."

"Like what?"

"A fake magazine article she's supposedly writing."

Flint raises his eyebrows. "And you think she's not playing you?"

There's nothing I can say to that, so I take another swig of whiskey.

"We need to find out more about her personal life," Flint says. "Like where she lives in Atlanta, who her friends are, and all about her family."

I don't like the sound of this. "Why do we need to know about her family?"

Jesse and Flint both look away from me.

"What are you two thinking?"

"We might need some kind of leverage with her down the road," Jesse says, still refusing to look me in the eyes.

"You would threaten her family?" I ask. "Like her parents?"

All she has in the world are two old parents, and the MC wants to find them.

The whiskey is beginning to burn a hole in my gut.

Why didn't I think this far ahead? Of course the MC would threaten her family. And threaten her. Maybe even hurt her or worse. It's what we do. It's what we've always done. What would be any different this time around?

Fuck.

The stakes in this game just got much higher. I'm not only playing for her, I'm playing to keep her alive and safe, too.

"Wait!" I say. "We don't need to go in that direction yet. Give me time to do it my way. I'm seeing her again tonight. Things are going well. We don't need to panic and do something rash."

"We have to hope for the best and prepare for the worst," Jesse says. "We can't be caught with our asses hanging out on this. She has to be stopped no matter what. You need to understand that if you can't take care of this, we'll be forced to handle it our way. There always has to be a Plan B."

"Club first," Flint says.

"Club first," the men say one by one around the table.

Everyone but me.

"Sam?" Jesse says, waiting for my answer.

I nod in agreement.

"Club first."

16

SAM

"You're early," Lila says when I arrive at her house. "I've been out for a run and I'm all sweaty. Don't look at me until I take a shower."

"No complaints from me about how you look," I say, pulling her in for a quick kiss. The tight sports bra and running shorts show off her curves perfectly.

"I'm serious," she says. "I have to take a shower first before dinner. If you want a snack, there is butter pecan ice cream in the freezer and chocolate syrup on the counter. I'll hurry."

"Take your time," I say. "I'll eat a bowl of ice cream or two."

"Don't spoil your appetite," she calls out from the hallway.

I wait until I hear the sound of the shower running before glancing around for her phone. It's not on the kitchen table, so I quietly sneak into the bedroom where I spot it on the dresser. With any luck, I'll be able to see how often she's checking in with the ATF.

I flip open the phone and immediately the screen prompts me for a four-digit code.

Shit!

This is hopeless, and I'm not even going to attempt it. I put the phone back where I found it and go back to the kitchen. Grabbing a bowl out of the cabinet, I add two scoops of ice cream and a generous helping of chocolate syrup.

I'm halfway through my second bowl of ice cream when Lila stomps into the kitchen with a pissed off look on her face. She holds up her cell phone.

"Did you try to get into my phone while I was in the shower?" she asks.

Damn!

Opening her phone was stupid and a mistake. Of course she would know if I touched it. She probably set me up just to see if I would try. One look at her face tells me that lying isn't an option.

"Yeah, sorry," I reply. "How did you know?"

She glares at me for a moment before answering.

"The phone has a program that alerts me if anyone tries to open it. Were you checking up on me?" She crams the phone in her back pocket. "Just so you know, I don't go for the jealous, stalker type of guy. I don't understand what you hoped to find. Were you afraid I was texting other men or something?"

Texting other men? Oh hell no!

The thought had never occurred to me until she mentioned it.

I feel like I've had the breath knocked out of me.

What if she has a boyfriend or even a husband in her real life? Here I've been thinking it's just the two of us involved in this game. A game that I'm enjoying way too much considering the high stakes involved.

If there is another man in her life, I need to know right now.

This puts an entirely different spin on things, and I don't like it.

Not one bit.

I can't let her see how unsettled I am by the idea.

"Hell no, I wasn't checking up on you," I say with a laugh. "That's the kind of shit women do. Drives me crazy. I hate it."

"So what's your excuse then?"

She is not letting this go about the cell phone. I calmly put the bowl of ice cream down on the counter and turn around to face her.

"Alright, if you must know, I was going to take a dick pic with your phone and set it as your background image." I grin at her. "It was a joke, that's all. I thought it would be funny if you opened your phone and there was a photo of my dick staring at you."

The look on her face is priceless. She's horrified.

I'm a little shocked myself at the outrageous lie that just came out of my mouth. It's over the top even for me. I've never sent a girl a dick pic in my life.

"Sam!" she says in exasperation. "Are you nuts? Women do not want to receive dick pics from men. Trust me, they just don't." She shakes her head. "I can't believe you are so crude."

I laugh at her disgusted expression.

"After last night, I thought you might want a photo," I lie again. "I didn't expect you to crawl all over my ass and accuse me of being a stalker."

"I didn't say you were a stalker," she argues back.

"You definitely implied it."

She lets out a long sigh and looks at me a long moment. I can't tell if she's buying it or not.

"Okay, you win," she suddenly says. She pulls out her cell phone, turns it on, then hands it to me. "So give me a dick pic. Maybe I'll love it as much as you seem to think I will. I've never had a man send me one, so who knows?"

I lean back against the kitchen counter and raise my eyebrows at her. What is she up to now?

"This sounds like a challenge. Do you think I won't do it?"

She laughs, and I realize this might be the first time I've heard genuine laughter coming out of her mouth.

Interesting.

I want to hear her laugh again.

"Oh, I know you'll do it," she says. "I bet you're the type that never turns down a dare."

True.

I glance down at her phone in my hand.

"Point and shoot, right?"

"Right."

Her eyes dare me to chicken out.

"I'll be back in a minute."

I walk away and head toward the bathroom.

"Whoa!" she yells after me. "Where are you going?"

"To the bathroom."

"Oh no, you don't," she says. "I want to watch this. Come back in here." She sits down in a chair and curls her legs under her. "Whip out that big boy and show me what you've got. You can take your time. I have all day. No pressure."

Her eyes meet mine. So she *is* daring me.

I feel my cock starting to swell. If she wants a fucking show, I'll give her one. And I'll enjoy every second of it, too.

I undo my belt buckle and reach for the zipper.

"Do you want it soft or hard?" I ask.

"This isn't a male enhancement ad," she says. "I don't need a before and after shot. Definitely hard, don't you think? But take your shirt off first."

"Why?"

"Just do it. Humor me."

I peel off my shirt and toss it to her. She catches it mid-air and laughs again.

Lila is actually enjoying this. I can't wrap my head around what game she is playing right now and really don't care.

I'm turned on as fuck.

Finally I'm seeing a glimpse of the girl behind the mask.

And I want her.

Like crazy.

The way she is right now...wild, sexy, and playful.

I switch the phone to my left hand and pull my already semi-hard cock out of my jeans with my right.

How the hell did I end up at this place?

I'm standing here with my dick in my hand while a fucking ATF undercover agent is curled up in a chair grinning at me like a Cheshire cat.

I say a silent prayer.

Dear dick, please do not fail me now.

Without taking my eyes off her face, I stroke my cock, feeling it harden and lengthen under my hand. When I suspect it is as big as it's going to get, I position her cell phone for a close-up and click the button.

My first and last dick pic.

I hope she likes it.

Something tells me she won't.

*MUCHACHOMAL

17

LILA

I jump up from the chair and grab the phone out of his hand to take a look.

"Oh wow," I say. "I'm at a loss for words."

Touching the screen with two fingers, I enlarge the shot and fail to stifle a giggle. The expression on Sam's face is killing me. I don't know when I've gotten so tickled by something. I turn the phone upside down so I can check the photo out from a different angle. His dick takes up the entire screen.

"Truly, Sam. There are no words. What exactly did you expect me to do with a photo like this? Show it to my friends? Post it on social media?"

I know he wasn't really planning to send me a dick pic. I caught him red-handed trying to prowl through my phone and he needed a quick cover story. When he gave me an opening, I couldn't resist taking him up on it just to see what he would do. I should have known he couldn't resist a dare.

"I take it you're not impressed then?" he asks with a cocky grin.

When I hesitate in answering, he gives his cock another long, slow stroke.

Good Lord!

Of course I'm impressed. What woman wouldn't be? I shrug and try not to stare with my tongue hanging out. His cock is getting even thicker and longer if that is humanly possible. How much longer can he keep this up? It's taking all of the willpower I have not to run over and tackle him onto the floor.

I wonder who is going to break first? I have a feeling it's going to be me. And I would bet anything that he knows it, too.

"At least now I can cross getting a dick pic off my life bucket list," I reply. "I'm deleting this photo by the way. I'm all about the total package. Don't move."

I back up a few feet and center the camera to take a photo of his whole body from his messed-up sandy blond hair to his black leather boots.

He's gorgeous and undeniably sexy.

All I ever dreamed of in one man.

The photo captures the essence of Sam perfectly.

No matter what happens, I will never forget how he looks at this moment. A big grin as always, bare muscular chest, deep blue eyes, unzipped jeans, and a tanned hand on the longest, hardest cock I've ever seen.

One hundred percent Sam.

Why couldn't we have met another way?

"Now this photo is a keeper," I say, turning the phone toward him. "I even managed to capture those beautiful blue eyes of yours. Regardless of what men think, it's not all about the size of the dick."

After turning off my cell phone, I place it on the table.

"Are you satisfied now, Lila?" he asks. "Because I'm beginning to feel a bit objectified."

He's teasing, and I laugh at the ridiculous thought.

"How many times have you and your biker friends made women feel objectified?"

"Two times, okay, maybe three at the most," he shoots back. "You didn't answer my question. Are you satisfied?"

I move so close to him that our bodies are almost touching.

"Not yet."

He inhales sharply. His blue eyes have gone almost black with lust.

"You had better stop playing with me," he warns.

"Or what?"

Sam is barely hanging on to control. I wonder how far I can push him before he snaps. I want to know what it feels like to be taken by Sam when he's not holding anything back. My hand reaches up to wrap firmly around the tip of his hard cock. I rub my thumb over the opening and then slide my hand down to meet his.

I lean forward and whisper in his ear. "So the player doesn't like to be played?"

"Okay," he growls. "That's it, young lady."

He grabs me with both hands and backs me up against the white oak kitchen island in the middle of the room. With one strong tug, he grabs the bottom of my shirt and pulls it up over my head.

"No bra? *Damn!* It's a good thing I didn't realize that or I would have been coming in my hand."

His teeth nip my shoulder gently while his hands slide up my stomach to knead my breasts.

"Take off your shorts," he says. "My hands are busy."

I push down my shorts and panties. They pool at my feet and he kicks them out of the way. As if I weigh nothing, he picks me up and sits me on the wooden island.

"Lie back," he says.

"Wait," I say in alarm. "We can't do this here. People prepare food where I'm sitting."

He grins back at me and reaches for the bottle of chocolate syrup on the counter.

"I know. So do I."

Before I have a chance to jump out of the way, he drizzles a line of chocolate syrup all the way from my nipples to my thighs. He moves in between my legs, slides me down closer to him, and wraps my ankles around his shoulders.

Leaning down, he starts at my breasts, slowly licking off the chocolate and tonguing my nipples until they are hard and erect. I grab his shoulders as he drags one nipple into his mouth, sucking softly at first before growing ravenous.

I squirm under his tongue as he trails down my stomach, licking and biting while murmuring how delicious I taste. When he moves lower, I grip his shoulders tighter and hold on for dear life.

"Oh Jesus!"

He chuckles and shoulders his way down between my thighs. Cupping my ass in both hands, he lowers his head. The intense sensation of his mouth settling between my legs and the friction of his trimmed beard nuzzling against my thigh makes me gasp.

He tugs and sucks on each pussy lip individually before settling his tongue flat over my opening. My thighs start trembling as he holds me down, forcing me to be perfectly still while he licks long strokes on my clit.

Sam's tongue is driving me out of my mind. What he's doing to me is the very definition of sinful.

When he hears my breath hitch, he glances up with those gorgeous blue eyes, slaying me with an unspoken promise of dark and wondrous things.

"My two favorite things," he says hoarsely with another long stroke of his tongue. "Chocolate and your pussy. I can eat you all day."

I'm melting.

He buries his tongue deep in my pussy, teasing me, before shifting back to my clit and sucking hard.

"Sam! *Oh my God!*"

I clutch harder on his head and shove his face even deeper. His growl of approval vibrates against my skin. My whole body starts to spasm, and I buck wildly against his face while my pussy ripples and contracts around his tongue.

I'm shocked by the intensity of sensations pulsing through me. Instincts take over, and all I can focus on is Sam's tongue and lips grinding into me with unbelievably delicious pleasure.

It is wicked and sizzling hot.

I cum for what seems like forever.

His tongue doesn't stop moving until I'm completely spent. While I try to catch my breath, he nuzzles his stubble back and forth against my inner thighs.

"Hot damn!" he murmurs. "Feeling you cum on my face was fucking fantastic. Ready for round two?"

"Yes...oh yes!"

He gently slides his hand down my leg wrapped around his shoulder and turns his head to kiss my calf. After moving me down to the very edge of the island, he places his cock at the entrance to my pussy. After waiting a split second, he thrusts all the way to the hilt inside me with one long movement.

"Oh God that's deep," I say.

I can't think and can only feel. Nothing and no one else could ever feel half as good as Sam buried deep inside me. He slides almost all the way out and plunges back in again all the way to his balls with a loud grunt.

"You feel so fucking amazing," he mutters.

With his strong hands holding my hips so I won't slide, he begins to thrust hard and fast. "Oh shit!" he suddenly says and stops moving. "Damn it! Hang on. I forgot the condom." He keeps up a steady stream of curse words as he moves to slide out of me.

"No!" I clutch the muscles on his back. "It's okay. I'm on the pill. Don't stop."

He hesitates, and a strange expression crosses his face. I tighten my muscles around him, causing him to suck in a sharp breath.

"Damn Lila, you're killing me. Are you sure? I have to move or pull out. I always wear condoms, so I'm safe. I promise."

I nod. "Yes."

He draws out slowly inch by torturous inch and then pushes back inside me in an increasing pace. Each thrust is angled to hit right up against my most responsive sweet spot. Wave after wave of pleasure rushes over me.

"Is this what you need?" he asks hoarsely as he pounds into me harder. "You feel so tight I'm not sure how long I can last."

He's watching me closely, and I can see the tension in his face. He's trying desperately to hold back for me. To know that he's putting my pleasure above his makes me desire him even more.

"You're what I need," I whisper back, amazed at how responsive my body is to his every movement.

Even now, I'm still hungry for one more thrust that will bring him closer. I run my hands over his chest, savoring the feel of his muscles under my palms. I can't get enough of the way every muscle in his arms is flexed and the heat of his skin pressed up hard against mine.

"I want to feel you cum inside me," I tell him. "Don't hold anything back, and don't pull out."

"Are you sure that's what you want?" he asks, pumping his cock faster into me.

The loud sound of our red-hot sex fills the kitchen.

"Yes, I'm sure," I pant.

His movements grow more driven and animalistic. This is exactly what I want and need. His pace grows almost manic, his grunts deep and loud. I know he is as close to coming as I am.

"Cum for me," he growls. "I need to see your face."

His words completely do me in. My orgasm slams into me and I cry out. He rides it out with me, still holding back, stroking and carrying me as far as I can go.

"Fuck!" he yells when he finally lets go.

His climax is as wild and powerful as he is, raging and intense. He fills me up with deep convulsive blasts and I eagerly take it all.

"*Lila*," he breathes huskily when his breathing finally slows.

The way he says my name lights me up from the inside.

"Thank you for giving me such a beautiful gift."

He closes his eyes and leisurely kisses his way down my leg still locked behind his shoulders.

"Am I still alive?"

Did Sam say that or did I?

I have no idea. I'm still in a fuzzy daze.

He removes my legs from his shoulders and wraps them instead around his waist. With one smooth movement, he picks me up easily and holds me against his warm chest. I bury my face in his neck. I love it when he carries me.

"I believe I might have missed some chocolate syrup," he says with a smile in his voice. "Feel like having your back washed in the shower?"

Round three?

Yes, please.

18

LILA

I wake up early and slip into the kitchen to make breakfast for Sam before he goes to work. I can't wait to see his face when he sees what I'm cooking. I'm a Southern girl, and my mother taught me how to make biscuits and gravy when I was ten years old.

Sure, I lied to him about not knowing how to cook. Something tells me he'll get over it.

The man can't eat at a greasy diner every day of his life. If it were up to me, there would be a few habits of his I would change. Like sneaking cigarettes when he thinks I can't smell them and eating unhealthy food every day of his life.

I would also try to get rid of those damn Sweet Butts. Trish and Kendra were on the right track where they were concerned. I didn't like the Sweet Butts that I met, and I don't like the thought of them hanging all over Sam either.

I would also suggest some major changes to how the Steel Infidels are conducting their business. The first thing I would tell them is to stop breaking the law though I doubt they would listen to me.

As I mix the biscuit dough, I realize it feels good to be fixing breakfast for someone else. I enjoy cooking, but it gets old cooking for one and sitting down to an empty table every night with a lonely glass of wine.

I roll out the biscuit dough and cut the biscuits with a glass turned upside-down. The rental house is furnished with only the bare kitchen basics, and that doesn't include a biscuit cutter. I guess most people renting a lake house for the summer don't plan on spending their vacation in the kitchen.

After sliding the pan of biscuits into the oven, I boot up my laptop. My boss thinks I'm working surveillance again today from the building down the street from the tattoo shop. I have a much better idea of how to spend my time. Like hacking into the local pastor's computer who tipped off the ATF about the Steel Infidels's bootlegging activities. Without his firsthand statement, I'm not sure there would have even been an interest in the Steel Infidels.

Everyone has secrets and something to hide. If he's hiding something, I'll find it.

Next on my list is the local judge who approved the wiretapping on the Mason brothers' landlines. He wasn't super eager to go along with it and balked at placing taps on the other Steel Infidels. At the time I was pissed off about it, but now I'm glad. It won't hurt to dig into his background too, along with the Bardsville Police Chief and any other high-level law enforcement officers in town.

A plan is beginning to form in my mind. I need time to think it through carefully.

Sam wanders into the kitchen barefoot, shirtless and sexy as hell. I glance at the clock on the wall. Not enough time to drag him back to the bedroom and feed him too before he goes to work.

He walks over to where I'm sitting at the kitchen table and places his hands on my shoulders.

"You're up early," he says, kissing my cheek. "Working hard on a story already?"

"Yes, but I'm almost finished with this paragraph," I answer. "Then I'll cook your breakfast."

"Breakfast?" he says in surprise. "I didn't know you were running a bed and breakfast."

"I'm making an exception today," I say.

He glances at the screen to see what I'm writing about, an article on Southern home remedies that I copied from the Internet and pasted into a word processing document.

"Do you need any help with that?" he teases.

"No, please. I'm begging you. No more help from you."

He wraps my hair up in his hand and nuzzles the side of my neck. I smile and close my eyes as he nibbles his way across my collarbone. Slipping his hands under the thin strap of my shirt, he slides it halfway down my arm and follows the strap with his tongue.

A delicious way to start the day.

I turn around in the chair and pull his head closer.

"Good morning to you too, stranger," I say before reaching up to kiss him slowly on the lips. "Maybe I should leave my door unlocked if hot men like you are going to come wandering into my kitchen looking for a cup of coffee."

"Don't you dare," he says. "Not unless you want me to beat somebody's ass. I don't share."

"Jealous?" I say.

"Insanely jealous. The thought of another man's hands on you makes me crazy."

I arch my eyebrows at him.

"And how do you think I feel knowing the Sweet Butts at your clubhouse are crawling all over you? Don't think for a minute that I'm too stupid to know what goes on there."

"If you want to be my girl, all you have to do is say so."

"Your girl?" I say with an indignant look. "I'm not sixteen."

He slides his hands down and cups my breasts, rubbing the nipples through the shirt with his thumbs.

"Want to be my girl?"

Yes.

"I don't want to be anyone's property," I say. "That's not my thing. I belong to no man."

"Okay then," he says. "Just remember that I offered and you turned me down. In case you change your mind, I'll keep asking you. I'm persistent and don't give up easily."

"Yeah, I know. What time do you need to be at work?"

"Same time as always. I have a long tattoo job this morning."

"Sit down and I'll pour you a cup of coffee. The biscuits are almost done and it will only take me a minute to cook the sausage gravy."

The expression on his face was worth getting up early for.

He's surprised and pleased.

"Let me get this straight," he says. "You crawled out of a warm bed to cook breakfast for me? I distinctively remember you saying that you were never going to do that. As in never *ever*. You stood right here in this kitchen and said 'Sam, if you think I'm going to get up and cook you breakfast...'"

He wags his finger at me and mimics my voice, causing me to laugh.

"Yeah, I know what I said." I shrug. "Never was probably a bad choice for a word." I reach up and run my fingers through his mussed-up hair. "I can't send you off to work without breakfast."

"I'm beginning to wonder what other skills you have that I don't know about," he says, suddenly serious.

I kiss him softly on the lips and stand up.

"Wouldn't you like to know?"

19

SAM

The last two weeks have rushed by in a blur. Every day, I rush to finish work early so I can be with Lila. Usually we grill out at her house or take long drives on my bike. At night, she falls asleep with her head snuggled on my chest while I lie awake for hours worrying about what the next day might bring.

Any minute now, I could lose her forever.

It's on my mind all the time.

The month is almost over, which means our time is winding down fast.

Tonight we're sitting out on Lila's back deck overlooking the lake where it's peaceful and quiet. She likes to sit outside at dusk every night to watch the lightning bugs when they first start flickering in the dark. I love seeing her face light up when they first appear.

"Do you want another glass of lemonade?" she asks, pointing to my empty glass.

"I'll get it," I tell her. "You sit still."

I stand up and out of habit reach for my cell phone in my back pocket. It's not there, and I realize I left it back at the shop. One rule of the MC is that we have to be able to be reached at all times in case we're needed. In my hurry to be with Lila, I forgot it.

"I left my phone back at the shop. Do you want to take a ride with me to go pick it up? It won't take but a few minutes."

She swings her long legs over the side of her lounge chair and stands up. "Sure. It's a nice night for a ride anyway."

After locking up the house, I hand her a helmet, which she buckles on as if she's been doing it all her life.

"Did you ever ride motorcycles before you met me?" I ask. She knows her way around a bike better than most women.

"Ride motorcycles as in ride behind someone else?" she asks. "No, I *drove* motorcycles."

"What? You can ride a bike? Why didn't you ever say anything?"

She slides on behind me and wraps her arms around my waist.

"What difference would it make?" she says. "Would you have ridden behind me and let me drive?"

I run my hand along her thigh. Damn, how I love her long, smooth legs.

"Uh...no, darling," I say. "Sorry, that is not happening."

"And that's why I didn't say anything."

Trying to discover the truth about Lila is like peeling an onion. The more layers I peel away, the more I find.

And the more I want to find.

I want to know all of her deepest, darkest secrets.

No, I want to *be* her darkest secret, because she's sure as hell mine.

I flick on the overhead lights in the tattoo shop and walk across the room to grab my cell phone. Lila follows behind me and sits down in my office chair. Several of my latest tattoo designs are scattered all over the desk. Most are only half-finished doodles since inspiration strikes me in spurts, sometimes even in the middle of the night.

She picks up the tattoo design I'm working on for Hazel and holds it up.

"This is amazing," she says. "Who is this for? I didn't realize your tattoos are this elaborate."

"That tattoo is a special design for a customer who had a double mastectomy. She doesn't have insurance to pay for reconstruction, and her doctor butchered her up pretty bad. My mom died from breast cancer, so I try to do my best to make the ladies feel pretty again. I get quite a few of them in here."

Lila glances over at me with a stunned look on her face.

I cock my eyebrows at her. "I bet you thought I only did skull-and-crossbones type of tattoos, didn't you? Most of my clients are women. Jesse does the typical badass tattoos for the men. Between the two of us, this place stays busy."

"What other kinds of tattoos do you design for women?" she asks.

There's a tone in her voice I haven't heard before.

Jealousy?

"I'm known for doing tattoos in private places," I say with a shrug. I don't want her to freak out on me. "You know...inner thighs, ass, boobs."

She does not look happy with my answer. At all.

I'm surprised she didn't know this already from her research on me. Maybe she doesn't know as much about me as I think she does.

She chews on her bottom lip. "So let me get this straight. Women come in here and strip off for you to do tattoos in intimate places? How far up on the inner thigh do you go?"

"As far as they want me to go."

Oh yeah, she's not liking this one little bit. I'm enjoying watching her squirm.

"Do they ever come on to you while you're doing the tattoos?"

"All the time," I answer honestly. "It's a terrible hazard of the job."

"I bet. And do you take them up on their offers?"

She's actually worried about this.

I reach out and tug her closer to me.

"Not since you came to town. I'm not even tempted. Not as long as I have you."

She tucks her head into my chest and whispers, "Will you do a tattoo for me?"

I'm shocked and thrilled. I wrap my arms around her tighter.

"Of course. I would love to. I thought you said the permanent nature of tattoos wasn't for you."

"Maybe I changed my mind."

Is she serious?

"I can do one right now," I offer.

I've been designing the perfect tattoo for her in my mind for days.

She smiles and tries to pull out of my arms. "But I don't know what I want yet. I would need to think about it first. Show me a few of your designs to get me started."

"Let me do a special tattoo for you." I hold onto her so she can't pull away. "Trust me."

My heart pounds in my chest while waiting for her answer. If she trusts me enough to do this, it means I'm not imagining what we have together. I can't believe she's even considering it.

Come on, Lila. Say yes.

"Where would you put the tattoo?" she asks.

I don't need to think twice about it. "On your gorgeous ass, of course. No one else will see it except me. Can you trust me enough to do this?"

20

LILA

Trust Sam enough to give me a tattoo on my ass?

Knowing what a devil he is, this might be a very bad decision. Then again, I need to know where his head is at.

"I trust you," I say after a moment. "Will it hurt?"

Sam slides his hands down my hip and cups my ass.

"I'm not going to lie. It will hurt. I'll work fast and try to be as gentle as I can. Are you sure about this? I don't want to pressure you."

I nod. I've never considered getting a tattoo before in my life, and I don't know why I suddenly want one now. All I know is that I do.

But only from Sam.

When he explained to me about the mastectomy tattoos, I was floored. I've never heard of those before, and the fact that he is willing to do them makes me so proud. Once again he's proven me wrong about him. Sam may be breaking the law, but he's a good decent person in many other ways that count.

"Can you draw it out first so I can see what you're going to do?" I ask. "Or at least give me a hint. Is it a flower or a butterfly? Tell me."

"It's a surprise. You'll have to wait and see. Now try to get comfortable and turn around so I can see your beautiful ass."

"Are the doors locked?" I ask. "What if Jesse drops by?"

Sam walks over and shuts the door to the room.

"You're going to need to take off your shorts and panties," he says. "It will give me more room to work."

"I bet that's what you say to all the girls."

The thought of Sam being locked up in this tiny room with a naked girl makes me cringe. I can only imagine how often they throw themselves at him. He's basically sizzling hot sex on a stick, and I can't be the only one irresistibly drawn to him.

"No, they always keep their clothes on," he answers. "I'm a professional."

Something tells me he's only saying that to make me feel better.

He positions me where he can reach my body easily with his tools and slowly caresses my right ass cheek with his hand.

I'm suddenly nervous.

"Still trust me?" he asks. "Last chance. Speak now or forever hold your peace. I'll do it right here." Leaning down, he kisses a spot and lets his lips linger.

I sense this is important to him. I can't imagine why.

"Go ahead. I'm ready."

While Sam works on the tattoo, he keeps up a steady stream of funny stories to keep my mind off the stinging pain. It hurts like a bitch. I can't help wondering what he's drawing. Maybe a little flower? A flower would be nice.

"Are you still hanging in there okay?" he asks after a while. "Not too much longer."

Finally, he stops working and stands back to take a look. He goes dead silent.

Uh oh. That isn't a good sign.

"Before you freak out, I need to explain about the tattoo," he finally says.

I close my eyes. *Oh my God.* What has he tattooed on my ass? And why did I let him do it? My mind is already thinking about booking laser treatments to get it off.

I'm terrified to look.

Sam grabs a big handheld mirror and holds it behind his back.

"You can yell at me all you want, just no slapping, okay?" he says, only half-joking. He's clearly worried about my reaction. "If you absolutely hate it, I can turn it into something else. Maybe. I can't promise anything."

"You're scaring me," I say. "Let me see it. Stop stalling."

He hesitates then holds up the mirror for me. The second I see the tattoo, tears spring into my eyes.

I love it.

The tattoo is a delicate infinity circle with the name 'Sam' in cursive within one side of the loop and 'Lila' on the other.

It's the most beautiful thing I've ever seen.

And the most wonderful present anyone has ever given me.

I look into Sam's worried eyes and my heart breaks.

What am I doing to him? To us?

I can't keep this up any longer.

"You hate it," he says. "I knew you wouldn't like it. I'm sorry. I should have asked you first. I'll turn it into a bird or something. All I need to do is add some feathers and a beak. And a couple of little feet." He makes a face. "I don't know. That probably won't work. A walrus might be better."

I grab his arm so he'll stop talking. "Sam, it's perfect. Better than perfect. I love it."

His face breaks into a huge smile of relief. "You really like it? I've been thinking about it for days. I wanted it to be perfect. Hop down and come over here to the full-length mirror so you can see it better."

I jump up quickly from the chair and everything goes black.

"Lila!" Sam's voice is calling me from far away. "Lila! Open your eyes."

I try to open my eyes and can't. They feel so heavy. My ass hurts, too.

"Lila, come on, baby," Sam says again. I can feel him sliding his arms under my legs and neck. What is he doing? He lifts me up and I struggle again to open my eyes.

"Sam," I mumble against his neck. "What are you doing?"

He backs down into a chair and holds me cuddled on his lap. Carefully, he brushes the hair back from my face.

"You fainted," he says. "Don't try to talk. Sit still a minute. I've got you."

His steady heartbeat under my ear is comforting, and I don't want to move.

"What happened?" I ask after a minute. "I've never fainted in my life."

"I don't know," he says, kissing the top of my head. "You jumped up to go look in the mirror and dropped straight down on the floor. I tried to catch you and barely managed to break your fall. Are you hurt anywhere?"

"My ass hurts."

"That's because of the tattoo. Do you remember that?"

I smile against his shirt.

"Yeah, I remember. I still love it."

"The tattoo must have caused you to faint. I'm sorry if I hurt you. When you passed out, it scared the living shit out of me." He tilts my face up. "Or are you sick and not telling me? If you are, you have to tell me."

He's worried I'm sick. Like his mom.

"I promise you, I'm not sick. I ran three miles today. How sick could I be? Don't worry. I'm feeling better now."

He doesn't look convinced.

"I'm afraid to put you on the back of the bike for the ride home. What if you fall off? I should call Jesse and have him bring a car."

"I'm fine," I say. "All I need to do is put my clothes back on. First though, I want to look at the tattoo again. Stop worrying."

Sam slips an arm around my waist and we walk across to the mirror. Turning around, I look over my shoulder at the tattoo. Sam reaches down to trace the tattoo with his index finger.

"It's an infinity tattoo," he says. "With our names."

I smile at him. "I know what it is."

"And you're okay with my name on your ass?"

I reach up to link my arms behind his neck and pull his face down to meet my lips.

"I love your name on my ass."

Now I'll always have something to remember you by.

21

SAM

Something is dead wrong.

I'm lying here wide awake in the dark with Lila curled up sound asleep against my side. She was acting weird tonight and then she passed out cold.

She keeps telling me not to worry, but I can't help it.

Would she tell me if she was sick?

I don't think so.

She doesn't share anything with me, and it's driving me fucking nuts. I want this investigation to be over. The lies and the deception are screwing with my head. We can't go forward until she comes clean to me about everything.

I keep waiting for her to say something.

Anything.

And she never does.

Why doesn't she tell me the truth? Even tonight, when I could see on her face how much she liked the tattoo. And yet not a word.

It was on the tip of my tongue to come right out and ask her about the investigation. To force her hand into telling me. And then she fainted.

All I could think about when she was on the floor was how fucking scared I am of losing her for good.

She wants me too. I can feel it.

Our situation can't go on like this forever.

I'm freaking out, and she's passing out.

The stress is killing us both.

Tomorrow, we're having a talk. I'm going to put everything out on the table.

Whatever shit happens is going to happen anyway.

How much worse can it be?

I'm almost afraid to find out.

I wake up before dawn and automatically reach for Lila. Her side of the bed is empty.

And cold.

Panic grips me immediately.

"Lila?" I call out.

The house is still and dark. There aren't any lights on, not even in the kitchen where she sometimes hangs out in the middle of the night to do God knows what on her laptop.

Throwing back the thin sheet, I walk into the kitchen without taking the time to put on clothes. Her laptop and cell phone are missing from the normal spot on the breakfast table in the corner. I open the front door and see that her car is gone, too. My heart starts racing in my chest as I run to the bathroom to see if her things are still there.

Nothing is missing except her makeup bag.

And her purse.

Everything she needs to make a quick exit.

She left everything else behind. All of her clothes, her personal things, and me.

Especially me.

I can't believe she took off without saying a word. Not even a 'fuck you Sam, you're going to jail, asshole,' as she slipped out the door.

Deep down, I felt something was wrong last night. Her every touch told me she was getting ready to run. And that she didn't want to go.

Why the fuck didn't I say something to stop her?

I was always thinking and hoping we would be able to work things out before it was too late. Waiting for her to open up and be honest. Tell me everything so we could both stop playing this fucking game and fight our way through hell to be together.

Maybe she thinks I couldn't forgive her.

Now she's gone and I don't know how to get her back.

I still can't believe this is happening.

Hurrying back into the bedroom, I dress quickly and reach for my cell phone on the bedside table. Out of habit, I turn it on and check for messages. There's only one message. From Lila:

"Goodbye Sam. I'm sorry."

Immediately, I hit her number and the call goes straight to her voice mail. The automated message says her mailbox is full.

"Fuck!" I yell.

I'm not going to let her just walk away.

This isn't over.

I unlock the door to the tattoo shop and flip on the lights. After crawling under my desk, I reach around and feel with my fingers for the surveillance bug.

It's gone.

Shit!

If I had doubts that Lila was gone for good, I don't now.

How the hell did she get in here without breaking the lock?

Obviously she's had a set of keys all along to the shop. I wonder how many times she's slipped in and out of here to switch out bugs or sift through our financial records. She probably made copies of every piece of paper in the shop and listened in on all of my conversations with customers.

Now she's taking all of that information straight to the ATF.

She's probably there already, unloading a carload of incriminating shit on me and the rest of the Steel Infidels. I bet she'll get a big promotion or at least a raise for fucking me over. Her bosses should be pleased with a job well done.

I can see them all now. Standing around the coffee pot in the office break room, laughing about how she sucker-punched a bunch of dumbass North Georgia bikers.

The facts can't be denied any longer.

She outsmarted me, and now we're all fucked.

It's time to head home so I can tell Jesse that I failed.

22

LILA

I check in my rearview mirror to make sure I'm not being followed before pulling up in front of a small house I rent in an older neighborhood in Atlanta. The house sits at the end of the block and is hidden from the street by a line of tall overgrown shrubs. Any other tenant would complain about the lack of upkeep on the house. For me and my purposes, it's perfect.

The owner and I have an arrangement that suits us both. I pre-pay six months of rent in cash at a time and hand-deliver the utility payments to her every month. In return, she stays out of my way and doesn't enter the house unless I'm there.

The house is untraceable back to me on paper, and that's why I like it.

As far as my co-workers at the ATF know, I live in a cheerful one-bedroom apartment two blocks from the downtown Atlanta office where I work. When I moved in, I furnished the apartment with all of the latest millennial accessories in case anyone decided to drop by unannounced.

A shiny espresso machine with matching red cups sits on the counter. Photos are scattered around the room of me and nonexistent friends doing fun activities, like hiking in the Sierras and white water rafting. It was easy to pull the photos off the Internet and Photoshop my face onto someone else's. If anyone visited my apartment, they would assume I live a normal life.

That's why I rented a second, secret place.

The house is the only place where I feel comfortable. I converted one of the large bedrooms into an office and filled it full of hacking gear. I'm a sucker for tech gadgets.

The room is my sanctuary.

As far as I'm concerned, it's nobody's business what I do in my free time even if it is illegal.

I don't hurt anyone and I only hack for fun.

There's something about the thrill of breaking into a computer system that I can't replicate, even with dangerous undercover work.

I tried to stop years ago. It didn't work.

So now I do it quietly and all alone in a dark, old house at the end of a run-down street.

Unfortunately, this time I can't work alone.

I desperately need help.

I unload the boxes of evidence against the Steel Infidels into the house and put them on the table. After picking up and putting down my cell phone a dozen times, I finally gather the courage to dial a number I haven't called in a very long time.

He picks up on the second ring.

"Erik?" I say. "It's Delilah."

There is dead silence on the other end, and I wonder if I've dialed the wrong number. It's been a long time since we last spoke to each other.

"What's wrong, love?" he finally asks. "Are you in trouble?"

"Not yet, but I will be."

"What do you need?" he asks. "Name it."

I'm weak with relief. Thank God Erik is willing to help.

"I need a team to clean up some audio and video tapes," I say. "I could do it myself, but I'm running short on time. I have to turn them in to the ATF Monday morning, so we only have the weekend. Can you help me?"

"Do you really need to ask me that?" he asks. "I would be rotting in jail if it wasn't for you. I'll pull a team together. Give me a few hours. Do you have a location for us?"

I give him the address of the rental house.

"See you tonight," he says before hanging up.

23

SAM

Jesse and Trish are sitting at the kitchen table having breakfast when I walk into the house.

"Look what the cat dragged in," Trish teases. "Rough night? You look like hell."

Jesse takes one glance at my face and puts down his coffee mug.

"What's wrong?" he asks.

"Lila's gone. She left in the middle of the night without a word."

"Did you guys have a fight or something?" he asks. "You said things were going good with her."

I pull out a chair and slump down into it. Trish pours a cup of coffee and silently hands it to me.

"Things *were* going great," I reply. "Or so I thought. Obviously I was wrong. We didn't have a fight. In fact, last night was fantastic. Couldn't have been better. Too fucking bad it was all part of her act. Has been the entire time. She outsmarted me."

"Are you sure she's gone for good?" Jesse asks.

I nod. "I'm sure. She took her laptop and a couple of personal things. Left all of her clothes and everything else back at the house. On her way out of town, she swung by the shop and picked up the surveillance bug. I've already been there this morning and it's gone. The bug was still under my desk yesterday when I checked."

"Are you fucking kidding me?" Jesse says. "How did she get into the shop? Was the deadbolt lock broken?"

"No. She must have duplicated the keys somehow. She's so damn smooth I wouldn't be surprised if she lifted them off me and made copies without me even noticing. There were plenty of opportunities."

"Did she take anything out of the shop? Papers? Bank statements?"

"I didn't take time to check. Hell, I don't know what she did or didn't do. Who knows? She's gone now and we're screwed. We need to call Flint."

Trish is standing quietly at the sink listening to our conversation.

"What's going on?" she asks. "What bug? What aren't you two telling me?"

Jesse lets out a long sigh. He stands up and walks over to put his arm around her shoulders. Pulling her tight against his chest, he kisses the top of her head.

"Nothing for you to worry about, sweetheart," he tells her. "I'll take care of this. Go on upstairs and feed Missy while we call Flint. I'll tell you everything later. Okay? Everything will be fine. We've got this."

She nods, but I can tell she's worried. As she should be. We all have a right to be worried. A hell storm is about to rain down on the Steel Infidels any minute.

I take a sip of coffee and wait until she walks down the hallway before speaking.

"Listen Jesse, I'm sorry," I say. "I know I let the MC down and the family. For Lila to do something like this completely shocks me. And I know what you're going to say. That I shouldn't have trusted her. And you're right. She fucked me over. I honestly did not see this coming."

He gives me a long look. I wait, expecting him to give me a good cussing out for being such an stupid idiot. I deserve it. Instead he grips my shoulder and squeezes.

"Let's call Flint," he says. "He'll know what to do next."

He punches in Flint's number on his burner phone and puts him on speakerphone so we both can hear.

"Jesse," Flint answers when he picks up on the second ring. "Why are you calling so early? Something wrong?"

"Lila has left town," Jesse says. "She picked up the surveillance equipment on her way out when she split. Sam is here with me now."

"Fuck!" Flint yells through the phone. "I knew this was going to happen. Sam, did she say anything to you before she left?"

"No," I answer. "She slipped out in the middle of the night. I didn't even hear her leave."

"We need to find her fast," Flint says. "Maybe we can stop her and coerce her into our way of thinking before she goes into the field office. If she isn't there already."

"Stop her?" I ask. "How? We can't stop her. She's hours ahead of us. I've called her a hundred times and her phone keeps saying her voice mail is full. What are you suggesting anyway? That we snatch her off the street? And then what?"

I glance over at Jesse and he looks down at his coffee mug. There's something he's not telling me.

"Lila is an immediate threat to us now," he says. "To the MC and to the family."

It takes me a minute to comprehend what he's suggesting. I stare at him, not exactly shocked but horrified all the same.

"You mean stop her as in physically stop her? You would hurt her?"

No.

They wouldn't do that.

At least Flint might not. Jesse would do it without a second thought if he had to. There's nothing he wouldn't do to protect the MC and to keep the family together. Especially now when we have the kids to look after.

"We've talked about this before," Jesse says. "You knew this was always a possible outcome if things went bad. And things couldn't get much worse than they are right now. She's every bit as dangerous to us as Big Roy and the Liberators were. And we all know how that ended."

"Lila is a fucking federal agent," I say. "We can't kill a fed. There has to be another way. Find her and let me talk to her. Just give me one more shot. I can convince her to come around."

"Hell no!" Jesse says in frustration. "It's too late for that. That ship has already sailed. Flint, can you talk some sense into him?"

"Sam is right about one thing," Flint says. "Before we do something irrational, we need to find her. Right now we're wasting time. I'll see if one of my guys in Atlanta can track her down. I'll also put someone at her field office to see if she enters the building and at her apartment. If we cover all of her bases, she'll be sure to show up somewhere before noon. Since today is Friday, maybe we'll be lucky and she won't go into the office until Monday. That would give us the weekend to track her down."

"Since when do we know where she lives in Atlanta?" I ask.

"Almost since the beginning," Flint answers. "I told my guy to keep digging into her background. We couldn't find out much. Only where she lives and the office she normally works out of. And where her parents live. It's really surprising though how much we couldn't find out about her. No friends, no pets, no activities. Basically she doesn't have a life outside of work."

"What's her address?" I ask.

"Don't even start with that shit," Flint says. "The last thing we need is you running off half-cocked and doing something stupid. Let me and Jesse handle it from now on."

I keep my mouth shut.

Flint is right.

The way I'm feeling right now, there's no telling what I might be capable of.

"What should we be doing in the meantime to cover our asses?" Jesse asks.

"Alert all of the guys," Flint says. "Call Toby and tell him to make sure everything is secure on his end with the suppliers. The merchandise needs to stay far away from us right now. It's time we informed all of the girls about what is going on, too. Even the Sweet Butts. If ATF agents decide to make a surprise visit and come bursting through the doors, they need to be prepared. I wouldn't be surprised if the ATF raided us before the end of the day."

"I'll head on back to the shop and double check everything," I say. "Call me the instant you find out something about Lila."

"No, I'm not calling *you*," Flint says. "I'll call Jesse. This is out of your hands now, Sam. I'm sorry. You have a thing for her. We get it. But you need to get the fuck over it. Frankly, I don't want to hear another damn word from you about Lila."

"I'll call the guys and then go over to the clubhouse to break the news to the Sweet Butts," Jesse says. "It's time to batten down the hatches and get ready for Hurricane Lila to blow back into town."

"This is a damn nightmare," Flint says. "Kendra is going to kill me when she finds out I didn't tell her about everything earlier. I'd better go grab her now before she heads out to the vet clinic. I'll call you later with an update soon."

Flint hangs up the phone.

I down my last sip of coffee and stand up.

"Don't you dare do anything stupid," Jesse says. "Trust me. She's not worth it."

Yes, she is.

24

LILA

I wait by the front window and watch for Erik and his team to arrive. When they pull into my driveway, I hurry out into the darkness to greet them.

"This way," I say to the group of muscular men in tight t-shirts piling out of the two cars. "Feel free to put your equipment anywhere you want. None of the rooms are off limits."

They quickly unload their equipment and file into the house to start setting up.

I wait for Erik to pull the last box out of the trunk. Even after all this time, he still looks exactly the same, only a few years older. Tall and big, with long wild hair, blue eyes, and a trimmed beard. A real life walking, talking Thor.

He walks up to me and engulfs me in a big, warm hug. My eyes unexpectedly fill with tears and I blink them back. What the hell is wrong with me lately? I cry over everything. It's been so long since I've seen my mentor. I knew he wouldn't let me down.

"Still as beautiful as ever, I see," he says. "Don't worry. We'll get this done with plenty of time to spare." He pulls back to look at me closer and tugs a loose strand of hair falling over my forehead.

"I like your new look and hair color. It reminds me of the girl I used to know. The boring librarian look you're rocking these days at the ATF is quite scary."

"I know. At least it keeps everyone off track about me."

"You always were a smart girl." He slings an arm around my shoulder. "So bring me up to speed on the mess you're in now, Delilah. Don't leave out anything."

"First, I want to thank you for coming," I say as we walk up the steps to the house. "I didn't have anyone else to call, and you're the smartest person I know."

"I'm glad you called. So does this have anything to do with the undercover investigation you've been working on?"

"How do you know about that?" I ask.

"Surely you realize I keep tabs on everyone in our old group? I had a feeling you might need my help one day. Think of me as your guardian angel."

"I always did. Too bad my parents didn't feel the same way. I refused to speak to them for months when they filed the restraining order against you and the rest of the group."

"You were seventeen, Delilah. A minor in the eyes of the law. As a parent, you would have done the same thing. They were only trying to protect you."

"I know. But you were only twenty-two, not forty-two. I'm still upset that you were treated no better than a child predator."

Erik smiles down at me and opens the door.

"No one ever believed us when we tried to explain it was all about the hacking. I miss those days. You learned so fast and challenged me to be better. Victor asked me about you the other day."

"You spoke with him? Where is he?"

"Amsterdam. Could there be a better place?"

I laugh and shake my head. Victor was the third lead hacker in our group. He made it through our numerous marathon hacking sessions by smoking weed and drinking energy drinks. Amsterdam would suit him perfectly.

Erik glances around the living room.

"My crew looks like they've all found places to set up," he says. "Tell me about these tapes that need cleaning. What are we doing?"

I let out a long sigh.

"I've been working undercover on an investigation of a motorcycle club in North Georgia. The ATF is trying to nail them on several different things, the two main charges being selling bootlegged alcohol without a license and gun running. The actual charges are quite a bit more complicated than that, but that's the five-second version. I need any evidence the ATF can use against them erased from the tapes. The job has to be clean so the ATF won't realize the tapes have been tampered with."

Erik gives me a confused look.

"Wait a minute. Back up. You're on the biker gang's side?"

"It isn't as bad as it sounds," I explain. "They live in a dry county, which is hard to believe in this day and age. Basically they bring alcohol and cigarettes in from other states, mark it up fifty percent, and sell a ton to the locals. Their volume is equivalent to a large metropolitan package store, and they're doing it without paying excise or sales taxes. The ATF has been watching them for a while. A local preacher turned them in for bringing sin into the county. His words, not mine."

"I've heard of worse things," he says. "It's not as if they're killing people." A concerned look crosses his face. "They're not, are they?"

"Oh no, of course not," I say.

I'll keep my suspicions about that to myself. There are certain lines of right and wrong that Erik would never cross. Even for me.

"What about the guns?" he asks with a frown. "That's a major problem no matter how delicately you want to spin it. Guns are bad news."

"I know," I say. "To be honest, I don't know much about the gun running, which is good because that means no one else at the ATF knows anything either. Just in case, if there is anything on the tapes about guns of any kind, I want it gone. As in completely erased or dubbed over. And anything else that sounds the least bit illegal. The case against the Steel Infidels needs to go away. I have to do this for them. They're not bad people."

Erik raises his eyebrows. "I'll take your word for that," he says. "In any case, this should be an easy enough job. Time consuming, but technically uncomplicated."

He walks over to instruct his crew on what to do while I put on a pot of strong coffee.

It's going to be a long night.
Things will be okay.
Erik is here now.
I trust him with my life, and more importantly, with Sam's.

Eight hours later, and we're all getting tired and blurry-eyed. I convince the guys to take a break while I put on yet another pot of coffee. It's 4 a.m. so nothing is open yet, or I would run out and pick up breakfast. It will be at least another couple of hours before the closest bagel shop opens their doors.

Erik walks into the kitchen and collapses in exhaustion into a chair. He runs a tired hand through his long hair and leans back to close his eyes for a minute.

"These all-nighters are harder than they used to be," he says while trying to stifle a yawn.

"That's because you're getting old," I tease.

"No, it's because we pulled an all-nighter last night, too. We've been awake for days."

He sits up again and pulls a box of photos sitting on the table toward him. After idly picking through the pile, he holds one up for me to see. The shot is of Flint, standing on the courthouse steps. He's dressed for work as a lawyer in an expensive suit and sunglasses.

"Is this the reason we're here?" Erik asks, pointing to Flint.

"No. Wrong brother. He's married with a baby."

"Ah...so I was at least on the right track then."

I pour him a cup of coffee. Black with one sugar. Just the way I remember he likes it.

He picks up another photo. This time it's of a bare-chested, muscle-bound Jesse.

"Has to be this man then, right? He looks about the age you go for. A little older than the last one."

I shake my head again and hand him his coffee.

"What? Please no," he says in surprise. "Don't tell me it's the younger one. Not this guy?"

He holds up a photo of a smiling Sam standing beside his bike. I reach across the table and take the photo out of his hands. I love this picture.

"Yes, he's the one. Sam Mason."

Erik takes a sip of his coffee.

"Your face lit up when you looked at his photo. Wow, I'm kind of shocked. Then again, now that I think about it, I can picture you as a ride-or-die kind of girl."

"You think so?" I ask.

"Sure," he says. "If that's what you really want. I hate to be a bummer here, but you know this might all go south on you, right? What's going to happen when this guy finds out you are working undercover? The motorcycle gang won't forgive you and go on as if nothing ever happened. This isn't a fairy tale. You could be in danger right now and not even know it."

I let out a long, tired breath and sit down at the table beside him.

"I realize this isn't going to end well, Erik. I'm not that naïve."

"Well then, I hope you have your exit strategy already planned. How do you see this playing out?"

"The best case scenario would be if the ATF closed the investigation and the Steel Infidels never knew about any of it. I don't want Sam to ever find out about me. It would be better for him if he thought I just left town and that was it. You know, like a summer fling that ends when it's time for everyone to go back home. Finding out about me would crush him. It's not worth it. I can't do that to him."

"Are you sure about that?" Erik asks. "What if there is a chance he'll forgive you? It's not like you to give up so easily. The only way you'll ever know is for him to learn the truth and then you try to work through it."

I shake my head in regret.

"Not going to happen in this lifetime."

"Then there will always be a place for you with us," he says. "Come back to the group. This life you've got going on with the ATF isn't for you." He waves his hand around the room. "Look at what you're forced to do to be yourself. You're renting two places so that you can lead a secret life and hack in a dark room alone. You deserve to be with people who appreciate you. People that can make you feel alive again. Think about it. We could hop on a plane in a few days and meet up with Victor in Amsterdam. It will be just like old times. Don't tell me the idea doesn't appeal to you."

"I'm not going to lie," I say. "It's very appealing, but I have to play this out to the end. I can't think about leaving town until I know Operation Thunderclap is shut down. I owe Sam that much."

"Always putting everyone else first," he says. "You're the most loyal person I know. Tell me this. Does he make you laugh, Delilah?"

I smile at the thought of Sam and his ridiculous banter that never stops.

"All the time," I answer. "I laugh constantly when we're together."

Erik reaches across the table and squeezes my hand.

"Then for your sake, I hope it works out. Above everything else, I want you to be happy again. But no matter what happens with Sam, you still need to leave the ATF. Promise me you'll do that. Your soul is slowly dying there. One day you're going to wake up and realize the girl you once were doesn't exist anymore. I don't want to see her evaporate."

"I'm planning to. I don't want to do this anymore. All I need to do is figure out how to leave without raising suspicions. Maybe I can fake an illness or something. Hack my own medical records and change them in case they check."

"So you'll consider coming back with the group if things don't work out with this guy?"

"I will definitely think about it," I finally say. "What is the group working on these days? Still hacking government websites?"

"No," he answers. "It's too risky and the reward is small. We choose our targets much more carefully now. I'm sure you heard about the last place we hit."

He waits to see if I can guess.

My mouth drops open. "You're behind the hack on the Ashley Madison website? I suspected that was you the moment I saw it on the news."

He smiles, and I remember a time when Erik rocked my world. Things are different now though. I will always have the deepest respect and affection for Erik, but my heart firmly belongs only to Sam.

"The men using that site had it coming," he answers. "And I gave them plenty of time and opportunity to pay up so their names wouldn't be leaked."

"You blackmailed them?" I ask, already knowing the answer.

"We have to make a living somehow," he says with a laugh. "It can't all be about social justice. We like to think of ourselves as modern day Robin Hoods. We were able to furnish an entire school in Africa with books from the hush money we received from one man alone."

"Who was he?"

"A television evangelist that shall remain nameless," he answers. "Our motto is to take from the idiots and give to those less fortunate. It all works out in the end."

"I have to admit that you make a very compelling case," I say.

"And you haven't even heard our plans for Black Friday this year. Denial of service attacks on all major retailers. We'll shut all the online stores down for the weekend. Force people to buy from the small local retailers. We're renting a chalet in Park City Utah for the week so we can snowboard during the day and destroy computer systems at night."

"I like the way you think."

"And we need you. The door is always open."

I make a trip to the bagel shop as soon as it opens and return with bags of bagels, croissants, and cream cheese.

"Breakfast is here!" I yell out when I walk in the door.

Erik hurries over to take the bags from me and helps me unload them in the kitchen.

"The guys have noticed something weird about the tapes," he says. "They thought I should mention it to you before they go any further."

I stop taking the bagels out of the bag and turn to look at him.

"What do you mean?"

"We started from the most recent tape and worked backwards. There's nothing incriminating on them so far. Not a hint of any illegal activity. No talk of guns, alcohol, or anything even mildly interesting. We're over halfway done and there's nothing to clean up."

I stare at him in shock.

"That's impossible," I say. "I put a bug in their tattoo shop where they've been selling the alcohol out of for years. The surveillance cameras were pointed at the back door of the shop. I watched the first week of tapes and there were tons of transactions."

Erik shrugs.

"I don't know what to tell you. When were the bugs and surveillance cameras set up? Did you do them all yourself?"

"Yeah, I placed the bugs because I was the only one who could get access to the tattoo shop without suspicion. And I placed the surveillance camera on a utility pole two weeks before I went there to capture the back alley."

"I have a suspicion about something," he says. "There's a possibility the Steel Infidels suspected at some point that they were under investigation. We need to look at the tapes and see when the illegal activity stopped. Maybe they were on to you."

"No way," I say. "And I swear I'm not imagining things. Take a look at the first week of tapes and you'll see what I mean." I follow him into the office and pull out the first day of tapes. He cues it up then fast-forwards the tape.

"There!" I say when the back door of the shop opens and Sam steps out into the alley. "Slow it down."

We watch in slow motion as a man walks up and hands Sam cash. Sam reaches back inside the door, pulls out a bottle, and hands it to the man.

"Yeah, you're right," Erik says. "Looks like we're in business now."

As the tape rolls, a steady stream of customers files in and out of the alley behind the shop. Every time I see this, I want to reach through the screen and throttle Sam. Watching him casually break the law right out in the open where anyone could see him is infuriating.

"Cleaning this up isn't going to be easy," Erik says. "Look at him. Half the damn town is swinging by after work to do business."

"Can we dub over it with another tape to make it look like the alley is empty with no activity?"

"That's the only thing we can do. There's no way we can fix each individual incident. There are too many. Has anyone else from the ATF seen these tapes?"

"No, thank God," I say. "It's my job to collect and organize all of the tapes. Then to go through them carefully and lay out the case."

Erik looks worried.

"You're putting yourself on the line here. Big time. If there's one tiny lag or mistake in the tapes, they'll trace it back to you. With your hacking background, they will suspect you right away."

"That's why I called you. You don't make mistakes."

"Obviously I do make mistakes, and you went to juvenile detention because of it," he replies. "I don't like the position you're putting yourself in here."

"Do you have any other ideas? Because I'm open to suggestions."

"Only one," he says. "I'll have the team fast forward through all the tapes and pull the ones that need doctoring. My gut tells me it will only be the time period before you arrived in town. Then I'll send the crew home to rest for a few hours. The only person I can trust to do this job is me. I can't take the chance of someone making an error and you paying for it again."

"You're already exhausted," I argue.

"I'll take a nap on your couch once everyone clears out. Don't try to argue with me about this. If I can pay back a tiny part of the big debt I owe you, then please let me. Okay?"

I nod.

"Deal."

25

SAM

I can't believe it's been over forty-eight hours and we still haven't located Lila. According to Flint's men in Atlanta, she hasn't made an appearance at her office, her apartment, or her parents' house.

I haven't slept more than a few hours since she left town. Now it's Sunday morning and I've worked myself up into a mental wreck, thinking of all the various possibilities of how this might go down.

Trish and Jesse finally chased me out of the house because I was driving them crazy with my constant pacing and 'what if' questions.

Something in the back of my mind keeps niggling at me.

It's hard for me to believe that Flint's men wouldn't have found out something by now. Lila couldn't have just disappeared off the face of the Earth. She has to be somewhere. I'm beginning to wonder if Flint knows where she is and isn't telling me. In fact, I'm almost sure of it.

On Sunday mornings, Flint keeps Josh while Kendra makes early rounds at the vet clinic. Maybe I should pay him a visit. Without telling Jesse where I'm going, I climb on my bike and head toward Flint's.

When I arrive at his cabin, he's already waiting for me on the front porch.

"I heard you coming up the mountain," he says. "Let's talk outside. Josh is taking a nap and I don't want to wake him. I just got off the phone with Jesse and you were my next call."

He's found Lila.

"Where is she?" I ask. "You found her, right?"

He hesitates a moment and motions for me to sit down in a rocking chair. I'm too nervous to sit and lean against the porch railing instead.

"Yeah, my guys found her Friday night."

"What?" I yell. "You've known since Friday night where she was and you didn't tell me? What the fuck, Flint! Tell me where the hell she is right now."

Flint holds up his hand. "Calm down. There are a few things you need to know first. It isn't that simple."

"Spit it out then," I say.

"My guys finally tracked her down to a house in Atlanta, not her apartment. She's been holed up there all weekend and hasn't left the place except to go out for bagels yesterday morning."

I pull out my cell phone. "What's the address?" I ask.

"I'm not giving you the address," he replies. "She's not alone."

"Not alone? What do you mean? Who is with her?"

"A man showed up Friday night. He hasn't left the house. They spent the weekend together."

I'm shocked.

Of all the things Flint could have told me, I wasn't expecting this.

Another man? Lila has another man in her life?

No fucking way.

I don't believe it. I won't let myself believe it.

There has to be a mistake. Flint's information is wrong. Maybe the guy is another ATF agent and they're working on the case together.

"Are you saying she was alone with another man in the house all weekend? Just the two of them?"

"No, that's the weird part. There were other men coming in and out. A group of four. They left last night though. All of them except for the one man."

I'm confused. Nothing makes sense.

"So Lila spent the weekend holed up with five men? What the hell were they doing? Going through the shit she has on us? They must all be ATF agents."

Flint shakes his head. "To be honest, I don't have a clue what the fuck the other men were doing there. All I know is that when they left, they took a shitload of equipment and computers out with them."

"So what about the one guy? Who is he? Do you know? Because you're acting like you do."

Flint runs a hand through his hair. It's a tell that he's never been able to control. Always a dead giveaway when we were playing cards. Flint could never bluff me.

"Can't you just drop it and write her off? Why do you need to know every detail? It doesn't make any difference at this point."

"It makes a difference to me, and no, I'm not letting this go. Who is he?"

He takes a few steps away from me on the porch.

"Don't kill the messenger," he says. "You remember me telling you about the information my contact dug up on her in the beginning? About how she went to juvenile detention to protect an older guy who was hacking with her? Well, he's the guy. Erik Dolan. They're back together and he's with her right now. Her parents had a restraining order against him when it happened, so maybe they've secretly always been together. For years."

And here I was stupidly thinking things couldn't get any worse.

Like an idiot.

If Flint had kicked me in the stomach, it would have felt better. I honestly thought that nothing else about Lila could shock me and then *boom*.

One more big fucking surprise.

To find out after all the time we've spent together that I never really knew her at all is devastating.

"Give me the damn address," I say.

"Why? So you can go in there with guns blazing and shoot people up? No way in hell. It's for your own protection. I can't let you run off to get yourself into the kind of trouble that even my legal expertise can't get you out of."

"Don't worry. I won't shoot anyone."

I'm not sure I believe that any more than he does.

"Oh really?" he says with a doubtful look. "How would you feel if you burst in there and see Lila in bed with another man?"

My gut tightens another notch. Flint isn't helping. The thought of Lila being with another man is killing me.

"You're about a quarter inch from a murderous rage," Flint continues. "It's written all over your face. You're mad as hell, and I don't blame you. And you have every intention of doing him bodily harm the first chance you get. Don't bother denying it."

"I need to talk to Lila. Not him. I don't give a shit about the guy. Lila and I have unfinished business that has to be dealt with. One way or the other, I'll find her."

"For the last time, I'm not giving it to you," he says. "Jesse is rounding up a couple of the guys now. We're going to ride down to Atlanta this afternoon and pay her a visit. Without you."

Fear catches in my throat. If Jesse is planning on paying her a visit, it might not end well.

"What are you planning to do?" I ask.

"Use our persuasive skills to make her see our point of view," he says with a shrug. "You know how this works. Threaten her and if that doesn't work, threaten someone she loves. Everyone has a weakness that can be exploited if they care about someone else. In Lila's case, the Achilles heel is her parents."

The parents who had a child late in life. Who were hopeless when it came to controlling a wild, unruly Lila. The parents who are now getting older and are the only close family she has.

"Lila is smart enough to know that she can't protect her parents twenty-four hours a day. She'll come around to our way of thinking."

"And if she doesn't?"

"Do I need to spell it out for you?" he asks.

No, I don't want to hear it.

I'm starting to panic now. The situation is spiraling out of control and I don't know how to rein it back in. I have to talk to Lila.

Just one more time.

That's all I need.

"At least give me a head start," I say. "Two hours is all I'm asking for. Give me one last chance to turn this around. What can it hurt at this point? You don't understand what Lila and I have. It is fucking real. Just like you and Kendra. We ran out of time. And she got scared. That's all."

Flint starts to deny it, then stops when he sees how serious I am.

"Jesse would never agree to it," he says. "The plan has already been made. It's not my place to change it. Jesse has the last word as President. You should be talking to him, not me."

"I'm asking you to do this brother to brother. For me. Please, just give me her address. You know as well as I do what Jesse is capable of."

"The answer is still no," he says in a firm voice.

Now I'm getting pissed at him. We're wasting time arguing when I could be on my way to Atlanta. I know the info is on his phone. If I have to, I'll take it from him by force. We're about the same size, but I'm a hell of a lot stronger and more motivated.

Shit!

He knows exactly what I'm thinking. I see him grip his phone tighter in his pocket.

"Damn it, Flint! You fucking owe me. I've never brought this up before, but you know what I'm talking about. You owe me and now I'm calling in the chip."

Flint's face looks stunned.

My words were a below-the-belt hit. I would have never brought it up if I wasn't so fucking desperate.

"I was just a kid and you ran off to chase your own dreams. You left me behind to deal with an alcoholic father who beat the shit out of me almost every single day. I didn't have anywhere else to go, and it wasn't like you didn't know what was going on. You left and turned your back on all of us for *years*."

He moves toward me. "Sam..." he starts to say.

"Save your fucking apology. Jesse was a brother to me. You weren't. If you do this for me, the slate will be clean. I'll never bring it up again. We'll be even. I swear. Please. I'm asking you to do this for me."

He looks at me a long moment.

"Jesse is going to give me hell for this," he says.

He walks inside the house and over to a table. After checking his phone, he scribbles down the address on a scrap piece of paper. He gives me the address and holds out his hand.

"Are we really good now? Because you've been mad at me for a very long time. And you're right about everything. All I can say is that I'm sincerely sorry. If I could do it over, I would have made different choices.

I wasn't much more than a kid myself, but it doesn't excuse leaving you alone in that situation. I've thought about it so many times."

I look down at the address in my hand. For the first time since Lila left, I feel hopeful. Now I finally have an opportunity to fix this fucking disaster.

"Yeah, we're good now," I say, reaching out my hand to shake his. He grabs it and instead pulls me close for a quick hug.

"I love you, bro," he says, clapping me on the back. "Don't make me regret this. You have a two-hour head start. I'll stall Jesse to give you time to get there. If you can work something out so that we don't need to come along behind you, call me."

I slide the paper into my back pocket.

"You won't need to make the trip. I promise you. I've got this."

26

LILA

I reach my turn around spot at the two-mile mark and stop running. Bending over at the waist, I try to catch my breath for the run back. The unbearably hot summer temperature and humidity are oppressive. I'm feeling queasy and wish I had started the run earlier in the day.

Then again, I find myself wishing for a lot of things.

Mostly I wish I was back in North Georgia sitting on the deck overlooking the lake with Sam. What I wouldn't give for just one more summer evening doing exactly that.

How I miss him.

I miss his constant stream of jokes and his devilish smile.

I miss hearing his laughter ring out loud and often.

And I miss the feel of his warm body curled up against my back in the middle of the night.

Sam Mason never leaves my mind for long. He's all I think about.

I stretch my leg muscles and start to head back when my cell phone beeps in my pocket signaling a text message. I pull it out to check. When I see the message from my security system app, my heart drops.

Motion detected by the security camera.

Someone is inside my house. It can't be Erik or his team because they're finished, and he would never go into my place without permission. I quickly touch the app to bring up the camera's view of my living room.

Oh no.

It's Sam.

He's walking around my living room, peeking into the boxes of evidence and looking at photos that I secretly took of him.

What the hell is he doing there?

Questions fly through my mind. How did he get in? And how did he find my address? At this point, it doesn't matter. He's inside now and surrounded by evidence of my betrayal.

I can't bear to watch him any longer.

Instead I turn around and start running back as fast as I can. Two miles will take me at least fifteen to twenty minutes based on how many times I have to dodge cars and wait for lights to change at crosswalks.

Twenty minutes is more than enough time for him to go through the boxes of photos and tapes. For Sam to find out about me this way is my worse nightmare.

My heart is racing so fast that I can barely breathe. Sam will never forgive me now, and I will never get a chance to make things right. I can't imagine what terrible things must be going through his head. To find out I'm an undercover ATF agent will be devastating to him. To know that I lied and even slept with him while gathering evidence to use against the Steel Infidels will be too much.

He is going to hate me, and he should.

I hate myself for letting things go this far.

I could have put an end to Operation Thunderclap sooner, but I didn't because I was selfish. I wanted more time with Sam. So I let the operation continue when I should have been back here fighting like hell to fix things for him. Now we've all run out of time.

I've screwed up everything.

The two-mile run back to my rental house is a killer. By the time I reach the entrance to my street, I'm panting and gasping for breath. I lean against the side of a stop sign and check my phone one last time to make sure he's still in the house.

The app brings up a blank error screen. He's obviously spotted the camera and unplugged it. There's no point in stalling outside. I need to get this over with.

I hurry up the front porch steps, reach for the doorknob, and step inside.

Sam is sitting in a chair facing the door with his gun pointed straight at me.

Shit!

This was a scenario that I never imagined in a million years. Instinct and training kick in. I turn and make a run for the bedroom where I keep a pistol in the bedside stand.

Sam lunges after me and body slams me into the wall. Grabbing my arms, he pins them high above my head.

"Don't even think about going for your gun," he says. "I've already found it."

His body squeezes me tightly against the wall. I can't move an inch or see where he put his gun.

"Sam," I whisper. "Listen to me. You don't have to do this."

"What is it you think I'm going to do?" he asks, his breath fanning my ear. "This?"

He wraps his left hand around both of my wrists and slides his right hand up my stomach, stopping right below my breasts.

"I can feel your heartbeat racing underneath my hand," he whispers, sending chills through my body.

I'm trying to catch my breath from my run and I gasp when his warm hand slips under my sports bra and tugs at my nipple.

"Lila," he murmurs slowly into my neck, breathing my name like a caress. "Why did you leave me?"

I close my eyes and lean back against him. How can I ever explain in a way that he'll understand? What can I possibly say at this point?

"I've been going crazy trying to find you," he says while kissing the side of my neck and nuzzling my ear. "I haven't slept. I can't eat. All I could think about was finding you. And now that I've found you, I can't think straight. My brain is fried. I know who you are, *Delilah*."

No.

My heart sinks.

He slides his hand down my stomach and underneath the waistband of my running shorts. I let out a moan as he moves lower between my legs and cups my mound.

"God help me, no matter how hard I try, I can't resist you," he says.

"Even now, after everything you've done to me. I want you as much as ever."

He rubs my clit in a circular motion and then sliding his hand further down, slowly pushes a single long finger inside my pussy. All the way up to his knuckle. I cry out and clench tightly around his finger.

"Fuck!" he mutters into my ear, sending shivers down my spine. "You are so wet and tight. Even now, you're melting for me. Just like all the other times."

He's right.

One touch from him and I'm a quivering mess.

Every single time.

No one has ever made me feel the way he can. To say I want him is a massive understatement. I hunger for him with everything that I am.

"I want to hate you so much," he says, his voice hoarse with emotion. "Why can't I hate you? Instead, all I want to do is sink my cock deep into your pussy and stay there forever. I can't stop wanting you."

I moan when he slides a second finger into my snug slickness. He fingers me slowly, his labored breath harsh in my ear. His body is tense and full of anger, yet he still physically wants me. Even after everything.

There might be a tiny sliver of hope.

I desperately clutch onto that hope and pray that I'm right.

Sam deserves to know how I feel. I have to tell him.

He suddenly removes his hand and I murmur in protest.

"If I turn your hands loose, are you going to run?" he asks huskily.

Run?

I shake my head, not trusting myself to speak.

He drops my wrists and slides his hands down my sides, pulling my ass tight against the hard erection straining against his jeans. I brace myself against the wall with my arms, not knowing what is going through his mind or what he is going to do next.

Whatever it is, I'm not stopping him.

"Do you know what I've been doing?" he asks. "Begging for your life. I begged and pleaded with my brothers to keep you alive and breathing because I can't bear the thought of a life without you in it. And now I need to hear you beg for me. I need to hear you say that you want me as much as I need you."

The sting of betrayal is raw in his voice.

My heart is breaking for him and for me.

If he only knew what I am willing to do for him.

"Tell me that I didn't imagine what we had together," he says. "I know you felt it too."

He grabs my shorts and slides them down to my ankles along with my panties. I quickly step out of them. Grabbing the bottom of my shirt, he rips it off over my head along with my sports bra.

Suddenly I'm deeply afraid that I've misread his actions.

"Is this a hate fuck?" I whisper, terrified to hear his answer.

"*God no*," he says, kissing a line down my neck and along my shoulder. "Never." He wraps his hand around my hair and pulls my head to the side so he can nibble on my ear.

I let out the shaky breath I'd been holding.

"Lean over," he says, putting his hand on the small of my back and positioning me lower.

He nudges my feet wider apart with his boots so that I'm spread wide, entirely his for the taking. I'm panting in anticipation and so weak with need that I can barely stand up. His hand rubs my ass and slowly lingers to trace the outline of the infinity tattoo with our names.

"Are you mine, Lila?" he asks.

"Yes," I answer honestly. "All yours."

"Then beg for me. Make me believe it."

He spreads apart my cheeks with both hands and plunges two fingers back into my soaking wet pussy.

Oh God.

I close my eyes and lean against the wall as he finger fucks me slowly. I shudder, feeling him stroke deeply in and out. His other hand reaches around and grasps my breast in his hand, kneading and tweaking my nipple in unmistakable entitlement. He's touching me like he *owns* me, and I love it. I nudge my ass back against him until his breath catches in a hiss. He's burning for me as hotly as ever before, maybe even more.

There's nothing more that I want at this moment than to feel him inside me, stretching my pussy walls and filling me up with his hardness.

I need him.

I'm not too proud to beg for Sam.

Ever.

Not if he needs to hear it, and I know he does.

Especially after everything I've put him through.

"Please, Sam," I plead. "I need you inside me. Now."

I don't need to ask him twice. He quickly unbuckles his belt, unzips his pants, and pulls out his cock. I feel him rubbing the tip along the rim of my pussy lips, teasing and tormenting me.

"Do you want me?" he asks.

"I've always wanted you, Sam."

With a loud groan, he penetrates me completely and slides all the way in. We both gasp out loud at the sensation. His arm wraps around me, bracing me up.

I'm waiting for him to start moving, and yet he's holding perfectly still.

"You take my breath away every single time," he says hoarsely. "Every fucking time. When I slide into your pussy, it feels like heaven wrapped around me."

I feel the anger slowly dissipating and his body relaxing. It's all about us now. Not the ATF. Not the MC.

Just us.

The way it was always meant to be.

Sam draws out slightly then pushes in again, deep and hard, stretching me to the limit. I close my eyes, unable to do anything other than gasp with each thrust. He moves now with long, slow, powerful strokes, filling me completely, claiming me as his own.

His breath is ragged in my ear. I know he's holding back and desperately trying to keep things under control. My hips will be bruised tomorrow where his fingers are gripping me so tight. I can't repress a shudder and a long, lengthy groan when his hand moves to cup my breast and rub the nipple with his thumb.

"Hearing you moan when I touch you is my favorite sound," he says. "I will never grow tired of hearing it." He continues to thrust inside me, his throat filled with growls.

When my climax hits, I'm moaning so loud the neighbors a block down can hear. I don't care. My body tenses and begins to shudder as the orgasm ripples through me in waves. Sam holds me up as I almost collapse against the wall, my body shivering. He rains kisses down my neck as I pant for breath.

I can feel him swelling inside me. I know he is close. His thrusts grow choppy, erratic, and then he groans, pushing in further. He buries his face against my shoulder while his body cums in release.

We don't move for a long time. I just stand there shaken to the core with his arms wrapped under my breasts and his breath fanning the back of my neck. After what feels like forever, I feel him gently pull out of me.

Instead of stepping back and moving away like I expect him to, his muscular arms tighten around my waist. He folds me into the warmth of his body and I never want to move.

"For God's sake, Lila," he murmurs hoarsely. "Say something."

I feel his heart hammering wildly against my back.

I'm afraid to look at him because I can't bear what I'll see in his eyes. The disappointment in me, all of the pain I've caused.

I turn around slowly in his arms and reach up to cup his face in my hands. Our eyes meet and my heart shatters in a million jagged pieces.

The twinkle in his beautiful blue eyes is gone. All that's left is a deep anguish that I put there. I'm devastated by the raw emotion in his eyes.

The pain is too much to bear.

God forgive me.

I've broken Sam.

The one man that means everything to me.

How am I ever going to make this right?

"Listen to me," I say, holding his face so he can't look away. "I'm going to fix this. I've already erased all the evidence from the tapes. I'll make sure this all goes away with the ATF. Don't give up on us. I can make things right."

"You can do that?" he asks doubtfully. "How is that even possible?"

"It's already done. I'm a hacker with friends who know how to do things like this."

I can see in his eyes that he doesn't believe me yet, but he wants to. His face is taut with tension.

"I begged for you because I love you," I say. "I'll scream your name until my voice is hoarse if you need to hear it. Whatever it takes for you to trust me again. Just tell me what you need for me to do."

He stands there quietly looking down at me while his mind tries to work out whether to believe me or not. I hold my breath and wait, almost afraid to push him too far. This is something he needs to decide for himself. I can't make him trust me.

Conflicting emotions flash across his face.

Words aren't going to be enough. Sam needs more so he'll understand how deep and lasting my feelings are for him.

"Come with me," I say.

I take his hand and pull him toward my bedroom.

27

SAM

I want to trust Lila and believe everything she's saying. And yet Flint's voice keeps ringing in my head, "*Don't trust her.*"

Her house is filled with boxes of evidence against the MC, and she expects me to believe that she can make it all go away with a snap of her fingers. She has to be lying to me still.

But why?

There's no point in keeping up the charade any longer.

Maybe she's afraid of me.

After all, I pointed a gun at her when she walked in the door. I didn't mean to scare the shit out of her. I didn't know who might be walking through the door, so I was prepared for anything. It didn't occur to me that she might think I was planning to harm her.

I could never hurt Lila and would protect her with my own life if my brothers tried to.

Now she's looking up at me with those big green eyes and saying she loves me. Right after I fucked her up against the wall and made her beg for the experience.

There's nothing to say she's not playing me now. She's certainly capable of it. She's proven that a million times over.

My insides are being shredded.

And yet my cock is already rock hard again with an insatiable thirst for her.

Will I never get my fill of this woman? Why can't I fuck her out of my system like every other girl I've ever met?

She's tripped me up, and I honest to God don't know what to do.

I love her desperately and I am completely, totally fucked.

Everything in me says she loves me too. But if I'm wrong, my whole family and the MC are going down with me.

I can't take the chance. Too much is at stake.

Don't trust her.

She reaches for my hand.

"Come with me," she says.

Fuck!

Why can't I ever resist her?

I follow her into the bedroom.

When we reach the edge of the bed, she pushes me down and I let her take the lead. I'm waiting and watching for a sign. Anything that tells me this is real.

I wish I knew exactly what I am looking for. I won't know until I see it.

"Why are you still wearing clothes?" she tries to tease as if I'm not freaking out.

She pushes my shirt up high on my chest and begins kissing her way down my abdomen. I inhale sharply when she reaches the top of my jeans. Without saying a word, she loosens them and slides them off, followed by my boots.

I hold my breath as she nuzzles her way back up my thigh.

My gut tells me she wouldn't slide my cock into her mouth if she didn't mean it. My head reminds me that she made a move for her gun when she found me in her house.

When she moves between my legs and runs her tongue along my balls, I grab her head with both hands.

That's it.

I can't take this anymore. I'm going insane trying to figure her out. I have to know right now where her head is at.

One way or the other.

"Lila, wait," I say.

I pull her head up. She blinks at me in confusion.

No wonder, since I just stopped what was most likely going to be a life-altering blowjob.

"You don't want me to?" she asks.

Of course I want her to.

"I hid your gun under the pillow when I was in here earlier," I say. "I'm going to hand it to you so you can put it away safely."

Giving her a loaded gun might turn out to be the stupidest thing I've ever done in my life.

I don't care.

If she's only fucking me because she's scared, I want to know.

The only way I'll know for sure is if I give her back total control of the situation. Even if things turn out bad for me and she calls the cops, at least then I'll know the truth. Anything would be better than this uncertainty.

The not knowing is making me insane.

"You stuck a loaded gun under my pillow?" she asks in alarm. "Be careful and put it on the side table."

She starts to lower her head back down.

"Lila! Please. Take the fucking gun."

Sitting up, she gives me a long look.

"Okay, okay. Calm down and hand it to me."

I slide my hand under the pillow beside me and pull out the gun. Pointing it away from us both, I place it firmly in her hand.

Now's her chance.

I'm completely at her mercy like I've been this whole damn time.

From the very first day, I've been in way over my head.

Now or never.

She holds the gun in her hands.

"What do you think I'm going to do now?" she says. Her eyes fill with tears. "Say it, Sam. Tell me honestly. What will I do? Am I going to hold this loaded gun on you and call the cops?"

I look at her face and I know the truth.

Lila loves me, and we'll get through this somehow together.

I reach up and rub my knuckles along her cheek. With my thumb, I wipe away a tear threatening to spill out of the corner of her eye.

"You're going to unload that damn gun and put it away. That's what you're going to do."

She nods and blinking back her tears, takes the clip out of the gun. Sliding off the bed, she walks to the dresser on the other side of the room and sticks the gun in a drawer.

By the time the drawer slams shut, I'm already across the room and right behind her. I whip her around and wrap my arms tightly around her, pulling her close against my chest.

"Sam! What are you doing?"

I tilt her face up and capture her soft lips in a deep, searching kiss. After a long minute, I pull back and touch my forehead to hers.

"You love me," I say.

Her eyes immediately fill with tears again that quickly flow out of the corners.

"You believe me?" she answers.

"Don't cry," I say, rubbing away the tears with my thumbs. "Everything is going to be okay. We're both in a hell of a mess, but we'll get through it together. We'll figure this out. I love you, Lila. You're the only woman I've ever loved."

She sniffles and wipes at her eyes with the back of her hand.

"I'm sorrier than you'll ever know. I have so many things to explain to you."

"We can talk about all of it later," I say. "Right now I need to make long, sweet love to my girl so I can calm the fuck down. For the last hour, my heart has been racing out of my chest. I may be getting ready to have one of those heart attacks you keep warning me about. And then I need to call Flint."

She smiles up at me through her tears.

"Is that what we're doing now? Making love?"

I scoop her up in my arms and carry her back to the bed.

"It's what we were always doing, sweetheart. You just weren't paying attention."

28

LILA

I slide out of bed quietly so I won't wake Sam. Even dead asleep, he looks exhausted. I'm sure I do too. Neither of us has slept much since the day I left him.

Even now, I can't take time to sleep. First thing in the morning, I'll need to return to the office with all of the tapes. I won't be satisfied with them until I go over the doctored evidence quickly one last time.

I can't afford any mistakes. Erik's work is flawless, but all it will take is one glitch in a tape to blow this whole thing wide open.

The truth is I won't be able to rest until the investigation is closed. The thought of Sam being arrested and taken away from me is unbearable. There's nothing I won't do to keep that from happening.

I shower quickly and then head to my computer room to keep working.

My worst fear is that I'll miss something on the tapes. A few extra days' time would help tremendously. While I'm watching the tapes, I start working out in my mind how I'm going to convince my boss to close the investigation. I'll need to play it cool. Act like it's nothing personal. That my time spent with the Steel Infidels was nothing more than a big waste of agency resources.

I also need to start planning my exit strategy. It's not like I can go in

Monday morning, suggest to my boss that Operation Thunderclap be closed down, and then turn in my resignation.

This is the time to be careful and methodical. No one can suspect anything is amiss. I wonder how long I'll need to stay at the agency before I can leave without drawing suspicion. A few weeks at least. Weeks that will feel like a lifetime while I'm separated from Sam.

I can do whatever it takes to pull this off.

All of our futures depend on it.

Sam slips up behind me in the dark room and slides his hands down my arms.

"So this is what you do?" he asks, leaning over my shoulder. "I'm impressed. This is quite an operation you've got going here."

I reach up to stroke his arm and then lay my head against it.

"Pull up a chair," I say. "I'll show you what I'm doing with the tapes."

He drags a rolling chair over and leans forward so he can see the screen.

I cue up the videotape. "Here is what the original surveillance tape looks like." I play him a few minutes of the video footage showing the transactions in the back alley. "And here is what it looks like now." The tape shows Sam stepping out the back door of the shop, walking over to dump a bag of trash in the dumpster, then an empty motionless alley for the remainder of the tape.

"Wow! How did you do that?" he asks.

"I called in help. An old friend who can do anything. Erik and his team spent almost two days here cleaning the tapes up for me."

"Erik?' he asks, with more than a hint of jealousy in his voice.

I reach over to rub his leg.

"Don't even go there," I say. "You never have to worry about me even looking at another man. Not going to happen. You'll always be more than enough man for me."

"Is he the older man you were involved with when you were caught hacking?"

"You know about that?" I ask in surprise. "How long have you known? How did you find out?"

Sam doesn't answer.

"You'd better tell me," I say.

He takes my hand in his and grips it tight. "We've known since the beginning. One of Flint's contacts alerted us about the ATF investigation the day after we met on the mountain."

My heart starts pounding and blood rushes to my face.

"I don't understand," I say.

Insecurity and doubt starts creeping into my mind. I thought Sam found out about me when he broke into my apartment. He's known this entire time? My mind starts going back over every minute we spent together. I'm afraid again.

I try to pull my hand away. Sam holds it tighter.

"Oh no, you don't," he says. "I won't let you pull away from me now."

"What was your plan if you knew who I was?"

He still can't look me in the eye.

"To let you get close to me and feed you false information. We were trying to minimize the damage you might do."

"So all the time we spent together was fake?" I ask.

I'm inexplicably about to cry again. Why am I always crying now? I never cry.

He brushes my hair back from my face and tucks it behind my ear.

"You tell me, sweetheart," he says. "Did it feel fake to you? Because it sure as hell never felt that way to me. Nothing ever felt as real to me as what we have."

Reaching over, he grabs me and slides me over into his lap. Wrapping his big arms around me, he cradles me like a tiny child.

"Come here where I can hold you," he says. "I can tell that you're freaking out. You're afraid that I played you. That I don't love you and that the bottom is going to fall out any second."

I nod and bury my face into his warm neck. That's exactly how I feel.

"I know because I've felt that way for weeks," he says. "I didn't mean to fall for you. I certainly didn't want to. I've always been a player, you probably know that. And I was absolutely sure that I could handle you. Whatever it took to keep my family and the MC safe."

I think back to the first morning at the diner.

"You already knew the morning we had breakfast together?"

He sighs and kisses my hair.

"Yes, I knew, and I wanted you even then. I don't remember a time when I didn't want you. Then along the way, things changed. I went from physically wanting you to needing you in my life. Something happened the day of the basketball game. I looked over and saw you sitting with my family. I knew right then that I wanted to keep you in my life forever. I kept thinking about how a future could be for us. With a house and kids. That's why I tattooed the infinity circle on your ass with our names. I wanted a forever after with you. The tattoo was my way of showing you our future."

I wipe my eyes. Damn! I can't stop crying.

"The tattoo was the most wonderful thing I've ever been given."

"Every day at work, all I could think about was hurrying back to you at night," he says. "You were on my mind all the time. And then when I woke up that morning and you were gone, I went berserk. Completely out of my head. I couldn't believe that you left me without saying goodbye."

I curl my fingers tightly in his hair.

"I won't leave you ever again," I say. "I promise."

"I'm glad to hear that because there's something else I need to tell you. You're going to be mad, but I don't want any more secrets between us."

I lean back to look up at him. He's dead serious. I'm afraid to ask.

"What did you do?"

"Remember the night when you were a little tipsy and I tucked you into bed?"

I nod.

"I went looking through your cabinet for some aspirin and I saw your birth control pills."

I don't have a clue as to where this is going. I'm surprised he recognized what they were.

"So I punched out the pill for that day and threw it away," he says in a rush of words. "I knew you might not miss it because of the tequila."

"Why on earth would you do something crazy like that?"

He slides his hand down to rest on my stomach.

"I wasn't thinking straight and...I wanted to get you pregnant. That's why. You're mad at me, aren't you?"

I let out a surprised laugh. "I don't even know what to say. If you knew I was an undercover ATF agent, why would you want to get me pregnant?"

He shrugs. "I love kids and I love you, so..."

"There has to be more to it than that."

He reaches up and rubs my bottom lip with his thumb.

"I was afraid of losing you, and it was the only way I could think of to stay connected when things ended," he says. "It was a stupid act of a desperate man. I was willing to do whatever it took to keep you from walking away when this was all over."

I shake my head at his screwed-up logic.

"That was seriously the worst plan ever. How did you know I wouldn't have an abortion and never tell you about the baby if I did get pregnant?"

"You wouldn't do that."

"No, you're right, I wouldn't. In any case, it's a good thing I can't get pregnant just by missing one little pill. A person would have to be seriously unlucky and the timing would have to be perfect to get pregnant."

"Or lucky," he says. "All according to how you want to look at the situation."

Suddenly I remember the queasiness I've been feeling lately and the uncharacteristic emotional state I'm constantly in. Considering our situation, I had attributed it all to stress.

Could I have missed more than one pill around the time when the investigation first started? Since I wasn't sexually active at the time or even planning to be, I wasn't really paying close attention.

Can I be pregnant?

"I knew you would be mad," he says. "I'm sorry. I know it was stupid. But no harm done, right? When we do get ready to have kids, I want a whole bunch. Maybe even an entire motorcycle club, which would be thirteen."

He stops talking when he sees the overwhelmed look on my face.

"Only when you're ready, of course," he continues. "No pressure. Maybe you should forget I mentioned any of this. Show me the tapes again. Let's talk about something else."

"And what would happen if your plan had worked and I was

pregnant?" I ask casually. "Did you think that far ahead in your grand scheme?"

His face lights up at the thought. "Then I would be the happiest man in the world. And honestly, that's about as far as I got with the plan."

I roll my eyes. "Figures."

"I can see that you need some warming up to the kid idea, so we'll take our time," he says. "No rush. If I have you, that's all that matters. I can wait for as long as you want."

"I don't want you to get your hopes up too soon," I say slowly. "But the dirty deed might have already been done. I haven't been feeling well and I passed out which was weird."

Sam's mouth drops open in shock. For once, he's speechless.

"Are you saying you might be pregnant?" he finally asks.

"Maybe. I should probably take a pregnancy test."

His eyes explode back to life. He's so excited he's about to jump out of the chair.

I hope I don't disappoint him again.

He gently slides me off his lap and stands up.

"Where's the nearest pharmacy?" he asks. "You stay here and keep working. I'll go get a pregnancy test."

I give him directions, and two minutes later he's burning rubber pulling out of my driveway.

While he's gone I think about what it would be like to have a child. I've never seriously considered it before because I didn't think it would ever happen for me. And now the thought of carrying Sam's child feels like the most natural thing in the world.

I love the baby already.

Please God, let me be pregnant.

Sam roars back minutes later and rushes into the house with two bags. He hands one bag to me and pulls a two-liter bottle of ginger ale and a box of saltine crackers out of the other.

"What is that for?" I ask.

"Morning sickness," he answers. "Trish lived off of this for a month when she was pregnant."

"Aren't you getting a little ahead of things here?"

He takes my hand.

"Come on. Let's go do the tests."

"Tests?" I repeat. "How many pregnancy tests did you buy?"

"Three. I couldn't decide between the different brands. So I bought them all."

"I can handle the test by myself," I say. "You sit here and have a glass of ginger ale and some crackers."

I take out the pregnancy tests and head for the bathroom where I place them all on the counter. After reading through the directions on all three, I choose the test where the actual words 'pregnant' or 'not pregnant' appear. Keeping it simple will give me the best chance of not screwing it up.

I sit down on the toilet and notice a shadow under the bathroom door.

"I can't pee if you're standing there," I say. "At least move down the hallway."

Sam sighs and I hear him walking a few feet away.

"Farther."

He chuckles and makes a point of stepping loudly down the hallway.

I take a deep breath and pee on the stick.

How did my life change so fast?

I would have never imagined being in this place. After carefully placing the test on the counter, I call for Sam.

"You can come in now."

He tentatively opens the door and steps inside.

"How long does it take?" he asks.

"Three minutes."

He leans back against the door, crosses his arms, and gives me that slow smile that I always find so damn irresistible.

"A few months from now, I bet I have a raging fetish for pregnant women," he jokes. "Or a pregnant woman, I should say. Your boobs are going to be gigantic."

"How can you think about sex at a time like this?"

He slides his arms around my waist and nuzzles my neck. "I'm always thinking about sex with you. Even when I'm asleep, I dream about it. I want you to know that even when you get as big as a cow, I will still find you as sexy and gorgeous as I do right now."

"Oh, thank you. That makes me feel so much better."

I lean back against him and trace the tattoos lining his forearm.

"I love you, Sam."

"Not as much as I love you, sweetheart."

He reaches over and picks up the test stick.

"And this is the absolute best day of my life," he says. "We're going to have a baby!"

"What? You're kidding! Let me see."

I look at the stick to double check. Sure enough, I'm pregnant.

How did I get so lucky?

"I know the exact moment it happened too," he says. "Remember the episode in the kitchen with the chocolate syrup?"

"Could I ever forget it?" I say. "I hope I never do."

"Just so you know I really did forget the condom that day. I wanted you so much that I couldn't think straight. And then when you told me not to stop, I thought my brain would explode. I knew there was chance that I could get you pregnant and I wanted that to happen more than anything."

My mind goes back to that moment. I remember every detail clearly.

"If I had known, I would have wanted it too," I say. "I wonder if we should offer to buy the wooden kitchen island from the people who own the house?"

Sam grins down at me. "We probably should. For more reasons than one. Now that we're having a baby, I have a very important question. Will you marry me soon? Like tomorrow?"

"Marry you?" I say with a laugh. "Is this your idea of a romantic proposal? Because it needs some work. You're holding a stick that I peed on."

He puts the pregnancy test back on the counter and tugs me closer.

"Better now?" he says. "I don't want to wait. If we're married, the Steel Infidels will have to accept you as one of our own. You'll automatically be under our protection. And I also won't have to worry about any blowback from the club against you."

"Is that the only reason you want to get married?" I ask.

"You mean besides the fact that I love you, I'm crazy about you, and I don't want to be without you for even a day?" he replies. "Maybe I should have said that first. So will you marry me? If you don't say yes, I'll keep bugging you until you do."

"Why doesn't that surprise me?" I tease. "Yes, of course I'll marry you." I slide a hand over my stomach. I still can't believe I'm actually pregnant. "This baby needs a daddy."

Sam looks concerned all of a sudden.

"Is that the only reason you said yes? For the baby?"

"I'm marrying you for me," I say. "I honestly think I fell in love with you before we ever met. I spent weeks studying you and looking at your photos. When we finally met on the mountain, it was like our future started that day."

"Do you want a wedding?" he asks. "The last Steel Infidels wedding was a fucking disaster. I'm not sure we want to go through that again. Jesse and Trish decided to go with a small private ceremony at the house for their wedding."

"I know all about Flint's wedding," I say. "No, I don't want a wedding. I'm not a lace and flowers kind of girl. All I want is a piece of paper that says Delilah Mason on it. The sooner, the better."

"Can I still call you Lila?" he asks. "You will never be Delilah to me."

"If I can call you 'all mine.'"

29

LILA

I arrive at the field office early on Monday morning with a car full of photos and surveillance tapes. I nod at the receptionist as I make my way to my cubicle with the first load of boxes.

"Delilah!" she says in surprise. "I almost didn't recognize you with the new hair color. I like it."

"Thank you," I say. "I dyed it for the undercover job I was working on. As soon as I get a chance, I'm going back to the old color."

That's a lie.

I'm never going back to mousy brown, and soon I'll never wear a drab business suit again either. My boss, Frank, spots me walking past his office. He hurries out to greet me in the hallway.

"Were you able to pull all of the surveillance equipment?" he asks.

"Yes, I got it. All of the cameras and bugs. There's nothing left to retrieve so we're out of there. Operation Thunderclap is no longer an undercover job. All I need to do is put a group together to help me go over the tapes and we'll nail these guys."

"You've looked at all the tapes?" he asks.

"Not yet," I reply. "I pulled them Friday and had a bunch of family stuff to catch up on over the weekend."

He's practically salivating over the thought of what he thinks is on the tapes. Little does he know that there is absolutely nothing worthwhile to the ATF on any of them.

"I'll need your full written report by the end of the week," he says. "I hope you documented everything."

"Of course," I say. "You know me. Always OCD about details. The Inked Dragon is a busy place. Lots of suspicious traffic going in and out of there. Would you believe even cancer patients?"

"That's odd," he says. "What would cancer patients be doing there? Are the Steel Infidels selling drugs too? As if illegal cigarettes, booze, and guns aren't enough."

I hesitate and make it look like I'm thinking hard about it.

"I can't say for sure. What other reason would the women have for being there? Marijuana for medical purposes would be my best guess. I took plenty of photos and tracked down IDs on a couple of the women if we need to interview them later."

The two women whose names I wrote down for the report would sooner run over a federal agent with their car than do anything to hurt Sam. One was a good friend of his mother and the other an old high school English teacher. He designed both of them tattoos to cover up their surgical scars. If ATF agents show up at their house to ask about Sam's tattoo shop, the women will probably shove boobs covered in flowers and dragons in their faces.

"We need to wrap this whole thing up by the end of the week," he says. "Most of the field agents are in the office today, so go pick a team to help you out. Tell them I said Operation Thunderclap takes priority over everything else they're working on. My ass is on the line with the suits up at the regional office."

I'm glad his ass is on the line because Operation Thunderclap will turn out to be a colossal failure for the ATF. Since my ass is technically on the line too, I'll make a big show of feeling terrible and embarrassed about how things went down when the time comes.

After a few weeks of being assigned grunt work for punishment, I'll turn in my resignation letter citing personal reasons. They'll believe me when I say that my elderly parents need more care. In reality, they're leaving soon for a two-month South American cruise and will be having the time of their lives.

While I unpack the boxes from my car, I give careful consideration to the agents who should work with me. I pick out the three most intellectually-challenged agents in the office and tell them to meet me in the conference room. After dividing the most current audio and videotapes between them, I settle down and pretend like I'm going through the first two weeks of the operation.

Even after knowing that Erik cleaned the tapes completely, I'm still on edge.

All it will take is one tiny slip up.

For the next five days, I'll sleep at the office if I have to. No way in hell am I leaving the evidence alone with any other agent. If a question were to arise, I want to be here to smooth it over.

Hell week, here we go.

My family is on the line.

"What the hell do you mean there isn't any evidence on the tapes?" Frank bellows several days later.

He's standing at the head of the conference table and is so furious the veins in his neck are throbbing. The three other ATF agents working the investigation are seated at the other end of the table near me. From the looks on their faces, they're all wishing they could crawl under the table and hide. Luckily, Frank's wrath is directed at me instead of them.

"I'm as upset and shocked as you are," I say. "I don't know how we could be so far off base about the Steel Infidels. Obviously our intelligence has been wrong from the very beginning." I pick up a file and hold it up. "Remember our source in Bardsville? The preacher who tipped us off about the illegal alcohol sales? Turns out he is screwing one of his church member's fifteen-year-old daughter. The local cops arrested him yesterday."

With my help of course. I hacked the man's computer and anonymously sent all the info to the local police department.

"Are you kidding me?" Frank slams his hand on the table and starts pacing back and forth between the table and the whiteboard.

I sit back and mentally prepare myself for the oncoming temper tantrum. He whirls around and points a finger at me.

"*You* were the lead agent on this investigation. *You* said they were shipping in loads of alcohol and selling it out of the back of the tattoo shop. I've never known you to screw up this bad before. Or screw up at all. What the hell happened?"

"It was all bullshit," I say. "The Steel Infidels are nothing but a bunch of weekend bikers. Riding around town on their noisy motorcycles, talking big and spreading rumors about how tough they are. None of it is true."

Frank opens his mouth in surprise and closes it again. "What are you saying?" he asks. "That they spread rumors about themselves to build a reputation as badasses?"

"That's exactly what I'm saying. Let me give you an example. Sam bragged that he knew a couple of moonshiners and offered to take me to meet them. When we get there, the moonshiners turned out to be his old aunt who makes apple brandy in her kitchen. Can you believe it? That's the kind of crazy stuff I went through the whole time I was working undercover."

I lean back in the chair and cross my arms.

The other agents snicker. Frank gives them an angry look and they immediately stop. I wonder how I've managed to work under him all these years.

"They're not running guns, either," I continue. "I don't think the Steel Infidels even carry guns. The entire time I was hanging around them, I never saw a single gun. Do you know what they do at their parties? They play basketball. What kind of a motorcycle gang plays basketball?"

"Damn it!" Frank says angrily. "Somebody better tell me what was on a month's worth of tapes then."

"Not much," I say. "Mostly talk about tattoos, boobs, and whose turn it is to pick up a gallon of milk on the way home. Normal brother stuff."

Frank suddenly looks suspicious of me and turns to the other agents to confirm. "Did all of you watch and listen to the tapes, too?"

"Yes, sir," they all say, nodding.

"All of them?" he asks again.

"We split them up," one of the agents says. "So between us, we went through every minute of tape. There's nothing suspicious on the tapes."

Thank you, rookie agent. I owe you a drink.

Frank glares at me. "I'm very disappointed in your work on this case.

For the next month, you'll be staying in the office and helping out with the paperwork on the other active investigations. I'll have to think long and hard about sending you out into the field again anytime soon."

I nod and try my best to look contrite. Everything is going exactly as I planned. All I need to do from this point on is mark time and keep my nose clean for a few more weeks, then I can kiss this life goodbye forever.

"What about Operation Thunderclap?" I ask. "Does this mean you're shutting it down for good?"

"What the hell do you think?" he yells in irritation. "Yes, I'm shutting the operation down today, and that includes the taps on their landlines. I'm taking enough heat about that already from the local judge. We've wasted enough agency resources on this case as it is. Operation Thunderclap is over."

Yes!

For the first time in weeks, I can finally breathe again.

I can't wait to call Sam.

30

LILA

I'm dreading this.

Seeing Sam's family again now that they know about me is going to be a disaster. He thinks his brothers and their wives will accept me because the investigation is over.

I know differently.

It's going to take a long time to gain their trust.

Maybe forever.

I wouldn't trust me either if the situation were reversed.

Facing his brothers will be bad enough, but it's Kendra and Trish I'm most worried about. From the first day I met them, they took me in and treated me like family, no questions asked. If Sam wanted me there, then it was good enough for them. They were both kind and accepting of me.

And I betrayed them in the worst possible way.

Now it's time for me to face them all again.

"Are you ready to go in?" Sam asks when we reach the door of his house.

"Ready as I'll ever be," I answer. "If nothing else, I'm ready to get this over with. They're going to hate me. I can't blame them."

"It won't be as bad as you think," he says.

Yeah, right. It will be worse.

He opens the door and ushers me through in front of him.

"Hey guys!" he says to the group sitting at the kitchen table. "What's going on?"

Jesse, Flint, and Toby all nod at us without saying a word. Kendra and Trish glance at each other across the table then at me. If looks could kill, I would be dead. I've never felt so uncomfortable and unwanted in my entire life.

Trish is holding Missy in her lap while Josh is hanging on to Kendra's legs under the table. All of the family is here.

This is not going to be fun.

Sam strolls to the refrigerator as if he doesn't notice the icy chill in the room and pulls out a beer for him and a bottle of water for me. He hands me the water and drapes an arm around my shoulders, pulling me close against his side. His warm, solid strength comforts me.

"I know Lila has a lot of explaining to do," he says. "But first we want to make a big announcement."

Oh no!

Why didn't he warn me he was planning to tell them? If I make it out of here alive, I'm going to kill him.

He takes a deep breath.

"We're getting married!"

Their shocked faces stare at us.

Kendra jumps up from the table and moves aggressively toward me, catching us all by surprise. "Oh hell no, you're not," she says.

Josh totters and falls under the table then lets out an ear-splitting scream.

Flint grabs at her arm. "Kendra, stop."

Is Kendra really going to try and beat my ass?

I think she is.

Wow! This situation escalated quickly.

"What are you up to now, Lila?" she asks. "It's not enough that you tried to destroy this family? Now you think you're going to marry Sam?" She shrugs loose from Flint's hand. "Let go of me, Flint. I'm not allowing this. We have to put a stop to it right now."

In typical Sam fashion, he bursts out laughing. I stare up at him in disbelief.

What the hell?

If this is a glimpse of my future, I'm in big trouble.

"You're fucking hilarious when you're mad, Kendra," Sam says. "Give Lila a chance. She put herself on the line trying to protect us all. You're not giving her enough credit."

He grins and hugs me tighter.

"We're getting married and you can't stop us. I'm not twelve and don't need your permission. So will you please listen to what Lila has to say? For me? Give her ten minutes."

Kendra plops back down in an angry huff and crosses her arms. Flint pulls Josh out from under the table and puts him on his lap for safekeeping. I guess he doesn't trust Kendra right now any more than I do.

I'm watching Jesse out of the corner of my eye because I know that of everyone in the room, he is by far the most dangerous. He catches my eye and I quickly look away.

Sam pulls out a chair for me and after I double-check the exit routes, I take a seat.

"Okay," I begin, taking a deep breath. "Here is what's going on with the investigation."

After explaining everything in detail, I excuse myself from the table to give the group some privacy to discuss the situation. Plus, I need to escape for a minute. The stress is getting to me.

I hurry inside the bathroom, shut the door, and lean back against it.

Safe at last.

I wish I didn't have to go back out there.

Kendra didn't hide the fact that she was considering doing me bodily harm, and I know enough about Jesse's past to be afraid of him too. On the bright side, at least Flint and Trish seem to be a little more calm and accepting of my relationship with Sam. I'll try to soften them up first. Trish is sweet, so maybe she'll eventually come around.

Thank goodness Sam didn't blurt out anything about the baby.

I splash cold water on my face and take a deep breath.

Finally feeling calmer, I open the bathroom door, and walk straight into

Trish. She's standing on the other side with Missy in her arms. She puts a hand on my arm and forces me back into the bathroom before slamming the door behind us. Normally I wouldn't allow anyone to push me around, but since there's a baby in her arms, I don't put up any resistance.

"I need to talk to you," she says. Her brown eyes are flashing in anger.

Terrific.

So she hates me too. The day keeps getting worse.

"I know what you probably think about me," she says. "That I'm the nice, easy-going one in the family."

Actually, I did until just now.

"Let me warn you." She shifts Missy to her other arm and points a finger at me. "Do not mistake my kindness for weakness. If you hurt Sam or hurt this family, I personally will cut..."

Missy lets out a big baby burp and spits up all over Trish's blouse.

"Oh no," I say, horrified by the volume of puke and the smell.

Is this what babies do?

"Missy!" Trish cries in frustration. "This is a brand new shirt."

Trish looks over at me and after a split second's hesitation holds out Missy for me to take.

"Here, can you hold her a second so I can wipe this off?"

I back up and slowly shake my head.

The sour smell of the spit-up hits me and I run for the toilet where I throw up my lunch.

Trish looks over at me in disgust.

"For heaven's sake!" she says. "What the hell is wrong with you? It's only baby spit-up, not vomit."

Oh God! Why did she have to say that word?

I bend over and throw up again.

She watches me silently, then reaches for a washcloth from the shelf above the sink, runs it under cold water, and hands it to me.

"Let me guess. You're *pregnant*."

She makes the word 'pregnant" sound like the worst thing in the world.

I wipe my mouth with the cold cloth before answering.

"Yes, I'm pregnant. What possibly gave it away?"

She wets another cloth and tries to wipe off her shirt while cradling Missy in her arms.

"Does Sam know?" she asks.

"Of course he knows."

"And?"

"And he's thrilled."

Trish sighs. "Of course he would be. He's always wanted a busload of kids. And you?"

"You're asking me this now while my head is in the toilet? I'm thrilled, too. Can't you tell by my cheerful enthusiasm?"

I scoot back on the cold tile floor until my back is against the wall and press the cloth to my face. Damn, I feel terrible. My morning sickness is turning into all day sickness that never eases up.

Trish is standing there silently watching me. Why is she still here? She's obviously waiting for something.

"I love Sam and that's all I can say, Trish. I'm in this for the long haul and I'm not going away. You and everyone else out there are just going to have to deal. I'm marrying Sam and we're having this baby. In other words, I'm *permanent.* If it makes you feel better to throw threats at me, go ahead, but it's not going to change anything. I don't scare easily."

I lean back, close my eyes, and try to will the nausea to go away so I can grab Sam and leave.

"Well," she says after a long moment of silence. "As far as I'm concerned, this changes everything. I might even like you. A little bit."

She smiles and reaches over to pat me awkwardly on the shoulder.

"Welcome to the family. The morning sickness will pass soon, I promise."

I pull my knees up and rest my head on them as she goes out the door. After a couple of minutes, I hear a timid knock on the door.

"Lila," Sam asks. "Are you okay? Can I come in?" He opens the door without waiting for me to answer. He steps inside and kneels down beside me with a worried look on his face. "Sick again?"

I nod.

"Let me help you up and I'll take you home."

He lifts me to my feet and slides an arm around my waist.

"Trish told you I was sick?" I ask.

"Yeah, she was worried about you. Considering everything, I think things went pretty well with them, don't you think?"

He smiles down at me just in time to keep me from slapping him.

"I'm kidding. Don't worry, they'll come around."

I look up at Sam's handsome face and it helps me to remember why I'm doing this. His family and the MC mean everything to him. I want to be a part of his life too, so if I have to crawl out of this hole I've dug on shards of broken glass, I'll do it.

Sam is worth it and I'm tough.

We'll get through this together.

31

SAM

I can't wait to see Lila. It's been a week and I'm missing her like crazy. We can't take any chances with the ATF finding out about us, so we're sneaking around on the weekends to be together.

I usually arrive at her house in Atlanta after dark and leave before daylight. It sucks, but it's better than nothing. Knowing that we'll be together soon keeps us going.

When I'm five minutes away, I call her on my cell phone to tell her I'm almost there. By the time I pull up in front of her house, she's already out the door and running toward me. I barely have time to take my helmet off before she's wrapping her arms around my waist. I grab her up in a big bear hug.

"Lila," I say into her hair. "I've missed you so much." I plant a long, slow kiss on her lips and hug her again. "Being away from you is torture."

"Tell me about it," she says. "All night long I reach over for you and you're not there. I have some good news though. Guess what?"

Lila is bubbling with energy and absolutely glowing.

"What?"

"The morning sickness is finally gone and I feel terrific."

She reaches up and pulls my head down to kiss me hungrily again.

"You must be feeling better," I say with a laugh. "I've heard a rumor about pregnant women and hormones. I don't know if it's true."

"What's the rumor?"

"That once the morning sickness leaves, you'll be horny all the time."

"It's true, so it's a good thing you're here. Leaving a horny, pregnant woman all to her lonesome can be a very bad thing."

"I'm here now and I'm all yours, darling. To do with me as you will."

She laughs and takes my hand.

I love seeing her relaxed and carefree. I knew all along the real Lila was deep down in there somewhere, just waiting to come out and let me love her.

When we step inside the house, she leads me to the kitchen.

"Are you hungry?" she asks. "I made lasagna."

"Hungry for you," I say, caressing her ass with my hand. She's already gaining weight and I love her new curves. "I need a shower first. I came straight from work."

She leans into me and buries her nose in my shirt.

"You smell like a man, and I'm sure as hell not complaining. But if you insist, I'll get you a clean towel."

I follow her into the bathroom where she hands me a thick yellow towel. Instead of stepping out, she stands there leaning against the door. She smiles when I reach around to tug the shirt over my head.

"Do you have some kind of a kinky thing for shirts?" I ask curiously.

"Maybe," she says slowly. "I'm definitely developing a kinky thing since I met you. But it's not about the shirt."

I don't have a clue what she's talking about. I drop the shirt on the floor and unfasten my belt. Grabbing the buckle end, I pull it out through the loops quickly and double it up in my hand. I start to toss it on the floor too when I look over and catch the hazy look in her eyes.

Whoa!

She's turned on by something.

The belt?

I slap it hard against my other hand and she jumps.

"Sam?" she asks hesitantly. "What are you thinking? Don't you dare."

She starts backing out of the bathroom when I move toward her.

"I saw something flicker in your eyes," I say. "Come here, Lila. You've been a bad girl."

She looks at me wide-eyed and shakes her head. "Oh hell no, you don't," she says before she turns and runs. She makes a mad dash for the bedroom and reaches the far side of the bed. I lunge for her, and she jumps up on the bed and rolls over to the other side. The king-sized bed is between us now, but I've blocked her escape out of the room.

"So this is the way you want to play it?" I say. "You can't run now. Time for your punishment. I've got you cornered."

I slap the belt against my leg.

"You know you've been bad. From now on, you have to call me Master."

"How about from now on you call *me* Master," she throws back at me.

An image of Lila handcuffing me to the bed floats through my brain.

"Okay," I say with a shrug. "Want to do that now? I'm game if you are."

Laughter spills out of her, and she tries to make a run for it.

"You suck at this so bad, Sam."

I crawl over the bed and grab her. Wrapping both arms around her chest, I attempt to drag her back down onto the bed with me. She struggles wildly, using all of her strength to fight against me. I'm being careful not to hurt her.

"Damn, woman! You're strong. Like one of those giant Amazonian women or something."

She's struggling with me and my cock is throbbing. We're both breathing hard and it's all I can do to keep a grip on her. Any moment now, I'm expecting her to pull some crazy martial art shit and knock me off my ass. I wouldn't put it past her to be able to do it. Underestimating her is always a mistake.

"Sam," she gasps. "Let me go, right now."

I tighten my arms around her lush breasts. They've grown bigger in a week's time if that's possible. I want to nuzzle my face between them.

"Nope. You're a bad girl, Lila. Call me Master."

"No! Never!"

I drag her across my lap so that her body is lying facedown and her head is hanging down.

"I mean it!" she says, her arms flailing wildly. "Turn me loose. I didn't know you were into BDSM." She tries to swat me and misses.

I chuckle and jerk her shorts down. Bright red lacy panties cover her beautiful ass.

Fuck! How I love a woman in red.

"I'm not into BDSM, sweetheart," I say. "I don't even know what it stands for, so why don't you tell me."

"If you don't know, I'm sure as hell not telling you," she yells with her head hanging upside down off the edge of the bed.

Is she really mad?

I can't tell for sure. Guess I'll find out. I toss the belt onto the floor.

"Whoops! I dropped the belt."

I would never touch her beautiful skin with a belt, even while playing. I've been on the bad side of belts too many times in my life. I rub my hand in a circular motion across the silky red panties covering her ass.

"If you won't tell me, I'll make up my own version of BDSM then. And as much as I love these pretty panties, they're coming off right this instant."

I hold her firmly with my left arm and pull her panties down to her knees.

"Okay, now let's get back to my poem."

"Sam, I'm warning you. Let me go."

After massaging both of her ass cheeks with my hand, I slap her lightly on one cheek and then the other. Not hard enough to hurt, only enough to tingle a little. Hell, it probably hurts my hand more than it hurts her.

"B stands for bad, and we both know you're a bad girl."

I'm transfixed by the color change on her ass where I popped her.

Maybe I should do it again.

"D stands for damn, I sure love looking at your ass. Have I told you lately what a beautiful ass you have? The perfect size for my hands."

She struggles and squirms against my cock, but not quite as forcefully as before.

I change the position of my arm to grip her tighter.

"Lila, I swear to God, if you don't stop squirming around in my lap, I'm going to cum in my jeans," I warn. "Be still."

"You can't make me," she challenges.

"Oh no, you did not just say that. Yes, I can make you do whatever I want."

I notice her movements have changed and instead of struggling against me, now she's rubbing on me. The blood roars in my ears. I'm losing my concentration.

"Let's see now," I say. "Where were we? S. That's an easy one. S is for Sam of course."

"Did you fail Creative Writing class?" she says. "That doesn't make sense."

"You're right, it doesn't. S should be for smack."

I smack her ass harder this time.

"You shouldn't have made fun of my word choices," I say. "It hurt my feelings, so I had to spank you. What's the last letter?"

"M," she whispers.

I slide my hand down the crack of her ass and push a finger inside her tight pussy. She is so fucking wet for me.

"M is for melting. My God, you feel like hot, melted butter."

She gasps as I finger fuck her slowly.

I want to taste her now.

To bury my face between her legs and stay there the rest of the night.

"I think you've been punished enough," I say. "Will you be a good girl now?"

She nods vigorously. "Oh yes. I'll be good, *Master Sam*." She giggles and I pop her ass again then lift her up to place her on the bed.

"Don't move," I tell her. "I'll be right back."

I go to the kitchen and grab the bottle of olive oil I had spotted earlier sitting on the counter. Uncorking the top, I walk back into the bedroom and hold it up for her to see.

"Sam? What are doing? Put that down right this minute. You're holding a bottle of expensive artisanal olive oil from Tuscany."

"So close your eyes and pretend I'm your own personal Italian stallion. Whatever makes it good for you, darling. It won't bother me one bit. I can be whatever you need me to be."

She rolls her eyes.

"As if I could *ever* think of another man when I'm with you? You're going to owe me a bottle of olive oil."

"I'll owe you a lot more than that," I say. "Roll over and scoot up on your knees."

She eagerly obeys and props herself up on her elbows, face down with her luscious curvy ass in the air. I can't help stopping just to stare.

How did I ever get so lucky to be marrying the sexiest woman in the world?

I place the bottle on the floor and quickly strip off my clothes before crawling across the bed to settle behind her.

"My plan just took a detour. I swear you get more beautiful every time I see you. Right now there's nothing I need more that to put my face deep in that sexy ass of yours."

My hands smooth slowly up and down the back of her thighs. She could never possibly understand how much I love touching her. Every time I look at her I'm in awe all over again that she's really mine forever.

My thumb skims over the infinity tattoo and I lean down to touch it with my lips. Her ass is getting a little plumper and I love it.

I grasp her ass cheeks, drawing them wide apart so I can run my tongue up and down the length of her crack. When she whimpers in appreciation, I nuzzle my face on her pussy then settle my tongue on her slit, lapping up her delicious taste.

Heaven.

She grabs the sheet with both hands and pushes her ass up higher. "Oh my God," she says breathlessly, squirming underneath my tongue. "You are so *wicked* bad."

I grip her ass tighter so she can't squirm away while I eat her pussy out the way I love to. She intoxicates me with her taste and her smell. I can't imagine ever getting enough of her. And now that she's pregnant she's even sexier than ever. I dip into her deeper with my tongue, savoring the burning moist heat on my face.

Her breath catches and I know she's close to coming. I recognize the sound and it thrills me every time. I vigorously rub her clit in a circular motion and she cries out, grinding her ass back into my face.

She's coming on my tongue.

Absolutely fucking amazing.

I can feel every pulse and contraction of her pussy as it goes on and on. My brain explodes and my cock feels like it's about to do the same. I don't stop until her breathing slows.

“We’re not done yet,” I say, reaching for the bottle of oil.

She watches me over her shoulder as I drizzle a thin stream of oil down the crack of her ass.

“Oh that’s cold,” she says with a shiver.

I put the bottle back down and start rubbing the oil into her skin with both hands.

“Don’t worry. I’ll warm you up again in no time.”

32

LILA

"Promises, promises," I say, knowing Sam will make good on his word.

He always does.

Minutes ago I was coming on his face and now I'm already burning hot again.

Between my crazy pregnancy hormones and not being able to see Sam often, I'm always in aching heat for him.

He rubs the oil all over my ass, down my crack and between my legs. The longer he caresses me, the harsher and more uneven his breathing becomes. The thick erection pressing against the side of my hip reminds me of the pleasure yet to come. When he wedges two fingers deep inside my pussy I gasp out loud.

"Oh...that's good."

I clutch around him with eager muscles, starving for any kind of penetration. My whole body trembles as he pumps in and out of me in a steady fucking motion. Just when I think things can't feel any better, he teases his thumb over my ass. Before I realize what he's doing, he pushes in past the knuckle until his thumb is embedded in my ass all the way.

A delicious fullness overcomes me and my brain starts to short-circuit. The forbidden sensation of his thumb fucking my ass and his two fingers thrusting in my pussy at the same time blows my mind.

"Oh...*fuck*!"

I've never felt a sensation so intense and I begin to grind my hips to match his relentless dual penetration. Bucking against his hand, I desperately seek more pressure, more burning friction. In this position I feel totally exposed and completely under his control.

"Lila," he mutters. "This is killing me. I need to be inside you *now*."

He slips his fingers out of me. The tip of his hard cock nudges me and I brace myself on my elbows as he plunges into my pussy in one long, hard power thrust.

"You're huge," I cry out.

His thickness threatens to split me apart in this position. He lubes a finger with the oil on my skin and slides it all the way up my ass. I bury my head in the pillow and whimper at the erotic sensation of being filled so completely.

"Tell me if you like this," he says, stroking the finger in and out of my ass while he holds perfectly still inside me.

"I don't like it, I love it," I whisper.

Oh Jesus he feels fucking fantastic.

His breathing is heavy and his body is taut with tension.

"Fuck me now like I know you want to," I say. "Fast and hard."

He moves his hand and begins slamming his cock into me with rugged thrusts. When I start to slip on the bed, he wraps one arm underneath me to hold me upright as he fucks me wild and powerfully.

Again and again he pounds me, his penetration so deep that he reaches all of my inner secret spots. Between the angle, the friction of our bodies and the intense pressure it's all proving too much to hold out. I cry out as my second orgasm hits, my body jerking uncontrollably.

"That's it, baby," he says. He grabs my ass and pulls me roughly back against him. His cock slams in deeper than I would have believed possible. "Let me feel you cum again."

He fists my hair and tugs my head back hard to bring my mouth closer to his. I moan in his mouth as he devours my lips hungrily. Deep within my core, I feel him swelling and throbbing. He intensifies his thrusts to lightning speed. Trapped beneath his muscular body, I'm overcome with a rush of sensations. He's fucking me into a hazy cloud of oblivion.

His body jerks raggedly several more times and then he cums with a loud groan sending an explosive rush inside me. I close my eyes, relishing how powerfully he loses control, just like everything else he does.

Holding nothing back.

Giving me everything I want and could ever need.

Making love with Sam is a mind-blowing experience every single time.

I love him more than life itself.

As always, he knows what I'm thinking without me having to say it.

"I love you too," he murmurs against the back of my neck. "I miss you so much, sweetheart."

He rolls off and stretches out close beside me on the bed so our faces are almost touching. Gently he touches my hair and trails the strands through his fingers.

"How much longer do we need to wait before you can leave the ATF?" he asks. "I need you and I want to be here for you too. I've hated being away from you knowing that you aren't feeling well. I worry constantly."

"I know you do," I say, snuggling closer to him.

Sam is going to be the most loving, considerate husband a woman could ever possibly hope for. I'm a very lucky girl.

"I'll give my notice this week. It's time to end this and put it all behind us."

I reach over and smooth my palm over the muscles on his chest and down his arm. To think I almost walked away from him for good. I'm so thankful that he didn't give up on us.

"Sam? Can I ask you something?"

"Sure. What is it?"

"What was the deal with the belt?"

He chuckles and his chest rumbles underneath my hand. "Why are you asking me? You're the one who was turned on. I saw it in your eyes."

I lean up from his chest and look at him in surprise. "By the belt? Uh..no. I was getting turned on by watching you take off your shirt. That's my kinky thing. I could watch you do that all day long." I lean in closer to kiss him. "You're ridiculous and a hot mess. And I love it."

"Does that mean I'll never get to call you Master?" he teases. "No fair."

"Oh yeah, we can definitely still do that. I'll make you take off your shirt over and over again."

33

SAM

"Are you sure you're okay with not having a big wedding?" I ask Lila for the hundredth time.

We're standing on the front steps of the Bardsville courthouse, and any minute now we'll be going in front of the justice of the peace to be married. I would have been fine with a wedding if she wanted one, but she insisted on a private ceremony. The 'sooner the better,' she keeps saying, which is okay with me.

"All I need is you, the justice of the peace, and two witnesses," she says. "And a honeymoon. I want one of those. We need some time alone and away from all the madness."

"Oh, you're going to get a honeymoon alright," I say. "Isn't that supposed to be the best part about getting married? The virgin bride?"

"Whoops! Sorry. There's something I haven't told you."

"You're not a virgin?"

"No, afraid not."

"Damn! Can we pretend you are?"

"Sure we can," she says, laughing. "I'll play any game you want to play. *On the honeymoon.* Are you ready to go in and do this? Or are you having second thoughts?"

I gaze down at her and brush her hair back from her face.

"No second thoughts. I've been fighting like hell to make you mine since the first moment I laid eyes on you. I feel like I've been climbing a big mountain and am finally at the top."

I step back to get one last look at her before the ceremony. She's gorgeous as always, dressed in an off-white linen dress and high heels. Her hair is longer than when we first met and now falls below her shoulders.

"You couldn't look more beautiful in a fancy wedding dress than you do right now. Being pregnant agrees with you. You're glowing."

"You might not think that in a few months."

"I will, and I'm the one that should be asking you about second thoughts. Are you sure you want to go through with this? Speak now."

She leans against me. "Don't even try to get out of marrying me. You're my Baby Daddy, so don't make me turn this into a shotgun wedding." She takes a deep breath. "Let's go do this."

I interlace my fingers with hers and we start walking up the long courthouse steps. The loud sound of motorcycles roaring down the street causes me to stop and turn around.

The Steel Infidels.

What are they doing here?

Jesse throws up a hand at me and parks his bike in the first parking spot. Flint pulls in beside him, then Toby. I count the motorcycles as they file in. All of the Steel Infidels are here.

Every last one.

Trish and Kendra are following behind the motorcycles in a car.

"Look who decided to show up after all," Lila says with a big smile.

I grin down at her. "You know something about this?"

Jesse runs up the steps and grips me by the arm. "What the hell are you doing?" he says. "A brother of mine can't get married without me. I'm the big brother, otherwise known as the best man."

"How did you know?" I ask.

I purposely didn't tell anyone about the ceremony because I was afraid they would try to stop me from marrying Lila. They haven't warmed up to her like I had hoped they would. She keeps telling me to give them time, but I've been worried. The Steel Infidels have been known to hold grudges for a very long time. I want my family to love her as much as I do.

"I called Trish," Lila says from behind me. "This is a big day. I wanted the Steel Infidels to be here for our wedding and for you. They're part of my life now too. We're all in this together."

"And I'm glad she did," Flint says, reaching over to shake my hand. "We would have been so pissed if you had gotten hitched without us."

Trish and Kendra make their way up to us. Trish is carrying a big bouquet of flowers and Kendra is holding a pretty blue box. Trish hands Lila the flowers and takes her arm.

"We're going to steal Lila for a minute," Trish says. "We brought along something borrowed, something blue, something old, and something new for you in the box. If you're going to get married, you have to do it right from the get-go." She slaps me hard on the arm. "I can't believe you didn't tell me you were getting married today, Sam. I am so mad at you right now."

"Give us ten minutes to fix Lila up and we'll be ready," Kendra says. "Sam, please tell me you brought rings."

"Of course I have rings."

"Just checking," she says, shaking her head. "I know how you are."

I watch the girls lead Lila into the courthouse. She's smiling ear-to-ear and seems genuinely happy to see Kendra and Trish. I love seeing the three girls together.

"Why didn't you tell us?" Jesse asks.

"I was afraid you would try to stop me," I answer honestly. "Kendra didn't take the news of our engagement well, and I didn't want to cause any more trouble within the MC."

"Are you kidding?" Flint says, slapping me on the back. "Lila saved our asses. We're indebted to her, not the other way around. Kendra was shocked and caught off guard. That's all. We're all over it now. Time for a fresh start."

The rest of the Steel Infidels walk up to join us on the steps.

"So the player finally gets caught," Toby says with a chuckle. "Never thought I would live to see this day. I wouldn't have missed being here for anything. I'm just mad we didn't get a chance to throw you a bachelor party. Think of all the fun we missed."

"I don't know about that," Jesse says. "You weren't here for the last bachelor party, Toby. We don't exactly have a good track record when it comes to weddings or bachelor parties."

"It means everything to me that you're all here," I say. "And Flint, I need to thank you the most. If it wasn't for you, we wouldn't be getting married today."

"Believe me, it was worth it," he says.

No one else knows what went on between us that day, not even Jesse.

Things are good again.

No.

Things are great again.

My girl, my family, and the Steel Infidels.

Life can't get any better than this.

EPILOGUE

SAM

Several months later...

"Hold my hand," Lila says as an intense contraction hits her. "I'm scared."

She grimaces and holds her breath to fight against the unrelenting pain. Her grip on my hand is so tight that I probably won't be able to use my hand tomorrow, but I'm not letting go.

"Breathe, baby," I encourage. "Stop holding your breath. Blow out like they taught us in the class."

She tries to breathe and lets out a cry instead.

I'm watching the monitor, carefully tracking every contraction.

"This one is almost done. Hang on a little bit longer and it will be over."

She nods and braces against the last wave of pain.

When the contraction is over, I wipe her forehead with a cool cloth. Watching her suffer is absolutely killing me. I would have never gotten her pregnant if I had realized how much pain labor caused. Why doesn't she hit me or curse at me or something?

"The childbirth classes we went to are all bullshit," she says weakly. "You can't breathe through these damn contractions. Trying to breathe is stupid. I could kill that instructor right about now."

"I know. I'll stop telling you to breathe."

"Thank you," she says, laying her head against my shoulder. "I'm too exhausted to breathe anyway."

I rub Lila's cheek with my thumb. Her face is unnaturally pale and I'm worried sick. No way am I letting her see it though. I have to stay upbeat and positive to keep her focused. The labor has been going on for hours, and the doctor keeps saying she isn't dilated enough for an epidural.

Whatever the fuck that means.

I don't understand why they can't give her something now to help her with the pain. Lila is such a tough cookie she would probably refuse it anyway. She hasn't taken any medications at all through the entire pregnancy.

"What can I do to make you feel better?" I ask.

"Stay with me. And don't get me pregnant again anytime soon."

"Believe me, I won't. I can't stand seeing you in pain. This is all my fault."

She tries to laugh. "Your fault? Like I wasn't right there with you? Oh shit! Here comes another one."

I almost remind her to breathe and stop. "You're going to be an amazing mom," I say instead. "Keep thinking about that. You can do this. It will all be over soon."

"Please keep reminding me because this seriously hurts."

"If I could take your pain away and give it to me, I would in a heartbeat."

She cries out again with the next contraction.

Fuck! This is awful.

Why did I ever think tricking her into getting pregnant was a good idea?

Three hours later, the doctor examines Lila and says that she can finally have an epidural. I've never been so relieved in my life. For her to finally get some pain relief is the best news I've ever heard. Her blood pressure keeps dropping and they've placed an oxygen mask over her face. I don't know how much longer she can hang on.

I knew labor was bad.

I had no clue it would be like this.

When the anesthesiologist comes in, he tells me that I will need to leave the room while he administers the epidural, but not before showing me the extremely long needle he will be inserting into Lila's spinal column.

If I wasn't freaking the fuck out before, I am now.

"I'll be right back," I tell Lila, then head to the waiting room.

All of my family is there waiting. Trish walks over and hugs me when I walk into the room.

"How is Lila?" she asks. "The nurses have been giving us updates."

"She's not doing well," I say, shaking my head. "I don't think she can go through much more."

"She is strong," Trish says, patting my arm. "Much stronger than I am both mentally and physically. I survived and she will too. She'll be fine. You'll see."

She holds out a fast food bag. "We brought you something to eat."

"I can't think about eating anything right now."

She shoves it into my hands.

"Eat. I don't want to hear any arguments. Lila will need you later, so eat the food."

I plop down in one of the metal chairs and unwrap the cold hamburger.

"Thanks, Trish. You're right. I'm starving."

By the time I finish the hamburger and drink a cup of stale coffee, the nurse is waving to me from the doorway. "Mr. Mason, you had better get back in here."

I jump up from my chair and rush after her. When I enter the room, Lila beckons me over to the hospital bed.

"The doctor says it's almost time. I'm numb from the waist down so I'm not in any pain. In fact, I can't feel a damn thing."

"Thank God," I say, leaning down to kiss her forehead. She already looks much better, and they've removed the oxygen mask. "That's good news. What am I supposed to do now?"

"I don't know," she says with a tired laugh. "Try to stay out of the doctor's way and don't distract the nurses."

"How would I distract the nurses?"

"Trust me, any woman who sees you will automatically be

distracted. Don't let them look at you. They might drop the baby on the floor or something."

"I got it. Don't talk to the doctor. Hide from the nurses."

A few minutes later, the doctor hurries into the room followed by several nurses.

"Are you ready to do this, Mom?" he says. "You won't be able to feel the contractions, but you can still push. Push with your mind and the body will follow."

"I'm past being ready to get this over with."

"Dad, hold her hand and encourage her to push," the nurse says.

"Dad?" I look over at Lila. "Is she talking to me?"

The nurse maneuvers the overhead mirror directly over the hospital bed so we can watch. I hope I don't do something stupid like pass out and fall on the floor. Flint and Jesse both assured me I would be fine. They also warned me to keep my eyes on the baby and try to block out anything else I might see.

"Here we go," the doctor says. "Time to push."

I'm holding Lila's hand in both of mine. We're both watching the mirror when the baby's head suddenly appears.

"Oh my God!" I say, squeezing her hand. "There he is."

"One more push and this little boy will be out," the doctor says.

"Come on, sweetheart," I encourage her. "You're almost done."

I'm overwhelmed with intense emotions that I've never felt before as my firstborn son comes into the world. His cry is loud and strong.

Just like Lila.

The doctor cuts the cord and the nurses quickly hustle the baby over to the table to clean him off.

Lila's green eyes flood with happy tears that roll down her cheeks. "Go over and check on him," she says, turning loose of my hand. "Make sure he's okay."

"Not yet. I'm not leaving you. He'll be fine. There's one more baby to go. It's you and me, sweetheart. All the way to the end." I grab her hand again and kiss it. "Are you ready?"

She smiles at me through her tears and nods at me.

"Okay," the doctor says. "Time for the second act. Baby boy number two is in a hurry to catch up to his big brother."

Several more long, intense pushes, and our second son arrives in the world, screaming and kicking louder than his brother. The nurses wrap up the babies in blue blankets and gently hand one to Lila and the other one to me.

When I look at Lila and our boys, I'm so happy and overwhelmed with emotion that I could burst.

"Do you have names for them yet?" the doctor asks.

"Yes, I do," Lila answers, smiling over at me.

"Daddy's Dangerous Duo."

TAKE DOWN
NEW YORK TIMES & USA TODAY BESTSELLING AUTHOR
DEZ BURKE

She thinks I'm her Guardian Angel. I know I'm her worst nightmare.
I thought I had everything under control. Until the day I saved Maggie's life.
Most men would *melt* if a girl like her looked at them the way she looks at me, as if I was her savior, her protector.
She sees the muscles, the tats, the hero the media makes me out to be.
I'd give anything to be that man, to hear her screaming my name as I showed her exactly what a Marine can do in bed, but I can't let her in.
What I had to do in Afghanistan made me a monster.
If I let *her* in… I might let *it* out.
I belong over there, in hell.
I don't know how to live in the heaven that is Maggie.
She doesn't realize how hard I'm fighting to keep her away.
She doesn't know who I really am.
I'm irredeemable.
She should run.
Before she unleashes a monster that can't be controlled.

1

TOBY

The food court in the Atlanta mall is hot, crowded, and claustrophobic.

Exactly the kind of place I don't like to be.

The tight crush of bodies and roar of conversation reminds me too much of the outdoor markets in Afghanistan. If my Steel Infidel buddies hadn't insisted they were starving to death, I would've suggested swinging by a fast food joint on our way back home instead. Being in a shopping mall on Valentine's Day is not my idea of fun.

As we squeeze our way between the packed tables, I can feel a bead of sweat slowly begin to slide down the back of my neck. Out of habit, I check for the exits. Floor-to-ceiling glass double doors at one end of the food court and restrooms on both sides in the middle.

I wonder if there will ever be a time when I can relax and stop being in 'fight or flight' mode every second of the day.

Probably not.

Being constantly on guard kept me alive for years when I was a Marine in the Middle East. No need to stop now. Though it would be nice to be able to sit down, relax, and eat a hamburger in peace every now and then. Like all the other men wandering around the food court with glazed-over, panicked looks in their eyes.

I wonder what their issue is before I realize they'd waited until the last minute to pick up a Valentine's Day gift for their girl. Most are wearing expensive business suits, fancy ties, and freshly shined shoes. They're carrying fast food trays in one hand and delicate little blue shopping bags from one of the mall's jewelry stores in the other.

More than a few of them glance at us with barely concealed disgust before quickly looking away without making eye contact. I guess our tattoos and black leather jackets with Motorcycle Club patches make them nervous.

I sure as hell hope so.

Luckily, I don't have to worry about shopping today. There isn't a little lady waiting at home for me tonight. I've managed to dodge Cupid's arrow for yet another year.

Unlike my two Steel Infidel buddies, Sam and Flint Mason.

My best friend, Sam, couldn't be talked out of buying lacy red lingerie as a gift for his wife. His brother Flint and I tried our best to convince him it wasn't the best or most original idea for a Valentine's gift. He laughed and said the gift was for him, not her, and that his wife's real present, her own motorcycle, was hidden back at the clubhouse.

Flint, the Steel Infidels VP, didn't do much better with his shopping. The best idea he could come up with was two pounds of peanut butter fudge from the candy shop. While fudge would certainly be at the top of my most wished for list, you would think a man smart enough to be a lawyer could think of something better for his gal.

If you ask me, both of the Mason brothers suck in the romance department. How they managed to snag two wonderful ladies, I'll never know.

"Hey Toby! What do you want to eat?" Sam asks from behind me. "Are you in the mood for pizza?"

I'm barely listening.

A bearded man on the other side of the food court has caught my attention. He's overdressed for the weather in a long trench coat that hangs almost to his knees. While I watch, he removes his coat and places it carefully on a chair next to him. Underneath, he's wearing a dark business suit.

Nothing to worry about.

Just another fancy ass preppie on his lunch break.

I seriously need to chill out.

"Toby!"

Sam suddenly punches my shoulder hard, and I flinch.

"What is wrong with you?" he says. "I asked you what you wanted to eat and you're just standing there staring off into space like a zombie. Damn man, why are you so jumpy today?"

I shrug.

"I don't like crowds. That's all. And it's hot as hell in here and stuffy. We should have made this trip to Atlanta yesterday. Why did you two wait until Valentine's Day to do your shopping?"

"I shop better under pressure," Sam answers. "And I had to keep the twins yesterday while Lila did some super-secret stuff on the computer. Speaking of the twins..."

Uh oh.

I shake my head and hold up my hand. I know what's coming next.

"Whatever you're going to say, the answer is a definite no."

Sam ignores me and keeps talking.

"Since you don't have a date tonight, would you mind keeping Travis and Trevor for a few hours?" he asks. "Just long enough for us to go to dinner?"

I let out an incredulous laugh.

"Are you kidding me? I can't handle those two little tornadoes by myself. What about Flint and Kendra?"

"No way," Flint answers adamantly. "We have plans. We lined up our babysitter weeks ago. Don't even think about asking us."

"Come on, Toby," Sam begs. "I promised Lila I would get a babysitter for tonight. The boys aren't that much trouble, I swear." He grins. "As long as you let them do whatever they want. It's only when you tell them 'no' that the trouble starts. Just remember that and you'll be perfectly fine. I swear."

Sam has no idea what he's asking. His twin toddlers are cute but are way too much for me to take care of. Dogs are my thing, not kids. Especially not the little ones.

"Why didn't you start asking around earlier if you needed a babysitter?"

Sam throws up his hands. "I did," he answers. "All week I've been trying. Everyone says they're busy tonight, even the ones who I know for a fact don't have a Valentine's date. I don't know why nobody is willing to babysit for us. I even offered to pay three times the normal rate."

"Well, I do. The twins are mini-Sams with sharp teeth. That's why."

Sam gives me a pitiful look and I roll my eyes. There's not much I wouldn't do for him, and he knows it. He's been my best friend since high school and we've been through hell together. I was one of the only people who knew what was going on back when his Dad was beating the crap out of him, and now he's doing his best to be here for me.

As much as I can let him.

Sometimes my demons are too scary to share with anyone.

I finally give in with a loud sigh. It's not as if I have anything better to do tonight anyway.

"If you want to bring them by the clubhouse I'll keep them there, but only if you get a couple of the Sweet Butts to help me out. Or maybe three. Pretty ones too. Not one of the Old Ladies."

"I'll make sure of it," he answers with a relieved smile. "Thanks man. I owe you big time."

"Damn right you do."

Flint points to a family getting up from a table on the other side of the room. "I'll go grab us a place to sit while you two order food," he says. "Buy me one of whatever you're having. And a large sweet tea."

As both a lawyer and the Steel Infidels VP, Flint could fit in as easily with the businessmen in suits as he does with me and Sam. The motorcycle club is lucky he gave up his position as an attorney in Atlanta to come back home and rejoin the MC.

His legal skills have come in handy more than a few times. For some unknown reason, the members of the club have an unlucky knack of getting into trouble.

When Flint snags the table, he throws up a hand and nods back at us.

"I wonder if he realizes the fudge is going to melt on the two-hour bike ride home," Sam says with a laugh. "All he'll have left is a gooey, peanut-buttery mess. Kendra will be so pissed. Sometimes my brother is a dumbass."

He peeks over my shoulder and points behind me.

"Hey look! Isn't that the girl from the evening news over there? She's setting up a live feed with her cameraman. What's her name? Mandy? Misty? She's a lot hotter in person than on television."

I turn around to see where he's pointing.

"Her name is Maggie," I say. "Maggie Turner from Channel 5."

"Why am I not surprised that you know her name?" Sam says with a hint of sarcasm. "She's exactly your type...long dark hair, nice curvy ass, big tits."

I shake my head.

"Nah, I don't have a type. As long as they're willing, that's good enough for me."

Sam laughs. "Bullshit! Every girl you date is almost exactly the same, so I would say you definitely have a specific type. And she's it."

Sam's right, though I'm not going to admit it. Maggie *is* my type and much prettier in person than on television, stunning really. She's shorter than I imagined, with long straight dark brown hair and green eyes. And curvier too with an ass just begging to be grabbed.

She's scanning the food court as if she's searching for something, and her eyes suddenly land on me. Catching me watching her, she smiles and turns to say something to her cameraman. He glances our way, nods, and picks up his gear to follow her.

"Aww...crap," I say. "I think she's headed this way. I wonder what she's doing?"

Sam makes a face at me. "Probably a thirty-minute segment on how bad men suck on Valentine's Day. Or a 10-hour documentary."

The line we're standing in to order food starts to move. Before Sam has a chance to step up to the counter, Maggie and her cameraman are in our face.

"Hi gentlemen," she says with a fake bright smile that doesn't quite reach her eyes. "Do you have a second? I'm Maggie Turner with Channel 5 and this is my cameraman, Bill."

I nod my head at the cameraman and look away, trying to appear disinterested.

"I was wondering if you would mind letting me ask you a few questions for the evening news?" she continues. "It won't take but a couple minutes of your time, I promise. I'm interviewing shoppers about their big plans for Valentine's Day."

We both stare at her blank-faced. I don't know how to respond or if I should. I can't imagine why she would want to interview a couple of bikers when there are tons more suitable men in the food court.

She looks at me, and I realize she knows exactly what I'm thinking.

"You're two of the most...interesting men in here at the moment," she explains. "Come on, fellas. Help a poor girl out."

I'm not sure if she means that as a compliment or an insult.

The word "interesting" could mean either.

I notice Flint watching us from across the room. He is not amused.

No wonder.

All three of us are carrying concealed weapons. Not to mention an outrageous amount of cash from an illegal gun transaction we made right before our pit stop at the mall. He is definitely not thrilled about a news team approaching us. He shakes his head at me and makes a motion with his hand at his neck to cut the conversation.

I nod back at him. I've got this.

"We're in a little bit of a hurry, ma'am," I say politely. "And we're not here to shop. We just stopped in for a quick bite to eat. Someone else would be a better choice for you. I don't even have a girlfriend. Valentine's Day isn't my thing."

I give her my best dumb country-bumpkin smile, hoping she'll take the hint and move along without any fuss.

She doesn't.

Her eyes narrow, and I get the distinct feeling she's determined now more than ever to drag us right into the six o'clock news.

This is bad.

Real bad.

The last thing the Steel Infidels Motorcycle Club needs is publicity. After being the target of a federal investigation last year, we've done everything we can to keep things quiet and clean. Not legal, just under the radar of law enforcement and anyone else who might be interested in the club's activities.

Maggie peeks at the bag Sam is holding. The strap of a lacy red bra is peeking out through the crinkly heart-covered tissue paper.

"What do you have there?" she asks Sam. "Someone has been shopping. Wouldn't you like to deliver a special message to your lady friend on air? I'm sure she would love it. You know how women eat up that kind of stuff. You'll make her day."

I try to catch Sam's eyes to warn him, but he's not paying one bit of attention to me. As usual.

"I'll make you a deal," she continues. "If you let me ask you a couple of questions, I'll let you give her a live on-air message. What would be better than that for a Valentine's gift?"

Sam's eyes light up and my heart sinks.

Dammit, Sam! What the fuck are you doing?

Of course he's going to do the interview. He can't resist. Sam always chooses the riskier choice. Flint is going to be so pissed at him.

And at me if I can't stop him.

"What about Lila's surprise?" I ask, hoping he'll get the hint. "You don't want to spoil it, do you? And we really don't have time for this. We need to get going and hit the road so we can make it back to the mountains before dark."

"The North Georgia mountains?" Maggie asks, turning back to me. "You're a long way from home. So you drove what? At least a couple of hours to do your shopping here in Atlanta? That's interesting. I'll be sure to add that in."

I frown at her and wish she would stop talking. I don't want her finding out where we're from. Or anything else for that matter. The less she knows about us, the better.

"North Carolina," I lie. "The North Carolina mountains."

Bardsville, our home town, is a mere fifteen minutes from the North Carolina state line, so I'm only fibbing a tiny bit. Georgia...North Carolina. Not much of a difference really.

She's already focused back on Sam, who is practically bouncing up and down on the balls of his feet in his eagerness to do this.

"So what do you say?" she asks him.

"Sure, I'll do it," he replies. "My wife will love it!"

Hell no she won't.

Sam's wife is the most guarded, secretive person I've ever met. I can't imagine Lila would enjoy having her name splashed across the news any more than I would. She's a computer hacker turned federal agent turned back to hacker. Once she hooked up with the Steel Infidels, she crossed over to the dark side and never went back.

"Terrific!" Maggie says, as if she knew all along that he would agree to be interviewed. "And what about your friend here?"

She turns to look up at me. The top of her head barely reaches my shoulder. She's petite and just the right height to wrap my arm around her shoulder, tuck her under my arm, and hold her close against my side.

Too talkative for me though.

"What are your big plans for tonight, big fella?" she asks me. "Dinner? Dancing? Maybe cooking dinner for your lady?"

"Nothing," I answer more gruffly than I mean to. "As I said before, there's no lady."

She blinks at me and seems a little surprised at my short answer then shrugs.

"Okay, well, we can still fit you in too. I'll tell the viewers you're available. Our phones will be ringing off the hook. All you need to do is stare deep into the camera with those soulful blue eyes. What do you think, Bill? Where would be the best spot to set up the camera to interview these two? Maybe over this way a little bit?"

She scoots out of the way of the line of pizza customers piling up and keeps talking to her cameraman about us as if we're not standing right there beside her.

"Wait a second," I say. "You misunderstood. I'm not doing an interview."

Maggie waves her hand at me dismissively.

"Oh, you'll be fine. Don't worry or be nervous. It's a short segment."

Sam snickers and shoots me a look. I know what he's thinking. That I'm letting this little slip of a girl steamroll right over me.

And he's right.

The situation caught me by surprise, that's all. It's not every day that a news team sticks a camera in my face. Meanwhile, Maggie is babbling on about camera angles and background shots while I wait for a chance to interrupt her without seeming overly rude.

It occurs to me that I don't particularly like her very much. She's abrasive and aggressive. Soft and pliable is more my taste.

Out of the corner of my eye, I see Flint stand up and start walking our way.

Good.

He'll put a stop to this craziness.

"Let's move down a little toward the doors," she tells her

cameraman. "That way you can get the wide angle of the food court behind us."

Maggie places a manicured hand on my upper arm and starts tugging me along with her to an empty wall beside the pizza place. Motioning for Sam to join me, she lines us up so that our backs are to the dining tables.

"Make sure to get a wide shot of the shoppers behind them," she says to her cameraman. "Is my hair and makeup okay, Bill? Let's get this over with so we can go back to the station."

She smooths down her white blouse and flips her long hair back over her shoulders.

"Beautiful as always," her cameraman replies before hoisting the camera onto his shoulder and backing up a few feet.

She turns to Sam. "What are your names?" she asks quickly. "I almost forgot to ask. We're running short on time."

"I'm Sam," he says.

Thank God he didn't give his last name. I don't answer. Not that she notices. She is focused on her mission.

Taking a deep breath, she puts on a bright smile and holds up the microphone. "Five seconds," she says to us before counting down to one.

Seriously? She's doing this right now? What an obnoxious, pushy woman.

I look over at Sam. He shrugs his shoulders at me and grins.

"Good evening," she begins, talking straight into the camera. "This is Maggie Turner reporting live from Northside Mall in downtown Atlanta. I have with me two gentlemen who have driven all the way from North Carolina to do their Valentine's Day shopping."

She turns to Sam and waves a hand at the pink shopping bag he's carrying.

"I see you've already made a few purchases. Are you impulse shopping today or were you searching for something specific for your sweetheart?"

Sam starts to give her one of his bullshit answers. Knowing him, there is no telling what's about to come out of his mouth.

Suddenly, a loud noise rings out and we all flinch.

A gunshot?

No, it can't be.

Maybe a truck backfired in the parking lot right outside the glass doors. I'm dreaming things up again. It wouldn't be the first time I've heard imaginary gunshots that turned out to be nothing.

I hate this PTSD shit.

Always thinking there's an improvised explosive device in every pothole or bag of trash on the side of the road. Jumping at every loud noise.

Then another pop explodes, louder this time.

Definitely gunshots.

Fuck!

The cameraman drops straight down to the tile floor right in front of us. His camera slides off his shoulder while blood gushes from a wound, quickly soaking through his shirt.

I can't tell where he's been hit. I hope the bullet missed any vital arteries. I'm not a medic, but it doesn't look good from where I'm standing.

The loud *boom! boom! boom!* of several more shots ring out. The sound echoes off the walls around us.

Jesus Christ!

A woman screams on the other side of the food court. The display case of a Chinese food takeout place next to us shatters in a shower of glass.

Maggie is standing there in shock, still holding the microphone up in front of her like she's expecting her cameraman to get back up and continue filming.

"Get down!" I yell. "There's a shooter!"

Sam runs four big steps to the pizza counter and leaps over.

In a split second, I assess the situation. Maggie is wearing a short skirt and high heels. There's no way she can make it to safety behind the counter on her own.

It's too risky.

I grab her with both hands and throw her under the nearest table. Diving on top of her, I cover her body with mine as much as I can. She's short and I'm able to tuck her head, arms, and most of her legs underneath me.

"Don't move," I whisper in her ear. "Stay down, keep your head covered, and don't make a sound."

Her body is trembling, but to her credit she doesn't let out even a whimper. I'm hoping she's tougher than she appears.

I'm not betting on it.

With any luck, she can keep her shit together and not draw any more attention to herself.

A surge of adrenaline quickly kicks in.

And a dreadful sense of familiarity.

As bad as the situation is, it feels like home to me.

I hate it.

When I left Afghanistan for the last time, I thought this crap was behind me.

The joke is on me.

As always.

Hell never gets left behind.

I reach for the gun in the side pocket of my leather jacket and carefully slide it out. When I tucked it into my pocket earlier this morning, I never dreamed I would need to use it today.

Well, maybe at the gun trade since there's always a chance those deals can go downhill in a hurry. Just not in a food court surrounded by a bunch of investment bankers who are crapping in their pants about now.

The shots continue to come, along with more screams and sounds of confusion. A baby is crying. He sounds more scared than injured. I try not to think about the casualties and injuries that no doubt must be mounting up.

All I need to do right at this moment is concentrate and focus on locating the shooter. The same thing I've done countless times before in Afghanistan.

The Marines called me the Guardian Angel.

I watched over my platoon through the crosshairs of a special rifle like a Border Collie guarding sheep. My buddies depended on me to keep them safe.

Kill or be killed was my motto.

Anything to keep my buddies alive.

I lift up my head slightly and glance around the food court.

Where are the damn shots coming from?

And where is Flint? The last time I saw him, he was walking across the food court toward us.

I glance up at the second floor overhanging the food court and see a man standing by the railing in a baseball cap and heavy winter overcoat.

The shooter.

I hope to God he's alone.

Something tells me he's not.

2

MAGGIE

I'm struggling to catch my breath and am on the verge of a full-blown panic attack. At least two hundred and fifty pounds of hard, packed muscle is on top of me, pressing my body down flat on the floor. My head is tucked under the biker's chest. I can feel his heart racing like mad through his flannel shirt.

What just happened?

One minute I'm standing there interviewing two tattooed bikers for another trivial news spot and the next my cameraman is shot right in front of me. My brain can't wrap its head around the situation. It's too much to comprehend.

When the shot rang out, I was turning around to ask a question and didn't see anything except Bill fall to the ground out of the corner of my eye. Before I had a chance to react, the biker was throwing me under the table and piling on top of me.

Thank God he had enough sense to step in and protect me. I was standing there like an idiot, frozen in fear and confusion.

As a reporter, we always prefer to think we're prepared during emergencies. That we'll be cool under pressure. Stay calm and get the story.

What a joke! That's all baloney.

I'm not a war reporter.

I do human interest stories about animal adoption events and pumpkin festivals. Not any real news. My station manager told me when he hired me that my job was to smile and be pretty. To pay my dues until my time came along. So that's what I've been doing the past five years. Biding my time until I get a chance to report on something big.

Not that I haven't tried to do more. I spend most of my free time tracking down leads on interesting stories. Hoping that someday, somehow, a news story I discover will take off and make me a star.

Now the big story has found me.

Hopefully I can live to tell about it.

I close my eyes and concentrate on pacing my panicked breathing. I'm scared. Terrified actually. I can't stay here doing nothing while waiting for the shooters to come closer. That's never worked out well for other people caught in terrorist situations.

My mind goes back to the past incidents of high school kids hiding under tiny desks while the shooter goes classroom to classroom or bar patrons crawling under cocktail tables in a gay night club.

The stories never have a happy ending.

Hiding and waiting isn't a good plan.

A plastic dining table won't stop men with guns or even slow them down.

A sob threatens to rise out of my throat. If Bill doesn't make it, I'll never forgive myself. There was so much blood spilling out of the wound in his chest. He has a loving wife and kids waiting for him to come home tonight. The whole family was going out for pizza for Valentine's Day because that's what his wife wanted. For the family to be together instead of the two of them going out for a romantic meal. He was working late because I asked him to help me out. Otherwise it would've been one of the less experienced cameramen tagging along behind me today.

I need to check on him to make sure he's still alive. I owe him that much. Pushing up with my arms, I try to wiggle out from under the heavy man crushing me so I can turn my head to see Bill.

"Dammit!" the man above me curses before curling a huge, muscular arm tighter around me.

A large tattoo of a magnificent lion runs down the length of his bicep. I'm momentarily fascinated by the lion's eyes. They're staring at me, looking straight into my soul. I wonder if I'm in shock.

"Do you want to die today?" he asks in a gruff voice. "Be still and be quiet. Don't draw attention to yourself. I've got you. Keep your head down flat. The shooter is above us on the second floor."

"What about my cameraman?" I whisper.

"Don't think about him right now. There's nothing you can do. Concentrate on keeping your own pretty little head alive. Your man is still breathing. That's something."

Thank God! Bill is still alive.

It occurs to me the biker might only be telling me that to keep me calm. For the time being, it's working. I need to trust that he's being honest. The other possibilities are too horrible to think about.

"How many shooters are there?" I ask. "More than one?"

"I don't know," he says. "Now hush!"

When he talks, his deep Southern drawl rumbles through his chest. Stupid as it might be, I feel safe underneath this big old biker in his leather jacket and tats even if I can barely breathe.

At least for now.

Who is this guy?

I didn't even get his name.

3

TOBY

D*amn!*

The girl is going to be trouble.

I can already tell.

If she had any sense at all, she would be still and stop wriggling around. I'm almost afraid to loosen my grip on her long enough to steady my gun. She might be stupid enough to try to crawl back over to her cameraman, putting herself right in the line of fire again.

The shooter on the upper level is too far away to see his face clearly, though the shape of his assault rifle is hard to miss. He's taking his time and leisurely picking out random targets in the food court below him.

Is he alone?

I can't tell.

He casually reloads and fires another fast round toward the front counters of the cinnamon roll shop on the other side of the room. Glass sprays everywhere, along with chunks of dough and sweet icing. I'll never feel the same about the smell of hot cinnamon rolls again. It's a shame because I love those damn things.

The random way he's shooting makes me think that his goal for the moment is to instill terror and fear rather than to rack up a quick body count. He is stalling, biding his time for some reason.

If so, this also means he has a plan.

I lift my head slightly again and scan the food court. Everyone is either lying on the ground or under tables. Whether they're dead, injured, or playing possum, I don't know. From where we're hiding, I can't see the whole room clearly.

When the shooter stops to reload again, gunshots ring out from another direction.

Fuck!

There's another one.

I figured as much.

The attack didn't feel like the work of one person. Shifting slightly, I turn to see if I get a better look. Where is that second shooter?

"Now you're the one moving!" Maggie whispers in a panic. "What are you doing? I thought you said to be still."

"Shhh...." I say and tuck her head back under my chest. "Don't worry. I'm not going anywhere."

I turn my head around and glance back over my shoulder to see if I can catch sight of Sam. He's crouched behind the corner of the shattered pizza counter. As soon as we make eye contact, he holds up three fingers and points toward the glass doors at the exit.

Oh shit!

There are three of them?

I turn the other way. Two men in hats and heavy coats are blocking the exit at the double glass doors. I wonder how many guns are hidden under their coats. Or god knows what else.

What a fucking nightmare!

We're all trapped here in the crowded food court waiting to be mowed down by bullets. I've never missed my rifle so much.

The words of the Marine's creed is playing over and over in my head like an old album that's skipping.

Without my rifle, I am useless.

I must fire my rifle true.

I must shoot straighter than my enemy who is trying to kill me.

I must shoot him before he shoots me.

I will.

Today my rifle isn't with me. My handgun will have to suffice. Improvisation under pressure is my specialty.

I take a closer look at the two guys near the exit. With their knit caps and scruffy beards, they seem almost familiar to me. They could be one of my old high school classmates or even a Steel Infidel on a bad hair day.

The men are around thirty, maybe not even that old, and white. They're not the typical stereotype of what I would expect a terrorist to be. They're cool and calm. Methodical with their movements. Nobody is running around yelling "Allahu Akbar" or acting delusional.

Which scares me even more.

Homegrown terrorists, they're called. Who knows what their agenda is or what they're aiming to prove? It could be anything these days. When their explanation for the attack comes out in the news, it won't make sense to anyone.

Another senseless shooting is what the news will say.

I wonder if they have bombs strapped to their chests. The heavy coats they're wearing could be covering up suicide vests. The thought makes me uneasy. If I get a chance to take a shot, it has to be to the head. Otherwise, if I hit their chest and they're wearing explosives, we're all going up in flames.

One of the men standing by the exit doors motions to the other then starts moving slowly in our direction.

"Oh shit!" I mutter. "They're heading this way."

"Oh no," Maggie whispers, her voice catching on a sob. "What if they're after me? I've been working on a story about street gangs in Atlanta."

I wonder if she's completely lost it and gone over the edge. Can't say I blame her. She's in shock after seeing her cameraman shot right in front of her. I would be too if I hadn't been through similar situations before.

There's no way any news story this gal could dig up would bring out the firepower these guys are pumping. Not unless she's about to expose the identity of a Russian mob or Columbian drug cartel operating in the area.

Being in the gun-running business myself, I know the identity of every organized gang in Georgia. Half of them are our customers. I can't imagine any of them willing to stage a terrorist attack of this magnitude over a simple news story told by a pretty girl in high heels and a short skirt.

I don't have time to persuade her otherwise, and maybe I shouldn't. As long as Maggie believes she's the target, then maybe she'll try not to draw attention to herself. It could be a good thing unless she does something stupid.

I'll play along with her if need be. Whatever it takes to keep her safe. I might not be able to save everyone here today, but I can save her.

Or die trying.

"If they're after you, then you'd better stay hidden," I say, trying to calm her down.

The shooters have stopped walking now. One has his automatic weapon pointed at a group of men in business suits on the floor in front of him. The other is watching the man on the second floor. They're waiting for him to give a signal.

It can't be good, whatever is about to happen.

The signal won't be to put down their guns and walk away.

If I'm going to make a bold move, now is the time. If I had to guess, I'd say the Steel Infidels are the only ones packing heat in the food court besides the shooters. With Maggie under me, I'll be taking a huge chance. The second I fire, I'm going to draw their attention and bullets our way.

Is it worth the risk?

I can't think about it because it's not as if I have a fucking choice.

Hopefully I can keep her body covered with mine. I'm big with solid muscle. Any bullets would have to go through me to get to her.

I hope.

What if I'm wrong? Damn! I hate making life or death decisions. I thought all that was behind me.

I don't have to see Sam to know that he's watching my every movement closely and waiting. He'll be ready to back me up whenever I make a move. For the millionth time, I wish I knew where Flint was. Since I don't, I can't depend on his gunpower.

Best case scenario, it will be two against three.

Me and Sam against the three shooters.

We can take them. We've been dealt worse odds plenty of times. And we have the element of surprise on our side now. The shooters believe they're in charge. They won't be expecting anyone in the crowd to try anything.

"Don't move a muscle," I say quietly to Maggie. "I have a gun." I feel her go dead still under my body. She's trying not to breathe.

Carefully, I ease my gun around with my right hand so it's in front of me yet hidden behind my left arm.

This is a suck-ass position to be firing from. Even for a sharpshooter like me. I'm almost flat on the tile floor, looking between the legs of a plastic dining table. A soft drink has turned over and is steadily dripping off the sides onto the floor. Since we're almost completely under the table, I'm hoping the guy on the second floor can't see the glint of my gun.

I focus on the shooter who has his automatic weapon pointed toward the group of men. He's farther away, and Sam would never be able to make the shot from his angle. I'm hoping the same thoughts are running through his head. We've been friends for so long that we usually know what the other is thinking. I hope he knows it this time. I wish there was a way to warn him about the chance the guys might be wearing suicide vests.

Too late to think about it.

Now or never.

I line up the shot and pull the trigger.

All hell breaks loose a split-second later. Sam immediately fires his handgun from behind the pizza counter, aiming for the other shooter.

My first shot hits its target right between the eyes.

A clean shot to the head.

The man falls to the ground, dropping his automatic weapon. A businessman on the floor awkwardly tries to be a hero and scramble for the gun. The shooter on the second floor sprays the area with bullets, and the businessman dives away in the other direction.

It takes me only a moment to realize all of Sam's shots have missed. I'm stunned. Normally Sam is an excellent marksman. The other shooter is running straight toward us now.

What the fuck?

Maybe Maggie was telling the truth. Otherwise why would he keep coming our way?

Sam continues firing and hits the guy in the leg. I wonder how many shots he has left before needing to reload?

The shooter stumbles and gets a round of bullets off, hitting the chairs and tables all around us. I suddenly realize why he's not going down. He's wearing a bulletproof vest under his coat, not a suicide vest. It's like shooting a knight in armor.

"Dammit, Sam!" I mutter. "Why do I always have to do everything?"

The man looks straight at me and makes eye contact. Time stops for a split-second. He's younger than I thought. No more than twenty-five. For a moment he appears confused, almost shocked. The realization has hit him that he's not going to live through the day. That their carefully laid plans contained a few loopholes. Holes that are going to get him killed. All for some stupid ideas that he probably doesn't even understand.

I can't think about his age or hesitate. He put himself into this situation. I'll get us out.

Lifting my gun a few inches, I aim for the guy's head.

Kill or be killed.

I never miss under pressure, and I don't miss this time either.

Two men down and one to go.

I turn my head to get the current location of the shooter on the second floor. He's moved almost out of sight. There's no way I can take him. He's too far away for my weapon, though not for his. Bullets rain down on the tabletops around us. He knows where the shots came from that took down his buddies, and he's pissed.

Maggie hasn't made a sound or moved at all. I'm terrified she's been hit. I'm afraid to find out. It wouldn't be the first time I've tried to protect someone and failed. My sleep is haunted by the past.

In the distance is the faint sound of sirens coming closer. The police and ambulances are on their way. I hope there's a lot of them and they get here quickly.

Sweat drops down into my eyes, blurring my vision. I blink to clear the sweat.

Dammit!

The motherfucker on the second floor is gone.

I slide off Maggie, who hasn't made a sound. Her cheek is placed flat against the tile floor and her eyes are squeezed tightly shut.

"Hey! Are you okay?" I ask her.

When she doesn't answer right away, I touch her shoulder and shake her lightly. She blinks open her eyes.

"I think so," she answers hesitantly.

"You would know if you weren't," I say. "Come on. We need to move now while we have a chance."

"Is it over?"

"I don't know for sure, and I'm not staying here in case it's not. Move your ass now!"

Grabbing her with my free hand, I drag her out from under the table on her hands and knees. A man suddenly slides down on the floor beside us.

Flint.

"Where the fuck have you been all this time?" I ask.

It seems like a lifetime since I've seen him when it can't be more than a few minutes. Ten at the most.

"Pinned down under a table in the middle of the food court," he says. "Where's Sam? I lost sight of him as soon as the shooting started."

"He's safe," I reply. "He dove behind the counter and was able to keep track of where the shooters were from there. Help cover me while I get this gal somewhere safe."

"I've got you," he says. "Go!"

"Move, Maggie!" I tell her, giving her ass a shove forward. "Get behind the pizza counter. Stay down low."

She quickly scurries across the floor on her hands and knees. We move along with her until we're all safely behind the counter. I prop her back up against the wall for support.

"What took you so long?" Sam asks when we crouch down beside him. "Where's the third shooter? I lost sight of him."

"He's gone," I say. "The bastard made a run for it."

"We need to get out of here too," Flint says. "I can hear sirens. The police are on their way. We can't be involved in all this. We need to go now."

I relax my hold on Maggie and move to stand up.

A few people are already making a mad dash for the exit doors or running in the other direction toward the inside of the mall.

Maggie grabs my jacket sleeve. "Wait!" she says in a panicked voice. "What are you doing?"

"I've got to go. Are you sure you're not hurt?"

She shakes her head slowly and gives me a dazed look. "No, I'm not hurt."

"You'll be okay then. I can't stay here."

"You're leaving?" she says incredulously. "Where are you going? I don't understand. You can't just leave. The police will have questions. Don't go."

Her big green eyes fill with tears that threaten to spill over. "Don't leave me," she pleads. "Not yet. What if they come back?"

Damn! Those eyes are hard to resist. For a split second, I start to waver before common sense sets in. We're bikers, we're carrying guns that aren't registered to us and tons of cash. Bullets from our guns took out two of the shooters. Hanging around to talk to the police would be a disaster. No way would we come out of it as heroes. The world doesn't work that way. We would all be arrested and thrown in jail before midnight on a list of charges a mile long.

"I have to go," I tell her reluctantly. "The police and the ambulances are on their way. The shooters are dead, so you're safe now."

"I'm not safe," she says. "There's one left. How can I ever feel safe now?"

"Come on," Flint says. "Let's move it. We don't have time for chit-chat."

Maggie lifts a trembling finger and points to her cameraman sprawled out on the floor a few feet from us. I can't tell now if he's breathing or not.

"What about Bill?" she chokes out. "Is he dead? You said he was breathing. I can't see him breathing."

I hate leaving her this way.

I shake my head.

"I don't know," I say honestly. "I can't stay. Help will be here soon. Don't leave this spot even to check on him until the police arrive. Do you understand? Promise me you won't move."

She lets go of my jacket sleeve and pulls her knees up close to her chest.

"I promise," she says dully.

"Fuck," I say when I realize she's given up on me. I'm such an asshole. "I'm sorry."

Without another word, I jump up and follow Flint and Sam through the stunned crowd of people and out the doors. Five minutes later, we're on the interstate and heading north toward home.

4

TOBY

We don't stop riding until we reach the Steel Infidels' clubhouse two hours later. Sam and Flint park their motorcycles in their regular spots. I pull in right behind them and cut the engine.

"Still hanging in there, Toby?" Sam asks casually as I unbuckle my helmet and slide off the bike.

"Why the fuck wouldn't I be?" I ask.

He doesn't answer. I know he's wondering if I'm going to freak out or have some sort of crazy post-traumatic stress meltdown. Sam knows a little bit about the struggles I've had since returning from Afghanistan.

Not everything though.

There are some things I could never tell anyone. Not even my best friend. But he's heard enough to know it's bad at times.

"Yeah, I'm okay," I continue. "Taking down a couple of asshole terrorists is all in a day's work for me. Or used to be. I'm still pumped full of adrenaline and ready to go again." I punch the air with my fists for emphasis. "The more of those bastards we can take out, the better. I'm just glad we were there. What if we hadn't been? Things could have turned out much worse for all those people. It pisses me off that one of those son of a bitches got away. He outgunned us. Plain and simple. At the last minute, it all boiled down to firepower. We need to talk to Jesse about buying more powerful weapons."

A concerned look passes between Sam and Flint.

"What?" I ask. "If you've got something to say, spit it out. Don't pussyfoot around me."

"I meant how are you doing with your post trauma shit and stuff," Sam says. "Don't tell me that didn't shake you up a little. One minute we're ordering pizza and the next all hell breaks loose."

I shrug as if it was nothing and start unzipping my leather jacket.

"Nah...I'm good. I'm over all that crap that happened back in Afghanistan. Time always takes care of things."

I wish.

Time hasn't taken care of it so far.

Not the nightmares or the panic attacks that come out of nowhere. Not the drenching blasts of cold sweat whenever a car backfires or when one of the Sweet Butts accidentally drops a glass on the floor. And time certainly hasn't taken away the overwhelming feeling of guilt every morning when I wake up and I realize I'm alive and some of my buddies aren't.

Nobody needs to know these things.

The guys in the MC would see me differently if they knew how bad it was. As a pussy. Or a liability. Maybe even kick me out of the motorcycle club.

I don't need their fucking pity. I can deal with this on my own like I've been doing all along.

I'm not worried.

I've got it all under control.

Sam gives me a doubtful look before leaning back against his bike and crossing his arms. He's not going to argue with me or push too hard. We've known each other so long that we know when to stop.

None of us are eager to go inside the building yet. We all need a few more minutes to decompress and get our thoughts together.

"I'll be honest," Sam says after a moment. "I didn't know what the fuck was going on or what to do. When I heard the gunshots, I dove behind the counter and saved my own skin. Meanwhile, you're gathering up women like the Incredible Hulk and throwing them under tables. Saving people and being a hero while I'm ducking down behind a drink machine."

"I'm a Marine," I say. "And was only doing what came natural.

That's what I'm trained for. It's what I've spent the past several years doing in the Middle East. Trying to stay alive and keep my buddies alive too. Today was more of the same with a different location."

Truth is, I'm torn up inside.

Anyone would have to be stone cold not to be.

Killing isn't for sissies.

I keep remembering the younger guy's eyes right before I took him out.

Scared, confused.

He didn't know what he was getting involved in. To him it might not have been much different than a video game. Until it was too late and there was no turning back.

I blame his leader, whoever the fucker is. For brainwashing a kid in the prime of his life.

And for making me kill him.

Killing someone not much older than a teenager was bad enough. Having to leave a terrified woman crying on the floor while she begged me not to go wasn't much fun either.

I felt like a fucking coward cutting and running. Any honorable person would have hung around and helped carry the injured to ambulances or something. Not disappear without a backwards glance.

My mind tells me we had to leave the scene. There wasn't a choice unless we wanted to end up in jail. Not only me, but Sam and Flint too. The rationale doesn't make me feel any less like dog shit.

I notice Flint being unusually quiet while methodically wiping down the chrome on his bike with a rag. He's doing some deep thinking, which means there's a problem that needs to be dealt with.

"What's going on in that head of yours, Flint?" I ask.

He crams the rag in his pocket and turns toward me. "This is going to be a fucking disaster," he says. "We're going to be all over the news. There's no way to avoid it. By this time tomorrow, everyone in the country will know who we are and where we are. What happened today and our part in it is going to go big. The Steel Infidels will be on center stage in the media."

"Does Jesse know yet?" I ask.

Jesse is Flint and Sam's older brother and the President of the Steel Infidels. He's a tough and fair leader.

"I called him on the way up and asked him to bring the crew in for a meeting," Flint says. "The girls too. Kendra is going to swing by Sam's house to pick up Lila and the kids. Everyone needs to be here so we can be prepared." He's pacing now and running a nervous hand through his hair.

"I can't believe we got ourselves involved in this," he says. "Why in God's name did we stop at the mall? We don't need this crap right now. Not when things are finally starting to settle down for the MC."

"Calm the fuck down," Sam says. "You're freaking out for nothing. Nobody knows who we are, and we slipped out before the cops got there. The whole scene was mass confusion. People running everywhere. I doubt anyone even saw us taking the shots."

Flint turns and stares at Sam like he's a complete idiot.

"Are you crazy? You think nobody noticed Toby taking out two guys?" he says. "The mall would have had security cameras, plus everyone carries a cell phone these days. You can't tell me people weren't recording from under tables or wherever else they were hiding out. I can guarantee that the two of you were being recorded from every angle. And the video clips will be played over and over."

"Don't forget about Maggie, the reporter from Channel 5," I remind them. "She knows Sam's first name. Considering what she does for a living, I'm sure she's an observant person. It wouldn't surprise me if she remembers seeing the Steel Infidels patches on our jackets too. She has two clues right there. The Steel Infidels and Sam."

I remember the fear on her face when she realized I was leaving her there alone. "On second thought, she seemed pretty upset. She might not remember anything."

"She doesn't have to remember," Sam says. "She was filming. All she has to do is play the video back and we're nailed right there. Why the fuck did I agree to that interview?" He slams a hand down on the seat of his bike.

"We're wasting time talking about this and how we all fucked up," Flint says. "None of it matters. We can assume that she'll find out who we are shortly. Along with all the other media. The question is what are we going to do about it? This could be very bad for us if the media starts digging into the MC's business. I don't know how we should play this when they come knocking. And trust me, they will come. This is too big of a story for them to ignore it."

"Play it how?" I ask.

"We have two choices," he replies. "As good ol' accidental heroes or badass bikers. We need to think this through. The way we handle this will make a difference not only how we're portrayed in the media, but also how we're thought of by the other MCs and our suppliers."

"Badasses," I answer without hesitation.

"Heroes," says Sam at the same time. "Or badass heroes as a compromise," he adds.

Flint lets out a long sigh.

"You two aren't worth a shit. I hope Jesse gets here soon."

5

MAGGIE

I swallow the last sip of cold coffee and toss the paper cup into the trash can. Pulling out my cell phone, I check the time again. Bill's wife should have been here by now. They live in a suburb forty-five minutes north of Atlanta, and the trip to the hospital normally wouldn't take this long.

It's been over an hour since the doctor told me that Bill needed to go straight into surgery. I've bugged the volunteer at the information desk so often about any new information that she finally told me politely to stop asking and to keep an eye on the pager she gave me. It's supposed to go off with blinking red lights whenever there is an update.

Which there never is.

It strikes me as ironic that the exact same pager is used at steakhouses to let customers know when their table is ready. Finally, after what seems like forever, I see Bill's wife rush through the sliding glass doors of the hospital lobby. She spots me and hurries over to engulf me in a big hug.

"Maggie!" she says, wiping away a tear. "Thank you for staying with him until I could get here."

"I wouldn't dare leave him here at the hospital alone. Bill is my friend, and I'm not leaving until I know he's out of surgery and going to be okay."

"Is there any news yet?" she asks.

"Not yet."

I take her by the hand and lead her over to the information desk. "I'll tell them you're here. Maybe they'll be more willing to share information with you than they were with me."

She takes a deep breath and grips my hand tighter.

It's going to be a long night.

Four hours later, I'm finally in my car and on my way back to my apartment. Shortly after Bill's wife arrived at the hospital, the doctor came out to give us the good news that the bullet had been removed safely. Luckily, none of his vital organs or arteries were hit and while he lost a great deal of blood, all signs pointed to a good chance of recovery.

I stayed at the hospital until they told us Bill had been moved to the Intensive Care Unit and that his wife could go in to see him. I didn't want to intrude on their private moment, so I took the opportunity to leave. There wasn't anything else I could do at that point anyway.

Bill would want me to get back to work and more importantly, to find more about the men who shot him.

Why were the shooters at the mall on Valentine's Day? And why did they go after Bill first? Not for the first time, the thought occurs to me that maybe their target wasn't random. What if their target was me?

The thought sends a chill down my spine.

The opportunity to gun down a reporter during a live television feed would be a prize to any terrorist, homegrown or otherwise.

My mind keeps going back over everything that happened in slow motion. Nothing feels real. It's like a nightmare I can't wake up from.

I keep thinking about the sexy biker who threw me to the ground and protected me with his own body without a moment's hesitation. If he hadn't been there, I would've been a goner.

I owe him my life, and I don't even know his name.

Who is he?

And maybe more importantly, why did he run out of there and disappear so quickly?

The man was a true hero today.

Then again, heroes don't run from the scene. Unless they're hiding something. There's a story here. I can smell it. I've got to find him. To thank him for saving my life, and to find out what he's hiding.

It shouldn't be too hard. His black leather jacket was covered with patches. One of them said Steel something or other. Steel what? Steel Outlaws? Steel Riders? Steel Rods?

Why can't I remember?

Normally I can recall every little minute detail about everything. I'm still too shaken up. Hopefully it will come to me out of the blue. As soon as I reach the house, I'll start searching the Internet for motorcycle clubs in North Carolina with Steel in the name.

By morning, I'll know who he is and where to find him.

6

TOBY

Less than an hour later, almost everyone is at the clubhouse. We're all gathered in the main room waiting for Jesse to call the meeting to order.

"What's up, Toby?" a female voice behind me purrs in my ear. "Any plans for later tonight?"

Before I have a chance to answer, I feel sharp teeth tugging my earlobe playfully while a cool hand slips under my untucked shirt.

I suck in my breath.

"Whoa girl!" I say with a laugh when her hand slides across my stomach and then stops at my belt buckle. "Easy now filly. Calm yourself down."

I don't need to turn around to know who the hand belongs to.

Danita.

One of the newer Sweet Butts who always aims to please.

Any way she can.

From making the crew sandwiches in the middle of the night to brewing strong cups of coffee the next day when we're all hungover. Danita is extra curvy in all the right places, sweet as sugar, and knows how to please a man in the sack.

Or men I should say, if I'm being honest.

She doesn't seem to have a preference among the crew, and we don't mind swapping. After all, that's what the Sweet Butts are here for.

Sharing is caring.

That's what we like to say.

She's one of a handful of regular Sweet Butts who hang around the clubhouse as many hours as we'll let them. The group of pretty girls make our life a whole lot easier. One of the best perks of being a member of the Steel Infidels is having a sexy young thing willing to do whatever you want, whenever you want.

It's easy to get spoiled by the adoring attention. Who cares if there isn't any love or even true affection involved?

I'm not all about that anyway.

Love is for suckers.

Her finger makes its way under the waistband of my jeans and strokes lower. My cock starts to stir. I chuckle at her nerve and grab her hand to hold it still. Danita wouldn't be past pulling my dick out right in the middle of a crowded room to jack me off if she thought it would gain her points with the MC.

"Why do you want to know if I have plans for tonight?" I ask. "Do you have something particular in mind?"

She laughs and nuzzles my neck. "Believe me, I have many naughty things in mind," she says. "I heard what you did today. Don't you think you deserve a reward, Toby?"

I chuckle at the thought. "Yes ma'am, I believe I do," I say. "But not here and definitely not now." Reluctantly, I pull her hand out of my pants and tug her around to face me. She purses her full red lips up at me and makes a duck face.

Is it supposed to be a pout? Or a sexy invitation to slide my dick between her lips? I can never tell. I'm hoping it's the latter. Either way, I don't know why girls are so fond of doing it. I playfully grab her ass cheek with one hand and hang onto the plump flesh. "I'll catch up with you later," I say. "Keep it warm for me."

A shrill whistle rings out and I drop my hand.

When a few of the Sweet Butts in the crowded room keep on talking, Jesse, the Steel Infidels Prez, puts two fingers between his lips and whistles louder this time. The noisy room immediately goes silent. When the President of the MC whistles, everybody had better listen up.

"Is everyone here and accounted for?" Jesse asks.

The crew all glance around the room, mentally taking count and nodding their heads.

"Jodi? How about the Sweet Butts? Are the girls all here too?" he asks.

Jodi, the oldest Sweet Mama, who is officially in charge of keeping the younger Sweet Butts in line, nods back at him. "Anyone who needs to be here is here," she answers. "And if they're not, they're out of luck this time around."

Jesse motions for Sam to lock the front door to the clubhouse and then makes his way to the pool table located in the center of the big open room.

Everyone involved with the motorcycle club is here for the meeting - the crew, the Old Ladies, the Sweet Butts, the wives, and even the kids. Normally our MC meetings are held among the twelve crew members in a room at the back of the clubhouse where we're assured complete privacy.

Not this time.

Jesse and Flint thought it was important to make sure everyone knew about the shit storm headed our way and how to handle it once it got here. The Steel Infidels can't afford to have one of the Sweet Butts running her mouth to reporters in hopes of grabbing her ten seconds of fame.

There is no telling what they would say or how much club business they would be willing to spill with a little prodding. The women that hang around the MC's clubhouse aren't always the smartest girls in the world, and it wouldn't take much to trip them up.

"Alright then," Jesse says. "Let's get started. By this time, I'm sure you've heard about what happened at the mall today in Atlanta. The details are sketchy. All we know is that at least three men came into the mall and started shooting up the food court. We don't know who they are and why they did it. All we know is that our man Toby right here..." He points a finger at me. "Managed to take down two of the shooters with a little help from Sam. Unfortunately, one of them got away. But two out of three ain't bad though, right? I'll take those odds any day. Who knew we had a real-live action hero right here in our own MC?"

A loud chorus of yells and clapping erupts. Rocco, one of the oldest crew members, reaches over to slap me on the back. His brother Donny grabs my hand tightly in his and shakes it.

"You did good, buddy," he says.

After a couple of minutes, I hold up my hand to get them to hush. "Just doing what any of you would have done," I say, more than a little embarrassed by the attention. "Nothing special."

"I don't know about that," Jesse says. "According to Flint, your quick thinking and actions saved a whole lot of people today. We're proud of you, Toby. And I'm honored to call you a Steel Infidel brother. You made us proud."

For a brief second, my gut is filled with a warm, fuzzy glow. A nice change from the way I usually feel.

Then I remember.

I'm not a fucking hero.

Nobody should be proud of me.

Not with the things I've done in my past.

And maybe even worse, the things I didn't do.

As much as I would love to have the admiration of Jesse and the rest of the crew, I don't deserve it.

Not today.

I don't want to be an ass, so I try to act normal and accept their congratulations while inside I feel like a big fucking fraud. I'm relieved when the attention turns back to Jesse.

"That was the good news," he says. "Now onto the bad. Since we have a national hero in our midst, the media is going to come calling. With a little luck, it will take them a couple of days to find us. Flint says we shouldn't count on it, especially with social media being what it is now. Photos are already being posted of the scene and crazy rumors being shared. People are marking themselves 'safe' on Facebook even if they're two hundred miles from the mall. Why the hell do people do that?"

"To let their mamas know they're safe," one of the Sweet Butts pipes up to say.

Jesse hides a smile. "I know. I wasn't really asking for an answer. Thanks anyway, Jessica. Here's the deal. No one is to talk to anyone, especially the media, about what went down at the mall." He slowly scans the room, taking the time to make direct eye contact with each person.

"If you run your fucking mouth and I find out about it, you're history. No questions asked and no excuses. This goes for everyone in this room. No exceptions. I don't care how long you've been with the MC or who is doing the asking. I don't care if it's Diane Sawyer calling your house ten times a day or the New York Times. Nobody talks until me or Flint gives the okay."

The room is so quiet that I can hear Rocco's steady breathing from several feet behind me. I can't think of a time before when Jesse threatened to throw people out of the MC. He means business.

I hope the Sweet Butts are listening and paying attention. I glance over at our two newest girls, Madison and Chloe. Twin girls in their early twenties with long blonde hair almost down to their asses. Their blank blue eyes are as big as saucers. Hopefully that means they're absorbing something. At least a few words maybe. While I'm watching, Chloe casually extends a manicured hand and checks out her nail polish. Then again, maybe not.

Jesse suddenly turns in my direction. "Toby, you're going to be the one in the spotlight, so be prepared."

"You don't need to worry about me," I say. "Because I'm not talking to nobody."

Jesse nods. "I'm not worried about you," he says. "Now Sam on the other hand..." he gives his youngest brother a stern look.

"Why are you always worried about me?" Sam asks in exasperation.

"Do I really need to explain why?" Jesse says. "Everyone in this room knows why considering your past history of getting into trouble."

Sam holds up his hands. "Okay, okay. Not one word from me either. I swear. Nada, nothing. Mum is the word. I don't know anything, didn't see anything. Hell, I'm not even sure I was there. In fact, I'm fairly certain I was in Victoria's Secret picking out Lila's Valentine's present when it all went down. A red lacy bra with matching panties. Except I don't think you can call them panties because the crotch is missing. Lila, what do you call those things? Bloomers?"

Lila slaps him hard on the forearm. He laughs before pulling her tight against him. "Don't worry," he says. "Reporters can come sniffing around here all they want, but they're not getting anything from me either."

"Good," Jesse says, looking relieved. "I'm glad you all understand. Flint, do you have anything to add to the discussion?"

Flint runs a hand through his brown hair and shakes his head slowly. "Not really. Just be prepared when the media shows up and let me do all the talking. Which there will be very little of. I'm the club's spokesperson and the only one with permission to talk. We still haven't worked out exactly what we're going to say or when to say it. Everybody got it?"

When everyone agrees, Jesse claps his hands together. "Alright then. This calls for a round of drinks. I know Valentine's Day plans were spoiled for many of you, and I appreciate you all showing up. Jodi, can you and the girls get some drinks going around? Make sure our man Toby gets the first shot. Hopefully this will all blow over and things will be back to normal in no time."

I hope so too.

7

TOBY

The squeaky sound of my bedroom door opening jars me awake. I open my eyes and squint against the bright sunlight streaming through the window blinds. My head is pounding like a motherfucker and my mouth tastes like I've been chewing cigarettes. After they've been rolled around in cow shit.

Groaning, I cover my head with a pillow.

"Want some coffee?" Danita asks from the doorway in a perky voice. "I can make a pot before I go to work. Or even breakfast if you want it. I'm handy in the kitchen."

I hate morning people.

And mornings.

"No," I mutter. "Just leave me alone and let me die in peace."

Now she's standing beside the bed, hovering over me. She's dressed for work in a white and pink striped waitress outfit. "You drank a lot last night," she says.

"No kidding."

I slowly become aware of the fact that I'm still wearing my jeans. I guess I didn't get lucky. A pity.

"Jesse told me to follow you home last night to make sure you got here safely," she says. "You shouldn't have been driving at all, but you insisted."

"Thanks," I say. "Appreciate it."

I wish she would go and leave me in peace. Even on a good day it takes me a while to get going in the morning, much less when I'm hungover.

My golden rule is to never let a gal spend the night at my place. Mostly so I can avoid awkward scenes like this one. I could kick my own ass right about now. I must've been super wasted last night to break my rule.

"Why I didn't crash at the clubhouse if I drank too much?" I ask out loud.

"You said you needed to get home for Sadie. I tried to call your dog sitter for you. She didn't pick up the phone. I guess she was out for Valentine's Day dinner."

Ahh...Sadie.

That explains it.

I try to recall the previous night's events. There's nothing but a blank space in my brain. "Did you sleep here?" I ask, dreading the answer. I live in fear the one time I let a girl spend the night that I'll wake up to a bathroom full of feminine products, makeup, and straightening irons.

"No. I just followed you home and waited until you got inside. Your house is on my way to work at the diner so I just dropped by to check on you. To make sure you're still alive and breathing."

"Barely," I say. "Thanks. I'm good now. Maybe I'll see you later tonight at the clubhouse."

Hint, hint.

"Okay," she says after a moment. "Sadie is in the backyard running around. I fed her already. She kept hovering around the bag of dog food in the kitchen and gazing up at me with those big brown eyes."

"Can you let her back in before you go?" I ask. "She's been digging under the fence lately and running off to play with the neighbor's dogs."

"Sure, I'll do that."

I hear the front door slam and thirty seconds later, a wriggly ball of yellow fur jumps on my bed. I know what's coming next, so I pull the pillow tighter over my head. When a moist nose pokes its way under the pillow and into my cheek, I can't help but laugh.

"Stop it!" I say, trying to push Sadie off me. "Go away, you mangy mutt."

We both know I don't mean it. She keeps digging under the covers until both of our faces are completely under the pillow.

Her hot breath stinks.

So does mine.

At this point it would be a toss-up on which one is worse.

I open one eye to see her staring at me intently, willing me with everything she's got to get up and play.

Damn! I love this dog.

I found her shivering on the side of the road in an ice storm back in December. Brought her home, fattened her up, and tried to find her owner. When nobody claimed her, I called her mine. Reaching up, I curl my arm around her neck and pull her down on top of me.

"Hey baby," I say to the only love of my life. "Do you love your Daddy?"

A slurpy wet kiss is my answer. She wallows around on the bed covers until she finds a good spot then snuggles under my arm. In seconds, we're both sound asleep.

Thirty minutes later, she's had enough resting and is licking my face again. There's no sleeping late when there's a dog in the house. I know it's pointless trying to ignore her any longer.

As much as I hate to, it's time to haul my lazy ass out of bed. As soon as I sit up, she jumps off and lands on the wood floor with a thud. Running to the door, she turns around and play bows toward me. When I don't move fast enough, she starts barking.

I wince at the loud sound and rub my temples.

"Sadie! Not so loud. You're killing your Daddy. C'mon girl. Out you go."

She runs down the hallway in front of me. I open the back door and toss a tennis ball as far as I can throw it then wince in pain. Ouch! My shoulder hurts like a motherfucker from hitting the tile floor yesterday.

After the fifth time of me tossing the ball as far as I can throw it and her retrieving it, I quit to go inside and take a shower. If I waited on her to end the game, I would be waiting forever.

They don't call them Golden Retrievers for nothing. Sadie would willingly chase tennis balls as long as I was willing to throw.

In the bathroom, I step out of my jeans and into the shower stall. Closing my eyes, I turn on the hot water full force and let it pound onto my back. The old football injury aches painfully in my shoulder. I think about how lucky I am to walk away with nothing more than aches and bruises.

Other people fared far worse.

I vaguely remember watching a news update on my cell phone after my fifth or sixth drink last night. The news report listed several names of people who had been shot. Everyone was still alive at midnight, which is a miracle all by itself. A couple of the victims were still in intensive care. The cameraman Bill was one of them. I hope he makes it. He was a decent enough fellow. Maggie was certainly concerned about him.

I'm dreading checking my phone to get an update. I don't want to see any bad news. I already feel guilty enough as it is. If anyone dies, it will be my fault.

I should have done more yesterday.

Moved faster.

Thought smarter.

Every second I stayed down and did nothing gave the shooters more opportunities to injure an innocent bystander.

I hated hearing everyone at the clubhouse talk about what I did when all I can think about is what I didn't do.

As always.

Same old story. Time after time I've walked away when others didn't. There's a fancy name for it. Survivor's guilt, they call it. The constant gnawing, guilty feeling that threatens to rot me from the inside out.

I've done my time with counseling and talking it out with the so-called experts. The Marines forced me to go. The counselors said all the right things and tried to reassure me that I'm not alone with my issues.

But I am alone.

The demons are mine to fight all by myself. The crazy thing is sometimes I think maybe I don't deserve to beat them. I never told any of the counselors that. They wouldn't understand. How could they?

They weren't there.

They've probably never even been to the Middle East. Or maybe even held a gun. It wouldn't surprise me. How could they understand what it's like to have to make split-second decisions that sometimes have irreversible and horrible results?

I'm good at hiding what I'm going through, and that's the way I want it to stay. I've become an expert at putting a big smile on my face and pretending as if everything is fine. Talking it out sucks. It only brings the pain to the surface. As long as I keep the emotions all packed down tight inside, I can make it through another day.

Keep moving. One foot in front of the other.

After all, today I'm a fucking hero, and I need to start acting like one.

I stay in the shower until the hot water finally runs out. When I turn off the shower, I hear someone knocking loudly on the front door. Sadie hears them too and is barking frantically in the backyard.

"Fuck!" I mutter. "Can't a man get any peace around here?"

Who would be knocking at my door? I live out in the middle of nowhere. Any of the Steel Infidels would just come right on in and make themselves at home. The Sweet Butts too. Which is the same thing I would do at their house. We have an open-door policy among the club members. What's mine is theirs and vice-versa. When the knocking continues, I sigh and step out of the shower.

Maybe it's something important. After what happened yesterday, it might even be the police. I hope not because I'm not in the mood to be talking to the police, and Flint isn't here with his lawyer skills to keep me out of trouble.

"Hang on!" I yell toward the door. "I'm coming."

Grabbing a towel, I wrap it around my waist and tuck in the ends. If it's the police and they're offended by my lack of clothing, I can use it as an excuse to come back inside and call Flint. I hurry to the front door and throw it open.

The person standing on my doorstep is definitely not the police and not someone I ever expected to see again, much less this morning.

"What the hell are you doing here?" I say in surprise.

8

MAGGIE

The biker is not happy to see me. Not that I expected him to be. From the irritated expression on his handsome face, I've arrived too early in the morning and interrupted his shower.

His jet-black hair is a damp, tousled mess and his blue eyes are sleepy and a little bloodshot. He's bare-chested, wearing nothing but a thin white towel that doesn't leave much to the imagination. The towel is tied around his waist on one side and hangs barely below his balls.

Could it be any shorter? Or the fabric more transparent now that it's wet?

His legs stretching below the towel are strong and muscular. The palms of my hands itch to reach down and caress his thigh. To feel the steel muscle underneath the pads of my fingers. Or trail my fingernails up his inner leg.

For a long moment, I'm at a loss for words. Not a typical scenario for me.

"What are you doing here?" he asks again.

"I'm sorry," I finally stammer. "Did I wake you up? I mean interrupt your shower?" I'm tongue-tied and screwing up my words.

"What the fuck does it look like, lady?" he growls. "And how did you find me so fast? I haven't even had a cup of coffee and here you are banging on my damn door first thing in the morning. Don't you sleep?"

"It's eleven o'clock," I say. "Not that early. Almost noon."

Why am I explaining myself to him?

He rubs his eyes with his fingers and leans against the door. The towel inches lower on his waist. He knows it and does nothing. Any second and the tiny piece of cloth is going to drop right down on the doormat. I'm halfway hoping it does.

It's taking everything I have in me not to stare at the v-line of muscles from his abs going down under the towel. I've heard my girlfriends talk about those particular set of muscles. I've never understood the fascination before.

I certainly do now.

I can't help wondering about the heat of his still damp skin and how those muscles would feel underneath my tongue. I would start at his ribs and run my tongue down the length of one side and then up the other. I would work slowly and wait until he begged me before I slid my tongue underneath the towel.

"Maybe for you," he says.

I've lost my train of thought and glance back up at his face. "Maybe for me what?" I ask, distracted by the magnificent maleness standing in front of me.

He frowns and crosses his muscular, tattooed arms. Now that he's shirtless, I can see the rest of the lion tattoo that I caught a glimpse of yesterday. The eyes of the lion are cool and blue. They remind me of his. I wonder if that was the intention. The lion tattoo will be forever branded into my brain.

"Maybe not early for you," he says. "What did you do, lady? Stay up all night researching me on the Internet? How the fuck did you find my house? It couldn't have been easy since I'm way off the main road."

I wonder what I should tell him. The truth is I don't know much. Not nearly enough. Only that his name is Toby and that he rides with a motorcycle club called the Steel Infidels. Other than that, I don't know one thing about him or the other guys. It took me all night to find out that tiny piece of information, and only because I had the station's video tape of the live broadcast.

Unfortunately, now the Associated Press has the tape too and television stations have been showing it all across the world. The other reporters are nipping at my heels on the story, and I'm only minutes ahead of them. Probably not even that now.

Back at the television station, my unpaid college intern is working as hard as she can to find out more. I'm not hopeful she'll dig up anything. She only works mornings and considering she's unpaid, it's not as if I can crack a whip and force her to work overtime.

If I'm lucky enough to get the jump on this story, it will be because of what I can dig up in person, not from searching through the same information on the Internet as everyone else.

"I didn't stay up the entire night," I explain. "I slept three hours and I had help from others at the TV station. You weren't too difficult to find. The Steel Infidel patches on your buddy's leather jacket gave you away."

He raises his eyebrows and gives me a dubious look. "And why would you want to find me?"

To find out why he ran instead of taking the credit for being a hero.

To finally have a chance to crack a big story of my own.

I don't say any of that.

Instead, I give him my most sincere smile. As a reporter, I have various practiced expressions for all occasions. This one is to reassure him that I'm genuine. To make him feel comfortable and at ease with me. It usually works well, especially with men.

"What you did yesterday was amazing," I say. "And heroic. Not only did you save other people's lives by your actions, you also saved mine. I drove up here this morning because I wanted to personally thank you. That's all."

I'm expecting him to duck his head, break eye contact, be bashful and say something along the lines of "golly geez, it was nothing. I'm just a good old country boy who loves America."

Or some other line of crap.

Instead he grabs the back of my neck and slams me against him in one quick, sudden movement. I yelp in surprise while my hands splay across his bare chest muscles for support. The heat from his skin still warm from the shower quickly seeps through my thin blouse. My nipples harden at the close contact.

He smells delicious and intoxicating.

Clean like soap instead of heavy cologne that masks a man's own masculine smell.

My head swims.

"Okay, so thank me," he says. His perfect lips twist into a smile. "Now that you're here."

His head looms lower, and he covers my lips in a kiss with such force and passion that I don't have a chance to protest.

Even if I wanted to.

Nothing prepares me for the blast of electricity ripping through me the moment our lips met. I'm too stunned to react. Instead I part my lips and he presses me impossibly tighter against him, robbing me of breath.

Gathering me closer still, he wraps a thick strand of my long hair around his hand like a cage fighter to hold me captive. My breasts strain and tingle against him. With a growl, he deepens the kiss and practically lifts me off my feet as his other hand closes around my hip. Backing me up against the side of the door, he begins to kiss me roughly, hungrily, with one hand moving up to cup my aching breast.

I couldn't fight him if I tried.

He's a tightly coiled lion whose wild energy has been unleashed.

The power of Toby is not something to tangle with lightly.

I should remember this and take caution.

For a brief moment, I close my eyes and allow myself to lean into him.

Just for a second.

A big mistake.

He feels me giving in and he grips me tighter.

"Wait!" I say breathlessly, reluctantly forcing myself to break the kiss. "Stop it! Let me go!"

I push against his upper arms. His hands tighten to cup my ass, holding me tight against his masculine hardness.

"Maybe if you sound like you really mean it," he says thickly. "But you don't. In fact, I think you're enjoying this as much as I am."

He leans down to kiss me again and I turn my face away. He chuckles and presses his lips to my neck instead, kissing and nibbling the soft skin wickedly. I shiver and he laughs knowingly.

Damn! The man knows *exactly* what he's doing to me.

This is going to spiral out of control quickly if I can't stop it. I place my palms against his chest to shove him away again and discover his heart is hammering as erratically as mine. I'm not the only one deeply affected by our kiss.

"What do you think you're doing?" I ask, my voice quivering.

He lifts his head and stares straight into my eyes. "A better question is what the hell do you think *you're* doing coming to my house uninvited and knocking on my door?" he replies. "For your information, I'm getting my thank you. You could have just sent a card, you know. Saved yourself a long car trip."

"A card?" I echo. "Who sends cards these days? Considering you saved my life, a drugstore card would have seemed inadequate."

"My thoughts exactly," he says with a devilish smile. "Since you mentioned it first, maybe I want more than a kiss for my thank you. Maybe I *deserve* more than a kiss. I believe I do. What is your life worth to you? It must be worth something good. Did you know we're miles from the nearest neighbors?"

"No, I didn't notice on my drive here. Why?"

"Just thought you should know there's absolutely nothing, or no one, to stop me from dragging you inside the house right now and throwing you across my bed." His blue eyes glitter dangerously. "Hell, we might not even make it to the bed. It's all the way down at the end of the long hallway. The sofa is closer. So is the kitchen table. I kind of like the idea of bending you over and sliding your tight little black skirt up around your waist."

He tugs my head back by the hair he has wrapped around his hand. Leaning closer, he whispers in my ear. "I could even make you scream my name. Do you know my name, Maggie?"

Is he joking? Would he really drag me inside against my will? I search for any sign on his face that says he's teasing me. His eyes are guarded, giving nothing away. The long, solid cock pressed against me through the towel tells me there's a chance he might be serious.

Now I'm worried.

What do I know about this man?

Not one thing.

He's right. I had no business showing up at his house. Not a single person knows where I am. He could be a murderer or even a serial killer.

He could drag me inside his house and do all kinds of unspeakable things to me, and no one would hear me yell.

Or scream his name.

I refuse to let myself think about that.

He loosens his grip with one arm and reaches down behind me to slide his hand under my skirt. His large palm cups my ass cheek and squeezes the flesh. One finger slides closer to my crotch. Unconsciously, I shift slightly to give him better access.

Oh yeah, he's dead serious.

I'm soaking my panties and detest myself for it. What am I doing? This is completely unprofessional and totally out of character for me.

I push against his chest again, harder this time, and it's like moving against a concrete wall. I bet he played a linebacker in football. He doesn't budge.

"You wouldn't dare!" I sputter in indignation.

"Lady, you have no idea what I would dare to do," he says, his voice cold. "No idea at all. It would be a good idea to remember that in the future and don't tempt me. Because once I get started, I'm a freight train and hard to stop. And don't lie to me either. I don't appreciate it."

He's screwing with me and enjoying every minute of it. He abruptly turns me loose and steps back, tugging the end of the towel tighter.

The chill of the February wind hits me with a blast. I already miss the heat of his big arms and warm chest. A part of me wishes he would wrap me back up again so I could snuggle into his delicious-smelling neck.

"Tell me why you're really here," he says. "And don't give me some bullshit answer again."

"As I said before, to thank you for saving my life."

"Is that a fact?" he says sarcastically. "Or were you hoping I would invite you in for a cup of coffee and answer a boatload of questions? The only reason you drove all the way up here is to interview me. So don't give me that horseshit about wanting to thank me and all that jazz. I know what you're up to, sweetheart. And I'm not talking. Not to you or anyone else you send my way."

"That's not why I'm here," I argue quietly.

My words sound flat, even to me.

"Right," he says. "And I don't have a hard-on the size of my forearm now either."

I swallow and will myself not to peek down at the towel since I know that's what he wants.

Do not look.

Instead I force myself to stare directly into his eyes framed by long dark eyelashes. Hmmm...probably another mistake. A woman could get lost in his eyes and never want to leave. I raise my eyebrows at him.

"The size of your forearm? Don't you think that's a little bit of an exaggeration? Even for a guy as big as you, that would be pushing it. Usually men that exaggerate penis size are trying to hide behind their own insecurities."

"Could be," he says. He rubs his two-day-old beard thoughtfully. "I know a way to settle it for sure. Why don't you feel under the towel and see if I'm as big a liar as you are? Or at least take a little peek? Come on. What's the harm? I know you want to. It's taking everything you have in you not to look down."

Is he really suggesting that I reach a hand under his towel to feel the size of his dick? How did this conversation deteriorate to this point so quickly? I've never had a man talk to me this way before.

So aggressively sexual and dominant.

From the moment his mouth touched mine, he gave me no doubt who was in charge here.

Then again, most of the men in my life were private school boys who were more intimidated by me than I was of them.

Toby is not a man to be intimidated by anyone - man or woman.

He's amused by my confusion. When he reaches out for my wrist, I jerk it away just in time. He laughs out loud when I childishly tuck my hand behind my back where he can't reach it. The lines around his eyes crinkle disarmingly when he smiles. Lines from years of working outside in the sun. Not from lying around a swimming pool as a lifeguard or on a sunny beach.

This is all a big joke to him. He's toying with me. I'm frustrated now in more ways than one. I don't have time for this nonsense and am getting nowhere fast.

"You need to leave now, little Miss Maggie," he says. "You came to say 'thank you' and I most graciously accepted. Now unless you want to give me something else, and I sincerely hope you do, it's time for you to go. Sorry you drove so far for so little."

"I'm not giving you anything else," I say defiantly, as if that was ever in question.

"Didn't think so," he says with a long sigh. He straightens up from where he's been leaning against the doorframe. "What a disappointment this morning is turning out to be."

Without another word, he turns around to go back inside. The towel slips loose and falls to the ground. My mouth drops open when he gives me a quick glimpse of his gorgeous bare ass before stepping back inside the house and slamming the door shut behind him.

Wait! Come back! I almost yell after him.

What just happened?

I'm not used to having people simply walk away and dismiss me. In fact, I refuse to let a man treat me this way. I raise my hand to knock on the door again when I hear the deadbolt turn in the door to lock it.

Is he watching me through the peephole?

He is.

I can feel his eyes on me with every pore in my body. I know he's standing there, silently watching me from the other side with a big grin on his face.

Fine.

Two can play this game.

"You can't get rid of me that easily," I say through the door. "I'll be back."

And next time, I won't leave until I get answers. He's hiding something. I'm sure of it, and I'm going to find out what that something is. As I walk away, I hear his deep rumble of laughter through the door.

9

TOBY

I'm less than a mile from the Steel Infidels' clubhouse on my bike when I realize the MC is in trouble. A Fox News truck with a tall antenna is poking along in front of me. The driver keeps hitting his brakes, obviously searching for road signs or mailboxes with street addresses.

I wish them luck since Bardsville still relies on an old route system. The mail carriers know everyone by heart, so street addresses are non-existent. My address is a simple Route 3, Bardsville, Georgia. The system works well so nobody has ever felt the need to change it.

The news team will be driving around all day trying to find the MC's clubhouse if that's what they're after unless one of the locals decide to help them out, which is always a distinct possibility too. After all, we're small-town heroes.

The takedown at the mall will be the biggest news to hit this town in ages. It wouldn't occur to anyone that the Steel Infidels might want to hide from the media.

I pull back on the throttle, duck my head down so the news crew can't see my face, and roar past them without glancing over at the driver. Immediately he speeds up and tries to tail me.

Trying to follow any guy on a motorcycle is a better prospect than driving around on country roads all day. It takes me only a couple of seconds to lose them on the curvy road. I'm almost to the cutoff for the gravel road where our clubhouse is located when I spot the second news van. I recognize the letters from a television station in Chattanooga, Tennessee.

My phone vibrates in my pocket and I ignore it. When it stops, then starts ringing a second and third time, I pull it out of my pocket and glance down to check the caller.

Sam.

Must be urgent, whatever it is.

I'm almost at the clubhouse when I see the dreaded media storm has beaten me there. The fenced perimeter of the industrial warehouse is surrounded by a caravan of media vans. Reporters with microphones and men with huge cameras are milling around outside their vehicles.

Waiting for something.

Or someone.

They're waiting for me.

Damn!

They have the driveway to the clubhouse blocked as well as to the metal entrance gate. How am I going to plow through this mess and get inside?

Then I see them.

Two of the MC's Sweet Mamas are standing right inside the closed gate. They're waving their arms in the air, motioning for me to keep on driving toward them.

Good God Almighty.

Who had the harebrained idea to put the Sweet Mamas out front to guard the gate instead of one of the Steel Infidels' crew members? Now that I think about it, it's not a bad idea since they're the toughest women I know. They would just as soon give a reporter a nasty beat-down as to not.

All of the crew are halfway afraid of them, though it's not something we ever like to talk about. We call it respecting the Sweet Mamas, when in reality they scare the living shit out of us.

I slow down and try to maneuver my bike between the vehicles. Suddenly the crowd of reporters and cameramen rush me from both sides. A young Asian woman with a microphone jumps in front of me to block my path.

What the fuck!

Is she insane? I grab the brakes to keep from hitting her. Flashbulbs go off in my face, almost blinding me.

Shit!

I'm not prepared for this. Everyone starts yelling questions at me all at once.

"Toby! Over here!"

"How does it feel to be a hero, Toby!"

Do they really expect me to stop and answer? The crowd swells around me, pressing tighter. I'm walking the bike now with the heels of my boots on both sides. The Asian reporter is walking backwards in front of me, talking rapidly in a foreign language into a microphone.

Chinese? Korean?

Hell, I don't know.

For the first time, I realize the shooting has made international news. A man shoves a microphone in front of my helmet and I push it away. Sweat breaks out on my forehead and trickles down into my eyes. The panicked feeling of claustrophobia sets in. The reporters are so close they're brushing my thighs with their coats and banging my shoulders with their cameras.

I do not need this right now.

Keep it together, man.

This isn't a fucking war. There are no bombs about to explode. Or shooters to watch out for. I remember telling myself the same thing yesterday.

Jodi keeps waving frantically at me. "Come on, Toby!" she yells. "Don't stop! Run over that bitch! Keep going! Break her leg! Gas it!"

For a split-second, I seriously consider doing just that if the gal doesn't move the fuck out of my way. "Move, lady!" I yell. "I'm warning you."

She is babbling non-stop and gesturing with her hands. She probably doesn't understand English.

Behind me, I hear the rumble and roar of several motorcycles, and I glance back over my shoulder.

Thank you, Jesus!

Here they come now. The whole crew of the Steel Infidels.

Everyone except for me. I guess I didn't get the memo. Then I remember the numerous phone calls from Sam.

Maybe I did.

No wonder the Sweet Mamas are guarding the gate. They're the only ones at the clubhouse. I feel a surge of affection for the two older ladies. Standing out here in the cold trying to protect the Steel Infidels. Their boys, as they call us. The first thing I'm going to do is hug both of their necks when I get inside.

I hear the threatening sound of the Steel Infidels revving the throttles on their bikes behind me. Next thing I know, the crew are clearing a path straight through the reporters. They're riding two-by-two except for Jesse, who is leading the way.

His face is full of steely-eyed determination. He means business. He's a tough badass, and the reporters seem to know this instinctively. Jesse wouldn't hesitate to run right over a reporter and break an ankle or an arm if they stood in his way.

When Jesse doesn't slow down or appear to even notice their presence, the group of reporters quickly jump aside to let him through. It's like watching Moses parting the Red Sea. The other crew members follow close behind him.

When he gets within shouting distance to me, he yells and motions me ahead of him, "Go, Toby!"

The Asian reporter still standing in my way takes one look at Jesse and her eyes widen. Oh, so now she's worried. I definitely need to work on my badass biker image.

"Move it!" I say again, and she jumps to the side.

Maybe she understands English after all. I gun it and drive past her. The Sweet Mamas slide open the gate and we all quickly roar inside. Jodi slams the gate shut and locks it behind Rocco, who is bringing up the rear. We don't slow down until we pull around the back of the clubhouse out of sight of the reporters. I park my bike beside Sam and tug off my helmet.

"What the fuck was that zoo all about?" I say.

Sam laughs and slides off his bike. "What was your plan back there, Toby?" he asks. "Man! You should have seen the panicked look on your face. Put you in a mall with terrorists and you're cool as a cucumber. Put you in a crowd with a bunch of reporters and you freak the fuck out. What's up with that?"

I frown at him. "What are you talking about? I wasn't freaking out. They caught me by surprise, that's all. Someone should have warned me. You obviously knew they were here. I drove straight into a hornet's nest. Those assholes were swarming all over me. There should be a law against that kind of crap. I wouldn't be a celebrity for ten million dollars if I had to put up with that every day. Makes me feel sorry for those poor little Kardashian girls."

"I called you a hundred times this morning," Sam says. "You might want to try leaving your phone on if you want to know what's going on. Don't blame me if you're in the dark. Where were you anyway? Why didn't you answer?"

"Still at home. Maggie, the reporter from yesterday, showed up at my door this morning. Said she wanted to thank me for saving her life. Can you believe that crap?"

"I can," Flint says, walking over to join us. "Don't talk to her. You know what Jesse said."

I hold up my hands. "Don't worry, I won't be talking." I grin. "I'll doubt she'll be coming back around anytime soon. Not unless she wants a piece of this." I grab my crotch.

Sam hoots in laughter. "Maybe she does," he says. "You're packing down there like a giant beast. What did you do to her?"

"Met her at the door wearing nothing but a towel and then planted a big, sloppy kiss on her. And I grabbed her ass. Which is very nice by the way. Just the right size to fit in my hand."

"What?" Sam says in surprise. "How did you manage to work that in? I always thought I was the one with the smooth moves in the MC."

"It was a piece of cake," I say, shrugging as if it were true. "She said she wanted to thank me, so I said 'come here and give me some sugar, baby.'"

I pucker up my lips for emphasis.

Sam gives me a doubtful look. "You really did that?" he asks. "And it worked? I'm finding that *very* hard to believe."

"Okay, so it didn't exactly go down that way," I admit. "You get the idea though. I made her uncomfortable enough that she probably won't be coming back around."

"Don't count on it," Flint says. "This is big news. All the major networks are here. We're prime time and there's no avoiding it at this point. Let's go inside before someone spots us. It wouldn't surprise me if the press is hiding out in the bushes behind the fence. They could be anywhere."

"Wait! Does anyone else hear that buzzing sound?" Sam asks, looking toward the sky.

"A helicopter?" I ask. "I don't hear anything. Then again, I'm half-deaf after having a grenade go off near me in Afghanistan. My ears rang for weeks afterward."

"You would have to be completely deaf not to hear this," Sam says. "It's coming from behind the pine trees over there."

He points to a wooded area of trees that goes on for acres behind the clubhouse. We all look up to where he's pointing.

"Oh shit!" Flint yells. "It's a drone with a camera! Everyone inside the clubhouse now!"

We hear him, and yet we all stand there like a bunch of idiots with our mouths hanging open watching a drone with little legs suddenly pop up over the treetops. It flies unsteadily our way, wobbling back and forth as if it's about to fall out of the sky any second.

"Toby, take it out!" Jesse yells from behind me. "You're our sharpshooter. Kill that son of a bitch now!"

That's all I need to hear.

When Jesse gives an order, I don't hesitate. I pull my gun from my holster and line up the shot. The drone is still quite a distance out, but I can hit it easily. No problem for a Marine sharpshooter.

"Wait!" Flint yells. "Shooting down a drone is a federal crime. I don't think this is a good idea. We're on camera right now, and we don't know who the drone belongs to. They're probably streaming live video."

"All the more reason to kill it. Do it," Jesse orders again.

I've never been caught in a showdown between Jesse and Flint. It's an uncomfortable position, and I don't like it. When push comes to shove though, Jesse is the Prez and his word stands above everyone else's. Even if Flint has the book smarts and a legal degree. I lift my handgun and fire. The drone splinters into pieces and falls straight to the ground.

When it hits, Sam bursts out laughing and slaps his leg. "Well, that escalated quickly," he says. "You were all so serious there for a minute."

"Shut up, Sam," Flint says. "This can't be good. Let's go inside."

Sam can't stop snickering. I've known him forever and once he gets a case of the giggles, he's hard to calm down. His laughter is contagious and the whole crew starts cracking up at the ridiculousness of our situation.

I shake my head.

"How did we end up in this mess?" I ask.

"That was hilarious," Sam says. "I hope they send up another one. This is going to be one fucked-up day."

"You can say that again."

10

MAGGIE

"Cindy, do you have anything new yet?" I ask my intern over the phone. "I don't have Internet access here because of the mountains, so you need to get your butt in gear. All the other stations are getting a jump on us. Take a look at what's happening. The Steel Infidels are already inside the building."

I turn my cell phone away from me and slowly scan the crowd of reporters so Cindy can see for herself.

"Wow! That many news crews are there already?" she says. "I'm sorry I don't have any new information for you. There isn't a whole lot of info on the Steel Infidels or on Toby. It's as if the Internet has been scrubbed clean. Also, I hate to tell you this. I have a big college exam this afternoon, so I need to leave the station early."

Of course she does. I rub my tired eyes and let out a long sigh. "That's fine," I say. "Let me know if you find anything interesting before you leave."

She won't. My college intern is basically useless. I'm on my own here. If I want a story, I'll have to get it all by myself. I hit the off button in frustration and lean back against a steel pole holding up the chain link fence surrounding the clubhouse. It occurs to me that it might possibly be electrified, and I quickly move away from it.

It's burning me up inside to be this close to a big story and still blow it. Not only am I close to the story, I was physically *in* the story and yet I'm still failing miserably.

I screwed things up with Toby too. I should have known he would see right through me. Taking the direct approach might've worked better rather than the "I came to say thank you' excuse for showing up at his house. Now he doesn't trust me at all, and I can't blame him.

"Hey look! It's a drone!"

A young cameraman standing next to me taps my arm and points to the sky. A wobbly drone is making its way over the trees behind the clubhouse.

"I wonder if that thing has a camera mounted on it?" I ask.

"I'm sure it does," he replies. "What other reason would it be up there?"

I frown. "Are drones legal?"

I'm ticked off if they are. Someone else is getting the camera footage I want.

"Who cares? As long as they get the story, right?" the cameraman says with a laugh. "I'd do it too if I had a drone. Anything for the story. It's what makes us feel alive."

He winks at me and I smile back. Yeah, we're all suckers for the story. Nothing beats the adrenaline rush of being ahead of the pack. And the despair when you're bringing up the rear.

He gives me a closer inspection.

"Aren't you the reporter from the attack yesterday? You were filming in the food court when it happened."

"Yes, that was me."

"What's the story? Who are these guys? You must know something. What's the inside scoop?"

"Wouldn't you love to know?" I say teasingly.

As if I know anything either.

It's better to keep the rest of the media guessing. Journalism is a cutthroat business when a hot story is waiting to be told.

I hold my hand over my eyes to block the bright sunlight and watch the drone fly closer to the clubhouse. The sudden loud crack of a gunshot rings out in the crisp air, startling everyone.

The cameraman flinches and dives down behind me for cover. I roll my eyes. A big help he would be in an emergency. The drone explodes into pieces and falls. The crowd of stunned reporters stand there in silence, then immediately rush to their vehicles to go live with their news feeds.

I can't stop the smile spreading across my face.

Toby shot down the drone.

I instinctively know it.

I'm loving these mysterious Steel Infidels more by the minute.

11

TOBY

"Do you see anything interesting out there?" Sam asks from the doorway of the upstairs office. "Any new hot chicks? I spotted the blonde girl from Fox News earlier. She's a sexy babe."

He pulls out the wooden chair beside me, whirls it around, and straddles it.

I hand him the pair of binoculars I've been using to watch the crowd of reporters so he can see for himself. We're sitting in front of a small window in Jesse's office located on the second floor of the clubhouse. A sheer curtain blocks us from view of the reporters.

"Not really," I say. "Same group of people who have been hanging around all day. I wonder how long they're planning to keep this up?"

"Until something more interesting happens," Sam says. "You would think the crowd would be thinning out by now. They must be starving. I see your girl from Channel 5 is still out there waiting for you. There's a cameraman standing beside her looking bored. Does he work with her?"

"No idea," I reply "And she's not my girl. Maggie wouldn't stop to give me a cold drink of water if I was dying on the side of the road if it wasn't for her wanting to get a story. She's one of those high society city gals. I can smell them a mile away. You know the type...nice clothes, expensive shoes, makeup applied just right."

"That's too bad," Sam says. "Because she's a hot one and definitely fuckable. Don't tell me the thought of sliding between her legs hasn't crossed your mind? I saw the way you were checking her out at the mall before the shooting started."

"I'm not denying it. Except I don't like her attitude, and she's already tried to snooker me, so I don't want any part of her. Got to keep my distance."

"Yeah, it's best not to get mixed up with that kind of girl. They're too much trouble and it always ends the same way, so why bother? Eventually you'll have to send her packing and she'll be pissed off. Then the phone calls and the angry text messages will start. At some point, you'll have to change your phone number. It's not worth it. Stick with the Sweet Butts. They're warm, wet, and willing. The Three Ws is all you need. For now."

Sam pulls out his cell phone. "Unless you want two or three of these of your own? Then forget the Sweet Butts. You'll want to set the girlfriend goal a little higher."

He hits the screen a couple of times and brings up a photo of his blond-haired, blue-eyed twin sons. They're sitting in the middle of the kitchen floor surrounded by every pot, pan, and kitchen utensil that was previously stashed in the lower cabinets.

"This took all of three minutes," he says with a sigh. "The time it took me to walk out to the mailbox, get the mail, and bring it back inside. I don't know what the devil we're going to do when they start climbing. The night this happened, Lila and I spent hours putting child safety locks on everything in the house. Sometimes I look at their faces and can see their little twin brains communicating back and forth. Travis will glance over at Trevor and they'll both start giggling for no reason. They know what the other one is thinking. It's a constant mental battle. Me and Lila against them."

"Who's winning the war?" I ask, already knowing the answer.

"Who do you think? They are. It's too exhausting trying to keep the score even, so we eventually gave up. At this point, the best we can hope for is to keep them alive. Lila installed security cameras in every room of the house so no matter where they are or what they're doing, she can see them. Protecting the twins is a very high-tech project. I'm telling you, it's hell having kids. Absolute hell." He bangs his head on the top of the chair.

I snort because I know him better than that.

"You're not fooling me," I say. "You love every minute of being a dad. Admit it. And not only that, you're proud of the fact that they're little badasses."

Sam puts his phone away and looks serious for a rare moment. "Yeah, I am. It's the best feeling in the world. Nothing like it. Not even close. The timing has to be right though." He puts the binoculars back up to his eyes.

"Oh no!" he says, jumping up and moving closer to the window. "It's Aunt Leona! What is she doing here? She must've seen us on the news reports. Someone should have called her to let her know we're okay."

"Your Aunt Leona is out there with the reporters? This can't be good. What's she doing?"

Sam pulls the curtains back and puts the binoculars against the glass. "Best I can tell, she's handing out cookies." He frowns. "She never brings me cookies."

"What? Why would she be doing that? She shouldn't be encouraging the press to hang around. Let me see."

I grab the binoculars from him. Sure enough, there Aunt Leona is in her blue- flowered dress hanging below her knees, her sturdy brown shoes and her white hair wrapped up in a bun at the back of her head. She's smiling and carrying a big tray in both hands. The hungry reporters seem glad to see her and are eagerly accepting whatever it is she's handing out. Her tray empties out in a couple of minutes and then she strides purposefully toward the gate.

When she's a few feet away she stops, looks to the side, and starts walking away in the other direction. I follow her with the binoculars to see what caught her attention.

It's Maggie.

Oh crap! "Now she's over there talking to Maggie," I say. "Call your Aunt Leona and tell her to come inside. She probably recognized Maggie from the news station. What channel does your aunt watch?"

Sam is already hitting the buttons on his phone. "She doesn't have cable and the antenna on the top of her house only picks up two channels. I'm calling her now. I'll put her on speakerphone." Aunt Leona's phone starts ringing. "Come on," he says. "Answer the phone." The phone keeps ringing.

"Doesn't she have voice mail?"

"No, she says she doesn't know how to retrieve the messages," Sam says. "Why isn't she answering? I know she carries her phone with her and she always takes my calls. I'm her favorite nephew."

"She hears it ringing," I say. "I can see her digging around in that big purse hanging from her shoulder looking for it. There! She's got the phone out now."

I watch as Aunt Leona pulls the phone out of her purse, glances at it briefly, then drops it back inside.

"Damn! Your good old Aunt Leona just hung up on you," I say with a chuckle. "And now she's got Maggie by the arm and is leading her toward the gate. Is she really going to bring her inside? What the fuck? The one person I'm trying to stay away from and your Aunt Leona is inviting her in."

"Don't panic," Sam says. "I'll call Rocco. He's at the gate. He'll stop her."

"It's too late for that," I say.

In frustration, I watch as Aunt Leona says something to Rocco. He lets out a big laugh and slides open the gate just wide enough for her and Maggie to slip through.

"They're both inside. Now what?"

"We had better go downstairs and warn Flint the media is coming inside the clubhouse."

12

MAGGIE

I can't believe my luck.

For once, I might be catching a break. As soon as I see the elderly woman climb out of her old beat-up truck and start handing out cookies to the reporters, I suspect she's connected to the Steel Infidels.

I'm hoping she might recognize me from TV so when she heads toward the gate, I push my way through the crowd so she can see me. The moment she glances my way, I wave at her as if we're old friends.

"Lord have mercy!" she says, heading my way with a big smile. "You're that Maggie girl from the six o'clock news. Are you okay, hon? I saw the video of the shooting. To think that you and my boys were right there in the middle of it all. It's a good thing they were there with you. Otherwise I don't know what would have happened. Were you hurt?"

I shake my head. "No, thankfully not."

"The good Lord was watching over my boys yesterday, and you too. Thank you, Jesus! I pray for them boys every day of my life and I know it makes a difference."

"Yes ma'am, it does," I say, agreeing with her.

I'm not very religious. She doesn't need to know this.

I wonder who she is. A mother? A grandmother? I hate knowing so little about the Steel Infidels. I'm flying blind here.

"You're every bit as pretty in real life as you are on television," she says. “Maybe even prettier. You could use a little more flesh on your bones though. Why do all of you young gals think you need to be so skinny?”

Her compliment pleases me. Truth is, I’m a little self-conscious about my weight. When they say the camera adds ten pounds, they aren’t kidding. I already have more than an extra ten pounds on the lower half of my body. Luckily my cameraman knows to shoot me from the waist up whenever possible so my extra pounds rarely show.

“Why didn’t you take the day off?” she asks. “You must be terribly shaken up. How long have you been standing out here in the cold?”

“Since about noon,” I reply. “I’m just doing my job, same as everyone else.”

She frowns and hugs her brown coat tighter around her. “You’ve been hanging around out here for hours? What’s everyone waiting on?”

“We’re hoping someone from the Steel Infidels might come out and give us a statement,” I say. “My station manager told me not to leave here until I get something to put on the news tonight.” I’m stretching the truth here and don’t feel one bit guilty about it.

“Well, you should tell him to come stand out in the cold if he wants something,” she says. “It’s too dang chilly out here. And you were almost killed yesterday. Come with me, child. Let’s go inside the clubhouse and I’ll get you something warm to drink. The boys might have a pot of coffee on and if they don’t, I’ll make us a fresh one.”

I’m surprised when she places a wrinkled hand on my arm and leads me straight up to the gate. I shoot the cameraman a shocked look over my shoulder.

“Go,” he mouths silently and motions me on with his hand.

“I can’t tell you how much I appreciate this,” I tell her. “It’s freezing out here. What’s your name? You already know I’m Maggie.”

“I’m Leona. The boys call me Aunt Leona. Even the ones who aren’t my nephews.”

For a second I’m worried we won’t get through the gates when a menacing-looking biker with a full beard steps up to the other side.

“Hurry up and open the gate, Rocco,” Leona orders. “We haven’t got all day.”

“Where’s my cookies?” he asks gruffly, hiding a smile behind his dark beard. “I saw you giving them out to everyone else.”

Leona reaches way down in her purse and pulls out a couple of cellophane-wrapped cookies. He opens the gate wide enough for us to squeeze through. She hands the cookies to him and pats his arm.

"I've got plenty more in the truck," she says. "Can you get someone to bring my vehicle inside for me? I don't want it to get banged up out there. There's plenty of cookies, but be sure to only eat the ones that are wrapped in cellophane. The other batch of cookies on the seat are for the reporters hanging around out here blocking your way."

"Oh no," he says with a knowing smile. "What did you do this time?"

"Nothing," she replies. "I don't know what you mean."

She hands him a big, heavy set of jangly keys.

"I'll take care of your truck," he says. "Thanks for the cookies."

"Remember what I said now. Only the ones individually wrapped." She winks at him and he lets out a big belly laugh.

I realize there's something happening that I'm not picking up on. Maybe Leona isn't as sweet and innocent as she appears. Now I'm wondering why she's being so nice to me. When we get to the front door of the clubhouse, a woman with tired eyes and short grey hair swings it open and quickly ushers us inside.

Leona reaches over to hug her neck. "Hey Jodi, how are you?"

"I'm good," the woman replies. "The boys are already waiting upstairs. They said to tell you that they need to talk to the girl for a few minutes and then they'll come down to see you."

"You got any hot coffee for this little gal first?" Leona asks. "She's freezing to death out there."

"Let's go in the kitchen and check," Jodi replies with a smile toward Leona.

She doesn't acknowledge me at all. I feel completely invisible. I take a quick glance around the large room that is empty except for us. There's a large pool table in the middle. Half-filled cups of coffee are scattered around, as if everyone jumped up and hid right before we came in the door. Hot steam is still coming off one of the cups.

I suspect that's exactly what happened.

They must have been watching the gate and knew Leona was bringing me in with her. Naturally, they wouldn't want a member of the press inside the clubhouse. It will be a miracle if they let me stay five minutes. I'd better check out the place and absorb everything I can while I have a chance.

I fall back a few feet and slide my hand in my pocket, curling it around my cell phone. If nothing else, maybe I can sneak a few photos before they make me leave. Carefully, I start to inch it out.

A large hand reaches around me from behind and covers my hand tightly in its warm grip.

"What the fuck do you think you're doing?" an angry voice mutters in my ear.

I would recognize that deep Southern drawl anywhere.

Toby.

His breath tickles my neck. The familiar smell of his soap from this morning's shower is still lingering on his skin. The image of him leaning against his doorway, looking cocky as hell in nothing but a towel, is permanently imprinted in my brain.

He squeezes my hand tighter, almost hurting me now.

"Planning on taking a few photos of our clubhouse?" he asks. "Or videos to run on tonight's news? I don't think so, missy. Give me your phone."

He snatches the phone from my grip and drops it into his leather jacket pocket.

"It's mine now," he says with a smirk. "You're in our house and you have to follow our goddamn rules."

Leona stops walking and whirls around, her hands on her ample hips.

"Toby!" Leona scolds. "How many times have I told you boys not to use the GD word? Especially in front of a lady! I don't like it when you use the Lord's name in vain. You should know better than that."

He appears contrite for a moment.

"Sorry, ma'am," he says. "I'm working on it. I picked up some bad language in the Marines. It's an awful habit. I'm trying to quit. I promise."

"You probably picked up lots of nasty things," she replies. "Doesn't mean you need to be spreading them around. Jodi, do the boys use that kind of language in the clubhouse all the time?"

Jodi looks over at Toby and winks, then back at Leona.

"No, not much," Jodi says. "Occasionally they'll slip up now and then. Otherwise they're pretty good about the cussing." She waves toward the stairs. "Toby, why don't you take the girl on up to the office? I want to sit down and have a chat with Leona in the kitchen. Catch up on some things."

Toby curls a hand around my upper arm and tries to tug me toward the stairs. I don't budge and lean in closer so Leona can't hear me.

"Give me my damn phone back," I say. "You can't expect me to let you take it."

He raises his eyebrows at me. "You obviously don't know much about the Steel Infidels, do you? If you did, you would know that yes, I can take whatever I want, when I want. You'll get it back when the time is right. Not before. Unless you want to leave right now? If that's the case, I'll gladly have Jodi walk you to the gate. If you haven't figured it out yet, you're not welcome here. We didn't invite you in. By the way, how in the world did you manage to trick Leona into bringing you inside?"

I frown at him. It ticks me off that he thinks I conned an old lady.

"I didn't do anything," I say defensively. "She came up to me and offered to bring me inside to get out of the cold. That's it. She recognized me from the news. What is up with your attitude?"

His hostile blue eyes stare down into mine. He doesn't like me. I can feel his distaste and can't help but wonder why. What did I ever do to him?

For a second, we stand there staring at each other in a stand-off, neither one wanting to give an inch.

"Are you going upstairs with me or leaving?" he finally asks. "Make up your mind now, woman. I haven't got all day."

Phone or no phone, being inside the clubhouse with the Steel Infidels is better than being out on the other side of the fence with the herd of reporters doing nothing.

"I'll stay," I say without hesitation.

"Suit yourself then," Toby says. "I'm keeping your phone. They're waiting for you upstairs."

He ushers me up a narrow staircase and into a small office on the second floor. The room is barely furnished with a small table and a few wooden straight chairs. Three men are sitting at the table. They all glance up when we walk in.

I recognize Sam from yesterday and the other guy who practically dragged Toby out of the food court. The third man I've never seen before. He stands up and holds out a hand to me to shake.

"I'm Jesse, President of the Steel Infidels," he says, giving my hand a firm shake. He points to Sam. "This is Sam, who I believe you're already met."

Sam throws up a hand in greeting.

"And our other brother, Flint, the VP."

Flint nods at me without smiling.

I notice Jesse and Flint are the spitting image of each other, except Jesse is older and quite a bit more muscular. He's big and intimidating. They both have dark brown, almost black hair, and are strikingly handsome.

Sam is smaller and covered in tattoos running down both arms. With his blue eyes and blond hair, he clearly inherited his looks from a different side of the family. There's something about his eyes that remind me of Leona's.

So they're all brothers...Jesse, Flint, and Sam.

I wonder how Toby fits in with the group and how he became involved with the Steel Infidels.

"Where's your phone?" Jesse asks. "We'll need to take it for now."

"I've already got it," Toby answers, patting his pocket. "I grabbed it before she had a chance to take photos. She wasn't inside two minutes before she was going for her phone. I don't know what your Aunt Leona was thinking bringing her in."

Jesse stares at me without speaking. He's dangerous. I can feel the scary vibes coming off him. It makes me uneasy.

"Did you take any photos inside the clubhouse?" he asks.

I shake my head. "No, I didn't."

He turns to Toby. "Check her phone," he orders.

Toby pulls my phone out of his pocket and hands it to me. "Type in the passcode," he says.

"Are you crazy?" I ask. "I'm not letting you prowl through my phone. There's personal stuff on there."

Toby grins. "Nude photos?" he asks. "Or maybe you've been sexting your boss at work? I can't wait to see this."

"All we want to do is check for photos of us," Jesse reassures me. "Type in the passcode and give Toby back the phone."

For the first time, I'm realizing the Steel Infidels are for real. Not a fictional group of men who ride motorcycles through the mountains on the weekends as a hobby. Or men who hang out at a clubhouse occasionally to drink and play pool. These are men in a real-life motorcycle gang that I know absolutely nothing about.

They could be criminals for all I know.

Probably are.

Drug dealers or pimps.

Criminals who happened to be caught in the wrong place at the wrong time.

If they didn't have anything to hide, they wouldn't have all run so fast from the scene.

And now here I am.

Alone with four of them in a room by myself.

Smart move, Maggie.

What was it that Toby just said to me? That he could take anything he wanted, whenever he wanted? Just because he didn't try anything earlier this morning doesn't mean that he wouldn't.

If I yelled, would anyone hear me or even care? Leona might. Then again, Jodi made a point of taking her off somewhere else in the clubhouse.

My heart starts beating faster. Taking a deep breath, I type in my passcode and reluctantly hand the phone back over to Toby.

"Smart girl," he says.

I stand there quietly while he flips through my phone.

"I see a few photos of my house on here," he says. "I'm going to delete those. If I ever get a hint that you're taking photos of where I live again, you won't have a phone left. Do you understand?"

His eyes are hard and cold. Not a flicker of warmth in them now. He's furious with me.

"I wasn't going to use them for anything," I say in defense. "I swear."

He isn't convinced. "Why did you take them then?"

I shrug. "Mostly out of habit," I reply.

"Are there any photos inside the clubhouse?" Jesse asks.

"Not that I can see," Toby replies. "The last photo was taken outside the gates."

"I told you I didn't take any."

"We've learned that it always pays to double check," Jesse says. "Now that we've got that cleared up, why don't you take a seat." He waves a hand at the table.

When I hesitate, Flint stands up and politely pulls out a chair for me.

"There's nothing for you to be afraid of," Jesse reassures. "We're not going to hurt you."

I laugh as if the thought is ridiculous. Never let them see you sweat is my motto.

"Of course you wouldn't," I say. "Half the nation's media saw me walk inside here. And you guys are heroes. I'm honored to meet you. Truly, I am." I'm babbling nervously now.

All four men stare back at me without speaking. Toby rubs the tiny spot of beard on his chin.

They're making me uncomfortable.

What is going on here?

13

MAGGIE

When the silence stretches to an unbearable length, I walk over to the table and sit down. Toby settles down into the wooden chair beside me. We're so close our legs are touching under the table. I move my legs away and Toby shifts, moving his so that they're still touching mine.

"Obviously we weren't expecting you to show up in the clubhouse," Flint says. "But now that you're here, there's something that we want to run by you. A proposal of sorts. It could be a good deal for you if you're willing to agree to our terms. Please hear me out before you say anything one way or the other."

My ears perk up. I'm very interested in what he's about to say.

He waves his hand toward the window.

"We're in over our heads with the media circus out there. This is way beyond what we expected. We need someone to help us navigate the press. Someone who knows and understands these things. We're aware that there will be lots of things said and written about the Steel Infidels that simply aren't true. The media is going to try to dig up every last bit of dirt they can find on us. The worse things they can find, the better the story. We're not stupid. We know how it works."

I nod my head to show him that I'm following his line of thought. Everything he's saying is true.

He leans forward and spreads his hands out on the table.

"The truth is we're good guys," he continues. "Sure, some of us have beards and a few too many tattoos. We realize that can be a little scary and off-putting to some people. That's just our style. It doesn't mean we're criminals."

"I personally don't have anything against tattoos," I say.

In fact, I suddenly seem to have a fascination with tattoos. Particularly the ink covering the tanned arm barely touching mine. I wonder about the stories behind Toby's tattoos and if I'll ever have a chance to find out. He doesn't seem to be the sharing kind, so I doubt it.

"That's good to know," Flint says with a quick, charming smile. "The members of the Steel Infidels also own several successful businesses. We do charity rides every spring. In the past, we raised over $20,000 for a wildlife rescue center here in Bardsville. My wife, Kendra, is a veterinarian, and she runs the place."

Okay, that surprises me.

"We're very involved in the community and don't want any bad publicity to come to our beautiful town because of us. We know the media isn't going away, so we need someone to help us manage what gets put out there. Since you're already involved, we were hoping you might consider helping us."

"Me?" I echo in surprise. "Why me?"

The question pops out before I think. Who cares why?

Flint smiles again. "You're a reporter, aren't you? And you were with us yesterday. You saw and heard everything the same as we did. Who better? You're local too, right here in the state. We would feel more comfortable working with you than a news anchor from ABC or one of the bigger networks."

"Have they already contacted you?" I ask.

"ABC Nightly News? Yes, along with several other major media outlets. Even television shows in the UK, Mexico, Australia, and Japan. The calls keep coming in. We're out of our league here. What do you say? Do you want to work with us?"

I'm shocked. This could turn out much better than I expected.

"What exactly are you proposing that I do?"

"We'll give you the first exclusive interview," Flint says. "When the press finds out we've already contracted with a specific media outlet, maybe they'll back off. That's what we're hoping for anyway."

I almost fall out of my chair. Instead I smile back at him.

"I would love the opportunity," I say, trying not to reveal how excited I am. "If Toby will hand me my phone, I'll call my boss at the station so he can set aside a time slot for the interview to air."

Toby snorts and then bursts out laughing.

I glance over at him in confusion. "What's so funny?"

"Nothing," he says. "Just that I told the guys you would try to run right over us if we gave you an inch, and here you go. Zero to ninety in two seconds. You haven't even asked what our conditions are."

"What conditions?"

Toby tilts his head at me.

"See what I mean?" he says.

"There are a few conditions before you agree," Flint says. "You might not like them."

I shift in my chair and cross my legs. In the process, I accidentally kick Toby with my shoe. "Oh sorry," I say automatically, trying to move my leg away from him under the table. He slides a possessive warm hand down my thigh and holds my leg still without looking at me. I try to ignore it.

"Okay, let's hear your conditions," I say. "I'm flexible."

"I just bet you are," Toby says under his breath while stroking my knee with his thumb.

Irritated, I try to push his hand firmly off my leg. He's distracting me. He grips my thigh tighter. I stop fighting him, realizing that he's only trying to aggravate me. Ignoring his juvenile tactics is the best option.

At this point, I'm realizing I don't like Toby much either. What happened to the guy I met yesterday? Maybe he wasn't real and was only a figment of my overactive imagination brought on by a horrifying event.

This Toby is rude.

And crude.

The twinkling eyes, bulging muscles, and interesting tattoos can't make up for a serious lack of class.

"For starters, you must work alone," Flint says. "We're not agreeing to a cameraman until we say he can join you. And you have to give up your cell phone when you're with us. It's the standard club rule for all outsiders."

I shake my head. "No way! I'm not agreeing to those conditions. I can't possibly work without my cell phone. And I need it to access the Internet for research purposes."

"Why would you need to do research if you're personally interviewing us?" Toby asks. "Isn't that the whole point? To get our side of the story? If you're researching the Steel Infidels on the Internet, then your opinion becomes biased, if it isn't already."

He has a valid point.

"I'm not going to make a fool out of myself by doing an interview without fact-checking before it goes on the air," I say. "My career would be ruined if I did something that stupid. I could lose my job."

"That's not what we're suggesting," Flint says calmly. "After the interview is finished and we sign off on it, then you'll be free to do your fact-checking before it goes live."

This sounds like a win-win to me.

If I find out they're manipulating me, I'll re-work the tapes and run whatever I want.

"Wait," I say when his words start to sink in. "What exactly do you mean by sign off on it?"

"If you want to run the story, you'll need our sign off on approval first," Flint explains. "If you decide not to run the piece, then you can kill it. What we won't allow you to do is change it substantially without our permission. We need final approval on anything you put on the air about the Steel Infidels."

"Last time I checked, that's not the way reporting works," I say.

Toby leans back in his chair and crosses his muscular arms. I wonder how he finds shirts with sleeves big enough for his arms to fit through.

"This is a ridiculous waste of time," he says.

"Maggie can take the deal or leave it," Flint says. "It's the only way we'll agree to being interviewed. I'm an attorney, so the agreement will be legal and binding. If you break it, we'll sue your ass off. And we'll need a separate non-disclosure agreement signed as well."

Flint's a lawyer? I didn't see that one coming either.

I should have suspected something was off, especially with the smooth, calm way he presented their offer to me. I've been thinking they're nothing but a bunch of hillbilly redneck bikers.

There is much more to the Steel Infidels than what I ever imagined.

I need to be more careful.

What they're suggesting is ludicrous. I've never let a source sway my story. Then again, I've never had this kind of opportunity either. A chance to do something really big that will make the national news stations.

It's not the first time for a journalist to agree to restrictions on an interview. Sean Penn went into the jungle to interview El Chapo for Rolling Stone Magazine. I'm sure El Chapo placed many restrictions on what he could ask about or see while he was there.

Sometimes sacrifices have to be made for the greater good.

Which, in this case, is the bigger story.

I consider their offer carefully then nod at the three brothers watching me intently from the other side of the table.

"I'm all yours, gentlemen," I say. "When do we start?"

14

TOBY

"Damn!" I mutter under my breath.

I'm not surprised at Maggie's answer. She would have agreed to any terms for the chance to get the lowdown on the Steel Infidels.

Flint's plan is fucked up.

I thought he was smarter than this. Just because I saved Maggie's life doesn't mean that she's blind to my flaws. He's hoping that if Maggie hangs around us for a couple of days, then she'll see the Steel Infidels in a positive light and be willing to do an interview slanted our way.

Right now, everyone wants to see us as a bunch of fucking heroes.

Because that's what they want to believe.

Even Maggie.

It's a stupid plan and too quickly put together for it to make sense. We panicked when Leona brought Maggie inside the clubhouse, and this idiotic idea is the result.

First, Jesse was threatening everyone not to run their mouth off to the press, and now they want to work with Maggie.

I'm confused as hell.

All it would take is one tiny slipup for her to catch on to us. Sure, we're a motorcycle club of family men with wives, children, and adoring aunts. We also have a huge gun-running and bootleg alcohol operation going.

Over the years, the Steel Infidels have been involved in numerous motorcycle gang shoot-outs with casualties on both sides.

We're no fucking angels.

We've been under investigation by federal and state agencies for various suspected activities. Most of their suspicions were true. A few activities we were charged for, and others we walked away free from.

Even if the interview goes perfectly, as soon as she gets back out in the real world, Maggie is going to know that she's been had.

I don't want to be anywhere near her when that happens. Especially not if it screws with her precious career.

"Where do we start?" she asks again.

Flint waves a hand at me.

"You'll need to stick with Toby," he says. "If you want to call someone like your family or your boss, he'll lend you one of our phones. If there's anywhere you want to go, he'll drive you."

"Whoa! Wait a minute," I interrupt. "We didn't discuss this part of the arrangement. I've got work to do. Why is it my job to babysit her? Can't one of the Sweet Butts do it?"

Flint raises his eyebrows at me. "Really? You want to trust the Sweet Butts with this? You're the hero. The one the media wants to know all about. You have to be the one to do it. Don't be an asshole about this."

Maggie holds up a hand to interrupt us.

"What are Sweet Butts?" she asks. "I don't know the lingo."

"They're the women that help out around the clubhouse with snacks, cleaning, that kind of thing," Sam patiently explains. "Like a part-time job. They come around for a few hours a day."

Maggie frowns. "How old are these girls?"

Do we know? I've certainly never asked or even thought about it.

"Not old," Sam says, making a horrified face at the thought. "We don't want any old women hanging around with wrinkles, saggy boobs, and all that other shit. That would be bad for the Steel Infidels image. Like we always say, 'we can teach a pretty girl to sweep, but we can't teach a good housekeeper to be pretty.'"

Flint shoots him a 'shut the fuck up' look.

"Except the Sweet Mamas," Sam says, trying to backpedal quickly.

"It's perfectly okay if they're old. They've been around a long time and can't help it. It's not their fault and we don't hold it against them. We're not prejudiced against old ladies."

"Sam..." Flint says in a warning tone.

Sam's eyes are wide and confused. As usual, he doesn't know when to quit and just keeps rattling on. "We believe in equal opportunity for women," he continues. "Of all ages. We are an equal opportunity employer, except we don't pay them anything."

Maggie rolls her eyes. "I wasn't concerned with how old they are," she says. "I was wondering how young they might be. Are they all over eighteen?"

Hell! I don't know.

Some of the Sweet Butts seem awfully young. I always thought someone else was keeping track of that kind of shit. Maggie hasn't been here an hour yet and she's already tripping us up.

She looks over at Jesse for clarification.

"Yes, they're all over eighteen," he says. "In fact, none of them are younger than twenty-one. The Steel Infidels doesn't need that kind of trouble, so we check IDs on everyone who hangs with us. There's alcohol in the clubhouse, and we can't have any underage drinking going on."

"That's good to know," she says with relief.

It sure as hell is.

"We're getting off track here," I say. "Would someone tell me again why it's my job to play chauffeur? What time length are we talking about anyway? Tonight? Tomorrow? How long is this little project going to take?"

"It's up to Maggie," Jesse says. "What's your schedule? Would you be up to hanging around for a couple of days? Help us work through this mess?"

"Two days?" I say, outraged by the idea. "This is some bullshit. What am I supposed to do with her for two days? I have people to meet and places to go. And where is she spending the night? Here at the clubhouse?"

The clubhouse has a couple of tiny rooms with beds for the crew to bunk in when they're drunk or hiding out from their Old Ladies. Maggie strikes me as the type of gal who doesn't like to rough it. I doubt she would appreciate being stuck in a spare room that smells of stale beer and other unmentionable things that I prefer not to think about.

Maggie glares at me.

"I wish you would stop talking about me as if I'm not sitting here," she says. "It's condescending and annoying."

"I'm condescending?" I say. "Like you're not looking down your uppity nose at us even now? Thinking how you're better and smarter? I see the way you look at us. Admit it. You're slumming."

"Where did that comment come from?" she asks. "The only thing I think is that you have a huge, ugly chip on your shoulder. What is your problem?"

My problem is that I want her.

The way she is now, with her green eyes angry and feisty. I had one taste of her sweet lips and now I'm craving more.

Much more.

I kissed her as a joke, to teach her a lesson about fucking with me. I don't like people who play games and knew she was trying to con me. What I didn't expect was how good it would feel to wrap her up in my arms.

One taste, one touch, and she had me hard and throbbing.

Hell, sex is all I can think about when she's sitting this close. It doesn't help matters that she's even hotter when she's mad, like now with her eyes shooting daggers at me.

I would be very surprised if she wasn't a wild spitfire in bed. Willing to do and say things that could blow a man's mind.

"Maggie can stay at your place," Jesse says. "Your house is way out on a private dirt road. We can put up roadblocks if needed to keep the media from getting anywhere close."

"No, sorry, that's not going to work for me," I say, shaking my head. "Sadie doesn't like people staying over."

It's true.

Sadie loves everyone, but she doesn't like it when people get physically close to me because she's a jealous little shit of a dog.

Maggie's body goes still beside me. The change isn't enough for anyone else to notice. I can feel it though. Her breathing has gone slightly shallow. My sniper training taught me how to pick up on almost imperceptible changes in body movement.

"Who is Sadie?" she asks nonchalantly.

Is that a hint of jealousy I see flashing in her pretty eyes? More than a hint maybe?

Ha! Now this is getting interesting. I sit up straighter in my chair.

"My girl," I reply with a straight face. "And she isn't particularly fond of other women coming over to the house."

"Oh," she says, clearly caught off guard by my answer. "You have a girlfriend? I didn't realize. That might be awkward then."

Now she's wondering why I kissed her this morning if I have a girlfriend staying in my house.

"I guess you could say that. I'm fond of her in my own way. She has these big, expressive brown eyes and when she looks at me, I know in my heart how much she loves me." I touch my chest. "She never has to say a word. I just know it. Right in here. Have you ever had that feeling?"

Out of the corner of my eye, I catch Sam struggling to keep a straight face. He's enjoying my game. I hope he appreciates my technique. He was a master player until Lila caught him. One of the best there ever was.

Jesse stands up and walks over to gaze out the window.

"Sorry, Toby," Jesse says over his shoulder. "She's staying with you, and Sadie will just have to deal with it. Your house is the best location."

I sigh heavily and lean back in my chair.

Game over.

Jesse is being quite the party-pooper today. At least he didn't give my ruse about Sadie away.

"If you're sure this Sadie person won't mind," Maggie says. "I'll try not to be a bother. It will only be a couple of days."

"I'll deal with her," I grumble while trying not to catch Sam's eye. "She'll get over it." A few dog biscuits will do the trick. Or maybe a tiny piece of cheese.

Jesse leans over and picks up the binoculars on the table then moves back to the window. "This is odd," he says. "Several of the reporters are getting in their cars and leaving. I wonder why they're clearing out all of a sudden?"

15

MAGGIE

The door opens without warning and Aunt Leona sticks her head inside. "Sorry to interrupt," she says. "The clubhouse phone has been ringing off the hook. Jodi sent me up here to find out what you want her to tell these folks." She holds up a piece of paper covered with scribbly writing. "Jodi's been taking down all the messages for you."

When she can't see the words clearly, she holds the paper out farther from her eyes and squints over her glasses.

"Okay, let's see if I can read her writing. So far you've gotten calls from ABC News, Nightline, 20/20, Inside Edition, Oprah, and..." She takes her glasses off and wipes them with the bottom hem of her dress. "You're not going to believe this one...Dancing with the Stars."

Sam lets out a hoot and slaps the table hard.

"Dancing with the Stars!" he says. "That would be a sight to see. Especially since Toby has two left feet. Our boy is going to Hollywood to be a fancy movie star."

"Fuck no!" Toby says, glowering at him. "This boy isn't going anywhere. Except maybe fishing. I'm already sick of all this mess."

"They're interested in you too, Sam," Aunt Leona says. "So you need to stop making fun of Toby."

"Hot damn!" Sam says, clapping his hands together. "We should do it! I can square dance with the best of them." He jumps up from the table and grabs his Aunt Leona's hand. In a deft move which she obviously knows well, he twirls her under his arm before sliding an arm around her waist and promenading her across the room. "Swing your partner round and round. Do si do and don't fall down."

"Stop it, Sam," she says, laughing and out of breath. "You're going to cause me to break my glasses. Whew! This old gal is out of shape."

"You've still got mad moves," Sam says, giving her hand one last squeeze before turning her loose. "Maybe you could be my partner on the dancing show." He looks over at Toby. "Do you remember when they used to hold square dances in the high school gym during the Sorghum Festival? There would be so many people dancing at one time that they'd open up the doors and run the line all the way out one door and back through the other."

Toby laughs and his face lights up from the inside. "Those were the good old days," he says. "The best. Doing the same thing every weekend. Friday nights meant making a beer run across the mountain and Saturday nights were the square dances. The whole town would be out there having fun."

Beer runs? Square dances? What strange land have I stepped into?

"Let me guess," I say dryly. "At least one of you owns either a Trans Am, a Mustang, or a Corvette."

Toby chuckles again and his possessive hand on my leg tightens. For someone who doesn't like me, he sure seems determined to keep me within touching range.

"Guilty as charged," Sam says with a grin. "And proud of it."

"I've got to go, boys," Leona says with a regretful sigh. "I would love to hang around longer, but there's been too much excitement today and I'm worn out. Are the reporters still out there?" She walks over to the window and pats Jesse affectionately on the back while peeking out behind the curtains.

"Most of them are getting into their cars and heading out," he says. "Must be dinnertime."

"That or my special cookies," she says, trying to hide a giggle behind a wrinkled hand. "I thought it was time they moved along and gave you fellas some breathing space. There's too many vehicles out there blocking the way. You can't stay holed up in here all night."

"Aunt Leona, what did you do this time?" Jesse asks, giving her a stern look.

"Nothing too bad," she says innocently. "Nothing criminal in any case. I handed out a batch of my oatmeal cookies. A special recipe with a couple of added ingredients. Let's just say they're good for the digestive system. Similar to fiber cookies, except a whole lot stronger. And works much faster."

She gives Jesse one more pat on the back and turns to leave. "If you want to make an escape, now is the time," she says. "I told my good friend Myra who runs the gas station down the road to lock the bathroom doors, so the reporters will need to drive all the way back into town. When things calm down, bring the kids over and I'll show them my new baby calf in the barn."

Toby pokes me in the ribs with his elbow. "How many special cookies did you eat, Maggie?" he asks while trying not to smile.

He thinks that I don't see him wink over at Sam.

"None," I say. "Are you disappointed? You want to be rid of me that bad?"

"You know I wouldn't give her any of those cookies," Leona scolds. "Here, I have a few good ones left in my pocketbook."

She digs down in the bottom of the big brown bag on her shoulder and comes out with a handful of cookies wrapped in cellophane. They're nothing but crumbs now after being dragged around in her purse. She drops them onto the table, and the guys snatch them up like starving wolves.

"Nice meeting you, Maggie," she says, slinging her purse back over her shoulder.

"It was my pleasure," I say. "I hope to see you again soon."

Toby waits until she leaves the room before speaking. "I don't have time for all this silly shit," he says. "Being stuck in this room all day is making me go stir-crazy. I've got to get out of here. You all know how I can't stand being cooped up." He stands up and stretches his arms over his head. I notice him wincing in pain and rubbing his shoulder.

"Did you get hurt yesterday?" I ask in concern.

He turns to me, surprised at my question. "Nah...it's just an old football injury acting up. If I woke up in the morning and wasn't hurting all over, I would think I was dead. Are you ready to make a run for it?

Because I'm leaving. My bike is parked around back. Now that it's getting dark out there, we should be able to make our getaway without too much attention."

"I'm ready," I say, standing up. "I'll follow you in my car. It's parked outside the fence with all the rest of the news vans."

"Leave it," Toby says. "You can ride with me on the bike. I'll grab an extra helmet downstairs for you."

The thought of being stuck with him without transportation of my own makes me nervous. "Why can't I take my car?"

"Because you'll be followed by the other media," he says. "Right to my house."

"What about my stuff? Like my overnight case? I'll need clothes."

"Rocco can drop it off at the house for you later," Flint offers. "Where are your keys?"

I take them out of my purse and hand them to him.

"Alright, let's get out of here while we have a chance," Toby says.

Five minutes later, I'm standing beside his motorcycle with the borrowed helmet strapped on my head. My head feels weird and heavy. It's too big for me and I can barely see out of it. The sun has gone down and it's getting darker.

"Here's the plan," Toby says. "If the press hears a motorcycle engine, they'll know we're coming. I'm going to roll the bike right up to the gate. We've cut all the outside lights on the building, so hopefully they won't see us until we're right on top of them. When I say the word, jump on behind me and grab my waist. Or anything else that you want to hang onto."

He glances over at me for my reaction to his lewd joke. I ignore it.

"Rocco will open the gate and then we'll make our way through the mess of people out front the best we can. Once we're on the road, be sure to hold on tight. I've been known to drive faster than a bat out of hell."

"Nice time to tell me," I say.

I'm not looking forward to this. Riding on a motorcycle on country roads at night without street lights isn't my idea of fun. I'm a city girl all the way.

"Have you ever had a wreck?" I ask.

"That would depend on your definition of 'wreck.' Do you mean laying the bike down on the road and skidding across the asphalt at sixty miles an hour?"

My eyes widen and I nod.

"Not lately," he says. "Why? Are you scared? Don't be. You've been through hell already, and you made it out alive. A little bike ride isn't going to hurt you. Besides, I never drive faster than my angel can fly."

"You don't believe in guardian angels, do you?" I ask.

I can't tell if he's serious or joking.

"The proverbial proof is in the pudding," he answers. "I'm still here, aren't I?"

I walk alongside him as he pushes the bike quietly around the side of the building and through the front parking lot. A few members of the press are still hanging around their vehicles outside the fence. Obviously the ones who missed out on the special cookies. With any luck, they won't see us until we're on our way through the gate. When we're within a few feet of the fence, Toby stops walking and climbs on the bike.

"Are you ready?" he says. "Let's do this."

I nod and climb on behind him. He scooches up a little to give me more room. Tentatively, I place my hands lightly on his waist. There's something intimate about being on the bike behind him and I'm almost too shy to touch him. Especially since I already know how appealing those ab muscles would feel underneath my fingertips. Reaching down, he grabs hold of my forearms and pulls them tighter across his rock-hard stomach muscles.

"When I said hold on tight, I wasn't joking," he says. "Don't loosen your hold or fall off. I hate scraping girls off the pavement. It's not a pretty sight."

"Wait a second! You didn't mention anything about falling off!"

He sighs loudly in exasperation. "Damn, girl! You're not going to fall off. I'm joking. Just hang on and lean with me when we go around the curves. You'll get the hang of it in no time. It's no different than riding a bicycle. You'll be a badass biker girl before you know it."

I wrap my arms around him as tight as I can. He's warm and the heat feels good against my face in the cold February night air. Snuggling up against his back, I place my cheek against his leather jacket.

"Maggie, I appreciate you listening to me for once, but now I can't breathe," he says over his shoulder. "Loosen up a bit, darling."

The word 'darling' slips off his tongue like warm butter. I could listen to him talk in his deep Southern voice all day.

And night.

Too bad he's not my type.

It's not fair.

How come preppy guys in business suits never have voices like his? Or call me 'darling' and make my insides melt when they look at me?

"Sorry," I say, relaxing my hold a little.

"It's show time," he says. "Now or never."

Rocco is watching us silently from the gate. When Toby throws up a hand to signal him, he steps up quickly and swings the gate wide open. Toby starts the bike and revs the engine. Though I was expecting it, the force of the bike underneath me catches me by surprise as we lunge forward.

"Whoa!" I say.

"Hang on," he warns again sternly.

This is going to be scarier than I thought. My grip tightens on Toby's waist. I'm sure he can breathe just fine. And if not, he'll let me know.

We roar through the gate and head for an opening between the vehicles. When the reporters spot us, they begin yelling out questions while scrambling to shoot video. Bright lights click on from every direction and shine our way. They're blinding me.

I don't know how Toby can see where he's going. Maybe he can't and is driving blind too. He doesn't slow down or look their way. Keeping his eyes straight ahead, he maneuvers through the parked vehicles and finally clears the last one.

"Dammit!" I hear one of the reporters yell when we zip past him.

Before the media has time to realize what is happening, we're free of them and on the gravel road leading out to the main highway. A quarter of a mile down the road, Toby slows down and glances over his shoulder.

"Ready to do some real riding?" he yells. "If you're scared, just close your eyes and trust me. That might be the best thing to do because I'm in a hurry to get home."

"Trust you to do what?" I say into his ear.

He doesn't answer. I wonder why. It wasn't a deep, thought-provoking question.

"Keep you safe," he finally mutters.

"I trust you," I answer automatically.

Because I do…

16

TOBY

When we hit the highway, I roll back the throttle and drive the same speed I usually do on my bike which is flat-out, wide-ass open.

Mostly to gauge Maggie's reaction.

It's a test for all my lady friends. If they try to slow me down, I know they're not the right gal for me.

I'm not all about living slow.

Not anymore.

Live life to the fullest is my motto.

As far as I know, this is the only one we're guaranteed, so we'd better make the most of it.

Every fucking day.

I live my life to honor those who aren't here to enjoy theirs any longer. It was a promise I made to my buddies in the Marines.

To her credit, Maggie doesn't squeal or carry on for me to slow down like most women do. Maybe she's too terrified to open her eyes. In the darkness, I can't tell if they're squeezed shut. The only thing I know for sure is that her body feels good tucked up close behind me.

Almost as if she belongs there.

When we turn off the main highway and start up the dirt road to my house, I feel her tense up. The only thing illuminating our way is the bike's shaky headlights, and that's not saying much. For a city girl, I guess the country could be a little scary. Except for the headlights and a few stars peeking out from behind the clouds, we're in complete darkness.

She doesn't say a word until I pull up in front of the house and cut the engine. "Home sweet home," I say. "That wasn't so bad, was it?"

"I survived," she says wryly. She slides off the bike before I have a chance to offer her a hand. "All I can say is that I'm glad it was a short trip."

"You did good for your first time. The Steel Infidels are going for a ride to Las Vegas this summer. Want to ride with us?" I ask jokingly. "You might enjoy it. We're taking the whole month of August off to ride."

"No thank you," she says emphatically. "I can't imagine anything worse."

I wonder how it would be to take her with me. In my imagination, the trip would be several days of long, hot bike rides and nights filled with long, hot fucking.

If I was a lucky man.

I rub my eyes to clear my mind of the image of her naked and warm underneath me with her long hair splayed out on the bed.

Damn!

This green-eyed beauty is going to be trouble for me. I knew it from the start. And now I'm stuck with her for two days. I'm hoping that's all.

"Come on inside and meet Sadie," I say.

Sadie heard us pull up in the driveway and is barking non-stop in the backyard. Maggie hesitates beside the bike.

"Are you sure this is okay? I feel uncomfortable barging in someplace where I'm not wanted. This doesn't feel right. Now that I've had time to think about it, I'm not sure this is a good idea."

I reach up and untuck the strands of her long dark hair that was caught in the neck of the jacket. "Who said you weren't wanted? It will be fine, I promise."

She throws off my hand without responding and sets off ahead of me toward the house. I know it's evil for me to enjoy aggravating her. For some reason, I can't seem to stop. Though I'm a little surprised that she hasn't caught on yet about Sadie.

I unlock the front door and flick on the lights. Maggie steps inside and glances around my place. It's small and sparsely furnished. Plenty comfortable enough for me and Sadie. We don't need much to make us happy.

A brown recliner sofa takes up most of the living room along with a big-screen television against the wall. A small oak dining table sits in the corner of the kitchen. My one splurge was the king-size bed for the bedroom, because I'm a big guy and need room to stretch out.

In the military, I spent too many nights hanging off the side of tiny cots. A bed was the first thing I bought when I returned home. It was my way of saying to myself that I was finally back.

From the guarded expression on Maggie's face, she isn't overly impressed with my humble abode. Not that I expected her to be. I'm guessing her place is a high-rise apartment with modern furniture and fresh flower arrangements on every table. On the weekends, her apartment is probably filled with well-dressed friends who come over for cocktails where they stand around a big glass window that overlooks the Atlanta skyline. Everything would be perfectly designed and proper. The kind of place I couldn't spend five minutes in before I would be itching to leave.

"Everything to your liking?" I ask. "We weren't expecting company."

Not that I care one way or the other.

She doesn't have to like my house as long as she doesn't bitch about it. I'm not in the mood to be dealing with a prissy-ass woman tonight. I'm tired, hungry, and need a beer. In fact, I'm bordering on hangry.

"Your place is great," she says, waving a hand at the room. "I like your big television. Do you ever watch our news station?"

"No," I lie.

She's trying to be nice and humor me. That'll work because it sure beats trying to piss me off.

I hurry into the kitchen and unlock the back door where Sadie is waiting impatiently. She jumps up on me in excitement, getting red clay mud all over my jeans, then runs into the living room to check out who I brought home.

"Hey there," Maggie says with a big smile. She immediately squats down to scratch Sadie's head behind her ears. Sadie sniffs her hand then leans against her legs, closing her eyes in contentment.

"You like dogs?" I ask. I'm not sure why I'm surprised.

Maggie gives me a genuine smile. It's the first I've seen from her. "I've never met a dog I didn't like," she says. "I wish I didn't work crazy hours so I could have one of my own. Maybe someday. Who is this pretty girl?"

"That's Sadie," I say with a straight face. I wait for the inevitable hammer to fall. She's going to be pissed. Now I'm feeling a tiny bit bad about deceiving her, since she's a dog lover and all.

Maggie's green eyes shoot to my face.

"Sadie is your dog?" she asks. "You intentionally let me believe Sadie was a girlfriend."

Yeah, she's mad at me and I deserve it. I shake my head and study an imaginary spot on the ceiling. "No, I didn't. You must have jumped to conclusions. I don't know how you got that idea. All I said was that Sadie has big, brown eyes and that she loves me. Don't you, girl?"

Sadie leaves Maggie's side and runs back over to me with her big, fluffy tail wagging. After licking my hand to tell me she's glad I'm home, she turns right around and goes back to Maggie for more ear scratches.

"Sadie likes you," I say. "She usually takes a little more time to warm up to strangers."

"Dogs know when people like them," Maggie says. "What does Sadie do all day when you're gone?"

"I have a lady who comes by every afternoon to check on her. To make sure she hasn't turned over her water bowl or dug under the fence again. One time she got out and didn't come home for two weeks. I almost went out of my mind looking for her. Called every place I knew and put up posters. It turns out a nice couple miles away from here found her and took her home with them. She had lost her collar with the tags, so they thought she had been abandoned. I never want that to happen again."

"Is she a good guard dog?" she asks. "Because I have a feeling I might need one. Against you." She stands up and pats Sadie's side. "I'm going to ask you again because I need to get this straight and I'm still confused. There isn't a girlfriend that lives here with you?"

"That's right. As I told you yesterday at the mall, there's no girl."

"We're alone here in your house? Just the two of us."

"Except for Sadie," I say, nodding.

Is Maggie scared of me? I hadn't considered it until now. I'm not sure how I feel about that.

"Are you afraid of me?" I ask. "If you remember, this wasn't my idea. You could have backed out at any time. Stop looking at me like you think I'm the Big Bad Wolf about to eat you alive."

"I'm not worried," she says unconvincingly. "However, I would like my phone back. For safety reasons. Can I have it?" She holds out her hand. "I wouldn't have agreed to stay here alone with you without access to my phone. A woman can't be too careful these days. Anything could happen."

She's playing me.

Trying to make me feel guilty about bringing her here to be all alone with me. Except it wasn't my idea and I was very clear about that. I don't feel one bit guilty.

"No, sorry. You can't have it."

I reach into my pocket and pull out my phone instead and hand it to her.

"Here's mine. Call anyone you want. I don't care. As long as I'm sitting here with you."

"Any nude photos on here?" she asks with a smirk, mimicking the questions I asked about her phone.

"Maybe," I reply. "Go ahead and check." I know there's not because it's a clean burner phone with nothing on it. No call records, no texts, and definitely no nude photos. "I'm more than happy to take a personal one just for you," I offer.

She hesitates then hands it back to me with a tired sigh.

"I'm too exhausted to talk to anyone, and I'm starving. Do you have anything to eat here? I apologize for even asking. If I wasn't desperate, I wouldn't."

"When was the last time you ate?" I ask. "You're not going to pass out on me, are you? You're a little pale."

Now that I'm paying attention, I can see that she truly is bone-tired. I wonder if she got any sleep last night. It couldn't have been much considering she was researching the Steel Infidels all night and then driving to see me early this morning. Not to mention she must have gone to the hospital with her cameraman after the shooting. I've been afraid to ask her how he's doing.

"I had a yogurt on the drive up here from Atlanta this morning," she says.

"Yogurt? That's not real food. Anything that comes in seventy-five artificial flavors can't be good. Let's go into the kitchen and see if we can scrounge up something. I don't do much fancy cooking, so our choices are limited." I take her into the kitchen and open the refrigerator. "I know there is a couple of steaks in here that I bought this weekend." I pull the two rib eyes out of the meat bin and stack them on the counter. "We can grill those. And there may be enough fixings for a tossed salad."

I dig around in the refrigerator until I find a head of lettuce along with a red bell pepper and a bag of baby carrots. After piling them all on the counter, I turn around and keep rummaging through the fridge in hopes of finding something better.

She's standing there watching me, clearly uncomfortable in my kitchen. I'm wondering how long it will take Miss Prissy to offer to help. As if she's reading my mind, she walks over to the kitchen sink and washes her hands.

"Tell me what to do and I'll help," she says.

"Can you make a salad? We'll have to make do with what I have."

"I believe I can manage," she says with an amused smile. "I have a feeling you don't think I'm capable of much."

I stop prowling through the crisper and glance at her over the refrigerator door. The way she said it makes me think I've hurt her feelings. Why would anyone think she isn't capable of doing anything she set out to do?

"No, you're tougher than you appear," I say grudgingly. "It's just that if I'd known you were coming, I would have bought groceries. And cleaned up the place a little too."

"Do you cook for yourself?" she asks.

"No, my personal chef comes in three nights a week," I joke. "I cook if I want to eat something besides takeout. Most nights it's just me and Sadie here by ourselves. I usually hang out at the clubhouse for a couple of hours after work and then come home to watch a game. The life of a biker isn't always as exciting as it may seem."

She raises her eyebrows at me. "Is that so? What about the Sweet Butts?" she asks. "I thought bikers were supposed to have a limitless supply of women. Surely there's no shortage of girls willing to keep you company at night? Or at least to cook you a meal occasionally."

I don't want Maggie knowing too much about the Sweet Butts. She might turn on us later and use it against the Steel Infidels.

At least that's what I tell myself.

Truth is, I don't want Maggie discovering the truth about the Sweet Butts for my own personal reasons. She wouldn't understand how they're part of the biker culture. Not many women would.

If I want to fuck her, and I've decided that I most certainly *do*, then the less she knows about my personal life, the better. She'll be in and out of my life in no time. The same as all the other women in my life.

"That's pretty much an old myth about the Sweet Butts," I say, counting on the fact that she won't be around long enough to find out I'm lying. "They hang out around the clubhouse until they get tired of the biker life. Then they're on to something else. You know how women are. Occasionally the girls will date one of the crew. It usually doesn't last long."

Like one night. Or five minutes.

All according to what they're offering to do at the time.

"You don't date any of the girls?" she asks with a knowing smile on her face.

"Not usually, they're not my type."

"And what would that be?"

17

MAGGIE

Toby leans on the refrigerator door and stares at me with those mesmerizing blue eyes that I find so fascinating. Who knew the color of blue could have so many distinct hues? I wonder how they look first thing in the morning when he's still groggy from sleep. Or late at night in the heat of passion. I imagine they go dark blue, almost black.

"You really want to know my type?" he says. "Okay, I'll tell you. Long, dark hair, green eyes, and lush lips." His eyes drop to my chest and I cross my arms protectively. "Large breasts," he continues, "At least a C-cup. All those guys who say more than a mouthful is a waste are lying through their teeth when it comes to boobs." He holds up his big hands and pretends to squeeze. "And a big ass. The bigger the better. None of those skinny ass girls for this country boy."

He's describing me.

"Is that descriptive enough for you? Or do you need more?"

I want more, and he knows it.

"Oh, do go on," I say, waving my hand. "I want to hear this."

"Why?" he asks. "For your interview? I don't see how my preference for women with a big old booty would be relevant to your viewers."

"You might be surprised," I say. "I'm all ears."

"You're a lot more than ears, sweetheart," he says.

I roll my eyes. He never stops with the sexual innuendos. Usually this is a sign the man isn't going to perform up to expectations. In Toby's case, I doubt I would be disappointed. The sizzling heat coming off him is impossible to ignore.

"I meant keep going with your ideal girl story."

"Sweet and sassy," he says, getting wound up now. "I like a girl with spunk. One that's not afraid to put me in my place when I need it. To speak their mind if I'm getting out of line." He rubs the stubble on his jaw thoughtfully. "Not a bitch though. I don't have much patience for that. And not a fancy girl either. I need a woman that's comfortable getting down and dirty. Who is willing to crawl up in the back of my pickup truck to help me bale hay in the summer. Or go fishing with me."

He holds up both hands.

"Only occasionally though. Not always. A man needs some alone time by the river. To think."

I wish I was writing all this down. For research purposes. So I can remember every detail later.

Not that I'm likely to forget.

"You like to fish?" I ask.

"I don't just like to fish," he says. "I *need* to fish. Like a man needs air to breathe. Sometimes it's the only thing that calms me down. Those are the most peaceful times I have these days...me, Sadie, and a fishing pole alone on a river bank. No cell phones, ear buds, or other people around to bother me."

"Why do you need calming down?"

The question slips out. I regret it immediately when his mask goes right back up. Where his face was animated a split second before, now it's blank and impossible to read. He turns away from me and takes the steaks out of the plastic wrapping before rinsing them under the water.

"Doesn't everyone need it at times?" he says. "We've all grown accustomed to so much noise in our lives. Cell phones, computers. It's almost as if we can't function without them. We're convinced we need constant stimulation. To be multi-tasking every second of the day. It's a bad habit and nothing but a big cover-up."

"For what?"

"The noise and activity prevents us from feeling alone. When it's dead quiet and there's not a device to pick up, we're forced to look inside ourselves. And sometimes it's not pretty what we see there. At least I know it's not for me."

Toby is surprisingly insightful and haunted by something. I want to know what is going on inside his head. And where the deep sadness comes from that peeks out when he thinks no one is watching.

"I know what you mean," I say. "Most days I need to be doing three things at once or I'm not working hard enough. Even when I'm driving, it feels like a waste of time if I'm not talking on the speakerphone to my station manager."

He whirls around and points a finger at me.

"See! That right there is what I'm talking about," he says. "Next time you're in the car, turn off your phone and turn on the radio instead. Full volume. It doesn't matter what station it's on. Country, rock, rap. They're all good. Roll down the window, let your hair blow in the wind, and sing at the top of your lungs. If you don't know the words, make them up. You'll feel much better, I promise you. Try it."

I shake my head at the thought. "If I did that in Atlanta traffic, everyone would think I was crazy. The police would pull me over for disturbing the peace."

He winks at me and picks up the platter of steaks with both hands.

"They might pull you over. Only to get your number. Everyone else would just be jealous because you would be enjoying life while they're stuck in misery."

"You sing in the car?"

"In my truck," he corrects. "Hell yes I sing! Every chance I get. Loud and off-key. Sometimes Sadie howls along since she goes almost everywhere with me, riding shotgun in the passenger seat."

He's relaxed and smiling now. As he's talking, I realize I would love to hear Toby sing. Or see him standing on a riverbank with a fishing pole in his hand. I might even volunteer to drive the truck if I could watch him pick up bales of hay and throw them into the back. Shirtless, with drops of sweat rolling down his back. I blink my eyes to clear the fantasy that is building up in my brain.

He tilts his head at the back door.

"Open the door for me. I'll start the grill and put these on. If you want to grab us a couple of beers from the fridge, we can talk out on the deck."

I open the door for him and rub my arms when the cold air blasts me.

"Whoa! It's chilly out there. Do you normally grill in the dead of winter?"

"If I'm doing steaks," he says. "I tried to cook them in a pan once and my house was filled with smoke for days. Plus the smoke alarm scared Sadie." He nods at a heavy coat hanging on a hook beside the door. "Bundle up in my coat. You'll be fine."

I slip on his coat and zip it up. The coat smells of Toby. After checking to make sure he's gone outside and can't see me, I take a deep breath of the collar. Maybe I'll steal his soap when I leave. I slip my hands in the deep pockets and my fingers touch a piece of paper. Curious, I pull it out.

It's an old faded photograph of Toby and three other men in the military. Toby has his arm draped over the shoulders of the man standing next to him. Both of their heads are shaved, and it's hard to recognize the much younger Toby except for his bright blue eyes. The men are all wearing big smiles. They're happy and carefree.

The edges of the photograph are worn thin from handling. I wonder how many times Toby has pulled the photo out to look at it. The men must mean a great deal to him for him to carry the photo in his pocket.

"Are you coming out here or not?" he yells from the deck.

Quickly I stuff the photo back into the coat, grab two bottles of beer from the refrigerator, and follow him out onto the deck. Sadie is excited to have company and is running around in wild circles trying to get one of us to play with her.

"Are you sure you can see well enough to grill?" I ask. "It's pitch black out here. Doesn't anyone believe in outdoor lighting up here in the mountains? You must save a lot on electricity bills." I'm freezing cold, so I jump up and down to stay warm.

Toby reaches over and hits a switch behind me. A dim, single-bulb porch light flickers on. "Better?" he says. "Don't worry, I can see just fine. I have grilling down to a science."

I nod and hand him his beer. He unscrews the top and places the cap on the picnic table in the middle of the deck. Closing his eyes, he takes a long sip. "Damn! This hits the right spot after the day I've had," he says. "There's only one thing in this world I like the taste of better than an icy cold beer."

"And what's that?" I ask, then immediately realize my mistake.

The mischievous glint in his eyes and the smile playing around his mouth gives away what he's referring to. "I'll show you sometime if you want," he replies. "Or if you want to hop up on the picnic table right now and slide up your skirt, I can show you now." He pats the table beside him in invitation.

My face flushes with heat. The mental image of Toby's head between my legs is making me go weak. Especially with that mouth of his and those full luscious lips. I have no clue how he is getting to me so quickly. He needs to stop it.

Before I do something I'll regret later.

"Either way, it's a standing offer," he says, giving me a sexy wink. "I'll let you think it over. How do you prefer your steak? It won't take long for the grill to heat up. Let me guess...medium well for you, and almost charred to the point of being burned all to hell on the edges."

"Try rare," I reply.

He cocks his eyebrows at me. "Oh, so you're an adventurous type?" He takes another sip of his beer while leaning against the deck. He studies me quietly from head to toe. Then he nods slowly. "I can see that in you. Interesting." He rubs the tiny spot of beard under his lips.

I have an urge to replace my fingers with his. Why does he leave that one little spot of beard on his face? It's unusual and immensely sexy. It makes him look mysterious. Naughty and oh so very bad.

I like it.

No, I take that back.

I love it.

"What do you do for fun?" he asks. "Tell me what adventurous, wild Maggie does on a Saturday night."

"Work," I answer truthfully. "Most of my time is spent either working or thinking about work. It's where I get my thrills."

Or I always did in the past. Now I'm mostly bored if I'm being honest with myself.

"That's what I thought," he says. "Doesn't that get old? Life isn't supposed to be about work. No matter how exciting or important you think your job is."

"I love my work," I say. "I go to interesting places and meet new people. It's exciting."

"Are you trying to convince me or yourself?" he asks with a knowing look. "How long have you been at the station?"

"Five years. They hired me right out of college and put me on the air a year later. I was lucky to be offered such a great opportunity. Other people would love to be in my position."

"I bet," he says, unimpressed. "And yet there's something missing."

"What do you mean?"

"There's a yearning in your eyes for more," he says. "You're still searching. When was the last time you felt alive? Think for a second before you spurt out some glib answer. Feeling truly alive is rarer than you might think."

I'm quiet for a moment while I think about his question.

My life *is* getting old and stagnant. I can't remember the last time when I truly felt alive.

Up until the shooting.

I felt more alive in that ten minutes than I have in years. Maybe everyone feels that way when they're faced with death.

"I felt alive yesterday," I answer. "For the first time in my life, I was faced with the chance of dying. I never knew how much I wanted to live. I've never been suicidal or anything. Don't get me wrong. I just didn't appreciate the mere act of breathing until I almost lost it."

He nods in understanding. There's a far off look in his eyes.

"I know what you mean," he says. "It's a life-altering experience, and it should be. To make you appreciate what you have. The first time our platoon came under enemy gunfire, reality hit me like a freight train. The knowledge that I could die at any time, on any day, was life-changing. You start to think about how you would want to live your life if you only had one more day. Or even another ten minutes. All the things you would do differently if you had a chance."

"What did you come up with?" I ask.

Toby is slowly but surely drawing me into his spell, sucking me into a world where I want to be right at this moment, listening to him talk about his life, his wants, his needs.

Or to show me if he can't find the words.

"I realized that the simple things in life are what brings me happiness. Not money." He lets out a short laugh. "Not that I would ever have a ton of it anyway. Don't get me wrong. I don't want to be dead-ass broke and go without food or a roof over my head. I've been at that place too when I was young, and it wasn't a cakewalk. All I need is enough money to have a decent life."

"Do you realize you're sitting on a gold mine right now if you need money?" I ask. "The publicity might be good for you and the Steel Infidels. You could make a lot of money off this if you play your cards right. What about social media accounts? Are you on Instagram? Facebook? You and Sam could also make a ton from public appearances. Maybe even hire a ghostwriter and write a book."

Toby grows still and stares at me like I've grown devil horns.

"Didn't you hear what I just said?" he asks in exasperation. "Do I strike you as the type of man who gives a fuck about money? Whatever you're trying to get me to do, I'm not interested. Stop right there." He holds up his hand. "No way, no how. I don't want people snooping around in my business. I'm not interested in fame or publicity. I want this all to go away."

"It wouldn't be forever," I say. "These kinds of things tend to burn out quickly. That's why they call it 'ten seconds of fame.' Make some fast money now while you have a chance." I wave a hand at his house. "You could fix up your place or buy a bigger house. Put some money aside for the future. What would be so bad about that?"

"My house might not be fancy, but it's home," he says curtly. "It's good enough for me. And besides, I'm not fond of change. I like things just the way they are now. The grill is ready. Time to put on the meat."

He stabs the steaks almost angrily with a fork and places them on the grill. The fat on the steaks drips down onto the flames, causing them to flare up. They sizzle loudly and smoke floats my way.

"I'm sorry," I say, realizing my words rubbed him the wrong way. "I didn't mean to offend you. I was only trying to help."

"I don't need your help," he replies. "Sadie and I are making it just fine. We were fine before you got here and we'll be fine after you leave in two days."

Well...damn. He's prickly.

Toby has shut me out tight. I guess I learned my lesson about mentioning money to him. I didn't mean to sound as if I was criticizing him or making fun of his house. I was enjoying listening to him talk. Now I've screwed things up with him again.

This isn't going well.

The smoke causes me to cough and I move my chair. Toby flips over the steaks and the smoke changes direction, coming my way again.

"I see smoke still follows beauty," he says with a hint of a smile.

"Is that your awkward way of trying to say you think I'm pretty?"

Did I really ask him that? Now I'm sounding like a high schooler.

"No, it's an old saying whenever someone changes position and the smoke still follows them," he explains. "Not a personal statement on my part."

Now I feel awkward and stupid.

"I don't need to tell you you're beautiful," he says after a minute. "I'm sure plenty of other men have told you that before in your life. I'm more of a show-not-tell kind of guy anyway. Certain words are used so much that they don't mean anything anymore...beautiful, love, I'm sorry. The list could go on and on. They're just words that need actions to back them up."

Toby is slowly warming up to me again. I don't want to screw it up and have him shut down completely.

"How would you show a woman that you think she's beautiful?" I ask. "If you don't tell her."

"Is this another one of your interview questions?" he asks. "I have to admit, I don't know much about news stories and investigative reporting. Even so, your interviewing tactics seem a bit strange. Don't you want to know about the motorcycle club instead of me? Not that I could tell you much. Flint or Jesse would be better to talk to about that."

He's right. My interview questions have gone completely off track.

"Flint's offer to interview the Steel Infidels caught me by surprise," I admit. "I wasn't expecting anything like that when you guys agreed to talk to me." I shrug. "I'm not sure which direction the interview will take, so I want to cover all my bases. Since you took my phone, I haven't talked to my station manager. In the meantime, I'll try to gather as much background information as I can. Starting with you. Then I'll work my way on to Sam and the other Steel Infidels."

"I've said more than enough for one night," Toby says. "And it's been a long day. Let's just sit here in peace for a minute, relax, and finish our beers." He pulls down the bill of his baseball cap and closes his eyes.

In other words, please stop bothering me with questions. Okay, I get it. I'm tired too. The last twenty-four hours have been crazy and I haven't stopped for one second.

I dust off one of the lawn chairs on the deck and sit down. Closing my eyes, I lean my head back to rest. After a minute, I notice the loud sound of insects coming from the woods behind the house.

"What on earth is that sound?" I ask, sitting up. "Bugs?"

"Spring Peepers," Toby replies.

I raise my eyebrows at him. "Which are?"

"Frogs. Hush for a minute and listen."

I stay silent as the sound of frogs get louder and louder until it's almost deafening to me. "Are they going to hop up here on the deck?" I ask, imagining a plague of toads creeping closer by the minute. I'm seriously getting freaked out by the thought.

"The frogs? Hell no!" Toby bursts out laughing. "Girl, where have you been living? Have you really never heard frogs before?"

I shake my head. "Not like that. Can't say that I have."

"That's hard to believe. They're one of my favorite sounds in the whole world. You should learn to appreciate them. One of these days, the frogs will all be gone and then there won't be sounds like this anymore."

Appreciate the sound of frogs? I don't think so.

"Do they quiet down enough at night for you to sleep?" I ask. I'm wondering how in the world anyone could sleep through the loud racket. Thankfully I always keep an extra pair of earbuds in my purse.

"Wouldn't know because they lull me straight to sleep," he says. "Always have. Ever since I was no bigger than knee high to a grasshopper." He holds his hand about a foot off the ground. "When I was in Afghanistan, the sound of frogs was one of the things I missed the most. And all the other night sounds of Georgia. Nothing else like it in the world."

My ears perk up and I lean forward. Now that he's brought up the subject of Afghanistan, he might be willing to talk about it. There's a hidden side to Toby that I want to know more about, especially after seeing the photograph.

"You were in the military?"

"Marines."

"How long were you in for?"

He's studying the label on his beer as if it's the most interesting thing in the world then slowly starts peeling it off from one corner. "Years," he answers vaguely. "Several long, hard years. I enlisted when I was eighteen."

"Were you in Afghanistan the whole time?"

"For the most part. We would come home every seven months. It didn't seem right though to sit my ass on a couch when some of my buddies were still there. I was always glad in a way when it was time to go back. When I was there, I wanted to come home. When I was home, I didn't feel comfortable until I went back. It was a fucked- up situation. I felt anxious and uneasy no matter where I was."

"Are you home now for good?"

I hold my breath and wait for his answer. I can't imagine how it would feel to be with a man like Toby then to send him off for seven long months. Waiting for him to return home would be agony. Or worse, not knowing for sure if he would come back at all.

"Yeah," he says. "I'm back for good."

Relief washes over me. Why do I care about a man I only just met?

"The steaks are ready," he says suddenly, putting an end to our conversation. "Let's eat. I'm starving. Enough talking for one night."

18

TOBY

Maggie's questions caught me off-guard.

I normally make it a rule not to say much about my time in the military to anyone, and yet here I am running my mouth off to her as if we're old friends.

She's easy to talk to and a good listener. Before I knew it, I was telling her my thoughts on everything from my time in Afghanistan to my love for big asses. Even when we weren't talking, the silence between us was comfortable and easy. Not strained or weird the way it can be when you first meet someone.

She's different from the other girls I've hooked up with lately. None of them could stand to be quiet for two minutes without blabbering on about absolutely nothing. Usually I don't have a clue who or what they're talking about and don't want to know. Generally along the lines of what the latest social media star is doing. Or how much they love their new pink lipstick. My head hurts thinking about them. Then again, talking isn't the reason I keep the girls around in the first place.

It's for the pussy.

Plain and simple.

A simple fact of life is that while chasing pussy serves an important purpose, it can be a fucking drain on a man's soul.

"Would you mind passing the salt?" Maggie asks, interrupting my soul-searching thoughts.

I pick up the salt shaker from its permanent place on my side of the table and hand it over. I've forgotten what it's like to enjoy a sit-down meal with a woman. Especially in my own house. Come to think of it, I don't remember that ever happening. Seeing a pretty woman across the dining table from me is nice.

Real nice.

Something I could get used to if I was given the chance. Maggie is out of my league though, so I need to put that right out of my head.

"How is your steak?" I ask. "Cooked to your satisfaction?"

"Perfect," she replies. "Nothing better than a steak from a grill. This is delicious. I was absolutely famished."

"I can make some mean barbecue ribs too," I say. "I'm the Steel Infidels official rib man."

"Really?" she says. "What exactly does being a rib man entail?"

"I'm in charge of the ribs when the MC throws parties. I make up my own special rub for the meat and prepare the slabs the night before. The day of the party, I get up early and stoke the smoker. If you want tender ribs, they need to cook all day...low and slow. Cooking ribs is a long ordeal. It takes a lot of patience. I don't know how I got roped into doing it in the first place."

She smiles at me. "You love it or you wouldn't do it. The parties sound fun. How often does the MC throw these parties?"

"Often," I reply. "At least once a month or more. When warm weather gets here, the MC and their families are together every weekend doing something. There's always a reason to celebrate...the kid's birthdays, Memorial Day, Fourth of July."

"It's weird," she says. "I always thought motorcycle clubs were about bar room brawls, drinking too much, and playing pool. I never imagined bikers as having families, wives, or little kids."

My mind goes back to the numerous times the Steel Infidels have been involved in everything from drive-by shootings to wild bachelor parties gone terribly wrong. We're hardly a bunch of innocent saints.

Far from it.

Maggie doesn't need to know. Maybe Flint had the right idea all along with this plan of his. It seems to be working out just fine now. I'm realizing I can make this work. Nobody ever called Flint Mason a fool. I need to remember that.

"The kids are great," I say. "Sam has twin toddler boys."

"Aww..." she says, "I bet they're cute as can be."

"Not really," I reply. "They're awful. Total terrors. I was supposed to babysit them last night. If the shooting hadn't happened, I would have spent Valentine's night chasing two little Tasmanian devils around the clubhouse."

"That bad, huh?" Maggie says. "You don't fool me. You adore them. I can tell by the tone of your voice."

"Yeah," I say with a sigh. "I guess I do. The little terrors are something else. Jesse and Flint both have kids too, that are a little older. The whole bunch is spoiled rotten from all the attention they get. They're little Steel Infidels mascots with t-shirts and everything."

Maggie yawns and tries to politely hide it behind her hand.

"You're flat worn out," I say. "Do you want to take a shower? I can show you where everything is at. The bathroom is small, but it's clean." I'm not used to having guests and don't know how to treat her.

"No, I'm fine," she says. "I wonder if one of your crew is still going to drop my overnight bag off here? All of my things are in it."

"I'll call Flint and find out."

We quickly clear the table of dishes and stack them in the dishwasher. Maggie excuses herself and heads toward the bathroom while I call Flint.

"How's everything going?" he asks me over the phone.

"Good," I reply. "Exactly as planned."

"I knew we could count on you," he says. "Charm the pants off her and we'll be home free. I'll be glad when this is all over and done with."

"Me too," I say with a tired sigh. "I'm already sick of the attention, and it's just started."

"Don't worry. Fame is always fleeting. This will all blow over before we know it. I give it two weeks tops and the Steel Infidels will be back to normal."

"I hope you're right. Has Rocco headed over this way with Maggie's bag? She's about ready to fall over from exhaustion."

"He'll be heading that way soon."

"Great. I'll talk to you in the morning."

By the time I finish talking to Flint and walk back into the living room, Maggie is already sound asleep. She's curled up on the sofa with my heavy coat spread over her. I don't know if I should wake her and offer to give her my bed or to let her sleep where she is.

Now that her makeup has worn off and her hair is messed up, she looks younger and more vulnerable. With everything going on, I haven't stopped to think about how the shooting must have affected her. Neither one of us mentioned it. It's almost as if we can pretend it didn't happen if we don't bring it up. Of all people, I should know that never works.

Maggie puts on a tough act. She's probably traumatized inside and doesn't even know it.

The way these things work is that it might not hit her until later. Right out of nowhere. Seeing her cameraman shot had to be terrifying. Then to not know if she would survive the attack herself. She must've felt completely defenseless and at their mercy. She had no way of knowing the lengths I would have gone to keep her safe.

I bet she hasn't let herself stop moving for one minute to think about the attack. To remember the sound of the gunshots or the screams of terrified shoppers. By throwing herself into her work and focusing on the Steel Infidels, she's been able to keep the bad memories at bay.

Sooner or later, she's going to have to talk about it. To work through the terrifying images in her head. Not tonight though. She needs the sleep.

I sit down carefully beside her on the sofa and gently touch her shoulder. "Maggie," I whisper. When she doesn't stir, I move her hair back from her face. My knuckles linger on her cheek. "Wake up, Maggie," I say again.

She curls up tighter into a ball and tugs my coat closer, still half-asleep.

"Do you want to take my bed?" I say. "I'll sleep on the sofa. You might be cold out here in the living room."

Opening her eyes sleepily, she gazes at me for a long moment. "I'm too tired to move," she says. "I'm fine here. I don't want to take your bed. You're too big to sleep on a couch anyway."

"Don't you want to at least change into something more comfortable to sleep in? Rocco is supposed to be here soon with your bag."

"No, it's fine," she mumbles. "I didn't pack anything to sleep in anyway. I usually sleep nude."

I'm sure that was a slip. Her eyes close again.

"Stay here," I say. "I'll find you something to wear. Your clothes can't be comfortable. You can't sleep in a skirt."

I go into the bedroom and search through my dresser drawers to see if I have something that will fit. Any of my clothes will swallow her whole. Finally, I choose my tightest fitting black t-shirt and a pair of grey sweatpants with drawstrings at the waist. She looks so comfortable sleeping on the sofa that I hate to bother her again.

"Here," I say to her, trying to nudge her back awake. "The shirt might work. I don't know about the sweatpants."

"Okay," she says sleepily. "I'll put them on in a minute." Her eyelashes flutter down and she's out cold again.

There's nothing else I can do except fetch a blanket for her and wait outside for Rocco. I feel bad for making a lady sleep on my couch.

It's not as if I didn't give her a choice though. I'm not going to beg a girl to let me give up my bed. The king-size bed is plenty big enough for two and I'm always willing to share. Maybe I should have offered the option to her.

I'm smart enough to know she would've turned me down flat. I'm not Maggie's type, whatever that might be.

I grab a quilt from the foot of my bed and spread it over her, being careful to tuck the ends in so it won't slide off. She mumbles something I can't make out in her sleep.

I should be feeling grateful that she fell asleep so quickly. First thing in the morning, she'll be up bright and early. Asking me a ton of questions that I don't want to answer, bugging the crap out of me, and prying into my personal business.

I prefer to keep my life a secret.

From my time in Afghanistan to my association with the Steel Infidels, none of it is anything I want to share. Eventually she'll realize that and will move on to something more interesting.

Or someone.

The thought leaves me feeling empty.

19

MAGGIE

The wet sensation of a tongue licking my hand startles me, waking me from a deep sleep. I reluctantly open my eyes to find Sadie sitting on the floor beside me. She's whining and nudging my hand with her nose.

"Sadie," I moan. "I'm too tired to pet you. Go back to sleep."

It's pitch dark outside. Now that I'm awake, I can hear the loud sound of the frogs again. I'll never be able to fall back asleep. Once I'm awake, that's usually it for the night. Insomnia is my curse.

At the end of the sofa, I spot the neatly folded t-shirt and pants Toby found for me. I was so tired at the time that I couldn't wake up enough to change. Sitting up, I quickly slip out of my clothes and put them on. I'm hoping my bag was dropped off, but I don't see it.

The t-shirt is big and hangs below my waist while the sweatpants are almost unusable. They're too long for me, so I roll up the legs and pull the drawstring as tight as it will go. I'll make it work. It was an unexpected gesture for him to take the trouble to find something for me to sleep in.

Sadie whines again and I rub behind her ears in hopes of quieting her down. She paws at my arm with her foot.

"Someone needs their nails trimmed," I say. "What do you want, girl?"

Then I hear him.

Muttering and cursing is coming from the bedroom. Loud enough that I can hear Toby through the closed door and all the way across the living room.

"Get down!" I hear him cry out. "The fucking bastards are everywhere."

Is someone in the house? Have the shooters found us again?

My first thought is to get to Toby. He'll keep me safe.

Run to Toby now, my brain tells me.

Jumping off the sofa, I sprint across the room and burst into his bedroom with Sadie right on my heels.

I realize my mistake immediately. There aren't any terrorists in the bedroom or anywhere else that I can see. Toby is alone in the room.

And completely naked.

Not a stitch of clothing or sheet covers him as he thrashes about on the bed, still cursing and murmuring fitfully. The light of the full moon streaming through the window lights up the room enough for me to see him clearly. He's sprawled across the bed on his stomach with one leg drawn up near his chest.

How is it possible for one man to take up all the space on a king-size bed?

Toby is a big guy with hard-packed muscles all the way from his neck down to his feet. There's not an ounce of fat anywhere. My eyes land on his well-defined ass and travel down his thighs to his calves.

For the first time, I'm able to see the tattoos clearly that I've only gotten a tease of before. A massive tattoo of an eagle in flight with spread wings runs across his back from one shoulder to the other. Various intricate tattoos cover both arms. The large lion's head tattoo goes all the way from his elbow to his shoulder.

His breathing is labored and stressed. Sweat has dampened his curly, jet-black hair.

"Fuck!" he mutters again as if he's in pain.

He's having a terrible nightmare. A horrendous one that he can't pull out of.

I don't know what to do. I act before I think, running across the room and grabbing his arm. "Toby! Wake up! You're having a nightmare."

A split-second later I'm on my back and his large hands are wrapped tightly around my throat.

20

TOBY

"Get down," I yell. "The fucking bastards are everywhere!"

The insurgent's bullets land all around me, hitting the walls of the building behind our platoon and sending chunks of concrete flying past my head. What started out as a simple ordinary patrol mission has turned into a cluster-fuck of massive proportions.

Don't go near the bazaar.

How many times have we been told this?

The large outdoor market is a no-go zone known to be under the command of the insurgents. To make it worse, the locals who buy and sell their goods there act as look-outs for the enemy. I've no doubt our every movement is being watched and transmitted back to forces wanting to do us harm from the time we arrived.

We know the rule.

And yet here we are pinned up against a wall with snipers firing at us from every direction. The order came in from intelligence higher up, so we had no choice but to do what we were told. To take out a small group of Taliban meeting at the far end of the bazaar. Our commander said the operation would be low risk and high reward if we could knock them out all at one time.

Low risk for who was my first thought.

Then I put it out of my mind. It's not my place to question an order.

Ever.

Even when I'm in a fucking disaster of a situation like this one.

I spot a sniper perched high on the windowsill of a building across the road. There's two more ducked down behind a truck near the street corner with four flat tires. The vehicle looks like it hasn't been driven in years, and the only thing it's good for now is cover for the enemy.

The snipers have my platoon cornered up against a concrete wall. We can't go back down the street the way we came. Our only option is through the shell-shocked building behind us where God knows what is waiting inside. What appears to be a safe solution could turn out to be a booby-trapped compound filled with improvised explosive devices.

The insurgents are known to plant IEDs in areas where the Marines might take cover. Behind a lone rock wall in a barren landscape. Or in an empty truck like where the snipers are currently hiding.

Any place is suspect.

Nowhere is safe.

My team goes ahead of me to clear the first floor of the building. They move room to room checking for hold-outs. I wonder how many times this same building has been cleared before by other platoons of Marines during their seven-month stint of duty.

Day after fucking day, we clear territory. As soon as we finish, the insurgents flood back in.

Over and over.

Like the ocean washing away a sandcastle.

Sometimes it takes a few weeks or months for the enemy to regain control of an area. If we're super unlucky, they regroup and are back in days.

I'm beginning to wonder if anything we're doing is making one bit of difference. I can't let myself think that way though. For me to be effective, I must believe one hundred percent in our mission. Any sliver of doubt will start breaking me down mentally, and I can't afford that.

Neither can my buddies.

I'm the platoon's Guardian Angel.

They depend on me to keep them safe.

Armed with my Mark 12 Special Purpose rifle, I'm expected to watch over and protect my platoon like a Border Collie watching their sheep through the lens of a telescopic sight.

My job is to constantly scan the barren, godforsaken landscape for threats. To size up every civilian and decide if they're a killer hiding in plain sight. To watch every hand movement of anyone coming near my troops.

When I was given the role of designated marksmen, nobody told me my job would also be to make split-second decisions on whether there was military justification to kill civilians.

Farmers, women...even kids.

After a few weeks in Afghanistan, I became nothing more than a well-oiled machine. Taking care of business and doing what needed to be done.

No second thoughts.

No regrets.

This is just another fucking day in hell.

I wait for the signal from my buddy, Fred, before I move. He motions, telling us the room ahead is clear, so we keep shuffling forward in heavy flak jackets with our rifles raised. In the stifling heat, the jackets and heavy combat boots weigh an extra eighty pounds.

Once we make our way to the roof of the building, I can set up a rifle position to watch the insurgents on the ground. If they're anywhere within 400 yards, I can take them out with no problem once they're in my crosshairs.

Fred carefully swings open the door of the next room and steps inside with his rifle raised. Terrified screams erupt. We all rush forward into the room with our guns pointed. Several women with their heads covered in the traditional hijabs are holding onto each other and crying hysterically.

"Get down!" Fred yells, pointing to the floor with his rifle tip. "On the floor. Let me see your hands."

They don't understand English, but they know instinctively know what he means. Their wailing only gets louder as they kneel in terror and hold out their empty hands for us to inspect.

Shit!

Do they really think we're going to shoot a bunch of unarmed women and children? The Marines have been stationed in the area forever and the locals still don't trust us.

Probably never will.

The scene becomes more chaotic by the minute.

The women are praying loudly. One has a baby who is sweating in the miserable fucking heat and flailing around in his mother's arms. He's so wet and slippery, I'm surprised he doesn't slide right out of her arms. A couple of small children with big, dark eyes are hanging onto their mother's legs, too terrified to make any noise.

I can't look at them.

Their scared little faces make my guts twist up inside. The horrible things these children must have already seen.

I don't think about it. For me to be distracted by any emotion could turn out to be a fatal mistake.

"Hold your fire!" our platoon leader yells. "It's just women and kids." He holds up a hand.

We don't shoot, but we don't lower our weapons either. Until proven otherwise, they're still a threat.

"What are they doing here?" I yell back. "The building is unoccupied. They shouldn't be here."

There's no reason for them to be gathered up in a room together. They obviously don't live in an abandoned building and aren't carrying goods to sell at the bazaar.

"Why are you here?" I yell to the oldest woman in the group.

I know she doesn't understand English.

I let loose a string of curse words at her anyway in pure frustration, which isn't helping the situation. She's clearly terrified of us. Her weak, watery eyes remind me of my Grandma. The last letter I received from her caregiver told me she was being put into a nursing home. By the time I return to Georgia, she won't remember who I am. If she dies, her favorite grandson won't be there for the funeral.

What would my Grandma think if she saw me now? Screaming and cursing at scared old ladies? Would she be disappointed and ashamed? Or would she realize I'm doing the best I can under the circumstances?

I honestly don't know.

I hate this fucking shit.

I would give my left ball to be back in the green Georgia mountains. Riding my motorcycle on the curvy roads and drinking shots of cheap whiskey with my friends. Or even better, to be between the legs of one of the blonde, big-boobed high school cheerleaders I knew from years ago.

Instead I'm in hell on earth.

Where the low temperature every day is over 100 degrees and the taste of sand never leaves my mouth.

The old lady keeps glancing toward the door. To underestimate her would be a mistake. I've made errors like that before and won't again. Everyone is a threat. She's watching and waiting.

Something isn't right.

Out of the corner of my eye, I catch sight of a dark-haired young man, no more than twelve or thirteen, step into the doorway of the room. He's thin and small, wearing tattered clothes and sandals.

I whirl around.

We never leave our backs exposed. Where the fuck are the guys watching the door?

I notice the glint of the gun in his hands as he raises it to fire without fear or hesitation. Fred doesn't see him because he's preoccupied with one of the women who is refusing to get down on the ground.

Fuck!

There's no time to think or second guess my actions.

I open fire, unloading my weapon into the kid.

He crumples to the ground.

"Motherfucker!" the Marine closest to the doorway yells. He takes a step and kicks the gun away from the kid's body.

One of the women scrambles across the floor and cradles the boy's head in her lap. She rocks back and forth, holding him and crying.

Is that his mother?

Did she know all along what was going to happen and did nothing to stop it? Maybe she couldn't.

I'm physically sick.

It takes everything I have in me to swallow down the hot bile coming up in the

back of my throat. I feel like puking up everything I've eaten the last three days.

He's just a kid.

And I've killed him.

The insurgents probably didn't give him a choice. Go in with a gun and take out as many Marines as possible.

Do it or die.

Or they might have threatened his family. His mother or siblings. One way or another, the kid was a goner. The knowledge doesn't make me feel one bit better.

My heart is pounding so hard and fast it feels like it might explode. Sweat and concrete dust drips into my eyes. The tension has gone sky high in the room. What happens next could mean the difference between life and death for everyone. Any movement could set off a rain of bullets.

Fred shoves the woman he was wrestling with onto the floor and puts the tip of his gun to her head. Whereas a minute before it was a shoving match between them, now she's dead if she makes a wrong move.

Just another fucking day in Afghanistan.

A hand grabs my arm, catching me by surprise.

I spin around and react. Reaching for the insurgent's throat, I wrap my big hands around it and squeeze hard.

Shocked green eyes gaze back at me.

It's a woman.

Kill or be killed, my mind tells me again, and I continue squeezing.

The woman grabs my forearms and tries to pull me loose from her throat. She struggles with me, scratching my skin with her fingernails and gasping for air.

It won't do her any good. She can fight me with everything she's got. In the end, I'm much bigger and stronger. I could easily snap this woman's neck in two with my bare hands.

And I will.

After what went down here today, it will be a justifiable kill. If there is any question, my buddies will back me up, just like I would them.

There is no black and white in Afghanistan. Only lines of gray that we cross every day to keep each other alive.

Something familiar about her frightened eyes slowly registers in my clouded brain and causes me to loosen my grip a tiny bit. The faint scent of her perfume floats into my nostrils.

I inhale deeply. It's been so long since I've smelled a woman.

I close my eyes for a second and drink in the sweet aroma.

She smells of fresh dew on the morning grass and wild honeysuckle growing on the side of country roads.

She smells like home.

Why?

I don't understand. How can she?

Now I'm confused. I can't breathe, and I'm struggling to draw in air the same as she is. Still, I can't turn her loose. Hesitation means death.

My throat is parched from the heat and sand. I'm suffocating to death in this hellhole. A dog barks incessantly way off in the distance.

I've never felt so lost and alone.

I struggle to open my eyes so I can finish the task. My team depends on me to do my duty, no matter what.

The beautiful woman I'm holding in my hands is already limp.

She's gone.

21

MAGGIE

I tug at Toby's large hands in a wild panic, trying with all my strength to pull him away from my neck. My windpipe is being squeezed, cutting off the blood flow to my brain. I might as well be trying to snap a beam of steel in two because he isn't budging an inch.

Fighting him is futile.

His eyes are open and focused on my face, but he's not seeing me. The dream he's in is so intense and real that he can't snap out of it.

I'm a living, breathing part of his nightmare, and he's become mine.

As terrified as I was during the shooting, it wasn't anything close to how panicked and scared I am now. I felt safe when Toby was shielding me with his body, protecting my life with his own. Somehow I knew things would be okay as long as I was with him.

Now Toby is going to kill me with his bare hands.

Except it's not Toby.

It's someone else.

Or he's somewhere else.

Far away from reality.

Either way, I'm dead.

I can't breathe. My vision is narrowing and black spots float in front of my eyes.

Is this how it feels to die?

My last thought is how devastated Toby is going to be when he wakes up and realizes what he's done. I look straight up into his confused, tormented eyes.

My world goes dark.

22

TOBY

I wake up from the nightmare with a jolt, gasping for air.

My brain is in a fog, and I don't know where I am or what I'm doing. Maggie's eyes are closed and she's limp in my hands.

Oh my God! What have I done?

This isn't a dream. At least not now.

It's real, and I've done something so terrible my brain can't wrap around the horror of the possibilities. There's no doubt I've hurt Maggie.

Or killed her.

I would never in a million years put my hands on a woman. Southern boys are taught from an early age to treat women with respect. Yet my big hands are circled around her neck.

What the fuck did I do?

All I can remember is a nightmare that felt so real.

Too real.

This can't be happening.

I shake her shoulders, hoping she has just passed out. How long have I been choking her? Seconds? Minutes? How much time has passed since she took her last breath?

As long as I live, I'll never forgive myself for this.

How could I?

My life as I know it has just ended with hers.

"Maggie, wake up," I yell in a panic. Shaking her shoulders, I try to rouse her. "Please God, don't let her die," I pray out loud. "I swear, I'll do anything."

How many times have I prayed the exact same thing before?

Please don't let them die...

Only to watch my buddies and even my best friend in the platoon bleed out on the ground right beside me. Why would God listen to me now when he didn't before?

There's always a chance. I refuse to give up. I start mentally bargaining with him. Pleading for her life. I swear to clean up my act. To go to church. To cut back on my partying.

I can't give up on her.

She just came into my life. I *saved* her life. God wouldn't be so cruel to take her now before we even had a chance. All these thoughts fly by in a jumbled blur. No more than a few seconds. Suddenly her eyes fly open and she coughs, trying to suck in air.

To live.

I quickly reach an arm around her back and pull her forward into a sitting position.

"Breathe, Maggie," I urge her frantically. "Just breathe. Slow and steady. I've got you."

I wrap both arms around her, holding her against my chest as if she were a tiny child.

She's alive.

I didn't kill her. I'm weak with relief. I've been given another opportunity to make this right.

I'm not going to fuck it up again.

23

MAGGIE

I open my eyes and suck in a deep breath. I'm dizzy and disoriented. Strong arms are wrapped around me, holding me tight. My cheek is pressed against a warm, bare chest. I feel safe until I remember.

Toby tried to kill me.

He's dangerous and deranged.

I panic and struggle against him, pushing against his chest. He immediately drops his hands and I scramble to the other side of the bed.

"Don't touch me!" I yell. "I'm warning you."

I'm breathing hard and trying to assess the situation. Is Toby going to come after me again? To reach the door, I'll have to run past him. He's fast and big. There's no way I can make it if he comes after me.

He's a killer.

Toby doesn't say a word or offer any explanation as to what just happened. Instead, he's sitting there on the bed watching me carefully. His face is filled with utter and complete despair. I've never seen so much pain in a man's eyes. He holds up the palms of his hands slowly to show that he's not going to hurt me again and tugs the sheet up around his waist to cover up.

"Maggie...," he whispers quietly, as if he no longer has the right to say my name. "I'm so sorry. I didn't mean to hurt you. I swear. Are you okay? Please tell me you're okay."

He starts to move across the bed toward me.

"Stop!" I cry out, holding up a hand. "Stay right there. Don't come any closer. Please." I'm physically shaking.

He freezes. "I won't move," he says. "I'm awake now, and I promise I'll never hurt you again. That wasn't me, Maggie. I'm almost afraid to ask, but I need to know. Exactly what happened here?"

He's awake and lucid now. His eyes are wide and clear.

"You really don't know?" I ask.

Toby shakes his head. "No. I can only imagine. I remember going to bed last night and the next thing I know, I woke up with my hands wrapped around your neck."

"You were having a terrible nightmare," I say. "I could hear you all the way through the walls into the living room. Muttering in your sleep and thrashing around on the bed. It was freaking Sadie out, so she woke me up whining. I came in here to see what was going on. You seemed very agitated so I tried to wake you up by touching your arm. That's when you flipped me over, pinned me down on the bed, and started choking me."

My hands unconsciously rub the painful spots on my neck where his hands were. "I tried to stop you," I continue, my voice trembling. "To fight back. You're too strong. I couldn't breathe and the next thing I knew, I must've passed out cold."

He turns away from me and drops his head in his hands. "I can't bear to look at you," he says. "Your neck is covered by bright red marks left by my fingers. It kills me inside to know that I put those there. What kind of a monster am I? I've never laid a finger on a woman before and never would. Not if I knew what I was doing."

We sit there for a minute breathing heavily, with neither one of us saying a word. The incident has shocked and traumatized us both too much to speak.

"We should get you to a hospital," he finally says. "To make sure you're okay. Are you in pain? I'll drive you in my truck. Or if you're afraid of me, I'll give you my keys. What am I saying? Or course you're fucking terrified of me. Either way, you should have a doctor examine your neck. And get an x-ray or something."

For a moment, I consider going to the emergency room then decide against it. All they would do is quickly separate me from Toby and ask a million questions about what happened. ER workers are trained to spot domestic abuse. If I didn't look like a victim right now, nobody would.

There's no way we could show up at the hospital together. The media would be there in minutes, and what a nightmare that would be. There's nothing they would love more than this story.

The savior turned abuser in twenty-four hours.

How could I explain the incident to anyone when I really don't know what happened myself? If it came right down to it, would I tell them the truth? Or would I protect Toby?

One look at his devastated face and I know the answer.

"No, I'm too upset to go to a hospital," I say. "There's nothing they could do anyway. Except maybe arrest you and cart you off to jail."

He nods and looks away. "That's what I deserve. Or far worse for what I did."

"Did you know it was me you were choking?" I ask.

He doesn't answer and rubs his bleak eyes with the palms of his hand.

"I know you don't want to talk about this," I continue. "I understand. But considering you almost killed me, I think you owe me an explanation. Make me understand what happened here. Right now, I'm scared to death of you. Being in the same room with you is freaking me out."

"I didn't know it was you," he answers. "I thought you were the enemy. Like you said, I was having a nightmare. They call them waking nightmares. Or reliving a real-life experience. It's hard to explain. The nightmares I have are so real. They go on for hours and I can't wake up. I've never had this happen before though."

"What about when other girls have stayed over?"

"I've never let that happen," he says. "Not since I came back home from Afghanistan. My number one rule is I always sleep alone." He lets out a rueful laugh. "I had no idea something this bad could happen. Turns out it was for a good reason."

I've read enough about servicemen coming home with PTSD to recognize the symptoms. Toby is a classic case. He's been adjusting his actions to hide what he's going through.

"You were basically sleep-walking," I say. "And perfectly capable of going through the motions of anything you normally might do while technically being asleep. Do these nightmares come often?"

"Often enough."

"What are they about?"

He starts to say something then stops. "I can't tell you." He lets out a long sigh. "I'm sorry. To talk about it brings everything up again. I'm afraid of losing control if I go there. I know I owe you an explanation. Something to make you understand that I'm not a bad person. A reason why I'm capable of doing something as horrendous as throwing a lady down on the bed and choking her."

His voice breaks and he stops talking. I quietly wait for him to go on at his own pace. He rubs his hands down his face and blows out a long, shuddering breath.

"The truth is, I think I'm a bad person," he says. "I've done terrible things in the call of duty. Every day I live with deep regret for the things I've done."

The anguish in his voice grabs my heart deep down inside and won't let go. I need him to keep talking. To let me in.

"I've killed innocent people," he continues. "And I've lost men who were close to me. The ones that didn't die are half-gone now, too. Nothing but empty shells of the men they once were. Nobody can understand unless they were there. We spent months in the Middle East trying to stay alive. Going out every day on patrol hunting for explosive IEDs in potholes or routing out enemy insurgents. The work kept us pumped full of adrenaline, day after day. It was a rush. We were a family, a tight-knit group. Then one day we came home to stay. Alone without each other's support. And now, everything is different. The world is not the same. Not for me and not for them."

My heart is breaking for him. To know that he went to Afghanistan a young, country boy full of hope and energy only to return home with pieces missing from his soul.

My head is telling me that staying in the room with a clearly dangerous person is crazy and insane.

My gut is telling me to wrap my arms around him, hold him tight, and kiss his pain away.

If only I can.

I'm not sure.

Toby is broken and damaged, maybe beyond repair.

It might not be possible to soothe his pain away. Even for a night. And he might not want me to try. There is a huge protective wall around him to keep people and the pain at bay. If he lets a crack happen in the wall, the whole thing will come tumbling down.

"I came back a different man," he explains. "I'm not the same person that I was when I left. And I never will be again. I don't even know how to begin to get back to that place."

In his husky Southern voice, I hear every fear he has and every regret.

All this and more.

Toby needs me.

He might not realize it right now or want to admit it. He's a Marine. To show fear or weakness would be against their basic principles. If I wait for him to reach out a hand to me, I'll be waiting forever. I have to take a chance and make the first bold move.

I slide across the bed until I'm right behind him. The mattress sinks down with my weight, yet he still doesn't turn to look at me. Both of his hands are clenched at his sides as if he's afraid to relax them for fear of what they might do.

"That's okay," I say. "Because the man right here and now is the only one I know."

24

TOBY

I glance down at the small hand reaching over to cover mine. Maggie gently pries my clenched fingers apart and laces her fingers through them without speaking.

The small gesture is a gut punch to my insides. I struggle to swallow past the pain I'm feeling inside.

It's almost too much to hope that she's willing to give me a second chance. Especially after what I just put her through. I'm nothing but a total stranger. She doesn't know me at all. Yet she's willing to take a risk.

On me.

For me.

It's hard for me to believe someone would be willing to do that. Most of my life I've been alone. Scraping by and making it the best I can by myself without help from anyone.

"Why?" I ask.

I don't elaborate. I don't need to. She knows what I'm asking.

"Because I see something hidden in you deep down below all the pain," she says. "I know it's there. I feel it. You're a good man inside, Toby. It doesn't matter what you've done in the past. Or even tonight. I can look past all that. I know who you really are."

I feel the tension I've been holding in my body for what seems like forever slowly start to melt away. Lifting our hands to my lips, I gently kiss her fingers. My lips linger a long second.

"Look at me," she says.

I can't.

Not yet.

I'm afraid if I do, she'll see me for what I really am. When I don't, she places a hand on my cheek and turns my face toward hers.

"See?" she says. "Take a long look. I'm still here, and I'm okay. A little freaked out and bruised, but I'll survive."

I'm not so sure.

There are bright red welts on both sides of her neck left by the imprint of my fingers. They must hurt like hell. It makes me sick inside to see them. And terrified that I'll do it again.

"How can you ever forgive me?" I ask, reaching up a gentle hand to lightly touch her neck.

"I already have," she says softly.

"Fuck...Maggie."

With a defeated groan, I pull her close and crush my lips against hers in a desperate kiss. All of the emotions I've fought so long to keep in check come flooding out. I close my eyes and drink in her intoxicating sweetness until my head reels.

Knowing that she's willing to take a chance after what I did makes me crazy. She should run out into the night screaming for help. Instead here she is, her lips soft and eager against mine.

I need her tonight.

She'll never know how much.

I wanted her the second our eyes met across the food court and never imagined in a million years that I'd get the chance to be this close. She sighs against my lips, clutching my shoulders.

Taking her arms, I link them behind my neck. My heart pounds erratically as she opens her mouth willingly to my hungry onslaught. The taste of her drives me mad and immediately has me so hard and thick that I'm throbbing.

I slide one hand under her t-shirt and hear the quick catch of her breath. Instead of stopping me, she places her hand over mine and guides it up her stomach until my hand cups her heavy breast. Her nipple goes hard when I graze it with my thumb. Moaning, she leans closer.

Tentatively, she slides her hand under the sheet that I've pulled over my waist to rest it on my thigh. I suck in my breath when her hand moves up. The instant her hand touches my dick, it impossibly hardens and lengthens even more.

"Maggie," I say, tearing my lips from her moments later, my breathing ragged. "Push me away. *Please.* I'm no good for you. You should run out the door right now and never come back. You have no idea of what you're getting into with me."

"No," she whispers. "I'm not going anywhere."

I bury my nose in her sweet-smelling hair, drinking her in. "I want you so fucking much," I mutter. "You can still say no and I'll stop right now. Even though all I can think about is how much I need to sink my cock deep inside you and stay there forever. I'm warning you. Stop me now. Before it's too late. Because God help me, I can't be the one to do it. I'm not strong enough."

25

MAGGIE

"Nobody is stopping anything," I say.

I gaze into his eyes and love the dangerous heat I see reflected there.

"Damn Maggie...I need you to tell me this is okay," he says hoarsely. "I need to hear you say that you want me as much as I need you."

He tweaks my nipple into a stiff, aching peak while his tongue ravages my mouth. I whimper in part agony, part ecstasy at his bold touch. His roughness turns me on more than any gentle caress could.

I'm unable to fight what is charging at me like a herd of bulls, and I'm quickly losing it. He wants to drive me straight out of my mind, and it's working. It's obvious there's no going back now.

Not that I want to.

I'm gripped by an insatiable craving to feel the raw hunger of Toby that I know is simmering right below the surface. To surrender to his dominance.

With no stopping and no holding back.

I want him this way.

Wild and powerful.

Overcome by my undeniable responses, I have no plans of running tonight.

He rocks his hardness against my hip, and the carnal gesture triggers a flood of heat to soak my panties. My hands clutch his head as his lips lower to seal around my nipple and suck with insistent tugs. Nothing has ever felt so good as his soft hair touching my skin while his mouth teases my breast.

His hands cup beneath my ass, half-lifting me off the bed as he reaches for the band of his sweatpants that I'm wearing.

"As good as my clothes look on you, they're coming off now," he warns.

In a single wrench, he tugs the sweatpants off and then my panties before tossing them onto the floor. His hand moves down over my waxed mound and between my legs. Finding my clit, he rubs it in a circular motion.

"You like that?" he rasps with his lips against my ear. "Your skin is so soft and warm. Are you wet for me?"

I nod feverishly, and he slides a finger into my dripping pussy. Gasping, I buck and writhe against his hand.

"Oh yes, you are," he groans against my mouth. "So wet...and *tight*."

He shoves in a second finger, and my muscles tighten around him as he finger-fucks me slowly, then faster.

"If you keep doing that, baby, I'll be ramming my cock into your hot pussy long before you're ready," he warns.

"I'm ready now," I cry.

"No words have ever sounded sweeter," he murmurs in that deep voice of his that grips my insides every time.

Toby knows what I want.

What I *need*.

It could've been minutes since I burst into his bedroom. It could've been hours. I've lost track of time.

All that matters is now.

He grabs the corner of the sheet and throws it off the bed so we won't get tangled up then settles his lower body in the cradle between my thighs. My fingers dig into his muscular shoulders as he braces his tattooed arms on either side of me, his knee nudging my legs far apart.

I feel the head of his thick, long cock rubbing against my thigh. I moan deeply and arch my back, stunned by how desperately I want this man.

Toby swears beneath his breath as he hesitates. "Shit! Almost forgot the condom," he says before quickly reaching into the bedside table and pulling one out. In two seconds, he has it unrolled on his cock and is back between my legs.

"Maggie," he whispers huskily against my lips. "I need to be inside you now."

I feel him position the tip of his cock at my opening and I hold my breath. Just as I thought the waiting would drive me insane, Toby flexes his hips and takes me in one body-splintering power thrust. As he slides in to the hilt, stretching and filling me, I gasp at the sweet-hot pleasure.

"Oh fuck!" he says hoarsely, holding perfectly still to give me time to adjust to his thickness. The pleasure of Toby settling deep inside me is intense. A single shudder sweeps through his body, and I can see every muscle standing out in his arms and shoulders. His grimace tells me that he is holding on tight to self-restraint.

"So good," he murmurs in my ear as he starts to plunge, his movements precise and solid hard.

Not trusting myself to speak, I tell him what I want and need with my body, locking my legs around his sides tightly while my hips writhe beneath him, urging him on. I hear him mutter another harsh expletive before slowly moving.

I reach up to fist his thick hair. He groans roughly when I tug harder, mirroring my hunger for him with his next round of thrusts.

I can't hold back my sounds of pleasure. Each time he bottoms out, it makes me squirm and moan beneath him.

"You're making me insane," he says through clenched teeth.

He cups my swollen breasts with both hands, fondling the flesh and teasing the tips until they tingle and burn with pleasure.

I close my eyes and feel his touch *everywhere.*

I can't tell where my body ends and his begins. We're joined together perfectly and completely. We both need this, to lose ourselves hopelessly in each other. We cling to each other like there's no tomorrow.

"Don't stop," I beg.

I'm close to climax, closer still when I hear his hot, rough breaths in my ear. He tweaks my nipple with such force that I gasp. Angling his hips, he thrusts deeper, igniting the fire raging within me. I buck my hips up to allow him to go even further, which pushes him over the edge. He grunts, the controlled, graceful slides of his thrusts turning ferocious and erratic.

I let out a cry and stiffen, my muscles clenching tightly around him as wave after wave of pleasure engulfs me. An instant later, Toby cums with me.

We don't move for a long time and I lay there beneath him, loving the feel of his strong back underneath my fingertips while he supports his weight with his elbows on either side of me. With his chest heaving raggedly, he touches my forehead with his

"You're fucking unbelievable," Toby says when our breathing slows to a normal rate. "Not even five minutes and you've got me hard and ready to go again."

26

TOBY

The sound of water running in the shower wakes me. I stretch my tired muscles, stiff and sore from sleeping the last few hours on the sofa. Sleeping isn't the right word, since I spent most of the night wide awake and staring at the ceiling.

Staying in the same bed or even the same room with Maggie last night wasn't an option. I was too terrified of what I might do again if I fell asleep.

For years, I've come up with every excuse in the world to run out the door as quickly as possible after I've fucked a woman. Snuggling up for hours after sex was never my thing. Something about the simple act of spending the night with a woman seemed too intimate for my comfort zone.

Love them and leave them. Plain and simple.

I was always honest with the ladies and never made promises I couldn't keep. The women knew what they were getting into with me.

You want to fuck? Fine.

You want a relationship? Keep walking.

Things stayed simple and uncomplicated.

This morning, I'm finding it cruel and ironic that the one time I would've loved to spend the night with a woman cuddled up under my arm, I couldn't. Now I don't know if I'll ever be able to do that.

How could I drift off to sleep when there was a chance of waking up with my hands around Maggie's throat again? And God knows how she would ever close her eyes with me in the room.

Sometimes life is a fucking bitch, delivering a low blow out of the blue just because she can. Showing you something beautiful then jerking it back when you reach out and almost touch it with your fingertips.

Like Maggie.

From the first time she smiled at me, I was lost. Then last night, she showed me how it felt to be accepted for who I am now. I haven't felt that way in a long time.

If ever.

Just the memory of her warm body underneath mine is making me grow rock hard all over again. Considering the number of times and ways we fucked, I should feel sated and be done with her. Instead I'm hungrier than ever for her touch.

I consider joining her in the shower and decide she might appreciate a good cup of coffee instead. Hopefully I'll be able to talk her into hanging around for more than a couple of days.

Now that I've gotten a taste of her sweetness, there's no way I'm letting her go.

27

MAGGIE

"What do you want to do today?" Toby asks. "Since I've been anointed as your chief bodyguard, chauffeur, and short-order cook," he says. He winks at me and my insides do a flip-flop.

He's standing at the kitchen counter measuring out coffee beans for the grinder, wearing nothing but a pair of black sweatpants. I lean against the refrigerator with a contented smile on my face, happy to do nothing but watch him. It's not every day a hot guy like Toby makes coffee for me.

"Are you still ticked off at me about that?" I ask. "You weren't pleased last night when Flint asked you to take me in. Just so you know, I'm still half-mad at you for making me believe you had a girlfriend living here named Sadie."

"Were you jealous?" he asks.

"No," I reply. "Not really. Uncomfortable with the thought of staying here with you and your girlfriend? Yes. Jealous? No."

He's not buying my lie.

"Liar," he says. "You were a little bit jealous. I could tell."

"Is that so? How?"

"I'm a master at reading body language, and I'm not giving away my secrets. I might need to use them on you later. Just admit it and we'll move past this topic of conversation. You were jealous."

I roll my eyes. "Okay, maybe a bit. Only because you had already kissed me, and I couldn't understand why if you had a live-in girlfriend."

"You said you wanted to thank me," he reminds me. "And a kiss was the best way I could think of. Okay, maybe not the absolute best way because we both know what that would be after last night. You can do things with those luscious lips of yours that a man would never forget. I know I won't."

He leans over and plants a long, lingering kiss on my lips before turning back around and hitting the brew button.

I'm liking the happy, carefree Toby. This is a side to him I didn't know existed.

"Take a deep breath and smell those coffee beans," he says. "I love the aroma of freshly ground coffee in the morning. Don't you? One of life's many pleasures."

I slip up behind him and place my hands on his shoulders. With the tips of my fingers, I trace the wings of the eagle tattoo on his back and down across his shoulders. Resisting the urge to touch him is impossible. I feel like a kid in a toy store to be able to touch him as much as I want, anywhere I want.

"I'm loving everything this morning," I reply. "Especially the muscles in your back and this amazing eagle tattoo."

I would love to know when and why he got it. I'm sure it has something to do with his time in the military. I'm afraid to mention the Marines in fear of spoiling our light mood, so I don't. There will be plenty of time for questions later.

"Are you hinting for another round of hot sex?" he jokes. He glances over his shoulder at me. "Or do you want a cup of coffee first? I should warn you. I'm an all-American male and always ready to go. All you have to do is say the word, sweetheart. Or give me a signal. Any kind of signal. And I'm there in a heartbeat."

I nuzzle into his warm neck and inhale his scent. "What kind of signal?" I ask.

"Similar to what you're doing right now," he says.

"I'm sorry, I really need coffee," I reply regretfully. I bury my face once last time between his shoulder blades and place a light kiss there before stepping away. "Besides, we can't stay in bed all day." I look at him and know what he's getting ready to say. "Or in the shower or on the kitchen table."

"The floor?"

"No, not that either," I say.

"Well, that's a terrible shame," he says. "Would you be willing to hand out a raincheck for later?"

"For you? Absolutely."

"Alright," he says with a sigh. "We might as well cook a big breakfast then. I'm starving after the workout you gave me last night. Hand me the bacon and eggs out of the refrigerator. There's some canned biscuits in there, too. I prefer homemade biscuits made from scratch but in a pinch, the canned ones aren't too bad."

Fifteen minutes later and we're sitting down to a huge breakfast. Normally the smell of bacon frying makes me almost gag. I don't have a big appetite in the mornings, and it's all I can do to eat a small cup of blueberry yogurt before noon. Today, the bacon and eggs smell delicious to me. It must be the fresh air, the country setting, or the handsome man across from me. I eat as much as I can and then get up to put my dishes away in the dishwasher.

"Would you like more coffee?" I ask.

"Sure, since you're already up."

I grab the coffee pot and return to the table. Toby holds his chipped ceramic mug up for me, and I refill it carefully as if it's something I've done a thousand times before.

The action feels familiar and comfortable.

"Thank you, darling." Toby glances up at me with those bright blue eyes and smiles.

My breath hitches in my throat.

He's getting to me.

I sit back down and enjoy my second cup of coffee while watching Toby eat. He easily finishes off a half pound of bacon by himself and three fried eggs. Considering the muscle he's packing, the need for enormous amounts of protein doesn't surprise me.

"How many eggs do you eat a day?" I ask curiously.

"Usually about six," he says with a laugh. "Three for breakfast and three boiled eggs for a snack later on."

"Seriously? That's a lot of eggs to put away. Even for a man your size."

"I've got to keep my muscle somehow. I don't eat store-bought eggs. Only fresh ones from a farm. I have friends with chickens running around their yards. They usually bring me a few dozen eggs a week. I'll come home some nights to find cartons of them stacked up on my doorstep. One time, Sadie found them first. There were cracked eggs and eggshells scattered all over the yard."

Sadie hears her name and comes over to nudge Toby's hand.

"You're a bad girl, aren't you?" he says to her while patting her side. "Such a little troublemaker." He's speaking in a low voice and she's eating it up.

"She's a lucky girl to have found you."

"The other way around," he says. "She saved me. I didn't know how much I needed Sadie until the day I found her. Sometimes life is like that. You're sputtering along, thinking you're doing just fine. And then bam! Something happens to make you realize what you were missing the whole time."

He drains the rest of his coffee and stands up. "Did you decide what you want to do today? I'll take you anywhere you want to go."

"I would love to know more about you," I say. "What your normal days are like in the Steel Infidels or what you do on a lazy Sunday morning. Show me what makes Toby tick."

"Okay, that's easy enough. It might be boring though. Do you mind if Sadie comes with us? She can ride in the back seat of the truck. I'll take you to see my fishing spot first. One of my favorite places in the whole world. You'll like it too. We'll figure out the rest of the day from there."

"Give me ten minutes to get ready," I say.

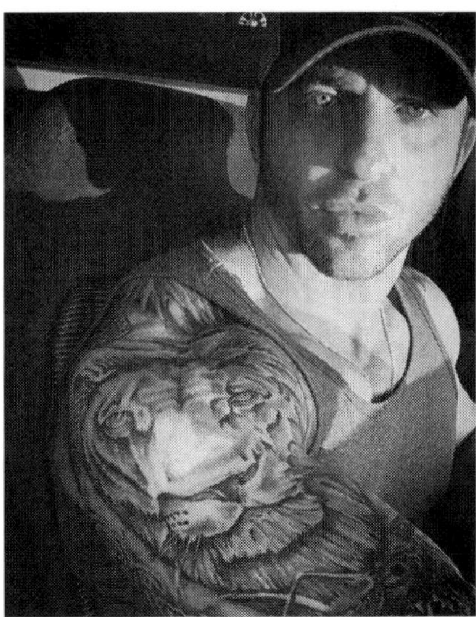

Toby opens the back door of the truck and Sadie eagerly jumps in. When I reach to open the door of the passenger side, he grabs my arm to stop me.

"Wait a second," he says. "Give me time to put a blanket over the seat. Sadie sheds like crazy and I don't want you covered in dog hair."

I wait while he spreads a clean blanket out on the seat of the truck for me. I'm wearing black jeans and a black turtleneck sweater. I was glad I packed the sweater. It covers up the purple bruises on my neck that I'm trying to hide from Toby.

If he sees them, he'll be so wracked by guilt that he'll shut down emotionally again. Today is about getting to know him, and I don't want anything to interfere with that. Hopefully the bruises will fade by tomorrow.

Toby pats the blanket. "Okay, now you can get in," he says.

Sadie shakes in the back seat and hair flies everywhere.

There's no way I won't be covered in yellow fur by the end of the day. I'm not worried. A little dog hair never killed anyone.

"Thanks," I say, climbing in.

Toby slides into the driver's seat and looks over at me. "Why are you sitting so far over there on your side? Slide over this way, darling. Where I can keep my hands on you." He pats the vinyl seat between us. "That's the best thing about this old truck. There aren't any bucket seats with a console in the middle. Just one big, long front seat."

Really?

He wants me to sit right beside him as if we're high school sweethearts? I resist the impulse to giggle and unbuckle my seatbelt.

Okay, no argument from me.

When I slide closer, he takes his right hand off the steering wheel and places it comfortably on my leg.

"Much better," he says. "And don't worry. I can drive just fine with my left hand. Even a straight shift if I have to."

I snuggle closer and run a hand down his forearm.

Yes, much better.

Fifteen minutes later, after several twists and turns on a one-lane dirt road, we arrive at the lake. Toby stops the truck and goes around to let Sadie out. She takes off chasing a squirrel and disappears out of sight.

"Sadie!" I yell after her. She ignores me and keeps running.

"Let her go," he says. "She's okay."

"Aren't you afraid she'll run off?"

Toby laughs. "Are you kidding? She'll be back in five minutes to check on me, then she'll take off again. She's too insecure about her Daddy leaving her to be gone for long. Don't worry. She'll be fine." He waves a hand at the lake in front of us. "What do you think about my fishing hole?"

Except for a few crows flying overhead, there isn't a sound to be heard. The clear lake water is still without a single ripple. Tall trees stripped bare of their leaves line the banks on all sides. There are no signs of human activity anywhere.

"The lake is beautiful and peaceful. I can see why you like it here."

"Most days it's so quiet I can hear my own heartbeat," Toby says. He takes my hand. "Come on. I'll show you the dock. If I'm only here for an hour or so, I'll fish straight from the bank. Otherwise I'll pack a cooler with lunch and walk out to the end of the dock. Sadie and I like to sit on the edge. She's a strong swimmer, so it's a good place to bring her for exercise in the summer."

"What kind of fish do you catch? Do you keep them or throw them back?"

"Most of the time I throw them back. I only keep the ones I'm planning to fry or grill for dinner. They're never wasted. Striped Bass is my favorite. The sweetest, cleanest fish you've ever tasted. Do you eat fish?"

If I didn't, I sure wouldn't tell him.

"I love fish," I say. "Every kind except swordfish. I can do without that one. And I'm glad to hear you have a few healthy foods in your diet. Something besides eggs and bacon."

We walk around a curve in the riverbank and he points to a long, wooden dock that jets out into the lake. "There's my sweet spot. You're the first person I've ever brought here. It's my secret place."

I'm pleased that he felt comfortable enough with me to share his special spot. The wooden dock is long, going several yards way out into the lake. It's narrow without railings on either side.

He looks down at me in concern. "You can swim, right?" he asks. "I didn't bring a life jacket, and the water is deep at the end of the dock."

"I was on the swim team in high school."

"Just wanted to make sure in case you fall in. Some people get dizzy walking on boat docks and fall off the edge. If that happens, I need to know if I should jump in after you or wait and see if you can get out on your own."

"I hope you would jump in to save me either way," I say wryly.

He laughs. "I'm just messing with you. I would *always* protect my queen. No matter what."

His queen.

I love the sound of those words.

28

TOBY

When Maggie said she wanted to know more about me, the first thing I thought of was bringing her here...to my happy place. The one spot where I feel peaceful, calm, and normal. Or let's be honest, as normal as I can be under the circumstances.

I wanted her to see the man I hope to be, not the out-of-control monster I showed her last night.

A fucked-up, damaged disaster.

Even after the horror of what I put her through, she managed to find a glimpse of something worthwhile deep inside me. It's hard for me to comprehend while at the same time gives me hope in myself and the strength to try my best to keep it going.

Disappointing Maggie is not an option.

She could be my queen.

The special one.

I felt more than a physical connection when we were fucking.

The word makes me wince as soon as I think it. I shouldn't call it that because it was so much more. The word 'fucking' when talking about Maggie sounds crude and just plain wrong. If someone else used the word in reference to her, I'd knock the shit out of them.

What we had last night was more than sex.

After being screwed up in the head for so long, I needed a soft place to fall and she was there with open arms. The intense emotional connection when we made love was something I've never experienced before.

Deep, emotionally intense, and scary.

I'm terrified.

I've kept my emotions bottled up for so long, and now they're pouring out like water over a dam spillway in the spring.

I'm scared that if I let Maggie *in*, I'll let the monster who lives inside me *out*.

"You're quiet all of a sudden," she says, glancing up at me. "Is something wrong?"

We're walking down the long dock and are almost at the end. The dock is narrow, not more than four feet wide. Plenty wide enough for two people to walk side by side as long as one of them doesn't stumble or trip. I let go of her hand and slip my arm around her waist, pulling her close against my side.

"Don't walk so close to the edge," I say. "It's making me nervous."

"You're really afraid I'll fall into the water?" she asks with a laugh.

Truthfully, I am. What the fuck is wrong with me?

I don't want to lose her.

"I was only trying to find an excuse to put my arm around you," I say. "And to grab your gorgeous ass." I slide my hand down and cup her ass with my hand. "You fill out a pair of jeans perfectly."

When we reach the end of the dock, I sit down on the edge and dangle my legs over the side. "Be careful and climb down here with me," I say. "If you're real still, we'll be able to see the fish in a minute."

Maggie sits down close to me and waits. "Oh look! There's one." She points down at the clear water. There's a big fish swimming around the wooden poles of the dock below us. "Do you come here more for the fishing or the solitude?"

"What do you think?" I ask.

I had no more than got the words out of my mouth when my phone rings in my pocket. Damn! I forgot to turn it off. I pull it out and check the caller.

Flint.

Must be important, since he rarely calls unless it is. He's not a man known for silly chit-chat.

"I'm sorry, I've got to take this." I stand up and walk several feet down the dock away from Maggie.

"What's up?" I say into the phone.

"There's been a change of plans," Flint says. "Bring Maggie back to the clubhouse and I'll fill you in on what's going on."

I'm not happy about leaving the lake right away and putting an abrupt end to our peaceful morning. It's the first time I've felt content and hopeful in a long time.

"Are you kidding? We're out at the lake with Sadie. We just got here."

"Tough titty," he says. "We're calling all of the crew back in. It's time to ride."

I click off the phone and reluctantly turn around. Maggie is listening to my end of the conversation. She's already standing up to dust off the back of her jeans.

"What's going on?" she asks.

"We need to go," I say. "We'll drop Sadie off at the house, pick up your things, then head on over to the clubhouse where you can pick up your car. You should probably go back to Atlanta."

"My car?" she asks in surprise. "Why? I thought I was supposed to hang around you for a couple of days? Are you in a big hurry to get rid of me?"

"Things have changed," I explain. "Flint is calling all of the crew back to the clubhouse. I'm not sure what is going on."

I whistle for Sadie, and she comes running full blast out of the woods. She goes ahead of us to the truck and waits impatiently until we get there.

"I'm not leaving and going back to Atlanta," Maggie says when we're all inside the truck. "I need to be here where the action is and besides, I don't want to leave you yet."

I blow out a long breath and grip her knee. She's as stubborn as I am.

"What do you mean by yet?" I ask.

"We're in this together," she says firmly. "I'm not going anywhere."

That's what she thinks.

29

MAGGIE

Toby is worried. I can tell. His leg muscles are tense bands of steel under my fingertips. The second he received the phone call from Flint, his entire demeanor changed. He went from happy and carefree to badass biker mode.

Both sides of Toby are equally attractive to me. Every woman wants to be loved. Every woman also needs to feel protected.

Toby is capable of doing both easily.

After dropping Sadie off and picking up my things, we drive to the clubhouse where the crowd of reporters are still hanging around the gate. From the number of vehicles parked along the road and on the grass, there appear to be more here today than last night.

If that was even possible.

"If you don't want to be seen with me, duck down in the seat," Toby says when we approach the clubhouse. "I can toss the blanket over you until we get through the gates."

"Why wouldn't I want to be seen with you?" I ask curiously.

"I don't know. I thought you might not want the other press to see you in my truck this morning."

"Who cares? They will only be jealous and wish they were me. After all, I'm getting dibs on the first interview with the Steel Infidels."

Toby has a valid point. If people suspect I'm sleeping with him, my interview will come across as biased or unprofessional. For the time being, it might be better to keep the private part of our relationship to ourselves. Or at least secret from the press and the public.

Up ahead, two of the Steel Infidels crew members are working the gate. I recognize Rocco from last night. The other guy I've never seen before.

"Who is the other man?" I ask.

"Donny, Rocco's brother," he says. "They own the auto repair shop where I work."

It hasn't occurred to me to ask Toby about his job. I assumed he worked full-time for the Steel Infidels doing something. I'm not sure what. Maybe I didn't want to know for certain. I'm relieved to hear that he has a regular job to go to every day instead of just hanging around the clubhouse.

Or doing whatever it is motorcycle clubs do.

The crowd of reporters try to film us as we drive quickly through the gate. I suspect my face will be on their news stations tonight. That's okay. All it will do is drum up publicity for my interview. When we're inside, Toby drives his truck around the clubhouse so we can go in the back door.

"Where's Flint?" he yells out to a tall, leggy blonde girl leaning against the pool table in the main room.

She straightens up and flips her long hair over her shoulders. "Upstairs," she says. "With Sam."

Her round, baby blue eyes cut over to me. The extra-long fake eyelashes she's wearing make her look like a china doll. "You're Maggie Turner from Channel 5," she says, her eyes growing bigger. "I'm so excited to meet you! I heard you were here yesterday. Will you be hanging around long? I would love to talk to you about how to become a newscaster. Or a weather girl. I've always wanted to be one of those. How hard could it be, right? I'm sure they tell them what to say."

She motions with her hands, pretending there is a map of the United States behind her. "Today we have storms in the South," she says, waving her hands in the general direction of where she thinks Georgia should be. "While the Midwest states are clear and cold." She holds out her hands. "What do you think about my nails? Should they be shorter if

I'm on air? I bet with your connections you could get me an interview at Channel 5."

I blink at her in surprise. The girl seems nice enough, and I hate to be the one to squash a person's dreams. On the other hand, she's seriously delusional.

"I'm not connected enough to do that," I say. "If you'll give me your email address, I'll send you the name of the station's personnel director."

No way am I giving this girl my cell phone number where she can text me ten times a day asking about a job.

The blonde claps her hands. "Thank you!" she squeals. "Maybe we can work together. That would be so much fun!"

No, not happening.

Toby raises his eyebrows at me in amusement. "Maggie doesn't have time for this today," he says. "We're going upstairs. Can you bring some soft drinks and snacks up for us?"

The blonde smiles at him. "Sure. I'll get them now."

Something about the way he casually orders her around rubs me the wrong way. I'm not sure exactly what's going on with the Sweet Butts. I need to find out.

"All you have to do is snap your fingers and they fetch you snacks?" I grumble on the way up the stairs.

"You should be thankful I saved you," he replies without answering the question directly. "Unless you want Chloe as your new intern."

"No, I don't. Not that my college intern is much better."

On the way to the clubhouse, Toby had let me borrow his phone. The first thing I did was check in with my intern. Her excuses were the same as yesterday. That she couldn't find any new information on the Steel Infidels because it was as if the Internet had been scrubbed clean. Since Toby was listening in, I didn't ask her too many questions. It would be pointless anyway.

From what I've seen so far, the members of the motorcycle club lead a normal, somewhat boring life in Bardsville.

Up until yesterday.

Flint and Sam are both waiting for us upstairs in Jesse's office. They're standing by the window watching the crowd of reporters. "Hey Maggie," they call out with a nod when we walk into the room. "Toby."

"Maggie, I'm sorry to have to bring your interview to an abrupt close," Flint says. "There's been an unexpected change in our plans..."

The ringing of his phone cuts him off mid-sentence.

"What did you find out, Jesse?" he asks into the phone. "You got us all a place?" He listens for a moment then nods over at Sam, who dashes out the door. "Are you sure it's secure enough for the women and kids? Okay, we'll be on the road in ten. I'll tell everyone to be at the meet-up spot in thirty minutes with whoever they're bringing."

He hits the off button and turns to Toby.

"Time to move out," he says. "We can't stay here with the media circus growing bigger every day. It's already getting old. They followed Kendra into the veterinary clinic this morning, and Lila spotted them hanging around in the woods outside Sam's house with telescopic lens trying to take photos of the twins."

"Where are we headed?" Toby asks.

Flint glances over at me.

"We can trust Maggie," Toby says firmly, taking my hand in his. "She's with me now."

"She's also media," Flint reminds him. "No offense, Maggie. I'm sure you understand our need for secrecy. The last thing we need is for the press to beat us to where we're going. We can't afford a leak. At this point, we need to think about the girls and the kids."

I nod. "Sure, nothing personal."

"You're more than welcome to ride along if you don't mind not knowing the location until we get there," Flint adds.

"I would love to," I say with a hopeful look at Toby.

"Do you remember where we spent the July 4th weekend last year?" Flint asks him.

"Sure," Toby replies.

"Jesse talked to the owner of the motorcycle lodge. He said he had enough empty rooms for all of us. We can stay there until the smoke clears. The women and kids are coming too. It will be a big family weekend getaway. We can leave all this behind for a couple of days. Nobody will be able to find us if we're discreet."

"Sounds like a good plan." Toby turns to me. "You need to go back to Atlanta and get some rest," he says. "You can't come with us."

He holds up a hand to stop me when I start to argue with him.

"Besides, shouldn't you go back and check on your cameraman?" he asks. "I'm sure he'd love to see your pretty face. It might cheer him up."

"He's going to be fine," I say.

I'm filled with disappointment. Didn't he just tell Flint that I was with him?

"Why can't I go with you?" I ask defiantly. "I want to go."

Toby sighs and rubs a tired hand through his black hair. "You won't enjoy it, that's why. Why are you arguing about this? Bike rides in February are rough. You can't come."

"I'll leave you two to work this out," Flint says, heading toward the door. "I need to let Kendra know so she can pack up Josh and the SUV. They're riding up with Lila, Trish, and the rest of the kids."

"I wouldn't want to be in the car with them for the whole trip," Toby says, making a face. "What a nightmare that would be. Do they sing children's songs?"

"I thought you loved singing in the car," I remind him.

"Not that kind of singing," he replies. "I'm more of a AC/DC kind of man. Not Twinkle, Twinkle, Little Star. About five minutes of that and I would be ready to jump out the window."

"Oh yeah, they sing," Flint says with a laugh. "Lucky for me, there's a Steel Infidels rule that says the VP is required to ride with the crew. We're wasting time. You two make up your mind what you're doing. Either way, be at the meet-up point in thirty minutes."

"We'll be there," I say firmly.

"No *we* won't be there," Toby adds. "I'll be there."

Flint shakes his head at us and goes out the door without another word.

Thirty minutes later and we're sitting on Toby's bike at the meet-up point waiting for the rest of the MC to arrive. After ten minutes of arguing back and forth and me adamantly standing my ground, Toby finally gave in. I knew time was on my side, and all I had to do was wear him down.

We quickly drove back to his house, where we called Sadie's dog sitter to come pick her up, then packed a duffel bag of clothes before hopping on his bike to meet the crew.

He cuts off the bike engine while we wait on the side of the road and then rubs my leg vigorously with his hand.

"Are you cold?" he asks. "Maybe I should get an extra sweatshirt out for you. The temperature will drop at least another ten to fifteen degrees before we get there. Maybe more when we get to the top of the mountains. The weather forecast said there is snow coming in tonight."

"No, I'm fine," I say. "Your jacket will keep me warm enough. Thank you for lending it to me." I snuggle deeper into the soft leather.

"My jacket looks good on you," he says, glancing back over his shoulder at me. "Black is your color. Maybe you're a 'ride or die' girl after all."

"I don't know about that," I say with a laugh. "Seeing as this is my first official bike ride. Talk to me about it again tomorrow. After straddling a bike for hours, I might not be able to walk in the morning."

"That's not the only thing you'll be straddling tonight," he says with a chuckle. "And if you can't walk tomorrow, trust me, it won't be because of the bike ride."

"Promises, promises," I tease back. "Let's see you put your money where your mouth is, big fella." I slide my hand lower and hover below his belt buckle. His rock-hard erection throbs underneath his jeans.

"Instead of talking about where I'm going to put my money, let's talk instead about where I'm going to put my mouth," he says, his voice growing huskier. "All this dirty talk is making me want to turn around and take you back to the house. We could sneak in a quickie and catch up to the MC down the road. It would mean driving a little faster. Okay, if I'm being totally honest, a helluva lot faster. We could definitely do it though. What do you think? Are you up for it? I'm game if you are. Live dangerously with me, Maggie."

"How much faster are we talking about if we take this little sexy detour?" I ask.

"No more than an extra fifteen miles an hour," he replies. "Or twenty tops," he adds after a moment of thinking.

"On a motorcycle?" I ask incredulously. "No way. As enticing as your offers sounds, I also want to live to see another day."

"Then you need to remove your hand, sweetheart," he says.

"Because when you're stroking my dick the way you are right now, sinking down between your pretty legs is all I can think about." He covers my hand with his and moves it away from his crotch. "I hear the MC coming down the road now anyway. You missed a golden opportunity."

"I'll make it up to you later. I promise."

"Don't think I won't hold you to that."

Several bikers pull in to a quick stop beside us, causing the loose gravel on the side of the road to fly up. It's hard to know who everyone is underneath their helmets. One of them throws up a hand at me and I recognize Sam's devilish eyes.

I count them quickly. Nine bikers including Toby. A few of the crew members have girls riding behind them. Matching long blonde hair flows out below two of the helmets. I see that Chloe, the future weather girl, made the cut for the bike ride.

Joy, joy.

She waves excitedly when she spots me. I hesitantly wave back.

"Who are we waiting on?" Toby yells out to Sam.

"Rocco and Donny stayed behind to stand guard at the clubhouse," Sam yells back. "Someone has to be there. Here Jesse comes now." He points to the road behind us where a lone biker has crested the hill.

"Hang on," Toby says over his shoulder. "Time to ride."

Jesse doesn't stop or slow down when he reaches us. Instead he twirls his hand in the air as he passes by, and the bikers all fall in line behind him. There's a set order in which the crew rides based on hierarchy in the club. Toby has hinted to me that the MC has many unspoken rules, least of which is who rides where.

I take a deep breath and hang on.

I hope this bike ride isn't a huge mistake.

30

TOBY

When Maggie insisted on accompanying me, I knew she didn't have any clue what she was in for. She is *way* out of her comfort zone.

The Steel Infidels ride hard and fast.

The same way we fuck.

Today is no different.

The ride from Bardsville to the motorcycle lodge in the Great Smoky Mountains where we're spending the night normally takes a little under three hours. That's in perfect summer weather conditions with dry roads and no stops along the way. Riding through the mountains in mid-February changes everything.

The first hour of the bike ride flies by quickly on the smooth, well-traveled road. Once we arrive at the Nantahala Gorge, things start going downhill quickly. The curvy road is treacherous and damp. An icy-cold river rushes alongside the left-hand side of the road with a strong wind blowing off it.

Maggie must be freezing, yet she doesn't complain or say a word.

I'm regretting giving in to bringing her along. She would've been safer back in her own cozy apartment in Atlanta. Instead she's wet and cold, with another two hours left to go.

"Are you making it okay?" I yell back over my shoulder.

"I'm fine," she says, tightening her arms around my waist.

"If you can hang on another thirty minutes, we'll make a pit stop in Cherokee. Give you a chance to stretch your legs for a few minutes and grab a cup of coffee."

"What's Cherokee?" she asks.

"The Cherokee Indian Reservation," I reply. "It's the last stop before we start over the Smoky Mountains. We need to keep moving if we're going to make it to Gatlinburg, Tennessee before dark. It's on the other side of the mountain range."

"Don't worry about me," she says bravely. "I'm good. Just keep your eyes on the road. These sharp curves are scaring me a little."

"Nothing to be worried about," I say. "I've driven this road plenty of times before and know every curve in the road. Relax and enjoy the ride."

I don't tell her that the drive will only get worse and that fog will be covering the tops of the Smokies before we get there. She's being quite a little trooper. I'm proud of her.

The other MC members will be watching her closely to see how she holds up. Something tells me she won't let me down. She's a tough cookie.

Once we reach Cherokee, we don't waste time. The crew knows we're racing against daylight, which will end in less than two hours. We line up to refuel our bikes quickly at a local gas station.

When Maggie excuses herself to the restroom, Sam makes his way over to me. "How's your girl doing?" he asks with a sly grin. "The two of you are already fucking, I see. How in the living hell did you pull that off so quickly?"

I hang up the gas nozzle and rip my receipt out of the pump. "None of your damn business," I say.

He snorts and throws his soft drink into the trash can beside the gas pumps. "You mean it's true? Whoa! I was joking. Tell me all the juicy details. How is she between the sheets? A tiger I bet, with those big titties and full lips. I can't believe you're already hitting that."

"Don't start with me," I say in warning. "I'm not in the mood."

His eyes grow wide. "Touchy, touchy," he jokes. "Boy, am I glad you brought her along. It will definitely make the trip more interesting." He grins. "For me anyway."

"Where's Lila and the kids?" I ask.

"About thirty minutes behind us. I just talked to her. One of the twins managed to figure out how to get out of his car seat, fell to the floor of the SUV, and threw a temper tantrum when they tried to strap him back in. They had to pull over on the side of the road until he calmed down."

"Which twin?"

"Travis."

"Figures. My god, I don't know how you take it on a daily basis."

"I'm paying for my raising," Sam says. "Or at least that's what Aunt Leona tells me. Apparently, I wasn't a perfect little angel growing up either. Here's Maggie now."

Maggie walks up to us and smiles at Sam. "Are your twins coming along for the trip?" she asks. "I can't wait to meet them."

Sam cuts his eyes over at me. "Oh yeah, we were just talking about how much fun they're having in the car," he says. "On the return trip, you should ride back with the girls. It would be the perfect opportunity to get to know all of them. They would love someone new to talk to."

"No way," I say quickly. "Maggie is staying with me."

"I was offering her a warmer ride, that's all," Sam says. He points to Jesse, who is strapping his helmet back on. "Everyone is saddling up. Time to go. See you on top of Old Smoky. Maybe it will be all covered with snow. I always loved that song."

I'd pulled out an extra sweatshirt for Maggie while she was in the gas station. "Put this on under your jacket," I say, handing it to her. "It's going to get a whole lot colder. Are the gloves keeping your hands warm enough?" My spare pair of black leather gloves look huge on her tiny hands.

"Warm enough, considering it's February," she replies. "I'm okay, I promise."

"Once we get where we're going, I'll warm you up in no time," I say.

"And where would that be exactly? You can tell me now that we're halfway there."

"A motorcycle lodge in Gatlinburg, Tennessee. We're in the Great Smoky Mountains now."

She quickly shrugs out of the jacket and pulls the sweatshirt on over her thick black sweater. "Thanks for letting me come along," she says, suddenly serious. "I want to be here. With you."

"I'm glad." I reach over to zip up her jacket tighter and pull the collar up around her neck. "I hope you can relax enough to enjoy the next part of the ride. We're entering God's country. The scenery is out of this world. Have you ever been on vacation here in the Smokies before? Maybe on a camping trip with your family?"

"A camping trip?" She rolls her eyes. "If you only knew how ridiculous that sounds. My family doesn't camp. In fact, I don't remember having so much as a picnic in the backyard. My parents are more about dinner parties and charity galas. I always thought the idea of camping sounded fun when I was a kid."

"That's a shame," I say. "You don't know what you've been missing. If you hang around long enough, maybe we can come back in the spring. Have you ever seen a wild black bear?"

Her eyes widen in alarm. "There are bears here? You didn't mention that fact before."

"Lots of bears. We won't see any this trip though. Not the time of year for it. In the spring, we might spot a Mama Bear and her cubs wandering around the open fields and split-rail fences of Cades Cove. Along with plenty of deer."

"Can I bring my camera?" she asks. "Photography is a hobby of mine."

"You bet your sweet ass you can," I say. "Cades Cove is a photographer's dream. Climb on. Next stop is Newfound Gap at the top of the mountain."

She eagerly slides on behind me for the next leg. I meant what I said about hoping she can relax enough to enjoy the ride. There's something about being on a bike that makes everything more vivid. In a car, the windows and roof block the view, along with the smells and the sounds. When I'm on a bike, I notice things I would never be aware of in a car.

It's nice having a girl to share it with. Unlike most of the other men in the MC, I was never fond of dragging along Sweet Butts on road trips. The pussy wasn't worth having to deal with them the rest of the time. They were more of a nuisance than anything else.

Maggie slips her arms around me and squeezes me once in a quick hug before loosening up. We roar onto the road behind the other crew members. I glance into the mirror and catch her smiling from ear to ear.

My girl is going to fit in just fine.

31

MAGGIE

Toby was right.

The scenery while crossing the Smoky Mountains is spectacular. I hope he was being sincere about me coming back with him in the spring because I would love to.

The sun is setting quicker behind the mountains than the crew expected, so we don't stop at the top of Newfound Gap. No matter how gorgeous the panoramic overlook view might be, I'm not eager to linger there either after overhearing the clerk at the gas station talk about sleet coming in.

It's dark by the time we reach the other side of the mountain.

Instead of driving toward the tourist town of Gatlinburg, we turn off onto a two-lane road and go straight to the motorcycle lodge.

Jesse parks in front of a rustic, Swiss chalet-style building and the rest of the MC pull up alongside him.

"We made it," Toby says after turning off the engine. He unbuckles his helmet and slides off the bike before helping me with mine. "Are you sore?" he asks with a knowing look.

"A little," I admit, swinging my leg over the bike and stretching. "It's similar to riding a horse when you're not used to it. It'll probably be a lot worse tomorrow."

"I hope not. Let's go inside and get warmed up. Would you like a hot coffee or cocoa while I get us checked in?"

"I would love something hot to drink. Anything."

Truthfully, I'm frozen and chilled straight down to the bone.

No way am I complaining about it. Toby doesn't need to tell me that the other Steel Infidels will be watching me for any sign of weakness. I don't want to be an embarrassment or source of ridicule for him.

We step inside the lobby of a huge biker bar and restaurant. On one side of the room is a stone fireplace with a roaring fire. Flat-screen televisions line the other wall. Pool tables are tucked into all the corners. Wooden oak dining tables and chairs stretch from one end of the room to the other.

No private romantic dining table for two here.

An older man with long, grey hair that looks as if it hasn't been washed in five years and a red bandana wrapped around his head hurries over to greet us.

"Jesse!" he says, reaching for Jesse's hand and shaking it. "Welcome, welcome. I'm glad you arrived before the bad weather."

"Barely," Jesse says, grabbing the older man in a bear hug. "Good to see you, Jeb. How have you been? We appreciate you giving us a place to hide out for a couple of days. The amount of media hanging around the clubhouse is nuts."

"We're proud to have you," Jeb replies. "When I saw your boys on the news," he points over to Toby and Sam, "I jumped up from my chair and ran to get Tina. I was like, 'Look! There's those Steel Infidels right in the middle of trouble again!' I was tickled pink when you called and asked for a place. I would've made room for you even if I had to throw someone else out."

"I hope we're not too much trouble," Jesse says.

"Not at all. My girls fixed your rooms up for you. This is our slow season, so I put you in the chalets down by the creek. Normally they're booked months ahead of time. Years in advance for the summer months. Before you all scatter and run off, I want to tell you now about the meals. The family-style dinner starts tonight at eight. Meat, potatoes, all the regular country side dishes. I closed the restaurant to the public so you'll have the place to yourselves. We'll serve a buffet breakfast in the morning whenever you want it."

I stopped listening at the word 'chalet' and walked over to stand alone in front of the fireplace to warm my cold hands. I'm liking the sound of that. I'm already picturing a hot tub to soak my aching back in and a big, comfortable bed for us to stretch out on. I wonder if they have room service here?

After Jeb hands out the keys, we grab our one bag from the bike and follow his directions down an unlit dirt path running alongside the creek. At this point, I realize I might have been overly optimistic about the lodging accommodations.

It turns out my definition of a chalet is a little different than Jeb's.

"Here we go," Toby says. "This chalet is ours." He points to a small, pre-fabricated wood building that looks as if it was rolled to its current location.

Four steps lead up to a front porch that is hanging precariously over the edge of the creek. If Toby wanted to go fishing, all he would have to do is stand on the porch and drop his fishing line straight down to the water.

Toby opens the door and turns on the lights. The chalet is one room except for the bathroom and is barely big enough for the full-size bed located in the middle. Knowing how Toby took up the entire king-size bed, I can't imagine how we're both going to sleep in this one.

"I'm not staying the night," Toby says as if he read my mind. "It's not safe."

"You're worried about having another nightmare?" I ask. We hadn't discussed sleeping arrangements and I assumed we would be together.

"Not the nightmare. I'm worried about what I might do to you. I'll bunk with one of the crew who doesn't have a gal with him."

I jump onto the bed and pat one side in an invitation. "There's enough room if you don't mind snuggling up with me. I'm a light sleeper. If it makes you feel better, I can lock myself in the bathroom if I hear you having a nightmare. I don't want you to sleep somewhere else."

He takes off his jacket and sprawls out on the bed next to me. The soft mattress sinks down with his weight and I roll against him.

"I don't mind snuggling. What do you think these big old cuddle-straps are for, if not to cuddle my girl?" he jokes.

He throws an arm around me and pulls me close against his chest.

I reach over to squeeze his huge biceps. "I can't think of a better use.

How did you get such massive arms anyway? They're muscles on top of muscles. Do you work out?"

"Occasionally," he says. "Mostly to keep my strength up, not for show."

"Strength for what? Lifting cars?"

"Car parts," he answers. "You're not too far off track."

His fingers trail up and down my arm. It feels *so* good and I close my eyes.

"Did you enjoy your first bike ride?" he asks.

"I loved it," I answer. "It was a thrill. Were you serious about coming back in the spring?"

"Absolutely! I'll drive you anywhere you want to go, if you're willing to ride," he says. "We can even ride to California. I've never been, and it might be fun. We can drive down Route 66 and stop at all the tourist traps."

"What about the Grand Canyon? Or Yellowstone National Park?"

"That sounds good, too," he mumbles sleepily. "I've heard the Rockies in the fall are spectacular when the Aspen trees start to change color. We could go to Jackson Hole, Wyoming. Maybe even cross over into Canada."

"I've always wanted to see the Grand Tetons," I say. "We could make a big loop. Go north first and work our way down and around the country to see everything. How does that sound for a summer vacation?"

I'm rambling, dreaming out loud and only halfway serious. As fun as it sounds, I could never take that much time off work to travel around the United States.

When he doesn't answer, I raise my head and look at him. He's asleep with his long eyelashes touching his cheeks. It should be a crime for a man to have eyelashes so long and dark. Most women would kill for them.

He is peaceful and calm for a change. His heart is beating steady and slow underneath my ear. I would love to gently push his hair back from where it has fallen across his eyes, but I don't want to wake him.

It's weird how fiercely protective I feel for a big man more than twice my size.

I know why.

Toby is special.

Unlike any man I've ever met before. A true, one-of-a-kind, once-in-a-lifetime kind of man.

I wonder how he's managed to escape being snatched up by another woman before now. They must've tried, especially the Sweet Butts. Toby thinks he's fooling me about their role in the MC, but after watching the girls, I'm onto the truth about them.

I slide my arm over his chest, snuggle up closer into his warmth, and close my eyes.

It doesn't matter how many other women came before me.

I'm the one that's here to stay.

I wake up to the sensation of warm lips pressing against my neck. When I open my eyes, Toby is leaning over me.

"We're late for dinner," he says. "Are you ready to meet everyone? The wives and the kids are here at the lodge now too."

I roll over and bury my face back into the pillow. The pace of the last twenty-four hours is catching up to me, and I'm exhausted. "What time is it?"

"Eight-thirty. If you want something to eat, we'd better head over to the bar. Jeb serves the meals family-style, and the Steel Infidels can pack away food like you wouldn't believe. If we wait too long, there won't be anything but crumbs left. Plus it's almost bedtime for the kids, and I want you to see them before they go to sleep."

"What's family-style?" I ask.

"It's similar to eating at your Grandma's house," he replies. "Jeb brings out platters of food and we all pass them around the table. Sharing the bowls like one big family. Which we are."

"I've never eaten family-style in a restaurant before," I say. "It's an interesting concept. Though I can't see it catching on in the fancier five-star dining establishments."

"First time for everything," Toby says, slapping me playfully on the ass. "Stick with me and there'll be lots of firsts."

"Ouch, that stings!" I yelp.

"Sorry, couldn't help it," he says, his tone conveying he's not sorry at all. "Your ass is too delicious not to be smacked." He laughs when I rub where he spanked it. "And worshipped," he adds. "Every day."

I reluctantly swing my legs over the side of the bed and sit there a minute without moving. The inside of my thighs and butt are already sore, almost numb, from the bike ride.

I dread standing up and trying to walk. I'm in good physical shape and try to work out on a regular basis. This is a different kind of soreness.

"You're feeling the ride now, aren't you?" Toby asks, frowning. "Anything I can do to help? I warned you our bike rides are rough. You've got to break your riding legs in. Like a new saddle. Unfortunately, there's no easy or quick way to do it. Nothing except time on a bike. I promise you, it will get better."

I stand up and feel the burn throughout my body. "When?" I groan.

"Three days?" he offers.

I walk stiffly around the room and do a few stretches for my back and legs. It's not getting better. I'll fake it until I make it. No matter how much pain I'm in, I'm not letting the other Steel Infidels know.

Toby watches me struggle then snaps his fingers with an idea. "You know what you need?" he asks. "I have just the thing."

"A deep-tissue massage?" I reply with a hopeful look.

"A double shot of strong whiskey. That'll help more than anything."

"It can't hurt," I say. "You've already talked me into it. If I get wasted, promise me you'll carry me back. I'm a lightweight when it comes to alcohol."

"Deal," he says.

We leave the cabin and start down the dark path back to the bar. Toby slips his arm around me for support so that I won't stumble or trip over a tree root. Considering the circumstances, I should be relieved that we're not camping out in a tiny tent underneath a tree. At least we have a bathroom, heat, and running water.

Things could always be worse.

Once we reach the front door of the bar, he removes his arm and ushers me in front of him into the cavernous room. The dinner is already in full swing.

If it can be called that.

The scene in front of me reminds more of a huge beer hall in

Germany than the quiet family dinner Toby led me to believe would be happening. I was expecting the Steel Infidels to be seated at the big tables with the kids strapped into high chairs, passing around bowls of food and making polite conversation.

Boy, was I wrong.

At least, Toby had the food part correct. One long table is covered with big platters of everything from fried chicken to squash casserole to homemade blueberry pies. The food smells scrumptious.

It's all the other stuff going on that confuses me.

Loud rock music is blasting through the bar's surround-sound stereo system. Our future weather girl, Chloe, as I've come to think of her now, is standing in the middle of a pool table doing a slow, grinding dance. Her eyes are closed and with the sexy moves she's making, I could swear she's a stripper.

A handful of bikers are gathered around the pool table, holding bottles of beer and egging her on. I don't see the man she rode over here with. I guess it doesn't matter. She obviously belongs to the whole group. The thought is disturbing.

"Show us your tits!" one of the younger men yells up at her. "Let us see those fat nipples."

Chloe smiles at him and reaches for the hem of her tight white sweater and starts to pull it over her head.

"Whoa! Hang onto your shirt!" A short woman with curly dark hair standing in front of the fireplace rushes across the room and stops at the pool table. She puts her hands on her ample hips and looks up at Chloe, who has abruptly stopped dancing. "Chloe! What are you doing? Get down from there this instant. The kids are here. Show some decency for once."

Chloe appears more confused than ashamed. "Sorry, Kendra," she tries to explain. "It was their idea." She waves a hand at the men hanging around the pool table.

Kendra rolls her eyes and shakes her head in dismay. "Chloe, it's perfectly okay to think for yourself sometimes." She turns around and smacks the oldest man in the group hard on his arm. "Tom Brewer, I'm surprised at you. You're too old for this silliness. How old are you now? Almost fifty? Help her down for heaven's sake. What are you all thinking? Do you not see little Josh and Missy over there trying to eat dinner? Can't you at least wait until they go to bed before you start this foolishness?"

She points to a table in a corner where a curly-headed little boy about three years old and a younger, blonde-haired girl are sitting. They're giggling and stealing food from each other's plate.

I glance up at Toby. "Who is she?" I whisper. "I love her already."

He chuckles. "That spitfire would be Flint's wife, Kendra. She's hell on wheels and doesn't put up with any shit from nobody. Especially not from one of the Sweet Butts."

My kind of woman.

"She's the town veterinarian. I've lost count of how many times I've called her in the middle of the night after Sadie has eaten something she shouldn't. Usually popsicle sticks or a roll of paper towels."

"Are those her kids?" I ask.

"Josh belongs to Flint and Kendra, while Missy is Jesse and Trisha's pride and joy. Missy is named after their mom. She passed away several years ago from breast cancer when Sam and I were in high school. It's a shame because she would have loved her grandbabies."

He motions to a pretty young woman with long brown hair sitting with the kids. "That's Trish, Jesse's wife. Jesse met her in Panama City Beach, Florida. The Steel Infidels went down there for Flint's bachelor party and all hell broke loose. I was in Afghanistan at the time, so I missed out on all the fun."

"So almost everyone in the Steel Infidels is taken except for you?"

"Who says I'm not taken?" he jokes. He slings an arm around my shoulder and pulls me tight against him. "Let's get a drink at the bar and I'll introduce you to everyone."

We make our way over to the long wooden bar that stretches along one wall. Several crew members and Sweet Butts are crowded close around it instead of sitting on the bar stools.

"Be careful!" I hear one of the bikers suddenly yell. "Watch out and don't fall!"

The group goes dead silent, then applause breaks out. Something is going on that I can't see through the crowd. Maybe another Sweet Butt is performing a specialty act, like standing on her head or something equally ridiculous since there's a risk of falling.

Toby squeezes us in beside Sam, who is leaning on the bar with a beer in his hand. "What's going on?" he asks. He positions me in front of him so I can get a better look.

"See for yourselves," Sam says, waving his bottle toward the end of the bar. "You would think the long car ride would've worn them out. But no..."

I peek over his shoulder. One of Sam's toddlers is charging full speed on chubby little legs down the middle of the bar that has been cleared of all glassware. When he reaches the end, he fearlessly dives off without hesitation into his Uncle Jesse's big, tatted arms like he's crowd-surfing at a rock concert.

He squeals in delight when Jesse tosses him high up into the air then stands him back up on the bar to run in the other direction. When he's halfway there, he passes his twin brother who is doing the same thing, only slightly slower. The twins briefly reach out to touch fingertips as they pass and then keep going. Flint is working the other end of the bar, grabbing and throwing them the same as Jesse.

"This is what the Steel Infidels do for entertainment?" I say to Toby over my shoulder. "Toddler juggling?"

"They're only getting started," Toby replies with a laugh. "The twins could do this all night and never get tired. I told you they were spoiled. The kids have the entire MC at their disposal. It takes all of us to keep them out of trouble. Look at Lila over there, playing defense and trying to make sure they don't fall off the other side. The poor woman never gets any rest."

Guarding the other side of the bar is an edgy-looking woman with shoulder-length red hair with bright purple streaks. She's wearing a pair of tight jeans and a t-shirt that says, "Fear the Honey Pot." Her arms are crossed nonchalantly. She isn't the least bit concerned that her twins are in imminent danger of breaking a bone if they fall off or if they're dropped. She's cool and calm.

The computer hacker.

"Is that your wife?" I ask Sam in surprise, nudging him with my elbow.

She's nothing close to what I pictured her to be. I can't imagine how the two of them hooked up together. They appear to be wildly different. I would love to know their story.

Sam looks over the bar at his wife and winks when he catches her eye. I can feel the smoldering heat passing between them. "Yep, that's my Old Lady," he answers, not taking his eyes from her.

"You'd better watch out," Toby warns. "The last time Lila heard you call her that, she took you down to the floor in a split-second with one of her karate moves." Toby makes a slicing motion with his hand. "One chop and you were on your knees. It was funny as hell. Lila didn't give a second thought about who was watching or anything. Just bam! Knocked your ass down to the ground right in front of everyone."

Sam snickers. "You should see what Lila can do when she's not mad," he says. "I never cease to be amazed by that woman."

"There are many smart people in this room," Toby says to me. "Lawyers, veterinarians. Except Lila takes smart to a whole different level." He raises his hand way above his head. "Freaky, scary smart. She can do things other people can't even dream up as a possibility."

"And that's *exactly* what terrifies me most about the twins," Sam says. "Think about it. They've inherited my troublemaker genes and her off-the-chart brain power. Not a good combination in my way of thinking."

"Bardsville had better watch out when those boys turn into teenagers," Toby says. "The place will never be the same."

Sam sighs and takes a long swig of his beer. "You can say that again."

The toddlers run two more laps, then Jesse grabs the fastest one and sits him up high on his shoulders. The child grips onto Jesse's hair and squeals, showing four little baby teeth.

"Time to eat," Jesse says. "We don't want Jeb's good cooking to go to waste. Everyone head on over to the table and dig in."

The family-style dinner turned out to be how Toby described it once we all sat down at the tables. Jeb's wife and girls brought out bowl after bowl of food that we quickly passed around. Just when I thought I couldn't possibly eat another bite, they came out with the desserts.

After everyone enjoyed second helpings of pie and the plates had been cleared, the men begin leaving the table and heading over to the fireplace.

"Did you get enough to eat?" Toby asks politely.

"Are you kidding?" I reply. "I'm stuffed. If I hang around you for much longer, I'll be fat as a butterball."

"You'll never hear me complaining about curves," he says. He reaches over and pushes my hair back over my shoulder. His fingers stroke the nape of my neck, sending a delicious shiver down my spine. "When you get finished, come over and watch," he says before standing up and pushing his chair back under the table.

"Watch what?" I ask curiously.

"You'll see," he says with a cocky grin.

I turn to Jesse's wife, Trish, on the other side of me and ask, "What happens now?"

She glances over at Lila, who is finishing up a piece of pie. "I don't know. The boys must have a game in mind. What would you guess they're up to this time, Lila? A game of pool isn't action-oriented enough for them when they're in a competitive mood. Darts, maybe?"

"Possibly," Lila says, frowning at the thought. "It always makes me nervous when they play around with sharp objects. Especially with the kids in the room. I'm going to put the twins to bed before it starts, whatever it is. The last thing I need is the twins getting their grubby little hands on darts. I should try to grab them now."

She gets up quickly and tries to corral the twins, who had escaped from the table several minutes before. They see her coming their way and duck under the tables so she can't reach them.

Her mission appears hopeless until Sam rushes over to help. He grabs onto a squirming leg to keep one of the twins from going farther under the table while Lila scoops up the other one into her arms. Sam finally gets a good grip on the twin he has and pulls him out. They hurry toward the front door with each of them carrying an unhappy twin over their shoulders, both of whom are kicking and screaming.

"Don't start without me," Sam yells back to the men. "We could use some help if there are any volunteers."

Nobody steps forward.

"Hell no, not me," the men mutter and hold up their hands. "No fucking way."

Trish waves as they pass by our table on their way out. "I pulled the lucky card in the family with our daughter, Missy. I don't know how I would handle those twins on a full-time basis. Lila is incredible. She never breaks a sweat or complains. She calmly does what she needs to do and never gets flustered. Sam is the same way. They make quite a team and are amazing together."

"I can see that," I say. "I'm exhausted just from watching them."

"Oh, here we go," she says. "They're getting ready to start."

The men have moved to an empty table. Two of the youngest Steel Infidels are taking seats on opposite sides of each other.

"The competition of the night is arm wrestling," she says. "If you hang around long enough, you'll learn how super competitive the Steel Infidels are in everything they do. It borders on ridiculous. They never have a get-together without competing in something. The drinking contests are the worst. When they say the winner is the last man standing, that's exactly what they mean. They drink until they pass out dead drunk."

Jesse walks around to stand at the head of the table. "Okay, gentlemen," he says. "You know the rules. As always, we'll start with the newest members in the MC. Pair off in order. The winner goes into the next round. Let's begin."

The two men put their elbows on the table and grab each other's hands. From the determined glint in their eyes, I can tell this is serious business. If I was a betting person, I would go for the guy with a Steel Infidels tattoo running down the length of his neck.

"Wait!" Kendra calls out loudly. "Don't start yet. You know the ground rules when the wives are present. Shirts off, bikers. Let's go." She makes a beckoning motion with her fingers. "Throw those shirts this way. Come to Mama!"

Jesse holds up his hand to stop the men from beginning the competition. "Kendra, it's twenty-five degrees outside," he says patiently. "Not a hot summer day at a picnic."

"Ask me if I care, Mr. President," she snaps back, firmly standing her ground. "The rules are the rules. And it's plenty warm enough in here. If you fellas are cold, you can move the table over there by the fireplace. You've got to give us ladies something good. After all, you dragged us all the way up here into the Smoky Mountains in the dead of winter. Make it worth our time."

The men are watching Jesse carefully. I'm not sure if Kendra is stepping out of bounds or if this is something the wives can get away with. I raise my eyebrows at Trish. "What's this all about?"

"Sex," she replies with a giggle, leaning closer. "I mean ultimately, that's what it's about. They'll give in if they want to get lucky tonight. Pay attention. All we have to do is wait them out. Works like a charm every single time. They'll play hard to get, but they'll take the shirts off. It's a game we love to play with them. And it's so *hot* to watch."

Kendra crosses her arms and stares pointedly at Flint. He sighs heavily and then starts unbuttoning his flannel shirt. When he finishes with the last button, he shrugs it off and walks over to hand it to her.

"Happy now?" he asks, raising his eyebrows at her.

She runs her hand slowly down his muscular pecs and back up again. "You bet I am," she replies in a low, sexy voice. "I'll show you how much later. You're such a handsome devil, Flint Mason. This kills me every single time."

He leans down and kisses her slowly on the lips before turning around to walk back to the group. A large Steel Infidels tattoo stretches the length of his back.

I love this rule.

It's *brilliant,* whoever thought of it.

"Do all the shirts come off?" I ask Trish.

"Yes. We call it paying to play."

"Okay," Jesse says to the group. "You know how we aim to please our ladies. Let's go." He tugs off his shirt and tosses it across the room to Trish.

"Told you," she whispers to me.

The other Steel Infidels quickly follow his lead in a blur of shirts, hard muscles, and tattoos. All the guys are incredibly sexy, except for Tom Brewer. We could've gone without him removing his shirt, but he's being a good sport and removes his too, which brings on good-natured teasing from the other crew about his beer gut.

Even in a room full of delicious man candy, all I have eyes for is Toby.

He's the only one who still has his shirt on, and I don't understand why. He gives me an expectant look. I don't know what I'm supposed to do, if anything. Biker club rules are unbelievably vague. There should be a handbook to help a girl out.

Trish nudges my arm. "If you want Toby's shirt, you're going to have to step up," she says. "Lay your claim on him. If you don't, one of the other girls will beat you to it."

I blink at her in confusion.

"What do you mean? Step up, how? You mean one of the Sweet Butts would take Toby's shirt?"

Oh, hell no.

"But I'm the one who rode up here with him. That wouldn't be right." I sound as if I'm whining about the unfairness of it all, which I am.

Trish shrugs. "They can and they will. Make a move, hon," she urges. "And do it fast."

She doesn't need to tell me twice. I stand and motion for Toby to throw me his shirt. That's all he's waiting on. He rips it off and walks over to loop it behind my neck. Tugging both ends of the shirt, he pulls me closer and leans down to grab my lips in a hard, hungry kiss. I cling dizzily to his bare shoulders as he kisses me with a force and passion that steals my breath. The men laugh and cheer him on until he reluctantly breaks the kiss.

"You're mine now," he breathes against my ear. "Every man in this room wants to be me."

He turns and walks back to the group, leaving me panting and weak.

"Aren't you glad I talked you into stepping up?" Trish asks. "That was intense."

All I can do is nod. My eyes can't leave the sight of Toby standing there in riding boots and jeans that fit him perfectly.

"Are the womenfolk happy now?" Jesse asks. "Because we would like to get back to the arm wrestling competition if we may."

"I'm deliriously happy," Kendra says.

"Me too," Trish pipes in.

"Good. Now where were we?" Jesse points to the two youngest men. "Are you two ready?" They nod. "Okay, go!"

The first arm-wrestling match only lasts a couple of minutes before an arm slams flat onto the table, signaling the end.

"Next," Jesse says.

Two more men step up. The competition goes quickly. At one point, Toby and Flint square off with each other. They're similar in height, but

Toby's arms are more muscular and bigger. He plays with Flint for a couple of minutes and lets him think he has a chance before easily putting his arm onto the table.

The competition finally comes down to Jesse and Toby as the final two. Both of their arms are unnaturally massive, with bulging muscles and tattoos. Their chests are bright red from all the blood pumping into the pec muscles from the previous matches.

The competition begins and neither arm moves. Not even an inch. They're equally matched for strength. The bicep muscles bulge on both arms and yet the strain doesn't show on either of their faces.

During the previous matches, the men were yelling and cheering on the competitors. Now they've all gone quiet. It would be disloyal to cheer against the MC's leader.

I wonder what Toby will do. Will he let Jesse win because he's the President of the MC? Or will he try his best to beat him?

After several minutes, Jesse begins to show the strain of holding Toby's arm steady. An almost imperceptible tremble runs down his arm. Toby sees it. He glances over at me and winks. He's not even trying hard yet.

My money is on Toby.

Every single time.

A split-second later, Toby catches Jesse in a moment of weakness and slams his arm to the table, winning effortlessly.

Jesse laughs and immediately reaches over to shake his hand. "Good match, brother," he says. "I would've been so fucking pissed at you if you had let me win. Always take the victory if it's yours."

"Amen," Toby says. "To the victor belongs the spoils."

He looks over at me, and the dark gleam in his eyes sends my heart racing.

I'm not sure if he's the victor or if I am.

I win either way.

32

TOBY

A loud banging on the cabin door wakes me.

"Toby!" Flint yells through the thick wood.

"Who is that?" Maggie whispers sleepily. She tugs the quilt closer around her neck and snuggles closer to my back.

"Stay here," I murmur to her. "I'll take care of it."

"Wake up, buddy!" Flint yells again.

"Shit!" I grumble. "Hang on! I'm coming, Flint. Hold your damn horses."

I slip on my jeans and pad to the door in my bare feet. Flint had better have a good reason to drag me out of a warm bed with a naked, sexy woman curled up next to me. I was planning to work in another round of hot sex before breakfast. Or two.

Throwing open the door, I glare at him. "Why the fuck are you banging on my door?"

Daylight is barely breaking across the mountains above the lodge. A heavy fog coats the treetops and the grass around the cabin is frozen with frost. It would be a perfect morning to stay in bed. I'm pissed about being disturbed.

"They've identified the terrorists," Flint says. "It's all over the Internet and the news. I wanted to let you both know. Maggie might want to check in with the television station."

I blink at him and lean against the doorframe. "You mind telling me why we give a damn who these fucking terrorists are? What are we now? Homeland Security?"

"Because they live right in our back door," he says. "That's why."

I rub my bleary eyes, sure that I heard him wrong.

"What are you saying? We live in bum-fuck Georgia for God's sake! That's hardly known as a hotspot for terrorist groups. Who the fuck are you talking about?"

Sure, we're involved up to our necks in an illegal gun-running operation and we've worked plenty of deals with other motorcycle gangs. But none of them would come close to what could be considered terrorists.

They're certainly not men who would shoot up a shopping mall full of innocent people. I can't imagine who Flint might be talking about.

"Do you remember Eric Rudolph, the Centennial Park bomber?" Flint asks.

"The guy who set off the bomb at the Atlanta Olympics years ago? Sure I do. Everyone around home knows about him. I don't remember much about the actual bombing since that was in 1996 and we were all just kids. I've heard plenty about Eric Rudolph though. All of the old-timers talk about him. That was the biggest news to have ever happened around the area."

Not only did Eric Rudolph set off a bomb at the Atlanta Olympics, he also fire-bombed an abortion clinic and a gay bar. After setting the bomb at the Atlanta Olympics, Eric Rudolph hid for years in a town right across the Georgia-North Carolina state line. He was finally caught digging through a trash dumpster no more than twenty miles from the Steel Infidels clubhouse.

"According to the statement they made, they call themselves the Army of God. The same as Eric Rudolph. News reports are saying they're a bunch of crazies. Home-grown terrorists with radical ideas ranging from anti-abortion to anti-media to anti-government."

"If they're against everything, what do they stand for?" I ask.

"Who knows?" Flint replies. "You saw the look in the kid's eyes at the mall. He didn't know what the fuck he was doing there. They're just a bunch of wackos. The point is they live close to us. Within fifteen minutes' driving time. Or closer. You can bet your ass they know who we are and where we are. We took out two of their men."

"Unbelievable. This is all we need right now. What are we going to do?"

"Go back home," Flint says. "And take down those sons of bitches once and for all."

33

MAGGIE

"I'm sorry, darling," Toby whispers in my ear before planting a soft kiss on my lips. "We have to go. Hurry and wake up."

I open my eyes groggily and reach up to pull his handsome face down to mine for another kiss.

"No," I protest. "Don't say that. Stay in bed with me. I don't want to get up."

He sighs. "Believe me, I'd love to. We don't have a choice. They've identified the terrorists." Reaching into his zippered jacket pocket, he pulls out my cell phone and hands it to me. "Here's your phone back. It feels stupid to keep it now. I'm sure you'll need to make some calls."

I quickly sit up in bed when I notice the frown on his face.

"This sounds serious," I say. "You're scaring me. Who are they?"

He quickly fills me in on everything Flint told him about the terrorist group.

"The important thing is they know who *we* are," Toby says. "And like a bunch of idiots, we're all up here in the Smokies, except for Donny and Rocco. We've left ourselves exposed back in Bardsville: the clubhouse, Sam and Jesse's tattoo parlor, our homes...everything. We have to get back there immediately."

I'm already up and heading for the bathroom. "Give me five minutes to brush my teeth and comb my hair," I say. "Then I'll be ready to go." I stop at the door and whirl around. "What about Sadie? Is she safe?"

"I've already left a message for the dog sitter to keep a close eye on her. She'll be safe there until this is taken care of."

My eyes widen. "What do you mean by taken care of? This is a police and FBI matter, not something the Steel Infidels should be involved in. You're not planning to do anything, are you? Please tell me that you're not."

Are they crazy?

I can't imagine why the Steel Infidels think they're equipped to take on a terrorist group head on.

Toby doesn't answer. Instead he reaches for his gun on the dresser and slides it into the holster on his leg.

"Nothing for you to worry about," he says, pulling his jeans leg down over the holster. "We can take care of ourselves. There's a lot you don't know about us."

"And I suppose you don't have time to tell me now," I say with a questioning look.

He shakes his head reluctantly. "No, I really don't. Hurry up."

Ten minutes later and we're waiting by Toby's bike for the return trip. The other Steel Infidels are in front of the lobby building too, hanging around their bikes and downing quick cups of strong coffee. Most of them are extremely hungover and groggy. I hope they're okay to ride.

I'm thankful Toby and I cut out early and didn't party until the middle of the night. I wouldn't want to be on the back of a bike with someone who was dead drunk five hours before.

Jesse and Jeb come out the front door of the building together.

"Sorry you couldn't stay longer, but I understand," Jeb says, shaking Jesse's hand. "You boys be careful on your ride back to Georgia."

Jeb walks over to Toby and reaches out to shake his hand too. "Listen here, son. If you find those fucking terrorists, you kick some *goddamn* ass. We're counting on you."

"Don't worry," Toby says. "We plan to."

34

MAGGIE

When we arrive back in Georgia, instead of going to their homes, the MC rides straight to the clubhouse. Now that the announcement has come out about the identity and potential location of the terrorists, the number of press around the clubhouse has grown exponentially. I suspect news crews from all across the nation have driven through the night to be here.

"Look at this mess," Toby says over his shoulder as we drive up to the clubhouse gates with the rest of the crew.

If we thought it was a madhouse before, it's nothing compared to now.

"I don't see this going away anytime soon," I say. "My advice to the Steel Infidels would be to hunker down and be prepared for the media to hang around for a long time."

After parking the bikes, we head inside the clubhouse, then go upstairs. The Mason brothers are already gathered around the table where lunch has been laid out for them.

"Wow! Who did all this?" I ask, glancing around at the big plates of sandwiches, chips, and chocolate chip cookies.

"The Sweet Butts who didn't go on the ride," Toby answers. "Grab yourself a plate. You must be starving."

Hmmm...those darn Sweet Butts again.

"I want a Sweet Butt of my own," I joke, picking up a potato chip and biting into it. "They come in handy."

"Did you tell Maggie about the shooters?" Flint asks.

Toby nods as he fills up his plate with food. "Maggie checked with her boss at the station to see if he knew anything we didn't before we left the lodge. There's nothing new. If the police have any leads, it hasn't been released yet."

"My boss reminded me that there were two guys arrested on Interstate I-75 in Atlanta last year who were carrying explosive materials in their van," I say. "It could be connected to this group. They're tracking down every lead they can find."

"That makes sense," Flint says. "It would be easy for a small group to work undetected in North Georgia for years. The locals would never suspect someone from Bardsville of making bombs or doing mass shootings. That's how Eric Rudolph stayed hidden in plain sight for so long. Nobody suspected him. Even after he'd been identified, people couldn't believe it. What else did your boss---"

Toby's phone interrupts him.

"It's Rocco," Toby says apologetically. "I'd better take this." He opens his phone and hits the button. "What's up?" he says. A worried look crosses his face. He quickly gets up and walks over to the window. "Which white van? How long has it been there?"

He leans over to pick up the binoculars from the table and goes back to the window. "Yeah, I see it now. It's unmarked. Are you sure it's been there this whole time? When did the guy show up?" He listens for another minute. "Is he the one wearing a dark jacket and red cap pulled down low over his eyes? Stay put. I'm coming out." He slides the phone into his front pocket.

"What is it?" Flint asks.

"Rocco noticed a suspicious white van that's been sitting there by itself all of last night and today. There were so many other vehicles around that he didn't think much about it until now. Nobody has been anywhere around it until a few minutes ago when a man showed up without cameras or a crew. He sat in the driver's seat for a few minutes then started walking away through the crowd."

"You can't go out there," Flint says firmly. "It's just a van. I'm sure it belongs to one of the news stations. We've already put together a plan with Maggie about how we're handling the media. You're going to blow it all to hell if you step outside the fence and wade right into the middle of them."

Toby scratches the stubble on his face and blows out a long breath. "Something doesn't feel right," he says. "I don't like it." He holds the binoculars back up to the window. "Damn! Now I've lost the guy. I can't see him."

Flint pulls out his phone. "I'll tell Rocco to go check it then," he says. "If it will make you feel better. I know how you can be about things once you get a bee in your bonnet."

Toby reaches over and grabs his arm. "No! Don't do that. Rocco wouldn't recognize an explosive if he was sitting on one."

"An explosive!" I say in surprise. "Aren't you overreacting? I realize the media doesn't have a great reputation. We hardly go around blowing things up just to have something for the six o'clock news."

"It's not the media I'm worried about," Toby says. "It's the Hand of God people."

"Army of God," Flint corrects.

"She's right," Sam mumbles with his mouth full of cookie. "You really should calm the fuck down. You're overreacting and freaking me out. This isn't Afghanistan. I know the shooting shook you up. No need to get all whacked out about it. It's just your PTSD acting up again. That's all. You're blowing this way out of proportion. It's an empty van." He shrugs. "Big fucking deal. Nothing to get your panties in a wad about. Maybe a news crew had to split up and left it behind to pick up later."

Toby takes a deep breath and leans his forehead against the cold glass window. "Fuck it!" he says suddenly, slamming his hands down on the windowsill. "I can't rest until I check it for myself. I'm going out there." He heads for the door in a rush.

I jump up and run after him. "Then I'm going too!"

"Jesus Christ!" Flint says. "We might as well all go then. Sam, you run interference with the media if you can. Charm their pants off and distract them from Toby. This is turning into a colossal clusterfuck."

By the time I catch up with Toby, he's already at the top of the stairs. I'm glad I'm not in high heels because for a big guy, he's incredibly fast on his feet. Jodi is on her way up the narrow stairwell. Toby almost knocks her over in his hurry and she grabs the banister to keep from falling.

"You all need to come down and watch the news on the TV," she yells. "I was just coming up to get you. Come quick. They're threatening to do it again."

"Do what again?" Toby asks as he moves past her.

"The terrorists!" she says. "They've released a video saying they're going to do something else. It's on the news."

"Did they say what?"

"No," she answers. "They were ranting about being anti-media, getting revenge and some other stupid stuff that didn't make any sense."

"Fuck!" Toby yells.

He moves past Jodi and runs toward the front door of the clubhouse. He's almost at the door when he realizes I'm right behind him. He whirls around, causing me to bump straight into his chest.

"Where do you think you're going?" he asks. "Stay here, Maggie."

"I'm going out there with you."

"Hell no, you're not!" He grabs my shoulders and holds me still. "Stay here in the clubhouse. I'm not asking, I'm telling. I can't lose you. *Please.* Do what I say."

I open my mouth to argue when I see something in his eyes. He's worried. For real. A connection passes between us. An unspoken word.

I nod my head. "Okay," I say reluctantly. This isn't the time to butt heads.

He drops his hands from my shoulders and goes outside. Stepping into the doorway, I watch as he sprints full speed across the parking lot toward the gate.

"Rocco!" he yells.

The bearded man at the gate turns to Toby and starts walking toward him. Before they meet, the white van on the other side of the fence explodes.

35

TOBY

The massive explosion of a car bomb in the white van throws me face down onto the ground. The car windows of the other vehicles parked nearby blow outward, sending glass and metal pieces flying in every direction. Flames from the van shoot high into the air.

I try to lift my head and can't. My ears are ringing in a constant buzzing roar. I draw in a breath and choke on smoke. My hands are raw and burning like a thousand angry wasps are stinging the shit out of me.

No, it can't be wasps.

I force my eyes open. The stinging is from tiny pieces of glass embedded into my exposed skin; my hands, arms, face, and the back of my neck.

Fuck! I was too late.

Where is Maggie?

I lift my head and look back at the clubhouse. Thick black smoke and debris fills the parking lot, and I can't see the doorway where she was standing thirty seconds before.

"Maggie!" I try to cry out.

My voice barely makes a sound and comes out as a hoarse whisper. I need to find her, to make sure she's okay. I push myself up onto my knees and attempt to stand. I'm dizzy and my ears are still roaring. Shaking my head, I try to clear my vision.

"Toby!" I hear her screaming frantically from way off in the distance. "Toby! Answer me!" Her voice sounds as if she's coming closer. "Where are you? I can't see you! Toby!"

"Maggie," I yell louder this time. I manage to stand, though unsteadily. "Maggie! Stay put."

I don't want her coming closer because of the threat of a secondary explosion. There's almost always a second bomb placed nearby. Suddenly I see her through the smoke, and then she's beside me with tears running down her terrified face.

"Are you okay?" she says in a panic. "Oh my god! You're bleeding all over. You're injured!"

"I'm okay," I manage to say.

My brain isn't working quite right yet, and I'm having a hard time forming words or thinking straight. Is this what it feels like to have a traumatic brain injury? To feel as if your insides have been squeezed like toothpaste out of a tube?

"What the hell just happened?" she asks shakily.

"Car bomb. The van. Are you hurt?"

"No, I'm fine."

"Thank God," I say, trying to see through the smoke. "Where's Rocco? He was right here."

She turns around to look behind us toward the gate. "Rocco!" she yells loudly. "Rocco! Can you hear me?"

"Over here," a faint voice calls out. "My leg's hurt."

"Hang on, Rocco," Flint calls back. "We're coming to get you, buddy."

Flint and Sam appear through the smoke, along with Rocco's brother, Donny, and several more of the Steel Infidels. Donny and the crew run toward the sound of Rocco's voice.

Sam hurries to my side, grabs my arm, and slings it across his shoulder to hold me up. "I've got you, buddy," he says. "You look like shit."

"Are you alright?" Flint stops to ask me.

I nod back at him.

"There's no telling how many injured people are outside the gates," he says. "You've had experience with this kind of thing. I haven't. Tell me what to do."

I look at the scene of devastation and tragedy unfolding in front of us.

The terrorist's target was the media all along.

We should have known.

What better spot to take them out than right here? Where they were all gathered up in one place, prime for the picking. Along with the Steel Infidels, the very men who killed two of their own.

A perfect evil plan.

Take out the media and get revenge on the Steel Infidels at the same time.

I'm angry and ready for vengeance.

I can't believe the motherfuckers managed to pull this off right at our front door. My auto-pilot kicks in, clearing the fog from my brain. I no longer feel the pain from the glass shards shredding my skin.

"Have the crew bring the injured into the clubhouse," I say. "We'll need to set up a triage unit until the ambulances get here. The local hospital only has two, so it will be a while before they can transport the injured. We'll also need to put the word out for any local nurses or anyone with medical experience to get here fast. Maybe even extra vans for medical transport to the bigger hospitals in Atlanta."

"I'll call Kendra," Flint says. "She can alert her veterinary staff. The girls haven't made it back to Georgia yet."

"The Sweet Butts are going to have to step up and help," I say. "They're capable of doing more than we give them credit for. Go inside, Maggie, and tell them to get ready to take care of the injured. Clear a space in the main room and gather up anything we can use for medical supplies."

"You should come inside too," Maggie pleads. She tugs gently at my hand. "Look at your arms and neck. You're bleeding all over the place. Please. Let me patch you up."

"No," I say firmly. "There's something I need to do first. That fucker in the red cap hanging around the van seemed familiar, and he's still out there in the crowd somewhere...dead or alive. Either way, I need to find him and put an end to this madness. Even if all that's left of him is charred pieces."

Flint gives me an incredulous look. "You recognized him? Who do you think it was?"

"I don't know for sure. I think it might be the third shooter at the mall. The man on the upper level."

"Son of a bitch!" Sam says. "I'll go with you. Are you sure you're okay to do this? Because you don't look so good."

I remove his arm that's holding me up and wipe off the blood that's streaming down into my eyes with the back of my hands. "As fine as I'll ever be," I say. "Come on, Sam. Let's find this bastard."

We make our way toward the direction of where the gate used to be. From the splintered metal pieces crunching under our boots, I suspect the fence surrounding our clubhouse has been blown to bits. It's hard to see more than a few feet in front of us to know for sure how much damage has been done.

Now that I have a plan, adrenaline is flooding my body and clearing my mind. I'm focused and calm.

"Where did you last see him?" Sam asks.

"When he was walking away from the white van," I say. "It was parked to the right of the gate. He must've set a timer and then took off. He either went into the woods on foot or had someone else pick him up in a car down at the main road."

"What's your best guess? Woods or the road?"

"My gut tells me the cocksucker is in the woods," I say. "His plan is probably to stay put and then make his way to a pick-up location when the coast is clear."

While others are rushing away from the multiple burning vehicles, we run toward them. If there was any justice in the world, the fucker would have exploded with the car bomb. When we get closer, I realize nobody could have survived the blast if they were anywhere near it. We won't find his body. I figure he set a five-minute timer and ran like a motherfucker.

"Go toward the woods," I tell Sam. "If we can get beyond the smoke, maybe we can spot him."

The wooded area to the right of the clubhouse goes straight up a mountainside. To an outsider, it would appear to be no more than a densely-wooded hillside. In reality, the climb up is rough, with big boulders and thick, tangled underbrush to crawl through. Over the years, Sam and I have hiked it so many times we could do it blindfolded.

Which is basically what we're going to have to do today through the dense smoke.

If the shooter is ahead of us, it's only by a few minutes, and he doesn't know the area. Visibility is low, like walking through a forest fire. When my throat starts to sting, I tug off my shirt and tie it around the lower part of my face to filter out the smoke. Sam does the same.

"We're never going to be able to spot him in this smoke," he says. "He could be five feet in front of us and we won't see him."

"That's why we have to get above him. To the top of the mountain. We'll be able to spot him once we get above the smoke level. And then we've got the son of a bitch right where we want him."

"Lead the way," Sam says. "I'm right behind you, as always. Seems like my life is spent looking at your lard ass."

We start climbing straight up the steep mountain, using tree saplings to pull ourselves up. As we climb farther, we instinctively follow the worn path our own boots had made many years before.

The first time Sam and I climbed this mountain, we were in high school. His Dad was beating the shit out of him on a regular basis. Flint had run off to Atlanta to be a big-city attorney. Jesse was taking over as leader of the Steel Infidels. My home life was an unstable mess.

We were too young to be in the Steel Infidels. The bikers in the MC treated us like a joke whenever we were around them, which wasn't often. That didn't stop us from dreaming.

We'd sneak up the mountain with a six-pack of beer so we could sit and watch the crew work on their bikes in the parking lot of the clubhouse. We'd talk about what kind of Harleys we'd buy and the cool tattoos we'd get. What badasses we were going to be once we were two of the Steel Infidels' chosen twelve.

We didn't find out until much later that the MC knew what we were doing the whole time. Nothing got past them. Certainly not a couple of teenage wannabes hiding out on the mountain to play 'I Spy.' They played along with the game and sometimes even put on a little extra show in the parking lot for our benefit. Sam and I were the little kids in the Steel Infidels family, the brats. The crew patiently waited for us to grow up and take their place one day.

And now we have.

The brats are all grown up with a job to do.

"The smoke is starting to clear," Sam says, breathing hard. "Damn! I don't remember the hike being this fucking difficult when we were younger. I'm out of breath." He leans against the side of a tree and bends over to try to breathe. He looks at me with concern. "You're still dripping blood. Are you sure you're okay? I can't carry your big ass down off this mountain, so don't even think about passing out on me."

"We're almost at the top. Keep going. Remember the rocks that we used to sit on where we could see the parking lot?"

"Sure," Sam says. "Didn't we hide a six-pack of beer up there years ago? Even a green beer would taste good about now. How long will beer keep outdoors? Ten years?" He pushes off from the tree and starts climbing again. "Okay, I'm good."

We hike five more minutes and then we're finally above the smoke line. The mountainside is as clear as ever. I take a deep breath of the fresh air. Sam is energized now and scrambles to reach the boulders first. He climbs up on the tallest one and stands to scan the area below us.

"Damn," he says in a solemn voice. "It's looks like fucking Armageddon from up here." He points to the black cloud of smoke hanging over the clubhouse and the surrounding area. "Doomsday."

I sit down beside him and use my shirt to wipe the blood from my face, neck, and arms.

"You're all glittery and shiny," Sam says. "Is that glass in your skin?"

"Yeah, it's all over me. And in me."

"Anything I can do to help? I can try to scrape it out with a credit card."

I roll my eyes at him. It's a good thing he's not a medic. "No, thank you," I say. "I'll manage fine without your help."

"Do you still think he's on his way up?" he asks. "I would hate to think we walked all this way for nothing on a stupid hunch. They could use our help at the clubhouse."

"We'll know in a few minutes one way or the other," I say. "Where's your weapon?" I remove my gun from my leg holster and stand up again for a better vantage point.

Sam slides a gun out of his jacket pocket and holds it up for me to see.

"You watch that side and I'll keep an eye out over here," I say. "The second he clears the smoke, we need to act. If he sees us first, one of us is a goner."

Sam holds up a finger. "One question," he says. "Are we planning to haul this motherfucker back down the mountain with us alive and hand him over to the police or...?" He raises his eyebrows at me in an unspoken question.

"What do you think? Are you in the mood to be carrying an injured asshole back down the way we just came up? I know I'm not. If we take him alive, he'll go to jail. Big fucking deal. He'll become an even bigger hero to his freaky followers. They'll carry on his work to avenge him. It will never stop. You know what Jesse always says. 'Cut off the head of the snake and the body dies.'"

"Guess that settles it then. No argument from me on that point. So now we wait."

Several minutes go by without any sign of the man. I've almost given up hope when I see movement down below us. The man is grabbing onto tree trunks to pull himself up the mountain the same way we did. He's moving slow and steady. Every time he grabs a tree, the leaves shake on top. By watching the treetops, we're able to pinpoint his location.

I motion to Sam and hold a finger to my lips for silence. The man will exit the tree line any minute now. When he does, he'll be well within my target range.

I take a deep, steadying breath to calm my nerves.

I'm tired of all the killing.

I'm ready to start living.

The man staggers out of the woods, limping badly with a hurt leg. He's cut up all over the same as I am from the explosion. It warms my heart to know that he feels pain in the last minutes of his life. I would love to make him feel more, to avenge everyone he hurt, but it wouldn't serve any purpose.

Strength isn't about destroying those you hate.

True strength is about building up the ones you love.

Life is about the living.

And loving.

I line up the shot and fire. He drops to the ground.

"Let's go home," I say to Sam, who's watching me quietly. "It's over."

36

MAGGIE

Three weeks later...

"Are you getting bored with me now?" Toby asks me.

We're on video chat where we can see each other as we talk over the phone. He chuckles, and I'm reminded again of how deeply I miss him when I hear his deep rumble. I trace his face lovingly on my phone screen with my fingertips. I wish I could reach out and touch him for real.

"How could I be bored of you when I never get to see you?" I ask. "I miss you more than you can imagine. I hate being apart from you."

It's been weeks since the shooting. In the first few days, Toby and I were together constantly. Between the shooting, the bike ride to the Smoky Mountains, and then the car bomb, it was as if our lives were on high-speed overdrive. Every minute was spent fighting to live another day.

After the car bomb, I refused to leave Toby's side. He wouldn't accept medical treatment until the last injured media personnel had been evacuated from the clubhouse several hours later. Even then, it was a battle to talk him into letting Kendra tend to his wounds and remove the glass deeply embedded into his skin.

I'll never forget how terrified I was when he took off after the terrorist into the woods. The thought of losing Toby forever was something that I couldn't let myself even begin to imagine. When he stumbled back into the clubhouse with Sam, bleeding and exhausted, but alive, I grabbed him in a bear hug and burst into tears of relief.

That night we clung to each other desperately until both of us finally fell asleep. There were no nightmares that night. Or so he said. There would never be any way to know for certain.

The next few days were a whirlwind of activity. The clubhouse was now the scene of a terrorist crime, so federal officials took it over and set up headquarters there while Flint legally fought to get it released back to the Steel Infidels.

Eventually the feds allowed the MC to begin cleanup around the building and to rebuild their security fence. We all pitched in and worked day and night to put things back the way they were the best we could. Everyone was eager to get back to normal as quickly as possible.

My station manager was understanding about my situation and the trauma I had been through up to a point, and then he gave me an ultimatum. Either I come back to my regular work, or start using up my sick days.

I reluctantly returned to Atlanta, back to my job and apartment. With both of our busy schedules, Toby and I haven't seen each other since. Being apart from him is tearing me up inside.

"I can't wait to see you this weekend," I say. "I hope you're planning to stay the night with me after the award dinner."

"You bet I am," Toby says. "If you'll let me. My bed is cold and empty without you beside me."

"Where is Sadie sleeping these days?"

"In the bed," Toby admits with a laugh after a moment's hesitation. "Don't worry, we'll change that when you're around. Or try to. She can be stubborn."

"I hope so. You take up an entire bed. I can't imagine trying to sleep with a Golden Retriever on top of me, too."

"Are you sure this award dinner is mandatory?" he asks. "I would rather order pizza and have a night in with you instead. Fancy dinners aren't my thing."

"Receiving a heroism award from the Atlanta Mayor is a big deal," I say. "You're a hero, and the city wants to thank you for stepping up to save lives."

He goes quiet. "It doesn't feel right though. I don't like being the center of attention and receiving an award for being a hero when people are still in the hospital. Couldn't they wait until summer or forget the whole thing entirely?"

"I understand how you feel. Keep in mind it's election year. The Mayor is doing this as much for him as you."

"Well, at least it gives me a good opportunity to see my girl," Toby says. "I miss you."

"Miss you too, babe. You have no idea how much. So we're on for Friday night then?"

"I'll be there right on time."

37

MAGGIE

"What time will you be arriving at the county club tonight?" my sister Nicole asks me over the phone. "Brad was excited when I told him you snagged us extra tickets to join you at the Mayor's table. Are Mom and Dad coming too?"

"Yes, they'll be there," I say. "You know Dad wouldn't miss the chance to hobnob with the Atlanta Mayor. He mentioned a new development he's working on that needs special zoning. I hope he doesn't bore everyone with business talk all night."

Nicole lets out a knowing laugh. "Well, it wouldn't be dinner with Dad if he didn't. When have you ever known him not to talk business at the table?"

"Never," I say.

Our father is well-known in Atlanta's social circles as a construction and real estate success story. He began his business with nothing as a young man by buying older homes, fixing them up, and selling them for a higher price. Eventually his business progressed into building large-scale shopping malls and apartment complexes scattered across the Atlanta area.

Now he's a pillar of Atlanta society. My mother does her part by frequently volunteering as chairman for various social committees and charity fund-raisers. She puts in as many hours as he does without complaining. They've built a good life for themselves, and for my sister and me.

My dad brought us up to work hard and to never accept anything less than total success from ourselves. No excuses, Dad always told me.

When I chose to major in Communications in college instead of following Nicole's path into the Science or Math field, my parents pouted for months. Dad was certain I would never be able to support myself doing something as frivolous as news reporting. To this day, he still brings it up every time we're together. Always worrying about my job security. Nothing would make them happier than if I found a rich guy who Dad deems to be successful and worthy enough to be his son-in-law.

Like Nicole's husband, Brad.

Dad was thrilled when Nicole married him. Brad was quite a catch, being a partner in one of the large accounting firms located downtown. Dad immediately found ways to involve him in the family business, first by sending him the firm's CPA work then by asking him to join the Board of Directors.

Sometimes when I'm listening to one of Brad's dull conversations that usually involve upcoming changes in the tax code, I wonder why my sister married him. She used to be lively and full of fun. Now she's almost as bland and boring as he is.

No matter what, I'm not going to end up in the same situation.

Life is too short to settle.

"Will seven o'clock be too early to arrive?" Nicole asks. "Brad wants to work in a bit of networking during the cocktail hour."

I roll my eyes, glad that Nicole can't see me. Everything is business with my family. Tonight's dinner is supposed to be about honoring Toby for saving people's lives at the mall. Not an opportunity to wheel and deal.

"Seven will be fine," I say. "We'll see you then."

"What do you mean by we?" Nicole asks, suddenly more interested in what I have to say. "Who is we? Are you bringing a date?"

I haven't told my family yet that I'm seeing Toby personally. Somehow the time hasn't seemed right.

"Toby, the guest of honor, is swinging by my apartment to pick me up," I say. "I thought it might be easier for him if he arrived with someone he knew. The country club can be intimidating to newcomers."

"Surely you're not coming to dinner with the guy from the mall shooting?" Nicole sounds aghast at the thought. "Doesn't he have a bunch of ugly tattoos and ride a motorcycle? Mom will throw a hissy fit. If you need a lift, we can pick you up on the way."

"No, we've already planned to ride together," I say. "And Toby is sitting at our table, so please be nice. For my sake. Don't forget he saved my life and the lives of others. That's the whole point of the dinner. It's an award ceremony, remember?"

"I know," she says. "I'm grateful to him. You're the only little sister I have. It's just that I'm sure this Toby fellow will be fine on his own. You shouldn't feel obligated to ride with him. What does he drive anyway? A pickup truck? The valet parking guys will get a kick out of that."

Here we go, just as expected.

I bite my lip to keep from going off on my sister. My goal is to just make it through the dinner tonight without any issues between everyone.

My sister's superior attitude is already showing. I expected it, so it's not a surprise. She's never been one to be able to look past a man's checking account to see what's inside.

"He's a good man," I say. "You'll like Toby."

I'm not certain she will. Not that it matters to me what she thinks. I'm past the point in my life of asking for permission of who I can date.

"Are you sure I can't talk you out of this?" she asks again. "Think about how it will reflect on Dad's image in the community if you show up with a motorcycle gang member."

"I don't care," I snap in frustration. "And Toby is not a gang member."

Nicole is getting out of line and pushing the limits of my patience.

"Don't get all snippy at me," she says. "I'm trying to be helpful. At the very least tell me the guy is hot. There must be a good reason why you've taken him under your wing. You always were the type to bring home every stray animal you could find."

Now she's trying to placate me in her weird way.

"He's a very attractive man," I say. "If there's one thing we can agree on, it will be that."

"Now you've perked my interest," she says. "I can't wait to meet him since I haven't seen you really into a guy in a long time. We'll wait for you in the lobby."

"See you then."

38

TOBY

I'm hoping Flint is at home and that I haven't made the long trip to his mountaintop cabin for nothing. The drive is up a winding gravel road with steep drop-offs on both sides. I tried calling his cell phone and didn't get an answer. Considering the reason for my unexpected visit, it might be better if I showed up in person rather than try to explain it over the phone anyway.

The loud muffler of my motorcycle gives my approach away a long time before I reach the cabin. Flint and Sam are both standing on the front porch, leaning on the wooden oak railing, waiting for me when I pull up in front.

In the summer, the big wrap-around porch is a popular spot. One of the first things Kendra did after they were married was to line the porch with old-timey, white rocking chairs. The Steel Infidels spend plenty of summer evenings there drinking whiskey and trading wild tales of motorcycle club life.

"What's up, Toby?" Flint asks when I climb off the bike. "Is something wrong? We heard the bike coming up the road. Come on in. Sam and I were having a beer."

He opens the screen door and I follow him inside.

"What's going on?" he asks. "You normally don't drive all the way up here without calling first. Is everything alright? Sam, go get him a beer out of the fridge."

I clear my throat and look at the floor, a little embarrassed to tell him why I'm here.

"You know that Mayor's dinner that I'm supposed to be at tonight in Atlanta?" I ask.

"Yeah, what about it?" Flint asks with a frown. "You don't want to go? It's too late to back out now. They're expecting you, and it will be good for the club's image. Take one for the team, Toby. Suck it up, do it, and get it over with. It will only last a couple of hours and then you'll be out of there."

"No, it's not that," I say. "I was just wondering...what should I wear?"

Flint lets out a surprised laugh. "You're asking me this now?" he says. "Hours before the dinner? Why didn't you say something two days ago? What were you planning to wear? Haven't you thought about this?"

"Nothing fancy," I reply. "That's not my style. Probably just jeans and a nice shirt. And my black boots. Then I started thinking that maybe I should put a little more effort into it."

Thankfully, Flint isn't the type of man to judge, and he doesn't now.

"What changed your mind?" he asks.

"I'm taking Maggie, so I don't want her to be embarrassed by how I'm dressed," I tell him. "Her family is going to be sitting with us, so I'll be meeting them for the first time too."

"And you want to make a good impression on Daddy Dearest?" Sam asks, grinning broadly. He's caught the tail end of our conversation. He walks across the room from the kitchen and hands me a bottle of beer.

"Well, I don't want to make a bad one," I reply dryly. "Are you two going to help me or not?"

Flint is the only man in the MC who owns a business suit or a tie. The rest of us live in our jeans, leather jackets, and riding boots. Up to now, I've never had a reason to need anything else to wear. I'm sincerely hoping the dinner tonight is a one-time deal. The thought of putting on a suit makes me itch and break out in a sweat.

"Lucky for you, I have a closet full of expensive suits that might fit," he says. "I knew they would come in handy one day, so I kept them all in suit bags when I left the District Attorney's office. I might even have a pair of shoes because the boots you're wearing are definitely not going to work."

He points down at my boots that are scuffed on the sides and dusty from the ride up. I hold up one foot to take a better look.

"What's the issue? I think they're alright. There's not any holes in them. I can shine these up to be good as new. Don't even think about handing me a pair of expensive loafers. These will do just fine."

He motions for me to follow him into his bedroom, where he opens the door to a closet. Both sides are hanging full of business suits and fancy dress clothes that I've never seen Flint wear.

"You weren't kidding," I say. "You were a regular fashionista."

After an hour of going through all the suits in his closet and Sam making jokes about every single one, we finally give up on the idea of my massive legs and muscular arms ever fitting into one of Flint's suits. We're the same height, but where he's lean and mean, I'm all bulk and muscle.

I realize now it was a stupid idea from the start.

"Now what?" I say. "Got any other ideas? I need to be on the road soon to Atlanta."

Flint carefully tucks the last suit back into a bag. "You must have another pair of pants in your closet," he says. "You can't wear jeans. Not to a country club dinner with the Mayor of Atlanta. Even for a biker, you need to show a bit of class."

I try to think. When was the last time I had to dress up in anything besides my regular work or riding clothes? I remember.

"I have a pair of black pants that I wore to my Aunt's funeral a couple of years ago. They might work if they're not too tight."

Flint thinks a minute, then nods. "That will be fine. What about a white shirt?"

"With buttons?" I ask.

"Preferably," he replies dryly. "If you're going to wear a tie."

"Yeah, I have a white shirt. Dammit! I hate things around my neck. I feel like they're choking me. Do I have to wear a tie?"

"Depends on how much you want to impress this girl. We're talking two hours here, not a lifetime of suits and ties. Suck it up and wear the damn tie. It's not going to fucking kill you."

He reaches way back into the closet and pulls out a large black blazer.

"This was Jesse's. Try it on."

I slip on the black blazer. It's a perfect fit.

"Now you're in business," Flint says. "It looks good on you." He takes out a hanger with several colorful ties and starts holding them up to my face one at a time.

"What the hell are you doing now?" I ask. "I think you might be enjoying all this clothes design stuff a little too much. Do you have a secret life you want to tell us about?"

I'm joking and he ignores me.

"I'm trying to match the color of your eyes," he says. "Trust me. Your girl will appreciate the extra effort I'm putting in here."

He holds up his final choice, a blue striped tie.

"I remember the last time I wore this tie," he says, serious for a moment. "It was my final day in the District Attorney's office in Atlanta. Jesse called me during my lunch break to say that it was time for me to come back home. The Steel Infidels needed me. And more importantly, my brothers needed me too. I knew Jesse would never have made the call if it wasn't necessary."

"Was that when the Liberators killed Tommy? Sam told me about it in a letter."

Flint nods. "I cancelled my appointments for the rest of the day, drove home, and stripped out of my suit and tie. My Steel Infidels black leather jacket was hidden way back in the closet. I put it there where I couldn't see it. Where I wouldn't be reminded of what I'd left behind. I remember pulling it out that day and slipping it on. The minute the soft leather touched my bare skin, I knew I was home again."

"Do you ever regret leaving Atlanta and coming back home?" I ask. I've never talked to Flint about his time there or why he went in the first place.

"Never," he replies. "Not for a moment. I'll never leave the Steel Infidels again." He presses the tie into my hand and grows quiet for a moment. "We're family, which means we're always here for you. Your last name might not be Mason, but you're still our brother just the same. Right, Sam?"

Sam slaps me on the back. "Toby knows that already. You don't need to tell him. We've been brothers since what? Seventh grade?"

I nod, knowing I don't need to say anything. I feel the same way about all of the Steel Infidels. I don't know how I would have made it this far without them.

I wouldn't have. No way.

"You had better get going," Flint says. "Your girl is waiting for you. Make us proud."

39

TOBY

I pull up to the gated entrance of Maggie's apartment complex and punch in the four-digit code she gave me. The double gates slowly slide open and I drive my truck through. To the right is the entrance to a 15-story parking deck. I'm supposed to enter the code again and then park on the 10th level.

I drive into the dark garage and start making my way up the levels. The lighting is dim and every corner is blind.

Just the kind of place I hate to be.

By the time I've rounded the corner for the third floor, my anxiety level begins to rise. It's been happening too much lately. Ever since the shooting, I've been on edge.

I can't imagine why Maggie would want to live in an apartment where it takes twenty minutes to get from her door to the ground outside. What an ordeal to go through every time you want to leave a place. I don't like the parking deck. It doesn't feel safe. Maggie works crazy hours, and the thought of her driving home alone every night makes me uneasy.

I breathe a sigh of relief when I finally reach the 10th level and find a parking spot where my big truck will barely fit. When I walk up to the door of the building, there's yet another code to be entered before it will open. I wander down the quiet carpeted hallway searching for 703 and hesitate in the hallway when I find it.

I straighten the jacket of my Marine uniform, take a deep breath, and knock lightly. At the last minute, I changed my mind and decided to wear my uniform instead of the blazer and black pants we'd decided on. Somehow it seemed more appropriate for the occasion, and it's the only dress outfit I feel comfortable wearing.

Maggie opens the door and her mouth drops in surprise. "Oh my God!" she finally says, grabbing my hand and tugging me inside. "You look incredible." She steps back to carefully study me over from head to toe and places a hand over her chest. "My heart stopped when I opened the door and saw you standing there in your uniform. Wow...just wow." Her voice trails off and she stands there staring at me. "I can't tear my eyes off you."

"Is the uniform okay to wear tonight?" I ask. "I didn't have a suit that fit."

There's no point in telling her about the wasted hour spent at Flint's cabin putting on a fashion show for Sam.

"Believe me, the uniform is more than okay. It's perfect." She leans up to kiss me lightly on the lips. "I'm so happy you're finally here. I can't wait to show you my place. I hope you like it. If you do, I was thinking we could swap out weekends. You know, one weekend in the country with you, and the next weekend here in the city with me. That way we would have the best of both worlds."

I glance around the beautifully decorated, spacious apartment. Everything is exactly as I imagined.

Which doesn't bode well for me.

Every furnishing, from the expensive leather sofa to the modern art on the walls, has been carefully chosen and arranged. The white modern-style furniture is too fancy and clean to sit on, so I stand awkwardly just inside the front door. Maggie doesn't seem to notice and keeps talking excitedly about all the fun things there are to do in Atlanta.

"There's a wine-tasting next weekend at the Atlanta Botanical Gardens if you want to come back," she says. "It would be fun, and I could introduce you to some of my friends from the TV station. They would love to meet you."

I try to pay attention and appear interested in what she's saying because I should be. I care about her happiness and this is Maggie's home, where she lives and works.

Yet I have this unbearable urge to bolt out the door, hop in my truck, and burn rubber trying to drive back to the country as fast as I can.

I can't see myself being comfortable enough to spend one night here, much less every other weekend. A car alarm blares out on the street below her window and I flinch.

"What the hell is that?" I ask.

She waves a dismissive hand at the window. "Atlanta traffic. There's always car horns or sirens going off. You get used to it after a while."

I don't see how.

"So what do you think?" she asks, whirling around to show me her low-cut, slinky, black cocktail dress and three-inch-high 'fuck-me' shoes.

"I think you're beautiful," I say, already forgetting about the apartment and how uncomfortable I am.

Like every other time I'm with Maggie, my mind always immediately goes straight to sex. All she needs to do is look at me or lean against my arm and I go rock hard. I wonder sometimes if she has any idea of the intense effect she has on me.

Probably not.

She links her hands around the back of my neck. "Aren't you the guy who doesn't use the word beautiful?" she teases me. "I distinctly remember you saying the word is overused."

"That's why I reserve the right to use it only for you," I say. My hands reach down to touch her silky hair and let the tendrils drift through my fingers. "Because you are. Unbelievably so. And sexy. Like now, with your tight little dress just begging me to do unspeakable things to you."

I slide my hands down to cup her ass through the soft fabric and pull her against me. She laughs and presses her abdomen closer against my hard-on through my pants.

"What kind of bad things are we talking about?" she asks, her voice dropping lower. "Tell me."

40

MAGGIE

I wasn't sure how Toby was planning to dress for the dinner. I didn't ask him because I didn't want him to think it was something I was concerned about.

No matter what I expected, it wasn't for him to be so devastatingly handsome.

Dressed in a blue Marine uniform with six gold buttons going down the front, dark pants, and a white cap, he could sweep any woman off her feet with just one look. The deep pride he takes in his uniform and everything it represents is evident from the stiffly starched collar to the freshly-polished shoes. This is another side of Toby that I haven't seen, and I find it immensely appealing.

Who wouldn't?

A gorgeous, blue-eyed, drop-dead hunk of a man in uniform.

Doesn't get much better than this.

When he stepped inside my apartment, I felt as if all the oxygen had been sucked out of the room. Even though we text several times a day, I forget how overwhelming my attraction to his physical presence can be.

Now he's threatening to talk dirty to me, and I'm melting.

His gaze swings to me, the blue of his eyes darkening when they rest on my black dress tightly clinging to every curve. Something primal and dangerous passes between us when I feel the full laser heat of his scrutiny.

Oh yes...this is going to be worth the wait.

"Talk to me, Marine," I say in my sexiest voice, leaning closer into him. "Tell me all the dirty, bad things you want to do to me, because you're the most dashing, handsome man I've seen today."

Not just today.

Any day.

Something about the sight of Toby grabs my insides and won't let go. Never more so than at this moment.

I've felt physical attraction to men before. It was nothing compared to the intense longing I feel every time he walks into the room. From a burning need to trace the intricate tattoos on his arms or to run my fingers through his dark hair that curls at the nape of his neck, I can never get my fill of him.

He slides a hand slowly up my bare leg. His fingers hover at the edge of my black silk panties.

"How much time do we have before we need to leave for the dinner?" he asks huskily.

I glance at the wall clock. The dinner starts in less than an hour.

"Fifteen minutes," I say.

Toby slips a finger down inside the front of my panties and strokes my clit in a circular motion, just the way he knows I love it. I'm already soaking wet. He goes lower and slides a finger up into me, all the way to the knuckle. I gasp at the penetration and lean into him.

Oh...that's deep.

I suddenly become aware of how harsh and uneven his breathing has become as he caresses me. His thick erection presses against my hip. He slides two fingers in this time...once...twice. I clutch at his arm.

"Fuck...Maggie," he groans. "Why did I do that? Now I'm going to be stuck sitting there at dinner all night with blue balls while trying not to think about how dripping wet your pussy is right beside me. I don't suppose it's appropriate to finger-fuck you under the table at the Mayor's dinner?"

"Not at all appropriate," I whisper. "Tell me how you would do it. If you could."

Toby knows I love it when he talks dirty to me in his sexy Southern accent. I could listen to him talk non-stop for days about anything and never get tired of hearing it.

He presses his lips against my hair. "I would reach underneath the tablecloth and slide my hand up your thigh," he murmurs. "At first you would look at me wide-eyed and shake your head 'no.' Then you'd casually take a sip of wine and willingly spread your legs just a little where no one else could see. I'd slip my fingers inside the rim of your panties. Or if you're a bad girl, you won't be wearing any."

"No panties then," I say.

"I would finger-fuck you slow at first, like this, so no one would notice."

He slides his fingers in all the way up to his palm. I'm holding my breath now.

"Then I'd lean over and whisper into your ear how tight and wet your pussy feels. And how much I wish I could bend you over the linen tablecloth and sink my cock deep into you from behind."

He pumps his fingers in and out of me harder now, each time more forceful than the last. I close my eyes and buck onto his hand, unable to constrain the low sounds coming from my mouth.

"You wouldn't dare do that at the table in front of everyone," I say, dying to hear more.

He chuckles. "You're right. So we politely excuse ourselves from the table and rush to the nearest restroom. After locking the door, I drag you over to the sink, twist you around, and slide up your sexy black dress up around your waist. You're watching me in the mirror now, with your face flushed and your lips begging to be kissed. I want you so fucking bad it hurts. We don't care if we're in a bathroom or who might hear us. We can't wait another minute to be together."

He nips my ear with his teeth and groans in anguish. "Dammit, Maggie! I can't keep talking about this. It's fucking killing me."

"Don't stop," I beg. "Please."

I press my hand against his cock through his pants for encouragement, feeling it harden and lengthen even more under my touch.

He takes a deep shuddering breath and continues. "I stop for a moment and gaze at you in the mirror just so I can remember you for my wildest dreams. Your dress is low-cut and your tits are falling out. Then I reach down and spread your luscious ass cheeks with my big hands and place the tip of my cock at your pussy. You're already soaking wet and ready for me."

"Oh yes," I whisper.

"Our eyes meet in the mirror as I slide my hard cock all the way into you in one slow push. As deep as I can go, all the way to my balls. You feel so fucking amazing. I wrap your long hair around my hand, holding your head back tight, forcing you to watch us in the mirror as I begin slamming into you from behind. You moan so loud I know the dinner guests can hear you through the bathroom door, but we don't stop. We *can't* stop. Not now. Because nothing else matters."

Suddenly he slips his fingers out of me and I cry out.

"Fuck, Maggie!" he says. "A man can only take so much." He rubs his hand down his face in frustration. "And here I am fully dressed in my uniform. Don't worry, this will only take a second."

Quickly he strips all the way out of his uniform, carefully folding and hanging each piece on a nearby chair so as not to cause wrinkles. The last thing he removes is his white cap. I would've liked for him to keep it on, but I assume that would be wildly inappropriate. Watching him undress only increases my anticipation. I'm almost drooling at the sight of his ripped, muscular body and tattoos.

When every last stitch of clothing has been removed, he strides back toward me like a panther on the prowl. He grabs my shoulders, whirls me around, and bends me over the back of my white sofa. "I hope you want it hard and fast, darling, because that's the way it's happening this time," he warns. "I'm going to explode if I can't get inside your hot pussy now. All this talking is driving me insane."

"Fuck me now," I urge, my voice shaky and uneven. "Just the way you described."

I don't tell him to be careful with the dress or not to mess up my hair. I have a closet full of clothes, and my hair can always be quickly pulled back into a ponytail. I want this as much as he does.

Who am I kidding?

I want it more.

He spreads my ass cheeks wide with both hands and pumps two fingers into me one more time. "God, how I love the sound of your wet pussy," he murmurs. "I can't stop touching you. My fingers, cock...I want everything inside you."

The tip of his cock nudges me from behind and I hold my breath. I barely have the chance to brace myself before he plunges into me in one long, powerful thrust.

In this position, his massive width almost splits me apart. His muscular thighs push against the back of mine, holding me up so that I don't slide down onto the floor in a limp puddle. I gasp out loud as he begins to slam into me with rough, rugged thrusts, holding nothing back.

His callused fingers grip my hips so tight I know there will be bruises there tomorrow. He fucks me savagely, taking me to a place where pleasure and almost pain blend together masterfully. Each lunge of his hips jolts me against the sofa while my insides feel ready to disintegrate. Again and again, his pelvis rocks against me, his penetration so deep I can feel his balls swinging against my ass.

Our lovemaking is like two long-lost lovers coming together after years of separation. It is our most desperate sex ever. I can't stay still or quiet.

This is rough sex personified, and I'm loving every second of it. I delight in the way he takes me mercilessly with just the right amount of force and dominance. I feel so helpless, my lower body completely exposed. He holds onto my hips, forcing me to take him over and over.

Toby *owns* me.

His mouth slides to my neck, nibbling and sucking, right before nipping me with his teeth with enough pressure to make me cry out. Everything feels impossibly good: his cock buried at the perfect slant to reach my secret spots, his large hands molding and squeezing my ass with possessive passion. Reaching around with one hand, he slides it down the neckline of my dress and squeezes my breast hard before tweaking the nipple between his thumb and forefinger

I bite my lip to keep from moaning.

"Don't hold back with me," he commands. "Say my name when you cum."

He drives into me faster, deeper, showing his power in every ferocious, unrepentant lunge. The friction, the angle, and the pressure proves too much. Trapped beneath his muscular body, I can't fight the delicious rush of sensations as he fucks me into oblivion.

"Yes," I pant as an intense orgasm hits, causing my muscles to clench and release spasmodically around him.

"That's it, baby," he mutters through clenched teeth. He slides an arm underneath me, holding me up as he grinds into me harder. His whole frame strains against me while deep inside me he swells and throbs, intensifying his thrusts.

"You feel so fucking good," he says, his breathing harsh. "How do you do this to me?"

His body jerks out several more uneven thrusts as he cums with loud grunts. I feel every pump and pulsation he makes as he explodes deep within me. I clench my muscles around him, wanting to feel every last throb. He continues moving slowly inside me until he's completely spent and exhausted.

He collapses against my back and we stay joined together until our breathing finally slows. I make a sound of regret when he eventually pulls out.

Turning my face around, he kisses me leisurely and slowly. "As much as I would love a round two, we should probably get dressed and head out to the dinner," he says. "Unless you want to blow the whole thing off, stay here, and order pizza?"

He's halfway serious.

"No, this is something we have to do," I say reluctantly. "Much as I hate to. Besides, I want to show you off in your uniform. Give me five minutes to repair my hair and makeup and I'll be ready."

"I'll need at least ten to dress and recover," he says. He grins when I reach down to pull my panties back up from around my ankles.

"What is so funny?" I ask.

"Your hair is tangled and your lipstick is smudged," he says. "You look like you've been thoroughly fucked."

"I have been, and it was *so* worth the wait."

41

MAGGIE

"Do you want me to drive my car?" I ask Toby on our way out to the parking garage.

"Why?" he replies. "Are you ashamed to be seen in a pickup truck? Or afraid of my driving?"

"Neither," I say.

"I washed the truck this morning and vacuumed the inside thoroughly," he says. "It's clean as a whistle."

I give him a doubtful look since the last time we rode together in his truck, the passenger seat was covered in Sadie's yellow hair and smelled of wet dog.

"I swear," he says. "I wouldn't put a girl looking as fine as you do right now in a dirty truck. Give me some credit. Do you see any dog hair on my pants?"

He turns around to give me a view of his fine backside.

"I don't know. Let me feel and see." I slide my hand across his muscular ass. "No hair here. I thought it might be easier for me to drive since I know the way," I explain. "I can give you directions. Luckily it's not too far. Only a couple of miles down the road."

We reach his red truck and he grabs the door handle before I have a chance to open it myself.

"Hang on," he says. "Let me get the door for you."

He opens the door, and I grab the top of the doorframe to try to climb in. The truck is tall. Getting into the truck in my heels and tight dress is not going to be easy or graceful.

Toby laughs when I struggle to put one foot up inside the truck and my dress slides up my ass. He scoops me up with an arm around my waist and the other under my legs to deposit me gently on the seat.

"All you had to do was ask for help, darling," he breathes against my hair. "I'll pick you up and carry you wherever you want to go. Just say the word. I'm all yours."

"Is that true?"

"What? That I'll sling you over my shoulder and haul your pretty ass around like a sack of flour? Absolutely, I'll do that in a heartbeat."

"No," I reply. "That you're all mine."

He grins and instead of answering shuts the truck door after making sure I'm all tucked inside. Going around to the driver's side, he slides in and turns on the radio.

"What kind of music are you in the mood for?" he asks. "How about Waylon Jennings? Do you know him?"

I don't have a clue who Waylon Jennings is. Apparently a country music singer from the woeful, sad song now playing on the radio.

"That's fine with me," I say.

He seems satisfied with my answer. I notice his arms tensing up on the drive down out of the parking garage, but he doesn't say a word. Once we exit the parking garage and are outside in the sunlight, he visibly relaxes again.

"Whew!" he says. "Glad to be out of there."

"Do you have something against parking garages?" I ask.

"I have something against dark spaces and driving around blind corners," he replies. "Now that I've seen where you live, I'm worried about you. It doesn't feel safe for a woman. How often do you work late at night?"

"Most of the time," I reply. "Don't worry. There's multiple layers of security. I'm perfectly safe."

Secretly I'm thrilled Toby is concerned for my welfare. It makes me feel good to know that my man cares about me.

My man.

Is that what Toby is now?

It's certainly how it feels to me.

"Tell me what to expect at this shindig," he says. "And remind me again of why I need to be there. Couldn't the Mayor just mail my award to me? How big is this thing? Three feet tall?"

"Most people would love to have an invitation to dinner with the Mayor at the country club," I remind him. "It's an honor to be selected."

He shakes his head. "I'm not most people, and my definition of honor is a little different than having dinner with a bunch of fancy people trying to impress each other."

"You're right," I say. "And everything is about politics these days. If holding a fancy dinner and giving you an award didn't win the Mayor points, he wouldn't be doing it either. I realize this isn't your idea of a good time. If nothing else, think of it as an opportunity to meet my family. Mom and Dad will there along with my sister, Nicole and her husband, Brad. They're all looking forward to meeting you."

Toby glances over at me. "Should I be worried?"

"Not at all," I reassure. "They'll love you. How could they not?"

"Maggie!"

My sister Nicole squeals loudly when she spots us walking into the lobby of the country club. "We've been waiting for you," she says, rushing over and tugging her husband behind her.

Nicole grabs me in a big hug then turns to Toby. "I'm Nicole, the big sister. And you must be the one and only Toby. I've been dying to meet you. Maggie has told me so much about you."

Not true.

I've barely said one word to Nicole about Toby, which was intentional. It's not that I wanted to keep Toby a secret. It was more that I wanted to keep him all to myself. I'm still trying to get to know him, and sharing didn't seem right. Not yet.

Toby gives Nicole a polite, guarded smile. He's been here two minutes and is already uncomfortable. He reaches out to shake her hand then politely shakes Brad's as well.

"I'm Toby. Nice to meet you both."

"Same here," Brad says. He takes off his black eyeglasses and cleans them with the handkerchief tucked into his suit pocket. "You're quite the hero, Toby. I can't imagine being the center of all this media attention. It was incredible how quickly the video of the shooting went viral." He glances over at me. "How many views did it get, Maggie? Fifty million views in twenty-four hours? That's quite a coup and amazing exposure for you. I hope you turned that into some big dollars."

I've been around Brad enough to know that he can be a complete asshole at times without even trying. To compare the terrorist incident to a viral video is thoughtless to say the least. Toby's eyes have gone chilly. This is going to be a long evening.

"Saving lives was my priority," Toby replies coldly. "The media attention has been more of a pain in the ass than anything else. Except for Maggie."

He reaches behind him to take my hand. When he touches it, he links his fingers through mine.

Nicole's eyes drop down at our interlocked hands.

Okay, the secret is out. No point in denying or hiding my relationship with Toby any longer. I tighten my grip on his hand. We're in this together now. One way or the other.

I stare back at her, defying her to say anything.

All she does is raise her eyebrows imperceptibly in a question. "Mom and Dad are already at the table," she says, waving her hand toward the ballroom. "The Mayor is about to make his opening remarks in a few minutes, so we should be seated. You're running late by the way. What kept you? I thought you said you would be here at seven, and you're always so prompt. I was about to send out the rescue squad to search for you."

"Heavy traffic," Toby answers while giving my hand a little squeeze. "Lots of stopping and starting. You know how it is. You speed up and then have to slam on the brakes. Over and over."

He winks at me behind Nicole's back, and I try not to giggle as we follow them down the hallway. I love the feeling of the two of us against the world.

Dad sees us coming from across the room and stands up to greet us. He is distinguished as always with his thick grey hair and tailored dark suit. Mom is seated beside him in a demure light pink dress. She's wearing her favorite pair of pearls with matching earrings.

Her face appears younger than when I saw her at Christmas. At first I can't figure out why, then realize it's due to her bi-monthly Botox shots and fillers for the lines in her face. As soon as the wrinkles start to show, she books an appointment at the day spa. Mom tries her best to maintain a youthful appearance. She says it's because they're photographed frequently for Atlanta's society pages. I know it's because she can't stand the thought of getting old.

When we approach the table, Dad's eyes slide from Toby's freshly shined shoes, to our linked hands, all the way up to Toby's curly hair that is a little too long and touching the collar of his uniform.

Dad never misses anything.

When I was growing up, I could never get away with the slightest bit of mischief because he could take one look at me and know I'd been up to something. "Maggie," he would always say. "What have you done now?"

It wouldn't surprise me if he'd already guessed before tonight that Toby and I were an item. To Dad's credit, he is careful not to show the disapproval on his face.

He doesn't need to.

I can feel it coming off him in waves.

Standing up on my tiptoes, I kiss Dad's cheek then lean down to kiss Mom too.

"Dad, this is Toby," I say, placing a hand on Toby's arm. "I lived to see another day because of this man's courage."

Dad smiles warmly and reaches out to give Toby a firm handshake. "You don't need to remind us of that," he says. "We owe you our utmost gratitude, son. I don't know how we would make it if something happened to one of our daughters. Thank you for protecting her."

"I was thankful to have been there where I could," Toby says.

"Come over here, dear, and have a seat beside me," Mom says to Toby. "I want to hear all about you." She pats the empty chair beside her.

We move around to her side of the table. I notice Toby glancing at the doors, which are directly behind where we'll be sitting. He pulls out a chair for me and sits down beside Mom. After a second, he shifts his chair, angling it sideways where he can talk to her and still have a clear view of the doorway. I wonder what he's going to do when the meal is served and he has no choice but to turn around completely to eat.

If given a choice, I would've preferred to put myself between him and my family. Hopefully he can hold his own with them. At least Mom can always be counted on to be polite and sugary sweet.

She's one of those Southern women who can convincingly say "bless your heart" in a sympathetic voice while mentally fantasizing how she would stab you in the heart. Mom wouldn't dare be rude to Toby no matter how she might feel about our relationship. It's the rest of the family I'm worried about.

Nicole and Brad take their seats directly across the table from us. Brad makes a big show of carefully straightening his designer tie. Does he really think Toby will be impressed by his seven-hundred-dollar tie? Then I realize it's not Toby he's trying to impress, it's Dad.

"How is the zoning for your new construction project going?" Brad asks Dad.

"Slow," Dad replies. "Hopefully a little faster after tonight. All I need is a few minutes of the Mayor's time to light a fire under the zoning commission. He knows where his bread has been buttered all these years. And if he doesn't, I'll remind him."

We all laugh politely. Dad has been a heavy political donor to the Atlanta Mayor's campaigns for years. If he wants something, he won't stop until he gets it.

"So Toby," Brad says. "I understand you were a Marine in Afghanistan. I assume that's why you're dressed the way you are."

Toby clears his throat. "That's right," he says. "I was. I've been back a while."

I slide my hand under the table and place it lightly on Toby's leg. I can feel the tension in his thigh muscles.

"And what are you doing for a real job now that you're back in the States?" Brad asks. He turns to peer up at the waiter beside him, who is pouring a sip of Chardonnay into his wineglass. After testing it, Brad nods his approval. "Very nice. Thank you. The wine has a nice, smoky finish." The waiter turns the bottle so Brad can read the label.

I'm not sure why Brad is tasting the wine since he's not paying for it.

What would he do if the wine was awful? Send it back and demand a better bottle?

The waiter beams happily as if he stomped the grapes to make the wine himself and finishes pouring Brad's glass. Brad takes another sip. "Excellent wine," he says. "From one of my favorite vineyards in Napa Valley. We should go there again this fall for a weekend, Nicole."

"Definitely," Nicole replies emphatically.

She leans forward, giving Toby a clear view of her ample breasts across the table. A gift from Brad after her last baby to ward off post-partum depression. According to her, nothing beats breast implants and a vaginal rejuvenation procedure to lift a new mother's mood.

"Last year we shipped home cases of wine from several boutique wineries in Napa," she says. "Specialty wines that you can't buy here. It was well worth the trip to stock our wine cellar. You two should come over one night for a wine tasting."

What fun that would be. I resist the urge to roll my eyes at Toby.

"I'm sorry," Brad says, turning his attention back to Toby. "With all this talk about wine, we didn't give you a chance to answer. What is it you do now for a living?"

Toby clears his throat again and drinks half a glass of water before answering. "I work on cars. You know...detailing them. Fixing them up for resale. That kind of thing."

"Sports cars, I presume?" Brad asks. "I know a man in Buckhead who runs a shop...Ferraris, Porsches. The occasional Lamborghini."

"No, Buicks," Toby replies with a straight face. "Ford trucks, Nissans, just normal cars that need body work done for regular people."

"Oh," Brad replies, clearly disappointed the conversation didn't shift to sports cars, where he could wow us all with his vast knowledge. "You own the body shop then? I can imagine there would be good money in that. The last time someone dinged my car door with a shopping cart, it cost over two thousand dollars to fix. It's outrageous what the body shop charged for repairs."

Toby shakes his head. "I work for someone else. My buddies Rocco and Donny own the shop. They're good guys and easy to work for."

Dad is appalled. "Surely you must have plans to start your own shop one day?" he asks with a frown. "Owning your own business is the best way to make it these days, son. There's no need to work for someone else only to line their pockets. I started out as a young man with nothing."

Oh no. Here we go again with Dad's spiel. Nicole catches my eye and winks at me. We've heard it so many times before.

"I borrowed fifty dollars as a down payment on my first tiny house in a run-down section of Atlanta. Fixed it up, sold it for more. The rest is history. Now I own apartment complexes and office buildings across the city. Never limit yourself by just being an employee. Don't work for the man, *be* the man. That's what I always told myself."

Dad is only getting started on his business philosophy. I've heard it so many times that I can recite it by heart. Now that he has a new audience to listen to him, he won't stop all night. I squeeze Toby's leg to let him know I understand this isn't fun and I'm right there with him.

"I can't abandon my bosses right now," Toby says firmly. "They gave me a job when nobody else was willing to when I returned from Afghanistan. They depend on me and they treat me right. I've got no complaints. I'm not going to leave them to start a competing business. It wouldn't be the right thing to do. Especially since we're in a small town. There's no room for two body shops in Bardsville."

Dad leans back in his chair. I can tell by the resignation on his face that he's already written Toby off. I doubt he'll be asking him many more questions tonight. He glances over at me and I can see everything he's thinking in his eyes.

That Toby is below us.

That I deserve someone better.

For the first time in my life, I'm feeling ashamed by the fakeness of my family. I've lived with it so long that I never questioned it before.

Brad nods as if he understands perfectly what Toby is saying. "I've heard about the servicemen having trouble finding jobs when they come back home," he says. "It's understandable when you think about it. For one thing, they don't have any real skills or training. The military should offer them night classes in accounting or coding while they're stationed over there in the desert. I'm sure they have lots of extra time on their hands. All they do is drive around in convoys hunting for Taliban who aren't there anymore. I mean, Osama Bin Laden is long gone. What's the point? It is such a waste of our resources. Wouldn't you agree?"

Toby picks up his fragile crystal water glass and twirls the stem between his thumb and forefinger. I'm half-expecting him to snap it. "They're still around," Toby says calmly. "Along with other enemy insurgents. There's plenty enough work to keep the troops busy and not a lot of free time."

He glances over his shoulder again toward the doorway for the umpteenth time. I can tell it's making him nervous to sit with his back to the door, and it's making me anxious to watch him fidget.

"Nicole, would you and Brad mind switching places with us?" I interrupt. "Toby prefers to sit where he can see the door. Because of the shooting and everything. You understand, don't you?"

Nicole's eyes widen. "Sure," she says with a tiny smile. "Whatever makes Toby feel more comfortable." I'm the only one who can pick up the hint of sarcasm in her voice.

Brad looks confused and points to his glass. "But the wine has already been poured," he says. He waves a hand at his plate. "And the waiter has taken our orders."

Nicole stands up and taps his shoulder. "Grab your glass and let's switch places with them. Stop arguing. It's not a big deal. They gave us two choices, chicken or pasta. Surely the waiter can figure it out if we move." She rolls her eyes at me over his head.

Toby doesn't say anything when we play musical chairs and all switch places. When we're settled into our seats again, I mouth a 'thank you' across the table to Nicole. On rare occasions, my big sister has been known to come through for me. This is one of those times.

Brad makes an exaggerated point of glancing back over his shoulder at the door as Toby was previously doing. "Is there anything back there I should be watching for too?" he jokes. "If men come in with guns blazing, I prefer for Toby to see them first. Since I left my shotgun at the house." He laughs loudly at his joke that nobody else finds funny.

I take a deep breath and try to give Toby a reassuring smile. I'm ready for the night to be over and the first course hasn't even been served. I'm relieved when the Mayor steps up to the podium to give his opening remarks. This isn't the first award ceremony I've attended since covering similar events is part of my job description. I know what to expect, and I've briefed Toby so he'll be prepared.

The Mayor's speech is almost word-for-word the same as always except for copying and pasting a few additional details. He thanks Toby for his heroism and reminds the crowd of how heroes are the ones who step up even when it means putting their own lives at risk.

When he calls Toby's name and asks him to come up for the award, I hold my breath. All Toby needs to do is accept the award, thank him politely, and walk back to the table. I've gone over all this with him before tonight. He doesn't need to give a speech or even to say a few words. Nothing but a 'thank you' and he'll be done.

When Toby steps up beside the Mayor in his uniform, a surprising and overwhelming feeling of emotion comes over me, causing unexpected tears to spring into my eyes.

I'm so proud of him.

And honored to be with him, to call him mine.

Toby is everything I've ever wanted in a man.

I'm hopelessly, completely in love with him. I have been since the very first day.

The Mayor says a few words and hands him the plaque. Toby shakes his hand, thanks him in his husky, deep voice, and walks back to his seat. I stand up to greet him. He wraps his arms around me and kisses my hair. Closing my eyes, I melt into his warm chest. I don't care who sees us or what they think.

This man is mine for keeps.

42

TOBY

When will this fucking nightmare of a dinner be over?

I wish I had never agreed to do this. What was I possibly thinking?

The main course has just been served, and the dinner has dragged on for hours already.

Or so it seems.

I've lost count of how many times the waiter has leaned over the table to refill the wine glasses. In the last hour, Maggie's mom has turned into a silly, giggly mess, and Nicole isn't in much better shape.

Maggie never mentioned her mom having an alcohol problem. Maybe she doesn't and is only trying to make it through the night any way she can. The same way I am. If I wasn't wearing my Marine uniform, I'd be sucking down the wine too. Anything to make it stop.

To make things worse, the pathetic excuse for a man sitting across from me will not shut the fuck up.

Brad.

Why do all pricks have names like Brad or Chad? Do their parents know they're going to grow up to be assholes the day they're born?

He's enjoying needling me. Constantly digging at me with little comments about everything from my shiny shoes to my truck. Has no one ever warned him about the dangers of poking a wild animal?

I'm sure he was a bully in school. Picking on kids much younger than him and always hiding behind his Daddy's money if he got called out on it.

Someone needs to teach this asshole a lesson.

As much as I'd enjoy it, it won't be me. Not tonight anyway.

Seeing the way Maggie looked at me when I was standing beside the Mayor made the whole night worthwhile. Her eyes were glowing with pride.

In me.

I've never had that feeling ever before in my entire life.

Even Brad can't take that away from me. As difficult as it is, I'll keep ignoring him the best I can until we can get out of here.

"How soon can we leave?" I whisper to Maggie.

She gives me an understanding smile and squeezes my hand underneath the table. "Not yet. After this they'll serve dessert, coffee, and after dinner drinks. It will be over soon, I promise."

Great.

That's all we need to make this shit fest better. More alcohol.

"Toby, you never did explain exactly why you didn't want to sit with your back to the door? Why is that?" Brad asks, his voice starting to slur. He's carefully cutting his steak, holding the knife and fork in what I assume would be the perfect position. I sure as hell wouldn't know. Half the time I use my pocketknife to cut my steak if it's handy.

"I need to see who is coming into a room," I explain. "Basic common sense if you ask me. To always be aware of your surroundings."

Brad nods and pops the bite of steak into his mouth. He chews and looks at me thoughtfully until he swallows.

"Isn't that one of the classic symptoms of post-traumatic stress disorder? Always thinking you're about to be bombed or attacked? I guess in your case PTSD was a handy disorder to have the day of the mall shooting and the car bomb."

I sincerely hope he chokes on his steak.

With my luck, there would be ten doctors in the room who would jump up and run over to do the Heimlich on him if he did.

"One of the symptoms," I reply.

Anyone with any brains would get the hint this is not something I'm comfortable talking about. My blood pressure is starting to rise.

"That's one of the things I don't get," Brad says. He holds his fork in the air as if he's directing a symphony. "These guys graduate from high school without a clue what they're going to do with their life, so they enlist in the military. Okay, fair enough. They're only in the service a few years and when they come back, they expect the government to pay for everything. College tuition, health care. It's ridiculous."

He's seriously treading on dangerous territory now. Maggie knows it too. She's gripping my knee so tight, I'm surprised there is still circulation left in it.

"Why should the government pay for all that?" he continues. "They claim their time in the Middle East is stressful and they deserve it. My job is extremely stressful too. You want to know stressful? Try being a tax accountant between the end of January and April 15th. You don't know stressful until you try that. And yet the government is not offering to pay anything for me." He shakes his head slowly and holds up his fingers to tick them off one by one. "Not my college. Not my medical bills. Certainly no housing allowance. Or retirement benefits. Why should they be special? I don't get it."

"Maybe because they're risking their lives for this country?" I argue. "Bad things happen over there. The men aren't the same when they come back. It changes them. They're not asking for handouts. They need the help. Especially healthcare."

I'm wasting my breath. Why am I trying to explain anything to this guy?

Brad waves a disgusted hand in the air. "I think that's all just a big excuse for them to get hooked on painkillers or drugs," he says. "Most of the ones I've met are nothing but a bunch of burned-out drug addicts. They would be losers no matter what they did in life."

"Brad!" Maggie's dad reprimands him sharply.

Too late.

I've heard enough.

I'm already stretching my big frame across the table and grab Brad by the necktie. I lift him up and jerk him toward me, dragging his expensive tie through mashed potatoes and brown gravy. My arms knock over both of our wineglasses, spilling the Napa Valley wine with the smoky finish onto the white linen tablecloth and into Maggie's mom's half-finished plate of food.

Brad's eyes are wide with shock and something else.

Fear.

"Don't you ever say anything like that to me again," I warn through clenched teeth. "Do you understand me? Those men have gone through things a weak pussy like you would never be able to withstand. You're not fit to even speak of them. You disgust me. Living in your fancy house, driving your expensive sports car and wearing designer clothes while the real men are out there fighting for your right to do exactly that. Never speak of them again. Not one word. Do you understand me?"

Brad's skin has gone three shades paler, and he's about to puke up his steak right into Nicole's lap.

"You're not nodding," I say. "Nod if you comprehend what I'm saying."

He nods once.

I tighten my grip and start to smash his nose into the table when I feel Maggie's hand on my arm. "Toby," she says quietly.

I shove him back down in his chair and let go of his tie. He grabs his throat and coughs. The room has gone dead still and quiet. Everyone is staring at me, wide-eyed with their mouths open in shock and confusion.

The hero turned unhinged psychopath.

I catch sight of Maggie's face and wish I hadn't. Her eyes are filled with hurt and embarrassment. I've humiliated her in front of her family and friends.

Without another word, I walk away from the table and head quickly for the door.

Fuck!

I can't fix this now. Things have gone too far.

I was a fool to think this could ever work out between us. We're too different, from entirely opposite worlds. It was only a matter of time before the fairy tale came crashing back down to reality.

Me and Maggie were never meant to be.

"Toby! Wait!" Maggie yells after me.

"Sit down, young lady," I hear her dad order sternly. "Let him go. He's not worth it."

I'm almost at the truck before I realize she's right behind me, running through the country club parking lot to catch up in her high heels and slinky dress.

"Wait!" she yells again. "Please! I'm coming with you."

When I reach the truck and hit the unlock button, she climbs into the passenger seat and tugs on her seatbelt. I start to argue with her and realize this isn't the place for the conversation we need to have.

43

MAGGIE

Toby pulls up into a parking space in front of my apartment building marked "Ten Minute Parking Only" and cuts the ignition. He crosses his arms and slumps back in his seat.

"What are you doing?" I ask. "Why aren't we driving up to my floor? You can't park here. The security guard will come out and make us move the truck in a few minutes."

"I can't do this anymore," he says softly.

"Do what?"

"Any of it, Maggie. I can't pretend I'm a normal person when I'm not. I can't be in a relationship. It's never going to work. Not now or ever."

I frown at him. We were both silent for the short drive from the country club back to my place. I didn't know what to say and was waiting for him to speak first. His outburst surprised me, but it wasn't as if Brad didn't have it coming.

"I don't blame you for being upset," I say. "Brad is a prick. He always has been. That doesn't mean you need to take it out on me. It wasn't my fault what happened tonight. Please don't make this about us. We're fine."

Toby doesn't answer. Instead he slips a finger inside the front of his stiff collar and tugs, then makes a frustrated sound when it doesn't budge. He starts trying to unbutton his uniform. "Dammit!" he says. "This uniform is choking the crap out of me." His big fingers can't maneuver the tight button at his neck.

I unbuckle my seat belt and slide closer. "Let me help you." Reaching up, I gently try to move his hands away. He grabs my hand firmly in his to stop me then drops it.

"I'm fine," he says tersely.

"Are you sure? Because you don't seem fine."

He nods and blows out a long breath.

"Okay," I say with a sigh. "Maybe it was partially my fault tonight. I know what a jerk Brad can be. I never should have invited him to the dinner. I'm sorry. He's blunt and obnoxious. The worst part is I doubt he realized what he said was wrong. He's an idiot. Always has been. I'm sorry he ruined what should have been a special night for you."

Toby places both of his muscular arms across the steering wheel and leans his forehead on them. He's exhausted. I wonder if he's sleeping or if the nightmares are keeping him awake at night.

"I'm not blaming you," he mumbles. "None of this is your fault. It's mine. I should have never started this up with you. I knew I was a mental mess and I did it anyway."

"Where is this coming from?" I ask. "We were having a great evening until Brad opened his big mouth. You seemed fine at the apartment before we left for dinner."

An uneasy feeling is forming in the pit of my stomach. Subconsciously, I know what's coming and don't want to face it.

"You have so much going for you," he says. "A career. A nice place to live." He waves a hand at the apartment lobby where the security guard is giving us the evil eye through the glass doors. "And a well-to-do family. I can't offer you anything. All I am is a biker who works on cars in a dirty garage. That's it."

I haven't heard Toby talk this way before. Alarm bells start ringing in my head.

"You're a lot more than that," I say. "Stop putting yourself down. You're more of a man than anyone I've ever met before."

"It's not that really," he says flatly. "If it was only a matter of money or a lifestyle, I would fight for you." He takes my hand and turns it over so he can trace my palm with his finger. "With everything I have in me. I would fight for my queen. I could work harder. Or go back to school. Get an education. Whatever it took to make you mine. I would try my best to get you whatever you wanted or needed. And our kids too if we ever had any."

A cold chill goes through me. Why is he talking about how things could have been instead of how things will be?

"Fight for me then! You're confusing me. What is so bad that it can't be worked on and fixed?"

He turns his head sideways and looks directly at me. His eyes are full of raw pain. This is the second time I've seen them this way. How much sorrow is hidden deep inside this man? I would do anything to make it go away. I've never felt so powerless.

"I can't be fixed," he says. "I'm damaged goods. No, correction. Not just damaged. I'm broken inside beyond repair. Completely shattered into pieces. And dangerous. Let's not forget that. What kind of a man almost chokes a woman to death before their first date?"

"You were having a nightmare. I don't blame you for that."

"How does that make a difference if I had killed you? I can't stop thinking about what I did. Can you imagine what your father would say? Or your mother? Or the police?" He puts his hand to his chest. "Personally, I wouldn't want any daughter of mine within one hundred yards of a man like me. I'm too unpredictable. Tonight I wanted to kill Brad. I honestly did. I felt a murderous rage take over me when he started criticizing my brothers in the military. As if they were less than nothing. Men who have lost their lives for assholes like him."

"Don't feel too bad for wanting to kill him," I say. "He deserved your rage. Nobody would have blamed you for putting him in his place. My parents were horrified by the thoughtless things he was saying too. I could tell."

"There's a difference between being mad and actually wanting to kill someone," he says. "I saw your face tonight. You were embarrassed by me when I lost it. I don't blame you. A fancy dinner isn't the place for a bar room brawl." He shrugs. "I couldn't ignore him and just let it go. Not about that. He could've called me dog shit and I might have turned the other cheek to keep the peace at the dinner table. But to put down the men in the military was more than I could swallow. I'm sorry the night didn't turn out better and that I made such a terrible first impression on your parents."

"It doesn't matter," I say, trying to reassure him. "You don't have to be around Brad again if you don't want to be. And my parents will understand if I tell them about your PTSD."

Or would they?

This conversation is quickly taking a downhill turn, and I'm starting to panic.

"We can work through this," I say, talking faster now. "We can work through anything together. Let's drive up to my apartment and park your truck. We can go inside my place and talk all night if we need to. Just don't leave when you're upset."

Toby slowly shakes his head. "You still don't get it. The reason we're sitting here outside your building is because I can't make myself drive into that parking garage again. I just can't. And I don't expect you to understand that my mind is telling me that there's danger around every dark curve. When I drove in there earlier today, my adrenaline level was through the roof by the time I knocked on your door."

"I'll drive the truck up," I suggest. "You can take the elevator from the lobby on the first floor. Then I'll drive your truck down in the morning. It's not a big deal."

"See what's happening here? You're already making accommodations for my mental instability. My craziness is affecting you. Did you know that yesterday I almost hit another driver head on? I saw a black trash bag that a volunteer clean-up crew had left on the side of the road for the next crew to pick up. When I glanced at it, I didn't see a trash bag. I saw a hidden IED that could explode at any moment. So I instinctively swerved away from it the same way I'd been taught to do. Except I wasn't on a dusty, desert road in Afghanistan. I was on a two-lane highway. I ran the other driver right off onto the shoulder of the road before I corrected. It's a miracle I didn't kill someone. Next time I might. Or you might be riding behind me on a bike when it happens. There's zero room for error on a bike."

Why hasn't he been talking to me about this more? Toby's PTSD is worse than I could've imagined. He's trying so hard to keep it hidden when he should be letting people help him through it.

Always the tough guy.

The protector.

Never a man who asks for help.

"How often does this kind of thing happen?" I ask. "Every day? Occasionally?"

"Often enough lately," he says, tiredly rubbing the back of his neck. "For a long time, I had my shit together. Or at least I thought I did. Maybe it was always simmering right below the surface, ready to boil over at any time. The shooting at the mall triggered something in me."

He slumps back against the seat and leans his head against the window.

"I hate the word 'trigger' since it's so overused. The truth is that's what happened. The attack put my brain right back in Afghanistan where every day was a fight for survival. Where danger could be hiding anywhere. Now that I'm back in that fucking dark place, I can't find my way out again. I'm going crazy. And I'm dragging you down into the nuthouse with me."

"We can get you help," I suggest. "I'm sure there are counselors who specialize in PTSD."

He snorts. "You think I haven't been to counselors already? I have. I'm not one of those men who think it's a weakness to ask for help." He lets out a humorless laugh. "Okay, maybe I am. My commander forced me to go. Said it was an order. Otherwise I wouldn't have gone either."

"What did they say?"

"That I wasn't alone. That PTSD is more common than people know. That I needed to find a way to work through it. They suggested all kinds of things. Support groups, talk therapy. Even a weird kind of exposure therapy where you wear a virtual reality headset that mimics going on patrol in Afghanistan. I said a big 'fuck no!' to that one. I didn't like the thought of any of it."

"You stopped going to the counselors?"

"Hell yes I did!" he answers. "I went a couple of times and that's about it. The last straw was when they started pressuring me to take medication. I have friends who are so drugged up on anti-depressants and mood stabilizers that they can't function. I can't be doped up on meds and ride a bike or carry weapons. That's not happening. All the talking was making things worse too. It brought everything back up to the surface where it felt raw. I handle things better when I can put it out of my mind. The less I dwell on my time in the military, the better."

"Your technique obviously hasn't worked so far," I remind him gently.

"It was working fine. Until the day at the mall. God, how I wished that hadn't happened. It turned my life upside down."

"Then we wouldn't have met."

"Which for your sake would have been for the best," he argues. "We can't keep on this way. There's no point in dragging things out when I know it's going to end badly for both of us."

"What exactly are you saying?"

He regretfully lets go of my hand. "That we're over. This is the way it has to be. And it doesn't mean that I don't care for you, because I do. Too much. That's why I'm letting you go. And please don't argue with me about this. I can't expect any woman to be with me when I need to do so much work on myself."

Now I'm beginning to feel angry. I can't believe he would walk away from us so quickly. Without putting up a fair fight. I thought we were more than that.

"I think you're trying to find an excuse to dump me," I say, fighting back tears. "I'm nothing more than another Sweet Butt to you. You're making up excuses to let me down easy."

Toby reaches over to tuck my long hair behind my ear and cups my cheek. I close my eyes and lean into his hand.

"Maggie, please don't. You know what I'm saying is the truth. Deep down inside you want to believe I'm your Guardian Angel when I'm your worst fucking nightmare. I'm doing this to protect you. From me. From who I am now. If we stay together, something bad is going to happen. I can feel it."

"We can work through this together," I say again.

A single tear oozes out of the corner of my eye and starts sliding down my cheek. He brushes it away with his thumb.

"You know how much I love Sadie, right?"

I nod because there's no doubt in my mind how much he loves his dog. If there's one thing I know for sure, Toby adores Sadie.

"Be honest," he says. "What do you think I would do if I knew I couldn't provide food for her or give her the love she deserves? I would try my best to find a loving home where other people would take good care of her. I wouldn't want to be without her, but for her sake, I would do what was best. Do you understand what I'm saying?"

"That you're comparing me to a dog?" I say, trying to laugh and failing.

"No. That I'm willing to make personal sacrifices for those that I care about."

"If you care about me so much, then you wouldn't walk away."

"There isn't a choice," he says. "Not with the way I am now."

Toby's voice is dead, flat, and without emotion. He's shut himself off from me now. I know him well enough to realize that things aren't going to get any better tonight. Maybe he just needs some space and time. I can give him that.

I'm willing to give him whatever he needs.

The security guard is walking toward us now. Any second and he's going to be tapping on Toby's window.

I wipe away my tears with the back of my hand and hit the unlock button on the truck door.

"This isn't over," I say. "I'm not giving up on you."

I slide out of the truck and tug my dress down before walking over to meet the security guard who is halfway to the truck.

"It's okay," I say. "He was just leaving."

I don't turn around or look back.

44

TOBY

The two-hour drive back to the North Georgia mountains from Atlanta is long and tiring. At the halfway mark, it starts to pour down an icy mixture of sleet and freezing rain. The truck's wipers are partially broken and make a loud, scraping sound every time they clear the windshield. It wouldn't surprise me if they quit completely. It would be a perfect ending to a mother-fucking disaster of a day.

I want to get home and take a long, hot shower. Forget about tonight and try my best to forget about Maggie.

I did the right thing.

I'm sure of it.

It's better to hurt her a little now than to have something awful happen to her later. When I completely snapped tonight, it scared me. This is the second time I've done something completely crazy, dangerous, and unpredictable. If Maggie hadn't been sitting beside me, I would've beaten Brad into a lifeless pulp. Knowing she was watching me was the only thing holding me back.

In the Marines, I was known for being cool and collected under pressure. Always accurate with a rifle. Precise and emotionless.

Now I'm a loose cannon going off and out of control. Since the shooting, I'm slowly but surely becoming mentally unhinged. Instead of getting better, every day I'm progressively getting worse.

I can't be with Maggie when I'm this way.
She deserves better.
And I don't deserve her.

45

MAGGIE

My cell phone rings, waking me from a fitful sleep. I grab it and hit the accept button, hoping it's Toby.

"We need to talk," Nicole says firmly.

Damn. The last person I want to talk to this morning. I close my eyes and plop back down on the pillows.

"Do we have to?" I ask. "What's to say? Brad was an asshole the entire night and Toby got sick of it. Brad had it coming. He should be thankful Toby didn't drag him outside and beat the crap out of him. If he did, I would have been right there cheering him on."

"Brad has a nasty bruise on his neck this morning," Nicole says. "We're thinking about taking him to the emergency room. What if there is permanent damage? And how is he supposed to go to work and meet with clients looking as if he was in a bar fight?"

Nicole is being overly dramatic as usual.

"Put some ice on it. He'll be fine. His pride is hurt more than anything. You and I both know that. I'm surprised this hasn't happened to him before now. He's been pulling this crap for years."

"Last night was humiliating," she whines. "It was an embarrassment to Mom and Dad too. Their friends and business associates were there to witness the whole thing. You can't go around physically assaulting people. Can you imagine what everyone at the country club thought? Toby is lucky we're not filing charges."

I bolt straight up in bed.

"Nicole, I'm warning you right now. If Brad files charges against Toby or causes trouble for him in any way, I'll never forgive you. I'm serious. Brad is a pompous jerk and always has been. Let it go. And as far as being humiliated, you *should* be humiliated by the way Brad acts. I don't know how you tolerate him. Mom and Dad were probably more embarrassed by his obnoxious behavior than by Toby causing a scene."

Dead silence comes from the other end of the line.

"I'll talk to Brad," she says after a moment. "I agree it would be better for everyone to forget this ever happened." She sighs. "I know he can be an ass sometimes. On the drive home, he kept asking me what he said to set Toby off. He really didn't have a clue."

"Why does that not surprise me?"

"There's actually another reason I called. I'm worried about your relationship with Toby. He has a weird psychological hold on you, and I'm concerned."

I frown. "What do you mean?"

"He saved your life, and you were together during a very traumatic event. It's only human nature that you would continue to cling to him after it ended. I think you should talk to a psychologist about it. I'm sure there's a scientific term for it."

I let out an incredulous laugh. "No way. You want me to see a shrink because you don't understand my feelings for Toby? That's not happening. Sure, he's not my usual type and we never would have met under normal circumstances. I'll admit that. What we have together is real and good. Better than anything I've ever felt before with another man. You make me sound as if I'm psychologically unstable. I'm not."

"Are you trying to convince me or yourself?" she asks quietly. "No matter what, you know that I love you. You're my baby sister and I want only the best for you. Your relationship with Toby scares me to death. What do you really know about this man? Be honest. Not for me. For yourself. My suggestion would be to take some time apart. Let the physical heat die down for a bit and see where things stand. A month from now, you might think back on this and wonder what you were ever doing with him."

"It doesn't matter because he broke up with me last night." I choke the words out. "You don't need to worry about me. It's over now."

"Are you upset?" Nicole asks. "I can tell that you are. I'm sorry about that. It's for the best. Toby sees it too. You come from two different worlds and it would never work out between you. You've dodged another bullet with him leaving. Let him go. I know you can be a bulldog when you want something or believe in a cause. There are times when it's better to leave things alone."

"It seems I don't have a choice now anyway," I say. "I've got to run. I'll talk to you soon." I click the phone off without waiting for her to say goodbye.

I can't help wondering about what she said. Could I be infatuated with Toby in some weird way because of the circumstances that threw us together? I know what I feel for him and how I feel when I'm with him.

Nothing has ever felt so real.

Or have I been so taken by the intense sexual chemistry between us that I never thought past the present? Our living arrangements would be one of the many hurdles to overcome. I have a great job in the city that I don't want to give up. Toby is happy living in the mountains and could never be comfortable in Atlanta. He's a country boy and I was raised in a high-society family.

Last night was a perfect example of the collision course we were on. All it took was a match to ignite the meltdown of our relationship. I couldn't keep Toby hidden in a box forever. Whatever issues we have would've popped up sooner or later.

Still though, it's hard for me to accept. If Toby didn't care about me, it would be different. Last night I could see the love for me in his eyes and feel it in the way his hand caressed my cheek.

No way is this over.

My Daddy didn't raise a quitter.

Nicole is right about one thing. There are still so many things that I don't know about Toby. Especially about his time in the military. I wish I could talk to someone who knew him then. The boy soldier who returned a shattered man.

A man that I love with all my heart.

If I can't talk to someone who knows him, I'll do the next best thing.

I'll talk to men or women who have had personal experience fighting in the Middle East. Maybe they can give me insight and help me to better understand what Toby is going through.

There's a veteran's hospital on the other side of the city. I'll pay a visit today and see if anyone would be willing to talk to me.

I'm not giving up on Toby.

Not now.

Not ever.

46

MAGGIE

"This is great stuff, Maggie," my station manager, Roger, tells me over the phone. "I'll switch some things around and make room this week to air the segments during the evening news. Come in as soon as you can to tape the promo spots and we'll start running them."

"Really?" I'm so shocked I almost run my car off the road. Another driver blows his horn at me when I get too close to the middle lane. "Are you serious?"

I can't believe it.

After years of doing fluff pieces, I'm finally getting an opportunity to do a news segment reporting on something worthwhile.

"Yes, this is your best work by far," he reassures me. "If you keep this up, I can see big things in store for you here at the station."

"I'm in my car now, so I'll be there in fifteen minutes," I tell him. "Thank you for approving the piece. It's an important issue and something I feel very strongly about."

"And it shows," he says. "Sometimes all a news story needs is heart, and this one has it. I always knew you had a great reporter somewhere inside you."

A few minutes later and I'm at the news station to do the promos. After checking my hair and makeup, I head to the taping room.

"How are you feeling today, Bill?" I ask my cameraman, who is setting up the video shots for me.

This is his first week back to work after the shooting. His recovery has been long and slow. We've talked almost every day because he didn't want to be left out of the work loop and I missed having him around.

"A little weak still," he says. "I'm making progress. My wife is tired of me hanging around the house, so she said I had to come into the station, if only for a few hours a day."

I smile fondly at him. "I don't believe that for a second. She adores you. I've missed you and I'm glad you're back. Take it easy though and don't push yourself too hard. The work will always be here."

"Isn't that the truth," he says. "It's certainly not worth dying for, I've discovered." He positions the video camera for the perfect angle. "Are you ready?" He stands back from the camera and closes his eyes.

"Are you sure you're okay?" I ask in concern.

"I'm having a déjà vu moment," he says. "The last time we did this, it didn't end well."

"Take your time," I say. "When you're ready."

He counts down from three and points to me when he reaches one.

I gaze directly into the camera and begin doing the voice over for the promo spot. The station will add footage of men fighting in the Middle East behind me before it airs.

"The military taught them how to shoot," I say. "Afghanistan taught them how to kill. Nobody taught them how to come home again. Tune in at six tonight for our latest segment on PTSD and the ways our military and their families are learning to cope with this all-too-common issue."

Bill nods at me when I finish.

"Is this segment about the biker guy?"

I shake my head. "No, I've spent the last week interviewing anyone and everyone that was willing to talk to me at the VA Hospital. Most of them wouldn't speak to me at all. Luckily, there were a few who were eager to share their stories. To hear them talk is heartbreaking and at the same time inspiring."

Bill nods. "I can tell you feel very strongly about the subject. I have an uncle who came back from Vietnam. It was hard on him for a long time."

"These men and women are strong and have been through so much," I say. "They wanted to let others know that it's okay to talk about PTSD. That it's not something to be ashamed of or to hide. I'm hoping the news segments will help someone who might be going through the same thing. Even if it's just one man or woman."

"I hope so too," Bill says. "What happened to the big interview you were doing on the bikers? Weren't you hanging around them for a while? I was expecting you to deliver a juicy, investigative exposé or something. I know you can be relentless when you're prying for information. I find it hard to believe they're the white knights the media has made them out to be."

No, the Steel Infidels are definitely not white knights.

Not in a legal sense anyway.

"The interview with them fell through," I reply with a casual shrug, as if I've already forgotten about it.

It didn't take me long to figure out the Steel Infidels were involved in a variety of illegal activities. Toby never told me exactly what they did in their spare time, and frankly I didn't want to know.

The longer I was with the Steel Infidels, the more I realized doing an exclusive feature interview on the MC would open them up to all kinds of other sticky questions.

Before I returned to Atlanta, I pulled Flint aside and expressed my concerns. Without either one of us mentioning any specifics, we agreed that going forward with the interview wasn't in the best interest of the Steel Infidels.

Or for Toby.

The man who I would protect with everything I have in me.

We killed the interview on the spot. Luckily, I hadn't built it up too much to my station manager, so it wasn't a big deal when I told him the exclusive interview fell through.

After the car bombing at the clubhouse, the press wasn't eager to hang around there anymore, so eventually the attention on the Steel Infidels died a natural death.

Their ten seconds of fame slowly faded away as it always does.

Which was the best thing that could've happened to everyone involved.

I wonder if Toby will watch my news segment and what he'll think about it if he does. I hope I've handled the topic respectfully and that he'll be a tiny bit proud of me.

I might never know.

47

TOBY

"Come on, Sadie," I say. "Let's go fishing."

I lean over the bed of the truck to pull out my fishing pole and the metal tackle box with all my gear. When Sadie sees the fishing pole, she takes off running ahead of me. She knows where we're going.

This is the first time I've been back to my favorite fishing spot since bringing Maggie here. I was full of hope that day and almost ready to believe there was a chance at a normal life for me. The feeling didn't last long before cold reality set in. I haven't had the heart to return.

What was once my favorite place in the world is now nothing but a reminder of what could have been.

Maggie never leaves my thoughts for long. When I'm around the other Steel Infidels, I'm the same happy-go-lucky, tough guy, while inside my guts are twisted up in a tangled mess.

No one knows the pain I felt the night I walked away from Maggie. It was for her own protection. Not for me. If I'd only been thinking about myself and being selfish, I would've kept her close for as long as she would have me.

Sometimes at night when I'm all alone, sitting out on the deck and gazing up at the stars, I let my mind wander. It's a forbidden treat and I've found myself doing it more frequently. It's the one thing that can't be taken away from me. As long as Maggie is in my memories, I'll always have her.

I think about what it could've been like to have Maggie in my arms forever. To wake up in the morning to find a beautiful, sleepy-eyed woman with tousled hair in my bed or to make her coffee and have her smile up at me when I hand her a cup.

If I close my eyes, I can almost imagine the touch of her fingertips tracing the tattoo on my back. Or the sweet smell of her hair when she steps out of the shower.

All the normal little things other couples take for granted.

Love is a bitch.

The chance of falling in love with another person and to have them feel the same is one in a million. Then to have it happen and still not be able to be together forever is a cruel fucking joke.

When I reach the end of the dock, I bait my hook and throw my fishing line into the water. Sadie sits down beside me to watch. Usually she runs around crazily, always full of energy, begging me to throw a tennis ball into the water for her to fetch. Today, it's almost as if she knows I need her by my side as quiet company. She's subdued, picking up on my mood.

I pat her head and she leans against my legs for an ear scratch.

"It's just you and me, girl. At least for now. But don't you worry because your Daddy has a plan. Things won't be this way forever. I promise you that."

48

MAGGIE

I'm nervous.

The closer I drive to the lake, the more I'm questioning if this is a bad idea. Rejection has never been something I've handled well, and to hear it twice from the same man will be devastating.

The only thing that gives me hope is that deep down in my heart, I know Toby cares for me. When we were together, I could feel it in his every touch and the way his eyes lit up when I walked into the room. As he told me once, he's a show-not-tell kind of guy and while he never came right out and said me he loved me, I'm sure I felt his love. Because he showed me in his own special way.

No more so than the night he told me goodbye.

I understood at the time that he did it for me.

And why.

He was afraid of hurting me again, emotionally or physically. His emotions were too raw and close to the surface. The shooting brought up everything he had tried so hard to keep clamped down under a lid. He was a pressure cooker, slowly and surely building up steam that had to be released before it blew up and destroyed him.

Toby needed space and time to work through his issues, both of which I was willing to give him. As much as he needed.

Up until a certain point.

I can't put my life on hold forever waiting for him to reach out to me. He won't do it until he thinks he's good enough, and that might not ever happen. It kills me to know that he feels this way.

Toby is more of a man than I could ever hope to be with. My greatest wish for him would be if he could see himself through my loving eyes. Just one time.

I know things might not be easy. There will be problems and issues that we'll need to overcome. Lots of them. Nothing that we can't handle together if we both want to try.

All I need to do is convince him that we're worth fighting for.

Up ahead at the end of the dirt road, I see Toby's truck parked under a tree near the lake. I'm relieved. I'd gone by the clubhouse first in hopes of catching Toby there. When Flint saw how disappointed I was to miss him, he took pity on me and suggested I try here instead.

I had my doubts at the time if Flint was really trying to help or to get rid of me. I never knew where I stood with the Steel Infidels. They were always polite, but guarded, never really bringing me completely into their group.

They had good reason to be leery of me. I'm a member of the press and a city girl. Trust from the MC is something that must be earned over time, not freely given. I understood and respected their attitude.

When we were in the Smoky Mountains, I was envious of the closeness within the MC. In my life, I've never truly felt as if I was a part of something. Even in my own family, I was an outsider, an oddball weirdo that the others simply didn't get.

The few days I spent with the Steel Infidels and their families, I felt a real sense of belonging. I realized I wanted that in my life. An extended family to care about, and who will care about me and the ones I love.

I want Toby and everything that goes along with him.

I hope he wants me too.

Now that I'm here, I'm scared. I pull my car up behind his truck and cut the ignition.

Oh well. Too late to back out now.

I grab the picnic basket from the back seat. Inside are a few of Toby's favorites: tomato sandwiches made with fresh garden tomatoes, homemade red velvet cake with cream cheese icing, and ice-cold Stella

Artois beer. Not a fancy menu by any stretch of the imagination. Hopefully he'll be pleased with my choices.

I take a deep breath for courage and start walking along the edge of the lake. The water is still and calm, similar to the first time he brought me here. It's a beautiful spring day, warmer than before. The leaves are budding out on the trees now and the lake is more alive with the sounds of songbirds singing to attract a mate.

When I walk around the curve of the lake, I spot him immediately. He's standing at the end of the dock, deeply tanned and shirtless, wearing nothing but ripped, faded jeans with a wide leather belt and old boots. On his head is a baseball cap turned backwards.

Typical Toby.

One hundred percent all-American male.

Everything I love about him wrapped up in one big package.

I stop walking and stand there quietly for a minute to watch him fish. He casts the line out and slowly reels it in. I could stand here all day watching him and never get tired of the sight.

Quietly, I pull out my cell phone and snap a few quick photos of him. If things go bad today, I want to have this memory of him preserved forever.

Sadie spots me and her ears perk up, yet she doesn't give me away by barking or coming my way. I step up onto the dock and start walking toward them. Toby still doesn't hear me. He's completely focused on the fishing line. The moment he turns around and sees me, I'll know everything I need to know. His face will give him away.

I'm almost halfway there when Toby feels the vibration of my footsteps on the wooden planks and whirls around. I put the picnic basket down and wait for his reaction.

"Maggie," he says in surprise, his voice hoarse with emotion.

Then he smiles and his whole face lights up like Christmas morning.

And I know.

He drops his favorite fishing pole and rushes to me. When he reaches my side, he picks me up in his arms, holding me tight against his chest and swinging me around.

"Be careful," I say, laughing and grabbing him tight around the neck. "We're going to fall into the lake."

"I won't let you fall," he says. "You came back for me."

He says it as a statement. His eyes tell me he means it as a question too.

"Yes, I came back for you. Didn't you realize I was never really gone?"

He buries his face in my hair and inhales deeply. "I've missed you," he says. "Every moment of every day. I never stopped thinking about you. I recorded your TV special and watched it many times just so I could hear your voice."

I pull back and look up into his gorgeous eyes that I've missed so much.

"Why didn't you call? I waited and waited, hoping you would." The hurt is evident in my voice, though I try to keep it out.

"I started to a million times. I didn't know what to say or how to ask for one more chance. It didn't seem right after you had already put up with so much from me."

"You were going to let me go forever?" I ask, disappointed. "To drift away, never to be heard from again?"

"No way," he says, tugging me close against his chest. "Letting you go forever was *never* my plan. I was coming for you, darling, with everything I had in me. And when I did, I wasn't going to take 'no' for an answer. You just beat me to it."

"When?" I ask with an incredulous look. "When we were eighty and grey-haired?"

He places his hands on both sides of my face. "When I became the man you thought I was," he says softly. "And not a day before. No matter how long it took. I needed to work through things before we could be together. I want you to be proud of me, not ashamed. The night of the dinner, it slaughtered me to see the embarrassment in your eyes when I fucked up."

"I was never ashamed of you," I say. "In my eyes, you've always been my hero. My feelings about that never wavered."

"You have no idea how much I want to believe that." He tilts my chin up so his captivating eyes can stare intently into mine. "The fact that you believed in me gave me hope. It made me think that maybe, just maybe, there's a chance I'm worth saving. I needed a reason to feel worthy again. Before you came along, I was drowning in darkness and didn't realize it until I was going under."

"I thought you had given up on us," I say shakily, holding back tears. "You told me so the night of the dinner."

"I had to tell you that so you would stay away," he explains. "For your own good. This whole time I've been fighting so fucking hard to get better, to *be* better, so that I could find my long way back to you."

"Why didn't you let me help?" I reach up to rub the tiny spot of beard under his lips with my thumb. "I should've been here with you. Surely there was something I could've done?"

"This is one journey I had to go on alone," he says. "The good news is, I'm slowly but surely getting better. I realized it was time for me to wake the hell up and start living again. The choice was in my hands and mine alone. Nobody else was going to do it for me. I've been talking to a counselor again."

I draw back to look up at him in surprise. "You have?" I couldn't be more shocked or pleased.

"I found one who actually knows what it's like to have been there in the Middle East. He's helping me work it out of my system. He's convinced me that I can't keep it bottled up anymore, so I've been talking, and then talking some more. About things that I thought I would never be able to speak of. Once I started, I couldn't stop. And I found a support group of screwed-up men like me. We meet once a week to hang out."

"I can't imagine how painful this must've been for you." I lay my head against his chest and close my eyes. It breaks my heart to hear the anguish in his voice and to know what he's been going through alone. I love him and should've been here. Why didn't I come back sooner? I knew he needed me, and I kept waiting for him to make the first move.

"It's been hard, no doubt, but some good has come of it too," he says, a smile creeping into his voice. "Would you believe I'm actually able to help some of the other men? I never would've thought a fucked-up guy like me could help anyone."

"Why would you think that? I can see how you would be a tremendous inspiration to other people. You've been through terrible things and yet here you are, stronger than ever. How are you helping them?"

"A few of the younger guys are in the same bad place where I was before. I've become a mentor to them, so they'll know they're not alone.

When they're feeling desperate, I tell them to call me. Sometimes we go out to a shooting range and work out the anger or just talk about sports. Along the way, I discovered that I enjoy helping people. It's an amazing feeling. To know that I can make a difference in someone's life. Sometimes it doesn't take much. Just a kind word or sharing my own personal experiences."

"I'm so very proud of you," I say. "You'll make an incredible mentor. I think you've found your calling in life."

"Maybe," he agrees. "And I haven't had a nightmare in a long time either. Now my dreams are mostly good. Do you know what I keep dreaming about the most?" He tugs my hair for me to look up at him.

"I can't imagine."

"Spending the night with you wrapped in my arms. Doing nothing but sleeping." He laughs when he sees my doubtful expression. "That sounds crazy, right? Especially for a sex-crazed maniac like me. To know that you feel safe and secure enough to fall asleep in my arms without worrying about nightmares would mean everything."

I raise my eyebrows at him. "I never really thought of the Steel Infidels as being cuddly teddy bears. Think of what it would do to your image if word got out."

"It will have to stay our little secret," he says with a wink. He leans down and picks up the picnic basket. Tilting his head toward the end of the dock, he says, "Let's go sit down and talk. We have a lot of catching up to do."

We walk hand-in-hand to the end of dock and sit down. Sadie comes over and drops down beside me, placing her head into my lap.

"She's glad you're back too," Toby says. "The house has been too quiet with only the two of us lately. It's funny how I thought it was fine the way it was before you came along. Then after you were gone, everything seemed empty and quiet."

I lean my head against his wide shoulder and slide my arm under his. With my fingertips, I trace the lion tattoo on his arm. Every time I look at it, I see an intricate detail that I've missed before. "Being here with you now is paradise. Do we ever need to leave this spot?"

"Not if you don't want to. We could always buy a houseboat and tie it up right here. I'm game if you are." He picks up his fishing pole and grabs the end of the line. "Would you mind opening the tackle box for me, sweetheart? I need you to hand me something from there. The fish are biting today."

I hide a smile. Even in the most intimate moments, Toby's mind is never far from fishing. I lean over to pick up his big metal tackle box and sit it beside me. "This thing is heavy! What do you keep in here? Bricks? What do you need?" I ask. "Not that I know what any of this stuff is anyway." I flip the latch and open the lid. It's crammed full of assorted fishing gear.

A black velvet ring box is sitting right on top.

My heart skips a beat.

"Never mind," he says with a sly grin. "I'll get it myself." He reaches over me and picks it up. "You might be wondering why I have this in my tackle box."

I let out a shaky breath. "Yeah, actually I was wondering that."

"From the beginning, I've always known that I wanted to propose to you here at the lake. What I didn't know was when the time would be right. Or even if I would get the chance. So being the Boy Scout that I am, I believe in always being prepared." He grins, and the lines around his eyes crinkle. "I've been carrying this ring around for weeks. Every night I take it out, shine it up, and think about how great our future can be."

Tears spring into my eyes. All this time he was thinking of me and planning for us while I thought I'd lost him forever.

He takes my left hand in his. "I love you, Maggie. I never said it before because I was a coward and afraid. I want you in my life forever because I *need* you by my side. To encourage and believe in me. You make me want to be a better man." He opens the box slowly and takes out a beautiful, sparkling silver ring with a solitaire diamond. "I'm not perfect. In fact, I'm seriously fucked up. We both know it, so no surprise there. I'm full of love though. I'm a big man with an even bigger heart." He spreads his arms wide to show me. "And I'll give you all that love inside me if you'll be mine."

Tears are sliding down my cheeks. I wipe them away with my hands. There's no point in trying to stop them.

"Should we stand up to do this proposal properly?" he asks. "I don't want to screw it up."

"No," I say, trying not to sniffle. The delicate ring is so tiny between his large fingers. I'm terrified he's going to drop it into the water. Knowing Toby, he would dive headfirst down to the bottom of the lake after it. "Right here is just fine."

Toby takes my smaller hand in his and slides the ring onto my finger.

"Will you marry me, Maggie?"

The most important question of my life, and I'm too choked up to answer. There's a huge stinging ball of emotion in my throat, and I can't speak. Toby is watching me carefully and thinking that I'm having second thoughts.

As if I would ever turn him down.

Never in a million years.

A dream man like Toby only comes along once in a lifetime, and only then if a woman is unbelievably lucky.

"Say yes," he whispers softly in encouragement. He takes both my hands in his. "Say you'll love me forever. Say you'll be my wife. Say you'll grow old with me and we'll raise a whole houseful of rowdy kids together. Say we'll sit on the front porch and watch our grandchildren play with puppies in the yard. Say we'll be there for each other through all the good times and the bad. Say all these things and I'll be the happiest man alive. Say that you love *me*, Maggie."

"Yes!" I say through my tears. "I'll marry you." I reach over to cup his face in my hands. "I love you more than I would have ever thought possible. Knowing that I'll be able to wake up next to your handsome face every morning for the rest of my life is all I want."

Toby suddenly scrambles to his feet, cups his hands around his mouth, and yells across the empty lake to nobody. "She said yes!!!"

The sound echoes back to us, startling a flock of migrating geese that have landed on the water. They take off and fly mere feet over our heads.

Laughing, he pulls me up beside him and wraps his big, muscular arms around my waist. "Our life is going to be better than either of us could ever imagine. Thank you for coming here today to light a fire underneath me, and thank God we don't have to waste another precious second being apart. I love you with all of my big heart, and I'll tell you that every day of our lives."

"I thought you were a show-not-tell kind of guy."

"Now that I'm going to be a husband, I'll work on being both."

Leaning down, he presses his perfect lips against mine. I cling to him as the kiss grows fierce, desperately clutching onto his wide shoulders. After a moment, he reluctantly breaks the kiss and pulls his lips away.

"Did I mention how much I've missed you?" he murmurs against my ear before pressing warm kisses down my neck and shoulder, sending delicious shivers through my body.

"I don't remember," I fib. "Tell me again."

"How about showing you," he suggests with a wicked grin that makes my stomach do flip-flops.

"Here? On the dock?"

He wiggles his eyebrows at me in question.

"Are you serious? You are so bad! I've never made out in a public place." I glance around the lake, checking to see if I can spot anyone who might be watching.

"Having a hot new wife would make a man want to have sex in all kinds of places. Don't worry. I don't think you could find a more secluded location for miles around. By any chance is there a blanket in the picnic basket you brought?" He points to the wicker picnic basket sitting beside his tackle box.

"A small, thin one," I reply. "Not much bigger than a towel."

"That works for me."

He bends down to open the latch of the picnic basket and quickly checks out the contents. A big smile crosses his face when he realizes I went to the trouble of packing his favorites.

"Stella Artois beer?" he asks, holding up a bottle. "How did you know?"

"As a reporter, it's my job to pay attention to details."

He digs down farther and grabs the red-checkered blanket from the bottom of the basket. Carefully, he spreads it out on the dock.

Sadie thinks the blanket is for her comfort and heads toward it to lie down. "Look. Sadie!" he calls out to distract her. "Go get that squirrel!" He points to the direction of the woods. She immediately takes off running and quickly disappears into the trees.

"There's one problem solved," he says. "Now we're all alone." He sits down on the blanket and takes up the entire space. "Why are you so far over there? Come closer, darling." He pats the blanket.

I give him a suspicious look. "What do you have in mind? Just to be clear, I don't want wood splinters in my ass."

"As your future husband, I vow to spend my life keeping your luscious booty splinter-free. Trust me. Now quit fooling around and come on over here, woman. I've missed you. Let me show you how much."

I slowly walk over to him and stop when his nose almost brushes my sundress. He reaches up with both hands to touch my thighs above my knees. Slowly he slides them up under my dress, with his eyes never leaving mine.

I grab onto his broad shoulders with both hands to steady myself.

"What are you doing?" I ask. "What if someone sees us?"

"They won't, I promise you," he reassures me. "I've never seen or heard another soul, and I've been coming here for years. It's just us, so you can make as much noise as you want."

"Why would I do that?"

"Because I'm going to make you cum so many times you'll be begging me to stop," he promises. "Turn around so I can unzip this pretty dress."

I hesitate for only a split-second before turning around and flipping my hair over one shoulder so it won't get caught in the zipper. He reaches up and tugs the zipper down, then slides the white cotton sundress off one shoulder and then the other before letting it drop in a pool at my feet. Placing his hands at my waist, he turns me back around to face him.

He's watching me silently, his eyes going dark blue, almost black, with lust. His harsh intake of breath tells me how much he loves what he sees, his body stilling as he stares at me.

He doesn't need to tell me what else to do.

I instinctively know what he wants.

I was made for this man.

49

TOBY

I can't decide whether to look or touch.

Or even where to begin.

Maggie is my fantasy girl, more lovelier and sexier than any calendar pinup or porn star. To be with her now is a gift that I will never take for granted.

Not for one single day.

Knowing how close I was to losing her forever scares the crap out of me.

The instant I heard her footsteps on the dock and turned around to see her coming my way, I knew in my heart things were going to be okay.

The last few weeks have been absolute hell.

The monsters trying to rip me apart inside didn't want to let go without a knock-down, drag-out fight. Maggie will never know the depth of pain I had to crawl through on my hands and knees before I could rise again.

Through it all, I always had a plan and kept my eyes on the prize.

Maggie.

I might not have been able to see where I was at the time, but I could sure as hell see where I was going.

My life has been like driving through one of those long, pitch-black tunnels in the Smoky Mountains, with only a glimmer of sunlight at the end. As long as I kept my focus on that shining light, I could find my way out of the darkness.

Now my light is standing in front of me looking more desirable than I could ever imagine. The sight of her almost nude body makes my heart hammer wildly in my chest. As gorgeous as her body is, it's nothing compared to the love I see shining in her eyes.

Maggie fills the holes in my damaged soul in a way only she can.

"Do you like what you see?" she asks in a low, sexy voice.

"I do because I love everything about you," I reply. "Your taste, your smell, the way you tremble when I nibble your ear. I would've waited forever for you to come along."

Smiling, she reaches around with both hands and undoes the clasp of her lacy bra. Slowly, she slides it off her arms and dangles it teasingly by one finger before letting it drop into my lap. Her firm, heavy breasts rise and fall with each shaky breath, swaying deliciously in front of my face. I can't resist taking a hardened, rosy nipple into my mouth, tugging and sucking until I hear her gasp.

Leaning in, I bury my face in the thin fabric between her legs and inhale the sweet smell of her warm skin. My hands slide to cup her ass, pulling her closer still.

"I'll spend a lifetime pleasing you and claiming you as mine," I say. "Starting right now."

I slip my fingers under the band of her panties and slowly peel them down over her hips and legs. She carefully steps out of them and I toss them aside.

"Spread your legs wider for me," I murmur. "So I can taste you."

She hesitates only a split second before willingly moving her feet farther apart to give me better access. I start at her knees and work my way up with my lips, rubbing my two-day-old beard stubble against her tender inner thighs. I close my eyes and linger, drinking in the essence of my girl.

"Oh *god*," she moans and grips my hair tighter with both hands.

My hard cock throbs and strains against my jeans when I hear that sound. Her responsiveness to my touch turns me on as nothing else can. I want to drive her wild, to have her grinding uncontrollably into my face until I'm smothering and can't breathe. To make her want me as much as I insanely crave her. As long as I live, Maggie will never have reason to doubt my love for her again.

When I move my lips to the juncture between her legs, Maggie spreads them farther apart and I drive deep with my tongue. The taste of her makes my brain explode. Her inner thighs start to tremble and I move up slightly to lick her clit.

She's on fire, wet and melting onto my eager tongue.

She bucks against my face and I grip her ass, holding her tight, forcing her to accept the relentless assault of my mouth.

I can never get enough of this woman. I'm insatiable where Maggie is concerned. If this means I'm an addict, then I never want to be cured.

When I hear her whimper and tense up, I glance at her face. She's watching me with her luscious lips parted and her glazed eyes half-closed. I blink twice to clear the fog of desire from my brain and concentrate on her clit, flicking my tongue faster.

"Oh...*Toby*!" she cries out.

She tugs harder on my hair, grinding her body against my mouth as she cums in a series of spasms.

Fucking hell!

How I love the feeling of her orgasm around my tongue.

Nothing can beat it.

The absolute best sensation in the world.

She moans and closes her eyes until the last tremor passes. I support her with my arms so she won't collapse, then lie back on the blanket and pull her onto my chest.

After a minute, her breathing slows. She raises her head and places her hands on either side of my head.

"Now it's your turn, big fella," she says, licking her lips.

Oh fuck!

I've been dying to feel her hands on me. She flattens her palms on my chest and moves from my pecs to my abs, lovingly touching every muscle. My cock throbs painfully.

"One day, will you tell me what all of your tattoos mean?" she asks, leaning down to trace the lines with her tongue.

"I'll tell you anything you want to know. All you have to do is ask."

When her hands reach my waist, she slides her fingers just inside my jeans, teasing and tormenting. My stomach muscles clench when her fingers graze the tip of my cock.

"Touch me and you'll feel how much I want you," I urge. "I need your hands on me everywhere because I swear it's been forever."

Moving downward, she unbuckles my belt and then lowers my zipper, freeing my hard cock. I close my eyes and suck in a deep breath. She circles it firmly with her hand and strokes the full length all the way down to the base and back up. I groan loudly, straining into her hand.

"Why are you the only one still wearing clothes?" she asks with a breathless laugh. "I want to feel your bare skin against mine." Quickly she tugs off my jeans and boots and then straddles me.

Growing bolder, she wraps her hand around me again. I place my hand over hers, guiding her, as she strokes up and down. She looks up at me to make sure I'm watching her before licking her lips slowly and lowering her mouth to the tip.

I swear loudly and grab her head before it goes any further. "As much as I would love your mouth on me," I say regretfully. "I want to be deep inside you more. And once you start sliding my dick in your mouth, there won't be any stopping."

Moving my hands down to her waist, I raise her up so that she's positioned right above my cock. She reaches down and guides the tip into her, sliding all the way down to my balls in one, long smooth motion until I'm completely buried inside her.

I've suddenly forgotten how to breathe. I can't take my eyes off her naked beauty or where our bodies are joined. Neither one of us wants to make a move. I reach up to slide a hand from her cheek, down her neck, and over her heavy breast. My thumb teases the nipple and she arches her back into me.

"Fuck," I mutter when she braces her hands on my chest and begins to move slowly, riding me. I take a deep breath and steel myself not to rush her, to let her move at her pace, when all I want to do is drive up into her, over and over in a mad frenzy. She rises and sinks down, again and again, driving me to insanity.

"I can't hold out much longer," I warn. "You feel *so* fucking tight and amazing."

It's sweet agony trying not to completely lose control. I want to make it last forever even when I know it's an impossible task. Especially when holding out another three seconds seems just as unlikely.

Maggie is close to coming again. I can see it in her eyes and feel it in the way her body is tensing up. She closes her eyes and cries out as she climaxes around me. I hold her steady, driving into her deeper, as wave after wave of her orgasm ripples throughout her body.

Watching her cum causes something primal and untamed to snap inside me. Losing my last remaining shred of self-restraint, I quickly flip her over onto her back, still buried deep inside her. Propping her up with one arm underneath to protect her tender skin from splinters, I thrust into her hard and fast. When I know I'm about to cum, I cup the back of her head and draw her up to meet my lips in a hot, breathless kiss. I drive into her harder and deeper. The friction and angle prove to be too much to endure.

"*Damn...*" I grit out, straining inside her as I cum.

I bury my face in the soft spot of her neck and stay there until my breathing finally begins to slow. Rolling over onto my back again, I drag her on top of me where she collapses in an exhausted heap. Reaching up with a gentle hand, I push back the hair that has fallen across her face.

"Are you sure you can handle me every day of your life?" I ask in genuine worry. "I'm a rough and rowdy beast."

"If not, I'll gladly die trying," she says with a sigh against my chest.

"Maggie?" I say after several more minutes of bliss, lying with her in my arms. "Were those slices of red velvet cake I saw in the picnic basket?"

She raises her head to kiss my lips. "Why? Did you work up a beastly appetite?"

"Afraid so," I say.

She reaches over a hand without moving from my chest and drags the picnic basket closer. After taking out a piece of cake, she unwraps it halfway and holds it up to my mouth. I take a big bite, and she leans down to slowly lick the cream cheese frosting off the side of my lips.

"Heaven couldn't be any sweeter than this," I say. "What we have right here, right now, is just the beginning for us. We're blessed, and we can't ever forget it."

"I swear I never will," she promises.

50

TOBY

"Do you still have the rings?" I ask Sam. "Show me."

Sam rolls his eyes in irritation and pats the pocket of his black leather jacket. "Right here, buddy. For the last time, I won't forget the rings. Or lose them on the way to the wedding. Or drop them in the water. Trust me, okay? I've got this."

"Alright, if you say so."

"Here's your tie," Flint says.

He tries to hand me a dark blue necktie. When I don't take it, he steps closer and starts to loop it around the back of my neck. I grab his wrist.

"What the hell do you think you're doing?" I ask. "I'm not wearing a tie. I thought we already discussed this."

"Maggie asked me to try one last time with the tie, so I told her I would." Flint shrugs and grins. "I tried and you said no. I did my part."

He tosses the tie onto my kitchen table. It lands among the empty beer bottles and paper chip bags from last night's party.

"Personally, I think we're all stunningly handsome in our boots, black pants, and white shirts," Sam jokes. "We don't need ties. What girl wouldn't want to marry us fine-looking gents?"

"Every woman in the world except the four who were crazy enough to say yes," Jesse says from the open doorway. He walks over and claps me on the shoulder. "How are you holding up, Toby? Any last-minute regrets? It's never too late to back out. All you have to do is say the word and we'll ride out of here together. Right now."

He's joking.

The Steel Infidels know how I feel about Maggie, and they've been supportive of our upcoming marriage.

"No...I'm not backing out," I say. "Marrying Maggie is something I want to do." I wave my hand at the three Mason brothers. "I want what you have. An Old Lady, kids, a family of my own. You're all lucky sons of bitches. Now I am too."

"I hear you," Jesse says. "We hit the jackpot of this thing called life. Do you have everything you need for the wedding? Who has the rings?"

"Damn!" Sam says, throwing up his hands. "For the love of God! Would everyone please stop asking about the rings! For the last time, I've got them."

"Are you sure you trust Flint to officiate the service?" Jesse asks. "I'm finding it hard to see my VP and little brother as an ordained minister."

"It's not as if I've suddenly become a Baptist preacher overnight," Flint explains. "It's merely a legal formality. For only this one special occasion."

"It is legal though, right?" I ask, suddenly worried.

"One hundred percent," Flint assures me.

My nerves are acting up again. When Flint volunteered to become an ordained minister to marry us, I felt honored that he would be willing to go to all that trouble just for me. I couldn't imagine anyone else that I would want to perform our ceremony.

Plus, Flint has an uncanny way of keeping everyone's shit together. He's calm under pressure. He won't let me down and even more importantly, he won't let me screw up either.

The other Mason brothers will be right there with me too. When I walk up to take Maggie's hand at the wedding, Sam will be beside me as my best man. Jesse will be my groomsman. I might not be a Mason brother by blood, but I'm their brother in every other way that counts.

They're the family I never had, along with the rest of the Steel Infidels. Our bond is stronger than any blood brothers could ever be. I would lay down my life for them and they would do the same for me.

No questions asked.

Flint glances at his watch. "The ceremony starts in an hour. The rest of the crew should be here soon so we can ride over to the lake together."

He'd no more than gotten the words out of his mouth when we hear the roar of motorcycles coming up the road to my house.

"That's our signal, boys," Jesse says. "Let's ride, Toby. Enjoy it, brother. This is your final trip as a single man."

I take a deep breath and blow it out. When he puts it that way, it makes a man stop and think for a second.

Only for a second though.

"Now or never," I say.

I grab my Steel Infidels jacket from the back of the dining room chair and slide it on. When Maggie and I talked about wedding attire, I assumed she knew my black leather jacket with the Steel Infidels patches was always part of the plan. If not, she'll know when we show up at the wedding.

The rest of the Steel Infidels crew are sitting on their bikes in the driveway waiting for us. I walk over and shake each man's hand individually to thank him for being there. I'm trying my best not to get too emotional, but it's getting harder with each passing minute. Especially when I reach Donny and Rocco at the end of the line.

Rocco acts like a tough, bearded badass biker who doesn't take any shit from anyone. Underneath it all, he's a big old softie who gave me a job when nobody else would hire an ex-Marine that was fucked up in the head. Donny brought me into the shop and patiently taught me everything he knew. I owe them for giving me a chance at a real life.

"Don't fuck up today and embarrass us all," Rocco says gruffly when he shakes my hand.

"I'll try my best," I reply.

They wait until I climb onto my bike and buckle up my helmet before starting their engines. Jesse nods at me then holds up one hand in the air and makes a circular motion.

"Let's ride," he says.

A chorus of loud whoops and hollers fills the air, and then we're off to a wedding.

51

TOBY

When the Steel Infidels arrive at the lake in our typical noisy fashion, a large crowd of wedding guests are already waiting for us. Instead of filing in and parking in our normal order, Jesse motions for me to ride to the front of the line and park my bike first.

I'm shocked and pleasantly surprised at how different the lake looks today in preparation for the wedding. Rented white plastic chairs are lined up in two sections on either side of the long wooden dock. On one side, I see the MC's large extended family along with several members of other friendly motorcycle clubs in the area. On the other is Maggie's family and friends.

I notice Brad is not among them. Maggie told me he made a lame excuse about an out-of-town tax conference he needed to attend. Something tells me I won't be seeing much of him in the future, and that's okay by me.

Maggie's guests are dressed in pretty, pastel-colored wedding attire while my guests are wearing motorcycle club jackets, jeans, and boots. There won't be any need for an usher to ask anyone if they're guests of the bride or the groom because one look will give them the correct answer.

The Sweet Butts, under the strict guidance of Aunt Leona, have been working hard all week on wedding decorations and food for the reception. When Aunt Leona volunteered her catering services, Maggie graciously accepted her help on the one condition that her special oatmeal cookies would *not* be served.

I search for Maggie and can't find her in the crowd. She told me it was bad luck to see her in her wedding dress before the big day, so I don't have a clue what she'll be wearing. I'm pleased that she wanted to keep to tradition since I'm a big old sucker for it myself.

A man near the front row of chairs begins strumming softly on a guitar to signal the wedding is about to begin. His long blond hair is pulled back into a man-bun and both arms are covered in tattoos. I recognize him as a regular client of Sam's tattoo parlor. The country music song he's playing is one of my favorites. I know Maggie chose it just for me.

Like most men, I've stayed out of the wedding plans and let Maggie handle everything. Whatever makes her happy, makes me happy. As soon as we announced our engagement to the members of the MC, the other wives and Old Ladies gathered around her and accepted her immediately as one of their own.

Just as I hoped and knew they would.

They're a fine group of gals, and I love them all as the sisters I never had. If I step out of line with Maggie, they'll be the first to slap me right back into shape.

Sam steps up beside me and pats his jacket pocket. "Before you ask me again, the rings are right here," he says with a grin. "Are you ready? Your feet aren't getting cold in those black boots, are they?"

"I'm ready," I say. "I hope Maggie shows up." I look around anxiously for her again.

"Don't worry," Sam reassures me. "She's hiding around here somewhere. Lila and the rest of the girls are with her. If she tried to run out on you now, they would drag her back by her hair if they had to."

Flint squeezes my shoulder in a sign of support. "It's almost time for the wedding to start. They're waiting on you, buddy. The first move is all yours. Maggie won't be coming down the aisle unless you're standing at the other end."

I take a deep breath. "Okay, let's do it."

When we start walking toward the dock, the wedding guests stand up and turn toward us. I make my way slowly between the two groups of guests with Sam, Flint, and Jesse right behind me. So many familiar faces are here to wish us well. Half the town has turned out for our wedding.

I wish my buddies in the Marines could've been here too. My eyes water when I think about them. I touch the photo I always carry with me in my pocket.

They're here.

In spirit, if not in physical body.

They would've been happy that I finally found peace in my life. I'll keep trying to live a full life the best I can to honor their sacrifice.

When I reach the front row, I reach over and shake hands with Maggie's dad. It's taken a while, but he's slowly warming up to me. It means a lot to know that Maggie's parents and Nicole showed up to support her today, especially since things started out so rocky in the beginning. Her mom reaches up to hug my neck, then impulsively kisses my cheek.

At the entrance to the dock, I hesitate for just a second under the wooden arch one of the MC members built as a wedding present for us. The Sweet Butts have carefully wrapped blue and purple hydrangea blossoms through the lattice work. I believe they've enjoyed putting this wedding together as much or more than Maggie.

My life will be changing in a huge way in a few minutes' time. I need to take a moment alone to let it all sink in.

Suddenly I feel a wet tongue lick my hand.

Sadie.

Where did she come from? I sink down eye level to her and scratch behind her ears. Maggie must've sent someone back to the house to pick her up and bring her over to surprise me.

Knowing she's here with me makes everything complete. I couldn't do this without my faithful girl.

I take a step up on the wooden dock and walk to the end with Sadie trotting along beside me. When we get there, I turn around to watch for Maggie.

"Sit, Sadie," I say.

I'm surprised when she listens and minds me for once. I hope the ceremony is short because she won't behave for long.

Flint moves over to stand on one side of me to perform the ceremony while Sam and Jesse line up on the other.

My heart is beating so fast.

But in a good way this time.

Not in a PTSD panicked way.

Hopefully not like that ever again.

When I catch sight of Maggie stepping up on the dock in her long, ivory wedding dress, I'm overwhelmed by emotion.

How did I ever get so lucky?

A country boy biker with a truckload of issues marrying the most gorgeous, sweetest girl in the world.

I'm truly blessed.

Maggie walks slowly toward me, carrying a big bouquet of colorful wildflowers. Her long brown hair is curled in ringlets and flowing free the way I love it.

She smiles at me and I know.

I'm finally home.

RIDE HARD AND CARRY ON!